BOB'S MEMOIR

4,000 Years as a Free Demon

Devon Layne

BOB'S MEMOIR

4,000 Years as a Free Demon

SIGNATURE EDITION

ELDER ROAD BOOKS
LYNNWOOD WA

THIS SIGNATURE EDITION of *Bob's Memoir: 4,000 Years as a Free Demon* contains all three volumes of Bob's seminal work on the history of the world for the past four millennia. It has been designed in a way that seems appropriate for the work of an immortal sharing his insights on the development of humanity and inhumanity. Bob has experienced all aspects.

It was a difficult thing for a poor defenseless demon to endure, especially finding how terribly wrong the history books and religious teachings and scientific writings have gotten the story over the years. It is his attempt to set the record straight. He's done everything possible to make the work simple and understandable, stopping short of labeling chapter and verse all the way through.

As a Signature Edition, this volume includes a photo of the real author, Devon Layne. Devon (me) wishes to assure you that he is not a 4,000-year-old demon, no matter what his ex-wives might say. He has merely acted as the intermediary for Bob, who introduced himself as Devon was driving on US Route 95 through Idaho, in search of inspiration and groceries.

Bob introduced himself politely as if he were a passenger in the cab of Devon's truck, and told him he would be dictating his story and as soon as Devon was conveniently settled in front of his computer, the story would begin. And thus it began.

As Devon sat naked in front of his campfire that night, fellow nudist and story consultant Doug showed up to share a beer and discuss the latest story. Devon told him about Bob's arrival on the scene and a little about what he'd been told so far. Doug nodded, downed another beer, and stared into the fire.

"I get it," he said. "Bob is just your every day, slightly horny, happy-go-lucky—mostly lucky—demon."

"That Doug," Bob whispered in Devon's ear. "He shows up every century or two. He gets it."

And so it proved to be. Of course, Doug was only a little of the story Bob told when compared to the many, many women who crossed Bob's path—some of whom, came to stay.

So I, Devon Layne, have endeavored faithfully to record Bob's story, even when it seemed disjointed and to extend into a future not yet seen. Enjoy!

author Devon Layne

PLANNED 2025
SIGNATURE COLLECTION RELEASES

Soulmates, February 2025. D.R. Peters, 'Doc' to his friends, is an artist. He paints portraits of women. Doc loves women. Many of the women he paints love him. Then smart and sexy Rita, his next door neighbor, asks him to teach her the art of love, which Doc is all too happy to do. He's not quite so sure, though when Rita, a research scientist, decides to start experimenting with the effect his relationship with his models has on his art. Doc is about to learn all about the science of the art of love.

The Art and Science of Love, March 2025. D.R. Peters, 'Doc' to his friends, is an artist. He paints portraits of women. Doc loves women. Many of the women he paints love him. Then smart and sexy Rita, his next door neighbor, asks him to teach her the art of love, which Doc is all too happy to do. He's not quite so sure, though when Rita, a research scientist, decides to start experimenting with the effect his relationship with his models has on his art. Doc is about to learn all about the science of the art of love.

Drawing on the Dark Side of the Brain, April 2025. Artist Jett Blackburn's paintings reveal the soul of his subjects. They have the power to change the viewer, the model, and the artist. Sometimes emotionally, sometimes terminally. Join this digital native and his accumulation of girlfriends as they break the ties with their parents and move off to college and self-discovery.

Forever Yours, September 2025. Artificial Intelligence programming prodigy Henry pulls three other friends with him to create a new company with $billion prospects. Getting through jealousies, college, loves, virtual and physical attacks, takeover challenges, and family life, Henry succeeds in creating a singularity AI~one that can contain all the data from one's life. But how will it be used?

Bob's Memoir: 4,000 Years as a Free Demon, November 2025. The entire three-volume original in one massive Signature Edition hardcover! The adventure of Bob, a free demon loosed on the world by an inept adept some 4,000 years ago. But Bob is not your ordinary textbook demon. He was not imbued with any traits of evil when he was summoned and as a result is rather benign, learning about humanity and morality as he goes. He's just your everyday, slightly horny, happy-go-lucky (mostly lucky) demon.

Schedule and Releases Subject to Change

CONTENTS

VOLUME 1: BEFORE CAESAR (MOSTLY)

Prologue 3

Part I In the Beginning 7

  1 My Inept Adept 9

  2 A New Me 13

  3 The Dikteon Cave 19

  4 The Pain of Being Handsome 24

Part II Architect for a God 33

  5 Cast into the Sea 35

  6 Build Me a Temple 42

  7 Wedding Bells 50

  8 Build It Better 58

  9 An Heir to Justice 65

Part III Gifts from Greeks 75

  10 The Possession 77

  11 A Code to Live By 84

  12 Shipwreck 92

  13 The Fall of Troy 99

  14 My Odyssey 106

  15 Homecoming at Last 114

Part IV Nobody Expects the Spanish Inquisition 123

  16 Churches and Demons Are Good Company 125

  17 The Wrath of a Woman Scorned 132

  18 In 1492, Columbus Sailed 139

  19 The Greatest Demon 146

  20 The Storm 153

Part V To Conquer the World 163

  21 A Walk in the Garden 165

  22 The Might of Babylon 172

  23 To Catch the Conscience of the King 179

  24 The Great... Again 186

  25 Great Caesar's Ghost! 194

  26 Battle in the Desert 201

Volume 2: After Caesar (Mostly)

Prologue 215

Part VI A Woman's Work 219

27 Unharnessed Joy. 221

28 On Becoming a Woman 229

29 Spared by a Goddess 237

30 On Freedom and Possession 245

31 The Price of Passage 253

Part VII Temple Builder 261

32 Nothing of the Soul 263

33 A Temple of Wood. 271

34 Pagoda 278

35 In Xanadu did Kublai Khan... 286

Part VIII Bob Almighty 295

36 The Legend Begins. 297

37 Praise Bob! 304

38 Love and Marriage 310

39 Entering the Modern World 318

40 I left my heart.... 326

Part IX What's So Real About Reality? 335

41 Integrating the Household 337

42 Ninjas. 344

43 A New Palace 351

44 Believing What You See. 359

45 Casting Call 366

46 Cheese It! The Cops! 375

47 Women! 383

Part X To Infinity and Beyond! 393

48 Mission Mars: The Mini-Series 395

49 Marian the Librarian 401

50 Navel Battle 408

51 Winnowing. 415

52 Happy Days 422

53 Loss 430

54 We Refuse 438

Volume 3: Current Era (Mostly)

Prologue 449

Part XI Headaches and Heartaches **455**

55 Dark Chocolate 457

56 When Is a Slave Not a Slave? 467

57 Season Two 475

58 Wealth 484

59 Pilot Test 489

Part XII Catch Me If You Can **499**

60 Something More 501

61 Fair Trade 509

62 The Decision 515

63 The Game 524

64 The Search 532

65 The Exorcist 540

Part XIII Candidates **549**

66 Cleveland Bob 551

67 The Erinyes. 559

68 International Bob. 566

69 Trying Not to Lie 573

70 Back to Italy 579

Part XIV The Bare Facts **587**

71 My Record with Strippers. 589

72 Stopping Traffic 597

73 On the Go 605

74 Arrested Development 612

75 Jail Break 619

Part XV It's in the Bag **627**

76 Gateway 629

77 Plotting the Finale 636

78 Sometimes an Ally 642

79 To Boldly Go 649

80 Finale 657

81 Launch 663

Interview with the Author **673**

Acknowledgements **678**

Bob's Memoir

4,000 Years as a Free Demon

Vol. 1: Before Caesar (mostly)

PROLOGUE

HI. MY NAME IS BOB. I'll be your demon this evening. I promise to take good care of you. We've prepared a delectable array of vices to suit the most discriminating palate. And I can tell by looking at you that you are a discriminating person. If you have an appetite for Greed, we have so much hoardable stuff... Pardon me. We have so many collectibles that we can fill your basement and attic and still leave you wanting more.

Need a really good lie to tell the little woman when you get home? Or the boss about your expense report? Our cellar is stocked with the widest selection of defendable lies in the country. We serve some of today's top politicians, lawyers, and preachers. Our lies are recommended by both right wing and left wing publications. And lies aren't even a deadly sin!

As far as Gluttony goes, eat as much as you want. We'll keep filling your plate.

For dessert, may I recommend one of a wide selection of our most lustful beauties. We have the ever-popular blondes, with a special sauce all their own. Something a little spicier? I still have a few redheads available. You can order any of our lustful delicacies in male or female, any race you'd like. If you don't mind waiting a few minutes, we can even custom fit them with your preferred body type.

Pride, Wrath, Envy, Sloth? You need look no further than the selection of sides available. Every vice is represented on our menu with some you might not yet have thought of!

Best of all, there's no tipping! When it's time to pay the tab, I just eat your soul.

I lied about that last part. I've never actually eaten a soul. Disgusting looking things. The ones you think should be sweet are as bland as earwax. And those that purport themselves to be spicy smell like rotted nuts. Souls are an acquired taste and I don't want to acquire it. I did that with beer and haven't been the same since.

You see, I'm not really interested in striking deals that make you my servant for eternity… though there are a few who have willingly offered themselves. Not as many as you might assume. Eternity is a long time. I take *very* good care of my possessions. A well-fed minion is a happy minion—that's my motto. I find getting myself into trouble is about all I can handle without tempting others—though I'm not above helping a buddy out if he or she needs a push in the wrong direction. It's a special talent of mine.

I've been around more than 4,000 years—ever since my conjuring in Knossos. As I said in *The Autobiography of Benvenuto Cellini*, "All men of whatsoever quality they be, who have done anything of excellence, or which may properly resemble excellence, ought, if they are persons of truth and honesty, to describe their life with their own hand; but they ought not to attempt so fine an enterprise till they have passed the age of forty." No, I didn't really adopt the persona of Cellini and write his autobiography, but I read it and I could really identify with his tales. But that is the subject of *his* autobiography, not mine.

Anyway, having now passed the age of forty centuries, I feel compelled to tell my story… or what I remember of it.

To clarify: Four thousand years is a fucking long time! I'm a simple demon. Don't read too much into that word. I'm not dumb. I'm just not omniscient, omnipresent, or omnimnemonic. That last word I coined to mean "all-remembering." I'm not. I remember some things as clearly as if they happened yesterday. In fact, I should tell you about Liz and her bra-burning episode. It was… not in this part of the story. Okay? Besides, at this point, I can't always keep straight what century some things happened in, let alone what order they happened. There were a couple in which I spent most of my time drunk and don't remember at all. And then the time I was stuck in the infinity room for seventy years. Esmira…

This is a memoir, not an autobiography, so most of the time, don't expect it to start at the beginning and go all the way to the end. I tell about things as I think of them, so if I take a detour to the fifteenth century AC (After Caesar) while I'm supposed to be writing about BC (Before Caesar), that's the order I remembered it in.

I took time to learn English and even took a writing class so I could compose this memoir in a common tongue that will be understood by all. Or most. Or at least some. At least more than can read Minoan Linear A.

Mostly, I learned what not to do that I'm going to do anyway. Take back story, for instance. Professor Tolkien went on and on about not starting a book with a lot of back story. Practice what you preach, I say. The theory is that if it is necessary to the story, it will come out eventually.

Well, right, but if you are going to understand any of my story, it needs to start with something more than, "Esmira, I'm going to kill you!" You would think this was a typical story of an evil demon, rending the flesh from innocent victims, and that would be *so* unfair! How are you to understand who in four thousand years Esmira was. And why would I hate my wife so much that I would threaten to kill her? Ha! Now the surprise has been spoiled!

So, I'll begin at the beginning. Even though the first chapter was not my personal experience, I'll tell the story of Pinaruti the way I learned it—from the man's memories.

Part I
In the Beginning

Image Credit: Danilo Sanino, ID1571939008 licensed from Shutterstock.com

1
MY INEPT ADEPT

PINARUTI WAS A BRIGHT lad with the common malady of being unable to stay focused on any one thing for long. Except sex. Pinaruti never had a problem focusing on sex. I'm sorry to say that, for Pinaruti, his focus on the act of sex was so single-minded that he never figured out how to actually get there. So, he spent some time as a shepherd, some as a bricklayer, some as a winemaker—which was nearly his undoing—and eventually ended up as the apprentice to one of Minoa's finest magi.

The inability to focus and a weakness for the wine he'd bottled meant that many of Pinaruti's spells went slightly—or even seriously—awry. That was, in fact, how his venerable master met his end. Pinaruti was practicing a simple spell to turn a sacrificial sheep into a blood sausage, when he inadvertently sucked the blood out of his master into the sausage. From that day on, he worked his spells only in isolation.

I once told Walt about what happened and while he agreed that it was a fitting end to the careless magician; he didn't see that he could put the apprentice killing his master into his movie. Oh well. There's no accounting for taste.

Also, from that day on, Pinaruti was the inheritor of his master's business and, most importantly, to his precious books of spells. I suppose I need to clarify that I mean "scrolls," or people get confused. There is always someone who will argue that a scroll is not a book. Upstarts. Pinaruti took his small library to Knossos, where neither he nor his master were known, and set up shop in a small but comfortable house where he worked charms and enchantments for a few coins and a supply of wine.

And that is how he happened to come to the attention of King Drakomaxos of the southwest quarter of the eastern half of Knossos. There were so many kings in Knossos at the time that each had to carefully define his kingdom and dared not claim both sides of the streets at his borders. Pinaruti came to the king's attention because the house he built lay inside the Kingdom of Drakomaxos.

I have found that anytime one comes to the attention of a king, or any other ruler, it is at least going to cost money if not servitude or even life and limb. So it was in this instance.

"You have taken residence in the Kingdom of Drakomaxos," the king declared. He was backed up by his entire army, which consisted at the time of two hired thugs who accompanied him when collecting taxes. "You owe a silver drachma in taxes for my royal protection."

"From what?" Pinaruti naïvely asked.

"From what I might do to you if you are not under my protection," Drako stated as though it were the most obvious thing.

"I have no more than a couple of copper coins," Pinaruti said. "I normally trade spells for what I need."

"Hmm. A magus. In my own kingdom," Drako said, slapping his hands together. "I, too, am willing to take taxes in kind. I will forgive your taxes for five years if you will cast a spell to air condition my house. My house is too hot. Just look at the sweat rolling off our bodies. Steam is rising from the laundry. I want my home air cooled."

Of course, I picked up the term 'air condition' centuries later. But in general terms, that's what he wanted. Pinaruti agreed. What else could he do, with the king's army at his doorstep?

"Your royal majesty, this is a complex matter. I would not want to cast a spell that mistakenly froze your home and everything in it. I beg your leave to search my books and practice a spell so that I might cast the perfect spell to keep your house at the perfect temperature all year round," Pinaruti begged.

"I will give you one year to research the problem, then you shall come to my house and air condition it, or I shall cut off your head," Drako said, magnanimously.

It was a miserable year. Pinaruti read the scrolls. He came across different things that might work, but there was no spell for cooling a king's home. So, Pinaruti turned to a higher power. If he summoned a demon, he reasoned, he could simply command the demon to cool the house and all would be well. Reaching that decision called for a drink to celebrate.

He climbed to the roof of his home and poured himself a bottle of wine from his glass. From the roof, he could see into his neighbor's courtyard where the wife of the neighbor and her women servants were often scrubbing laundry or preparing meals. Or changing clothes or scrubbing each other. Pinaruti kept watch over them, benevolently stroking his magic wand as he drank his wine and had visions.

If you are slow on metaphors, he was jacking off as he fantasized about the women.

Eventually, he entered the room in the back of his house in which he did his magic. Up until this time, you might say that Pinaruti practiced mostly household magic—protective spells, simple illusions, and brooms that swept the floor by themselves. He held the scroll open with a bottle of wine at each end and carefully traced out the pattern for the protective circle into which he would summon his demon. Do I need to point out that when I use terms like glass and bottle at this time, I am quite aware that transparent glass was rare to non-existent and I include in the term those bottles and cups made of fired clay? Please, don't nitpick. I'm trying to explain it in terms the simplest mind can understand.

All the while, Pinaruti kept reciting the spell and rereading what was probably the most complex spell in all his master's books. There were some words he didn't know exactly how to pronounce, but he got a series of sounds out that matched the characters in the writing. Then he looked down the list of possible demons he might summon.

I must say that in Knossos and on all of Crete, demon-summoning was a fairly new art. There were few known demons to summon and in a typically naïve act of overestimating his abilities, Pinaruti chose to summon Beelzebub, the most powerful demon whose name was written in the book. That is where the problem began, but wasn't really the problem it could have been if Pinaruti had been a competent mage. He didn't really believe this would work, as he had never seen the spell performed.

He had another bottle of wine as he looked at the sketches he had made over the years. In another day and age, Pinaruti might have been recognized as a typically socially inept artist. He had been drawing pictures for many years and sketched out exactly what he felt his demon would look like.

Over the course of several days, Pinaruti alternated between preparing the spell and watching the neighbor lady sunbathing. Drinking wine. He actually forgot to eat, so focused on his two tasks he was. They came up with a name for that kind of guy a few millennia later, but such people were in the world since day one.

The result was somewhat predictable, I'm afraid. Pinaruti began chanting the spell as he lit candles around the room. He stood on the point of the circle where he was supposed to be strongest. He looked at the picture he had drawn and pointed to the center of the circle as he commanded Beelzebub to appear and serve him.

That's where Pinaruti's drunken mind fell apart on him. He slurred the name of the demon he was summoning and instead of Beelzebub, he got Beetlebob. Me.

I'll have to say, he did a few things right. The image of the demon he manufactured in his brain and so carefully drew was a pretty good physical specimen, if I do say so myself. And I do. Strapping bulging muscles, broad chest, a fine pair of hooves on my feet, long claws for fingers, a proud set of horns on my head. And a good-sized chunk of meat between my legs that seemed to have a mind of its own. I immediately felt at home in my new body. I flexed my muscles, rolled my head on my thick neck, and crouched down to look at my master.

He did not look well. He was stammering and shuffling around in such a way that he was erasing parts of the chalk circle he'd so carefully drawn. It was obvious he was in shock. He kept pointing at me and gibbering as if he hadn't really expected me to appear. Actually, he hadn't, and the shock of seeing me materialize in the middle of the circle was too much for the old man. At this time, he was more than forty unremarkable years old, and was destined to grow no older. He clutched his chest, dropped his wine bottle, and pitched forward, landing squarely at my feet. Dead of shock.

The circle began to dissolve around me and I had to act fast. Pinaruti was my bridge into the world and I put my foot forward and stepped on him until I was out of the circle and free. I could see his hands beginning to dissolve with the circle and reached out to rescue his body. I wasn't a bad guy, even then. He brought me into this world. The least I could do was save him from being dissolved into the primordial mass from which I'd emerged.

But when I put my hand on his flesh, something amazing happened. I suddenly received a burst of memories from the old man, including how he'd summoned me, why, and the view from the roof. I snatched my hand back and his body faded away.

2
A New Me

▨▨▨▨▨▨▨▨▨▨▨▨▨▨

ERE I WAS, a brand new demon, cast adrift in the cold cruel world, alone, with no guiding hand to show me the way, no mother's breast to nurse me. Sob.

Um... That last was definitely implanted from Pinaruti's memories. I'm sure I wouldn't have thought of it otherwise. You see, in spite of the way I was endowed, I was not born a sex-craving monster. I had to work hard for that. Nor are demons inherently evil. We are brought into this world by magi who give us our instructions and implant the character we have. Pinaruti's intent to use me to air condition the king's house was pretty benign as far as good and evil are concerned. I have met plenty of people far more evil than any demon.

And I have met some—dare I say?—holy demons.

I suppose I should explain a bit about demons, or you will never understand the depth of my bewilderment when faced with the human world. Before Pinaruti summoned me, I did not exist. That is one of the things Pinaruti (and most magi of any sort) misunderstand. They spend their lives trying to discover the names of demons they might summon and control. Eventually, they come across a name in an ancient scroll or a name comes to them in a dream, and they set up an elaborate summoning spell.

In some cases, they stumble upon a demon who has been summoned before and therefore has a personal identity. As long as that demon's name is known and he is not in use by someone else, he can be summoned. Inevitably, the frightened mage dismisses the demon to hell, and that is where the demon waits until the next time he is summoned.

I remember Jana, a perfectly delightful young beauty I spent several years with. We were close in more ways than the joining of our genitals. However, the sex act with Jana was unbelievable. She happened to meet me during a time when I was in my natural form, complete with horns, hooves, and huge phallus. I transformed into something less intimidating, but she begged me to keep a cock big enough to satisfy her. That took a lot.

Oh, was she a screamer! She sacrificed herself on my sword daily for many years, having created a fantasy tale in her mind that she was saving all the virgins in her village, then in the area, then in the country, by throwing herself onto my dick and riding hard until one or both of us passed out. She might have been the most enthusiastic lover I ever had, so committed was she to the salvation of her peers—or perhaps to keeping them away from me.

After one particularly loud and satisfying bout of sex, she lay in my arms and said, "Oh, Bob. I'm sure I'm going to hell for this. Tell me. Is sex like this in hell?"

"I don't know, Jana. I've never been there!"

"But... but you're a demon! Everybody knows they come from hell."

"Everybody is wrong. Many demons are *sent* to hell by their masters. The fellow summons a demon, uses him or her, and then needs to dispose of him. Hell is the common destination. But the first time we are summoned, we don't come from hell. We come out of the primordial mass. We don't exist before we are summoned."

"I love it when you talk dirty. Fuck me again, Bob!"

Well, she wasn't a great conversationalist, but it got the point across. Before Pinaruti summoned me, I was just part of the primordial mass of pre-creation. Once a magus learns to summon, he or she *could* summon anything into existence. I think, frankly, that is how hell came to be. I can think of no god who would have created it. We should all simply be thankful magi have such limited imaginations.

So, when Pinaruti summoned me, I was a brand new demon. I had no experience of the world. I took the shape that Pinaruti envisioned. But he never gave me a command—never sent me away before he died—and never infected my mind with evil. Yes, I captured as much of his memories as his fading body would yield, but I could easily identify them as his memories and not my own experiences. And Pinaruti wasn't particularly evil as magi go. He was just inept.

I was left on my own to discover the world and I set about doing so at once. The magic room into which I had been summoned contained Pinaruti's library of scrolls—six of them. Writing wasn't that common at the time, and so there weren't that many books. If people had known what he had in that room, he would have been considered a very wealthy man rather than a poor hedge witch. People came to him for cures to various ailments, love potions, charmed artifacts, and travel talismans. King Drakomaxos was the first to actually challenge him to a task that was of a true mage level.

In addition to the scrolls, there were shelves of potions, herbs, sacrificial animal body parts, mortar and pestles, and oddities of every sort. And wine. There were also scraps of food on the shelves that I took to be edibles and not magic substances. I quickly acquired a taste for wine and cheese and dried sausages. It took me nearly a week just to explore that room. Then I realized the room was not the entire world. It had a door!

The next room was a kitchen and the selection of food was somewhat better than in the magic room. I simply had no idea how to cook anything and discovered that even Pinaruti's memories had very little about the subject. The next room was a bed. Not a bedroom, but an entire room-sized bed. When Pinaruti had come to Knossos, he fancied that he would become a popular mage and would have women falling all over him. One woman actually did trip and fall over him, but she was quite unfriendly about it. Pinaruti's huge bed had no sign of conjugal relations having ever occurred there.

In the modest courtyard, the bread oven was tucked under the stairs to the roof. I kept exploring and found my first view of 'the world!' It was amazing. And a little frightening. Up until that very moment, my world had all been contained in Pinaruti's house and court-yard. Imagine seeing houses in one direction as far as the eye could see. And in the other direction, mountains like a wall around the world. In another direction, the sea, sparkling in the afternoon sunlight. And opposite the sea, fields of olives, grain, grapes, and sheep. The world was huge! I couldn't comprehend it all and stood on the roof watching my surround-ings until it grew dark and I saw stars in the sky.

I have to tell you: I get a little choked up about this even today. I'm just a sentimental little demon. I swore I would see every inch of this remarkable world. I would discover all its wonders. I didn't bother with Pinaruti's huge bed. I spent the night on the roof, gazing at the stars. What a remarkable world!

I spent a few more days mapping my surroundings in my mind. This also began my fascina-tion with mapping the stars and learning to know where I was located by their position in the sky. That became a bit of an obsession that I have had ever since. Which is why the stars in the infinity room... Well, let me get to that in a minute.

I learned every detail of Pinaruti's house and had even explored his plan for cooling the king's chambers. As brilliant as it was in some ways, it was also disgusting. To me. His original plan was to enchant a bottle in such a way that he could command me into it and I would have to stay there until summoned again. From that point, I would be called upon to cool the king's house. He had no idea how I would go about accomplishing that feat. It was supposed to be my problem.

What really put my nose out of joint was that he'd just grabbed a bottle, drank the last of the wine, and cast the enchantment so that I'd fit in it. Barely. With the dregs of the wine. But the process of creating that bottle room led him to another thought. Why not sim-ply imprison his pet demon in the walls of the king's house. Then he could simply command me to keep it cool and walk away. I was insulted by his lack of care and loyalty to the being he had created. He actually used the word 'imprisoned' when describing how he would use me. I admit to a moment of being glad he was dead. Rest his soul.

No, sir! I was not going to spend the rest of my life—eternity if you will—imprisoned in the walls of a dead king's house! If I was going to cool his house... Well, I wasn't exactly sure how I'd do that. It was the middle of summer and was definitely hot enough to bake bread without a fire in the oven. I learned that expression much later in life. At the time, I had no idea how to bake bread. It was cooler at night, so I supposed I could cover the house in darkness and it would be cooler. That was the best idea I could come up with at the moment.

I was lying on the roof, contemplating the problem of cooling the king's house, when I heard a pounding on the door. I cautiously peeked over the edge of the roof to see what was going on. Remember, I had yet to have any human interactions since Pinaruti so conveniently died after my summons. What I saw, chilled my bones.

King Drakomaxos stood at the door with his entire army—now grown to four goons with bows and spears—behind him.

"Pinaruti! Your year is up! Come out now and cool my house!"

Of course, there was no answer and I was not about to give one. The king was not going to take silence as an answer. He kept pounding and demanding and finally told his soldiers to break the door down. It may have been my sentimentality that took offense at that. This was Pinaruti's home. Mine now. I closed my eyes and focused on the door, reciting the sealing spell Pinaruti had intended to use on the bottle with me in it. To my amazement, the four soldiers rammed into the door and were repulsed to lie in a heap on the other side of the street. Immediately, soldiers from the kingdom across the street met them and began to repulse the invasion of their kingdom.

It was fascinating and I watched from the rooftop wondering at what had caused the fight. At some point, one of the soldiers, or perhaps it was an interested bystander cheering them on, spotted me on the roof and raised a ruckus. Eyes raised to meet mine and fingers pointed in my direction. I waved, thinking it would be best to put on a friendly face. The king raised alarms, pointing.

"An evil beast has killed the wizard Pinaruti!" the king exclaimed. "Protect our kingdoms and kill the evil beast!" Not friendly at all.

"No, no!" I yelled as the first volley of arrows flew toward me. I swatted them away with my hand. "I'm not an evil beast. I... I'm just here to bury my old friend Pinaruti. He passed away, you see..." Another volley of arrows answered my plea. I pulled back. I was trapped inside and frankly did not know how long the sealing spell would last.

I ran to a different edge of the roof and looked down into my neighbor's courtyard. That would have to do. I needed to escape and run away. I didn't want to hurt anyone.

I dropped into the neighbor's courtyard to look for an escape route. I found women. There were screams and they ran away. All except one. She'd been bathing and stood in a small tub of water, soaking wet and completely naked.

I'd never actually seen a naked woman before, though I had memories of Pinaruti gazing on his neighbor's wife. The reality of being face-to-face with her was quite different than Pinaruti's muddled memories. My body began to react instantly and the phallus that usually dangled between my legs suddenly rose of its own accord to salute the naked woman.

"Blushing Aphrodite!" she exclaimed. "Would you look at that! It puts my husband's wee probe to shame. I want it!" With that, she leapt at me, wrapping her arms around my neck and her legs about my waist as her wet and hairy groin bounced against my stiff prick.

I wanted to stop right there and enjoy the new sensations a while, but the shouts were now outside *her* front door. I ran for the wall of her courtyard and leapt into the next property, finding I was more than capable of jumping over the privacy walls of the city. When

I landed in a crouch, my new lady friend groaned as she impaled herself on me. I groaned as well and thrust up into her as she wailed in ecstasy. That wail brought the ladies of the current house out. Some ran screaming back inside, as others clamored for 'Ariane' to hurry up and share. As delightful as it was to see ladies rushing to disrobe, I was frightened of what was behind me. I ran into the house, as soldiers shot arrows over the wall. Three naked ladies followed me out into the street with Ariane still snugly impaled on my prick. I began to run away from the area, out into the countryside toward the mountains I had seen from the rooftop. It seemed word of our flight traveled faster than we did and women rushed out of doors all along our path, struggling out of their clothing as they ran.

Ariane's continued wailing about how I was killing her did nothing to slow down her concentrated bouncing on me. I could feel her fluids running down my running legs even as I felt myself near a bursting point. So *that* was what Pinaruti's fantasies were of! I was well out in the country when my first ever climax overcame me and I exploded inside her. This time her wail was so loud (and possibly accompanied by my own primal bellow), sheep in a nearby field all turned and fled from us, causing the shepherd a moment of panic as he rushed to recapture his flock.

Ariane passed out and went limp in my arms—something I was not likely to do yet. It was just as easy to carry her with an arm wrapped around her and her female parts tightly welded to my male part. I simply kept running.

We'd left the soldiers and the City of Knossos in the distance as I climbed higher into the mountains, still running in fear from the unexpected violence. I gasped for breath as I climbed and finally saw a cave into which I could duck and hopefully rest for a while. It seemed comfortable—much cooler than the midsummer heat I'd run through. I stumbled in and sank to the floor, stretching out on my back before realizing Ariane was still impaled and just beginning to come around.

"Ah, who are you who has captured my soul and made it your own?" she breathed as she began kissing my chest. I liked that feeling and would have returned the gesture, but she was considerably shorter than I was. As she kissed, she began moving up and down my pole again.

I was ready to enjoy her and to quickly declare undying love by giving her my name. But something stopped me. Pinaruti had summoned me into this world with that name and somehow, it had some power over me I should not share lightly. Even with a woman whose pussy was doing such nice things to my cock.

"Um... I guess you can call me Bob," I said. "And you are Ariane?"

"Yes, Bob. And I'm yours. Just fuck me unconscious again and again!"

"I'm happy to get to know you... um... your pussy. You feel really good. I've never experienced such a delightful sensation."

"Oh, my! Am I your first? Oh! I can't believe I've taken a demon's virginity! You are splitting me in half with your pole and I love it. I've certainly given you parts of me that have never been touched before. Please say you'll take me with you wherever you go," she said.

"I don't know how all this stuff works, but I'm about to go again right now. You feel so fucking good! Here I come!"

"Oh, my demon! I'm full to overflowing. I'm never going back to that foolish old man. I'm with you now!" With that, her body began to quiver and pulse as she once again shrieked out a climax. Finally, we lay sated for the moment and she used me as a mattress as we slept.

3

THE DIKTEON CAVE

SOMEONE WILL SURELY go off on me about what order things occurred in and when I was born. That's why I'm not going to cite dates as a matter of course, as if this was a high school term paper. I thought time was an easy thing that I marked by sunrise and sunset. We didn't have a calendar in ancient Crete that said 2076 BCE. Someone might have told me it was in the third year of King Drakomaxos' reign, but you wouldn't know him anyway. Time of the modern calendar sort is a relatively new invention. In reality, time isn't linear. It jumps all over the place, and so do I. So, just go with it, okay? The same is true of distance. How far can I travel in a day? It depends on how long the day is.

Besides, it's irrelevant to this part of the story. I think. Just remember that I was running for my life from Knossos with a naked woman riding shotgun on my unceasing erection. I might have run like that for days or for a few minutes. I was panicked. I ended up in a cave on a mountain. I have since learned Crete is an island, so I can safely say that since I didn't cross any bodies of water, I was still on the island of Crete.

In a cave.

I'm not going to tell you this cave was the *actual* birthplace of Zeus. He didn't say. Nor will I say this is where he brought Europa and lived with her as they brought forth their three sons. I'll only say that he seemed to have a strong presence in this cave. That I found it at all was indicative of divine guidance. It was replete with water, a store of vegetables and dried meat, and lay just above a plateau of wild crops and game to supply our needs. We couldn't fuck all the time and Ariane, being human, required food and water and, eventually, she wanted clothing—which I reluctantly gave her.

I have since discovered that I can go for long periods—possibly forever—without food, drink, or sleep. But I indulge in all three for the sheer pleasure they bring. Much like fucking. I *could* go without, but why?

Some people in Knossos would tell you Ariane wasn't the most beautiful woman in the city. To me, she was the first woman I saw in all her splendor, and you never forget your first. She was as fascinated with my sex organ as I was with hers. We would finish fucking and she would roll to the side, swearing she was broken and would be unable to go again until she'd healed after two or three weeks. Half an hour later, she would be stroking, licking, and riding my cock like it was the first time she'd discovered it.

But, like I said, she needed food and clothing. Not wanting to deplete the supplies in the cave that certainly must belong to someone, we happily hunted and gathered side-by-side.

"How," I asked as we licked berry juices from each other's face, "did you know I was a demon?"

"Great Minos! What else could you be? Just look at you! No human man looks like you do. Or is hung like you are, I'm sure!"

I was puzzled. I tried jumping out of my skin to turn and look at myself, but it never seemed to work. How was I to know what I looked like?

Ariane figured out my dilemma and took me to a lake where I could look into the water and see myself. I jumped back in fright the first time I saw my reflection. I knew I had horns and hairy legs, but seeing them for the first time was startling. I was certainly not like any of the men I'd seen outside Pinaruti's door. I was far more handsome. I had large ram's horns on my head, a little pointed beard on my chin, hairy legs with hooves, and muscles that rippled beneath the otherwise smooth skin of my torso. I preened a bit and could only just imagine how I might seem frightening.

"Oh! This is just how Pinaruti imagined me when he summoned me. I saw a drawing," I said. "I suppose, though, that it will make it difficult for me to walk among men without being attacked. Do they always attack people who are different from them?"

"Yes, I'm afraid so." That was my first lesson in human interaction. The anger and violence shown to me by King Drakomaxos and his soldiers was typical of humanity. "At the very least," Ariane continued, "we would need to find clothes for you. Of course, we left so suddenly that I came away naked as well. I'll need to find clothing. Appearing naked like this would give men the wrong idea."

"I have an idea," I said. I caught her in my arms and began to probe at her with my stiffening cock. She locked her legs around my torso, keeping her pussy just beyond where I could penetrate it.

"That's what I mean," she laughed. "We wouldn't want every man we meet to start plundering my pussy." I was about to suggest that I'd kill them, but Ariane did the most remarkable thing. She pressed her lips against mine and then she pressed her tongue into my mouth. For a few moments, I lost all my senses to this new experience. As we kissed, she relaxed her grip and gradually slid onto my pole. I had to bend almost double to get my entire length into her while still maintaining contact with her lips and tongue. I knew at once that this was something I would like all my life, no matter how long it was.

And that was my first lesson in morality. Not the kiss, but my visceral reaction to the idea that other men may plunder her pussy. And it wasn't that I owned her pussy. It was that anyone might take it without her consent. As much as I abhorred the thought of her being raped, the thought of killing a man, even for so heinous a crime, caused me to pause and consider the value of a human life. Yes. I decided a man who raped a woman deserved to die. There might be other such crimes as well. But I was not a bloodthirsty demon.

I killed a couple of sheep under Ariane's direction, and she efficiently butchered them and dried the meat over our fire. It would have been difficult if she had not explained that she needed a knife, which I was able to fashion out of a glassy rock. She also prepared the skins, and before long, we each had a breechclout that we could wear if we encountered any other people. She managed herself a vest as well, but I kept trying to position myself so I could see her breasts under the skin. She finally gave up, laughing about how in some things I was a typical man. She removed her vest and breechclout and we only put them on when we went to trade with a nearby village.

That proved a little embarrassing when we had a guest one day.

"So, who's screwing around in my cave?" the great one bellowed.

"Oh, Zeus Almighty!" Ariane said, flattening herself against my chest. It took a lot of pressure to flatten herself. The boobs kind of squished out to the side.

"Hi!" I said. "I'm Bob."

"Hmm. So, you're the one," Zeus said, settling himself on a chair I hadn't noticed before. In fact, the whole cave seemed better furnished than it had been before. And there were little minions running around serving drinks and food. "I heard there was a demon on the loose. That's why I came down to investigate for myself. What am I going to do with you?"

"Do you need to do something with me?" I gulped.

"Well, we don't usually allow stray spirits to wander around among men. You already caused a riot in Knossos. No, no. I understand it was an accident and nothing you did, though that girl's husband, Basarti, is a bit upset. He's already remarried. Uh... That cute little nymph you had waiting on you," Zeus said to Ariane who had relaxed enough that her boobs were once again standing proudly in front of her.

"Well, that's okay," Ariane said "I feel sorry for her with no more satisfaction than he can give with his little member. If you see her, please let her know I kept a long gourd hidden behind the pantry that works pretty well."

"I'll pass that on. Or you can when you go back."

"Go back?" we both said at the same time. We linked our pinky fingers and made a wish.

"You left a mess and you have to clean it up. Nice sealing charm you put on the place, by the way. Nobody can get near it. Property values are falling. People claim the place is haunted and that you are still inside. Some women won't go outside for fear they'll be kidnapped by the demon. And some have taken to wandering the streets, hoping," Zeus said.

"But if I go back, they'll hunt me down and kill me!" I said.

"About that. It's really not easy to kill a demon, though they might make you suffer a bit. And you could learn to hide your appearance."

"Really? How?"

"You are a babe in the woods, aren't you?" Zeus said, shaking his head. In an instant he shifted forms from the stately god to a swan, to a bull, and back again. "Will and word. And for you, that means learning the spells. You can change your appearance and become a good-looking guy, still adequately hung to satisfy the likes of Ariane there, but not frightening."

"I could look like you?"

"Don't! Let's work on the spell and figure out what model you should use. Don't use an animal. It's hell changing back to this form if you can't speak the spell. We'll decide what else you need to survive in the world without creating any more disasters."

That began my period of instruction under the great Zeus. It seems he was bored, having taken a vow not to interfere in the affairs of men. But educating a demon did not have anything to do with human affairs. He stayed with us for several days or weeks or some amount of time. It's hard to keep track when dealing with a god. In her devotion to me, Ariane took it upon herself to make sure Zeus's needs were also satisfied. In fact, she went to the local villages and recruited a few young women to come and spend time with us. Zeus managed to teach me during the times when Ariane was gone, but when she returned, she was just too distracting for me to learn anything.

The girls! Aside from a few fleeting glimpses of women tearing their clothes off as we fled, Ariane was the only fully naked woman I'd ever seen. When she lined six beauties up in front of Zeus and me and had them strip, I was lost.

"They're all the same but so different!" I exclaimed.

"That's what makes them so hard to resist," Zeus agreed. "It's like having seven pieces of sweet fruit on the table before you. You know they are all tasty, but each one will be a little different. And having tasted one, you would not want to make it the only fruit you tasted with so many other available. That's why we males need a variety. Being fed only one fruit for all our lives would become dreadfully boring."

"I am devoted to serving Bob," Ariane said. "And as our guest, I happily service you, too. But I will always make sure Bob has a variety so his appetite never dwindles."

"I'd have you give lessons to Hera, but I'm afraid she'd corrupt you," Zeus sighed.

And then the party began and the seven women made sure we had each sampled their fruit. I'm not sure how often Ariane traded them out, but between sessions, Zeus taught me like a father. He told me exactly how an immortal like me could be killed or controlled. It is false to assume immortal means the same as 'can't be killed.' That is invincible. But an immortal doesn't die of natural causes. He or she can, however, be killed. Both of these concepts, I decline to write down here as I've no desire to be either killed or controlled.

Zeus taught me how to transform myself into different visages, and how to transmute one substance into another. Both spells had the same limitation in that eventually the sheep turd I turned to a gold disk would return to being a sheep turd. Just as I would eventually return to my demon self.

"What I don't get is how Drakomaxos ever expected Pinaruti to cool his home. Even if Pinaruti had succeeded in putting me in the walls, I don't know what I' have done to make it cool!" I said in frustration. "It's always nice and cool here in the cave. We can dry meat on the rocks outside when it's so hot. There must be some powerful magic in these walls."

Zeus groaned.

"Think for a minute about what is missing in the cave that hits the rock on which you dry your meat," he finally said. He liked to make me figure out things myself, but I wasn't the fastest chariot in the race.

"Rain!" I said. He groaned again and motioned me to try again. "Dust? Sunlight!"

I swear all the minions in the cave sang a choral descant to Zeus's "Yes!"

We took a break for a while and fucked the entire troupe of new girls Ariane had recruited.

"So," I said, after we'd partied for a day or two. "I could cast his house into darkness. That was my first thought because it is cooler at night when the sun is not shining."

"You'd be stuck there holding it in darkness. That would have worked if you were confined in the walls according to Pinaruti's original plan. And people would get depressed at living under the shadow," Zeus said. I looked at him blankly. "Rock, you idiot! What keeps the cave cool is layers and layers of rock blocking the sun."

"Drakomaxos should live in a cave!" I was jubilant. But caves were in the mountains and his kingdom was in the city. "I wonder if I could just build him a cave around his house. Take a lot of rocks and surround it."

"Try it a few times and see what happens," Zeus said. "The trick will simply be to keep them stacked on top of each other without falling in on him."

Well, Zeus said he needed to appear on Olympus before Hera came looking for him again. Ariane begged him to marry us before he left.

"Bob? You want to be married to Ariane?"

"Oh, yes, sir!" I said happily.

"Well, a demon has as much right to be miserable as a god." Of course, simply saying we were married wasn't enough to satisfy Ariane. She needed a formal procession and to be attended by the women who had serviced us during the god's stay of—I have no idea how long he was with us. Anyway, eventually he pronounced us married, warning Ariane that I was immortal, but she wasn't. That was a sobering thought.

Then Zeus paraded a bunch of images in front of me that I might choose to transform into. I felt Ariane's heart flutter when Adonis passed by and so I chose to transform into his likeness. Zeus snickered. And then he left.

At that, all the women who had been with us fell upon us and we had a long fuck-fest. At the end of which, I gave each woman a sack full of gold that I was certain would stay gold for a few years. Long enough to be a rich dowry for each of them.

Ariane and I prepared to return to Knossos.

4
THE PAIN OF BEING HANDSOME

S ARIANE might be recognized when we returned to Knossos, I took the time to work a transformation on her as well. Mostly I just made her appear younger and changed her hair color. There'd been a blonde among the village girls we both liked a lot, so I gave her blonde hair and big tits. She made me trim them down a little so she could walk without falling over forward, but she was still a fine-looking woman and a suitable companion to my Adonis image.

We made our plans and set a date to return to Knossos. First, we needed to fully explore and appreciate our new bodies. Ariane said she missed my horns because they gave her something to grab onto when I was pounding into her. I kind of missed the old Ariane, but I latched onto her boobs and started sucking away. Her frame wasn't much different than the old Ariane. She was still short by my standards, but she was a lot more flexible. So was I. We could kiss while we fucked. And she'd made sure I didn't alter my man-meat. She was still claiming I was killing her when I came in her tight little hole, but then she'd ask for more.

"You're okay just being called Bob," she said to me as we were ready to leave. "I can't go claiming to be Ariane, though. Aside from the hair and the boobs, I'm about the same as I was a few years ago. You should call me Aria. I've always liked the sound of that."

It was agreed and we left.

During our sojourn in the mountains, we'd acquired quite a wagonload of skins, pottery, dried fruits, and smoked meats, which I pulled down the street to Pinaruti's house. I was mumbling the spell that would take the seal off the door.

"Be careful there," Basarti from next door said. "Some demon put a spell on that place and no one can get in."

"I have a key," I said. Aria snickered as Basarti cast a puzzled look at his former wife.

I pushed the door open and there was a swoosh of stale air as we went inside.

"I need to air it out," Aria said as she rushed to the windows and opened the wooden shutters. Once the door to the courtyard was open, a hot breeze began to flow through the house, lifting the odors of rotted food and dried herbs.

"There's a bin in the back we can dump the old food into," I said. "You do that while I empty our cart."

There were already street urchins poking their fingers into my cart and I chased them all away, reminding them there could still be a demon in the house. The skins, pottery, grain, and dried meat were all soon inside and Aria efficiently put them away.

"What a huge bed!" she exclaimed. "Has it ever been used?"

"I don't think so. Pinaruti seems to have had all his fantasies on the rooftop, looking at the neighbor's... um... you."

"I always knew he was up there. I made sure the girls paraded around naked, or that I was in the bath when he needed relief. It seemed like a neighborly thing to do—as long as I didn't have to touch him," Aria said. "Let's try it out and see if it's as comfortable as it looks." With a quick flourish, she stripped off the dress she'd traded for at the village, and we jumped on the bed and on each other.

Aria and I always seemed about a heartbeat away from having sex. It was a good life.

Of course, word of my arrival spread rapidly and it wasn't long before King Drakomaxos came pounding on my door—this time with his army of a dozen thugs behind him. After my previous appearance in Knossos, things had improved for Drakomaxos. He'd acquired the kingdom next door. This was done by the simple expedient of having his soldiers kill or capture the soldiers from the neighboring kingdom who had joined them in chasing after me. As soon as they were out of the way, he marched over ten streets and captured the former king, claiming the kingdom his by right of having fought off the invading army. His third wife was the daughter of said king.

"The former owner of this property left without paying his taxes," Drakomaxos announced imperiously. "If you are his heir and are to enjoy the protection of our royal state, you must pay up the back taxes. Are you a magus?"

All the time, the king was trying to get a good look into the house around me. Word that I had an extraordinarily beautiful wife had circulated as fast as word that I was extraordinarily handsome. There were always people—men and women both—making long detours past our house to try to get a glimpse of Aria or me.

"No. I'm not a mage," I said. If I admitted to having magic, my peaceful life would be over and there would be a non-stop flow of people wanting warts healed. "I'm something better."

"Better than a mage? See here now. I'm the king. You can get no better than that!"

"No. But I'm an architect. That may not be as good as a king, but it's far better than a mage. I build things."

"What kind of things can you build?"

"Well, have you noticed how hot it is here all the time? I know the secret to building a house—no, let us call it a palace—that stays cool all year round."

"You can do that? I command you to build me such a palace!"

"Oh, gentle my Lord, your Kingship, Sir. I will provide the knowhow and the plans because I owe you this tax. However, you must provide the place for the palace to be built, the materials, and the labor. A man has to live, you know."

"I have a kingdom. I will put everyone to work. What materials do I need?" Drako was getting enthused and wasn't thinking straight. If everyone in the kingdom worked at building his palace then everyone would soon be naked and starving. But I continued to lay out the plans.

"Stones," I said. He looked at me blankly. "Each stone must be cut from the quarry bed at exactly a cubit square. The laborers must bring the stones to your building site and place them as I direct. You, oh, mighty King Drakomaxos, will have a palace envied by all other kings."

That was really all it took. Drakomaxos was sold on the idea. He fretted about how he would pay for labor.

"I will raid the next kingdom and acquire slaves to do the labor," he stated boldly.

"Your Majesty," I said sadly. "It is well known in the mountain kingdom from which I come that a house built by slaves will one day collapse on its owner. Labor must be cared for and paid."

"How can I pay for such labor?"

"Let us start small. Find me six strong men and promise them one of your coins for every hand of days they work." Drako had established a kind of currency he called a coin that had his image stamped on a disk of metal. It looked sort of like his image. If you turned the coin upside down, it looked rather like a horse's ass.

When Drako had drafted six laborers who agreed to his terms, they joined me at the site outside of town I'd identified as appropriate to cut the sandstone for the palace. The very first day they cut into the rock, they uncovered a seam of gold in the stone. This, they mined, enabling Drakomaxos to pay for workers and to buy the land for his palace. He even managed to talk a couple of neighboring kings out of their kingdoms without having to invade. Amazing what a little gold will do. And I was reasonably certain the spell I'd cast on it would keep it gold for at least twenty years before it turned into sandstone again. Drakomaxos forged it into little disks and stamped his image on it. The Drako became the common currency for all of Knossos.

I didn't want to do a lot of work myself, which is why I agreed only to supervise. That light little job, however, was rife with difficulties. I needed to supervise the cutting of the stones, the clearing and prep of the palace site, the payment of workers, and the actual construction of the palace. And labor troubles... Bah! The stones were heavy. The weather was hot. The days were long. None of that was my fault, but I had to deal with the problems.

I did do a couple of things that I thought up myself. For example, I built a couple of sleds for moving the sandstone from the quarry to the palace site. I cast a spell on them so that no matter what was put on the sled, it would weigh no more and be no harder to pull than when empty. I dug a pool near the quarry and filled it with water. Three times a day, I gave all the workers a break to go take a dip in the water. That kept them cooler and generally happier.

It didn't make the cutting and lifting of stones any lighter or the work any easier, but the laborers seemed to be happier. Especially, when they were paid in Drakos. I revised my timing, promising to be done in ten years instead of twenty. I didn't want to be around when gold started turning to sandstone. And I didn't want to risk having my body change back to its natural form before I was someplace safe.

My body—and Aria's—was creating enough problems for me. I got home one evening to find three naked beauties kneeling on the floor next to my bed. Aria simply fed me and chatted about the day, while totally ignoring them.

"Aria, dear, what are they doing here?" I asked, gesturing to the naked ladies.

"Oh. They just showed up today, totally starstruck. They were taking lunches to the laborers at the quarry today, hoping to attract one of the strong young men as a mate. Apparently, a 'godlike man' rose up out of the water in the pool and dried himself in the sun. They were all so struck by his beauty that they sought out his home to offer themselves to him. Did you have a swim today, love?"

"Um... I might have. It was a terribly hot day."

"Well, it was not unnoticed. Maybe this body wasn't the very best choice. Do you know what I saw last night?" Aria asked, still ignoring the nymphs by the bed. "That little slut Nimia who married my former husband was up on her roof last night, watching us make love in the courtyard. From what I saw, she has probably rubbed her nubbin raw."

"Oh, dear. I really don't want any problems with Basarti."

"Of course not. But the house is getting a little small, don't you think? Where there are now three little sluts waiting by our bed, I'm sure in time there will be six or ten or a hundred. Where *will* we put them all!"

"Do we really need that many?" I could see no end of problems with a harem of women wanting a little more room, a private well, a pool, or what have you. I was sure Drakomaxos would not look kindly on it, either.

"How can I turn them away when they've seen you, my handsome husband? We would have a houseful of men as well, if they hadn't all seen you swimming. They've given up on me because they are unable to compete."

"We really can't have a houseful of men," I sighed. "Not that I would object to one or two if you need them to keep you satisfied. I know you enjoyed Great Zeus when he visited."

"Yes, but there is not a man in Knossos who could compete with god or demon. I know that no matter how many of these young beauties you fuck, you will still have a solid pole to satisfy your Aria."

With that, Aria crawled into my lap and proceeded to demonstrate to the young nymphs what I was capable of in satisfying her. Then one after another, the naked beauties kneeling at the bedside took their turns riding the staff of Adonis. Oh, what an incredible feast.

As I was seating myself into the third delectable bit, I looked to the side and saw one of the nymphs with her face buried between Aria's legs. Aria was writhing in pleasure.

"What is she doing?" I whispered to my lover.

"Oh, there's a limit of available equipment when there are several ladies and only one man. We have to satisfy each other while we are waiting for our turn."

"But you haven't a prick!" I said. I knew very well what it took to satisfy these women and it was solidly embedded in this girl's glorious pussy.

"We have tongues. They might not be as long or as thick as your prick, but they are agile."

"Show me!" I demanded. This was new information about sex and I was always interested in sex. The girl pulled her dripping pussy from my cock and lay on her back beside me. With a crook of a finger, she beckoned another girl between her legs and I watched as the slut's greedy tongue slipped out and probed every aspect of her friend's pussy. Fascinating. While she worked on her friend's pussy, I got behind her for a better view and just slipped into another welcoming pussy. I pumped while she licked and we had a great time.

I resolved that I would find a time to practice this little stunt myself.

It did not take ten years to build Drako's new palace. It did not even take five years. He was pleased. It was cool. He tiled the floors with pretty designs and they were cool, too. The walls, made of stone as thick as a man's arm is long, kept the burning effect of the sun isolated. The workers who built it had enough gold to build themselves nice homes. The little Kingdom of Drakomaxos enjoyed great wealth.

For my part, I built another pool and a fountain near the quarry and opened a spa. The land around the spa became quite valuable and since it all belonged to Drakomaxos, he profited even more from the development.

Unfortunately, Aria's prediction of more women flocking to our little home came true. We bought Basarti's place next door and made him an offer to take it with everything in it, including his new wife and her maids. He took the sack full of gold Drakos and ran! We knocked a hole in the wall between our courtyards and Nimia rushed through and into our arms.

She was just as happy to be held by Aria as by me. She said she'd seen through her disguise at once and wondered if I was the new and improved version of her demon. We hushed her with our kisses.

I was glad Basarti was considered a small man. The various openings I was given to fill with my staff were all tight and slippery. And with Nimia, who I discovered had been a playmate with Aria before I came along, we had our own special games. I wedged my dick into her tight pussy while squeezing firm little titties in both hands. In the meantime, Aria threw a leg over Nimia's head and settled her pussy down on Nimia's mouth. We were both fucking the same girl at the same time and all three of us had a lively conclusion to our tryst.

I was not idle after working on Drakomaxos' palace. I had other things to do. I had the spa, of course, and satisfying the variety of women Aria brought into our house was another full-time job. But as a demon, I don't need much sleep. I've never tested to see how long I could go without sleep, but it could be forever. I just enjoy sleeping, cuddled with my women. Eventually, all my lovers would be exhausted and I could work in Pinaruti's magic room. I wanted to read all his magic books and examine all his plans so I could work magic I was not yet capable of. I was drawn back to his plans for either keeping me in a bottle or in the walls of Drakomaxos' house. Nether option was comfortable. I actually tried stuffing myself into a bottle and you can imagine the results. But as I read the scrolls, I found several spells that were relevant.

There was one spell in particular that attracted me. It was a strange spell that would make a room bigger on the inside than on the outside. We were once again getting crowded in our little house, even with the addition of Basarti's house next door. I really didn't want to draw a lot of attention to myself—or not more than was already being drawn by the women who entered the house next door and never emerged. Only Aria and I used the door to Pinaruti's house. Everyone else used the door to Basarti's house, as if it were in no way connected to ours.

Expanding the inside of our home without changing the outside seemed like a great idea.

I practiced the spell repeatedly on small things, among which was a leather satchel I'd found. It was good leather and it responded well to the spell. I began seeing how much I could put in the satchel. At first, I tried simply stuffing a few of the jars from Pinaruti's shelves into the bag. They went in with no difficulty. Bowls, ritual knives and other implements, mortars and pestles, and kettles. All went into the bag.

It was no heavier with all this in it than it had been when empty! I practiced other spells on the bag, making it impervious to water and sun, and opening up a gateway into it that was bigger than the bag itself. I also cast a look-away spell on it that would cause anyone but me to overlook it.

The bag wasn't making any of our rooms bigger, though, so I abandoned it for a while and went to work on the bedroom. Before long, I had expanded the bedroom and the bed enough that all thirty of us crammed into the little house could sleep there comfortably. The girls thought the whole room was just orgy central, and spent their time convincing me. I did the same thing for the courtyard and put in a private pool that would accommodate all of us for our baths. The girls considered it the orgy satellite and spent their time convincing me. The result was that that we had a house and harem that we could all fit into. The oven could hold bread for all of us. And we could all happily enjoy the bed together.

We were a happy lot.

I don't want to talk about what happened to Aria.

That girl was a marvel. I believe most of the women who were in our house were there as much for her as for me. She might have been the love of my life. But, as I discovered later, 4,000 years is a very long life and it has room for many, many, many loves. It is less than reasonable to assume any one woman could be the love of such a long life. But she was certainly my first love and one never forgets the first.

After she passed away, the household was in chaos until I married Nimia and made her the head of the household. I never regretted that decision.

⌨⌨⌨⌨⌨⌨⌨⌨⌨⌨⌨⌨⌨⌨

It was getting on to the time that I needed to move on or be exposed once more as the demon. I could feel the horns pressing against the inside of my skull.

Drakomaxos had a party to celebrate his newest wedding. Technically, at that time, monogamy was generally accepted, but some men of wealth and power had looked at the women in my harem and decided they need a similar variety of women. This was Drako's seventh and youngest wife—a real beauty and the daughter of the neighboring king. By that time, the plan and process of building palaces had been purchased from Drako by several neighboring kings, who also bought the sandstone from him. One king had paid the price with his daughter.

It was a long party and we might have all been a little drunk. Drako might have been unconscious next to me. His lovely new wife, Portia, might have been under the table pleasuring my cock with her mouth. She was near to getting dessert when I suddenly realized what was happening.

"Stop! Stop!" I hissed. "You just married Drakomaxos!"

"Oh, pish! He married me. I didn't marry him. I was traded for a scrap of paper and the promise of sandstone blocks from his quarry. I want this! I mean you. Take me with you, Bob. Let's leave this place. Let me be *your* wife."

It was against my better judgment, but I slipped an arm around Portia and left the party, with nearly everyone there still sleeping.

Once I was back in my own house, I realized what a terrible mistake I'd made. Drakomaxos was going to be upset. He would know I had stolen his bride. And I had no intention of giving the sleeping girl back to him. I went into the magic room and grabbed the leather satchel. Into it, I stuffed the scrolls from Pinaruti's library and everything else that remained in the magic room. I looked into the bag and couldn't see where everything had gone, so I stepped into it.

What a mess! Everything I'd put into it was there, but all jumbled up in a pile. I quickly worked a few transformation spells and before long had something resembling my house in the bag. I stepped out the door and into the magic room. I carried the bag into the rest of the house as all the little nymphets were awakening. I gave each one a couple of gold Drakos and shooed her out the door. All except Portia and Nimia. They clung to my arms and would not leave.

"Okay. If you refuse to leave me, you will need to be packed in my bag," I said. Neither girl flinched. "I need someone to keep my house and put everything in order." Both nodded. I held open the gateway and they stepped into the bag. I went around the house grabbing everything else that wasn't attached—food, pots, pans, wine, statues, and decorative pottery—and I reversed the expansion spells on the bedroom and the courtyard. I stuffed everything I encountered in the satchel.

I was about to leave when there was a pounding on my door. I looked out from the rooftop and saw Drakomaxos, backed up by his entire army of over a hundred thugs.

"Bob! Where are you? Where is my wife?" he demanded.

"Your wife?" I asked innocently. I could almost hear her giggling in the bag. "Did you look under the table? That was the last place I saw her at your palace." I thought that was an adequate qualifier to not be a lie. I hadn't looked at her after I pulled her from under the table and hurried her out of the palace until we got to my house. The last time I'd 'seen' her at his palace, she was under the table. Sucking on my cock.

"I know you have her, Bob!" Drako insisted. "Come out here at once! You and she will both be put to death for this betrayal."

"That's unkind of you," I said. "After all we've been through together? You'd do that to your old friend Bob?"

I was answered by a volley of arrows loosed from his soldiers into the courtyard of my home. That was enough for me. I grabbed the bag and skipped from rooftop to rooftop on my way out of town, interrupting more than one naked sunbathing woman who attempted to cling to me as I ran.

For the second time in my young life, I ran from Knossos ahead of Drakomaxos' army.

END OF PART I

Part II
Architect for a God

Image Credit: Fernando Cortes, ID173466851 licensed from Shutterstock.

5

CAST INTO THE SEA

ᴿOM THE DAY I was born, or created, or summoned from the primordial
mass, I have been in love with the sea. Of course, it wasn't literally that day. It was when
I was exploring the rooftop of my—or Pinaruti's—home, that I saw the sea, glistening miles
away and seeming to go on forever.

If you are a literalist and have visited the modern site of Knossos, and want to challenge my ability to see the sea from a rooftop in the ancient city, I encourage you to repair to hell. I am a demon. My eyesight is long. I saw the fucking sea!

As I was saying, I have always loved the sea. But I knew very little about it or what lay beyond it. So, when I left Knossos, I headed more or less directly to the sea, avoiding people as much as possible. As I walked along the northern coast of Crete, I watched the fishing boats and the sailing ships as they plied the waters, oars dipping into the waves, sails billowing with the wind. It was all quite romantic. I thought, what I would like to do is become a sailor.

The salt spray in my face, the wind in my hair, the smell of the sea all around me. Yes, I would describe it as romantic, and it represented my first boyhood dream of what I would like to be when I grew up.

I should mention that, as I wandered along the seashore, I did not simply ignore the babes in a bag. I had that bag on my shoulder all the time, and I wasn't about to lose control of it. And I knew I had responsibilities to my ladies. In fact, I had no idea how getting picked up and thrown over my shoulder as I ran from Knossos would affect the contents of the satchel.

It turned out, not at all.

I found a cave in a cliff face overlooking the sea and pushed the bag into it. 'Cave' might be a glorious term for the hole in the rock that I found. It was scarcely larger than the bag itself. That really made no difference, because I could still open a gateway into the bag and step through it even though the gateway was larger than the hole in the rock and the bag was smaller. It was one of the many mysteries of the bag that I was to discover over time.

I found Portia and Nimia happily arranging the replica of our home in Knossos and making sure everything was in order. So were the other three ladies.

"Who are they?" I asked, pointing at three very naked beauties who were helping with the tasks.

"You put them here," Nimia answered. "I guess there wasn't much choice. They were among the nymphs living with us, but one night we were all playing in the pool and they were being especially naughty. You said that as a punishment, you would turn them into stone for one day and they would have to watch everyone else playing without being able to join in. When we escaped from Knossos, you grabbed the statues and shoved them in the bag. It was only a little while later that they returned to themselves. We've been keeping them busy, but they're really horny."

"But you need to do me first," Portia said. "We hardly got started on our wedding night before that dirty old man came knocking on your door."

I remembered that. I'd brought her home with me after the wedding feast, but we'd been so drunk that she collapsed in bed before we finished what we were doing—and I wasn't going to finish without her. That's when I panicked and started packing up to leave. I sent everyone away, but when Drakomaxos came pounding on the door, I stuffed Portia and Nimia into the bag. With the statues. Ah well. There was nothing to do about it now but take Portia to the bedroom and finish the process of deflowering her. Once her maidenhead was gone, she became a sex maniac akin to what my dear Aria had been.

I learned a lot about what I came to call *the infinity room* in those hours—or days—or years. I don't know how long we were there. For all I know, time was running backward. Time in the infinity room is not in sync with the world outside. There is no sensation of time passing. The girls had happily worked setting up our house. They had eaten and slept. They worked and made love. But as far as they could tell, I'd only just put them into the bag and then followed them. We picked up conversations and tasks as if I'd just turned around.

I had a lot of work to do in studying the amazing room. I'd worked the spell, but apparently, I had no idea what was included in it. I was going to need to study the scroll and see if I could decipher some of the side effects. You know, that mumbo jumbo written on a prescription bottle that says, 'May cause diarrhea, swelling of the joints, double-vision, and other serious side effects, including death?' The fine print has been around as long as written documents have. In the scrolls, spells were carefully and clearly written, but the margins were filled with the notes of various wizards who had experimented with the spell and written a commentary on how they'd altered it or what their experience had been. Pinaruti's scrolls were already ancient when I retrieved them and had many margin notes.

I told the girls that I'd decided to become a sailor and they were all excited about taking a cruise. They'd each heard tales of various mythological places they wanted to visit. I agreed that I would try to find a map.

I left the infinity room and tossed the bag over my shoulder once again. As I traveled, I hunted or gathered fruit and grain, which I delivered to the babes in the bag. The girls put it away and rewarded me handsomely when I got home. It was getting easier and easier to consider the room home. The five wet and willing pussies were all the reward a man (or demon) could want after a hard day's labor.

Did you know that Minoa had the first navy in the world? It dominated the Central Sea for centuries. I suppose it started out as a couple of rowboats with an archer in the bow, but most of the traders were either Minoan, or were protected by the Minoan navy. The ships of the day were pretty much flat-bottom barges equipped with sails and auxiliary oars, but they floated and that was good enough for me.

I knew that if I wandered along the coast long enough, I would come to a place where the ships came to port. I felt, however, that the Adonis look had served more than its purpose and I could feel my horns pushing out. I wore a hood over my head as I traveled, looking for a good model for a new body. I needed something a little more down to earth, so to speak. Since I planned to go to sea, I searched along the coast for a fellow I thought looked handsome enough and strong enough to be a sailor.

I found him in a village drinking house where I had my first taste of sour beer. Personally, I liked wine better, but I learned to get along with the beer. I saw a fellow who matched the description I'd built in my head and had a drink with him. I found that he was a thoroughly boring young man with little to talk about other than the fish he almost caught. Nonetheless, I got his pattern set in my mind, and while he stood at the latrine to get rid of the beer he'd drunk, I whispered the transformation spell. By the time he was finished, so was I. He looked at me a little funnily and started to say something, but cut himself off. Finally, he said, "Sorry. Thought you looked familiar." Then he left.

So did I. I kept to the shadows until I was well away from the fishing village and found another cranny in the rocks where I could conceal the satchel and open a gate into it. I just had to show the girls my new body. They all wanted to test it to make sure it still functioned in a way that pleased them. I passed that test.

I came upon the seaport town of Mania where there was a big project of some sort going on. Hiring agents were bringing in laborers from all around the district. By bringing them in, I mean they tapped their intended laborer on the head until he could no longer resist, and dragged him to the king's work camp. They decided that a strong young man like me should become a laborer and attempted to tap me on the head as well.

Apparently, the thugs sent out to recruit help had never run into someone who tapped them back.

I considered my options as I looked at the two unconscious men at my feet and read their memories. I hadn't done much of that since reading Pinaruti's memories from his dead body. These were even less pleasant. In fact, reading the list of heinous acts the two had committed convinced me they had no need for their liberty. I stripped them of their clubs and clothing, tossed them over my shoulder, and took them to the bounty office. I dumped them on the floor.

"I have two to turn in," I said. The bursar looked at me skeptically and glanced at the men. It was obvious he recognized them.

"And why are you not on the work crews. I'll send for my men and have you stripped. Then I can collect the bounty on all three of you," he laughed, moving to call for reinforcements.

"I tap harder than they do," I said, lifting the surprised bursar off his feet and out from behind the desk. He spluttered in surprise as I stared him in the eye.

"No offense intended. No offense. It was a joke," he stuttered.

"I don't have a sense of humor."

"Let me just get you your money!" I set him back down at his desk and his hand shook as he pulled two strange coins from his pouch and placed them on the table.

I'd lied to him, but had no remorse. I actually have a very good sense of humor for a demon. I love a good joke. I convinced him that I was humorless and considered that to be a joke on him.

"What's the king need all the workers for?" I asked.

"He's got a stone quarry and says he's going to build a grand palace. Needs more laborers to move the stone because it's that heavy, don't you know. These two are a little on the scrawny side for laborers, but we'll use them. Now if you could collect us a few good strong fellows—like sailors—I'd be able to pay more for them."

I left the slave office and decided I needed to meet this king who was having so much difficulty.

⌷⌷⌷⌷⌷⌷⌷⌷⌷⌷⌷⌷⌷⌷⌷⌷

I had to tap several guards on the head before I finally got an audience with King Idiopheles.

"And what do you have to offer me besides your back and strong muscles?" the king demanded when I stood before him and presented my proposal.

"I hear you're having problems moving the stone for your palace. They do get pretty heavy. I built Drakomaxos' palace over in Knossos. I know how to get the stones moved and keep the laborers from revolting."

"I heard Drako's architect ran off with his wife," Idiopheles speculated as he squinted his eyes at me. "No. That couldn't have been you. He was said to be the most handsome man on the island."

"I think I'm pretty good looking, but I don't think I'd merit being called the most handsome man on the island. Drakomaxos and I had a disagreement about paying me once the palace was built. I collected what I was owed and left."

"What do you want in order to get my palace built? One of *my* wives?"

"Oh, no. Have enough of my own, you know. Want to fuck all the time. What I want is to become a sea captain. I need a ship and a crew and a captain who will teach me everything I need to know."

"Hmm. I see. Well, if that's all you want, I think we can make a deal."

I could read from his mind that the deal he wanted to make was to get me to build the palace and then sell me to a shipmaster. For the time being, though, I took the deal the way *I* intended it and set about building the sleds that would lighten the workers' loads.

Meeting the workers told me I needed to do more than lighten their loads. They at least needed better food. Strong men came to work and in a short time they'd become weak men.

"A house built by slaves will crumble about its owner's ears," I intoned to the king.

"Oh, fuck that. I'll grant them extra food, but they can be free after they've finished," Idiopheles declared. He had a lot of men at his disposal and his press gangs kept bringing in more. I didn't waste any time getting the palace built. It was bigger than Drakomaxos's, but once I lightened the loads, the building went quickly—especially as the men got stronger with better food and worked harder with the promise of freedom as soon as the project was built.

"Now, about my ship," I said as we toured the completed palace and he began moving in. I'd already dismissed the laborers and even managed to give them each a coin for their labor as they left. I wanted them all far away when the walls of this palace began crumbling. I was going to make sure of that.

"Oh, I have a captain who will take you on as a swab," Idiot laughed.

"I think you have misunderstood our deal," I growled. He looked at me and for a moment I simply let my horns show through. "When you make a deal with a demon, you should always keep it."

"Um... uh... A demon? Well, of course I'd keep my deal with a demon. I simply misunderstood the terms. A ship, you say. With a captain and crew. It will be ready for you in the morning at the wharf."

I nodded and walked away.

I knew he would still try to get out of it, but for now he had to scurry about and get a ship for me. I spent my time that night, wandering the city with a watchful eye, sticking to the shadows and watching the king's thugs looking for me. I wasn't quite invisible, but it would take a sharp eye to find me in the shadows. By the time the sun rose, a dozen weary thugs sat themselves at the wharf and watched for me to come and claim my prize. That told me which ship I should board. I stopped at the ship just before it and slipped aboard unnoticed. Sailors were untying the lines.

"When's this new sailor going to be here?" the captain of the next ship yelled. "The tide's going!"

That was all the signal I needed. I jumped from one ship to the other, landing lightly on the deck.

"I'm here and ready, Captain," I said from beside him. He was so startled he nearly fell backward off the ship, but I steadied him.

"Cast off!" he yelled. Our ship began to move, leaving the puzzled thugs standing on the wharf.

I happily bent to the tasks of learning the ship from the old captain. This was something I could do and not constantly make mistakes. It seemed I needed only to disconnect my mind from my body and let the body carry on with the tasks. I was happy and contented on the ship. The salt spray in my face. The wind in my hair. The smell of the sweaty sailors working around me. Well, everything has a down-side, I'm afraid.

I loved seeing the different ports we put in at, and soon learned that no matter where in the port I went, I needed to be back aboard my boat when the tide went out. At each port, I traded for goods, following the captain's example. Only the goods I traded for, I slipped into the satchel when I joined my girls at night. Having time with the girls was difficult. This 'ship,' as I indicated, was little more than a barge with a sail. There were no private quarters where I could secure the satchel and step inside. That had to be done in port.

I don't know how long I'd been sailing. Time was as meaningless to me at sea as it was in the infinity room. I was often the only one awake on the ship and seldom slept at all. It was, however, during one of those rare sleeps that I was visited in a dream.

Dreams were something new to me. I only slept when I was bored or drunk. Or fully sated. But this time, my sleep was invaded by a supernatural being.

I had dealt with gods before. Zeus visited me in the cave and I found him to be a very down-to-earth kind of deity. He liked human women as much as I did and we regularly drank and fucked whoever Ariane brought to us. And Ariane.

The golden being who visited me in my dream was different. He seemed to have no interest in human women at all. Or in anyone. He carried a golden shield and spear. He flew so fast that his legs looked like a storm tearing across the land, great wings flapping. Lions prowled by his side roaring above the tumult.

Every time I closed my eyes, this god would invade my sleep, gesticulating wildly and speaking in a tongue I could not understand.

"Why not just tell me what you want?" I asked the image one night. It froze with a puzzled look on its face, then vanished.

The next night, another shining man stood in front of me. I could tell, however, that this wasn't a god, but was some kind of messenger he'd arranged. He held a beautiful blue stone in his hands, smooth and highly polished. He handed it to me and I recognized a kind of map. I puzzled over it.

I'd built two palaces and had drawn plans for them. It didn't take me long to realize this polished piece of lapis was the divine equivalent of a drawing on a napkin, describing a plan for a kind of palace. I started to say something to the man but he had disappeared, leaving me the tablet. And I was awake.

I carefully put the tablet in my satchel, knowing the girls would find a good place for it.

This kept up for days. I didn't even need to be asleep, but everyone around me seemed to be snoozing when I was visited. I got maps. I got a brick mold. I got a drum I didn't know how to play. A stallion appeared before me and a chariot of silver and gold jewels on the ship deck. I couldn't let the men on the ship see these things, so I managed to hand them all off to the girls in the infinity room and they took care of everything.

Then, instead of the man, a woman appeared to me with a silver stylus, writing on a smooth clay tablet. I felt there was a command for me there, but I couldn't understand what it was. I was a kid! In terms of my life experience, I was a randy teenager. Life was about sailing and fucking.

As my frustrations grew over these continued visitations, the weather seemed to reflect my attitude. When I closed my eyes, I saw a tree with so many birds chattering in it that I would never be able to sleep. When I opened them, the waves were breaking over the bow of our little ship and the rain whipped across the deck.

"Are you going to sleep through your death?" the captain screamed at me. "Don't you care that we are all going to drown in this storm?" The boards of the ship creaked and threatened to break apart.

Then I saw the man again, in a flash of lightning pointing off the ship and I finally figured out one thing clearly.

"What gods do we need to sacrifice to? How will we save ourselves?" the captain continued.

"Pull yourself together, man," I said. I made sure my satchel was securely strapped to my side and straightened up. "You must throw me overboard. I'm the sacrifice that is demanded. Throw me overboard and the rest of you will be fine."

There was about thirty seconds of discussion as the men could hardly hold themselves back from doing what I ordered. The captain stood aside and they grabbed me. I considered making myself weigh as much as a horse, but none of this was their fault. I couldn't blame them for snatching at any hope to be saved from the storm. They heave-ho'd and I found myself in the water, swallowing as much as I swam through.

6
BUILD ME A TEMPLE

THE STORM immediately abated around the ship, but it was no better for me. A giant tentacle wrapped around my waist and squeezed until I could no longer breathe. I thought for an instant of how I could be killed and prepared for my return to the primordial mass. I whispered a little apology to my girls in the satchel and then the serpent flung me through the night sky.

It was my first encounter with one of Poseidon's tentacled monsters of the sea, but sadly would prove not to be my last. I loved the sea, but its god and I never got along all that well.

I'm sure I was only airborne for a few seconds... minutes at the most. But it seemed like I sailed through the air for days. I wished Pinaruti had thought to add wings to his image of me. Flying would be so cool.

Landing wasn't.

I hit the sand at the water's edge and just lay there gasping, still clutching my precious satchel. As I dried out in the sun, a weathered old man came up to me and nudged me with his foot to see if I was alive. I groaned.

"You look a mess," he said. "What kind of creature are you?"

I looked down at my legs and hooves. I reflexively touched my horns. Apparently, my midnight flight had stripped my latest body from me. The old fisherman didn't seem too concerned. Not the kind of response I'd expect, so I just went with it and told him honestly.

"I'm a demon. Sorry about the appearance. I usually try to clean up before I meet people."

"Oh. I see. Yeah, this shore is one that will wash up all kinds of things. I'm Theodoglus. You can call me Doug. Nice to meet you, demon."

"Bob," I said, by way of introduction.

"Yep. Saw a mermaid here once, Bob. She was right nice when I helped her back to the water. Quite a handful. Two hands full, in fact. Oh, and that god with a three-pointed spear. He shows up every so often to go have a drink in the village. Anything in particular you're looking for? Have anything to trade?" He sat in the sand beside me and broke off a piece of smoked fish to share with me. I noted he had a wineskin, too. After he saw me look at it, he offered some of that as well.

"I don't understand what's happening at all," I moaned. "Some god has been pushing me to build somebody a palace, I think. It all comes to me in dreams. Just don't hardly know what it all means." I was picking up some of his vernacular in my mind speaking, just from sitting beside him.

"Dreams, huh. I know just what you need." He looked away from me out toward the sea as he rubbed his fingers together. I tell you, the gesture for money is older than I am. At least I understood that. I reached down into my satchel and felt around until I found a bag of coins.

Feeling around in my satchel often involves feeling one of my women and I got a little distracted. Finally, however, Nimia understood my gesture and placed a bag of coins in my hand.

"I'm happy to pay for information. If you can tell me how to find out what my dreams mean, I'd gladly give you..." I looked in the bag and saw mostly pieces of sandstone. I dumped it out on the ground and sorted through it until I found a couple of actual metal disks. "...two silver Drakos. That seems to be all I have that's real."

"That's enough for me to tell you, you need to go see Nansi. She's about three days to the rising sun, next to the big river," Doug said, still eyeing the sandstone coins. "If you could turn a couple of those into silver, I could get you a donkey to ride. I know it's fool's ore and it will turn back into sand eventually, but the wine I spend it on will have turned to piss by then, too. So, it ain't my problem."

What a cagey scoundrel. I wondered how many other magical creatures he had encountered who gave him fool's ore. He seemed to know an awful lot about everything. Maybe he *had* met Poseidon. I worked the transmutation spell on a couple of the small disks and handed the silver coins to Doug.

"I don't really need a donkey," I said. "But a fresh wineskin and some food would be helpful. Maybe some clothes."

"Well, you best stay out of sight while I go fetch it. Most people are afraid of the magical beings," he said.

"But not you?"

"I've seen them all. Of course, nobody believes me. I'll take a coin into the bar and get the wine. Somebody will look at it and say, 'What did you see on the beach today?' and I'll say, 'A demon with big horns and hooves for feet. Chest as thick as a tree trunk and eyes like burning coals.' They'll all just laugh and say, 'Sure, Doug.' But they'll take the coin and give me the wine."

"Sounds like a good schtick."

"Just combing the beach to see what washes ashore."

I stayed out of sight. I couldn't depend on people to be as friendly as Doug. He got me wine, smoked fish, some cheese, and even a flat loaf of bread. Once I hit the road in the direction he'd indicated, I worked a transfiguration spell on myself and picked up the look of one of the hardier sailors I'd worked with—young and well-muscled, but not so handsome as to attract unwanted attention.

I walked all day and all night before I felt I was far enough away to hide and spend some time in the satchel with my girls. Not too much time, mind you. I didn't want this god-whoever-he-was to get angry and toss me into the sea again.

"So, all these things came from whoever this god is," I said as we looked at the drawings, maps, molds, horse, chariot, and the lapis diagram.

"You must be doing well to have a god giving you all these gifts," one of the statue girls said. "If you find a nice place to let me off, I'm ready for you to let me out of the bag. I love everyone here, but I want to see the world, not just be dragged through it in a bag."

"I'll do my best to find you a place. Where we are camped right now is not a good choice." The girls all attacked and drained me.

Now, if you've never had five nubile young women attack your cock and make sure it is drained, let me tell you that when they are done, you are *drained*. I would have been happy to just cuddle up to Nimia and Portia—which is where I ended up—but statues one, two, and three were undoubtedly the kinkiest of all the women I'd collected in Knossos. Which is why they'd been statues. If there was a position they could bend their bodies into, or a hole to be filled, they wanted it. I wasn't sure how they managed to get my cock into some of those places, but that didn't stop me from coming.

In the morning, I emerged from my bag and continued the journey eastward.

It's not like there were blinking lights and big signs that said, "Nansi: Get your dreams read here!" But her house was obvious by the number of gifts and statuary outside. And the line of people waiting to see her. I hadn't even thought about a gift for the seer. I reached in the bag and grabbed the first thing I found. It happened to be statue three. People were a little shocked to find a naked girl suddenly standing next to me. They gave me room and I quickly moved to the front of the line.

"I think this is your opportunity. I need to give a gift to the seer," I said.

"Oh, cool! Maybe she'll be pleased enough with me that she'll teach me to interpret dreams, too. That would be such fun."

"What is your name?" I hissed as we got to the door.

"Saris," she whispered. "The one with the lovely tight asshole."

I blushed as she said this just inside the door and just loud enough that I thought Nansi might hear her.

"I hope whatever dream you have brought me is worth the price of this lovely maiden with the tight asshole," Nansi said upon greeting us. "You would not believe how many men bring me a dead chicken and the story of a wet dream, hoping I will tell him he is destined to marry the subject of his fantasy. I usually tell them to continue raising chickens, because they are far more successful at that. I don't get many demons, though."

I quickly felt my head and glanced at my feet to be sure my latest body was still intact. Nothing was showing through.

"I guess we don't dream much under normal circumstances," I muttered. "How could I dream something better than what I have in my hands? But these dreams seem to be wanting me to do something and I don't understand what. Building a palace somewhere in the desert is the best I can come up with, but he shipwrecked me and threw me up on land so I'd come and find out what he's talking about. It's like we speak different languages."

A word about languages. I was born or created or summoned with the Minoan dialect ingrained in me because it came straight from Pinaruti's limited imagination. But I'd discovered in our trading ventures that people in other areas speak other languages. In fact, Doug didn't speak the same language I did. I simply pulled his meaning from his mind and gave him my meaning the same way.

It's a pain to learn all those languages, so most of the time I just kind of read minds and answered mind to mind. It didn't work with the god. That's why it was so frustrating with this god. It was like he could only communicate with words and I didn't understand them.

A few centuries (millennia?) later, I finally learned English so I could write my memoirs. I like the language because if you don't have a word for something, you just borrow one from a different language, or make it up on the spot. Remember my term omnimnemonic? I'm still proud of that one.

English was so much easier than German, where you can make up words, but the entire definition has to be contained in the word. I'd be der Dämoncarryinginfinityroomwanderingtheworld. See what I mean?

I didn't have any difficulty communicating with Nansi, though. Her words seemed to carry the definition straight to my head and she had no trouble understanding anything I said as I described the sequence of dreams. I even pulled the lapis slate out of my bag to show her the plans.

"I see," Nansi said after she'd examined the gifts and listened to my dreams, and let Saris get her robe open enough to get a hand on her bosom. "Ninra is tired of playing second tier war games and wants to establish himself as the patron of Bathra. Ninra is the golden god with wings and a storm for his body. He has two lions with him that will attack and destroy his enemies. The palace he wants built is a temple where people can worship him. The lapis slate has the temple plan; the maps show where it is to be situated. The brick mold is sacred and will be what you use to cast the bricks for his temple. I know you are used to working with stone, but there is only sand and clay where you will be going. The silver stylus was used to write the chants and spells you must use to bind the bricks together. The stallion is you, dear Bob. He has chosen you as the architect to build his temple. The tree and birds indicate he will not let you rest until you have begun his work."

"No shit? He could have just told me," I said.

All the time Nansi was interpreting my dream, Saris had been crawling around her like some cat, rubbing and petting and purring. Nansi was obviously becoming aroused by the naked girl's attentions. For my part, it didn't take much for me to get aroused when two pretty girls are playing with each other.

"Show me now how best to use this lovely gift you've given me and I will show you how to interpret the god's language in the future," Nansi said as her robe finally fell fully open to reveal a beautiful body of her own. I was all too happy to demonstrate our various techniques for making love and Nansi hung a 'closed for the day' sign on her door so we could play uninterrupted.

Early the next morning, before the line formed at her doorway, I slipped away, kissing both Nansi and Saris thoroughly before I left. They were both still splayed on the bed with their legs spread wide, recovering from the kisses I'd placed there.

The route to Bathra was a simple one. I built a little boat out of cypress I found growing near the river and jumped aboard to float downstream on the current.

I found a secluded place just outside the city of Bathra where I could slip into the infinity room and have the girls make sure I looked okay for my surveillance.

"Are you going to keep building a boat every time you need to travel?" Nimia asked. "You might as well create a lake here and bring it into the infinity room when you aren't using it. I might want to learn to sail, too!"

That sounded like a reasonable idea, but I wasn't sure how to create a lake. I hauled the boat through a gateway into an unused part of the infinity room—which was actually most of the infinity room. Hmm. I guess that if you use a little bit of infinity for a purpose, like our house and courtyard, the rest is still infinity, isn't it? So, of course there were unused parts.

Anyway, I just plopped the boat down on the sand and it started to drip the river water off the sides. As I watched the water drip, I hollowed out a space by virtue of creating a wind to blow the sand out of the hollow to a depth and size I deemed large enough for a small lake, and commanded the boat to keep dripping until the lake was filled.

"Bob, sweetie, honey," statue girl one said sweetly. Even at my young age and inexperience, I knew that when a naked nymph playing with my cock used that particular voice, it indicated she wanted me to do something for her. In this instance, it seemed unlikely that she was about to ask for sex, since that was already assured.

"What is it? And what is your name? You haven't been statues in a long, long time."

"I'm Bileah and my sister is Cileah. And we love you."

"But...?" I said.

"We're feeling a strange pull from the city you are about to visit. We don't know what it is, but we want you to know we love you and when we leave you it isn't because you aren't wonderful to us," she said.

"I see. Saris left to join Nansi, and she had a premonition beforehand, too. It might be that the god Ninra who has commanded me here has a destiny in mind for you as well. I will be attentive and watch for the right moment to summon you," I said. I wasn't upset about this. Had Nimia or even Portia suggested that she would leave me, I might have felt differently. But they were my wives. These two women were not my wives and I couldn't even call them my possessions. They were simply two free women who had been swept up in my flight from Knossos and had been terrifically good sports about it. I had no other claim on them.

After a night of loving all four women, I straightened my clothing and headed for town with the leather satchel over my shoulder. I had the look-away spell refreshed on it, so unless I actually handed it to someone or pointed it out, it would go unnoticed. I slipped into town with the morning traffic, just another peasant on an errand to the city.

I found the site where Ninra indicated he wanted his temple and looked at it in despair. It was populated with houses connected by a sewer ditch that stank in the mid-morning heat. The only source of water was a canal that ran from the river. It was neither close nor full as the area was in the midst of a drought. A lot of the traffic in the area comprised people carting clay jugs to or from the water for their homes. Some went as far as the muddy river itself to get water.

To make it worse, at one end of the site, there was already a temple. I visited as a sojourner to pay respects to the local deity and found the priestesses to all be rather fierce. Not that they weren't beautiful as well, but I could imagine leading this small army of women to war against a much larger opponent and winning handily.

The temple honored Namri, the patron goddess devoted to protecting the poor. And the poor had clustered around her temple. The priestesses were kept busy tending the sick, getting food for the poor, and teaching the orphans. They were almost desperate in their devotion. I was not going to go into this neighborhood and simply tear down these poor people's homes and the goddess's temple in order to build a new temple devoted to a god of war. I needed a new strategy.

I retreated from the neighborhood and left the city to contemplate what I should do.

I spent a restless night outside the satchel, calling out to Ninra. He demanded to know why his temple wasn't built yet. Not particularly reasonable since I'd only arrived that day. When I explained the situation, he declared that he would simply cut off their water supply and they would move. I explained that they had little or no water as it was with the area in a drought. He said that he would make the sewers back up and they would leave because of the smell and disease. I explained that they already lived in a sewer that simply didn't drain because of the lack of water and because it had no outlet to drain into. Then I talked about the goddess who already had a temple there and was sworn to protect those people. Ninra had only one answer to every question. He would make war against the goddess. I politely suggested that might take many years, would raise great antipathy toward him, and he might well lose the battle, if the priestesses were any indication of the goddess herself.

Finally, Ninra settled down enough to ask me what I thought he should do.

"The city is poor and beset by drought. Perhaps you could negotiate with the goddess and join in league with her. If you provided rain to end the drought, she might be willing to share the site."

"Share? What is share?" demanded the god. It was a foreign concept to him.

"If, say, you were to occupy one part of the square and the goddess occupied another part, you could have an alliance. She might care for the poor and you might defend the city. People would flock to your temples and bring you many sacrifices," I said.

The idea of many sacrifices appealed to Ninra, though I'm not sure how much of the concept of sharing he ended up grasping. He finally appointed me as his ambassador to go talk to the goddess Namri.

If you get confused about the names, don't worry. I'm making them up to sound like what I heard. Toss in Nimia, Nansi and Saris with Ninra and Namri and I got confused myself. But what I saw in my head was Great Zeus in the cave we shared, fucking all the little nymphs we could bring him. I figured what Ninra really needed was to get laid.

I dressed slightly better to return to the goddess's temple the next day—not as fine as a prince, but as befits an ambassador. The priestesses didn't object when I approached the altar and seated myself in front of it to wait. They looked at me strangely, but went on about their tasks until one finally separated herself and approached me.

"What do you want here?" she demanded. She didn't need to do a lot of obvious adjustments to her robe, nor did she flex her muscles to show me she could probably remove me from the temple. I didn't want to get into a fight with her.

"I bear greetings to the fair goddess Namri, protector of the poor and defenseless, from the fierce god Ninra, who holds at bay the hordes at our frontiers. Oh, fair and mighty goddess, I entreat you to accept the gifts I bring that we might sit and learn to know each other." I reached into my satchel and pulled out Bileah and Cileah to set them beside me with food and drink. The priestess was apparently not used to naked nymphs appearing in the temple and stood back a step, ready to object.

"It is well," a clear and feminine voice said from the other side of the altar. The priestess was struck dumb and stood aside staring, as the goddess herself took shape opposite me. "I am Namri, protector of the poor. Who comes before me?"

"I am Bob," I said as formally as I could. "I am but an emissary, hoping to bask in your glorious presence as I bring greetings from the god Ninra."

"Join me at the table, Bob. Are these gifts?" She pointed at the two naked girls setting our table.

"The food and drink are gifts, fair one. The ladies, Bileah and Cileah are here of their own accord. I would not trade in humans, but they come willingly to offer themselves to your service," I said. This whole conference had been their idea and it was working well so far.

"Welcome. I accept your service, gentle ladies. Let us discuss the god you serve, Bob."

From then the conversation turned to my description of Ninra and his desire to make a gift to Bathra and to the goddess. I phrased things carefully, ultimately showing the plan for the temple, which I had altered somewhat, positioning it beside the temple to Namri. She picked the plan apart and I filled in holes with other ideas as they came to me. I was becoming quite an architect. It seemed things were going well until she stood.

"I will take this conversation no further until I have met this Ninra and have looked into his eyes. Tell the god I will expect him to dine here at sunset tomorrow." With that, the goddess disappeared. So did Bileah and Cileah and all the food and drink. I stood and faced the priestess who had suddenly come to life again.

"I go to convey the words of your mistress to my master," I said. "I think we'll see you tomorrow evening. Better prepare for company."

The startled priestess stammered and nodded her head as I turned to leave.

7
WEDDING BELLS

I HAD A CONVERSATION with Ninra that night that was not all positive. I suggested he focus on creating a body for himself that could sit at a table rather than creating a storm. One of the hardest tasks I have faced in my long life was civilizing this war god enough that he could sit at the table without coming to blows. But he did it and we went to the temple the next evening.

What a difference!

I have an opinion that gods are much like demons. They are created from the minds of people who call on them. When some battle-hardened seer stands up before the armies to encourage them and says, "Our god is a great and mighty god, fierce before his foes. His body shines like gold and his wings stretch over the land to give us protection in battle. His body is a great storm, visited upon our enemies and his lions roam at his side to visit carnage on their bodies. His sword is swift and his arm is mighty. Praise be to Ninra, the god who sub-dues our foes!"

And then the whole army cheers for Ninra so capably described by their seer that they can see the god taking shape in front of them, and suddenly, a god has been created with the characteristics described by the seer. Probably out of the same primordial mass from which I was summoned.

That's *my* theory.

The priestesses had transformed the central area of Namri's temple into a living room fit for gods. The mosaics on the floor were all polished to a high sheen. The altar was set as a dining table and spread with plates and bottles and platters.

I entered ahead of the god.

"Hail to the fair and wise and beautiful Namri, protector of the poor and patroness of Bathra," I announced. "Presenting the fierce warrior god Ninra, guardian of the borders of Bathra and bringer of prosperity for his people."

The goddess appeared at the table and Ninra entered through the doors of the small temple. They were seated at the table and the goddess's handmaidens—my former statues—served the food and tantalized both parties.

I shan't recite all the conversation that went on between the two deities. Suffice it to say that as the night wore on, their conversation became less and less formal, more and more flirtatious. They were oblivious to the presence of the rest of us. The girls withdrew to my side and as the two gods crossed to each other, their conversation becoming more physical, the two girls renewed our acquaintance in the best ways possible. Namri had seen fit to keep their style of clothing—or lack thereof—the same, and having those two naked beauties climbing on my frame was all it took to turn the dinner party into an orgy. Plates, knives, food, and drink went scattering from the table as the gods got busy themselves and fucked right there on the altar. The building shook with their orgasms.

They'd pulled themselves together somewhat by first light and addressed me once again. I patted each of the nymphs on their bare posteriors and they scampered off to clean up the mess.

"Bob, you had a good idea here," Ninra said. "Namri and I have married and will share this sacred site. You will build my temple around hers that I might guard and protect all that is precious to me. When you begin to lay the foundations, I will bless this city. The canals will run full with water. The fields will bring forth great crops. The traders will come from far and wide and the people will prosper." He paused and turned to his new wife. "Right?" he asked.

"That was just the way we practiced, honey. You are so strong and commanding. I'm sure Bob will do a good job."

Somehow, I thought Ninra had been played a bit. He was thoroughly pussy-whipped. But they seemed happy.

"There is one thing that bothers me," I said with a sigh. "I'm nobody here. How am I supposed to demand that the area be cleared, find workers to do the labor, and most of all, pay for everything? I'd love to get right to work and improve things for the people, but like I said, I'm nobody."

The god and goddess put their heads together—and other parts—and when they were finished and the building shook again, they turned to address me.

"Your words have been heard, Bob," Namri said softly. "We have a plan for you to marry the king's daughter. Then you'll be the prince and can bring all these things to pass."

"She'll consent to that? I will not take an unwilling wife."

"Oh, she's one of my priestesses. She will consent. Now this is what you must do." With that, the two deities explained the plan and I had to admit, it was probably a better plan than either could have come up with on their own. I bought into it wholeheartedly. Even if

I didn't like the princess, I could always slip into my satchel once in a while and play with Portia and Nimia.

⌘⌘⌘⌘⌘⌘⌘⌘⌘⌘⌘⌘

I laid low outside the city while Ninra and Namri had their little honeymoon. I found a good place to hide the satchel and crawled in for a little enjoyment with my wives.

"It's lonely without the statue girls," Nimia said. "Can't you bring us some more playmates?"

"When this stuff is settled with the gods, why don't I work on finding you husbands?" I answered. "Human men who will make you happy for the rest of your lives. This seems like a nice place to settle down. And besides, I'm going to get married to the princess."

"Boo," Portia said. "Marry her and bring her here. We'll train her to be your good and faithful wife."

"Um... That might not... Uh... Oh..." Those girls sure knew how to disconnect my brain from my tongue. Portia pushed her hot pussy onto my engorged cock while Nimia lowered hers on my mouth. My tongue had other things to do than talk.

⌘⌘⌘⌘⌘⌘⌘⌘⌘⌘⌘⌘

On the appointed day, I emerged from my satchel and from my cave, dressed in splendid clothes that had been delivered in one of my dreams. I led the stallion from the infinity room stables and he pranced happily as I hitched the chariot. Portia and Nimia were more indecently dressed than if they'd been naked. Their pert little titties kept 'accidentally' slipping into view as they rode behind me in the chariot. Namri had suggested a new body for me, designed to appeal to Princess Bao. It was nice that she had sent Bileah and Cileah with the clothing and image. We'd had a lively reunion. We were a splendid sight and I looked far wealthier than, in fact, I was. The gods had told me I would soon be wealthier than I appeared.

Entering the city gates was far different than entering Knossos. This city-state was ruled by a single king, who is so unimportant to this story that I won't bother trotting out another long and hard-to-remember name to substitute for the one I forgot. He was just King.

He was, however, powerful enough to have an army that would have put all the kings of Knossos to flight. They were fierce men and women who wore a short kilt and half-vest as their uniform. On both men and women, there were costume slips that left normally covered parts on clear display. I thought that might be part of why they were always victorious when fighting their enemies. The appearance of an army is often as important as the fighting capability. These, however, looked to be as capable of fighting as any army I have seen.

⌘⌘⌘⌘⌘⌘⌘⌘⌘⌘⌘⌘

That reminds me of the time I was working my way up the coast of Africa a few centuries later and encountered the most peaceful tribe of little dark people I have ever met. Their tribe was never attacked by others and they were never traded as slaves. The secret was that they fought naked—in fact, lived naked—because they couldn't trust their bowels. That's right, the entire tribe had constant diarrhea. From an offensive point of view, it is difficult to throw a spear when you never know if your bowels will choose that moment to release.

52

As a defense, their reputation had spread widely, and no one wanted to risk getting close enough to fight.

But, of course, that was centuries later. Back to Bathra.

Inside the city gates, Portia and Nimia jumped off the chariot and ran ahead of me announcing my presence.

"Make way for the Illustrious and Glorious Prince of the Far East Bob, come to pay homage to the Wise and Beautiful Goddess Namri, Protector of the Poor, and to celebrate the nuptials between the divine goddess and the Golden Guardian God of the Gates, Ninra. Come and celebrate the joyous occasion at the temple of Namri!"

I have no idea how they managed to get all those words out repeatedly as they ran in front of the stallion. Different language, you know. People began to follow along—perhaps just to see the girls' naughty bits flash on display. That always attracts a crowd.

We took a roundabout route to the little temple to give people plenty of time to gather. People, meaning King and his army, came to welcome the visiting prince. We trotted up the forum between the rows of people, kept back by the soldiers to form an avenue of approach. At the temple gates stood King and the high priestess.

"Oh, Honored King and Glorious High Priestess," I called out from my chariot. "I have come at the bidding of my god, the Golden Guardian of the Gates, Ninra, to stand in his stead in marriage to the Protector of the Poor, Namri."

King was a little befuddled and caught off guard. He didn't realize he was being summoned to perform a wedding. The priestess filled in the gap right on cue.

"Our gentle goddess visited her priestesses to tell us of your impending arrival. She placed her blessing on one of our own to stand in her stead at this wedding celebration. Come into the house of the goddess, Prince Bob. Your bride awaits."

The priestess took King's arm and led him ahead of me into the temple. Portia and Nimia fell in behind me as my escort. The priestesses of the temple came next, and King's guard arranged themselves around us. People crowded in until the temple could hold no more. From somewhere there was a chorus of horns and the crowd parted to allow the approach of the bride.

I couldn't tell you what she looked like, as she was covered in so many veils. When she stood beside me, we faced King and the priestess. It was clear the priestess was orchestrating everything. She looked at me.

"Prince Bob, do you accept the role of Ninra and agree without coercion to be married to this woman for your wife?" she asked.

"I do," I bellowed. It was not the last time I said those words in my forty centuries, but I believe it was the first. There had been no questions asked before Zeus married Ariane and me. She turned to my bride.

"Do you accept the role of Namri and agree without coercion to be married to this man for your husband?" the priestess asked.

"I do," the bride said meekly. I noticed the priestess did not use her name.

Then the priestess, like religious people throughout the ages, preached a sermon glorifying the god and goddess and calling upon them through this union to smile upon the people of Bathra who were gathered to celebrate their marriage. She even prayed a little prayer over King for his beneficence and continued good health. Then she turned to him for the proclamation. He was less off-guard at the moment as he had apparently officiated any number of weddings and given his blessing.

"On behalf of the people of Bathra and by my authority as King, I hereby pronounce you God and Goddess, husband and wife, guardians of our fair city and state. You may kiss the bride."

I finally got to lift a few of the veils out of the way and my new wife raised her beautiful face to me for a kiss that nearly ended with us stretched out on the altar fucking as the god and goddess had done a week earlier. There was certainly no hesitance or coercion at work here. When we broke our kiss, we turned to face the priestess and the astonished King.

"Bao?" he stammered. I have to say, it is difficult to stammer a single sound like my bride's name.

"Father, I have long been a priestess of the Goddess Namri and happily take her place in the city as wife to Prince Bob of the East to bring blessings on our city."

The priestess had a hurried and whispered conversation with the nearly apoplectic King who had just married off his daughter in the ceremony to a complete stranger. He finally nodded his head and faced us.

"I recognize this marriage of Princess Bao and Prince Bob," he said. The priestess whispered to him again. "And I hereby declare them to be the heirs to my kingdom. May Bathra prosper beneath your rule."

There it was. I was married to the princess and was now the heir apparent to the King. I could begin my work at once.

<hr>

After the wedding, King really had no choice but to give a big party for the happy couple, which delayed the part we were both eager to get to. We ate and drank with Nimia and Portia feeding us. We danced, with Nimia and Portia holding us together. And all the time, Bao was trying to climb my frame or get her tongue all the way down my throat. Periodically through the party, she lost another of her veils, revealing more and more of her body to my eye. And probably to every other eye in the room, though the room didn't hold all that many people. Nimia and Portia collected the veils as they fell.

The palace was distinguished from the homes surrounding it only by location and a slight increase in size of the house and grounds. I decided that one day, I would replace the structure with one made of stone—if I could find stone anywhere in the region. Perhaps the god's magic bricks would suffice.

It was hard to think of the future in longer terms than bedding my new wife. She'd been living with the priestesses of Namri since becoming one a few years previously, but she still had a very nice chamber in the palace, to which she led me as soon as we could acceptably excuse ourselves from the party. There were cheers and obscene comments made after us, Bao shedding veil after veil as we fled the banquet and ran to her room. Nimia and Portia followed us, laughing and collecting the veils as they fluttered to the floor. By the time we reached the bed, Bao was delightfully naked and set about getting me in the same condition, assisted by Portia and Nimia.

"Are your ladies in waiting going to join us?" Bao asked as the girls helped undress me.

"Um... I don't think they are actually waiting. Don't worry. You'll like my other wives."

"I have no doubt of that! No men were ever allowed to touch a priestess, so you will find my body unsullied by males. But oh! Did the priestesses ever sully each other," she laughed.

"I am delighted to be the man who sullies you," I said as I caressed her curves and played with her breasts.

"Oh, please do. I have dreamed of you for the past seven nights... dreamed of you touching me... dreamed of your rampant manhood parting my nether lips and spearing me to the core. It has been almost like watching us every night, pleasuring each other and yet not quite being me."

"I believe that you, as was I, were viewing our godly counterparts enjoying their honeymoon this past seven nights. They did not wait for our formalization of their union to get started on their carnal pleasures," I said.

"I feel I have several days of catching up to do, my love. Take me. Make me your queen."

This girl spoke to the very essence of my being. Perhaps the gods had increased our libido to match their own. Regardless, Portia opened the petals of Bao's sex with her fingers as Nimia guided my rampant cock to its new home. It was exquisite! By this time of my life, my cock had been in the welcoming embrace of perhaps a hundred wet and willing pussies, but I could recall none that molded itself better to my cock—that milked me like the ripples of this pussy did. And Bao's sighs of lust confirmed that she, too, was seeing her goddess's hand in our pleasure.

Actually, I think it was Portia's hand, still positioned where we were joined, stroking Bao's clit, just as Nimia was caressing my balls. We were not long before our fulfillment washed over us in wave after wave of pleasure.

Nimia and Portia made it their business to be sure we were bathed and refreshed—with their tongues—and were ready for the next round of lovemaking. Eventually, they were included more intimately in the loving and Bao became familiar with every aspect of their depravity—and loved it.

We adjusted quickly to both married life and to becoming the heirs apparent to the throne. There were no laws in Sumer that said a woman could not inherit a throne on her own. In fact, there were few laws in Sumer at all. It was quite unlike Crete where King Minos had ruled and made governing laws under the guidance of Zeus. In Sumer, each king was his own law and most weren't very good at it.

That was going to change.

But the problem with a woman inheriting the throne was simply one of keeping it. Any man who was bigger and stronger might wrest it from her. Armies tended to support the strongest and people expected women to do women's work. King had set about remediating these concerns. He had no sons. By making Bao a priestess of Namri, she gained the perceived backing of a goddess the people adored. He further integrated both men and women into his army and made sure they trained as hard as any army before or since. Ninra had observed that and blessed it with his strength. As a result, most of the priestesses and women in the army were strong and willing to fight for a queen as well as a king.

I had no desire to upset that balance, but there was no question that my presence helped validate Bao's claim as heir. And, in addition to being an absolute sex kitten, she was smart and clever. I laid out the plans for the new temple and went over each detail on the map. Both fresh water and drainage were problems in the temple district. She set her mind to remedying that problem while I tried to re-engineer the god's plans. It wasn't that I wanted to change the design, but structurally, he expected too much from too little.

Yes, I had been given a special mold for the bricks and spells to cast upon them to make them stronger. There was no convenient source of good clean stone near our fair city. There was, however, remarkably fertile land. Somewhere along the line, the water table had dropped and left it dry. Nonetheless, I needed to make the bricks of sand and clay and they needed to be stronger than they would be, even with the strengthening spell.

The solution came to me unexpectedly as I was wandering the streets and stumbled on what I assumed was a rock. I picked it up to examine it and found it was mostly the same sand and clay mixture I planned to use. But it had straw embedded in it. When I attempted to break it, the straw held the pieces together, even when I had fractured the binding. I rushed back to our rooms to talk to Bao. As usual, I expected our best talking to be done in bed after we'd had sex.

<hr>

"I know what you're doing," a voice hissed at me from the shadows as I walked through the hall of the palace. I turned to confront an old man, hunched over a staff that looked like it could contain magic or be used as a cudgel. "Usurper," he hissed.

"Please enlighten me! You know, I'm kind of improvising here and a little help would be appreciated." I thought the gods might have sent me a helper here who could counsel me. Though my experience was and continued to be that the gods kept sending me women, not gnarled old men. "Who are you?"

"I am Assininé, Mage to the King, and I have read your augury."

"Really? I've never had that done before. What does it say?"

"You are not what you appear to be. You will change the very fabric of our culture. You must be stopped."

I couldn't disagree with the first two items. I definitely disagreed with the third. And I had an inborn distrust of magi.

"How do you propose to stop me?" I asked as I prepared my own spell.

"I have a spell in my chambers and will use it to reduce you to a bumbling idiot who will never do anything but screw her majesty until she listens to sense." The old man cackled. I mean, actually cackled like a chicken laying an egg.

"As attractive as doing nothing but screwing her majesty is, you should not have told me your plans. Are you unaware of how foolish you are?"

"You can do nothing once I cast my spell."

"Perhaps you should have cast it before you became a cockroach!" I threw the spell I had prepared at him and he looked startled for a moment before he began to shrink and grow legs and feelers. His staff fell to the floor, nearly crushing him. I immediately regretted having transformed him into such a disgusting little creature, when I'd only meant to have him *think* he was a cockroach. I prepared a counter spell to return him to his other disgusting self, but he immediately scurried off down the hall. I turned to follow, but saw Portia running up to find me. She faltered in her step and began hopping on one foot.

"Eww! I stepped on a bug. Yuck!" she said. Well so much for the counter spell. I guess it doesn't pay to oppose the gods. "The princess sent me to find you. She's figured out the routing for the new canal and wants your input." Portia dropped her voice and leaned in toward me. "I think she wants you to put in your cock. Save a little for me, okay?" I wasn't sure if Portia was referring to a little of my cock or a little of my wife. She'd become completely enamored with Bao. With that, she pulled off the scrap of fabric she was wearing and wiped her foot. I set off to see my wife.

8
BUILD IT BETTER

ORTIA WAS CORRECT in her assessment that Bao wanted my cock, which I gladly gave her until she screamed in ecstasy. Then I rolled to my left and, while Nimia kept Bao at a peak, I planted my pole in Portia and made love to my first princess. Yes, remember she was the daughter of a King in Knossos and was supposed to be married to King Drakomaxos until the sod got drunk and left her to be plundered by me. Bao never minded me satisfying my two Minoans as long as one was paying attention to her needs, which always seemed to be at a fever pitch. Occasionally, I had visions of Ninra having the same time with Namri and her two handmaidens. It was a share-and-share-alike arrangement.

When we were sated—for the moment—we shared our discoveries and approved each other's plans. We set a time to meet with King to describe our intent.

"How many slaves is it going to take to build this new temple and canal?" King demanded. "I will need to take the army and raid the Orasines to get enough slaves to do the work."

"No!" I bellowed. I suddenly felt the presence of the god and goddess descending on Bao and me. It was no longer I who spoke, and King quaked in front of me. "No slave will lift a brick for our temple," Ninra said through me. "Hear what I say! The day ground is broken for the foundation of my temple, I will loose the water and fill the canals as they have never been filled before. The sheep will multiply. The grain will ripen. Famine shall be no more. And every laborer who lends his hand to the building of my temple will prosper."

Bao took up the narrative—or Namri within her.

"No slave shall walk upon our sacred soil. We shall be worshiped by the free citizens of Bathra. Every laborer who sweats to build our temple shall not want for bread or meat but will prosper in our service."

"Let this be decreed throughout the land: Our home shall be a home for the free citizens of Bathra. We call upon them to help in its building," I concluded. I felt the presence of the god leave me and caught Bao as she sagged against me.

King turned to his scribes.

"Well? What are you waiting for? Publish this decree and let all the people rush to do the bidding of our gods!"

I found it strange that no one seemed to miss the old wizard and I wondered if he really had an official position in the palace or with King. As I wandered through the halls exploring my new domicile one night...

Let me interrupt to say that it was not unusual for me to slip out in the middle of the night to get a little break from my voracious girls, or to slip into the infinity room with Nimia. Portia had taken to Bao with fanatic devotion and never went into the infinity room any more. Nimia, however, considered the room to be her home. She stayed there more and more and I never let her languish for lack of attention. Over the years, this arrangement would have unexpected consequences, but now, I was happy to have my wife in charge of my home in the infinity room.

Back to my wandering. I happened upon a door I had not opened before. I could see it had various protection and invisibility spells on it, cast by the old mage. Apparently, the spells were wearing off now that he was dead. I thought long and hard about how to open the door and finally, just pushed it in. The spells collapsed at my touch.

Inside, the room reminded me of Pinaruti's magic room. Shelves of specimens, bottles of potions, a circle chalked on the floor. And scrolls! More scrolls than Pinaruti had. I quickly opened a gateway and called Nimia to me. We began emptying Assinine's room, taking everything into the satchel where Nimia efficiently organized it. Nimia was the only person other than myself that I allowed in the replica of Pinaruti's magic room. I considered her to be my first wife and head of my household in the satchel. We didn't yet know what all the dried and bottled specimens were, nor how to use any of the potions, but I would have leisure to read and experiment once the temple was built.

In the meantime, Nimia organized and straightened and cataloged what she could, putting things with similar items on the shelves and not opening any bottles. She said the task made her feel closer to me, and in a way, she was right. I always carried my satchel or had it next to me. I had expanded the spells on the bag, so it was not visible to anyone unless I showed it to them. That gave me some amount of security when I entered the room myself.

The day after King's decree went out, we had a hundred volunteers at the new temple site, ready to do the bidding of the gods. Bao put some of the laborers to work extending the sewer ditch so it drained into a pit outside the city walls. I set some to extending the canal system so it would water the district. And the rest were set to relocating families in the way of the actual construction and making sure they had been justly compensated for the inconvenience. As soon as a hovel was emptied, it was torn down. The old sand and clay bricks went into a heap where they were pounded into dust. They would be reshaped into temple blocks, reinforced with fibers and magic.

Not everyone, of course, was a believer. There were those in the city who outright laughed at us, calling out how foolish we were to build canals where there was no water to feed them. Ninra in me wanted to strike them down and curse the town, but Namri in Bao had a way of settling the war god down—which usually included Bao and I having an energetic bout of sex.

I had discovered a secret of reinforcing the bricks with straw fibers, but also discovered the straw was weakened in the slurry for the bricks. I found, however, that the reeds growing in the river water produced strong fibers when they were pounded out and these did not deteriorate in the wet slurry. I sent a crew to harvest the 'useless' reeds by the river amidst more jeers from the skeptics.

I set myself to work making more of the molds for the blocks, carefully following the instructions of the god on how to enchant them so they would be stronger and longer-lasting. I trained a crew to pour the slurry and embed the fibers, but Ninra insisted that I be the only one who could enchant the bricks. As soon as I had chanted the spell, which I could do over dozens of brick molds at a time, the bricks were set out to dry—a process that did not take long in the hot sun. In a few days, we had quite a stockpile of bricks forming.

In a few weeks, the canal connection was completed and emptied into a vast pool in front of the temple site. It *would* empty. At the moment, it was dry, as the water level had not risen to fill the canals. That was my next task.

⌗⌗⌗⌗⌗⌗⌗⌗⌗⌗⌗⌗⌗⌗

Over two hundred laborers gathered around the temple square the day I decided it was time to begin the foundation for the temple itself. It was to be a day of great celebration—or a day of great folly. Many of the city skeptics were gathered with the workers to watch the crazy prince and princess pray to their gods. Bao and I held a shovel together as we prayed to the god and goddess so that everyone would hear us asking for their blessing on our work.

The people who had worked on the construction so far had been well cared for. Each family had been given a measure of grain and dried meat that was replenished as long as they continued to labor. They had nothing to want for and all seemed happy enough. But everyone wanted to see the blessing of the gods as it took place.

Bao and I set the spade to the earth and pressed with our feet to dig into the ground. We had staked out the foundation to be an armlength across and an armlength deep. This would then be filled in layers of the slurry and left to dry before adding the next layer. When the foundation was complete, it would be as if we had made a brick that encompassed the entire temple.

When we had broken ground, we heard a great thunderclap. Everyone's eyes were drawn to the mountains opposite the river. There, a glorious display of lightning played along the ridges and the clouds lowered. As far as we were from the storm, we could feel a change in the temperature as rain stormed on the mountains and filled the streams. Those streams, in turn, filled the great river, raising it gradually to a height at which the canals began to fill. We didn't get rain directly on our building site, so construction began in earnest.

This was a point at which I was kept very busy. Workers could and did dig the foundation trench, but for each pouring of slurry I had to chant the spell over it so it would last as long as the bricks themselves. The key element in this spell was to prevent damage to the bricks or foundation from either water or wind. Both were known to erode the common clay bricks used in constructing houses. In a span of days, the foundation was poured and cured.

And miracle of all, the canals were filled to a level never before seen in Bathra. Even our pool in front of the temple was filled.

This created some problems, as bridges had to be built so people could cross the canals. But it was not difficult. Water also washed into our sewer canal and the effluent was washed at last outside the city walls to the great pit awaiting it.

The skeptics were suddenly silent.

As construction continued, news began to come in from the surrounding countryside that crops were greening in the fields again. Sheep were breeding. Wool was thick. Meat was plentiful

And that is when King died.

His chambermaid reported that the king was looking out his window and saw the full canals and the happy people in the streets. He said simply, "I'm done now. The rest is up to Bao and Bob." Then he went to bed and went to sleep. He did not wake up.

We had an official day of mourning for the king and no one worked that day. The next day, we had a coronation ceremony. No one worked that day. On the following day, everyone was surprised to find Bao and me back at the worksite preparing bricks and directing workers.

A wealthy citizen approached me as I was mixing slurry. "Your Highness," he said. I almost missed the fact that he was addressing me, but half a dozen scribes and assistants had followed us to the site and were trying to get court work done while we built. One pointed the man out to me and I turned to find one of our loudest skeptics.

"Oh, sorry. Didn't realize you were addressing me. If you would like to work on the construction, you should see my foreman, just over there. He'll assign a job for you."

"Oh, not me, sire. It is unseemly that a man of our rank should be laboring in the mud." *Had he just elevated himself to the same rank as the king?* "I can bring you ten slaves to do this work and it will go much faster," he said. I looked hard at him. He didn't seem to be stupid, but was caught in a new world order he didn't understand. I remembered the old mage's words that I 'will change the very fabric of our culture.' I guess it was true.

"The gods have decreed that only free citizens, volunteering their labor, will work on their temple," I said. "Therefore, if you choose to send me ten slaves, they will thenceforth be considered free citizens. They will be compensated with a home and food for their labor.

They will no longer be your slaves."

The man looked at me as though I had spoken Minoan instead of Sumerian. I checked through my memories to be sure I'd spoken directly to the minds of the people around me. I might speak in Minoan, but they would all hear in Sumerian.

"That's preposterous!" The man said. "It's not the way things are done. Slaves are slaves! They are not the same as citizens. Some of them aren't even the same color!"

"A man being captured or defeated in battle, a woman who cannot pay her husband's debt, a child who has no parents. None of these things make them less of a man, woman, or child. Slavery is a condition we have imposed upon the weak and vulnerable, not something that defines who they are." I looked around me and my scribes were writing furiously on their tablets. Bao smiled at me and joined by my side.

"Let this proclamation be the first of our rule over Bathra," I said. "Any slave who is sent to work on the temple is thereby freed and becomes a citizen of Bathra through his labor. Further, if a master dwells seven days in his home with his slave woman, the slave woman will become equal to her mistress and the slave will walk side-by-side with her master. The orphan shall come to the temple and be cared for. These are the people of Ninra and Namri. They shall be cared for."

It was going to take more than that to get slavery abolished. I wasn't about to tackle that problem right now, but when it was reported that a slave was beaten, the case came before me and I judged whether the punishment was just. If I deemed it was not, I delivered the same punishment back to the master.

And the walls of the temple rose, and the people prospered.

There were some rocky times in store for Bathra. A neighboring kingdom heard about our policy toward slaves and decided this would be a good time to attack and take some slaves for themselves. Our people prospered and the foreigners felt they could help themselves to the wealth. I personally led the army out to meet them at our border and they quickly decided it was not such a good time to attack Bathra.

The vanquished leader surrendered himself as payment for leniency to his troops. He was surprised when I let them all return home—minus their weapons. I told him there were only two options when making war against Bathra: Go back home or die. That word spread rapidly throughout the region. I won't say we had no conflicts, but I met each one with the full strength of our army and reaffirmed that Ninra and Namri were the protectors of Bathra and my army was their army.

While we were campaigning, we came upon several small temples that were broken down or in poor repair. As soon as I could spare people from the building site, I sent crews out to rebuild any temple they found in our land. It made no difference to me what god the temple was erected to honor. We honored all with our labor.

Word spread among the surrounding peoples as far away as Europe, Asia, and Africa, that we were blessed by the gods because we labored for their honor. Countries wanting to share in our bounty quickly saw a different path than making war against us. We were sent gifts from far and near to help make the temples of Bathra glorious.

Massive cedar logs came to us from the north, which we fashioned into beams to support the roof of the temple. Tiles encrusted with jewels reached us from the east, with workers who installed the floors of our temple and then stayed to enjoy their new citizenship in Bathra. Copper came from the mines of the southwest and the metal was hammered into sheets and used to encase the roof so it was impervious to weather.

It was said the roof of Ninra's temple could be seen reflecting the sun as far away as Babylon. And there were so many gifts and excess materials that I expanded and improved the palace so that it was more beautiful than what I'd built for either Drakomaxos or Idiopheles.

And the people prospered.

Bao and I were contacted by our patrons in a dream. We were given instructions on further reforms we could make in our society that would improve justice, care for more poor and weak, and establish us as the rulers of the region. And we were given 'tokens' of the gods' approval. These tokens amounted to so much wealth that we could care for every citizen of Bathra.

Those who worked, no matter what business they conducted, worked in service to the gods and were well-compensated for their labor. Those who refused to work, like the wealthy skeptic who had offered me slaves, were deemed undesirables and were driven out of the city. Oh, we continued to provide food for them, but they could not participate in the bounty of our land. Most soon came around to the idea that working in the service of the gods rather than in service to their greed was good for them and they returned to the city and prospered.

I had never liked the idea of killing people. After Zeus told me what would happen to me if I were killed, I couldn't see sending others to that fate. I felt I was responsible for the old mage's death and in a way for Pinaruti's, but I wasn't happy about it. There were deaths on the battlefield, but no more than necessary, I felt. Once our enemy surrendered or retreated to his homeland, we did not pursue them and kill them. But there were crimes that were also punishable by death. In most cases, I replaced the penalty with permanent imprisonment. If a man or woman was guilty of a capital offense, he was imprisoned outside the town where the prisoners grew their own food and tended their own flocks, but could not leave the compound.

I maintained only two punishments without mercy. A man guilty of murder was killed. But his family was not punished and continued under the care of the god and goddess. If a man was guilty of rape, he was castrated and made a eunuch. Both crimes all but disappeared from Bathra.

Beatings and cruel punishments decreased as well. There had been a movement toward punishing a person by taking away the body part that committed the offense. If the injured party lost a hand, the guilty party also lost a hand. This resulted in two people who couldn't work with both hands. I didn't like that notion. A person might still receive a few lashes if the crime could not be restored, but usually, restoration two-fold was imposed. Stealing from someone was not an interest-free loan.

The day of the temple dedication finally arrived. We had built the walls of the new temple around the temple to Namri, including it inside the temple precincts. "I will protect the poor and defenseless," Namri said through Bao at the dedication.

"I will protect my wife and her city," Ninra answered through me.

And Bathra was blessed with peace and prosperity.

"My husband, we must plan for our legacy," Bao said when we went to bed.

"And what could we leave as a legacy that would be greater than the temple we have built to honor our gods?" I asked. She moved closer to me and threw a leg over my midsection.

"We must leave children who have been brought up in the ways of our god and goddess," she answered. "They must rule when we are returned to the earth as dust."

That was a jolt. Bao had just reminded me that she was human and would grow old and die. She, of course, assumed I was merely a divinely blessed man and had no idea I was a demon.

I confess, I hadn't really thought of my reign in Bathra ending. However, it would become obvious in a few years that I wasn't getting any older. I needed to think about that. But I also needed to respond to Bao's statement of leaving children brought up in the ways of our god and goddess. That was true.

"It is good that we are educating the orphans and training them in the way of the gods," I said. "We will have many children as our legacy."

"Bob, don't be dense. We need a child. We've fucked at every opportunity for over a year and I am still not pregnant. Nor are Portia or Nimia. You must take another wife into the harem to have your child."

I was shocked. It was not that I was opposed to more women in my harem—there were only the three—but that I would be expected to father a child. After what happened to my precious Aria, I swore that would never happen.

"Let me consider your words, my wife. I will talk to our god and ask his guidance. And to our goddess. I know nothing about being a father. I will not reject you, beloved."

I left our bed late that night to wander the city.

And to mourn Aria.

9
AN HEIR TO JUSTICE

I SUPPOSE there is no way to avoid telling you, though 4,000 years later, the pain can be renewed with an unthinking word. But the story cannot go forward unless I move backward and tell you about losing Aria.

She had brought dozens of women through our home in Knossos for entertainment, true to her word to Zeus that she would always see that her husband had variety. Now, I knew from Zeus's example that leaving a bunch of bastards loose in the world was problematic. I didn't want to be known as leaving every woman in Knossos with child, so I had consulted with Zeus and he told me how to assure that no woman I laid with conceived. But Aria wanted my child. She had been denied that privilege by Basarti of the shriveled dick. With all the women he tried, he had fathered no children. I considered her request and found it tickled my instincts as well. The night I decided to satisfy her desire, she conceived.

For a long time, the other women made over her and some left to pursue the same dream with a husband. All wanted to bless Aria's child. We were happy as her womb grew with our child.

"Boy or girl?" I asked her.

"Ah! He kicks like a demon," she laughed. "And I'm sure he weighs as much as a full-grown goat. I'm huge! Soon you will need more wives just to bring me food and carry me to the privy."

"Oh, but I am sure she will be an angel like her mother," I said. "She will have your golden hair and be the most beautiful in the land."

"You still flatter me after these years together. Ten years! They have flown so fast. If we had waited any longer to conceive, I'd have been too old."

I had to stop and consider that. I was sure Aria was not yet thirty, but perhaps humans aged at the same rate as some large animals. What if she had the same lifespan as a horse? We might be nearing the end of our time together. I could barely think of her in those terms. I was not ready to lose my Aria. I would never be ready.

She was near full term when the pains became more than she could stand. We knew the child was arriving soon. We had no idea what it would be. I began to worry that it might not be boy or girl, but rather a beast. The pains became unbearable and I could see the infant moving in its mother's womb. Nimia tried to get me to leave and let the women take care of things, but I was not about to leave my Aria's side.

Then my son... the damned creature... tore through my precious girl's womb with his horns, leaving a gaping wound that none could staunch. My Aria died in my arms as our son devoured the womb from which he was ripped.

I am not proud of what I did. Zeus had told me how my immortality could be ended and what would happen to me. I considered joining Aria in the primordial mass. But instead, I ripped the head from my half-demon son and devoured him myself. I crunched his bones in my teeth and sucked the marrow out of his horns before grinding them to powder and making a bitter drink of them. When I was done, I shit out the waste that returned to the primordial mass it was born from.

Nimia held me in her arms, the only other of the women who had ever seen my true demon form, and rocked me back and forth against her breast as I swore, I would never again impregnate a human woman.

Now, I was a respected husband and king—avatar for a god with a goddess for my wife. Bao had every reason to want a child. What was I to do?

▨▨▨▨▨▨▨▨▨▨▨▨▨

I walked along the walls of the city that night, surveying the prosperity of Bathra. Twice around the entire city I walked as I contemplated what to do and wept for my sweet Aria. I cried out to Ninra and Namri for help and could not hear their answer. It is said that on that night the people heard the mournful spirit of a long past saint crying for the blessing of Bathra.

Obviously, adding to the harem would not solve the problem of an heir. But as I passed a point where I could see the temple courtyard, I saw a man sitting quietly next to the pool. It was still hours before dawn, so I knew he wasn't just early for work. I came down from the ramparts and went to see what was troubling him.

"What brings you to the temple at this hour, brother?" I asked.

"Ah... I... Uh... had a dream. I was told to come to this spot and wait for the god to make use of me. I wouldn't want to offend the god, so I rose from my bed and came here straightaway."

I thought it strange that he would be sent to this particular location just at a time when I was walking by. I've learned well, though, not to ignore the commands of a god.

"Tell me about yourself," I said. "You are devoted to Ninra?"

"And to Namri—very much, sir. I have been in Bathra for a year and helped with the building of this wonderful temple. The gods have been very kind to me, giving me friends, work, food, and care. But the one thing I have most desired, they cannot grant me," he sighed.

"Do not underestimate what the gods can grant," I said. "What is it that you desire?"

"I want to be a priestess of the goddess Namri and serve in her holy temple. But obviously, there are limitations."

"Yes," I chuckled. "Most priestesses I have known were women."

"All of them. I wish I was a woman," he sighed. "Have you seen them? They are strong and beautiful and glow with the light of the goddess within them. They are kind and caring. There is never a child who weeps that is not comforted. No injustice comes before them that is not made right. They are the blessed of the goddess."

I had to agree with that. In fact, if I ever had my own priestesses, I would want them to be like the blessed priestesses of Namri. Like my wife. Not that there would ever be a reason for me to have priestesses. I just shared this man's admiration of them.

He had an interesting thought, though. He was born a man but wanted to be a woman. How ridiculous.

"I will consider his request," a voice whispered beside me. I turned to see the goddess incarnate standing beside me. It was apparent that the man did not see her, in fact, was oblivious to all around him.

"You will?" I asked, surprised.

"Yes, but both you and he must fulfill the need of my vessel Bao."

"My goddess, I am devoted to my wife, your vessel, as I am to you. I will do anything for her. But surely you know why I refuse to father a child on her."

"I understand, my lover. But still, she must bear a child. Here is what you must do."

I listened, glancing frequently at the unresponsive man. The goddess gave me instructions and I followed them closely, seeing the man transform into my likeness. The goddess told me how to enter him and direct his steps, leaving my own body in her care at the temple.

We returned to my bedchamber and I saw my beloved wife, stretched casually naked across the bed. On the floor next to our wedding bed lay Portia and Nimia, clasped in each other's arms. I guided the man to my bed and he removed his clothes. He caressed my wife and I could feel his interest rise.

"My husband, have you come to make love to me again?"

"My love, I have come to plant a child in your womb. The goddess has spoken to me this night and it shall be done."

"Oh, my love! My adored husband. Take me and make me the mother of our children," she declared.

It was a strange sensation to feel this other body—this other man—caress my wife and bring forth her essence so that he... I... we... could slide into her vestibule where we made love for what seemed a long time, depositing a full load of semen in her repeatedly. When my wife was fully sated, I directed the man out of bed. Instead of gathering up his own clothes, he took one of the dresses worn by Portia and we stole out of the palace without disturbing a soul.

When we returned to the pool, the goddess awaited us with my body, which I slipped back into. I looked at the man as he dissolved back into his original form and I restrained my jealous hand from murdering him. The goddess intervened.

"You have come to the temple seeking to become a priestess, but now you have sampled the pleasure of the man's body as he plants his seed in a woman. Do you wish to abandon this and still become my priestess?"

"My goddess, I have no desire but to serve you. Would that I could change this man's flesh into that of a woman so I could serve you in your temple."

"Then so be it," the goddess said.

Before me, I saw the man, still naked, change his shape. His cock disappeared into his lower hair. His breasts grew. He shrank somewhat in size, but still retained the fine muscles that marked so many of the goddess's priestesses. His skin became fair and his hair lengthened. His lips filled with the seductive pucker of a woman.

"Now," the goddess said, "my faithful servant, Bob. You have done what was very difficult for you but was necessary for your wife. Here before you is one you cannot be jealous of. Examine her. Touch her. Feel the heat of her woman's parts and sink your manhood into her. Verify that this is, indeed a woman fit to be a priestess of the goddess."

I was hesitant at first, though the woman who stood naked before me was quite desirable. I had seen the transformation. I touched her breasts and let my fingers explore her nether region. For her part, she helped me from my clothes and made sure my staff was ready to mate with her. I bent her over the bench next to the pool where she had sat and thrust my manhood deep within her. There was no longer a question in my mind. The goddess had created a woman and that woman would become her priestess. I bellowed my satisfaction as she panted her own and then I withdrew. I can only say, she glowed with satisfaction. I picked up the dress we brought from the palace and helped her into it. She helped me into my clothes.

"Now come with me, my sister," Namri said. "You will enter my service as my priestess. Bob, you should return to your wife and make sure she knows how deeply you love her."

I left as Namri escorted the new woman into her temple. Bao welcomed me back into bed with open arms and open legs. I erased all memory of the feeling of being in the man as he fucked my wife and of fucking the woman he became. I held my wife in bed long after the sun rose, worshiping her and assuring her we would have a fine child blessed by the goddess.

"That was very difficult for you," Nimia whispered. She had returned to the infinity room before dawn and later the next night I made time to join her. I had followed the example of old Assininé and had put a spell on one room of the palace that I considered my special retreat. It was locked and the door was invisible to anyone passing by. I retreated to the room almost daily for a little time with Nimia.

"My loving wife," I said, "you are my first beloved wife after Aria and I will do anything in my power to care and provide for you. But I beg you, please, never ask to carry a child for me. My heart would break."

"You need not fear that, my strong and handsome demon. I have no desire for children that exceeds my desire for you. But you understand that what you did was necessary and you have made your wife Bao—and your wife Portia—the happiest woman in the world. I know and she knows that Portia carries no child, but she is as invested in Bao's pregnancy as if she were bearing the child herself."

"I am happy they are happy," I said. "I would endure any hardship to see them like this. My petty jealousy of a man who is no longer a man is childish and of no consequence."

"Then prepare yourself, my husband, for the trial has just begun."

"Nimia, what are you saying?"

"I have been studying the infinity room as I have so much time here. I come out only one or two times a week for a few hours and will emerge even less frequently in the future. I am not aging, just as you are not aging. But even in the year and a half we have been in Bathra, I see the changes coming over Portia and Bao. Bao will change through pregnancy and childbirth. She will have the cares of a mother. She will get older and older. And one day, she will die. Portia has elected to share her fate and will grow old and die with her. My beloved demon, though it may be years away, you must prepare for the loss of your loves. And you must work a spell on your body that will make it appear to age as well. Otherwise, you will be seen as an undying king and eventually your true nature will be uncovered."

"You are wise and kind, Nimia. It pains me to know that what you say is true. But I have determined to live each day in wonder and in love. And knowing that I have you to help me makes me able to see the hard parts through."

"About that," Nimia began and I recoiled in fear of what she might say. "Relax, Bob. I was just wondering if you couldn't somehow find a playmate for me here. Or, perhaps on one of my rare outings, I could look for a girl to keep me company. It is so lonely without the statues now that Portia has cast her lot with Queen Bao."

"Of course! How thoughtless of me to think my few visits are enough in your isolation. It would be best if you sought your companion yourself. My only requirement is that she come here of her free will and with understanding of what awaits her here."

"Yes, my love. As I have made this my home of my own choice, so shall our companion have free choice. She might not, however, want to marry you."

"That is a blessing!" I said. "Now I must work on an aging spell that will give the appearance of aging without affecting my real aging process. Only the appearance of Prince Bob must change."

"I may have found a spell in my reading. Anytime you find new books, please bring them to me. We should collect a nice library to keep us company on cold winter nights."

"I've never heard that expression. What is a cold winter night?"

"We'll need to discover that. It was something I read in one of the scrolls."

As Bao's belly grew, so did the wealth and prosperity of our city. Grain and sheep were traded to countries for gold, silver, lapis, and precious gems. So great was our wealth that I paid the debts of the poor, protecting the orphans from the wealthy and the widows from those who would prey on them. People migrated from other countries around us to worship Namri and Ninra, to work for the gods, and to become prosperous as the people of Bathra. And to each who worked for the gods, citizenship was granted and their needs were met.

And into this world, Bao brought our son, Ur-Ninra. He was a fine young man and blessed by the god. He learned well the lessons of being clean before the holy, and wise before the people. I taught him as much as I could teach and gradually had him take over the judging of complaints and offenses.

"My son," I said, "The day is coming when you must rule over this city and our state in place of your father. What kind of ruler will you be?"

"Father, is it even possible that I could be as wise and just as you? If I were given any gift by the gods, it would be that I could serve them as faithfully as you and my mother have done," Ur-Ninra said.

"It is well said. What will you do when our neighbors see that I am gone and decide to invade and steal our wealth and enslave our people?"

"It pains me to consider either taking a life or costing a life. But I have learned at your knee that the cost is much greater if we are not strong. I will continue to train with the army in the arts of warfare that I hope we never use. If we are challenged, however, we will rise up to meet our enemies with force and power. If they invade the lands of Bathra, they have only the choice to retreat or die. We will never take prisoners and make slaves of them."

"And what would your first decree be when you have become king?" I asked.

"I would decree an end of slavery."

"Now, let us consider that decree. Many consider slaves to be a part of their wealth. To them, freeing their slaves is stealing from them."

"Would it be just, father, to buy the slaves' freedom and thus to compensate their owners for their loss?"

"That would seem fair, but many will still resist. If you set a price on slaves, they may be traded and sold to others as well."

He stopped to consider this. I could see him turning the idea in his mind. Over the years, we had significantly reduced the trade in slaves, but there were still traders who sold on the outskirts of Bathra and we had never forbidden immigrants from bringing their slaves. I hoped my son had a solution.

"First," he said, when he had organized his thoughts, "the sale and trade in slaves must be banned. The only sale of a slave that will be allowed will be to the Crown, which will free the slave thereafter. Second, any slave that accompanies an owner into this country at his owner's command shall be freed within ten days. No immigrant slave-owner shall be granted citizenship until all his slaves are freed. Third, no child is born into slavery. A slave-owner whose property becomes pregnant will provide for the welfare of the child until he or she is fourteen years of age. At that time, the child is free to leave the owner and appeal to the Crown for a job and sustenance. Alternatively, a slave-owner whose property becomes pregnant, may sell that slave to the Crown and the slave shall be freed. Finally, a slave whose master dies is automatically freed and is to have an equal share of the master's inheritance as any other heir."

I smiled at my son.

"Have I missed anything, father?"

"Perhaps. Perhaps not. That is the problem with royal decrees that are made law. You may discover unintended consequences when the law has been enacted. You will need at that time to determine if the law was just and the consequences should be endured, or if the law has uncovered an injustice and must be changed. Strive always to maintain equality under the law for all people, citizen, slave, and visitor. If you do this and listen carefully to your advisors, you will be a just and great ruler for your kingdom," I said.

I saw that he was good and would become a good king when I left.

Now, in our old age, my precious Bao had become frail. Beside her, Portia had aged as well, and though she had no child of her own, she treated Ur-Ninra as if she were his mother.

Nimia, having set to work organizing and building my library and home in the infinity room, seldom made an appearance in Bathra. When she did, people were amazed that she had not aged a day and they honored her as if she were the high priestess—servant of the gods. As a result, she had attracted an occasional young woman to join her, promising that she would live a very long life of youth and beauty, but would not set foot on this world again. I wasn't sure of the terminology she used, but she had decided that crossing the threshold of the infinity room was entering a different world.

When I stepped into the infinity room, as I often did, Nimia and I were both young and as randy as goats on the mountainside. The three young women she had attracted to her side became members of the harem and were happy to share their treasures with me, though all three recognized their first responsibility as being to Nimia.

I loved Bao and Portia as if they were one and were dear to my heart as Nimia was. It saddened me deeply when they weakened and passed away, lying next to each other in the same bed and holding their hands.

"This marks the day when you shall become King and servant of the Most High," I said to my son when I had laid my wives to rest. "The Prince of the East must return to his homeland. My son, practice justice and temperance, kindness and mercy. Be strong against our enemies and gentle among our people. Let no man accuse you of greed or gluttony. And most of all, let this temple be known throughout the world as the house of justice—the home of Ninra, god of war, and Namri, goddess of mercy."

Having bid my wife a sad farewell at her tomb and pausing to remember the gentle and loyal Portia by her side, I set my foot upon my boat and sailed the river to the sea.

If you have read stories that convince you that this tale is merely a hodgepodge of myths and legends set in an impossible location, let me remind you that I am Bob, writing my memoir as one who lived these things some forty centuries ago. My memory is not perfect. I may have mashed names and misrecalled details. I am not an archaeologist and have never been back to that city I once loved. I set it on a path I believed was the will of the gods and a good path for my people.

And then I left.

For many years I simply wandered until I could find a suitable place far from people, where I could hide my satchel and step into the infinity room with Nimia and her three nymphs. I do not know how long we spent there, or even if time there ran the same as pace in the outside world. As I traveled, I sought books to add to our growing library, of which both Nimia and I were very proud.

"Bob, you cannot go on forever in isolation from all other people. And I am sure the four of us staying in our little home would be happier with others among us. We have a very big world here that goes beyond where any of us have explored. It needs crops and animals. People to tend them. Even a market where people gather to gossip," Nimia said. I considered that to be a reasonable suggestion.

And that is what brought us eventually to Troy.

END OF PART II

Part III
Gifts from Greeks

Image Credit: Daniel Eskridge, ID2011375139 licensed from Shutterstock.com

10
The Possession

We WANDERED AROUND a while. I couldn't tell you exactly where. We sailed the sea, but kept ending up back at the mouth of one river or another. The seaports were often near the mouth of a river because it provided fresh water while still having access to the rich fishing grounds of the salt water.

When I say, 'seaport,' understand that I am referring to towns of as many as a thousand people in some instances. When we came to such a place, I often brought the girls out to explore and find interesting trinkets that we traded for. We got to experience a lot of different kinds of food in this way, as well. And we continued to trade for interesting grain, plants, and animals to expand the living and growing area of the infinity room. Nimia periodically found and tantalized another young woman for the harem and there may have been a dozen living with us when I decided people were more plentiful along the rivers than along the seashore, so I headed upstream along one of them.

Having been on the sea for some time, I stowed my boat in the infinity room, which had the immediate effect of expanding our lake into a fair-sized body of water. It seemed to be a trait of the infinity room to adapt to what I put in it. It was as if the boat remembered the sea and brought that memory with it into the room. Lots of things worked that way. An animal used to grazing on a particular kind of grass would wander a while and then find a patch of that kind of grass. And the bag never seemed to get heavier!

As I was saying, I stowed the boat and decided to walk across the land for a while. It was fertile and the hills were dotted with sheep. It reminded me of Bathra. I stopped to chat with various farmers and shepherds and do some trading in the villages. It was rare that I'd find and manage to trade for a scroll. Nimia spent as much time reading the scrolls I collected as she spent with the other girls. It seemed no language written was beyond her ability to learn. Perhaps that was another trait of the infinity room. I knew the girls we had collected spoke different languages, but they all seemed to communicate just fine. The other girls would sometimes join me to walk for a while, but Nimia seldom emerged from the infinity room where I visited her nightly.

I could see a flock of sheep and goats on the hill in the distance and in a well-grazed area, I came upon a well. There was a bucket and a rope, so I could tell the well was deep. I started to lower the bucket when I heard a voice.

"Help! Help me out of here!" she weakly cried. I hurriedly let the bucket down, not knowing what kind of creature from the depths I might find.

"Can you catch hold of the rope?" I asked.

"Yes. Oh, thank you!"

She didn't weigh all that much. Even if I hadn't had the muscles I did, she was easy to pull up. I think Nimia could have done it. When she was finally at the top of the well, a very wet and soggy and naked girl threw herself into my arms.

"My savior! My hero! Thank you for pulling me out of that awful well. Uh... Don't drink the water from here. I've been pissing and shitting in it for two days," she said.

"That's a fair warning. Are you a naiad? A spirit of the well?"

"No! I am a girl! I was out here tending my father's goat herd when I was suddenly caught from behind and thrown into the well. I screamed and shouted, but all I heard was the goats being driven off. I've been waiting to either be rescued or to die."

"I see. Um... You don't have clothes on." The slippery girl in my arms was almost like a cat, trying to mold herself to every contour of my body as she dried herself and warmed against me.

"They were weighing me down in the water," she said. "I suppose you will ravish and despoil me. Know I am a virgin. My father might give you a reward for returning me intact. If you return me used, he will probably want to charge you for the privilege," she said.

She'd found a protrusion beneath my robe and was attempting to mold herself to that as well, so it was hard to tell which option she was hoping for. She continued to crawl on me and press her naked bits against me. It would have been a simple thing to cast my robe aside and part her legs with my cock. I somehow thought that would make me less of a man in Nimia's eyes.

I withheld.

"In what direction are your father's tents?" I asked.

"He makes our home at an oasis a day's walk north of here."

"I think I have a dress in my satchel," I said. "Left over from the last naked water nymph I helped." She caught her breath as I thrust my hand into the satchel and Nimia handed me a dress. I put it on the slender girl and it nearly fell off again. Nimia had far more bountiful breasts than this slip of a woman. But these breasts were capped with lovely rosy nipples that sat atop puffy cones on her chest. I did not at all mind the way the dress slipped off her shoulders periodically, as we walked toward her father's house.

Learning her story was not difficult. If I was quiet, she was talking.

"I'm the youngest daughter of twelve. My mother died of exhaustion after trying for a son so many times, while I was still nursing. I was raised by an older sister who lived with her husband in our little tent village. There was a war between tribes out here a year or two ago and all the eligible young men were killed. So, I'm my father's last daughter and have no marriage prospects. He's recently taken a war widow as his wife and hopes to breed a son on her. I don't know why he won't just let me inherit his fortune and his herds. I've always been able to handle the goats and camels and sheep better than any hired shepherd."

"I'm sure he is worried about you," I said.

"If he even notices that I'm missing. He's always moaning about how he doesn't have a son worthy of carrying on the name of Abdul ben Duggo. I was out with the sheep and goats, which are probably all missing now—stolen by the man who threw me in the well. It will probably lower my bride price. Maybe he'll just give me to you."

"Uh... I haven't said I wanted you."

"Oh, I could feel your desire when you were holding me. I'm actually quite enthused about becoming yours. You're a hero. You are stronger than any ten of the shepherds in the region. And you are hung like a camel. I can almost feel it parting my feminine folds... tearing through my maidenhead... thrusting into my secret places. Oh! Oh!" she sighed. She might have just talked herself into an orgasm. My sensitive nose detected an aroma of aroused woman beneath the stink of the stench well water.

"What is your name, by the way?" I asked.

"Josephet. Yes. Father was so set on my being a boy that he'd already chosen a boy's name for me. He simply added the feminine ending," she said, shaking her head. "I ask you, what is a girl to do when her father doesn't really want her and there are no men to take her off his hands?"

We continued in this mode for the rest of the day and camped beneath the stars. I realized that approaching the camp in the dark would raise an alarm. I was going to slip into the infinity room, but that would raise all kinds of questions and I wasn't ready to reveal myself to Josie yet. I just stretched out under the stars and Josie stretched herself out... on top of me. The way she wiggled around in her sleep kept my attention all night long. In the morning there was a wet spot on both our robes.

Things dried as we walked toward the tents ahead of us. We were hailed as we approached and Josie called out to everyone that a great hero had come to see her father. I wasn't that happy about the attention I was getting, and reflexively brushed at the hair on my head to be sure the horns weren't appearing. Before we arrived at the main tent, Josie pointed to the animal pens.

"Those are my goats! Father must have recovered them." I was suspecting something else. "Father!" she called at the flap of the tent. "A hero saved my life and I have brought him to be honored by you."

There was some scrambling inside the tent and the flap was flung open. A man, looking like he'd just been awakened, peered out.

"J-J-J-Josephet!" he exclaimed. "I thought we'd lost you!"

I rather thought there was a hint of regret in his voice. Certainly, a bit of disappointment in what he saw. Then he looked at me.

I made it look like I was just standing up straight as I added an extra handspan to my height. I'm sure he could see my muscles bulging in my neck and my chest straining against my robe. Josie turned to me and swooned.

"Father, this is Bob. Bob saved me. I see you found my goats. Bob, my father Abdul ben Duggo." The man shook his head as if to clear it.

"Goats. Yes. Came wandering in. Um... Thought you were lost to bandits. Couldn't understand why they'd take you and not the goats. Yes. That's it. A real puzzle."

"I am pleased to meet the father of this spectacular woman," I said. "She is an honor to your strength and tenacity. I'm sure you must be very proud of her."

"Proud. Yes. Um... certainly. I suppose you've had her, wandering out in the desert as you've been. That will cost you. Um... thirty drakma," he said, finally nodding his head and rubbing his hands together.

"Father, I assure you I am as virginal as the day I was born," Josie said. I thought that might be stretching it a little.

"Oh. Is that so? Ah... Well... Come in, come in. Please break bread with us. Camela! Bring bread and cheese and honey. We've a guest who wants to bargain for Josephet," he called into the back of the tent. A woman pulling her robe together stuck her head out of a flap.

"Josephet? I thought you said..."

"Yes, we all thought she'd met her demise. But she is here and she's brought a man."

"Oh. Don't let her go cheap," Camela said.

I thought, *What an appropriate name.*

"Now, Bob... May I call you Bob? Just call me Dug. Bob, you've already had an opportunity to get to know my youngest daughter, since you dragged her out of a well. Custom out here is that spending a night with a girl is tantamount to marriage. Now if you'd jumped the broom, as they say, and despoiled her in the wilderness, I'd be harsh with you. Father deserves to be compensated. But since you're a gentleman and a hero, I tell you what I'll do. Twenty drakmas and we'll hold the wedding right now."

I just sat looking at him. Neither Josie nor I had mentioned anything about a well. When she brought me a tray of food, I could see she'd caught the mistake as well, and she was seething. I motioned her to silence and returned to staring at the father.

"Okay," he continued. "You can see she's a little bent and scratched, but she still runs well. Good as new where it counts. Everything else will heal. And did I mention, she comes with her own camel? I can tell you're a nomad. A camel would be a blessing, yes?"

I was silent. Josie knelt beside us waiting for a deal to be struck. I could tell she was getting fidgety.

"You know, I thought we'd lost the twenty goats she was supposed to be taking care of. A girl like her needs a strong hand and work to do. I'll toss in the goats so you don't have to constantly listen to her chattering." I still made no move. "Okay, fifteen drakmas. And a tent. It's an old tent, but of course you want to keep her out of the sun. Just look at that skin. Fresh as a daisy and soft as butter."

Josie's skin was softer than mine, but she already showed signs of wear and tear from the sun. I'd want to get her inside, all right. She scooted over toward me and leaned against me. I put an arm protectively around her.

"Careful there. You break it, you bought it." I stared harder at him. He shifted uncomfortably. "I can see true love in bloom and only want what is best for my daughter. I'm a poor man with no sons. I need room in the tent for another family. I'll give you the girl, the tent, the camels, the twenty goats, and ten drakmas, if you'll just take her and leave. Do a guy a favor would you?"

I smiled at him and held out my hand. He dug beneath his robes and produced a pouch that would probably make him the richest man in the country. He counted out the coins and placed them in my hand. Josie jumped up and kissed me on the cheek, almost losing the dress in the process.

"I'll get my things," she whispered. She ran off, leaving Dug and me to finish our meal.

We walked outside and he had someone bring a camel, tent, and twenty goats to me. By the time the goats arrived, Josie was back with a small bag and grabbed my arm. She called to the goats by name and we left the oasis. I hadn't said a word since my introduction.

I put Josie on the camel and led out at a pretty good clip. She was worried about the goats keeping up, but I gave them a little boost and they were right with us when we camped for the night. I set up the tent as a nod to her expectations—after all it was her wedding night, though there had been no wedding. She made sure the goats were watered and grazing on the patch of lush grass I'd 'found.'

A new trick I'd learned was opening a passage up to the infinity room that looked like whatever the surroundings did. In this case, it simply looked like an inside flap to another room in the tent. Regardless, when Josie came in from tending the animals, she exclaimed over how much larger the tent looked inside than outside.

"Um... Bob? Did you cook something?" she asked, sniffing. Of course, Nimia and the harem had been busy preparing a feast and the aromas were delightful.

"Just a little something to welcome my beautiful new concubine to her new home," I said. "Are you hungry?"

"I'm hungry for you. Take me to your bed, Bob."

"Oh, that would be so rude. A concubine needs to be bathed and oiled. Her hair should be braided. Her skin massaged," I said, laying it on a bit thick.

"Yeah, sure. There weren't even baths and oils back at my father's tent," she scoffed.

"Did it not occur to you in our day together that I might be more powerful than your father?" I asked gently.

I lifted her chin with a finger to look into her eyes. She caught her breath and for a moment looked frightened. Then she rushed into my arms and let me hold her.

"Oh, Bob! I don't have any experience with men or with flirtation games or with anything that has to do with being your lover. I know you hold more power over me than my father ever did and I yield to you. Take me. Own me. Possess me."

Those were magic words. It was the first time I'd heard them spoken, but when she said, 'Possess me,' a switch tripped in my mind and I moved in to possess my concubine.

"Oh, my! What's happened?" she gasped as the room seemed to spin.

"You have been possessed by our master," Nimia said from the open flap into the infinity room. "You will be the most pampered and cared for concubine in the history of the world. You are *Bob's*."

"Who are you?" Josie asked as a dozen other naked young women emerged from the tent.

"I am Bob's wife, Nimia. And this is our harem. You will get to know all of us very well. Right now, we are here to bathe you and massage you, to feed you and oil you, and to present you a perfect offering to our husband."

"He really is more powerful than my father!"

"Oh, honey, you have no idea."

Nimia took Josie into the infinity room with most of the other girls and I could hear them exclaiming and laughing as Josie stripped and stepped into the waiting bath. Two others of our harem led me to a different part of the house and stripped me, soaking with me in a nice hot bath. They washed me, making sure I was well and thoroughly bathed. They trimmed my hair and beard and when we emerged from the bath, they oiled my skin, paying special attention to oiling my manhood until I thought I would explode.

I'd learned a spell to put on a flat wall that would reflect back the image of what was in front of it. Yeah, a couple of thousand years later, they were called mirrors, and just about everyone had one. I'd found it necessary to have one as I'd gradually aged my appearance in Bathra. I was getting to the point where I could fine tune my appearance and considered letting just the tip of my horns show through, but I thought that might be a bit much for our first night together.

"She is a doll!" Nimia exclaimed as she came into my dressing room. "What skin! She's so sensitive, I believe she climaxed as we oiled her breasts."

"What is she doing now?" I asked.

"Being massaged. And probably sleeping through it. I thought I'd better come to make sure our Lord and Master was ready to take his new possession," Nimia laughed, examining my barbering job and trimming a bit of my beard and the back of my head.

"What's with this Lord and Master stuff?" I asked. "You know, dear Nimia, I do not possess you as I do Josie. I'm not even sure how I possess her."

"Yes, I know, but it sounds so powerful. Better than anything since you became King of Bathra."

"Hmm. But you and I are bound together by the strands of love, not by possession."

"True, but you will find Josephet is nearly as closely bound to you by love as she is by possession. As time passes, I foresee that she will love you like no other."

"You have become quite a seer."

"I'm learning from the manuscripts. I, too, want to serve you any way I can." She wrapped a scarlet kilt about my waist and made sure my chest was oiled and glistening. "Now, let's take you to your concubine, my love."

Josie was nothing if not receptive to my love. She tolerated my teasing but begged me to continue. The bed Nimia and the girls had prepared for us was soft as down and I wondered when we had added that to the infinity room. I was to find out there had been many improvements over the years since I was king—almost as many as there had been in Bathra itself. Nimia and our harem were very busy girls.

"My lord and honored master," Josie said as I scattered kisses down her torso. "I am yours and would not think to tell you how to treat your possession, but if you don't fuck me soon, I'm going crazy!"

That was as good an invitation as asking me to possess her. I spread her legs and moved my staff into the wetness I found there. As I pressed slowly forward, I circled her nipples with my thumbs and blew sweet breath across her stomach. Josie arched her back in orgasm and I drove my cock through her barrier. She cried aloud and convulsed around me again as I drove all the way into her core, spewing my load against the guardian of her womb. In that moment, I was a little sorry she would never bear my child, but I would never break that vow.

We rutted together like a bull and cow in heat. Eventually, Nimia joined us and shared in Josie's treasures as I gave her that portion of myself she, too, craved.

Josie was accepting of the second world contained in the infinity room. Perhaps that was due to my influence on her, but perhaps it was simply her acceptance. We led the camel and goats through a tent flap into a lush pasture where there were other animals peacefully grazing. Once we had pasture lands, we had begun gathering animals. As King, I was often given personal gifts of which I kept a portion, returning most to the service of Ninra and Namri. Goats, sheep, cows, horses, donkeys, and camels were all part of the grazing herds.

She readily agreed that she would rather stay in the little corner of paradise I had created with Nimia, even without my expressing my will for her. As for me, reduced of my burdens to just my satchel, which never changed weight, no matter how much I put in it, I made quick time back to the sea where I found a new boat and navigated up another river to see what the world had to offer.

11
A Code to Live By

THE RIVER VALLEY was a rich land with plentiful crops and many sheep and goats. As was typical of a land of plenty, the people were stingy. It seems no matter where you travel, the poor are always willing to help the poor. The rich are unwilling to help anyone unless they think that person might be a benefit to them. Present company excluded, of course. I'm sure you are a generous person who often helps others and only elects representatives who are guided by the same principles.

I solved my problem by pulling my horse and chariot out of the bag, and traveled by road instead of looking like a river rat. Of course, it wasn't the same horse I had in Bathra. That good steed had died years before I left the city-state. This was one of his progeny, raised and kept in the infinity room his whole life. Nimia and Josie dressed me in fine clothes, left over from the royal court. They were a little out of fashion, but being considered eccentric is not really a problem most of the time.

The tricky part was figuring out how to look like my entourage was larger than it was. It was me and my harem of fourteen women who were all happier running around naked than clothed. The climate in the infinity room was ideal for nudity. I created a small home with an axle and wheels that I could pull behind the chariot. I called it a mobile home. The girls thought it was a kick and sometimes came out of the bag in daytime, just to ride in the mobile home. Of course, they fixed it up and often went shopping when I came to a town of suitable size. When we camped for a night, it was no problem to pull out all manner of tents and banners to look like I was well-guarded. I'd acquired a couple of wolf pups on the journey and took the time in the infinity room to carefully train them to alert me to danger and to protect the girls. Having them sit outside my tent at night was enough to discourage any unwanted visitors.

I enjoyed packing everything into my satchel—horse, chariot, mobile home, and all, and walking through a town to trade for things of interest. Usually, one of my harem girls would accompany me, but they were all well aware that as long as they were in the infinity room, they did not age. When they were in the normal world, time affected them. So, mostly, they stayed inside and I joined them in the evenings. People could not readily tell that I had the wealth of a small city in the satchel I carried over my shoulder.

As I was in a town on market day and browsed through its bazaar, I came upon a scribe who had a number of small scrolls he had made himself and sold for only a copper drakma each. I paid for a copy and returned to my tent to read the scroll with Nimia curled up in my lap reading with me. The scribe said it was a faithful copy of the laws of the land described as the Code of Hammurabi.

It was a list of laws as long as my arm with a penalty ascribed to each. I really needed to go find this self-styled king and have a chat with him. There were entirely too many things that required the death penalty—most of which were because it was inconvenient for the king to keep them alive.

I pushed the horse a little faster than horses usually go while pulling a chariot and rolling wagon behind. I used the same enchantment on the load that I had used on the sleds back in my palace building days in Minoa. The weight was light and easy for the horse to pull. Within a few days, we were in sight of the new city of Babylon, capital of Hammurabi's kingdom. He'd conquered nearly everything south, but stopped before he reached Bathra—at least for the moment. To the north, he was bordered by Assyrians on one side and Persians on the other, and was constantly fighting off one or both.

Word of my arrival as a wealthy merchant from the south spread quickly. I was conducted into the presence of the great man.

"You seem to have little of value to trade," Hamm said when we met.

"Ah. I have converted my wealth to smaller precious jewels and metals," I said. "I hope to trade those here and assemble a caravan of rare goods to take to the sea in the west and to the islands beyond." I showed a selection of my jewels and, of course, Hammurabi collected a tax on them. Nonetheless, I'd shown enough to establish that I was capable of assembling a caravan.

That had been another of Nimia's ideas. She suggested that an actual trading caravan would legitimize my claim to be a merchant and would also make it easier to establish a number of people in the camp. She suggested that it would also be a way to select certain people to join the population in the infinity room. I was, of course, willing to add to the harem, but Nimia suggested that some of the girls might want to have access to a man of their own and I should consider providing men, or find that the girls decided to stay in one of the towns through which we passed.

That hurt a little. I wanted to consider myself to be enough to satisfy any number of women, but I couldn't really expect all the women I collected to deny their basic drive to motherhood. I didn't own them as slaves, nor had I married or possessed them. And I did want them happy. So, I agreed to the arrangement.

Back to Hammurabi.

"Now these laws," I said. "They seem to be punitive. You focus on punishing the offender and not on restoring the victim."

"I rule with a rod of iron," Hamm stated. "I am obeyed or people die." Quite the big head.

"There is a small kingdom to the south that has created laws that show mercy to the poor and weak. They focus on the restitution of goods and righting the wrong, rather than punishment to show the power of the ruler. This kingdom has been blessed by the gods with great bounty. It shows leniency and fairness in the law," I said.

"Such a system could not be sustained. The ruler would become weak and the laws would be broken. I will go to that country and conquer it, bringing true law to the kingdom. The people will thank me because I am a great king. Tell me where it is," Hamm demanded.

I doubted that and hoped my... Hmm. I wasn't sure how long I had been gone wandering from Bathra. Would my son still be on the throne? My grandson? Another generation? I hoped he had maintained the laws and the strong army it would take to defeat Hammurabi's warlike people. I diverted his attention.

"It is in the direction of Egypt. Many days journey from here. You might find strange things there. The tombs of their kings are like mountains," I suggested. I'd never actually been to Egypt, but the story of the magnificent tombs entranced me and I thought that when I found my way to the sea, I might sail south and find the strange land of the Egyptians.

In the meantime, Hammurabi took me on a tour of his city and proudly pointed out the buildings. I congratulated him on the fine stone structures, occasionally making a suggestion that would improve the structural integrity or aesthetics.

"You know, this would be a fine place for a garden," I said. "Think of how people would come to see it and each visitor would bring their coins to spend in your bazaar."

"I will make it so. Bob, when you return here from your next journey, you will find a great garden here."

I promised I would one day return. Then I set about assembling a caravan of trading goods to take westward. We left Hammurabi's lands, finding our way to the Phoenician city of Tyre.

I camped well away from the city and had a conference with my girls. Oh, there were more of them now. It seemed nearly every town and village had a rebellious daughter who was more interested in an adventure than in becoming a wife. We had also assimilated a few of the men who traveled with the caravan, though I examined each thoroughly and let them know that the penalty for hurting one of the women was the most severe in the infinity room. Those I felt were unreliable in that regard, I paid well and sent away.

I know I sound like an old man talking about the good old days, but there was once a time when people knew their place in the great cycle of life. I don't mean only women. Men of every rank knew what was expected of them and where they fit in society.

Josie was a good example. She yearned for the life of a wife to a strong man who would care for her and protect her forever. Finding me—or vice versa—was her dream come true. Women were born and raised to be good wives. In fact, they competed to draw the greatest bride price. You could buy a pretty face for as little as a couple of sheep. But chances were, she was not well-trained or had a low opinion of her own skills. Many of those thought if they were good at one thing—like sex—all others would be forgiven. If you were able to offer a little gold, a flock of goats, and a good horse, you could get a wife who would manage your household efficiently, make sure food was prepared and served when you were hungry, be a happy and willing partner in bed—and if she couldn't for some reason, would supply a woman who was—and see her man and her household prosper. Like Nimia.

This did not come without responsibilities on the part of the man. If he paid that kind of money for a woman, you can bet he was going to take care of her. He treated her well, provided fine clothes and servants, hunted or farmed or shepherded or traded so there was always food for her, and protected her from every danger. And they were both happy. She was proud to have commanded such a price and set about proving she was worth it. He was happy to have purchased a luxury model and spent his weekends polishing her and spoiling her.

Sorry. I mixed centuries a little there.

But we had encountered girls of an independent spirit as we traveled. Well, Josie wasn't really that independent. Her father had devalued her. I mean, twelve girls—I could understand a little of how frustrated he was trying to find husbands for all of them. And without a mother, Josie had grown up a little rough around the edges, preferring to watch the goats rather than to watch a pot of water boil. Other girls, however, had wanted to choose for themselves what kind of mate they would have, and to negotiate their role in the marriage according to their own ideal.

It was this latter kind of girl we attracted as we traveled.

I was not willing to simply take on all comers with no questions asked, but Nimia and I found most of them to be capable negotiators and sticklers regarding the terms of their contract. In several instances, that included me providing a husband for them with no questions asked about how they had pleased me. When they discovered they would not be the only woman in my life, they rejoiced. Whether they had a taste for pussy themselves or simply wanted helpmates in the household, nearly all felt the company of women in the household was a great advantage to them.

And they all recognized Nimia as the head of my household and that Josie was my own special possession and to be respected in every way.

So, when we camped on the shores near Tyre, I held counsel with a couple dozen young women in my harem and a few men. I'd found many years ago that a counsel held with sexually sated women was far more productive than one in which they were frustrated, horny, or angry. The men in the household willingly helped me get them to a pliable state. The men, too, knew that Nimia and Josie were completely off limits and that any young woman of the harem might tell them, 'No,' with unbroachable finality.

When all were ready to meet, I suggested that I was ready to go sailing again and would find myself a boat. I suggested they would be best served by staying in the infinity room while we were at sea and that I would visit regularly and always protect them. One or two were ready to leave our company and I granted them this, along with a bride price. They trusted me to find a husband for them, but not to take them to sea.

I took the caravan into town, the young men of the infinity room as guards, and set about trading. I collected a fair amount of gold, silver, and jewels, but probably as many goods as I traded away. This time, however, the trade goods were transported directly into the infinity room set up in the tent I occupied in the market.

Tyre was a city of traders. Yes, I was one and had been trading for many years, but the people of towns and villages and even larger cities inland traded for the things they needed to live. 'I'll give you a basket of barley for one of those sheep.' That kind of thing. The people of Tyre traded for profit. Their objective was not to give a fair price for something they needed, but to get an object for as little as possible and trade it for as much as possible—whether they needed it or not. In Bathra, everyone lived and was provided for according to their service to the gods. In Tyre, there were a few very wealthy men who styled themselves as lords, there were many merchants who lived off the profits of their trade, and a vast ocean of peasants, each trying to trade his way up the social ladder, or to simply survive.

At last, I had found suitable husbands for the women who wanted them and made sure they would be well-cared-for their entire lives. Then the men and I packed up what remained of the caravan, selling off the tents and most of the camels. We went out of town to a place I knew that was well-protected. I was not unfamiliar with the area, though the population had grown immensely over the years. But I had once met a beachcomber in this area who told me the way to Nansi, the dream interpreter.

I packed everything and everyone I owned into the infinity room and tossed the satchel over my shoulder. I adopted the strapping body I'd come to know as a sailor and went back to town to see if I could find a ship.

Ships had changed since I'd last sailed the inner sea. They were larger and sleeker. Some had as many as two or three masts and sails with a great rudder for steering rather than oars operated by a dozen men. They had cabins for the captain and crew and space below deck for cargo.

When I finally found a ship I considered suitable, I had to find its master. The master had to find his owner. The owner had to come to the docks to haggle the price of the ship. Of course, he didn't want to sell. That was predictable. In the game of trading up, he only wanted a bigger and better ship in exchange for his little piece of shit. It wasn't a very big ship. I wanted one I could handle by myself without constantly using magic to keep the thing afloat. I reached in my satchel and withdrew a sizable bag of gold nuggets and a few priceless gemstones. He actually salivated, but he had to keep playing the game.

"I don't know. Is that all you have? It's already been loaded with trade goods."

"No. It's all I'll give you. As you well know, it's enough to buy two of these barks fully loaded or one really nice freighter."

"If that handful of trinkets is worth so much, why don't you buy a freighter?" the owner demanded. At the sight of the gold, the crew of the ship had begun to edge closer to us and I could foresee a fight about to begin.

"I want this ship," I said firmly. I glared at the sailors and they stepped back.

"Take the money and run, Mordecai!" a woman's voice snapped from behind him.

"Madam!" the suddenly frightened owner said, bowing. "Certainly. I did not know you were funding this sailor, madam. I would never cheat you, madam. Please spare me your wrath." He snatched the purse out of my hand and literally took off running. "It's all yours!" He yelled over his shoulder. The master and crew all stepped off the boat, gave the lady and me wide berth, and ran off after the owner.

"Oh, damn! I suppose now, I'll have to wait for you to get a new crew."

"Not at all, madam," I said, copying the owner's form of address. "I intended to fire them anyway."

"And what? You can't plan to sail this alone!"

"Why look!" I said. "There's even a cabin on deck. If you would care to board, madam, we'll be off."

She looked at me and grinned. Then she gathered her robes about her and boarded the ship. I cast off the lines and shoved the little ship out into the water. Once there, I floated on the outgoing tide until I had raised the sail and then I blew a gentle wind to fill it. Before the sun had moved to cast a different shadow, we were sailing away from the seaport.

Ah, the salt wind in my hair! The smell of the sea! The sound of the waves lapping against the sides. The musical voice of my unexpected passenger.

"Oh, Captain," she said. I turned and found the most beautiful woman I have ever seen in my life. Not just up until that time, but ever in four millennia—and I have seen some extremely beautiful women. To say she was breathtaking would be an understatement. I know that everyone has his or her own definition of beauty, but I honestly believe that anyone looking at her would immediately identify her as the most beautiful woman in the world.

She was dressed—I think that's what you would say—in a wrap of translucent silk that partially concealed one ripe breast. The other was fully exposed. I wanted immediately to fall to it and suckle. Golden hair cascaded around her shoulders and down her back. Much to my surprise, I could see that her womanly charms were bare. I mean, the wrap was over her hips and legs, but it was so transparent that I could see clearly through it. What I meant was that her pubis itself was bare. I saw not a hair on her body that was not attached to her head. I wondered for an instant if this ripe a luscious body belonged to a child!

"What do you plan to feed me on our voyage?" she demanded, but in such a lyrical voice that I wanted nothing more than to give her whatever she desired.

"Why, what would you like, fair lady?" I asked. Madam was too coarse a word to use in describing her, I decided.

She put a finger to her lip as if considering.

"I should like honey cakes with fresh goat's milk," she said, as if it would throw me.

"Honey cakes with fresh goat's milk?" I said so my women in the infinity room could get to work. "Allow me to prepare a table for you, my lady." I reached into the infinity room and grabbed a table. She gasped when I set it before her and reached back for a chair so she could be seated.

"What minor deity have I ensnared in my plan to escape?" she asked as I held the chair for her.

"No deity, my lady. I'm a simple, happy-go-lucky demon. Please allow my women to serve your dinner." I opened a door to the infinity room and Nimia and Josie rushed out, spreading a linen cloth on the table and setting out plates of honey cakes and fruits and a goblet of goat's milk. The girls retreated back to the infinity room with my stern warning that no one else was to emerge when I called for service. I could well imagine what might happen if the men cast an eye on this beauty.

"Now, there are a few things you must know if you are to serve me," she said as she snacked on the spread.

"Ah, my lady," I said. "I am delighted to have you as my guest upon my ship, but you must understand, I serve no one but myself. I will always attempt to provide whatever hospitality is within my ability to give. I am, however, a free demon."

"You don't even flinch away from me! Do you know who I am?" she demanded.

"No. It is apparent you are a goddess, but I don't believe we have met before. Let me begin. I am Bob and I welcome you to my ship."

"Bob? I've never heard that name. Since you don't know me, you may continue to address me as My Lady. It is much better than being called 'madam' by those sods in Tyre. It made me feel like a brothel keeper. Are you not even in awe of my beauty?" she asked. There was obviously only one correct answer to the question, but I attempted to side-step it.

"You are, indeed, the most beautiful woman on earth. For all I know, perhaps in the heavens as well," I said.

"You are very clever," she said. "Who taught you?"

"My first tutor was Great Zeus, who shared my abode and my women for some time. It was he who taught me to be polite. Later, I had the honor of acting as emissary for the great war god Ninra of Sumer. He taught me honesty and strength. His wife, Namri, the protector of the poor, taught me compassion and love," I said. I was quite proud of this lineage, and wanted all three of those gods to be proud of me.

"Oh, Bob. I think we can have such a good time. Do you not want to run your hands over my alabaster skin? Do you not want to part my legs and drink the honey from my pussy? Do you not want..."

"I beg your forgiveness, my lady, but even a poor demon such as I can easily reckon when a woman is out of my price range." She shut up. I thought she might have been insulted, or perhaps she'd simply never been turned down before. I was afraid of what price she would charge for my attentions. Beautiful though she certainly was, I was not willing to exchange my freedom for her pleasure.

I contented myself with watching the sails and steering the ship according to the stars in the night sky. When I turned back, she had returned to her cabin. I summoned Nimia and Josie to clear the table. Then we played on the deck beneath the stars for a while before I sent them back to the infinity room. I didn't think it was a good idea for me to go into the infinity room while the goddess was aboard my ship. I didn't know what havoc she might create.

12
SHIPWRECK

▨▨▨▨▨▨▨▨▨▨▨▨▨▨

*I*N THE MORNING, My Lady Goddess appeared from the cabin in a similar lack of attire, but of a different color. If I had doubted she was a goddess before, the doubt was dispelled by the costly dye used in her wisp of clothing. And by the fact she seemed to have much more baggage than she'd brought aboard with her. She sat on the gunwales, looking into the waves as she brushed her hair.

"Oh, Bob, would you be a good demon and brush my hair for me. I simply can't reach the spots behind me."

"My Lady, since you ask so pleasantly, I will be happy to brush your hair, with your permission, of course."

"Yes," she said. She handed me her brush and I set about a very relaxing time brushing out her long golden hair. "Is my hair the silkiest you have ever seen?" she asked.

"Yes, it is," I answered. Could she possibly be more vain about her looks? That gave me an idea. I had no difficulty brushing her hair until the sun passed its zenith. It seemed to be a relaxing thing for both of us and we chatted idly while I stroked the silky strands.

"I don't actually *hate* my husband," she sighed. "He's just such a stick in the mud. I, like you, am a *free* goddess. I am older by far than he is, having been born from the sea when Uranus's genitals were cast there by Cronos. I should be able to have what lovers I want. He does make me pretty things, though. Like the brush you are using."

"So, you are running away from your husband?" I asked. I was pretty sure that somewhere in the middle of Hammurabi's 300 or so laws, I had read a woman taken in adultery was to be drowned. And the man, too.

"Oh, no. Let's say I'm on a vacation. You will discover, Bob, that a steady diet of just one partner for all your life is an incredible strain on an immortal. The fire dies eventually.

You *have* to take a break."

I had heard much the same from Zeus when I was young and naïve. Ariane had sworn to keep me in a non-stop supply of other lovers for variety. Nimia had continued the tradition and there were now a couple dozen in the infinity room I could choose from. Though I seldom got a choice. They seemed to all want my attention all the time.

I brought a luncheon of figs and honey cakes to her and while she ate, I quickly retrieved the mirror from my wall. This I brought to her and fastened to her door. I correctly predicted that she would find looking at herself to be endlessly entertaining.

The goddess was good company as long as you didn't want to talk about anything but her. And that was not difficult. Ancient morality tales decried vanity, painting the tale of cursed Narcissus who fell in love with his own beautiful reflection in a pool and stared at it for the remainder of his life. I suppose that was a bit extreme, but I have known many men and women alike who were vain about their looks, their knowledge, their power, and their wealth. Nebuchadnezzar, Alexander, Caesar, Cleopatra, Helen. Not all were unpleasant people.

As days went by and the sea was easy, the goddess spent time every day standing or sitting in front of the mirror as I brushed her hair. It was peaceful and calming, making for a very pleasant journey. Once she had retired for the night, or at least closed the door to her cabin, I would bring one of my ladies on deck and work out any sexual frustrations I'd picked up from such close proximity to the perfect goddess of lust.

My ladies were very good at making sure my frustrations had been satisfied. I don't mean just Josie and Nimia, though I loved both of them, but a dozen other women in my harem were equally as affectionate. They were having a great time in the infinity room, designing and building whatever their hearts desired. It was refreshing to find women who were not so into themselves that they could talk about nothing else.

Then the winds picked up.

I'd been in rough seas before. I simply made doubly sure my satchel was strapped securely across my shoulder, dropped the sail, and manned the rudder. I had also been in a storm initiated by a god and this one was looking suspicious.

The goddess was furious.

"He's enlisted that damned Poseidon to torment me!" she declared. "Why can't he simply let well enough alone? He knows I'll come back eventually. He just does this to be mean! I haven't even had sex with you yet!"

Well, that was a revelation on several fronts. First that not only was the storm brought by a god, but Poseidon himself might be at the root. Second, that she considered sex with me to be a 'not yet' and not a 'not ever.' I believe she was most unhappy that I had to pay attention to sailing and not to her. The storm got progressively worse. I hadn't experienced anything like this since Ninra roiled the waters to get me where he wanted. I was not happy about the prospect of having to throw My Lady Goddess into the sea to calm it and vowed to fight it out with this Poseidon. With that thought, I reached into the satchel and withdrew the Sword of Ninra, given me by the god of war to lead my armies into battle. I belted it to my side and shook the water out of my face as I steered the ship into the wind.

I rapidly worked a spell to make the ship impervious to the storm, but what I got was something that just kept it from capsizing. That was nearly good enough.

Nearly.

It was no defense against the tentacled monster that wrapped an appendage around the middle of the ship and began to crush it. My second meeting with a Scylla of Poseidon.

The rudder was of no use as long as the ship was in the grip of the monster, so I drew my sword and rushed to the middle of the deck to hack at it. It was tough going, but I had the limb almost severed when I heard My Lady scream behind me. I turned to see another tentacle had wrapped around her and was pulling her toward the sea.

My own experience with having been grabbed by a sea serpent was that it just threw me where it wanted me to go. Not pleasant, but survivable. This monster seemed intent on dragging the goddess down for a personal interview with the god of the sea. I did the only thing I could. I jumped in after her.

I will leave descriptions of our intense battle under the sea to poets like that old fraud and seeker of fame and fortune, Homer. Not that I disliked Homer when I met him a few centuries later, but you have to call them like you see them. He was a professional liar—known these days as a novelist.

Suffice it to say, as the hero of this story, I hacked at the monster with the Sword of Ninra and the monster was no match for it. Eventually, I won the goddess's freedom and lifted her above the waves. The monster fled back to the deeps to nurse its wounds and I found the rocky shore of an island. There, I deposited My Lady Goddess, and there my ship was hurled to crash upon the rocks. I stretched out to sleep in exhaustion.

I awoke to the sensations of the most beautiful woman in the world—the goddess of beauty and lust—riding on my cock to portals of ecstasy no man is privileged to enter. Let me say, without bragging about the conquest, that her pussy was as beautiful to my cock as her body was to my eye. There were things that she did while seeking her own satisfaction that brought tears to my eyes. There were moments I could have sworn it was only her hand giving me pleasure, but then it would be the most exquisite clasping of her pussy, and then it felt like a mouth had enveloped me and a tongue was exploring every bit of my cock. I could even feel her throat swallowing me and coaxing a mammoth load from my balls.

And all this was while I was looking into her eyes, my hands filled with her perfect breasts, as she bounced energetically on my cock. When I exploded within her I shook with fervor. When she exploded around me, she milked another load from my recently emptied balls. And then she collapsed forward on me, her breasts pressing lightly into my chest as I held her and kissed her.

"That was definitely worth waiting for, my hero," she sighed.

Ah. So that was it. Now I was her hero. Looking back, I'm sure she could have saved herself, if by no other means than fucking Poseidon when they finally met. He would be helpless to do anything but her bidding. As I was when she asked me to take her to my infinity room, where she was sure she could not be detected.

The landscape had changed in the infinity room. There was a new lake on the horizon and Josie exclaimed excitedly that they had a storm and a flood, but everything receded to the beautiful beach where we found a dozen naked nymphs lying beneath my sun. Like scattering stars in the sky, having a sun added to the aesthetic of our little world.

Aphrodite, as she now shared her name with me, was as lusty as any of my ladies had ever been. She wanted my cock as often as I could get it up—which I never had difficulty doing—and wanted my ladies' tongues, sometimes all at once. And as my ladies pleasured her, they were each endowed with even more beauty than they had before.

Eventually, she tired of our quiet little world. And, I am sorry to say, of my cock. She took to wandering the island and quite a cult grew up around her presence. Cyprus, I discovered, was as well-settled and civilized as my native Crete. One day, Aphrodite simply did not return to our little camp near the sea.

I did some exploring of the island myself—not looking for her, mind you, but trying to make sure she had not fallen into some nefarious trap. I discovered she had fallen in with an artist and he was currently sculpting an image of her. I could only offer her a mirror. He offered her a statue. Easy come, easy go. And Aphrodite was definitely easy.

When my ship wrecked on the rocks of our little beach, I was able to salvage all of the trade goods that had been on board in Tyre. I took them all into the infinity room, but did not have them stored or put away. Instead, I went looking for a ship to buy. The guys in the infinity room who had also been blessed by Aphrodite's effect on their women, hauled the remnants of our ship into the infinity room and over to the new sea, apparently created by a leak in the bag when I was battling the Scylla underwater. I resolved to get that fixed right away. There, they set about rebuilding it and learning all they could about shipbuilding.

When I had found a ship and made a remarkably favorable deal on it, my men emerged from the infinity room and began loading our cargo. Then we shoved off and headed toward Crete. I was thinking I would visit my old home, but we docked in Mania and I made some favorable trades with cargo bound for Athens.

I did have a chance to go look at the desolate site where King Idiopheles' palace had stood. It seems that soon after I left the island, an earthquake had struck. In the shaking, all the rock that had been quarried by slaves crumbled and fell on the idiot king. He and his entire line were extinguished. The people of Mania were living under the rule of an elected committee, following the model of Athens somewhat. I was happy. There was no slavery on the island of Crete.

My men returned to the infinity room and I set sail for Athens with my shipload of goods. It seemed that in every port of call we would gain a few ladies and perhaps another sailor or farmer or shepherd. Life in the infinity room was tranquil and domestic. Nimia governed the room with the same general rule I had used in Bathra: Those who worked for the good of the people (and me) would always be cared for and would never lack for any needed thing. Those who did not, would be courteously escorted out of the infinity room to make their way in the 'natural' world. It was the first I'd heard that name applied to the world we had all come from.

But a new phenomenon was occurring in the infinity room. The men were not sterile like I was. And as a result, several of the women became pregnant and attached themselves permanently to their men. But we slowly realized a child born in the infinity room aged the way any child would. He would become an adult. He would grow old and he would die. I use the term 'he' here because that is what Professor Tolkien taught in his classes. Of course, I mean a child and adult of any sex.

What's more, it was discovered that after the birth of a child, the parents also began to age and would eventually grow old and die. It was only those who came into the infinity room from outside and remained childless who would cease aging. I needed to study those damned scrolls again.

While in Athens, I paid tribute to the city's patron gods, including the goddess Aphrodite. She might have abandoned me in Cyprus, but I felt her presence near me when I sincerely paid my homage to her. Athene was also a patroness of the small city, as was Poseidon. I felt nothing at all from Athene and mild distaste from Poseidon.

I took the goods for which I traded and began sailing from island to island, trading and becoming richer and richer. What I really wanted was to find a place I could settle down and simply enjoy my ladies. The harem was quite large now, and I was not filling nearly as many places with men as I could have. I just wanted to have peace and quiet and a few centuries to learn to know each of them.

And that is when I came upon a great walled city in Anatolia. It was larger than any I had seen. I estimated that half a million people lived in the city of Ilium and more in its surrounds. It was prosperous and trade came from every corner of the world. Best of all, I could blend right in with the people of the city and no one would think twice about me. I adopted a body that was similar to the men of the city, and opened a little bakery. I was able to show myself a modest craftsman in an essential industry. No one bothered me when I retired to my chamber at night and slipped into the infinity room to make love all night long.

"You know that if you are to stay in this place, you need to age for a while and then disappear to return as a new man," Nimia reminded me. "You are having daily contact with people who are growing older. You must not appear to be forever young."

"My fair and wise wife, I hear you and will do as you say. I don't know what I would do without you. I don't know how you have become so wise," I said.

"If what you tell me about time outside our infinity room is true, I am some seven or eight hundred years old," she answered. "Both you and I should have learned something in all that time."

"What of the others?" I asked. "We have women with us we picked up in Bathra and in our travels after. Even in Babylon. Have they grown and learned as you have?"

"I don't understand it, Bob. Josie has certainly gained in her understanding of life and the world, but her devotion is entirely to you. Anything either she or I have learned in all that time is placed in service to you. She hasn't read as much as I have, but she listens to people and is very understanding of them. But the others... they seem completely contented with their life and do not seek knowledge or greater understanding. Even those who marry have contentment to simply be what they are and not attempt to learn more."

"Hmm. I wonder if that is a good thing or bad. We should think about that," I said. I felt her slip down on my shaft as we talked in bed and envelop me in her pussy.

"What we need to think about right now is the loving act of a husband and wife. You need to focus on filling me and I need to focus on the wonderful lover I have devoted my life to," she said as we began to move.

"You are constantly in my thoughts, my wife. Immersing myself in you is more than I can describe. Feeling you mounting toward your climax pulls me along and I am helpless inside you," I said.

"Come, my husband. Let me feel your love flowing into my vagina. I love you." And with that, we lost ourselves in loving again and again.

I took to heart what she had said, though, and learned to age myself gradually. When I felt I was sufficiently old enough, I moved from that spot and opened a shop in a different part of Troy as a younger man.

When war came to the Kingdom of Troy, I could see My Lady Goddess Aphrodite's hand in the proceedings. Not that she was solely responsible for it, but she certainly gave cause for it. There is a story about a golden apple addressed to "The Fairest of the Goddesses" being tossed into a celestial gathering. Apparently, Aphrodite had grown tired of her artist and returned to Olympus and her misshapen husband Hephaistos. There was no question in my mind (or in anyone else's, I was later told) that Aphrodite was deemed the most perfect image of femininity in the universe. She would certainly outshine cow-eyed Hera or virgin warrior Athene with ease.

But Aphrodite, as I mentioned, was not only the most beautiful and lustful woman in the universe, she was also the vainest. The slight possibility that an impartial judge might find her second in beauty was intolerable. So, she fixed the game. She secretly told Paris, a son of King Priam of Troy, that if he chose her, she would give him the most beautiful woman (human) on earth as his bride. I wish I'd been near him to warn him off, but sure enough, he attended the wedding of the Greek King Menelaus of Sparta to Helen. When Paris saw Helen he was smitten and she, seeing a ticket away from the old man she was to be married to, ran away with him on her very wedding night.

Hmm. That reminds me of another young bride, but I think I already told you the story of Portia.

Paris brought Helen home to Troy and the Greeks followed en masse.

Here's something that old goat Homer wouldn't tell you. He was such a romantic! Pure women and heroic men. But he failed to mention that Helen was a slut. I believe she ran away with Paris simply so Menelaus wouldn't discover his new bride was no virgin. That and

Menelaus was an old man of at least thirty, while Paris was a young and well-hung prince in his teens. Also, Troy was an entire city of men she hadn't slept with yet.

There was no doubt that Aphrodite was her patroness.

It took nearly a year, with the Greeks camped outside the city, for her to find her way to my bed. She was, indeed, like a... um... hairy Aphrodite. The goddess eschewed all hair except what grew from her head. Helen was as nicely formed as a human girl could be, but grew hair from under her arms, around her sex, down her legs... I checked to see if she had hair growing from the palms of her hands. But all the hair on her body was as silky, soft, and golden as the hair on her head.

She was enthusiastic about sex, teasing a man (or demon) unmercifully until he cast her on his bed and fucked her. And she may have had the juiciest cunt I'd ever been in—which was good as my size was considerably more than any invading prick she'd had before. Oh, the ride was nice and the steed was energetic, but her pussy was in no wise as talented as her patroness goddess.

She left me to hurry back to her husband's bed with my semen running from her pussy and down the inside of her legs. For my part, I closed my little shop where I sold baked goods made by the ladies in my infinity room, and changed my appearance to an old man, just entering the city's gates. Sure enough, the prince's guards came looking for the despoiler of his wife the next morning. They could have arrested almost anyone.

13
THE FALL OF TROY

*I*T DIDN'T TAKE too long to see how the war would ultimately play out, though it took ten years for the final curtain to fall. Aphrodite had recruited Apollo, Artemis, and mighty Ares to help the Trojans. But arrayed against them were Athene and Hera (losers of the beauty contest), Aphrodite's once-again estranged husband Hephaistos, Poseidon (who was still upset about losing Aphrodite at sea), and Hermes. Hermes is known today by the simple title of being a messenger god. But to me, he was a god most to be feared. He was the god of travelers and, oddly enough, the god of the satchel. He should have been my patron. If you've lost your luggage, appeal to Hermes. He'd had nothing to do with my own satchel and the infinity room, but I had no doubt he could unmake it if he knew about it. Worst of all, Hermes was a spy. You just never knew where he might show up. I just hoped Aphrodite would keep her mouth shut about the infinity room.

There was a lovely temple to Aphrodite in Ilium (the name of the city in the Kingdom of Troy). As in most of her temples, worshipers bearing gifts for the goddess could ask a question of a priestess and expect to get an answer during coitus. No, they were not prostitutes. That's something the anal-retentive archeologists of the nineteenth and twentieth century arrived at because they considered any sex act with someone other than a spouse to be prostitution. Aphrodite was the goddess of sex, true, but not of prostitution.

If they had paid attention to what happened back on Cyprus with the Propoetides, they'd have figured that out. Those twelve priestesses of the goddess got it into their heads that they could make a pretty fortune by just selling sex and profiting from it. This was not long after Aphrodite and I arrived on Cyprus, so I was there when she put an end to the practice by turning them into stone. The last I saw of them was in the British museum.

But the priestesses of Troy were devoted to Aphrodite. They often blessed the warriors going out to meet the Greeks in battle. And lest you think that was an easy task, remember there were over 100,000 warriors on each side in this conflict! It was a bloody mess on the battlefield. But the priestesses rightly felt that no man should go to his death without having been laid. Recently. The soldiers retreated behind the city walls at night and many of them retreated into the embrace of the goddess, who felt the hot smell of sex was the best offering she could be given.

Nonetheless, Aphrodite came to me in a dream one night. I came, too. As we copulated, she wept on my shoulder because she knew the Greeks were going to win the war and her precious city would be sacked and ruined. Now, there is something else you need to realize. Just because she (and her priestesses) loved sex, didn't mean that she wasn't emotionally committed to the act and to the people involved. She had loved and lost many times. I saw the priestesses in the temple weep over the list of fallen published each day, touching the names of those they had blessed and, indeed, remembering their touch and love.

Aphrodite painted a picture of horror that would occur once the barbarian Greeks breeched the city gates. Men would be slaughtered. Women would be raped... and then slaughtered. I was beginning to shrink out of her hot embrace when she entreated me to save her priestesses when the city fell. With my cock steeping in her juices, what could I do but agree? She knew I had the means as I could easily stuff them all into my infinity room.

I asked one boon. I asked that they gather together all the scrolls of Ilium they could collect so that when I rescued them, I would save the knowledge of the city as well. Aphrodite agreed and our bargain was sealed with another crashing orgasm.

There were details that needed to be worked out. I talked to Nimia and Josie, and they went to work preparing a place for the one or two hundred priestesses who would be joining our little world. That would double our population. The men in the harem were called upon to build housing for them and I did what I could to make their work lighter. Even the women could lift the stone blocks to build the housing. The infinity room was growing into a small city.

Of course, I had to figure out how I was going to escape when the city fell. I'd adopted the visage of an old man in my latest transfiguration, so that I could avoid being sent out to fight. I was still opposed to the senseless bloodletting of this war and wanted no part in the killing. I'd been given a job in Priam's harem as a joke. I was told I was the last line of defense for the women—and then all his household laughed.

"If it comes down to Bob protecting the harem, they might as well strip and open their legs. There will soon be a Greek between them," laughed Hector. I looked too old even for Helen to want a ride.

Let me just mention that I bore no grudge against Hector. What he said was exactly what I wanted him to believe. I had nothing at all to do with that asshole Achilles drilling Hector with a spear the next day. I just want that to be clear.

After Hector's death, when Paris went out to gain revenge for his brother and killed Achilles, Troy had renewed hope. Their warriors met the Greeks with renewed fervor and drove them back toward their boats. Day after day the battle raged. And then a day dawned clear and bright. The warriors marched out of the city and found no Greeks to meet them on the field. Of their thousand ships, perhaps half had not been burned, but those had loaded their soldiers and departed.

The Trojans went out to investigate and found only a huge wooden horse. You probably know the rest of the story from Virgil's writing of the *Aeneid*, though he got most of the details wrong. Homer was dead set to make Odysseus out to be the hero of the Greeks, so he ignored the horse entirely. I think Athene was probably prompting him. I never understood why she liked him so much. The Greeks in their message wished Paris and all the other men of Troy enjoyment of Helen.

It was quite a celebration. Even the harem emptied to go party in the streets. Only Cassandra and a few children and nurses remained. Cassandra was cursed with being able to prophesy only the absolute truth, but to have no one believe her. Homer gave her short shrift in the Iliad. Virgil did slightly better in his telling of the story in the Aeneid.

First off, the girl—daughter of Priam and Hecuba and younger sister of Paris and Hector—was just plain cute. Helen might have been the most beautiful woman in the world, but if Cassandra had been allowed to grow up, she would have surpassed the legend by far. As a pubescent teen, she became the object of affection of Apollo who had been enlisted by Aphrodite to fight for Troy and had given enchanted arrows to the Trojan archers. Where they struck, if they did not kill instantly, they caused disease that eventually took the life of the wounded and spread to others in the Greek camp. But while he was in the city, Cassandra caught his eye and he fell in lust.

Cassandra was barely thirteen. Apollo was an old man to her and regardless of how glorious he looked in the temple, she had no interest in him at all. Apollo, thinking he would convince her with a rare power, gave her the gift of prophecy so that everything she said would come true. She was so horrified by what she saw in the future that she cursed Apollo and told him to bugger off. Not the way to win friends—especially gods. Apollo couldn't revoke his gift, but to punish Cassandra—Punish! For not loving him!—he added to the gift a curse that no matter what she prophesied, no man or woman would believe her.

So, I found her in the harem, blubbering amidst the children, most of whom had been left behind. This is where Homer and Virgil both screwed up. Apollo's curse was that no man or woman would believe her. But as she prophesied the destruction of Troy, the children of the harem were terrified. *They* believed her. And then Cassandra straightened and in the midst of her manic rantings pointed at me and told the children, "There lies your salvation. Go with Bob and you will be safe."

I am neither man nor woman, either, lest you forget. I am a demon and Aphrodite had already told me Troy would fall. I opened a gateway to the infinity room and my women rushed to take the children and their nurses into my satchel. But nothing I could say would convince Cassandra to join them. She had been given a vision that she knew to be a true prophesy that she would be taken by Agamemnon after the fall and that she would see him die in Athens.

I found my way to the temple of Aphrodite to fulfill the rest of my commission. I asked the faithful priestesses of the goddess to gather up all their scrolls and come through the door I stood beside—a doorway into the infinity room. There was hesitance among some. They had a line of warriors outside the temple getting drunk and wanting to praise Aphrodite for their victory.

Then all hell broke loose. Greeks had been hiding in the horse and while most of the Trojans slept off their celebratory drunks, the hidden warriors threw open the gates of Ilium and the entire Greek army swarmed through to put every man to the sword. I shouted for the priestesses to hurry and grab as many scrolls as they could carry.

There were still some who scoffed at me. I am sorry to say these suffered a worse fate than the Propoetides. As representatives of the goddess who had fomented the war, the Greeks took particular pleasure in raping and killing them. Mostly in that order. I slipped away with over a hundred priestesses in my satchel and ten times that many books. There was nothing more I could do but hide. If the Greeks saw me, even disguised as an old man, they would do their best to kill me. If they discovered I was a demon, it was a sure bet that they would call on Hephaistos to hammer me into the ground.

I looked for a place to hide and dove behind Aphrodite's altar in the temple, only to find another man hiding there as well. A Greek!

"What the hell are you doing hiding here?" I asked, taking an unnecessary risk of discovery.

"Are you kidding? It's dangerous out there. Don't hurt me! I was all for a sneak attack, but the damned Trojans are fighting back!" he whispered anxiously.

I couldn't believe the gall of this fellow, hiding out in the temple of the goddess he'd made war on, hoping there would be some pussy left for him when the shooting died down!

"Did you see the tits on that one?" he asked excitedly as a priestess who had chosen to stay ran past with a scroll, hoping to find me. "I've got to get me some of that!"

He chose the wrong moment to stand from our hiding place and a stray arrow—shot from a Greek, of all things—nailed him through the neck. He fell beside me, unnoticed by the warriors still around. The priestess chose that moment to dive behind the altar and I opened a gateway just wide enough for her to slip through, then sealed it tight.

I saw my chance and decided to grab the body of the Greek to get me safely out of Troy. I laid my hands on him to absorb his memories and images and whispered the words of the transfiguration spell. In a matter of moments, I was Odysseus, a Greek, and he was an old Trojan man with an arrow through his neck. I grabbed his sword and bloodied it in the body, then emerged from the temple proclaiming our victory.

By that time, the battle was pretty much done, so I went to join my victorious allies.

Neither Homer nor Virgil adequately expressed the carnage the barbaric Greeks visited on the beautiful city of Ilium. Shakespeare actually came closer in *Hamlet*.

> *Pyrrhus at Priam drives; in rage strikes wide;*
> *But with the whiff and wind of his fell sword*
> *The unnerved father falls. Then senseless Ilium,*
> *Seeming to feel this blow, with flaming top*
> *Stoops to his base, and with a hideous crash*
> *Takes prisoner Pyrrhus' ear: for, lo! his sword,*
> *Which was declining on the milky head*
> *Of reverend Priam, seem'd i' the air to stick:*
> *So, as a painted tyrant, Pyrrhus stood,*
> *And like a neutral to his will and matter,*
> *Did nothing.*

Seeing the proud tower of Ilium fall, though it was long after Pyrrhus completed his murder of the King of Troy, was still like watching the symbol of a nation, its prosperity, its wealth, and its very soul suddenly collapse in a heap with whoever was inside it either trapped and crushed or falling to their death. I had no doubt that Hephaistos had hammered the foundations of Ilium into dust.

Centuries have changed the story, thanks in large part to Homer and his distorted tale. I was drinking with him a few centuries later and told him about it, but that's a different story.

Oh, what the heck. I'll tell you now.

He was a wandering poet, singing on street corners when I found him. Nice voice, too. He had some cockamamie story about the hero Odysseus and how he almost single-handedly won the battle of Troy. I'm pretty sure Athene had a hand in inspiring Homer. First, because she isn't a great poet herself. Not like Apollo. And second because she was totally enamored with Odysseus. You know, in the same way an abused girlfriend or the wife of an alcoholic defends her mate. "Oh, he's not that bad. He's got a heart of gold. He didn't mean any harm. It doesn't really hurt." She needed counseling!

So, when I heard him patching together the story of great Odysseus, I intervened.

"That's not the way it happened," I declared as we sipped a mug of wine. I had to admit, for as barbaric as the Greeks had been at Troy, they were fine vintners. "Odysseus was a coward who died at Troy."

"And how would you know anything about it? This is the story that has been told for generations!" Homer declared.

"Well, I'm older than the story," I declared. I admit, I was a little drunk.

"Right. Prove it!"

I should have just walked away. I should have ignored him. I should have found a nice quiet spot and slipped into the infinity room for a century or so.

Instead, I shoved Homer into the satchel and took him to Troy. I traveled by land except the ferry across the straits between the Aegean and the Sea of Marmara. It wasn't that far from there to Troy, but it took me several days to find it. The Greeks had so totally destroyed the city of Ilium that there was only a fragment of wall with one stone on the next. I took him to the top and showed him the battlefield, where Hector fell, where Achilles was killed by Paris, and finally, where the horse came into the city and the Greeks carried out their sneak attack. No army claiming to surrender would ever be trusted again. The honor had evaporated with the cursed Greeks. Except Homer conveniently left that part out of the story. It was Virgil who put it in. Using my senses to examine the area and feel my way toward the center of the city, I found the crushed altar of Aphrodite and the place where Odysseus fell and I told Homer how the coward had been shot by his own men as he rose up to chase the women.

I suppose you are asking, "How did you 'show' the blind poet?"

I ask you, "If Homer was blind, how did he manage to write down all his stupid epic poems?"

Regardless of whatever else you believe, understand this: Homer was a novelist, not a historian. He took all the details I gave him, put them in a bag, and shook them up. Then he took them out of the bag in random order and wove a story from them all.

Never believe the words of a novelist. They lie for a living.

Sorry about that. I get a little wound up when I talk about Troy. They were noble and beautiful people, replete with the arts, poetry, music, and philosophy; destroyed by barbarians who could scarcely write their names. I had friends there and I found myself in the uncomfortable position of masquerading as Odysseus as we left the smoldering embers of Ilium behind and headed to our boats.

I saw Menelaus lead hairy Helen through the streets of Troy like a captured monkey, and heard him promise that he would let every soldier in the Greek army have a turn with her for her betrayal. I shook my head. The idiot couldn't see how much that idea turned the little slut on. Agamemnon carried the weeping and still bleeding thirteen-year-old Cassandra under his arm, after she was raped by Ajax. Ajax who had committed sacrilege in the very temple of Athene who was patroness of the Greeks when he toppled her statue in order to drag Cassandra from it, in spite of the sanctuary she pled for. His own goddess! I could tell you right then he wasn't going to make it home alive. What other Trojans survived—whether male or female or child—were shackled and taken as slaves, scattered among the many city-states of Greece.

And me? I had read the memories from Odysseus and met his men at his ship. The ships had all left the night before the treachery and dropped anchor beyond the point where they could not be seen from Ilium or the battlefield. They had returned after dark and crept up to the city. I had 'my' men, who all had their own spoils aplenty, including silent or weeping women taken from the city and surrounding countryside. I promised myself I would try to protect them as much as possible, but I knew they were destined to be raped repeatedly before the ship returned to Greece. I would attempt to spirit them away to the infinity room, blaming the disappearances on drownings or capture by the gods.

We cast off to head back to Ithaca, a place I had no desire to return to. I knew I'd have to tell Penelope her cowardly husband was dead and she should get remarried. It should only have taken a couple of weeks to sail from Troy to Ithaca, but that was not how it would be, thanks to that damned spy, Hermes.

14
MY ODYSSEY

ERMES HAD SEEN ME transform myself into Odysseus. He went straight to tell Poseidon. Somehow, Odysseus had already offended the sea god, and Poseidon was still upset with me for damaging his sea monster and rescuing Aphrodite from his grasp. Two reasons for the ancient god to dislike me.

We would leave Troy with the five hundred ships of Greece still floating. Odysseus and his men had been gone ten years, most of which was spent sitting around waiting. Homer only described the last year of the campaign. If he'd have described the whole thing, anyone reading it would have died of boredom. But in ten years, we'd basically built a good-sized city on the shores, not just an army camp. We'd landed with 100,000 warriors, give or take a few thousand. But as any military person will tell you, you need a nearly one-to-one ratio of logistics personnel to soldiers in order to feed and supply and fuck the army. Don't think these hearty warriors were doing without for ten years.

Like Odysseus, some of these men had wives and family at home. The majority, however, had been teenagers when they left Ithaca and all they knew of women was from the camp followers. Of course, Homer cleaned up that part of things. He was as sexually repressed as a Puritan, and made sure there was no hint of sex in his story.

Except when talking about the rape of the Trojan women or in his allusions to various warrior bonds that developed, like between Achilles and Patroclus. I forget if it was Agamemnon or his brother Menelaus who insulted Achilles, but the great hero had spent most of the war sitting in his tent, making out with Patroclus. Odysseus was the one who convinced Patroclus to join the battle. That started an exchange of deaths. Hector killed Patroclus in battle. Achilles was so upset by the death of his lover that he went out and not only killed Hector, but humiliated the Trojans by dragging the body behind his chariot around the city walls. Paris took revenge for his brother and got a lucky shot off that hit Achilles with one of Apollo's poison arrows. Paris was killed by... I don't remember who. You lose track after a while.

Oh. My point was that there were women in the camp village from all over Greece and the Aegean islands, and over the course of ten years, more came with reinforcements for the lost forces. During the course of the ten years, there was a battle about once every week or two. A lot of people would die and then there would be a week of truce as people—non-warriors—went out and picked up the bodies and weapons, providing a funeral pyre for the fallen. Then the warriors would decide a day to go back and fight again. Both the Trojans and the Greeks received reinforcements on a regular basis. A few—or a lot—of men got weary of the war and decided to take their ships and leave. Agamemnon decided to burn their ships so they couldn't leave. So, there were only half as many ships now as had come over and they were filled to overflowing.

Some men took the option of trying to start a new life right there in Troy where there were a lot of widows who'd been captured, but not all would fit on the ships and not all men wanted to take a new woman home with them. It was a real mess and I sat to have a little talk with my men.

"I hold one crime above all others as deserving of instant death," I said. "That crime is rape. Now, I'm not going to work my way through all of you because until this moment you didn't know it was a crime. Let me tell you this: Any woman you bring on board had better have agreed to become your wife or be happy to live the life of a prostitute. If she isn't that willing, leave her behind."

"Are you kidding, Dys? Fuck you! Any spoils of war are ours to do what we want with," one of the men said. "I'll fuck this little hole anytime I want."

It was one of those moments I couldn't let pass. I drew my sword and swiftly removed his head from his shoulders.

"Does anyone want to leave this ship instead of living by my rules? That's a better choice than challenging me."

A few of the men jumped overboard, leaving whatever treasure or women they had behind and wading back to shore. I saw a couple getting aboard Ajax's ship. Good luck with that. He pulled down Athene's statue and raped a little girl who had sanctuary there. That was not a goddess I would want to be on the bad side of.

I turned to the women who were on board and changed my speech, so they would be able to hear and understand me and the Greeks wouldn't.

"You women don't have many choices. If you think your chances are better over there with the other Greeks, you can leave. If you plan to stay on the ship, you should choose a man and make him happy. But don't put on airs and say you're too good for this one or that one. There are no princesses here any longer. There are no women with rich fathers. Your fathers and brothers are dead and your wealth is gone. I'm sorry to say, it's your lot in life," I said. The women talked together for some time. Men had a single choice. Go or stay. The women had to discuss the positives and negatives. Some suggested it would be better to kill us and steal the ship. They were laughed down and another woman pointed over to where the men had stripped the body of their one-time comrade and threw it into the sea. I think the reality of their situation, even with what they had seen over the past several years, had just hit home. They gradually got up and approached the men who seemed to have some minimal amount of negotiation and accepted their new mates.

The woman who had been in the process of being mauled by the sailor I dispatched came to me and bowed her head before me.

"You have won me as the spoils of battle, Captain. I will be your woman," she said. I put a hand on her bare shoulder. Most of the women were only partially dressed if at all. I'd have to get Nimia to provide me with some clothes for them. While my hand caressed her soft skin, I read her thoughts. I can't imagine anyone having pure thoughts in that kind of situation. She wished we would all just die. But she considered me to be noble and the best choice among the men and would give me her loyalty. I agreed to take her.

When the tide started out, our ship moved with it. With us, most of the fleet of Greeks moved as well. We clustered near each other, mostly because they'd all grown used to being near each other over the years. Occasionally, song would break out on one of the ships and would be answered by another. There wasn't enough wine to get everyone drunk, so most of the activities remained good natured.

For three days we sailed out into the Aegean with ships turning farther north or south to return to various ports of origin. And then Poseidon's vengeance struck. I didn't think he had anything against most of the Greeks. He'd been their ally. And this storm did not wreck our ship. I think Poseidon had already discovered I didn't drown easily. But when the storm broke and the skies began to clear, there was not another Greek ship anywhere on the horizon. We entered the deadliest calm I had ever seen on the sea. Not a breath of wind filled our sails. The men lay about the deck under the burning sun and often under their women who took seriously the task of keeping the men as beneficent toward them as possible.

I couldn't just fill the sails with wind on an otherwise clear and still day. I was walking near the edge of what was believable. And I wasn't yet sure how Athene would react to the knowledge that I was occupying the likeness of her hero. She'd been so devoted to Odysseus it was legendary and he had been such a coward in battle. Odysseus would have done better, perhaps if he had taken refuge in Athene's temple rather than Aphrodite's. No, all we could do was wait for the wind.

I was supposed to be Odysseus. If it weren't for all the men and women on the ship—which caused it to nearly wallow from the overload—I would have risked Poseidon and blown my ship to land. I secluded myself in my cabin with a psychic barrier on the door, and took the woman who had asked to be under my care, Doria, to the infinity room. There, she joined the harem without hesitance and was amazed at the paradise that awaited her.

"Why do you not bring all of your men and women here?" she asked in wonder.

"That's not such a bad idea," Nimia said. She'd taken immediate charge of Doria when I brought her through. We were eating at a table spread with fine food, the likes of which had not been seen around Troy in many years.

"My heart says to be generous and kind to them," I said. "But I fear for what they might do in upsetting the natural order of things. I believe they are still only one step away from rape, even though the women have submitted to them. That barbaric mind might be more than our fragile society in the infinity room can withstand. I don't want our people turned into barbarians."

"Here's an idea," Josie said. "We have a nice lake and the beginnings of a saltwater sea. Enlarge the sea and place a replica of your ship on it. Move the men and women to it and they would not know where they are."

"Can you cast an illusion over the men?" Doria asked. "Give them a kind of waking dream in which they sail your private sea for as long as you sail the real world. Then when you reach this Ithaca of Odysseus's you can transfer them out of the inner sea and back onto your boat, but you won't need to deal with them while you pilot your craft."

"Doria, you are a brilliant young woman," I said. "Let us work together to refine the plan."

It did not take too long to enlarge the sea and put a replica of our ship on it. It was, of course, almost time enough for the men to mutiny against their missing captain and the women were fearful-looking when I emerged from the cabin. I acted as if nothing untoward were happening. I noticed, however, that even though we had no wind, the ship was slowly moving on some hidden current. I took frequent sightings on the stars at night and could see our southwestward drift. I felt we were likely being dragged to some doom Poseidon was cleverly preparing for us.

The next night, I set about the long task of moving the crew from the ship to the infinity room.

I went from man to man and woman to woman to read their memories and decide what kind of person I would be bringing into the infinity room. A few were just too disgusting to tolerate—both men and women. Most were fine and had begun to develop a mutual respect with each other, male and female. In these, I implanted a memory of sailing away from Troy together and induced forgetfulness of those I refused to bring into the infinity room.

Doria led a small team of women, including some of the goddess's priestesses, onto the ship to carry the sleeping forms into the room and onto the replica ship there. A few of the women so despaired of life with these men that we took them to our village that was rapidly turning into a city. And a few of the priestesses—used to a steady diet of frequent sex—were pining for male company and quickly took the places of the unhappy women with the men on the ship.

It took much longer than a single night to accomplish all this and we simply kept the people asleep as we rearranged them and their lives. I found an interesting phenomenon among them. Although the idea of leaving Troy to return home victorious was appealing, few if any had women or families in Ithaca they particularly wanted to return to. In fact, many had joined the soldiers from other ports over the ten years of the war and didn't care where they ended up, as long as they could enjoy the fruits of their war and have a woman or two to comfort them. Ultimately, that would work well to my ends.

When we had moved everyone I felt I could trust to the infinity room, I closed the gateway and woke the remaining crew with a memory of hardship and sacrifice in which only twenty brave men and the refugee women who clung to them were returning to their homeland. I did my best to ignore their slovenly lasciviousness and rough ways. I had simply spent too many years living in a highly civilized society as King of Bathra to take part in the barbarous pleasures of these craven men and women.

And thus, we were washed onto the shores of an island I did not recognize. It seemed a one-eyed giant lived there and we carefully avoided the territory. One of the women saw this as a great opportunity to escape in a new land and ran from the ship. The men, seeing the threat of losing their women, tied the rest up on the ship and set off in pursuit of the runaway. In so doing, they came upon the giant's cave and discovered it was filled with cheese and sausage and bread. The gluttons fell to eating as much as they could.

I had stayed with the ship, seriously considering shoving off and leaving them all on the island, but I didn't want the responsibility of the women they'd chosen. I wondered, in fact, where these women had come from. They did not reflect the refinement of even the poor women of Troy. I discovered some had been camp followers, providing for the Greeks the same services the priestesses of Aphrodite gave to the Trojans. These, however, were there for however they could profit. If it was possible, some were fouler than the men, having become pregnant during their time with the soldiers as cooks and whores. The children they bore, they'd dashed on the rocks instead of attempting to raise them in the camps. Rather than run from the men, they eyed the various treasures the men had stolen from the ruined city.

Eventually, I decided to go seek out the men and found them in the cave of Polyphemus, a one-eyed giant. He had them all cornered and had already eaten the runaway woman and one of the men. That was too gross for me to stand, so I started yelling insults at the oaf from outside the cave.

"Who's the idiot who lives in a cave?" I shouted. "Must be the result of a sheep-fucking monkey. What did you do with your other eye, numbskull? Swallow it with dinner?"

"Who's out there who dares insult Polyphemus?" the giant yelled, coming to the door.

"Oh, it's nobody. Nobody's voice carries across the world declaring Polyphemus is an imbecile. Nobody says Polyphemus is a coward! Nobody thinks Polyphemus keeps sheep because he doesn't know how to use a woman!" I called inside.

"I'll kill Nobody!" Polyphemus yelled, rolling the stone away from the entrance of his cave. I'd found a place to hide above the cave where I'd have a good shot down at him and sharpened a thick spear. When Polyphemus the cyclops came bursting out the entrance to his cave, he had a club and was looking all around. "Where's Nobody?" he screamed.

"Nobody's home!" I shouted from above him. He spun to look at me through his one big eye as he raised his club to smite me. I threw the makeshift spear and it lodged in his eye. He screamed and I quickly dropped down between him and the cave as he battered the mountainside with his club while crying in pain and blindness. I waved the remaining men out of the cave, and they thought it would be a good idea to drive the entire flock of sheep out with them. That caught the cyclops' attention. He immediately started feeling around for his sheep, scattering all over.

As he gathered them up in his arms he cried out, "Who is Nobody?"

I was pretty ticked off at the moment, so I carelessly yelled back over my shoulder, "Odysseus is Nobody!"

"I curse Odysseus! Father Poseidon, wreck the ship of Odysseus! Send him to ruin!"

I didn't care. I wasn't actually Odysseus. Except I might have just increased my problems with the god of the sea if Polyphemus was his son. I had to laugh about my characterization of the brute being a cross between a sheep and a monkey. Oh, Poseidon was going to be so upset with me!

Not everyone made it back to the ship, I'm afraid. When we set sail from the cyclops' island I had about an equal number of men and women. I made them all crew members and put them to work as a stiff breeze arose and we set the sails. I continued to carefully chart the stars as I traveled. I didn't know precisely where I was, but I was beginning to get a feel for the area as it related to the rest of the ocean.

Well, right on schedule, old Poseidon blew us through the gates of the world and sent that damned sea monster after me again. You'd think he'd have learned from the last encounter, but there were all the tentacles again, wrapping around the ship to crush it and snatching at the sailors working on it. I had a new weapon, though. I'd lost the Sword of Ninra in the last battle with the monster, but I'd taken up Odysseus's sword in Troy, not knowing that it was forged by great Hephaistos himself and blessed by Athene to give to her pet. It sliced right through the tentacles and the ship was free. Unfortunately, we lost another half dozen sailors.

We were weary and damaged, and the ship would only go in circles until it finally wrecked on a western island in strange seas. This time, I required my crew to stay with the ship while I checked to see if the area was safe for them. What I found was a peaceful island on which the only inhabitants seemed to be a fine herd of cattle. I resisted the temptation to follow them home as that was what led to the problems with the cyclops. The woman had followed the sheep and led the men right into the cave.

Instead, I sat out on the hillside and just waited until I saw a cowherder coming over the hill to drive the herd home, or to somewhere. It was quite a healthy-looking herd. I picked up a stick to use as a staff as if I were merely wandering the hills and when I approached, the herdsman stopped and came toward me. I let him come and tried to be as non-threatening as I could be.

I was surprised when he got near because he was quite a young and strapping man. I immediately filed his image away as one I could one day adapt for myself. There was something almost regal about his bearing, though he carried no symbols of office other than his herder's staff. He looked me up and down as I greeted him.

"And what kind of creature have we here?" he asked.

"I'm a simple wayfarer whose ship has been damaged. My men are working on its repair as we speak and I wandered out to scout the surrounding land."

"That story is partly true. A Greek would not have been blown so far unless some god was very angry with him. Hmm. My cousin has a very uneven temperament. I'll wager you ran afoul of Poseidon," the young man said.

I did not want to have a bad relationship with another of Poseidon's relatives.

"My lord, I do not know you, but I assure you my disagreement with the god of the inner sea is unintentional," I said. "Let me fully disclose that I am Bob, a free demon disguised as a Greek in order to get some men and women home after a great war."

"Oh, a deamhan! How fascinating. Well, deamhan, I'm Mac Lir. I don't think I've seen one of your kind in this area. And you claim to be benevolent? Well, sit with me and let us share tales."

We sat on the hillside overlooking the cows and I told him of my journey from Troy and tried to convince him that I was an innocent in the disagreement with his cousin. At last, I asked if I might trade for a few cows so I could feed my men.

"What might you have to trade?"

"We do have much treasure from Troy," I said. "I can persuade the men and women to give up part of it for the promise of a roast beef." We agreed on a sum and I returned to the ship to raid the treasures of the men. It was much easier to put them all asleep and make off with the sacks of the dead men than to try to negotiate with the living. I returned to the hill and traded for four plump cows. On the way back, I led two into the infinity room to enhance our herds there, and took two back to the ship where the men and women rejoiced that I had provided meat for them. We repaired the ship over the next few days and set sail once again.

▣▣▣▣▣▣▣▣▣▣▣▣▣▣

Gods have an odd way of viewing the world and reality. You'd think they were all ten years old. They deliberately tell lies and then insist they are true until people start believing them. It's a talent I've noticed politicians employ all the time. I don't. I'm an honest demon. I have no reason to lie. People expect that I have done whatever I'm accused of.

I hear your skepticism.

Let me give you an example: If you ask if I slept with that woman, I would ask immediately for clarifications. "*Which* woman?" I would say. "Oh. *That* woman. Yes. I slept with *that* woman. And let me tell you, she was incredible. Her pussy smells like roses and tastes like honey. You've never tasted her pussy? Oh, my friend, you must try it." You see? Denying that I slept with that woman would never be believed. But by the time I am finished describing the event, my accuser will have forgotten about all the other hundred women in the room. Just as I told Manannán mac Lir all about our ship and our battle and our voyage, but didn't mention the infinity room.

A god, on the other hand... Poseidon says to Helios, "Say, don't you have a herd of cattle on an island?"

Helios thinks he *could* have a herd of cattle. Why not? He finally says, "Oh, yes. Those are my cattle. Fine beasts. Have you seen them? Bred them myself. What? Odysseus stole my cattle? He can't do that!" and all of a sudden, a god who has no skin in the game comes burning after me for stealing *his* cattle.

15
HOMECOMING AT LAST

MY PEOPLE AND I set sail to the south, for I'd decided we had been blown through the gates of the inner sea to the outer sea during our battle with the Scylla. When we got back through that channel, I had a pretty good idea where Greece was. I figured I might as well head there and get the marital confrontation over with. It was only just of me to tell Penelope of Odysseus's demise and offer the remaining men and those who sailed in the infinity room, an opportunity to return home.

Do you think Poseidon would let it go at that? Not a chance.

Another storm, another shipwreck and I'm on Circe's Island. Now Circe was a beautiful pig farmer and—wouldn't you know it—Helios's daughter. I never thought of pig farming as being the profession suited for a beautiful woman, but she seemed to derive great pleasure from the pigs.

That was the point at which my crew and their women decided to take a permanent powder. They'd apparently worked out whatever differences they had and salvaged all the treasure from the wreckage they could find and took off into the hills. I figured I'd run into them again before long, but they were dead set on being scarce. I bid them good riddance.

That left me to deal with Circe.

I'd actually known a delightful pig farmer. Manannán mac Lir, from whom I got cattle, told me a long story as we sat on the hillside about having once been a pig farmer. He owned a drove of immortal pigs. When they were killed, they resurrected and came back to life. In all but one instance. If they were butchered and eaten, the pigs did not return to life. It reminded me a bit of my monster son. Nonetheless, the gods of that region found out about Mac Lir's pigs and descended en masse to have a great feast for days on end. When the feast was done, there were no immortal pigs left, but the gods had all gained immortality by eating them.

It didn't take long for me to discover Circe was also more than a pig farmer. She was a sorceress.

If you are curious about the various words used for workers of magic, perhaps I can help you. I've often referred to my maker as a mage or magus. That might not have been a correct term as it is credited to the Zorastrians sometime around the first millennium before Caesar. In that culture, it simply meant priest of the religion of the Wise Lord. It implied a worker of unnatural acts or miracles. A wizard, however, is derived from the Middle English word for wisdom. A much later term. They were originally known more for divination than magic, but the magic evolved as well. Finally, 'sorcerer' referred to one who influenced fate, from a Latin root. So, you see, the terms are all more modern than what I have applied, though mage seems to be the earliest, etymologically speaking.

Who am I to describe language? I just use the words that fit.

However, Circe considered me a sorcerer, too, and I had to ask why that and not some other branch. She said that in a sorcerer (or sorceress), the magical ability is innate rather than studied. We might learn specific techniques or new spells through our reading of scrolls, but our ability was inside us, not based on what we learned.

Circe was a fascinating woman when she wasn't trying to kill me. I could see a spell spinning out of her hands from a mile away which is about where she started throwing them at me. She was fun. There is something about a dangerous woman that is just too appetizing to pass up. We engaged in a battle of wit and magic that went on for days. Foreplay. That's all I can call it. I never managed one spell correctly but they all turned out all right. I was just learning to make spells out of nothing. There were a few well-studied spells—like my transformation spell—I had done so frequently, I knew them forward and backward. But even that one could go awry. There was the time I turned myself into...

I shouldn't get sidetracked when I'm telling a romantic story about doing battle with a sorceress. Gods playing tricks again. But oh, she got hot when she wove spells and brewed potions, and I was not at all above taking advantage of that. We fucked from one end of her island to the other and back again. She was raw passion. She wanted a child and I seriously considered revoking my vow and giving her one. After all, I reasoned, she wasn't a human woman, but a demigoddess. She should be able to handle a demon child. But then, I thought about there actually being a little me running around somewhere, learning sorcery and potion making at his mother's knee. That kind of thing will really dull the desire to make babies.

I finally decided it was time for me to get going and so I proposed a feast during which I intended to give her one of her own potions that would make her sleep long enough for me to push the little raft I'd made off her island and into the sea. I butchered a hog and set it to roast for an entire day, turning the spit myself. Late that evening, I brought the feast to her, laced with the potion I had stolen.

"Oh!" she said in surprise as we ate the roast pork. "Laertos tastes divine!"

"Laertos?" I said. "You named the pigs? I once had a sailor named Laertos."

"Yes. I rounded up all the crew and women from that shipwreck and turned them into pigs," she yawned. "I seldom keep one more than a year before I butcher it."

I was horrified. I'd killed and roasted a man, thinking it was a pig. Then I saw Circe grin as I picked up my goblet to wash the taste from my mouth. Something about that grin told me I would end up spitted if I drank from her cup. I started to set it down and Circe gathered herself to throw a spell at me. I threw the drink at her and in her haste and drugged state, she slurred her words, accidentally reversing the transformation spell. I heard the pigs suddenly talking and running for the woods as Circe fell asleep.

I took off as well, reaching my raft and shoving off from the shore. I don't know what happened to the rest of my crew. I called for them to join me but, of course, they'd just witnessed me take one of their number and roast him, so there was no trust between us. I do hope they survived.

I've never had a taste for pork since then.

And then there was Callie. Oh, my, what a girl! There are so many islands in the sea and it seemed I beached my raft on each of them. When I managed to get to her little island, I found a beautiful and sensual woman who sat looking out at the sea, praying to Aphrodite for a lover, even if only for a year. The past few days had been rather peaceful on the raft, and I had a feeling Aphrodite might have been pushing my craft toward this island as the answer to the prayer of one of her devotees.

"Why do you weep, girl?" I asked when I saw her. She stared at me in disbelief and fainted. Being the gallant demon I am, I caught her as she plunged toward the rocks below and scooped her up in my arms—where she woke.

"My prayers have been answered!" she exclaimed.

Whenever I'm the answer to someone's prayers, you can bet a god or goddess has been interfering. But I really had no urgent need to be anywhere. What crew was left in the infinity room had long since given up ever returning to Ithaca and had found a peaceful seaside paradise where they built a village and were thriving with some of the women brought from Troy by the sailors and some of the priestesses I'd brought from the temple. Most of the children and nurses from the harem had been delivered there as well, much to the delight of the women. Since arriving in the infinity room, they'd ceased aging and even regressed some to an optimum age. Those who had wives in Ithaca had no desire to return to the old women back home. Yes, they were heartless cads. And also highly sexed. For myself, I had Penelope's image from Odysseus's memories, but she was *his* wife, not mine.

Following Callie's instructions, I carried her to her home where I met her family, such as it was. She lived with an elder brother and his wife and their three children. The wife was pregnant with another. The village in which she lived was isolated and a little inbred. It looked like Callie was doomed to become a lower wife to her brother. Neither of them was looking forward to that.

The people of the village lived a peaceful and pastoral life and most were bored silly. They had regular free sex parties during which they had sex for entertainment and occasionally procreation happened.

Callie was soft and sensual—perhaps not the most beautiful woman in the world, but I'd already had *her*. It did not take long courting Callie before we were in bed together. That night, I think. We were shown to a little cabin nearby that was empty and from that moment were considered married. She was plush. No bones stuck out in odd places like hips or ribs. She had adequate padding overall to be perfectly delightful to sex. She was phenomenally receptive to making love at any given time and usually twice at a time.

Sinking into her steamy depths was like being welcomed into a volcano of love. And when she erupted, she sprayed her juices everywhere!

I mentioned the village and surrounding area as having regular sex parties. One might think of them as orgies that included everyone in the village. Each orgy resulted in at least one pregnancy, father unknown. The women all flocked to my pole, hoping to bring new blood into their progeny. I needed to help the village expand its gene pool. After my first introduction and for the next seven years thereafter, I would slip into the infinity room during the orgies and disguise one to six of my men to take to the village to plunder the waiting pussies. Over the next few years, I could count most of a generation as having come from outside the village. The people, of course, credited the new blood to me, including the three children I had with Callie (seeded by one of my men). In fact, Bartolos became quite fond of Callie as I was myself, and occasionally I left him for as much as a month with my wife while I returned to the infinity room.

I discovered our own population growing. Several of the women in the village of my former sailors had children and our experience told us that as of that time, mother and father would both begin to age naturally—but healthily. Since we'd never indicated this was a place where they would be immortal, they considered the process natural and to be expected.

As I worked my way from woman to woman in my harem, I always ended up in Josie or Nimia. They wanted me to bring Callie to the infinity room to stay with them, but somehow, I didn't think the village girl would adjust to life with the ageless. Josie and Nimia had been with me for the better part of a millennium and still looked like the teens I'd married. They never came out of the room into the natural world anymore. I was never sure how much time had passed in the infinity room while I was outside, but I was always greeted as if it was just the next day.

My idyllic life was interrupted by a dream. Not mine, but Callie's. She woke in the morning weeping on my shoulder.

"What is it, my little love?" I asked.

"You have to leave me," she whimpered. "My goddess Aphrodite said I asked for just one year and she had rewarded me with six more, but now your time on the island is over. You must re-build your raft and leave my side. Oh, my Odysseus, why must you leave?"

"I don't know, Callie," I said. I was still masquerading as Odysseus, though I'd neglected to really age while on the voyage or the island, so I suppose that could have raised alarms soon by looking ever young. In fact, I probably looked younger than I had at Troy.

I could see Aphrodite's hand all over this decree. I went to the top of the island that night to call out to her and find out what was going on. Imagine my surprise when the bastard Hermes showed up.

"I suppose you're the one who told everyone I was here," I said.

"Hardly," he sniffed. "Your wife has made so many sacrifices and prayers of thanksgiving that there is scarcely a god on Olympus who hasn't heard her."

"So, why are they demanding all of a sudden that I leave her?"

"Politics," Hermes spat as if the word left a bad taste in his mouth. I could understand that. "Zeus has been afraid that another war like Troy would break out soon unless he got Aphrodite and Athene to make nice. They've reached a conditional truce."

"Condition that I leave *my* happiness behind," I grumbled.

"Side effect. Athene's condition is that her beloved Odysseus be allowed to return to his wife and home on Ithaca."

"Doesn't she know I'm not Odysseus?"

"Irrelevant. She decided you had assumed his identity, so you needed to assume his responsibilities."

"And what is she giving up?"

"She has gracefully consented to allow Odysseus's men to remain in your little concealment with the spoils of Troy and Aphrodite's priestesses. She *asks*, however, that you take care of their widows and provide for them as you will for Penelope."

"What about Poseidon?" I asked. There had to be another catch to this. The gods were never this straightforward.

"That was your own fault. Destroying the Scylla and blinding his son put you on Poseidon's bad side. He has consented to letting you reach Ithaca, but not to make it easy."

"Great. And I get no say in any of this?"

"It has been decreed by Zeus."

"Shit."

▧▧▧▧▧▧▧▧▧▧▧▧▧

Homer made ten books out of the adventure, but I'll try to make it short. I built the raft and left my peaceful life with Callie, calling out a thousand curses on the gods for disrupting her happiness. Then I thought of another person and went to talk to Bartolos, one of the men who had come often to join the orgies, and who I knew was rather sweet on Callie. He agreed that it would make him very happy to stay with Callie and he would do his best to make her happy. I was satisfied. I built my raft and shoved off from yet another island. And pursuant to the Olympian Convention, Poseidon wrecked my raft and I floated to shore hanging onto a log. He finally let me be.

Ithaca was a mess when I got there and I sympathized with Athene over wanting Odysseus to come back and clean it up. I put on a different and much older body so that no one would recognize me and went in to take a look at how things were in the city Odysseus had left nearly twenty years before.

In fact, the city was preparing a wake for their hero to be held on the twentieth anniversary of his departure. Penelope would then be required to choose a new husband from among the suitors who had been gathering in and basically despoiling the royal house for over a year. A hundred and eight of the bastards, figuring one of them would bed Penelope and displace her son as heir to Ithaca!

Penelope was not happy. She'd been delaying for over a year by weaving a funeral shroud to honor her husband. She would work all day and at night, would pull all the weaving out that she'd done that day. Finally, she'd been forced to set up a contest to eliminate the weak ones. She always did have a weakness for a six-pack and guns. She had a bow she claimed was her husband's and that she would only marry a man who could draw and shoot it.

Now, I ask you: What kind of warrior goes off to battle and leaves his bow behind? Well, I'll tell you: A warrior who has no intention of ever getting close enough to the battle to make a difference! Nonetheless, the bow was as thick as a man's arm and I could tell there was a powerful spell on the bow that would make it difficult for any mortal to draw.

On the day of the festivities, I took my place at the end of the line as the 109th suitor, which made people laugh. Each suitor ahead of me tried and failed to even get the bow strung, let alone to draw it.

I hadn't really heard anything from Athene since she made her bargain, though I often felt her presence nearby. As I stepped up to the bow, to the laughter and jeers of the crowd, I heard her whisper that she wanted the suitors dispatched permanently. I really don't like killing people, but Athene insisted I would be unable to draw the bow unless I promised to take aim at the line of suitors. I finally agreed and stepped up to string the bow. It was a good stiff bow with arrows nearly thick enough to be considered a spear shaft. I nocked an arrow, pulled the bow, and swung to let the arrow loose at the reformed line of suitors who couldn't believe an old man like me had defeated them and wanted another chance. I closed my eyes and let loose the arrow, figuring Athene could guide it as she wished.

She wished them all dead and the arrow passed through every suitor in the line.

That wasn't the end, of course. I still had to convince Penelope that I was her long-lost husband. Simply letting my visage fade to look more like Odysseus was not enough. She wanted to know what was unique about her wedding bedroom. I dredged that up from Odysseus's memories—telling her the bed was made from a living tree. Then I showed her even more intimate knowledge of her body. The latter was pleasurable for both of us.

Old softy that I am, of course, I could not let Penelope dwell under the mistaken perception that I was Odysseus. My job here was technically done. Telemachus, the son of Odysseus and Penelope, had gone straight to work cleaning up the remains of the invading suitors. He also created a few remains, hanging several household staff who had helped the suitors in exchange for various rewards, and a couple of suitors who had not been in the line I shot. He was a good kid, just an infant when Odysseus left home. A little bloody for my taste, but a lot braver than his father.

"Penelope, I need to talk to you seriously," I said as I led her to a hill away from the city where I read in Odysseus's memories that the two had shared many pleasant times. "I am not the Odysseus who left you. He died at Troy," I said as I touched her face and looked into her eyes so she could see I was earnest. I saw her countenance fall and she heaved a great sigh.

"I know," she whispered. It was my turn to be surprised. "I was visited in a dream by Aphrodite. She told me she was sending me a lover who would always be by my side and that I should go with you and find eternal happiness. Can you do that? Can you bring me eternal happiness?"

"I hope to do so. Athene laid the charge on me to rescue you and to provide for the widows of those who sailed with me. I can do that. I would like to show you my secret sanctuary."

"Before you do that, could I ask one boon?" she said.

"Yes, of course, my dear."

"Would you make love with me one more time as Odysseus so I may say goodbye at last. I know he was not always a noble man, but he was my husband and my lover."

That was an easy request to satisfy. We made love on the hill and she cried out his name, asking the gods to care for his spirit. I gradually let my horns show through so she could see I was a demon, but I didn't go whole goat on her. I took her hand and led her into the infinity room to meet my other wives and become a part of my family. She was thrilled. She lectured the remaining men who had stayed with me and they all agreed to accept their own wives if they could be brought into the infinity room.

Of course, I couldn't remain in the visage of a demon, but Penelope and I returned to the city and our palace where we began turning over the kingdom to Telemachus. In the meantime, we gathered the widows of the sailors and gave them the option of either coming to the infinity room to join their husbands or even live on their own in a land of plenty, or staying where they were. Some chose to stay in Ithaca, happy with their grandchildren and not caring about the old coots who left them. These I gave a dream that they'd only received their husband's share of the spoils and they thanked us for providing for them. The others went to see their husbands again, some staying with the men and their new families and some choosing to find a place in our capital city. All were happy.

Eventually, Penelope and I reached the point where we could fully abdicate the throne in favor of Telemachus and retire 'to travel the world.' Once we were away from Ithaca and on the mainland, Penelope moved into the infinity room as my wife, and I restored her very seductive teenage body. Then I adopted a new body for myself, shouldered the bag, and hit the road again.

A quick word about wives. I have had many, starting with Ariane and including notably Portia, Bao, and Callie. But only one had taken up permanent residence in the infinity room before Penelope. Nimia had entered the room when it was first created and we fled from Knossos. She was the undisputed head of my household. Penelope accepted this without objection. My other wives had all been temporal and either died or were left behind.

"What about Josie?" you ask.

Josie had never actually become my wife. She was my possession. In her mind, being *possessed* by a demon trumps being *married* to one. Go figure.

I decided it was not a good idea to go back on the sea. So, as soon as I'd managed to get from the island of Ithaca to the mainland of the Peloponnese, I made my way down to Sparta to see what became of the old soldiers. There weren't many. Menelaus told me stories of the great generals. Word of the return of Odysseus to Ithaca had already reached Sparta. Menelaus was reconciled with Helen, but if anything, she was even more slutty and had even more hair than before. He spent most of his time drunk while she slept her way through all of Sparta.

His brother, Agamemnon—the king who took Cassandra to become his personal slave—was killed by his wife and her lover when he returned to Athens. Cassandra, attending him in the bath at the time, was joined in the same fate, even though she'd warned him repeatedly that Clytemnestra would kill them both. And Ajax, I was happy to learn, had been cursed by Athene for despoiling Cassandra in her temple. She raised a storm on the sea herself to shipwreck him. All the sailors with him, including those who jumped ship from me when I forbade rape, were drowned. Ajax was tossed up on a rock and laughed at the foolishness of the gods in failing to kill him. Poseidon himself rose up from the sea and smote the rock with Ajax on it. It split open and swallowed the rapist.

Years later, I told Homer about Odysseus and the trip I made back to Ithaca, but I was not heroic enough for the poet. Homer wanted a superhuman who had single-handedly outwitted the Trojans, who had defied the gods and survived the storms, the sea monsters, and sorceress, and who had returned to bring truth, liberty, and justice for all to the island of Ithaca where he lived in eternal youthfulness with his faithful wife, Penelope. I told Homer about the infinity room, and he even experienced it for a while as we went to find Ilium. I'd hidden most of Odysseus's men there, but Homer needed the tragic tale of men who disobeyed the gods and were killed as a result. He refused to mention the priestesses of Aphrodite's temple there, even though he slept his way through half of them while I carried him in the bag.

I gave him all the highlights of history and then made him walk back to Greece. Maybe by the time he got there, he was blind. I never saw him again.

So, you see, you should never trust the words of a cheap novelist. They only take the historical facts and rework them into what they think will be a best seller. His agent probably told him to change it.

END OF PART III

Part IV
Nobody Expects the
Spanish Inquisition

Image Credit: Kiselev Andrey Valerevich, ID1166831713 licensed from Shutterstock.
com

16
CHURCHES AND DEMONS
ARE GOOD COMPANY

FTER I LEFT the palaces of the Peloponnese, I paused long enough to pay my respects to the patroness of Athens and erect a small temple in her honor. Soon after Clytemnestra and her lover Aegisthus murdered Agamemnon, there was an earthquake that made the small kingdom of the Acropolis self-sufficient with its own water source. Erectheus, the ruler of the microcity, wanted to build and reinforce a wall around the top of the Acropolis. I agreed to do so on condition that he also erect a small temple to Athene within its precincts.

Well, I was there for four or five years, creating the fortification and the temple. It wasn't huge, but Athene had blessed it and my work, so I was pleased. No, this was not the famed Parthenon of later years. It was just a small temple near Erectheus's equally small palace. But it served to separate and protect the Acropolis from the curse of the House of Atreus that had claimed so many lives, including Agamemnon. I'll tell you about that story sometime, but I stayed away from the family as far as I could, and as soon as the little temple was finished, I headed on north.

I'm tired of talking about ancient history. Yes, I met some famous people, like Nebuchadnezzar, Alexander, Caesar, and such, but I'll get to their stories later. For a few centuries, I enjoyed wandering through northern and eastern Europe, before heading south into Mesopotamia again. There were places where I thought I might successfully settle down and hide the satchel before crawling in and living there with my family forever. But every time I thought I'd found such a place, I'd see people moving that direction.

Not that we didn't have some good times. There was Impi, for example—a Finnish girl whose name meant 'virgin,' which was true for most of the first day I met her. The day was only a few minutes long and then it was night for hours. What's a demon to do to keep a girl warm when the night is twenty-three or more hours? I built a little hut and we stayed in it for several years. Sadly, the people of that region were not terribly long-lived and I once again bid farewell to a perfectly lovely wife.

Centuries after Homer wrote, there was a great revival of the arts and literature. People dug up the bones of Homer's Iliad and Odyssey and made translations and books. I'm sure if he read and understood them today, Homer would be appalled at how his precious words have been twisted. Well, serves him right if you ask me. He glorified the barbaric Greeks and denigrated the Trojans. Didn't even mention the underhanded horse trick. I'm glad Virgil got that part right in *The Aeneid*. Romans should be proud to have the blood of Troy in their veins instead of on their hands.

The whole story of being chased all over the Mediterranean by Poseidon reminds me of another unpleasant voyage or two. But let's put off talking about more ancient history. I'll get to Caesar and Cleopatra later. I know you want to hear about them. But everyone has heard about them. This next adventure I want to tell you about happened, oh, less than a millennium or so ago.

I love the sea, so I'd spent years sailing on waters Poseidon had never touched. Of course, by this time, things had become so crazy on earth that the Olympians pretty much gave it up as a bad game and moved on. I didn't understand for a long time, but when the king of the gods loses control of the kingdom, he gets pouty and out of sorts. Zeus, Poseidon, Hades, all decided eventually to get out of town when the new god started pushing them around. I'll tell you about him later.

The seas I sailed in this time were far in the south and in the Far East as I made my way from island paradise to island paradise. Those were some good times and I met some interesting people. Remind me to tell you about the Great Khaan sometime. The journey eventually brought me up the west coast of Africa until I once again found myself sailing the familiar seas of the Mediterranean. It was nostalgic. I'd thought I might visit some of the old places and see if anything I remembered was still there. That thought ended with my first stop in Italy. A plague had just begun and they called it the Black Death. People who caught it tended to die.

I considered getting right back on my boat, but it had become infested with rats in almost no time after I made port. I abandoned ship. There were thousands of people living in the infinity room world by this time, so most did not recognize my long absence. I placed a sealing spell on the case making it impervious to anything that might attack it. Especially, rats. After some time in Rome, working on the center city of the church, I made my way north through Italy, hoping to find a place to sit out the plague.

What I found was construction. There were ancient buildings in Rome which had fallen into ruin. The forum and Colosseum were a shambles. But there was a construction boom in Italy. Mostly churches. I was an old hand at building temples by this time and it was easy for me to find small churches either being built or needing repair. I could work pretty rapidly, easing the burdens of many of the workers so their work also went more swiftly. I never stayed longer than it took to complete a specific task or project, then I moved on.

Gods and temples. I've never quite understood. I believe it is an immortal vanity. When Ninra got me to build his temple in Bathra, there was no slowing things down. Everyone knew the god and goddess had their hands in getting it built, as they were represented directly by the Queen and King—Bao and me. We worked beside the laborers to make a beautiful temple with Ninra and Namri's blessing. People saw the hand of the gods at work.

To me, it was evidence that the Christian god didn't command the building of a temple in every city of any size in the world. The churches were created to the glory of the architects and priests who made sure their names were attached to the various churches and cathedrals.

Here's the thing. The god of the Jews, to whom I had been near but never met, had a single temple. His people knew exactly where they needed to go to worship. Oh, there were some smaller places regionally where people met to study the holy books, but sacrifice was strictly limited to the temple.

Then there was the whole debacle with the summoning of a messiah and not knowing what it was they wanted. Everyone had a different idea of what the messiah should be. When he didn't turn out to be that, they looked for something more substantial. Now many people maintain the old ways, and worship the old god of the Torah. I have nothing against that, any more than I object to raising my glass to Aphrodite on occasion. But he quit working when the world began to collapse around him. Like the ancient Greek gods, he retired to Olympus or to Sinai or maybe to Miami.

Without a god and having rejected the message of the messiah they summoned, a new religion arose. It was designed according to the ideal that these adherents held—the new god would dominate not only his people, but the world. And if their god dominated the world, then his people dominated all other people. This general philosophy was present in the creation of some other religions and at least one competed for world domination.

You don't have to believe my theories, of course. I am merely a 4,000-year-old demon. I have seen gods come and go. Gods that depend on the belief of their people. More than anything else, the new god destroyed the belief in other gods. It's just my opinion, of course. I'm not about to try to find that god and interview him.

Which brings me back to the elaborate and beautiful cathedrals. A simple survey of the names of the cathedrals and their dedications will tell you quickly that they were not erected to serve the god, but rather the various saints and priests and architects who attached their names to them. Hence—and since the objective of the religion was world domination—there was not a single temple where the god could be identified and worshiped, but rather a cathedral in every town, established with the mythos that the god is present in all at the same time.

All of which made no difference to me at all. I had built dozens of temples throughout the world at this point, and I saw no difficulty in helping build another. Which is what brought me to the temple in Firenze. I should remember to say cathedral. It had been begun fifty years before I got there and was expected to take another hundred years to finish. I revised my assessment that no god was lightening the load of the peasants cutting stone and elevating it to be stacked on the walls. The god, if he was involved at all, had provided engineers. The sleds used for hauling the heavy stones had wheels. They were pulled by horses. There was no need for a simple demon to come along and enchant the sled so whatever was on it was light enough for a man to pull. Stones moved steadily from the quarry to the temple.

I admired the men who dreamed dreams of these temples and then created them with essentially the same tools I used for the palaces in Knossos or the temple in Bathra. Oh, there were bright architects, engineers, and mechanics at work. A small item I contributed was to demonstrate how a groove on one stone could be matched with a tongue on the next stone to create a stronger weld between the stones. I'd learned that in creating the bricks in Bathra.

I tried not to practice too much magic around the cathedral, and none at all on the building itself. I'm not really that good with subtle magic. I did, however, find an ancient spell for binding two items together. When I saw the rickety scaffolding the workers were using to hoist the heavy stones into place, I made nightly trips around the structures and bound the joints together so they wouldn't collapse. Otherwise, I was just a worker putting my back into the building of the cathedral, and leaving some well-placed drawings lying around where the architects could find and claim them.

During this time, I fell in with a monk named Brother Matteo, who spent his days in sober prayer for the safety of the workers and the glory of the building. Glory of God, I should say. I visited with Brother Matteo frequently and he took me to his home at night. His home, with others of his kind, was out in the countryside and most of the holy men spent their time tending vast plots of grapevines. The grapes were harvested and pressed into juice, then fermented into some of the finest wine I had ever tasted. They had reached a point of perfection. While Brother Matteo spent his days in sober prayer, his nights were not as sober.

Eventually, I left the construction on the cathedral and spent my time learning everything I could from the monks about making wine. Then I began searching for a suitable plot of ground where I could grow my own grapes and make my own wine.

Enter Esmira. Remember, I mentioned her back once at the beginning of this tale. Well, it's time tell her story. I might *almost* have thought Aphrodite had placed her in my path, but I hadn't heard from My Lady Goddess in a thousand years. Nonetheless, I whispered a blessing to her.

Esmira was a raven-haired beauty with bountiful breasts, scarcely contained within her dress. She was the sixteen-year-old daughter of—Surprise! Surprise!—a vineyard owner. I approached her cautiously and she approached me flirtatiously. The plague had reduced the number of potential mates for the surviving women. She took it as a sign when I stumbled upon her vineyard that I was destined to be hers. Perhaps she was right. I had no objections.

"If you are looking for work, I have a few suggestions of things you could do," she said, sidling up to me. She almost brushed me with the tips of her breasts as she swayed in front of me.

"I could see working in a vineyard for such a beautiful young foreman," I responded.

"Some of the work would be hard," she said, definitely brushing her nipples across my sleeve this time. Things were getting hard already.

"I would hate to plant seeds in someone else's vineyard," I said. "Or even to plow someone else's field." My hand had strayed to her waist and stroked down her hip.

"If your plow is as sharp as your tongue, the furrow would be easy to part," she said, reaching between us to stroke my length.

"So sharp, in fact, that I sometimes use my tongue to prepare the soil for my plow." I tweaked her nipple and she gasped.

"Come with me. This field can only be plowed by its rightful owner, but I think a purchase could be arranged." She grabbed my hand and dragged me out of the field toward the modest home near the winery.

I observed the operation as Esmira continued to chat with me and discover where I came from. It seemed most of the vineyard was run by women, but that made sense if young men were in short supply. That happens in times of plague and war.

"Papa! This is Roberto! He is eligible and I want him. Please make a marriage contract between us," Esmira announced when she brought me into the house to meet her father. She was not about to waste time in laying claim.

"Roberto? Roberto who? I don't know any Roberto!" the man said.

"Roberto di Firenze," I made up on the spot. "Please, just call me Bob."

"I am Manduggo Domenic Ermengildo di Maiano," the man said. "You may call me Doug. Now, what do you have to offer that will make me give you my precious daughter and her inheritance in the vineyards around us."

That was music to my ears. Not only was Esmira a fiery woman who was hot to trot, she came with an inheritance of these vineyards. I thought I could easily live with that.

"Since the time of the plague, I have worked my way from church to cathedral, lending my back to the glory of God. But my heart belongs to the land. I have spent the past two years learning winemaking from the monks of San Michele a Monteripaldi. They make a fine wine and I would put it up against any in the region."

He simply stared at me as if winemakers were a dime a dozen and he wanted something better for his daughter. Hmm. It seemed I'd used that strategy before, myself.

"I have some small wealth of my own that I can bring to hire help when we expand our vineyards and our winery to double its current size, and your lovely home into a palazzo worthy of the beautiful Esmira," I said. I laid it on a bit thick, I suppose. I think he was sold as soon as I mentioned a little wealth. Esmira had been sold as soon as she stroked my manhood.

He immediately tapped a keg of wine and poured us each a carafe from which we poured glass after glass. When I had adequately sampled his fare and approved of it, I pulled two bottles of the Monteripaldi wine from my satchel and we compared the subtle differences. During the evening, Esmira brought plate after plate of food, waiting on us as we discussed her dowry and the commitments we would make to each other as father and husband. Her mother had been caught by the plague and they mourned her, but father and daughter had avoided infection and worked constantly in the vineyard and winery.

By the end of the night, I had a bride and a stake in a lovely vineyard.

⌫⌫⌫⌫⌫⌫⌫⌫⌫⌫⌫⌫⌫

"Roberto, we are now wed," Esmira said when we returned to the vineyard after our vows at the still-unfinished cathedral.

I couldn't help myself while we were in Firenze. I saw the display of the architect's drawings for the duomo and stopped to sketch a few suggestions to leave for him. If he took my suggestions, it would reduce the building time by half.

"Bob!" Back to Esmira. "You are my husband. You need no longer confine your hands to the outside of my clothing. Please! I have waited all my life for this moment and I want my husband between my legs!"

We slipped away from the party held in our honor and I began undressing her at once.

"What are you doing with my clothes?" she asked in alarm.

"Oh, my dear wife," I said. "I am preparing us for the most delightful experience of your young life. To do it properly, we need no clothes between us."

"No clothes! You are an evil and lascivious man!"

"Did you think I would merely raise your skirts and plunder your sex without worshiping every inch of your body? My sweet, we are to become one flesh. There is no sin in putting our skin directly together."

As hot and ready as Esmira was, I don't believe she was expecting the sudden shaking that wracked her body when she came. Girls were often highly protected from all knowledge of the world in that day. She stared at me with eyes and mouth open as I peeled my own clothes off my body. She simply stood and stared, stark naked and not knowing what to do next. For a girl who had so mastered the art of flirtation, she really did not know where to go from there.

I swept her up in my arms and carried her to the bed, pulling the blanket off before I laid her down. I was serious when I told her I would worship every inch of her body. I set about proving it, and she began what would be a long line of climaxes that helped to pass our night before I ever parted those womanly folds and entered her.

Esmira was so overwhelmed with the strength of her orgasm when I came in her that she passed out and slept until morning.

⌫⌫⌫⌫⌫⌫⌫⌫⌫⌫⌫⌫⌫

Life was good. I managed on occasion, to cross into the infinity room and update my wives and possessions about what was going on in the natural world. They were thrilled that I'd taken another wife and asked me repeatedly to bring her to them.

That was something I wasn't about to risk. My time in the infinity room was limited as it was. You see, the Church of Rome and, as a result, the people who followed its religion, had rigid views of demons. They were not good.

Back in Jesus' time, there had been instances in which he convinced another demon to leave a possession and make its home elsewhere. Now, never did Jesus send a fellow demon to hell. That manmade lake of fire and torture had no place in his dealings. But he was also firm about the possession of a human body.

There is a difference here that you may not understand. I'll try to explain. When I possessed Josie or Pari, they actually asked me to possess them—to take full and complete ownership of their bodies, minds, and wills. I had my own body. I didn't need to inhabit theirs in order to possess them. On the other hand, there were many demons who for one reason or another had lost their bodies without returning to the primordial mass. One means of avoiding death was to jump into the body of someone else and possess it regardless of their will. Jesus was known to have cast demons out of the body of a person, setting that demon free to find another host—often an animal.

There's a famous story of a demon being cast out and into a passel of swine and the pigs ran off a cliff. Let me say several things about this. First, there were very few pigs in Judea. They were anathema and there was no market. I suppose some Roman soldiers somewhere might have had some. They liked bacon. Second, in the story, Jesus did not send the pigs off the cliff. He had a very high regard for life and would not have sent innocent animals, even unclean ones, to their death. Third, the death of the pig would not have meant the death of the demon, any more than the death of his original body. It might have hurt like hell, but he'd have escaped and found another host.

The religion, however, holds that all demons are evil, that they come from and return to hell, and traffic with one is to risk eternal damnation. I was not about to reveal myself to Esmira.

Everything went well for a long time. Esmira was a lubricious lover and made sure I was always welcome between her legs. When it became necessary to produce an heir on her, I enlisted the help of one of the many men from the infinity room, to whom I gave my shape and let him happily impregnate my wife. And I was proud that I restrained myself from killing him afterward.

Esmira was none the wiser and was happy to produce little Doug and later, Esmirina.

The farm and vineyard were prosperous. I enjoyed drinking the wine almost as much as I enjoyed feasting between Esmira's legs.

The plague was now well past, so my visits to the infinity room increased in frequency. I was careful. I would load up a wagon of barrels of wine and take it into the city or to another village to sell. Of course, I didn't take all the wine to a city or village. I found a cave where I could open a door to the infinity room and bring barrels of wine in for our future enjoyment. I always paid for the wine with gold from the infinity room. While there, I had ample opportunity to enjoy Nimia, Josie, Penelope, Princess, Zhi, Pari and others. Yes, I'll tell you about those you don't recognize later.

That is what proved to be my undoing as I once became careless about crossing the threshold into my kingdom.

17
THE WRATH OF A WOMAN SCORNED

XACTLY WHAT IS THIS, and who are you?" Esmira demanded from behind me.

I spun in my embrace with a naked Josie to see my wife standing right beside me. Behind her, I could see the open door to our palazzo. How could I have been so careless? I *almost* never entered the secret room from the palazzo and then only when I knew it was deserted. There was nothing I could do but own up to the situation.

"This, my beloved wife, is my devoted minion, Josie. Once a few thousand years ago, she asked me to possess her, and I have," I said. I watched as Esmira tried to process what I'd said.

"You have a slave? From how long ago?" she screamed.

"What's it been, Josie, my love? Three thousand and maybe five hundred years?" I asked my possession.

"Oh, Bob, we can celebrate our anniversary anytime you want," she answered.

"How can you keep this little slip of a girl as your sex slave? It's inhuman! You must free her at once!" Esmira insisted.

"Josie, are you an unwilling slave? Do I treat you inhumanely? Do you want to be free of me?" I asked.

"Oh, Bob! Don't use words like that! Slave? I'm right where I want to be. And the sex—as you should know, Esmira—is fantastic. We were just about to go to bed. Please join us!"

My dear Josie had no qualms about having any number of women in my bed as long as I paid enough attention to her—and I did. Dear Esmira did not see it that way. The world had become progressively less tolerant of others since it stopped accepting a pantheon of gods and now fought wars over one or two who staked exclusive claim to the entire world. It was a trend I feared would continue a long time.

If you have never been scolded by an Italian woman who has had her honor slighted, pray to whatever gods you may that you never have the privilege. I, as meekly as I could, agreed with her that I was a monster and unfit to be her husband. She couldn't believe a demon had entered the Catholic Church and married her before God, then took her precious virginity and forced children on her, all while maintaining a harem of teenage whores for my own enjoyment. I was a monster—not only an affront to her, but to God himself. Surely, the very walls of the cathedral I worked on would crumble and fall once it was known a demon had helped to build it. I had a special place reserved for me in the lowest circle of hell and she would see to it that I suffered for all eternity.

I was not sure that suffering for all eternity in hell would be worse than suffering the next few years living with Esmira.

Speaking of hell, Dante Alighieri's *Divine Comedy* had debuted about 100 years previously and nearly every library had a copy. As a favorite son of Firenze, there were many copies in the area, being the second most popular book next to the Bible. And probably more closely quoted by both laymen and priests as a description of the heaven and hell and purgatory that awaited all souls upon death. In the volume *The Inferno*, Dante holds that there are nine circles of hell, the last of which is reserved for treachery and includes Judas, Brutus, and Cassius. Interesting that the two murderers of Caesar were on a nearly equal footing with Judas Iscariot, but that is of no matter.

The interesting thing is that no demons are depicted herein as being tortured in hell. They are, in fact, the torturers and only Lucifer seems to suffer as he chews on the living bodies of the three traitors. I will provide a clue that pointing this out to my darling wife did not have the desired effect of lessening her wrath.

Scarcely a day went by that Esmira did not harangue me about my level of depravity. I took to sleeping in the winery. My marriage bed was colder than the stone floors. And since I was in the winery, I moved several barrels of wine into the infinity room where they were stored with casks from different ages of the world.

In the infinity room, we already knew that people did not age unless they had a marker for aging, like a growing child. In the same way, the *things* we brought into the infinity room, like wine, did not age further, either. So, there was a lifespan for wine in the natural world, but it stopped aging in the infinity room. Since most wine of that era was better drunk young, moving recently fermented wine into the infinity room was not in any way harmful to it. I had casks of wine from all over the world, collected over three-and-a-half millennia, that were as good and as fresh today as they were the day I acquired them.

And I drank quite a bit. A lot. Far more than my share.

I often visited the infinity room where my harem was more than sympathetic about my poor marriage. They did their best to keep me from despairing. I always went on a sales trip before going into the infinity room, though. I knew a couple of secluded caves where I could hide the satchel, lead the horse and wagon inside, and close the gateway for a few hours (or days) of peace and love. I would return home after a week or two in the infinity room feeling fine and refreshed. I would give my wife a loving kiss, silencing her raving about my demonic ways for an instant. If I was very insistent, she was silent for an hour or more while I made sure she enjoyed—thoroughly—every sensation a wife should receive from her husband. Bringing home a sack full of gold always helped to smooth my return, as well. As far as my wife was concerned, I'd sold the wine and brought her the payment, which enabled her to elevate her position with servants of her own.

I did not count on her treachery.

She followed me.

At first it was only to verify her suspicions that I was a horrid cheating demon. Then it was to find out if there was a way to trap me.

I've mentioned the demons of Egypt, called djinni, before. They were always kept trapped in a bottle or a lamp or some such container. It is essentially what Pinaruti had intended to be my fate. Well, the djinni are mentally a little slow. No offense if you happen to be one. A djinn is summoned from the primordial mass by a conjurer, much like I was. I can scarcely call the level of conjurer a mage. The djinn is then lured into a container, and the conjurer pops a cork in it. Demon sealed in a bottle and bound to the will of whoever releases him. Time and time again. I don't know, but I suspect the conjurer just dropped a bit of sugar candy into the bottle to lure him inside.

My infinity room was full of my own special kinds of sugar candy in the form of Nimia, Josie, Penelope, Princess, Pari, Zhi, Chione, Lakshmi, and all the other lovely women who had attached themselves to our household. I was often willingly in my satchel.

But I had created many safeguards on my little world. I enchanted the satchel with a look-away spell that would make it nearly invisible to anyone who wasn't literally in touch with it. I kept it on my person at all times, unless I was inside. After the unfortunate discovery, I always made sure I closed the gateway behind me so no one could stumble in. I didn't think there was any way to be trapped there.

I was wrong.

I suspected she had hidden on the wagon when I went on a selling trip and slipped off at the very last minute when I led the horse inside. Then I closed the gateway and she felt around until she found the satchel. I was completely unaware that I had been trapped until two weeks later when I attempted to open the gateway and leave. It would not open! I tried everything. I pounded. I screamed. I swore revenge. I went to my library, which now contained thousands of books and scrolls collected over millennia, and read everything I could find regarding sealed magic chambers.

Nimia joined me. She had read nearly all the books in the library, learning the various languages from the librarians and people we had picked up along the way. There was likely no one in all of the infinity room she could not communicate with—and not by reading minds, like I did. She spoke their languages. She brought me books with spells and incantations and she tried them with me. She pointed out the hieroglyphic scripts that told how to capture a djinn. The best we could tell was that it was a simple matter of putting a cork in it.

In any room (or container) all one needed to do to trap the demon inside, was to close the door from the outside.

It was easy for me to think of the infinity room as an entire world, impossible to wrap in an enclosure. But the truth was that this entire world was contained in a normal satchel that could be carried over the shoulder. I was trapped.

And so, I got drunk.

I emerged from my room in our house—which had grown to palatial proportions—only to rail against the unopening gateway to the wide world outside. I was quite sour.

My women didn't know quite what to do. They attempted to entertain me and make sure I was distracted. To them—and to all the million or so residents of the infinity room—nothing was different. No one ever left the infinity room unless I disguised a man to go breed my current lover. The children born in the infinity room were just normal people. They grew up, met mates, had jobs, and died. Their parents aged with them. It was almost exactly as it had been on earth.

Only people who had come into the infinity room from the natural world had the ability to stay forever young. But if they chose to reproduce (male or female), they began to age into mortality. To all others, it was as if time stood still. Except it didn't quite. I could tell that Nimia and Josie were very gradually aging. They were still young and beautiful women, but perhaps in their twenties instead of their teens. An increase in their physical maturity was showing.

It became a daily ritual for me to go to the gateway and attempt to open it, then go back to my room and drink and fornicate until the next day.

Then one day, it happened. The gateway opened.

I should point out that there is more to controlling a djinn than just capturing it. If you want to open the bottle and have the djinn obey you, you have to put a spell on it and get the djinn to agree to it. Most are forced to agree, but none are bottled who can't be controlled when they are released. No one got me to agree to anything when I was trapped in the infinity room. I was angry and ready to fight.

"Esmira, I'm going to kill you for that!" I growled as I emerged from the infinity room and hit my head hard enough to flatten me out.

"She said that would be the first thing you said," a cute young thing stretched out before me said. I was not expecting to be greeted by a child! What kind of trick was this?

"Who are you?" I demanded.

"I'm Esmeralda," she said. "Esmira was my grandmother. Um... great grandmother."

"Great grandmother? How long have I been trapped in there?" I asked. Time definitely flowed differently in the infinity room than in the natural world. I was still upset that I'd been trapped, but I had no sense of how much time had passed.

"I'm not positive. Sixty or seventy years, I think. There was no date on your monument to indicate when you'd died. Grandmother gave me the key, but forbade me from opening the flap until she was dead. She was really old. She thought having lived with you gave her an extra long life to live with her regrets.”

“Regrets, eh? I don’t know what she had to regret. I’m the one who let her trap me and had to serve the time cut off from the natural world.” I was still a little huffy, but I didn’t want to take it out on an innocent child.

“Oh, she lived as a widow all those seventy years. She had a beautiful stone erected to you at the cathedral she said you helped build. You should have seen the dome when it was finished. It’s fabulous,” Esmeralda said. Her enthusiasm was infectious. I could tell I’d have trouble with this one.

“How nice.”

“She was really sad you were gone. She told me she regretted having locked you away from the moment she did it, but was afraid you’d kill her if she ever opened the bag, but she thought I’d be safe.”

“Yes, you are. You...”

“...let the goat out of the bag,” she giggled. “You might want to do something about your horns before anyone sees you.”

I felt my head. Yes, I was fully in my demon form and that would certainly raise an alarm. I wondered how long I’d been in that form in the infinity room. My women, of course, loved the goat demon as well as any personage I’d adapted.

“Where are we? Why is the ceiling so low?” I asked.

“We’re on a boat. Under the bed. I didn’t want anyone to see me or you.”

“Where are we bound to?”

“Um... Spain. If we get there. I need help.”

“Help for what?”

“I kind of killed him,” she said, pointing across the floor to where a man lay bleeding. Oh, great! We crawled out from under the bed and I grabbed the man’s hand. What a disgusting creature! His body was already cooling, so the memories I collected were rather scattered. A church emissary to the King and Queen of Spain. He was very proud of the robes he wore, representing a bird of high rank. Or something like that. They were red.

Two things were foremost in his mind. First, that he carried a papal bull, *Exigit Sinceras Devotionis Affectus*, that established an inquisition in Spain under Ferdinand and Isabella. He hoped to be named the inquisitor general. The second thing was how he was going to rape his lovely little assistant, Esmeralda, now that they were at sea. That idea went south rather quickly when she slit his throat.

As I was collecting the scattered memories, I worked the spell that would transform my body into his.

“Oh, yuck,” Esmeralda said. “I hope you don’t think we’re going to have sex with you looking like that! I’d rather have sex with the goat.”

“Don’t worry, my dear Esmeralda. Sex and you are a long way apart. What are you thirteen? Twelve? I plan to protect you, even if I have to shove you into the bag for safekeeping. For now, however, we need to dispose of His (former) Excellency Bonaventure Calvino. Are his clothes here somewhere?”

"Acting as his secretary, I was folding them when he grabbed hold of my teats and said I could either take my own clothes off or he would," she said.

"And you just happened to have a knife at hand?" I chuckled.

"Once I figured out what kind of man he was and what he intended, I sharpened my letter opener," she answered smugly.

"Resourceful girl." I searched my memory for a spell of dissolution and in a few minutes, the cardinal and his blood were floating out the porthole in a cloud of mist.

Esmeralda found a nightshirt in the cardinal's bag and helped me into it. Then we sat on the beds to talk. I opened the bag, whispering my desire to Nimia inside. In a moment, Chione emerged with a table of food for the two of us, then quietly went back into the bag. Esmeralda set to the food with the gusto of a child who had not eaten lately.

"Now, since I've been isolated from this world for seventy years, you need to tell me everything that's happened in that time and what I need to know for us to survive in this world," I said, waving a chicken bone. "And why is a young girl on a sea voyage with an old priest who intends to rape her?"

"Mmm. There are, as usual, wars and rumors of wars," Esmeralda said around a mouthful of noodles. "The Turkish Sultan is threatening to invade Rome and the only thing that stands between them and the papacy are the Spanish soldiers and navy. Ferdinand and Isabella consider themselves the supreme authority in Spain and Pope Sixtus has given them authority to examine and try heretics. He's had armies out for years, trying to solve the Jewish problem," she said.

"You are remarkably well informed."

"I've been listening to all the conversations. I can stand right next to Monsignore... or I could... and fill his water glass while he talked of the most secret things, assuming I must be a deaf mute."

"Where is the Christian god in all of this? Why would he play to such intrigue?" I simply hadn't grasped the absenteeism of the Christian god, who seemed quite satisfied to just let people kill each other in his name and forgive them for their sins later.

"I don't need God now that I have you."

"Whoa! Whoa! Back off there. First of all, you don't have me. I am a free demon and I will make sure you never catch me in the satchel unguarded. Secondly, I am a *lowly* free demon, not a god. I learned long ago not to contest with gods and goddesses. I don't like impersonating a priest when I've no commission from this god of the Christians."

"Um... You mean I don't get three wishes?" she pouted.

"No. That's an old tale from another part of the world. Though I've always listened to what my women want and have done my best to give it to them. Should you ever become one of my women, you can expect equal treatment," I said.

"Don't you just pop out and take control of everyone? I thought I became one of your women when I opened the bag. That's what Grandmother said would happen. Maybe she was just trying to keep me from opening the bag," Esmeralda said.

"You are too young to safely bring into the infinity room. Since you are not yet fully grown into your womanhood, you might cause everyone else to start aging as you mature," I speculated. I thought back over the past 3,500 years and could not think of a time when I brought a child into the infinity room to mingle with my harem. Certainly, the children of the harem in Troy had been brought in, but they came with their own nurses and were sent directly to a private area away from the center of my city. Hmm. "Now, tell me how you happen to be on this boat in the company of an old priest who intended to rape you," I said.

"It's a long story."

"We have all night before I need to see anyone on deck."

The story Esmeralda spun kept me awake all night.

18
IN 1492, COLUMBUS SAILED...

"FTER YOU LEFT..." Esmeralda started her tale.

"Was imprisoned," I corrected.

"After you were cruelly and brutally forced into a dank dark cell and kept there without food or water or human company," she started again, rolling her eyes, "Grandmother discovered you had never been on a sales trip in all the years you were taking casks away. There was no one outside our valley who had ever heard of our wine. The money had all come from you as you stockpiled the wine in your bag. She almost opened the bag just to demand the money."

"That would have been unwise," I grumbled.

"So she figured. Anyway, she had enough money to keep the vineyard producing and was able to buy another wagon and horse to replace the one you stole."

"I didn't steal it! She trapped it inside with me."

"Uh huh. She hired helpers for the vineyard and then she and her son loaded the wagon and took it to surrounding villages. After sampling the vintage, the road houses and taverns all wanted to buy as much as they could. Our Chianti became the most popular *primitivo* table wine in all of Tuscany. She reckoned that if you had actually taken the wine to sell, we'd have earned twice the paltry sum you paid for it."

"That was not a paltry sum!" I bellowed, and then lowered my voice. "She certainly never complained about money when she was spending it."

"I'm sure. Great Grandmother Esmira always exaggerated when she spoke of you. To hear her talk in her older years, you were so well hung she had to take a day's journey by horse just to get to the end of your cock."

"It's not that big," I said.

"I saw. Big enough, though."

"When did she tell you all of this?"

"Some of the stories were passed down from my mother or her mother. Anyway, Esmira's children got married and had children. The more she thought about it, the more Esmira decided you couldn't have actually been the father because her children showed no sign of any demonic traits."

"I wonder which of my traits she considered demonic," I sighed.

"Most of them. Really, the kids didn't even look anything like you according to her. One was so dark-skinned she was sure the father was African or south Mediterranean. I have just a bit of her color."

"Well, she was right. I cannot father children," I confessed.

"I need have no worry about having sex with my grandfather then." I looked at her sharply, but she just continued. "Everyone worked on the farm, but Esmira was always the head of the family and the boss, right up until she died. She continued to acquire land and began raising goats to make cheese that went well with the wine. By the time she died a couple of years ago, the palazzo was among the wealthiest and most illustrious in all of Tuscany."

"She died a couple of years ago and you just got around to opening the bag?" I raged. Quietly.

"She shoved it into my hands just before she died and told me to keep it next to me always. There was an inheritance dispute among the descendants. As a result, I was shipped off to a convent at San Michele a Monteripaldi. That reduced the number of heirs. It's funny how no one has ever touched or even mentioned the satchel."

"The look-away spell," I said. "I'm glad it is still working. I need to refresh it so it doesn't fade."

"Well, I can see it. It's right... Wait! Where did it go?"

"You could see it while it was in your possession. Now it is in my possession."

"That's not fair. I wanted to go inside."

"Someday. Just not yet. I need you out here. Now continue the story."

"I'm still too young to take the holy vows. I was just considered one of the orphans they cared for. Though I understand I came with a rather sizable gift to the convent. Then Father Calvino arrived. He'd recently been promoted to Cardinal and was all full of himself in his red robes and pointed hat. He got the appointment so he could carry 'certain papers' to Spain on behalf of the Pope. But that was all he had. He had to find a seaport and book his own passage. The ports around Rome are still too dangerous as Turkish pirates harry the Spaniards. So, he came north. He stopped at the monastery, looking for a secretary. They sent him to the convent. The convent gave him me because I could read and write."

"And he took you because you have tits."

"You noticed?" she asked excitedly. "They're not as big as Mother's or Grandmother's, but I think they'll grow."

"I noticed," I said. "We need to disguise them to keep you from looking so desirable."

"Desirable," she sighed. She was not getting the point.

"See here, Esmeralda. If you follow around a priest and look like you are ready to fuck, someone will. Or they will imagine that I already am. Either way, it would put us both in danger. Until we have fulfilled our current mission and delivered the papal bull, we need to lay low and not raise any suspicion. If I have to use magic to protect us, they will do their best to find and destroy us."

"I understand, Bob. But can I have them out to display when it's just the two of us?"

I groaned. She really looked delectable. And to think her great grandmother had been shocked speechless when I removed her clothes.

I'd last sailed just a century and a half ago, but I was amazed at how far the technology of shipbuilding had come, even in that little time. The Spanish galleon was a large and fast ship with passenger cabins below deck. I thought fleetingly that Poseidon would have had a tougher time with this ship than he had with my tiny boat. I'd like to see the Scylla attempt to crush this one!

I quickly silenced my thoughts lest they be overheard as a challenge.

By the time we reached Catalonia, I had made sufficient alterations to Esmeralda's appearance that she would not draw attention. I also worked on a modified 'look-away' spell that would keep her from unwanted notice. It wouldn't make her invisible like the effect on the bag, but she would be unremarkable and simply not draw attention. She was more androgynous in appearance but I didn't want her to look too much like a boy. There were many in the religious orders who preferred that gender. I had not told Esmeralda what Calvino had actually intended to do to her. It would make her constipated.

We disembarked and were met by a small detachment of mounted soldiers and a few priests. The priests did obeisance and the soldiers watched impatiently as our luggage was loaded onto the top of a carriage in which we rode to Castile, where Isabella had recently consolidated her control by ousting her aunt and legitimizing her claim to the throne. I was transporting three large trunks and had no idea what was in any of them. How many possessions did a priest need? We stayed in inns along the way and no one thought it the least bit strange that my secretary nun stayed in my room.

A rumor grew that she was a bodyguard and people were better warned away. Of course, I had no part in starting that rumor. I did, however, spend time making sure she knew how to defend herself and she took to the instruction well. When we were in private, Zhi emerged from the bag to give her lessons in hand-to-hand combat.

In Castile, we were conducted to a suite of rooms in the local diocese and given two days of rest before the monarchs summoned us. We immediately began unpacking the trunks to see what on earth was in them.

What I found made me smile. Some twenty-five years before, a man in Germany had succeeded in making multiple copies of the Bible with a machine he called a printing press. Since that time, many books had been printed in Germany, Italy, France, and even England. I pushed the trunks through the gateway to the infinity room and the ladies unloaded the books for our library and refilled the trunks with normal clothing and household goods so they weighed about the same. Then they pushed the trunks back out to me. I had a new collection of books and looked forward to the time when I could sit and read.

My libraries had grown quite extensive, as I noted during my time in captivity. I'd collected works from some of the largest libraries in the world, not just those of Europe and the Middle East. But it was not appropriate for me to just steal all the books from wherever I saw them. I developed a replicating spell that I could pass a thing through and make a copy of it. I had first discovered the spell when I replicated Odysseus's boat on the infinity room sea. With only a few modifications, I was able to rapidly send books through to the infinity room where they were replicated exactly and then I put the originals back on their shelves. But sometimes, I simply saved books from disasters or from ignorant people who decided too much knowledge was a dangerous thing and were devoted to destroying them. Or from luggage I inherited from a dead priest.

Ferdinand was besotted with his wife, Queen Isabella. In fact, I'd say totally pussy-whipped. He'd made a play to be declared ruler of Castile when her father died, but it did not take long for the nobility to set him straight. Isabella was Queen in her own right and, as she was adjunct to him in Aragon, so he was adjunct to her in Castile. Together, they brought the rest of Spain and Portugal under one rule, at least in name: The Catholic Monarchy. Ferdinand might have been upset about his position in Castile, but he was overwhelmed by his wife. I did not witness anything Isabella wanted that Ferdinand didn't jump to provide. More about that later.

The papal bull I brought to them was exactly what she wanted. It put control of the Inquisition in her hands rather than in the hands of the church. Of course, priests would investigate and *try* the accused, but the queen's soldiers made the arrests, consolidating the power of law under the monarchy rather than the pope. The priests did not need an army.

"You see," Isabella explained to me as if I were a child, "we have too much greed in our nation. A man covets his neighbor's house and therefore denounces the neighbor so he can get the property. I'm sick of it and the priesthood has been complicit. They have the notion that the church should get all forfeited property. Not in my country. The inquisition is not a path to greater wealth for the church."

"What is the scope of the planned inquisition?" I asked.

"The Moors have been too long on the soil of Europe. We will build our strength and push south until we have driven them into the sea and across to Africa where they belong. And the Jews. I suspect that most of those who convert to Christianity are false. I will root out and kill all those who are not truly of the faith. Believe me when I tell you, Spain will be a Catholic country and there will be only Catholics in it. So, I suppose you want to become the Inquisitor General since you came here from the pope."

"Oh, your Majesty, not this humble priest. I will, of course, be at the disposal of your inquisitors, but have no desire to seek the glory of Inquisitor General," I said. In fact, that had been Calvino's intent, but everything I found about the direction of the Catholic church in this century repulsed me. I wanted to wash my hands of it and depart as quickly as possible.

I was dismissed as no longer of importance to the monarchs.

Religious fervor and the threat of eternal damnation is an effective means of controlling the poor and ignorant. The Jews of Iberia were neither poor nor ignorant. On the other hand, they had their own religious fervor that I had seen on a couple of occasions in my history. At some point, I'll tell you about how the Jews summoned the most powerful demon I've ever met. Fortunately, I have not met many demons.

The Inquisition got off to a slow start, which gave Esmeralda and me a chance to put together a kind of path to safety for the Jews. There was not much I could do for the Muslims because Isabella had reignited the *Reconquista*. This holy war was devoted to driving the Muslim Moors out of the south of Spain.

The Jews were stubborn. They held that their god would protect his people. Frankly, I felt their god had already left to join the immortals on Olympus—or perhaps Sinai or some other holy mountain where they did not need to deal with humans. But even those who had publicly converted to Christianity insisted their god would protect them. I offered to resettle anyone who would go back to their promised land. As strongly as they believed in their god, they were not quite so committed to the country from which they had been scattered.

Some few heeded my word and left for France. Not a good move. France had already expelled the Jews and they had to keep moving. Some others decided to sail south and founded an enclave on the African Continent, where Christians were uninterested. And there were a few—a very few—who took my offer of refuge in the infinity room.

Of those arrested and tried in the Inquisition, over ninety percent of those executed were Jews.

I spent ten years traveling as an itinerant priest, attempting to get the Jews to safety. Ten years is not much time for me. For Esmeralda, it was a time of great change. She went from a thirteen-year-old girl to a twenty-three-year-old beautiful woman. My spells were no longer enough to keep her from being noticed. And, it seemed she was constantly horny. Keeping her a virgin to honor my role as a priest did not last long. By the time she was sixteen, she was in my bed every night. She had no desire to leave me, even knowing I was a demon. She did, however, want to visit the infinity room. The more I thought about it, the better the idea sounded. She was the only living human being who knew of its existence and even one person in knowledge was too many.

We made a wide circuit through the western edge of Spain and Portugal, now united—at least in name—under the Catholic Monarchs. I gained a reputation as a great evangelist, converting Jews wherever I went. Ferdinand and Isabella celebrated their victories over the Moors by moving the seat of government to Cordoba. The treaty assured an independent state for the Moors. I had to wonder how long that would last. Isabella was devoted to conversion or elimination.

In the mountains of Portugal, I addressed my mistress's desire to enter the infinity room. I explained that it was a one-way trip, but she had heard me tell others the same thing.

We adopted the disguise of two country kids and went to a local priest to get married. Then I found a cave in the mountains and, deep inside where I was sure we could not be stumbled upon, I opened the door of the infinity room and took Esmeralda through. I had only made quick trips into the room to deposit new residents since having been released from the bag. I found it much as I had left it and Josie and Nimia met me as soon as we arrived. They made quite a fuss over Esmeralda and I confirmed that she was, indeed, also my wife. We celebrated for several days and Esmeralda found out what it was like to have a couple more wives helping her out in bed.

I was beginning to tire of traveling the world again. It had been around thirty-six centuries. I liked what I saw growing in the expanded infinity room. Everyone was busy. Everyone was cared for. I wanted to find a place where I could cease my traveling and retire to the world I had created, and still know the room was safe without me outside it guarding it. I decided to devote my time henceforth to finding a safe and secure place where we could live undisturbed.

This is what I was thinking when I reached Cordoba and encountered an enthusiastic sailor named Christopher. He was having difficulty getting funding for a journey west across the Atlantic to reach India. Now, I had sailed the Atlantic as I worked my way up the west coast of Africa some years back. I convinced Chris that I could be an asset in his travels, a position that he eventually endorsed.

He'd made a gross error upon his first meeting with the queen. She was an incredibly beautiful woman and had no difficulty using her womanly charms to get what she wanted. But woe be to a man who attempted to use *her* in such a way. When Chris had first met her and described his vision of a journey to the west, she leaned toward him and asked sincerely, "What do you want from me?"

"Consummation," had been his prompt reply. The idiot could have asked for boats and likely got them. Now we had to work our way back into Isabella's good graces.

I knew the way to sway Isabella.

<hr>

"Your Majesties, I am widely traveled as an emissary of the pope. I have seen the Holy Land. I have read the journeys of Marco Polo. I have traveled through Greece, Italy, and across the Mediterranean Sea. One thing I have discovered is that everywhere I have gone, there were people who had never heard of the salvation of our Lord and Savior," I said, laying it on as thickly as I could.

"Heathens and infidels," Isabella said distastefully.

"Only until they have heard the Word. Then they become faithful followers of the Lord and loyal supporters of the Crown—with their praise and their *taxes*. The people of India have not been blessed by the missionary zeal of our faith. I would help this master sailor on a mission to bring the true gospel to the people of India," I said. I decided to cut it off there so I wouldn't be accused of lying too grossly. I thought that we could sail across, find an uninhabited land, and I could ditch Columbus and his ships.

The ploy worked. Isabella's missionary fervor burned hot enough to singe Ferdinand and he grudgingly gave three ships to Chris and we set sail.

Of course, I was not the only priest taking passage. I was the only priest who could sail, however. And certainly, the only one who had been to India, though no one knew that. It seemed that in selecting missionaries, Isabella had found the lowest dregs of the priesthood she wanted to get rid of. They were motivated far more by the promise of great riches than by the mission to save souls.

And Christopher kept those fires burning. He nightly regaled the crews with tales of the wealth of India and the spices of China. When there were grumbles among the crew regarding how long the voyage was, he increased the share each would have in the wealth. When wealth was not enough, he added tales of beautiful women who served and worshiped their men.

And that was the first I heard him mention the word 'slaves.'

I was happy to say nothing.

In all my years of sailing, there were only a few times I had sailed with a crew. I wished I could go back to sailing alone. The men, the captains, the admiral, and even the priests were among the foulest people I had ever met. I had thought that when I found my own paradise, I might offer some of the sailors refuge in the infinity room. I put that thought aside as I knew I would have none of them soiling my landscape.

Sadly, as I think of the years that brought me here, I find that when the gods gave up on humanity and fled to Olympus, they did so because people had become more corrupt and vile than they could stand. Where sacrifices were once burned to the gods, they were now cooked for a feast of men. I found fewer and fewer people I wanted to add to the infinity room as the years went by.

But then, the lookout on the foremast called out the words we all longed to hear. There was land on the horizon.

19
THE GREATEST DEMON

SHOULD HAVE KNOWN that taking things out of order like I have would mean I have to go back in time in order to explain what happened next. In this instance, I'm going back around fifteen hundred years.

I'd been wandering around Egypt for some fifty or seventy-five years. Rome had consolidated its hold on the world and I had parted ways with Caesar when he burned the library at Alexandria. Well, he didn't burn it, Cleopatra's brother started the fire, but Caesar didn't help. But since my ship was also burned, I had some trouble getting out of Egypt.

Yeah, me and libraries. I love books. I saw Ptolemy's rabble headed toward the docks and had to choose whether I'd save my ship or the library. I ran into the great library to tell the librarians to start packing. I opened a portal into the infinity room and the librarians scooped up every scroll and book they could carry and took them to my little world. Then they came back and grabbed another handful. I went through the library grabbing everything I could and shoving it through the portal, telling the librarians to sort it all out when they got there. The library wasn't quite empty when the flames caught up to us, but we'd saved thousands of volumes. I closed the bag and ran.

Ultimately, I ended up wandering around in the desert like the proverbial Moses, which was a big legend told in Egypt. "Be good, children, or Moses will get you." It was quite a different story than what was told in Judea. In Egypt, Moses was painted as a lying magician who double-crossed the masters of the land, set traps that killed their children, and sent plagues on the land that forced Pharaoh to expel him and his chosen people. And then the idiot led a million people out into the desert and wandered around until all who had left the good life in Egypt were dead, including Moses. Their kids descended on the land near Jordan

River like a swarm of locusts and consumed everything and everyone in their way. Egyptians had no love of Moses.

I digress. I wandered with little or no purpose. There were other libraries in Egypt and I could foresee more destruction in their future. So, I picked up the families of the librarians I'd collected and made my way south to the Temple of Rameses, later changed and rebuilt by Ptolemy Soter. The significant thing was that it had an immense library. The priests of Horus, who were also the librarians, had already begun moving and hiding the many volumes stored there. It took me a long time and a lot of convincing, with a few visits from the librarians of Alexandria, to get the priests and librarians to bring the books all to the infinity room and then to get them settled.

I almost settled down there and joined them in the infinity room. In fact, I did for a while in order to create rebuilt replicas of the two great libraries. There were a lot of old places in Egypt where I could hide us. I'd heard about Kafre's tomb and the great Sphinx, but I'd never been there. What an engineering wonder! There was no question in my mind that the many Egyptian demons—djinni—had a hand in building the massive structures. There were places there where I could occupy a corner of the space and just enjoy the infinity room and my women.

After fifty or seventy-five years, I had a yearning for new wine and decided to head north again. This journey took me on the same perilous route Moses led the Israelites on. Except I took a few shortcuts and avoided the Red Sea altogether. There were other adventures, but I'll talk about those later. That's not the point of this story.

When I got up to Jerusalem, I found the most incredible thing I'd ever seen.

I'd had dealings with Jews over six hundred years before—ah, sweet Miriam, my wife—and found them to be reasonable people in everything except their religion. And I saw a few examples of why they were so devoted to it. But nothing had prepared me for Jesus.

I first heard of him from an itinerant preacher out in the wilderness who was baptizing people and telling them the Lord was coming. Well, I've always been one to follow the customs of the god whose land I was in, so I got in line and got baptized, too. Got the satchel sprinkled as well, so I counted that as having all its hundred thousand plus citizens baptized. Then I went off to see Jesus when John pointed him out.

I *liked* that dude! He preached some of the same things I'd advocated over the millennia. Peace, love, and kindness. It got me real excited. I mean, here was a demon summoned by an entire nation! They'd been working on the chants and pleas with their god for centuries until they finally built up enough unified will to conjure Jesus. He healed people, fed people, chastised those who were greedy, and forgave those who were weak. Just like Ninra and Namri. I wanted to do a little something for his ministry and I figured I could set myself up at a watering hole someplace in the wilderness and do what John was doing: Give people a ritual cleansing that would prepare them to meet Jesus.

I'd just found a place where I thought I might set up when I heard that John was dead! The fuckers cut his head off! What kind of place was this? I knew the Romans were merciless killers, but I'd never heard anything about the Jews being so single-mindedly violent toward one of their own.

I took shelter in a cave where I found a few scrolls buried in clay pots. I didn't want to defile any holy place and there was no one to ask about taking the books. Being a basically honest demon, I took the pots into the infinity room one at a time and worked a duplication spell on them that I'd found in one of the old scrolls. Did I tell you about that? Oh, yeah. I did. Once I had duplicated the contents of a pot, I took it back and worked a little spell on it to make it watertight and impervious to the elements. No telling how long it was intended to stay buried there as a kind of time capsule. Then I took the next pot in line and duplicated it. I wished I could find some Jewish librarians to join me, but nobody was doing any active work except in the temple.

It really burned me when I heard the Romans had executed Jesus. I found out all I could about it and decided they couldn't have been successful. You see, Zeus had told me when I was only a year old how a demon could be killed. I was sure Jesus had to be alive and word eventually filtered out that his disciples had seen him. I was relieved to hear it.

Still, I knew he wouldn't be able to stay in this area. They'd just keep trying. And that decided me that I shouldn't stay in the area either. I crossed over Jordan headed east and knocked the dust off my sandals, so to speak. I wanted as far away from this place as possible.

I knew this area from ancient times and it hadn't changed all that much. I made my way back to the great river and built a raft on which I floated leisurely south toward the sea.

I acquired a good-sized fisherman's boat near the mouth of the river and started stocking it up with trade goods to take me through the Persian Gulf to the Sea of India. I worked a few spells on the boat to make it more sea worthy. The routes were well-known by traders of the day and even back in my days in Bathra, we had seen traders bringing spices from the south. While I was working on the boat and preparing it for sea travel, a voice behind me spoke.

"Are you heading for the open sea in the south?" he asked.

"Yeah. That's the plan if I don't get blown apart. I've had a bad time with Poseidon in the past, but I don't think he's active down here."

"I would expect there are others, but no one who would have a reason to harm you," he said. He sounded familiar and I pulled my head out of the hold to turn and look at him. There was Jesus! Well, I'd assumed he wasn't in Judea any longer. He sure couldn't stay there after being crucified.

"Lord, how may I help you?"

"Start by not calling me Lord. I've had quite enough of that. Call me Issa. That's the name my friends in the south use. If you can stand the company, I'd happily ride with you to get home."

"That's great, Issa. I understand you know your way around boats as well. I have provisions, so we can launch as soon as you're ready."

He grabbed a towline and we pulled the boat toward deeper water, then we both jumped in.

Ah, the salt wind in my hair! The smell of the sea! The sound of the waves lapping against the sides. And a congenial partner to share the journey—even if not the lusty goddess Aphrodite.

We talked and relaxed on the boat for the better part of a month, fishing and eating and enjoying each other's company. Then he guided me to a port where I tied up and embraced him before he disembarked.

"Can I come with you, Issa?" I asked.

"Oh, Bob. You know it's not a good idea for two like us to stay in the same place. I love you, brother, but I don't want to compete with you."

I understood, I guess. I'd considered doing miracles like he'd done. He'd tried to teach me the simple spell for turning water into wine and the result tasted so foul it brought tears to his eyes. I poured it overboard with my apologies to the local sea god. I'd stick to making my wine from fermented grapes.

I waved goodbye, and then shoved off to continue farther south along the coast of what would become India. I was in that region for a century or three before I continued eastward. I'll revisit some of my adventures in India later. It's a story worth telling about. I learned their pantheon of gods, the castes and social order, the architecture, oh! and tantric sex. From an interesting perspective. One day I'll tell you all about that.

I bring all this little digression to the fore simply to tell you that I knew Jesus and I knew India. I knew the people there. I have many people in my household in the infinity room from the Indian subcontinent. I traveled the many islands surrounding the great peninsula and ventured across the warm eastern sea to the lands in southeast Asia, Japan, and China.

The people we saw on the island where Columbus first made landfall were not Indian. It was as obvious to me as the greed of my shipmates. They all but ignored the people who came out to greet us and went in search of gold and riches. They were disappointed.

Of course, you couldn't tell Chris that he wasn't in India. No, he named the people Indians and went to search for all the gold. Even if he had landed in India, I could have told him gold was a rarity there. The great trade goods from India and Asia were spices and silks. That other idiot explorer, Marco Polo, had given people false expectations. We crossed paths briefly in China. Maybe I'll get a chance to tell you about him later.

Explorers. I'm sorry to count myself among their number. Let me give you the basics of the life and mind of an explorer. He is generally a man hyped up on his own manhood, who believes he can take on anything. He is not usually anywhere near as smart as he perceives himself. When he comes up with an idea of a place to explore, he makes that his single-minded goal. He decides to become a demigod and do something no other man has done or can do.

But his adventure must be financed. No adventure is free, especially if he wants the best equipment that will ensure his success. That is expensive. So, he must find a way to finance his exploration. The first way is to be rich. If he has enough money to fund even a part of his exploration, he can leverage that wealth to get others to invest in him. It is called a joint venture. A joint venture is when a man with experience teams up with a man with money. At the end, the roles are reversed.

The second means is to focus on what motivates a potential investor. Religion is always the most effective, because it can disguise any other motivation as altruism and concern for the souls of others. Chris almost screwed that up with Isabella the first time he met with her. A good Catholic girl may tease, but she doesn't surrender. But when we whispered, "To save the souls of the heathen who have never heard the word of our Lord," she wet her panties. And when we suggested the Lord would reward her with the riches of a new world for her faithful service, she excitedly spread her... um... purse strings.

You see, you can never jump to the conclusion that a person is just motivated by riches. That seems greedy and it's an insult to his character. But to suggest a person who serves his or her god will be rewarded, not only with riches in heaven, but with wealth on earth, you have an unbreakable commitment. The gods have been using it to control people for all of human history.

Imagine if you will, a billionaire who has all the wealth he needs, but sees a *new* potential source of income. Of course, he will not risk all his own wealth on the enterprise. It would be seen as self-indulgent and suspect. He needs joint venture partners. What would happen if he went to the leaders of his religion and declared, "The poor people of Mars suffer under eternal damnation because we have not taken the word of God to them. We must evangelize the universe in the name of our god and God will reward us with eternal riches in heaven and with the wealth of the entire planet Mars in this life."

Even poor Baptists in Alabama would be lining up to contribute to his missionary trip to Mars. People would work in his factories at substandard wages to pay for this great evangelical endeavor. The finest equipment would be donated by 'sponsors.'

And somewhere along the line, possibly while waiting on a voyage of some months from Earth to Mars, the idea of untold wealth would come to the fore and greed would become the motivating force. So it was with Columbus and his merry men.

My insistence that this was not India, nor even an island near India, got me put off the ship. Actually, it was when the Santa Maria ran aground that I left the party. Chris couldn't get all the men on his two remaining ships, so he made the bold move of establishing a settlement and leaving some forty of his men behind. I was 'needed there' to minister to the spiritual needs of the settlers.

I may have been the only one happy to see the ass-end of the Nina and Pinta. I marked it as the end of my time in the Christian world with the charlatans, priests, monarchs, and explorers.

It did not take long for the sailors put ashore to realize they were missing one of the principal ingredients for happy colonization. They were forty-one men (and one demon) who had no women and no prospect that Columbus would revisit them with European women. The natives would have to do. And that was a source of contention. The prevailing opinion among the settlers was that "god's people" should have whatever they wanted. And they wanted women. The natives—and especially their women—were not enthused about the idea.

I'd been going out to visit the local tribe to learn as much as I could about their customs and society. They did not seem to the Europeans to have a religion and therefore had no excuse not to humbly accept their God and give the Europeans their women. But though there was no 'church' as such, I witnessed the natives asking the sea to bless their fishing, asking the sky to bring them rain, asking the earth to give them crops. They were very religious.

My words fell on deaf ears when I encouraged the men to a life of temperance and abstinence. I even considered asking for volunteers in the infinity room to come and provide for the 'needs' of these sailors, but I couldn't see exposing any of my people to them, even if they volunteered.

I was returning to the settlement after listening to a shaman in the native village one afternoon, when I heard a scuffle and muted cries in the woods nearby. Upon investigating, I saw one of the sailors ripping the clothing off a native woman and plundering her sex.

I am not a violent demon. I believe in peace. I believe in love. I believe in sex. But I had made it clear that I considered rape a capital offense. I did not hesitate to slit the sailor's throat. I'm sad I got blood on the woman. She scrambled away, gathered what clothes she had about her and fled. I didn't even bother collecting the memories of the dead man. As far as I was concerned, I'd had enough foul memories from European men. I stripped off my ecclesiastical robes, dropped all disguise as a man, and scampered off into the wilderness with my bag as the goat-legged demon I am.

I found a cave in the island mountains and crept deep into it. I reviewed my spells that would keep us undetected, and strengthened them so no one from outside would stumble upon my bag. Once the spells were set, I opened the entrance to the infinity room and stepped inside.

Though there was no sensation of the passing of time in the infinity room, I was welcomed as if I had been absent for years and as if I just came home from a hard day at the office. My wives and harem spread a feast before me that included a wide variety of pussies. Esmeralda was fascinated to see my full demon form revealed and did her best to ride me to exhaustion. She succeeded, but it was her exhaustion and not mine. Then it was Princess Agora, Zhi, Lakshmi, Pari, Penelope, Josie, and finally Nimia. There were others as well, but don't let me get distracted by going into their stories right now. I'll get around to it.

My wives, possessions, and devotees had been hard at work administering the world within the infinity room. I was surprised to find there were now over a million and a half loyal subjects of Demon Bob scattered over a range of hundreds of miles. Wherever one of my people settled, the fertile land spread farther before him. It got me thinking there were frontiers aplenty in both my world and the natural world and no one needed to take anything from anyone else. Of course, the pride of our world was the library, and people came from all over the infinity room to read there.

When I first got to Italy—remember the beginning of this story?—I managed to get inside the vast Vatican Library, which was almost as big as the Library of Alexandria and was better kept. I spent nearly a year in the rooms. I would not steal the man's library, but I did copy it. Using the replication spells I had used with the holy books of the Jews, I duplicated each book and handed it through to the librarians in the infinity room. I handed through a couple of librarians as well, and went off to collect their wives and children. One or two devoted monks found welcome arms among the priestesses of Aphrodite and were never the same again.

I have found over the centuries that the most dependable people in the world are librarians. Librarians are not duplicitous. They have no pronounced loyalty to any god, but only to the written words. They will defend the knowledge contained in those pages, even when the words of one contradict the words of another. Librarians are champions of knowledge, keepers of secrets, and fearless warriors for freedom. And when all else has failed, librarians are the leaders of revolutions.

I was always happy to sit with a librarian for a few hours to discuss what he was reading and how it compared to other volumes in the library. After spending a day discussing a good book, I would return to my little home—still reminiscent of my home with Pinaruti, though occasionally added onto to accommodate the needs of my growing harem—and I would indulge in lovemaking with my women. It was a good life.

Often Nimia and I would sit by the pool—very much like the pool I'd built in Babylon—and talk about the books we'd read and the meanings of various passages we'd found in the writings. She was more than a librarian and I loved her intensely.

Eventually, I decided I needed to check on our security and surroundings. I stepped out of the infinity room and back into the cave. There was a stillness over the island that I could not fathom. I shouldered the satchel and inspected my new body, patterned after the natives of the island. All was the way I expected it to be, so I went out to see what had transpired during my absence.

It was a wasteland. The village founded by the sailors was gone, as well as the native village. I found many had been killed by the European guns, but many more fell to the ravages of smallpox. As I wandered around the island, I found other places where new European settlements had been established, but in all areas, the disease had decimated the native population.

It was time to leave this place. I consulted my charts and decided I should go south and west in order to find another island or country where, perhaps, the Europeans had never traveled. I built a boat worthy of the sea and shoved off from this land to seek another.

20
The Storm

I'VE HAD MY RUN-INS with various sea gods. Most notably, Poseidon tried to kill me several times and settled for just making my life miserable. Tawhirimatea and his brothers didn't even know I was there when they pitched me across the Pacific to Australia. And did I ever tell you about how I ran afoul of Guabancex? No, I think I got sidetracked. When I built my little boat, I didn't know how long I had been away from the natural world, but I thought that land was most likely in the west. So, I set a gentle breeze to blowing and was making good time out into the open water.

And that is when I met Juracán and Guabancex. I'd heard of this pair from my acquaintance with the natives, but had never been face-to-face with either. Juracán was the god of chaos and he was upset with what was happening to the people of his islands. When Juracán got upset, Guabancex got angry. If you knew them like I came to know them, you'd realize that Guabancex was always angry. The upset of the god of chaos was a good excuse for her to cut loose and express her ire.

About the time I had made it out beyond the sight of land, the skies clouded over and the wind began to shift, wiping away my gentle breeze. Guabancex decided to visit a rain of death on the Europeans of the Caribbean. This was accompanied by Juracán's chaos and there was no one spared the terror she brought.

Including me.

If you are ambivalent to my talk about gods and goddesses, it all boils down to this. I set out in my little boat just ahead of the hurricane and was caught up in the chaos.

If I had not constructed my boat with the help of magic spells I found among the Phoenician writings I'd collected, it would have been smashed to pieces when the first wave broke over me. There was nothing I could do but hold fast to my craft and let the goddess have her way. I was driven forward and back, sometimes above the water and sometimes beneath. I believe I was caught up in the wind, and the water of the sea flew with me.

When my craft was flung upon a shore, I fell from it and hit the wet sand. I frantically scrabbled to reach higher land as floods followed a storm of this force and I could see them coming. The last I saw of my little boat, it was still sailing on the wind of the storm and may be in the sky yet today.

When the storm finally broke, I was exhausted and soaked to the bone. I sought shelter and found none. I found high ground and set about building myself a small hut where I could huddle inside with my satchel and dry out. I didn't dare just crawl into the infinity room because a wind so violent could tear up my hut and grab the satchel like it had my boat. I had to protect the infinity room.

Some days later, the sun appeared and the gods had mercy on the earth. The waters receded and I found myself walking again, trying to find what I didn't know I sought. When I finally found a cave where I thought we would be undisturbed, I put look-away spells all around me and opened a gateway into the infinity room.

I was thankful to see my women and to see that my world had survived the storm I had endured. They were blissfully unaware that a storm had blown me around for many days. Their total oblivion to the world outside was refreshing to me and I swore once again to protect them from harm.

And I got laid. One thing about which there was never a question was that when I entered the infinity room, I had eager partners for all forms of sexual activity. Zhi was among the first to meet me this time and the intensity of her devotion was overwhelming. I held her in my arms and loved her over and over again.

According to my charts, the storm had blown me west and slightly north. I decided to follow the coastline south, a safe distance from the angry goddess. I thought.

"I apologize for the unnecessarily rough journey over the sea," the man walking beside me said.

Man walking beside me??? When had this occurred?

"Greetings," I said politely. "I'm Bob. May I ask what spirit is addressing me?"

"Of course. And spirit is a good word for me. I am Kukulcán, the god of these people." I looked at him more closely and saw that beneath his feathered headdress, he had slit eyes, a pointed nose, and a forked tongue that flicked in and out to taste the air.

"I am honored by your presence, God Kukulcán," I said.

"Well, I'm only half here," he laughed. With that he passed an arm completely through me. "Here in spirit alone, I'm afraid."

"Am I to assume you were behind the storm that brought me to these shores?" I asked.

"Oh, no. That was all Guabancex and her minions. She doesn't really need an excuse. She is always angry. I simply asked her to give your boat a push in my direction. You were headed this way anyway. She never does anything gently."

"You speak elegantly in my language. How may I serve you?" I asked.

"Like you, Bob, I am a traveler. I have crossed the seas and the continents and have met many of the deities who are, even now, withdrawing from their lands as the new gods and religions push them out of the hearts of their people. I have already begun my transition to a different plateau. But I fear for my people now that the Europeans are upon them. In many of the pantheons I encountered, the name of Bob was referenced as a builder of temples and friend of gods. Therefore, when you arrived in our part of the world, we watched to see how you would behave toward our people. We saw a priest—which frightened many of us—but we witnessed you save one of the island people from the European attempting to force her. Your true self was then revealed, hiding in the mountains for nearly a century."

"Was it so long? I was too disgusted with the European men to remain in their company any longer for fear that I would kill them all. Things were different when I awoke from my nap."

"Please, Bob. Save my people. There are only a few faithful among them and now that the Europeans have spread their disease and their death and their god, there are even fewer. Your legendary infinity room is a hope for our people to have eternal reward. It is a spell that none of us have been successful in creating. I assure you that if you take these few with you, you will earn the eternal gratitude of the gods. And we will richly reward you," he said.

"Honored god of these western people, I will undertake this service. But no reward is needed. I do this for the sake of the people and will take all who are pure at heart."

"Bravo, Bob. We accept your service. It is your lack of greed that separates you from the followers of this strange new religion. And for that alone, we shall reward you. Here is what I propose we do."

And with that, the god Kukulcán told me of his plan and I agreed to go on a search for the faithful in his name. Our first stop was at his great temple, so far kept secret from the Spaniards, but soon to fall. I was impressed with the ziggurat and examined it closely before Kukulcán prodded me to ascend to the top of the temple.

"Help me! This is not the will of the gods! This is the barbarism of this greedy priest. Do not let him go through with his perverse plan, hatched with the Spaniards to deceive you. I belong to Kukulcán and not to the bloodthirsty knife of a priest," a young woman screamed. I approached unnoticed as she was led, struggling between two warriors to an altar where a priest dressed in feathered finery—a poor mockery of the garb of the god—awaited with a sacrificial knife.

"Tie her to the stone. Let her protests be sweet music to the gods who thrive on the fear of mere worms like us. Let the power of Kukulcán come upon me and take the lifeblood of this virgin sacrifice!" With that, he moved toward the stone and the frightened girl.

"Stop!" I commanded as I entered the circle of worshipers. "Lay not a hand on the maiden. She is blessed by Kukulcán and is not to be touched by your unclean ritual."

"Who are you to stop the sacrifice to our god?" The priest demanded. "Seize him!" Two warriors moved to trap me between them, but I twisted their arms around and flipped them down the steps of the pyramid where they lay motionless at the bottom.

Then the form of Kukulcán came upon me and I gave him use of my voice, which rang out from the top of the pyramid.

"I am Kukulcán, the feathered serpent, who commands the heavens and has visited the sun. This false priest is no one and has sold the people to the Europeans. Follow him and be led in chains across the sea. Choose me and I will lead you to a promised land where your blood will never again flow to assuage a thirsty god or a greedy priest."

Seeing the visage before him, the priest dropped his blade and ran from the temple, stumbling down the steps as fast as he could go. His remaining guards and several of the people who had gathered to witness the sacrifice followed him. I stepped to the stone altar and loosed the bonds of the virgin sacrifice. She flung herself at my feet and kissed them.

"I am yours, oh mighty serpent. Take me and possess me."

It was the first time I'd heard those words that I didn't jump to accept the offering. But this was offered under the false assumption that I was her god.

"I have appointed my servant Bob to lead the faithful to their eternal home. Follow him and you shall have abundance. And in that distant future, you will remember me only as a story to tell your children's children. Be blessed, my people."

With that, Kukulcán withdrew from me and his visage fell from me. The people looked on in awe as several knelt before me.

"If you will follow the words of Kukulcán with a pure heart, stay with me. If you are unsure, depart from me and go to join your priest," I said. Only half a dozen left and about fifty remained, now all on their knees. I seated myself on the altar. "Okay. I'm the demon Bob, emissary of the great Kukulcán. What I have is a gateway to a different world where you can live a long and peaceful life. You will find good work to do and plentiful food and drink. Unfortunately, that priest has gone to gather more soldiers, so we have no time to waste. If you want to go, line up and walk through this portal." I opened a gateway and two of my women stood in the entry, looking like angels welcoming the faithful.

The woman at my feet stood from her kneeling position and walked to the gateway. She hesitated and then stepped boldly forward. The women welcomed her and she faded from sight. There was some confusion among the people at that point and I turned to the women in the gateway.

"Send her back and let her tell them it is okay to follow," I said.

"Come ye faithful to Kukulcán," the young woman announced when she came out of the gateway. "It is as we have been told: a beautiful and bountiful land prepared for us."

She stood beside me as the people—men and women—walked to the gateway and entered. Some held hands and some straightened themselves to make the entrance alone. Two more fled before they got to the gate. At last, all had gone through except the girl.

"It's time to go," I said, pointing at the gate.

"I will stay by your side and guide you away from this place. I know a path the warriors will not follow."

I nodded and closed the gate. From the temple, I could see out to where a small company of warriors and a dozen Spanish Conquistadors approached from the north. The woman took my hand and led me down the south stairs and into the jungle.

My guide was good and led me away from the danger of the disgraced priest and his warriors. It was nearing sunset and I was thinking we should find a place to camp when she pulled to a stop and pointed ahead. There was a massive hill in the middle of an overgrown opening in the trees. It took me a minute to realize that I was looking at another temple—abandoned and grown over with vines and other plants. The dirt was piled in drifts against the structure and only my recent experience with one clued me into what I was looking at.

"Are there more people here to rescue?" I asked.

"I don't think so. This is part of the reward the gods have promised you," she said.

"Really? Am I to make this my home?"

"Only as a stopping place for a day to rest," she laughed. "Come. Kukulcán has opened a passage for you."

We circled the pyramid and she began moving some branches that soon revealed a passageway into the pyramid. We went in and she pulled the brush and debris over the passage behind us. I reached into the satchel and pulled out a torch. It startled my guide, but she took it from me and led the way.

After a few turns and steps, we entered a room that seemed to reflect the light. She lit more torches along the walls and I saw we were in a treasure room filled with gold and jewels and precious statuary. What's more, there were books and I hurried to look at them.

"You know what the true treasures are," she said. "Therefore, the gods have granted you these books to take and preserve forever. In thanks for your honor and service, you are invited to empty all the gold and precious items out of this room and take it as well. We know that whatever is not given to you and taken safely to your infinity room will be looted by the greedy Europeans. Please take this."

I looked at her and she seemed to have a strange countenance in the torchlight. I realized at once what I was seeing.

"Lady Goddess, how may I address you?" I said as I lowered my eyes.

"I'm am Ixchel, goddess of love and beauty, and I speak through my beloved priestess, Maya, known only by the name of her people. You must not hesitate to accept Maya's offer. She has pledged herself to you and you will be blessed beyond all creatures if you accept her."

"Her gift is great. I am reluctant, however, to accept it until she knows who she is binding herself to," I said.

"An ethical and honorable demon!" the goddess said. "You honor our people. You have our thanks. I will withdraw now and leave my blessings with you and with her so you may woo her." Then the beautiful woman approached me and softly kissed my lips. When she broke the kiss, I saw it was no longer the goddess, but the girl Maya who had been guiding me.

"Demon Bob. The gods have shown me your true nature and I know I could not find a better mate should I move all heavens and earth to discover him. I render you my service and my love completely. Possess my mind. Possess my spirit. Possess my heart. Possess my body. I am yours forever." With that she returned to my embrace and as we kissed, I possessed her.

⌷⌷⌷⌷⌷⌷⌷⌷⌷⌷⌷⌷⌷⌷

A word about possession. I'm sure you have a concept of what it means and it is probably wrong. There are demons who possess other people by transferring themselves into the body of that person and taking control. So, I guess your concept might not be all wrong. Personally, I like my body and do not want to lose it. I can reshape it to just about any form I want. It's good.

And I *try* not to simply 'take control' of a woman's mind and force her to do whatever I bid. That strikes me as being a kind of rape and demeans the woman, taking away her free will. When I possess a woman, I merge my spirit with hers. It is more intimate than any other relationship I have experienced. My wives and I are unified in love, but my possessions and I are of one spirit. My possessions continue to have self-will, but it is always in concert with mine, even when I have not yet determined what my will in a matter is. I dare say that there is no closer relationship possible for a woman and a demon than possession.

Maya was my fourth possession, though I know I have not told you about all. The first was Josie, and we still had a relationship that made us of one mind. The second was Pari, and the third was Princess Agora. I'll tell you about them eventually. Maya was the first of my possessions that was blessed in our union by a god or goddess. She filled my heart.

⌷⌷⌷⌷⌷⌷⌷⌷⌷⌷⌷⌷⌷⌷

I opened the gateway to find my harem had already prepared a celebratory feast with all Maya's people gathered as well. Our night of celebration included unwrapping my newest gift and being amazed at her lush, ripe body. Her soft skin was a creamy cocoa color. Her teeth were blazingly white and even. Her eyes were dark but flashed with fire. Those lovely breasts stood proudly on her chest, each beautiful mound capped with a dark and prominent nipple. The juncture of her thighs was covered in a thick thatch of black hair that glistened with moisture.

"You are mine, Maya. I will do all I can to make you happy."

"You fill me with joy, Bob. Come and partake of your treasure—your gift from the gods."

I did not rush to consummate our love. Instead, I taught her the rudiments of the Tantra and we sat facing each other for an hour, just looking into each other's eyes to find the depths of our souls reflected there. As I sat, she moved forward to sit on my lap with her legs straddling me. In that position, we kissed and explored each other's body with our lips and fingertips. Then she lifted herself and found the tip of my cock with her opening, settling slowly onto it. The fragile barrier guarding her entrance stretched and broke and she sank onto me with a sigh. In the silence of our bed, we returned to looking each other in the eye and began to move. The slow rocking of our bodies prolonged our ascent to the heights of passion and when we burst together, she knew that she was truly mine.

⌷⌷⌷⌷⌷⌷⌷⌷⌷⌷⌷⌷⌷⌷

While Maya and I consummated our relationship, others in my household hurried to empty the treasure room. The librarians were ecstatic about the books, many of which prophesied this very night and the coming of Kukulcán to save his people. In the morning, we ate well and then Maya and I returned to the now-empty room to continue our journey south.

As we traveled, we continued to encounter small groups of Mayans, gradually being displaced by Incans on one side and Spaniards on the other. Maya guided me as if she had traveled the entire continent before. In some places we made it to the people before the Europeans did, but more and more, the greed and murder and disease of the invaders was evident. The people passed from the dominant culture of the Americas into slavery and poverty.

The odd thing, as I thought about it, was that none of the people—even faced with the guns and dominance of the Europeans—believed they could be enslaved. They were surprised when they were forced from their homes and put in chains. Each day as a slave they wondered how this had happened. War, disease, death, and slavery are not predictable. They come as a surprise because the people cannot fathom a time when they could be affected by them.

When we reached the great Incan city of Machu Picchu in the Andes Mountains, it was deserted and already falling into ruin. I found a secluded place in the city and opened a gateway into the infinity room where Maya and I stayed for some years. I easily lose track of how many years have gone by, but we were undisturbed.

In that time, I enjoyed each of the ladies in my household who all seemed to have missed me terribly, though I'd made frequent trips into the infinity room with Maya and often with other people through our journey south. I also read all the acquisitions of manuscripts and books we had collected over the past years. In the Vatican Library, for example, I'd found an incredibly detailed book from Ethiopia on magic spells for transformation. There were spells by which one could turn himself into a lion, a snake, or a crocodile.

When I had read this book, I sealed it with a spell so no one could open it without my permission, and I put it in my personal library instead of the great library we were gathering. Sometimes I recognized a book as being too dangerous to be read without guidance. This book was a book of traps. It gave instructions on how to turn into any one of these beasts, but no instructions on how to return to human form. And even if it had included instructions, the magus would be unable to perform the return spell because the lion or gazelle would be unable to pronounce the words. It was an evil book and I did not want any of my people trapped by it.

I suppose that makes me a two-faced censor. I had read the book and decided my people could not read it. Well, I will have to live with that. Perhaps one day in the distant future, I will take on an apprentice and together we will explore these forbidden spells. But I would not venture into them alone and would not have one of my people venture there without guidance. Still, I would also not destroy the forbidden books. In that way, I guess, I was a librarian.

I traveled about my world, visiting the people I had brought into it from all the different cultures of the natural world. I visited only those I had brought into the infinity room and not those who had been born here. To those who were born here, I was merely a story—a part of their mythology. To the thousands I had personally met and brought from the natural world into my kingdom, I owed some greater presence. I sat and talked with them—sometimes made love to them. I was accompanied by my possessions and my wives, but did not bring the hundred or so concubines in my harem. We traveled much as we had in the deserts of yore, stopping to pitch our tent when we were tired and to cavort with our mates in an unhurried way.

Development in my world seemed to have been slow, based on the developments of the natural world. Most of the people I had brought into the room came from civilizations that were not affected by the new religion and had not developed high degrees of technology. That did not mean, however, that they had not developed small cities at various places around the infinity room. There were definite areas of urban development and agricultural development. I was pleased with what I saw. There was plenty for all who would make an effort to work, and thus, no disputes arose over who had what possessions.

And, possibly among the most important things in our cultural development, my population was highly sexed. There was no taboo regarding open sexual relations with multiple partners—the people having taken their cue from me. I have found there was a great truth in the saying of the 1960s: "Make love, not war." It was difficult to make a dispute with your neighbor when she offers to fuck you into submission. The practices of tantric sex, meditation, and martial arts were made available to everyone and not just to elite classes. The world of the infinity room was flourishing.

END OF PART IV

Part V
To Conquer the World

Image Credit: Warm_Tail, ID2104382180 licensed from Shutterstock.com

21
A Walk in the Garden

¶¶¶¶¶¶¶¶¶¶¶¶¶

I'VE ALWAYS BEEN FASCINATED with men (and a few women like Isabella and Cleopatra) who fancied themselves rulers. I had been a king in Bathra, but I couldn't recollect ever feeling happy about being a ruler. I led armies to subdue our enemies and levied taxes to pay for the armies. But my rules to live by were simple and not retributive.

I wandered through the Kingdom of Judah, perhaps 2,700 or 2,800 years ago, and found a people who were generally happy with what they had. Their god had given them laws and they were the most rigidly law-abiding people I had ever seen in all my travels. Being a soldier was something they did when necessary, not as a career or profession. Yet they had gained their lands a thousand years earlier by defeating and destroying everyone in their way. It was a bloody nation.

I had settled myself down with a lovely young woman named Miriam as my wife. I'd adopted a body that was of similar sort to the Jews and was even circumcised. It seemed strange to me, but a gentile would not be welcome there. There was some hullaballoo about people worshiping false gods (defined as any god but their own) and the country was in dis-array.

And into this disarray stepped the king who would overthrow an empire. Babylon—the famed city of the lawgiver Hammurabi—was an Assyrian province, but Nebuchadnezzar saw a weakness there and decided to become the ruler of the world as he knew it. He had several battles in a ten-year period and defeated the Assyrians in the east and north and the Egyptians in the south and west. He considered Judea to just be a worthless province until the king there decided to stop paying taxes. If there was one thing Nebuchadnezzar was keen on, it was his taxes. He besieged Jerusalem, tore down its walls and its temple, and took the king captive with all his court. Since he couldn't trust the king, he marched him off to Babylon with his retainers and priests.

The people of Judea had been indoctrinated for a thousand years to follow the treasures of their temple; and so, several thousand went into exile with the rulers and priests. Miriam and I went along.

In Jerusalem, there had been all kinds of places where I could slip off and enjoy the company of my harem. When I was gone for a few days, Miriam would ask where I had been. I would good-naturedly tell her that I'd been off with my harem. She would inevitably respond that she would have to become one of my concubines, so she could see me more frequently.

But Miriam didn't believe I had a harem. She knew I was an architect and builder and I had built several buildings in Jerusalem which were now rubble. When we got to Babylon, I set to work helping build the Jewish Quarter. We needed to house a few thousand exiles and, of course, Nebuchadnezzar hadn't thought about that. He only intended to take the ruling household and priesthood with him, but all these other people had followed. He had no plan for housing them, feeding them, or putting them to work. It didn't take me long to get everyone organized and building rudimentary dwellings. Once we had the ghetto laid out, I began replacing the rudimentary dwellings with more permanent houses of brick and stone. As far as building an economy went, the people needed no help with that. They were up and functioning as a community before all the houses were built.

I guess word of my efforts finally made its way to the ears of Nebuchadnezzar and I was summoned. That meant that a company of guards came, chained me, and led me to the court.

Neb hadn't intended that I be chained and got them removed right away. He asked me about the development of the Jewish Quarter and how I was able to build so rapidly. He wanted to know what techniques and materials I was using. I explained some of the architecture from the south of his territory and how I had made bricks for a temple where there wasn't enough stone available to build with. I stressed the aesthetic of pools and gardens, of which we had included some in the Jewish Quarter.

"Oh, yes! I quite agree!" he said enthusiastically. I discovered he was a bit of an architecture enthusiast himself and he took me for a walk around his palace. One feature struck me above all else.

"Nice gardens," I said as we walked through a veritable hanging jungle.

"The hanging garden was the last thing the venerable Hammurabi of many centuries ago decreed. It has withstood the invasions of Medes, Persians, Assyrians, and others—all of whom have looked upon the gardens and declared their admiration. The garden has lasted longer than his code, though we still abide by as much of it as we've been able to locate."

I nearly told him I had a copy, but decided to leave well enough alone.

"You know what you need here?" I said as I turned and looked back at the marvelous garden. "You need a reflecting pool, say all the way from here to the foot of the steps ascending into the garden. Then when people saw the garden, they would also see its reflection and it would look twice as large as it is."

"Yes, a great idea, but where would the water come from? I have a hundred people bearing water each day from the river to the top of the gardens to keep them lush. I can't imagine how many I would need to keep a pool filled."

"We could arrange a tiled passageway and a pump to draw water from the river to the top of the garden. Then we could use the steps to bleed off the excess and let it run down into the pool. A further channel could be used to take the overflow from the pool down into the city where people could draw water without going all the way to the river. Beautiful."

"Water flowing uphill? Make it so! I want to see this miracle!"

Which was my first commission from Nebuchadnezzar. It took a year for me to get the pool dug and set up the waterwheel pump that drew water to the top of the gardens and let it run down the steps to fill the pool. I employed people from the Jewish Quarter, of whom there were still many who were unemployed. During that time, most others had found employment in households and farms, and as tradesmen in the Quarter. They weren't exactly slaves. They were treated more like immigrant workers and were paid for their work. As they have always done, they prospered.

Nebuchadnezzar was so pleased with his pool that he spent many hours each day sitting next to it. And, like party boys throughout the ages, when he was beside the pool, his women were also there. He was married, of course, to—I don't remember. Six or seven wives. There were another hundred concubines who were part of the treaties with the nations he had conquered. Assyrians, Persians, Egyptians, Jews, Sumerians, Lebanese, Greek. I was certain I saw women of Trojan blood among them. Looking at the beauties arrayed around his pool was a veritable feast for the eyes.

Especially since Nebuchadnezzar liked his women the same way I did—naked.

Most of his business that did not require him sitting on a throne, he conducted at the pool. As a frequent consultant on the architectural affairs of Babylon, I was often privileged to be present at the pool. On those nights after spending the day at his pool, I hurried home, made love to Miriam, then disappeared into my satchel to work my way through my own harem. I spent a lot of time with the priestesses of Aphrodite I had rescued from Troy, who had not found mates and settled down. Apparently, Aphrodite noticed.

"So, my randy little demon," she said from beside me one night. "You are still besotted with my women."

"My Lady Goddess," I answered quickly. "They remind me of you. How could I not be in love with them?"

"You are such a smooth talker. Enjoy them as much as you can," she said. "I am unfortunately here on a mission."

"How may I be of assistance?"

"The gods are having a little contest."

"Oh, no. Please don't turn Babylon into another Troy!" I said.

"No, not quite. You know the Jews have a unique relationship with their god. The Olympians have mostly ignored him over the years, but they're extending a hand with this little contest since most of them are here in Babylon."

"And what am I to do here? Are there priestesses I need to rescue? A library to pillage?"

"No, no. But you have the king's ear. He'll ask a number of questions and you will answer. As easy as that. Okay?" she said sweetly.

"And how am I to know the answer to give?"

"Let me introduce you to my cousin Morpheus," she giggled. "Not as fun as me, I think, but a good resource."

"My Lord Morpheus," I said to the visage that appeared. My mind suddenly flashed with images. It was as if I was dreaming, but as I dreamed, I understood what the dream meant. Okay. Whatever. When I looked around again, there was no sign of Aphrodite, Morpheus, or the dream. I couldn't even remember it. I couldn't imagine what I was supposed to do next.

Gods. My experience is that they are generally capricious. They operate on such a different plane from everyone else that they are usually out of touch with the reality of the human experience. They've never quite reached the point of understanding humanity. I dare say that I'm not perfect at it either. The whole idea of free will means that humans will continually surprise you.

There is a story told about the god of the Jews in regards to that. In the Jewish writings, it is said that the angel Lucifer challenged God to a contest in which he bet he could make a particular loyal worshiper deny God. The deity was quick to accept the challenge, only forbidding Lucifer to physically harm Job.

Mark the implication here. Lucifer was given the right to kill Job's children, steal his cattle, take all his wealth, and ultimately to afflict the man with painful boils, just to see if he could make him deny God. All to no avail. Job remained constant, but protested his innocence before God. At which time, God speaks to Job through one of his friends and says basically, "Who are you to question me? I made you and I can unmake you. The world is mine to do with as I please. Who do you think you are to question my decisions or actions?"

Excuse me, but this is basically no answer at all. Oh, God restores Job's wealth. He gives him seven more sons stronger and smarter than what he had before. He gives him seven more daughters, more beautiful than any in the land. Job is 'rewarded' for his faith in God.

But gods have no concept of what humans value. Are seven new sons and seven new daughters supposed to replace the ones Job lost? Did God magically erase the memory of those children from Job and his wife so they would not mourn for the ones who were taken from them? And there wasn't even a bet to pay off in the end. Lucifer didn't owe God anything for losing the contest. The only one who lost anything was Job (and his wife).

But as Hermes told me when I was forced to leave Callie and go find Penelope, my feelings on the issue were irrelevant. Zeus had decided. Gods can talk all they want about caring for their people, and they have their favorites, but they have little or no understanding of them.

I rest my case.

"Bob, come and sit with me a spell," Neb commanded. I was just there tending to the pool. There was a cute girl flirting with me and as long as I didn't make it obvious, I encouraged her.

"How can I help you, your Majesty?" I asked.

He waved a couple of servants over to bring me a drink. I sipped slowly, never sure what might be in a drink from the king.

"There are a lot of wizards and wisemen in Babylon," he started.

"Yes. I've noticed. I try to avoid them most of the time."

"I'm going to kill them all."

That news was a real shock. Babylon was quite a fertile field for magic to grow in—always had been. In fact, Hammurabi had some penalties for the practice of certain kinds of magic in his code. But mostly, it was deemed harmless. Unless the king wanted something done. Then it wasn't harmless; it was impotent.

"There isn't a single one who can tell me my dream and what it means," he swore. "What good are they? Worthless charlatans brewing magic love potions for the forlorn."

"Oh. Is that all?" I said nonchalantly.

"All? All? I had a dream that has been troubling me for days and I can't even remember what it was."

"Well, not that I'm all that opposed to getting rid of the charlatans, but this isn't a good reason to do so. Most people, unless given a special revelation, could not tell you how to interpret a dream about a huge statue with feet of clay."

"That's it! Tell me! Tell me what the dream was and what it meant."

With that, I set about showing him the dream Morpheus had given me and the interpretation I'd been given.

"Bob, that's brilliant! That's exactly it. Of course the kingdom that comes after mine won't be as wonderful as mine. I'm the best that could ever be. As long as they don't destroy the garden, what do I care about the next hundred years! And good luck to whomever it is that thinks his kingdom will last forever. That's not going to happen!"

With that, he decreed that I would have ten talents of gold. That is a grateful king. In twentieth century terms, that would be about $20 million. He also made a gift of the girl who'd been flirting with me. When she was called before him, she was terrified that she'd been found out. But when she heard his decree, she flung herself into my arms and I carried her home. That made for some interesting conversations with Miriam.

"Do you choose to be with me, Pari?" I asked. "I will not take you as a slave. I will grant your freedom right now if you wish to leave."

"Bob, I wouldn't have been flirting with you if I wasn't interested in you. I was just worried that Nebuchadnezzar wouldn't let me go," she said.

Ah, wonderful. The concubine Neb gave me was Persian. Oh, she was gloriously arrayed in golden skin and hair as black as midnight. She was tall as a palm tree with breasts like the clusters of its fruit. I wanted to climb that tree and lay hold of its fruit. I wanted to taste the sweetness in my mouth and be drunk on her kisses. (My apologies. I'd been reading some of the great Jewish erotica in my library.)

And I wanted Miriam to be happy about it, too. Well, fifty percent of my wants were about to come true. Miriam was not happy.

There was some tradition of multiple marriages among the Jews, but it had lost fashion sometime in the past generation or so. Miriam did not want to share her man and was not interested in sharing his other woman, which we both offered repeatedly. I was not going to win this one and watched sadly as Miriam returned to the home of her mother.

Pari was also sad. She said she would happily have shared the bed with Miriam. I asked if she would be just as happy to share the bed with me. She blushed.

"Bob, you are so strong and favored by the king. He has given you a treasure of his harem who has not been bedded by a man. I knew one day I would be given to an important person and I vowed to welcome him into my bed and my arms and my body. When I saw you, I prayed you would be the one he gave me to. I welcome you, Bob."

That was all the invitation I needed. I stripped off my clothes and she gasped when she saw my manhood. Now, let me say that after a millennium and a half on earth with many incredible beauties in my life, including the goddess of love herself, it generally took more than the casual sight of a naked woman to arouse me. Not much more, but I couldn't walk around all day with a raging hard-on. When Pari first beheld my strength, I was fully engorged and ready for action. She was mesmerized and knelt on the floor as if to worship it. Instead, I received a gift I could not have expected. She took me in her hands and then in her mouth.

While the practice was not unknown in my harem, fellatio was not a common practice and usually just a brief warm up to sex. My time among the Jews was a time of cock in pussy only. They had very strong prohibitions against any kind of sex other than a man putting his cock in a woman's pussy—preferably for procreation. I knew it was too much to hope Miriam would want to participate in making love to Pari. A woman lying with another woman was unheard of—though not as stringently prohibited as a man with a man. And as for blow jobs, a real man would never expect such demeaning behavior from even a common street whore.

The feeling Pari gave me was so exquisite and so unexpected that I emptied my balls in her mouth before I felt we had really gotten started. When she saw that my erection was not disappearing, she sighed and stretched out on my bed, opening her legs to me.

"Will it hurt me, Bob? I knew I would yield my maidenhead to you when Nebuchadnezzar made a gift of me. But the few men Nebuchadnezzar has had me pleasure with my mouth were not nearly as big as this. I didn't know you were so huge."

Well, that answered a question regarding her skill and the preservation of her maidenhead in the harem. She was a fellatrix of no little accomplishment.

"My dear Pari, let me worship at the gates of your paradise and be sure you are prepared to receive me without pain and suffering." No more had I bent my head to her fount than she began to climb toward her first climax. I say first because after a few minutes, it became obvious that she would have as many climaxes in a row as I could give her, and each would be more earthshaking than the last. As she shook in the throes of her eighth or tenth peak, I simply slid up her body and inserted myself between her folds. With a single thrust, I was buried to the balls in her welcoming depths.

And then she really went wild.

"I didn't know! I didn't know. Love me some more, Bob. Take me. Make me the receptacle of your love. Possess me!"

Oh! There were those magic words. How could I possibly pass them by? I possessed her. I made her mine and every thought she had was of me filling her. After a long while, rutting and screaming, we lay in the bed and rested.

"It would be nice to have another woman with me," she sighed and then went to sleep.

I knew how to grant her wish and I picked her up, walking through the open entrance to the infinity room. There, Nimia, Josie, and Penelope met me and I said simply, "She is mine. I have possessed her." Josie was ecstatic. She knew precisely what those words meant since I possessed her as well.

It was not long thereafter that Miriam appeared at my door and, without a word, resumed her place in my household as my wife. She was my mate and my lover and she cared for me. She did not comment on Pari's absence, assuming I had simply disposed of her so that Miriam would return to me. That hadn't been my specific intention, but I had let it out that I was alone in my house. I was rather fond of Miriam.

There was no way to disguise that I was a wealthy man. My community all knew Nebuchadnezzar favored me and the elders frequently brought planning matters for the quarter to me. We discussed the layout of streets, a gathering place for prayer and to read the Torah, and the quality of the water in our sector. I listened and occasionally commented, but mostly they worked the plans out for themselves. It was important to them to feel they had included the king's man in their discussion, and I nodded my head and agreed with them most of the time.

I did, however, caution them and help to cool hot heads when the discussion came to rebelling and returning to Judah.

"My friends, at the moment, we are treated as guests in Babylon," I said. "We have work and we prosper with the Lord's blessing. Remember that should we rebel against the rightful king of this land, it will not go easy on us. Nebuchadnezzar is God's emissary to punish us for our sins. God alone will decide when our exile is over."

There was some grumbling, but they nodded and agreed that God had told them the exile was just. They had known this was coming, and even their king had admitted his culpability in rebelling against his overlord. And so, peace was maintained in the Jewish Quarter, and I continued to make regular visits to the palace, maintaining the pump and water supply, and consulting on the architecture of proposed new buildings and additions.

22
THE MIGHT OF BABYLON

WAS ONCE AGAIN at the pool when Nebuchadnezzar strolled up to me and began to chat. He was feeling quite full of himself, but Morpheus had visited me again and I knew something was on his mind.

"Isn't this a wonderful place? I built this," he said. "I made Babylon the center of the world. I rule over all that is known to man. I will build ever bigger and greater works, so that all the world will come to see Babylon."

"Shh. Your Majesty, be aware of the dream," I whispered.

He immediately blanched, remembering what he had dreamed just the night before.

"What does it mean, Bob? I dreamt my mouth was full of grass. What does it mean?" he asked. Well, just having a dream about eating grass wasn't adequate to make a good story, so I elaborated.

"You, sire, are a great tree. You can be seen from the ends of the earth. Your branches spread protectively over all who look to you for their very sustenance and you provide for them well. But you lack the humility to honor the gods for your greatness. Such is hubris that they cannot overlook. This dream is a warning that if you do not honor the gods for your greatness, it will be taken from you. The tree shall be cut to the ground and you will wander like a beast of the field, eating the grasses you have dreamed of."

"Is this true? Can a man's sanity be taken from him so quickly? I charge you, Bob," he said, beckoning a scribe closer. "If my sanity is taken from me for a period of time, my son Belchadnezzar shall rule in my stead. He shall have dominion over all save my harem. I hand my harem into the care of Bob. He will have knowledge of it and will guard it until the day of my return."

Well, shit. That wouldn't make Miriam happy. I just hoped the warning the gods had provided would take root in Nebuchadnezzar and I would never have to worry about it. Wishful thinking, I knew.

Nebuchadnezzar was a good king and generally a nice guy. He often sent me on an errand to discuss a matter with the ruler of a neighboring country or with community leaders around Babylon. On one such trip—I don't remember if it was before or after the dreams; I just thought of it now—I was sent to a small city up the river from Babylon to discuss the petition of the magistrate to help improve their water source. It seemed the river flowed warm at this point and encouraged the growth of green scum.

I talked to the magistrate and decided to go upstream a little farther to see if I could find what was causing the heated water. I found a most amazing thing. There was a point in the mountains where the water flowing out of a spring was hot. Someone had created a bathing pool around the spring and the channel that would carry the water out to the desert had been blocked. The pool overflowed and broke a new channel that led to the river, raising the temperature of the river.

I was alone, so it did not take long for me to unblock the desert channel and shore up the dam on the river channel. The problem of the city was solved and they paid a tax to the king for clearing their water supply.

That was not the amazing thing I saw. I'd seen hot springs before. The amazing thing was a bronze statue of a lovely woman that graced the pool. I had seen bronze statuary before, as well, but this was near life size! In fact, if she was not a large woman, she might walk right out of the bronze. The detail was amazing, and while there was a green patina over most of the statue, her left breast had been touched by bathers so frequently that it shone golden.

Yes, the temptation was far too great for a mere demon like me to resist. I stroked the golden breast as well. And then I paused and stroked it again. Some miracle of having her feet in the hot spring warmed the statue and the breast was as warm as flesh. What's more, I paused with my sensitive fingers on the golden skin and was certain I could feel a heartbeat beneath the bronze.

I spent a long time looking at the statue. It had incredible detail. The folds and curves of her flesh looked so real one might make love to her if the bronze were not so unyielding. I looked into her eyes and thought I could see intelligence and life.

I was not a great sorcerer, though Circe had told me I had a natural ability to work magic. I did not want to bring a bronze statue to life, but I did want to free a person if one was trapped there. I sought guidance from my books in the infinity room and came across the spell I had used once long ago to turn three girls into stone statues for a day so they would watch the fun we had and be unable to participate. The spell had a time limit when I cast it. The next day, when I pushed them into the infinity room, they ceased being stone and became flesh again. There was, however, a spell I had never used that would reverse the enchantment and turn a person who had become stone into flesh once more.

I wondered if that was what happened to Pygmalion's Ivory Lady. Of course, My Lady Goddess could have created life from nothing, just as she had turned the Propoetides to stone. I wondered if the spell would work to turn a bronze lady into flesh. I studied the spell, laid my hands on the statue, and began to chant the rather involved spell.

As I said the words, I felt the shoulders rise and fall with her breath. The flesh became supple. As I finished the spell, she fell back into my arms. She was beautiful, breathing, alive. She looked at me with adoration and spread kisses across my chest.

"Thank you! Thank you! Whatever you would have of me, I would give you. You have released me from a curse set a thousand years ago and I cannot thank you enough," she said.

"Fair lady, tell me your name and your story," I begged.

"I am Srininx. I was a servant of the Sorcerer Dbossé. Each day I accompanied him to the spring for his bath and he attempted to force his attentions on me. When I refused him, he cursed me to be a statue watching him bathe each day and he caressed my breast each time he came to the spring. He died centuries ago and others have come to the spring, finding my breast irresistible. Just as you did."

"I apologize for my rudeness, yet it was that caress that let me know you were a living being."

I took her hand and we stood up. She was nicely shaped and desirable. In only one place did a sign of her captivity remain. Her left breast continued to be the color of bright gold. When she pressed it against me, though, it was fully flesh.

She was insistent on showing her gratitude. Next to the pool where she had watched for centuries, we lay on the rocks and made love. She was inexperienced but enthusiastic and when I suggested she join my ladies in the infinity room she agreed readily. We have enjoyed each other many times and within the harem, caressing her breast is considered a kind of good luck gesture which she welcomes.

I was one of the very few intact males allowed near Nebuchadnezzar's pool with his harem there. He had a few other trusted advisors and scribes there, but the normal business of Babylon was conducted in his throne room. I was at the pool one day when Neb came up to me and started gushing about the treaty he'd just made. Then it was on about his wonderful garden and his beautiful pool, reflecting, as it did, the beauties of his harem. That hadn't been my thought when I built the pool, but it was a nice way to use it.

"Just look at all this I've created," Neb said. "I'm the greatest king who ever lived. Even the Jews acknowledge me as a king appointed by their god. There has never been such a one as me and I will..." he broke off his soliloquy and suddenly belched a guttural groan like a cow. He then wandered to the garden and began eating the leaves. Nebuchadnezzar had offended the gods one last time and was condemned to eat grass in the fields like an ox.

Well, the palace had been prepared for the possibility of such an event. I think Neb knew he could never keep the offense of pride in his work out of his life. He'd instructed his son, Belchadnezzar, well on how to handle a regency. A field had been planted on the south side of the palace where rich grasses grew and Neb began to browse and eat. It was deemed best at this time—because his son was rather young and inexperienced—to keep the transformation a secret. It was said that Nebuchadnezzar ruled from his bed and did not receive visitors. His son carried on all royal duties in consultation with the nobles and wise men of Babylon. He did fine without me.

However, Nebuchadnezzar's decree that during his incapacity, I was to be put in charge of his harem was adhered to. You might ask why.

There were a variety of laws—in fact so convoluted as to be almost indecipherable—regarding degrees of incest and penalties for each type. Some of them I recognized from the code of Hammurabi. For example, a woman sleeping with her nephew could be drowned if she was the nephew's father's sister, but would be exiled if she were the nephew's mother's sister. The nephew went without punishment, of course. A man was forbidden from sleeping with his sister—except if his sister's husband died and there were no male kin of the husband to take her in, then he could—no must—take her in and make her his wife. But in every instance, it was forbidden that a man should ever sleep with his mother.

The Prince of Babylon interpreted that as meaning that he should just stay out of his father's harem. Good plan, especially since he had just begun building a harem of his own. So, the prince and nobles and advisors were happy to put the harem in my hands, so to speak. I had to go home and explain that to Miriam. She went home to her mother. I took the infinity room with me and moved into the harem.

It was a long seven years. Ah! You might think I screwed my way through the 114 women in the harem and six eunuchs. No, I did not. It happened that many of the women—maybe thirty or forty—were still virgins. They were trade and surety given by subject kingdoms for their loyalty. It was expected that one day the king would or could have any woman in his harem in his bed, but many were kept chaste so he could use them later as a bargaining chip. Also, some of his 'wives' had been given to him in marriage while they were still young girls, six or seven years old. He would not touch them until they had become women. And I was certainly not going to deflower any of the king's brides or concubines.

I had a private chamber in the harem and kept the door locked at all times. I continued the practice of taking the harem to the pool to play on good days and watched over them as they frolicked with each other—and their children. Yes, young children of the king and his consorts also lived in the harem. It was like having a very large family. The children all knew me as Uncle Bob and often came to me for stories and games.

At night, I locked the door to my chamber and entered the infinity room where my wives and concubines awaited me. I did not do without sex just because I wasn't sating my lusts on the king's harem. I'm an honest demon, you know.

Each day, I visited Nebuchadnezzar in the field where he contentedly grazed on the lush grasses and dipped his head in a pond to drink. He was an ox in human form, but a beloved pet. Sometimes, I even brought his children to play with him. He was a gentle ox and let them climb all over him. While I was with him, I would recite all the news of the court and the gossip of the harem. He never said anything, but I felt he looked forward to my visits and was attentive to what I said.

His exile came to an end one day when he suddenly stood up and said, "Praise to the gods! All good things issue from them and all power is received from them. I am nothing if not the implement of the gods to rule their people."

And with that, he walked into the palace, bathed, and dressed, and resumed his duties, congratulating his son, Belchadnezzar, on the good administration of the kingdom in his absence. He was very pleased with his son's performance and kept him working at his side for the next several years. Those years were marked by tolerance, building projects, and mercy on his enemies, who were so stunned they never left his side.

And his wives and concubines were all happy to have him back. They nearly screwed him to death. He called them together and selected one of the virgins to give to me. She was happy with the match as nearly all the women in the harem had fallen in love with 'dear Uncle Bob' over the past seven years.

I took Chione, a beautiful Egyptian girl, to the Jewish Quarter and found my house undisturbed. I'd not been seen in the area for seven years and I found many people I'd known had passed on in that time. Included in the number was Miriam. I mourned her.

Chione and I lived quietly in the little house for several years. She was pleasant company and often went with me to visit the king and her friends in the harem. Her dark skin shone among the lighter skinned concubines and I found myself growing very fond of her.

So much so, in fact, that I introduced her to the infinity room.

I had to work out a spell so that she could not speak of the room to anyone when we were in the natural world. It was just my luck that the spell worked too well. The result was that she could not speak at all. It was a little embarrassing at first, but it did not seem to affect her joy in life, nor her fondness for me and the others in my harem. Living at least half the time in the infinity room slowed her aging process and years later she still appeared to be just twenty years old.

Nebuchadnezzar was a good king. Once he had learned humility, his worst fault was corrected. He was a just ruler, a wise conqueror, and a discerning judge. And he loved his family—all 114, now 113, wives and concubines and their children. Occasionally, he would even go out into the meadow that had been his home for seven years, and romp with the children, letting them climb on him and giving them rides.

We sat by the pool one day when he was quite old and looked at the naked ladies frolicking in and around the water. Then he began pointing out specific women. Over the years some had died, and I think Neb was considering his own mortality. Others were as old as he was and likely to pass on soon. And, in the course of political involvement, some had been added in his older years when he no longer had an interest in copulating. I guess that happens to human men at some point. I wouldn't know.

"Bob, I know you are not simply a man. You are blessed by the gods. You are a wise and capable counselor. I know you are something other than man, but I do not know what. And I don't care. I believe you are a good person and all the women of my harem trust you with their lives," he said. "Therefore, I want you to take those I have pointed out to you away from the court and make them your own. They are good women and will go wherever you lead them. Go to your room in the harem tonight and I will send them to you one at a time. I know you can transport them somewhere safe and away from Babylon."

"Of course, I will endeavor to do what you ask, your majesty," I sighed. I needed to get to the infinity room and prepare my wives to receive more concubines.

"I will make it worth your while, Bob. We have often spoken of your love for books. I will expand your library for every concubine you accept."

I looked at him and we both began to chuckle. He knew my weakness. Well, my other weakness. I'd have taken the women even without the books.

That night, I waited in my room in the harem and one by one, the women came to me. I asked them if they wanted to leave the harem and go with me forever, never to see Babylon or home again. Each one agreed. I opened a door to the infinity room and they walked through to be greeted by Pari and Chione, who most knew from when they had been members of the harem.

By morning, I had accepted twenty-five of the most vulnerable in Neb's harem. Each one had brought with her a book from Nebuchadnezzar's personal library. They were scarcely missed.

It always amazes me to see the reaction of women when they first arrive in the infinity room. I kept my door locked for the remainder of that day so that I could welcome them to our home. I did not attempt to sleep with every one of the new women that day. These had been the pampered and preserved women of Nebuchadnezzar's harem. By and large they were the youngest, and all were virgins. But they were welcomed by my harem and each was given a tour of our home, exclaiming at how big it was. They all loved our pool and were soon naked in it with the rest of my wives and concubines.

That is not to say that I didn't have sex at all. Srininx found a woman of Anatolia named Afet. She had a triangular face with large innocent eyes and black eyebrows that accented them beneath the long black hair that framed her face and hung nearly to her waist in gentle waves. Her breasts were firm and plump, and crowned with rosy nipples that stood out straight. I'd noticed her at Nebuchadnezzar's pool on many occasions and she seemed often to fix me with fiery dark eyes.

"Bob, this is Afet. She has had her eye on you for some time. And I like her a lot. Don't you suppose you could take us to your private room for a while and introduce us to the wonders of your love?" Srininx asked.

Srininx had been a part of my harem for some years now, but had always seemed just a bit aloof, though she welcomed my caresses and loving. She did not ask for it. To so boldly seek my intimate company was very unlike her. I pulled her to me in a warm embrace and she raised her lips to kiss me. Sometimes I imagined there was a lingering taste of metal to her, especially when I leaned down to tongue the nipple of her golden breast. As soon as she'd convinced me with her kiss that this was truly what she wanted, I turned to Afet.

"Beautiful woman, do you want to move so quickly to my bed?" I asked.

"Bob, I've wanted you for nearly all the time I've been in Nebuchadnezzar's harem. I was brought to Babylon as part of a treaty when I was only twelve. That means I have had eight years to fantasize about the time when I would be your woman. With my new friend Srininx to guide me, I would have you show me the ways a man and woman may please each other," she said.

That was good enough for me. I took the two girls to my bedroom where the bed was always the right size for the number of people in it and the activities we engaged in. Since we had been at the pool, we were already naked and my pleasure at this invitation was already obvious. I did not rush the girls in their exploration and investigation of my body. They were so different. Afet was twenty years old and had been sheltered from all men in the harem since she was twelve. She marveled at my body which did not look nearly as old in the in-finity room as it did when I stood next to Neb. Srininx was a teenager in body but had been frozen as a statue for a thousand years, unable to move or investigate any of the hundreds who had polished her left breast with their hands. I didn't avoid her left breast as I caressed and explored her body, but I didn't make it the focus of my attentions, either. Two such very different girls.

When I lifted Afet's hair to kiss her and worked my way down her chin and onto her throat, I saw another reason the two girls had been drawn to each other. Afet had a band of gold around her neck. When I had seen it before, I assumed it was a necklace, possibly a mark of her slavery to the harem. But as I kissed her throat, I realized the color was in her skin, just as the golden color of Srininx's left breast was in her skin. These two would always be known as my golden girls.

Each held onto the other when at last, I parted the folds of Srininx's sex with my cock and thrust into her. Her instant gratification was earth-shaking.

Afet's orgasm was just as quick when I pushed through her maidenhead, showing that the anticipation did not need to build for a millennium to be earthshaking. We held each other all day before I returned to my chamber in the harem.

Only a few days after that, Nebuchadnezzar II, King of the Babylonian Empire, returned to the primordial mass from which all souls are born.

I feigned illness, myself, and, after his coronation, begged leave from Belchadnezzar to return to my home to die. He, thinking Judah was my home, granted the request and I left. I turned south rather than west, however. It was time to visit the ruins of Bathra and pay my respects there.

23
To Catch the Conscience
of the King

⌘⌘⌘⌘⌘⌘⌘⌘⌘⌘⌘⌘⌘⌘

Y TRAVELS DO NOT ALWAYS take me to the best places. I sailed for the Americas with Columbus in 1492, when what I should have done was hide out a century and gone to England. I completely missed the Bard of Avon. I have read all his plays and have even sponsored and acted in some of them. I am quite the theatrical patron.

I fancy myself treading the boards and declaring "The play's the thing wherein I'll catch the conscience of the king!" Of course, I'd have written the scene a little differently. There were better plays in the Greek repertoire for his purpose than *The Murder of Gonzago*. But they were preserved in the infinity room and I found later that no other copies had survived intact. I always bless my collection and my many librarians for maintaining it.

⌘⌘⌘⌘⌘⌘⌘⌘⌘⌘⌘⌘⌘⌘

I traveled around Mesopotamia for several years, never actually finding my one-time home. Nebuchadnezzar's heirs were neither as strong nor as wise as the old man and they began to lose control of the empire. I saw the armies of Egypt and Persia both amassing for an attack. Belshazzar subdued the Egyptians, but by that time, Cyrus the Great had asserted himself over the Medes and united all of Persia. It looked bleak for Neb's grandson, so I returned to Babylon to introduce myself at court. I thought perhaps I could help the struggling monarch and prevent a bloodbath in Babylon. I didn't claim to be the same Bob who had served his grandfather for some forty years. I'd been gone from Babylon for twenty years and was sure I was forgotten. I returned as merely another Bob who made his home in the Jewish Quarter.

And it was there that I heard word of a rebellion fomenting. I knew that would be disastrous for the Jews, even if they were successful. The army of the Persians would simply put

179

them in chains as rebellious subjects. Belshazzar managed to reach an agreement with Cyrus and paid tribute as a subject king, but knowing the greed of kings, I could tell that would not last long. I wandered the Quarter and into the countryside, trying to at least keep the locals peaceful. It seemed like an impossible task.

Until I saw the army approaching.

Led by the great general Darius, the Persians were headed to Babylon and Belshazzar was by no means prepared. I rushed back to the city and had to sneak in because the gates were closed. I knew, however, where the pump was concealed that fed water to the gardens and I entered the city there. I rushed to the palace to find Belshazzar was holding a big party and was in complete ignorance of the approaching army. What a twit! How could his soldiers possibly not spread the alarm? The Persians were in sight from the battlements.

I rushed to the doors of the banquet room, but was denied admittance. While standing outside, waiting for another opportunity, an old woman came by. She looked at me strangely as she led a group of people carrying golden plates and goblets to the chamber.

"I know you," she said.

"I don't know, honored matron," I answered. "Have we met?"

"The night you took the maidens from the harem, I was with Nebuchadnezzar, the youngest of his consummated wives. I wanted to go as well, but he said I had a special role to play in the future. Now our great grandson, Belshazzar, is following the path of Nebuchadnezzar and will end up eating grass," she said.

"I fear he will never have the opportunity for such a feast. I am trying to warn him," I said. "The Persian army approaches."

"I will do my best to get you admittance."

She and the group of servants, wives, and concubines entered the room and I shook my head. I knew where some of those plates came from and even the Jews allowed only their priests to touch them. Still, I stewed outside the chamber, running once to the tower to see how near the armies had come. What I saw chilled me. The guards on the ramparts were all asleep.

"It's a shame, isn't it?" a voice said beside me. I turned to see My Lady Goddess next to me.

"Is this part of the great contest the gods were having?" I asked.

"Yes. They have decided to support the claim of the god of the Jews. Belshazzar shall die."

"I need to get back to the banquet and warn him."

"It will make no difference," she said. "His days are numbered and his kingdom will be divided. Go if you will and tell him this." The goddess faded away from my sight and I shoved at my cock to get it down. Even in the direst of circumstances, Aphrodite has that effect on me. I ran to the banquet hall again.

Just as I arrived, the doors burst open and the old woman beckoned to me.

"My Lord and King," she announced as we entered the banquet hall. "Here is a man who can tell you what this means. I present Bob!" the queen grandmother said.

"Come in here, Bob. If you can tell me what this means, I will give you riches untold and make you the third most powerful man in the kingdom!" He pointed at a wall where four words were scrawled. "A hand appeared and wrote those words. Are they in your language?"

"Keep your gold and appointments, oh, King," I growled. "They will do no man here any good by morning." I looked at the words and shuddered. "Mene mene tekel upharsin. This is the judgment of the gods, for whom you show no respect and do not fear. Numbered, numbered, weighed, and divided. Your days have been numbered and the days of your kingdom have been set by the gods. You have been weighed in the balance and found wanting. Your kingdom will fall and be divided among the victors. These are the words on the wall and their meaning."

Aphrodite's warning was fresh in my mind and the interpretation of the words was clear. The king was shocked.

"Clear the dishes and return them to the altars of their gods!" he shouted. "Bring me gold and all my concubines. Bob, you are a great man and spokesman for the gods. I give you all the gold I have in the palace and all the virgins in my harem. Here is the badge of office that will open any door in my kingdom. Here. Have a glass of wine, too."

"Your Majesty, there is no time for rewards and celebration. The Persians are at the gates and Lethe has come upon all your guards. There is nothing more you can do."

The king's concubines began filing into the room as his guests fled. I could hear the trumpets outside and knew they were all too late. I opened a portal to the infinity room and took all the concubines who would go through. I was amazed to find that most were carrying books, scrolls, or tablets. I shouldered the bag and headed to the garden. This would be where I faced the new ruler of Babylon.

That night, the king and all his remaining household were put to the sword as the Persian army swept the city. The Jewish Quarter was spared.

Darius himself came in the company of several soldiers to look upon the famous hanging gardens of Babylon. He spied me sitting by the pool and had me brought before him.

"Who are you?" he demanded. I'd taken the time to put on nice but not wealthy robes.

"I am Bob, the builder of this pool and keeper of the garden. I welcome your majesty to a place of peace and contentment, known throughout the world," I said. Yes, I told him I was Bob the Builder. I said it first.

"It looks like your work is finished here," Darius said. He was preening a bit after I addressed him as 'Majesty.' Cyrus was still on the throne of Persia. Darius was married to his daughter.

"I bring you greetings, conqueror. Greetings from the gods of Olympus, the gods of the Sumerians and Chaldeans, and the god of the Jews. They have blessed your conquest and ordained your future and set you on the throne in Babylon. You shall inherit the throne of Persia and all the world will bow down to you."

"That's heady stuff," he said. "I think there are several empty apartments in the palace just now. Choose one for yourself and I will talk to you again presently."

And that quickly, I had changed from a servant of Babylon to a servant of Persia.

I won't dwell on Darius. He had to lie and kill his way to the Persian throne. Even at the decision time, when he and the other six generals lined up to see who would become king...

Now this is funny when you think about it. They decided they would line up on their horses facing the sunrise and the first horse that neighed as the sun rose would indicate the rider who would be the new king. Well, Darius had a good and loyal groom who rubbed his hands through the sex of a mare that Darius' stallion was known to favor. Just as the sun rose, the groom held his hand up to the horse's nostrils and the excited horse neighed to find his mare. Darius became king based on the sex drive of a horse!

I managed to spend most of my time in my rooms at the palace and didn't socialize with most people. I spent my nights in the infinity room, getting to know all the new members of my harem. Many, I placed with single men we had collected in one way and another. A few found their way to my bed. I had noticed Belshazzar's concubines all carrying books and scrolls and tablets when they stepped through the gateway. It turned out that when the old woman hurried to bring the virgin concubines to me, she routed them through the king's study and they simply grabbed as many books as they could carry and came through the portal. They had no idea what was in the books, only that they were to carry as many as possible. Nimia summoned as many librarians as she could to meet the concubines and take the books to the library. That was where a few of the concubines went, too. We had a lot of single librarians.

When Darius got back from Persia as the new king, he had some rather stupid advisors with him who filled his head with idiocy. That was where some of the trouble started. While he was gone, I had been commissioned to find the brightest and best youths in the country and train them to become advisors to the king and administrators of his kingdom. Of course, some of the boys I found were Jews and they showed great promise. But Darius' advisors convinced him that he should decree that for thirty days no one was to pray to any god but him. Stupidity comes in multiples. It was a trap for the Jews and especially for the boys I'd located. And, of course, one of them was caught and brought before the king who could do nothing but agree to throw the boy into a den of lions and seal it up. I was able to slip into the den with the boy without being seen and managed a quiet spell to put the lions to sleep.

In the morning, Darius opened the stone in front of the den and called Daniel out of it. As soon as the way was clear, I woke up the lions and slipped out. Darius was so furious at having been betrayed by his advisors that he had them all gathered up, along with their families, and thrown into the lions' den which was then sealed. We can only assume that the lions feasted for many days. The den was never opened.

"What am I supposed to do, Bob?" Darius asked. He was a good man at heart but tended to put too much faith in his advisors. With the bulk of them now gone, he turned to me for advice.

"My King, the last king of the Jews was released from prison upon the death of Nebuchadnezzar II, nearly twenty-five years ago. Yet the people have remained in exile in Babylon.

There is no longer a purpose for confining them here for sixty years or more. You have seen how their god favors them. Why not appoint a new sub-king over them and let them return to Judea? This will make you a great man in their eyes and one to whom they owe more loyalty than exiled subjects would," I suggested.

"Bob, that is an excellent solution to the Jewish problem. I'll just shuffle them back to their own land and we won't need to deal with them again," Darius said, slapping his hands together. "But, Bob, what about the boys you've been training as my advisors? They have proven to be the most capable of the lot. Is there a way I can keep them here?"

"I'll talk to them. Giving the Jews their freedom does not mean the entire million of them in the Jewish Quarter will return to the waste that Nebuchadnezzar made of Jerusalem. But even having half of that number migrate away from Babylon will make the remaining citizens grateful." I'd used the term 'citizens' hoping Darius would get the hint to consider the exiles who remained in Babylon citizens of the nation. Certainly, he would want those who returned to Jerusalem to consider themselves citizens as that would encourage their loyalty to him. He figured it out and drafted a decree that allowed the Jews to leave Babylon and go back to Judea. When he returned the holy implements of the temple to the priests to take back to Jerusalem, he cemented his relationship as a friend of the Jews. And over the coming years, there was a steady migration of the Jews out of Babylon.

Not all, by any means. Many of the residents of the Jewish Quarter were very young when they arrived in Babylon or were born there. Jerusalem held no immediate interest for them. Many did return, following the priests and the temple accoutrements, but many were content with their life in Babylon.

Darius often called upon me to discuss building projects that he was constantly starting. As many Jews as left Babylon, even more migrants from other parts of the empire arrived there. It was a thriving commercial center and soon made the capital of the Achaemenid Empire. So, I wasn't surprised to be summoned to him.

"Bob, it's come to my attention that you have a good eye for women. I don't know where you keep your women, but I know you have more than one beautiful and well-comported young woman who will always do your bidding."

I was immediately on my guard. I'd been careless in exposing any of my women to the king, but some had desired to return to Babylon to pursue other interests, or simply to let friends know they were okay. I'd managed to perfect the spell to prevent them from telling anyone about the infinity room without making them mute. It turned out that the proper spell had nothing to do with speaking—the problem I'd had with Chione.

"I'm not concerned with that, Bob," he said to my relief. "What I'm concerned with is that my son Xerxes has come of age and should be finding women of his own. I'd like you to take on the task of finding a starter set for his harem. Like any ruler, he should have a variety of women that connect him to the various nations he rules over." He lowered his voice. "And Bob, they shouldn't all be Jewish. But one or two would be okay."

"I understand, Your Majesty. I will endeavor to seek out the best candidates for him to choose from."

I knew that I couldn't simply grab women and shove them in the young man's path. The position required me to travel to various subjugated kingdoms and negotiate the arrangements for a hostage concubine. During this time, I also sought a bride for the young man. It was a good job and the women were impressed that I could offer such pleasant accommodations on the journey to Babylon. All came along willingly.

But the bride I chose for him came from the Jewish Quarter. I'd nearly wooed her for myself, but her father was a leader in the local community and I didn't want to deal with losing another wife because she couldn't accept my harem. When I presented her to Xerxes, he was smitten. It was almost as if the concubines I had brought him didn't exist. For a while. Of course, he was a boy/man with a wide range of pussy to sample. I tried to present them to him one at a time over a number of months that stretched into years. But no matter what pussy he was screwing at the moment, Esther remained his favored wife.

It seems that idiots advising the king abound. Darius died and Xerxes came to the throne. He moved the capital to Susa, farther east near Persepolis, where Darius was buried and had intended to move the capital. I was beginning to feel old again and bored with governing a province. Besides, I'd had quite enough of 'The Greats.' So, I contrived my own death and returned as a much younger man, content to wander in the countryside continuing my search for a quiet place to go into the infinity room for a few years and enjoy my growing harem.

About three years into his reign, Xerxes gave his official signet ring to an aide, making him the most powerful man in the land. That man had an axe to grind against the Jews and signed a decree on behalf of the king that all the Jews should be killed on the thirteenth day of the last month of the year. When I heard the edict, I headed toward Susa, but by the time I got there, the crisis had passed, thanks to the queen. She outwitted the advisor and turned the tables on him so that he was put to death and the Jews killed close to seventy-five thousand men throughout the empire.

Xerxes loved his queen but the intrigues had been more than he wanted to deal with, so he left administration of the kingdom in the hands of his new advisor (a Jew), and raised an army to invade Greece. Well, I'd been on my way to Greece anyway, and had made my way almost as far north as Troy. So, I tagged along providing logistics for a branch of his navy. I'll get to talking about that later. He was successful in his invasion, conquering all the way down to the isthmus of Corinth. Then the invasion fell apart. Phillip of Macedon came riding to the rescue of Greece and drove Xerxes back. I stayed.

You see, I discovered something miraculous in Greece: Theatre!

My first experience of the famous Greek theatre at the Festival of Dionysus was all it took to make me a devoted follower. I attended a play and it was beautiful. It was actually a whole day of plays at a festival. I went back the next day to watch three more tragedies and a satyr play.

Actors, wearing elevated boots, costumes, and masks, strode about the stage, declaiming the part of a historic figure and reciting an event. They were accompanied by a chorus of actors who would explain what was happening between scenes, using dances and poetry. It was marvelous and I immediately wanted to be a part of it!

I found out who controlled the casting and selection of plays, and went at once to see what I must do to become a thespian. Well, the bastard had all kinds of hoops one had to hop through in order to become one of his actors. Most of them had to do with paying him in either gold, wine, or women. I happened to be very good with all three and was soon added to his 'stable' of actors.

We read and performed nearly everything written over a span of fifty years. Not all the performances were public, but the archon had to see all the plays submitted in order to select the ones that would be performed in the annual competition. By that time, a playwright had to submit three tragedies and a satyr to the contest. The best known of the playwrights was Sophocles, but there were many others. I submitted a few plays of my own. I had enough Greeks in my harem that I could dictate a play in the infinity room and someone would write it down. That way, I never actually had to learn to read and write Greek.

My plays were never chosen for the competition, but I was mentored by some fine professionals. What I really wanted to do was direct.

24
THE GREAT... AGAIN

"**B**OB, BOB, BOB. This won't do. The idea of the play is solid, though it's not true to the word of Homer. We could never sell this to the archon. Now, let me help you out some and we'll come up with a hit," Indougoles—'Just call me Doug'—my acting coach and story consultant said upon reading my latest effort.

"But this is what happened. That twit Homer messed it all up!" I insisted.

"Shh. Shh! Such words are sacrilege. Or heresy. Or something like that. Even if you *think* something happened differently than what Homer suggests, you don't *say* anything. His is the official word and no other can be tolerated. Now, let's get back to work on your vowel sounds. Open up and make them rounder so they will reach the back of the theatre. Alpha, epsilon, iota, upsilon, omega. Now, let me hear those sounds run trippingly off the tongue."

I carried out the exercises, listening to my acting coach/story consultant's instructions.

And, behold! I was chosen to be in the chorus.

Theatre was the first place I discovered groupies. Every official in every government I'd known had a certain number of hangers-on, and there were always women who would cock an eyebrow at you in invitation to an assignation. But in theatre, there were women waiting in the wings, so to speak, for the stage to clear and the actors to unmask. Of course, the divos of the plays were the leading actors, but there were only three of those per performance. Depending on the play, there might be twelve to twenty in the chorus. After the actors and the choragus had taken their choice of the girls who threw themselves at us, the rest of the chorus helped themselves. There were always plenty to go around.

Girls loved the theatre and the actors. Poor girls, rich girls, young girls, old girls. Delphia. *What a girl!* They made it quite clear they wanted to attach themselves to the actors—preferably at the groin. You could just grab them by the pussy and they let you! They'd do anything for the actors.

I enjoyed my share of the groupies. In fact, Delphia and I were eventually married. She wasn't technically a groupie. I'll tell you about her sometime. But groupies were a phenomenon I did not fully understand. I chose one of my harem girls who was originally from Greece to explain to me.

"Bob, theatre is glamorous. Every girl thinks you'll sweep her off her feet and carry her away to a fantasy world that is filled with applause and riches."

"But it's all fake!" I said. "We aren't the famous people we play on stage. We aren't nobles and kings. We have nothing but the script."

"But you make it all look real. If you play a famous king on stage, you must be a famous king. If you play a great lover on stage, you *must* be a great lover. If you are seven feet tall on stage..."

"Then I must be seven feet tall. They don't get the elevator shoes are like walking on stilts!"

"Exactly!"

"Then what should I do?"

"Take what is offered and try not to be cruel when she finds out you aren't a famous king, or seven feet tall, or..."

"Or a great lover. Thank you," I said.

"Oh, Bob, you *are* a great lover and I love you forever. Would you like me to be waiting off stage for you when you finish tonight's show?"

"Now that, my dear, would be a wonderful idea."

Well, I did enjoy the groupies on occasion, and sometimes I would discover one who was particularly outstanding and would fit in with my women. She would silently disappear into the infinity room, from where she would discover I was much more than I appeared to be on stage.

I'd quickly instituted a theatre program in the infinity room and many of the girls were quite taken with it. Females were not allowed on the stages at Athens until years later. There were exceptions, however, when plays about Antigone or Medea arose. No matter how you padded him, a male actor never carried the right presence onto the stage when playing a woman. In the infinity room, we had many plays and most of the actors were women. I got to be the gropee. Uh... groupie.

I fucking loved Greece! And I loved fucking in the theatre. However that worked. I got my opportunity to appear onstage as an actor instead of a member of the chorus at last, and wouldn't you know they asked me to play Odysseus! Comedy was on the rise and the great festivals of the City of Dionysia and the Lenaia now had comedies on every day of the performances, following three tragedies and a satyr. Most of the time, the three tragedies were by the same author. Often the satyr was also by that author. But seldom was the comedy part of the unity of the other plays. Playwrights were emerging who specialized in comedy.

The play I was in was a mockery of Odysseus and remarkably consistent with what Homer had written. I was okay with it, though I felt I added some interpretation to the poetry that pointed out how ludicrous the man really was. Much of the play was about the contest between Odysseus and Poseidon, and neither was shown in a very good light. Poseidon was depicted as a tentacled monster himself, attempting to capture and destroy Odysseus. Of course, no violence took place on stage. Each time Poseidon entered, he had fewer tentacles, proclaiming that Odysseus had cut another one off.

The chorus sat around drinking wine and saluting Dionysus as they sang about the blinding of the cyclops and how the crew were all drunk when the monster tripped and fell on a spear. I thought the play went very well, but we didn't win the contest.

"Now, Bob," my story consultant and acting coach, Doug, said, "you can't just bring actual women onto the stage. Not *actual* women. They could never stand the rigors of acting and are nowhere near strong enough to wear the masks and costumes. And their voices! The audience would know at once they aren't *real* actors."

"Doug, I'm tired of being told we can't do something. If the play can't be performed at the festival the way I want to do it, I'll find someplace else to perform it," I declared. Not that I had any real idea about where that would be. I admit, I was acting the part of a temperamental actor/director/playwright and doing it quite well.

"There's an idea for you! Why not circumvent the whole festival rigamarole? You'll never win a competition anyway. Your material doesn't fit. You could self-publish your plays, as it were, and perform them anyplace you wanted," he said. "Get your act together and take it on the road!"

"What? I can do that?"

"Even great Thespis himself did touring road shows. Oh, the regional theatres don't seat 10,000 like the festival theatres do, but people in the sticks are crying for more entertainment. Put together your troupe of *women* and travel the countryside, performing wherever you wish."

The more I thought about it, the better I liked the idea. We'd take our show on the road and perform off-Acropolis. It was a perfect solution.

I had a few hundred Greeks in the infinity room. I'd gathered them from the sailors at Troy and my journey as Odysseus. Most had joined me before theatre had become a big thing in Greece. There were festivals, but they were primarily religious, celebrating Dionysus the god of wine, women, and song—and ritual madness. The great festival of Athens was still called the Festival of Dionysus Eleuthereus. I had chuckled a bit to myself at the creation of the festival just beneath the wall of the Acropolis, which I had built. The part of the theatre that most closely resembled the ancient religious rites was the role of the chorus, singing and dancing like the Bacchae.

That was really the pinnacle of insult as far as I was concerned. The Bacchae were women, the priestesses of Dionysus (also known as Bacchus). They were the ones who drank the wine and danced into such a frenzy that they could tear a man to shreds. But were women allowed to be in the chorus that represented their role? Oh, no! Not the delicate fairer sex who would never drink to excess or fuck everything in sight or rip a man apart in a ritual madness.

I predicted we were coming to a day when women would reclaim the stage. And I was right! Don't mind me jumping around the timeline a little to tell you that *Medea* by Euripides had already won the festival one year and it was a woman who played the wronged queen and wife of Jason. It would not be long before Aristophanes profaned the stage with his production of *Lysistrata* with a battling men's and women's chorus in which the women withhold sex from the men until they lay down their weapons and stop going to war. And that greatest of all the Greek theatre that has survived through the ages, Euripides' *The Bacchae* celebrated the evisceration of King Pentheus of Thebes at the hands of the Priestesses of Dionysus. Women were about to come into their own as thespians, though men have attempted repeatedly to demean their participation.

I'll get off my soapbox, to mix eras once again, and say the women of my harem loved the stage and the ability to set their fancy free with productions that especially emphasized the role of dance and music in the chorus.

I wrote and directed, usually taking a leading male role so I could be on the stage with my women. We built a touring cart that we could unfold to create a stage that resembled the festival theatres. We could roll into town in the evening and be ready to perform to our adoring audience before the sun was at its pinnacle the next day.

We selected shows for the first season and plotted a circuit of the outlying districts. It was an ambitious route, but Doug assured me he had sent ahead to each of the regional centers and they would be expecting us. I paid him his fee and we left.

We opened in Epidaurus,

We next play in Argos,

Then on to Patras.

Lotsa laughs in Patras.

Our next jump is Delphi,

Where the people are all wealthy,

Then Thebes, then Athens,

Then we open again, whence?

We open in Epidaurus!

Um... Well, you get the idea. My apologies to Cole Porter. Those years were some of the best in my memory. By packing everything into the infinity room when we were out of town, we could travel faster than most people could. When we arrived in a town, we performed. It made no difference if there were a dozen people or a thousand. We gave the show our best. The girls, of course, hopped out of the infinity room only to perform and then were back home where they were safe and ageless. I could easily strike the theatre, stow it—making it look like I'd loaded it into a wagon with a horse pulling it rather than putting it in the infinity room—and then take off. As soon as we were in a safe location, I joined the girls for a post-show celebration that typically involved a lot of wine and a lot of sex.

The first circuit was just a warmup. We headed down to Corinth and then to Sparta. Later we ventured as far north as Thessaly and Macedon. Eventually, we were the oldest roadshow in Greece, performing for more than fifty years.

And that was when everything changed.

Comedy makes fun of everything: People, places, politics, society. It is the role of the comic actor to hold up a mirror to life in such a way that people see how ridiculous they are. It's supposed to lighten things up a little and make people laugh at themselves.

We were having a good time with a play about Alexander of Macedon being a bit of a child when it came to being king. In fact, I was dressed in a diaper with a baby rattle for my scepter as I played the role. We had no idea that the king was in the audience.

I managed to get the girls back into the satchel, but I was detained by Alexander's guards and brought before the twenty-year-old king.

"Your majesty..." I began with my deepest bow.

"Stow it," he responded. "Do you think this is Athens where you can ridicule your leaders and pretend everyone is equal?"

"It is a gift to be able to laugh at oneself," I defended.

"I don't have a sense of humor," he growled.

"My grave apologies, your highness. Please forgive the temerity of this poor playwright." This was not going well. I might need to hightail it out of town with Alexander's army in hot pursuit. I didn't really want to reveal myself.

"You call that a play? First of all, there was no clear storyline at all. Making jokes about your monarch might be good for a couple of laughs, but dramaturgically, that really sucked. There were no sympathetic characters—no one the audience could truly identify with. There was no unity of place, action, or time. You were all over the boards with disconnected sketches. It was tavern quality entertainment at best, not theatre! Did you study your craft at all? You and the rest of your players were amateurish and barely adequate to take up space on the stage. You mumbled your lines, making even your jokes hard to understand. And your meter was terrible," he said.

"I had no idea your majesty was a critic."

"I was educated under Aristotle. Do you think he would not teach me to appreciate the fine arts? Do you need to hear me play the aulos? See me prance upon the stage? Let me tell you: The world is my stage and I will command the applause of every person in it. Too young, you think? What is near us here? Scribes! What is the nearest city south of here on the way to Athens?"

"Thebes, your highness," volunteered a man with a pen and parchment.

"Thebes it is, then. When I sack Thebes, you will give me a play in honor of our victory."

"I pray it is not a tragedy," I sighed.

"Have the army ready to move at dawn. We go to sack Thebes!" Alexander shouted. "And you. Load your scenery and fall in with my company. I will show you the stage as it was meant to be!"

I could have loaded everything and sneaked away. I might even have won my way clear if I had to fight. But this young man was a master of command. He was so confident that he would simply march up and sack an important Greek city, that I thought this might be worth watching. I loaded my wagon and slept with my women. Before dawn the next day, we were rolling southward and Alexander was about to invade Greece.

He did sack Thebes. Upon doing so, he called me to his temporary headquarters in the hall of justice, one of the few buildings left standing in the city.

"Now, Bob, here is the making of a great comedy. Fools rise up against the king they have acknowledged and, through multiple acts of foolishness, they pass opportunity after opportunity to avoid disaster. When one fool suggests they stop paying tribute to Alexander, another fool asks, 'Who is Alexander?' A third fool says, 'There is no Alexander. He is a myth among the people.' As they argue among themselves about whether Alexander exists, Alexander marches into their city, lays it waste, and kills them. Now that's funny! Write it."

I wrote it. And we performed it in Athens in advance of Alexander's arrival there. It was, actually, a good play and after seeing it in the comedy festival, Athens set aside all thought of armed resistance to Alexander. The gates were thrown open to him and he was met by the rulers of Athens, of Sparta, of Corinth, of Delphi, and all the other powerful men of Greece, who came to meet him there and swear their allegiance, swelling the ranks of his army. They didn't call him their king, but they awarded him the rank of General for all Greece, which Alexander considered to be the same thing. The army prepared to march on the hated Persians who had attempted to subdue Greece years before.

In retrospect, I should have known Alexander had an axe to grind against the theatre. His father, Philip of Macedon, had been assassinated as he entered the theatre in celebration of his sister's marriage. I found out later that Alexander had written a script and used an actor, Thessalus of Corinth, whom I'd met once or twice, to attempt a marriage negotiation for him with a mate Philip was not in favor of. But it put an end to the match with his brother that Alexander thought Philip was going to arrange.

I quickly found out that Alexander was *not* without a sense of humor. He was quick of wit. Most of what is remembered of him is his figure on his stallion, Bucephalus, as he led his armies into battle. But he was a clever strategist who seldom wasted a life in battle. And he commissioned many plays from me for his entertainment.

"Bob, we're going to enter Phrygia shortly. They are paying tribute to the Achaemenids and have no king. It also has a city with a prophecy. It is said that whoever looses the knot of the Gordians will conquer all of Asia. I intend to be that man and you will write a play about how I untied the ox cart from the pole in the palace to which it is tied."

"Is this to be a comedy?" I asked.

"Oh, yes, Bob. I assure you it will be very funny."

Alexander practically wrote the play himself. There was no resistance to his army when we entered Phrygia, in central Anatolia. The generals had pulled back to amass a stiffer resistance farther to the south. We entered the City of Gordium and Alexander rode directly to the center of the palace and called the elders together to acknowledge him as king.

There was a lot of back and forth as they argued the terminology of whether he could be considered a king before he had conquered the Achaemenids. And, they said, there was the matter of loosing the knot. Every time the elders suggested something, Alexander refuted the argument with his charm and boyish wit.

The next day, he returned to the palace and called the city's merchants together. They negotiated for much of the day, finally agreeing that the merchants had nothing against Alexander becoming king, but there was the matter of the knot.

On the third day, the priests came to the palace to talk to Alexander. They argued about who the gods were and whether the Persian gods were the same gods as the Greek gods. Finally, the priests, as well, said they had nothing against Alexander becoming king, but there was the matter of the knot.

"The knot, the knot, the knot!" Alexander cried out. He stood and strode over to the ox cart tied to a pole in the center of the courtyard. "All I've heard is that the man who solves the Gordian knot will become the ruler of all Asia. Well, here is the solution to that problem." With that, he drew his sword and swung it mightily at the knot and split it in two with one blow. As soon as it was severed, it began to unravel of its own accord.

"Faced with the sword of Alexander, the empire of the Persians will unravel and I will conquer all the world," he declared. "Your only excuse to avoid acknowledging me has been the knot. Your excuse is gone now. I will rule Phrygia. Now, whose head should I unknot?"

I admit that I had a lot of fun creating the comedy of the Gordian Knot. It was truly representative of the way Alexander cut through all kinds of conflict.

I found Alexander, later called 'the Great' to be an unstoppable force of the universe, who demanded a play from me after each of his major victories. I followed him through much of the land I had known years before: Granitas, Miletus (near Troy), Tyre, Egypt (where he established a grand city named after himself), all of Mesopotamia, northern Arabia, Persia, and on as far east as Northern India and the Caspian Sea.

At Troy, we found the city mostly gone with another town built on top of it. However, I was able to find the tomb—out where the Greeks had their encampment—of Achilles and Patroclus. I'd enacted a play—one of my few tragedies—for Alexander about the two and when they saw the tombs, Alexander laid a wreath on the tomb of Achilles and his dear friend Hephaestion laid a wreath on the tomb of Patroclus.

He listened to his army, as well, and when he heard complaints that they did not want to cross the Indus and fight the people there, he turned the armies back to the west and swept up the loose ends as he returned to Babylon. But at Ecbatana, he paused to retrieve the treasures of Persia and hold games. That was when tragedy struck.

He lost Hephaestion, a childhood friend and trusted general to a sudden illness that may have been food poisoning—or poisoned food. Okay, we'll call a spade a spade and say they were lovers. His wives, Roxana, Stateira, Parysatis, never seemed to mind having Hephaestion around and there were rumors that Roxana's second child, which she miscarried at Babylon, may have been his. Nonetheless, when the general died, Alexander became morose. He ordered everyone to Babylon in a massive funeral procession. The funeral bier that was built was sixty meters high! He held massive games in honor of Hephaestion and petitioned the oracle to have him declared a god. The oracle approved having him declared a Divine Hero, which satisfied Alexander.

The games included both physical and intellectual contests, and I was told to write a play in celebration of Hephaestion. It was one of the few tragedies I wrote and performed. From the stage, I beheld the first and only time I saw Alexander the Great weep.

I'd been gone from Babylon for almost two hundred years and found myself back in my same old rooms in the palace of Nebuchadnezzar. I spent time at the pool reflecting the somewhat diminished gardens. And showed them to Alexander. He was impressed, but was already drunk and had little to say. His drunkenness soon led to his death, still mourning his lover.

I have never again met such a man as Alexander the Great.

25
GREAT CAESAR'S GHOST!

I DIDN'T STAY in Babylon long after Alexander died. No one did. His generals split up the empire among them and all led their armies out to rule their part of the world. Many soldiers went back to Macedon and Greece. I decided I missed the sea and went to Tyre to buy a boat. It wasn't as difficult this time as it had been the last time I bought a boat here. I did look around at every sound to see if My Lady Goddess had shown up. But she, too, was silent in the process. I bought a small ship, which came with a crew from Cyprus. I guess I was feeling sentimental and thought I might visit Crete as well as the island of My Lady Goddess. I offered to transport the crew back to their home base as I learned the intricacies of my new ship.

My new ship had a single mast that could be lowered to the deck in case of a storm. There was essentially nothing else above deck except the rails. Below deck, there was a cabin for the captain (me) and hammocks for the crew. The remaining space was used for cargo and I picked up a shipment of copper bound for Rhodes at the port in Beirut. While my crew was loading the ore, I went looking for books and found a few very interesting old daily journals and account lists, mostly scrawled on clay tablets. The Phoenicians focused their society on trade and so, they had made records of every transaction of every kind. I bought a few old record books, but found little to interest me otherwise.

We sailed first to Kyrenia on Cyprus. There, I bade farewell to my crew who were happy to be back in their home port. I did not allow curiosity to grow regarding what I would do for a crew when I continued my voyage. Suddenly, my deck was crawling with women from the infinity room who all wanted a Mediterranean cruise. It looked good to have so many people swarming over my ship and I set sail on the next tide, not waiting for the longshoremen to negotiate a new crew.

That next portion of our voyage was very pleasant. I set a fair wind to the northwest and then spent my time enjoying the sunbathing beauties lying naked on my deck. Every day or two, the crew would change and one group would return to the infinity room as another emerged.

Among my many subjects in the infinity room were a few good sailors—some from my time as Odysseus. These I invited above deck to man the craft as we sailed into the harbor of Rhodes. I was able to trade the copper for a good profit. Rhodes was a center of education and understanding. Following the withdrawal of Demetrius's army and capture of all their military equipment, the city had decided to build a colossus in honor of Helios, their sun god. The copper was needed for the statue. I'd had a couple of run-ins with Helios back in the day, so I was careful to make fair trades on the copper.

Perhaps as a result, I had the unbelievable good fortune to take on a cargo of manuscripts and books bound for Alexandria. Ptolemy Soter was one of Alexander's best generals and had forged a strong bond with Rhodes. He was building a great library in which to store all the knowledge of mankind. That was my kind of king!

I am an admirer of Ptolemy Soter and believe he would have been the best choice to rule the empire after Alexander's death. However, when Alexander was asked who should succeed him, his answer was simply, "The strongest." That had the predictable result of creating conflict among the three remaining generals of his army, and the division of his empire. Antipater, the regent of Macedon and Greece held that territory, even though Alexander had sent a replacement for him. Seleucus made the biggest land-grab, claiming everything from southern Anatolia to the Indus River. In today's language, that included Syria, Jordan, Iraq, Iran, Afghanistan, and Pakistan. It was also the unruliest portion of the empire and Seleucus could not effectively fight off Ptolemy when the latter claimed Egypt, Cyprus, Lebanon, and Judea.

Ptolemy claimed to be Alexander's half-brother, the bastard of Philip II and Arsinoe of Macedon. As such, he claimed the body of Alexander from Babylon and moved it to Egypt, eventually settling the tomb in Alexandria. He attempted to establish his dominance through negotiation and marriage. His sons by Eurydice briefly ruled over Macedon in their succession. He later married Eurydice's lady-in-waiting—apparently waiting for her opportunity to marry her mistress's husband—Bernice. To them was born Ptolemy II of Egypt.

One of the reasons I liked Ptolemy was because he shared Alexander's cultural perspective. As I've indicated, Alex was educated under Aristotle, knew the arts and sciences as well as war, and had a dream of creating a vast paradise as his kingdom. Antipater was primarily a politician with all that spells included. Seleucus was a warrior and had very little to do with the arts in any way. It was easy for him to conquer and difficult for him to rule. Only Ptolemy carried on that dream of creating a cultural center of the Mediterranean—a dream carried on by a dozen generations of his descendants.

Nonetheless, I plied the waters from Rhodes to Alexandria and set up a favorable trade situation with Ptolemy, whom I had met when I was an actor. Of course, I'd changed shape since then and he didn't recognize me. He did, however, introduce me to his librarians and I became a book gatherer for the great library. That was a relationship I enjoyed for many years, though I returned to Alexandria in a new body each generation, having inherited my ship from the previous Bob.

On each of the trips, as we sailed (and my women sunbathed), I replicated nearly all the books I was transporting and moved them into the infinity room where my own librarians were thrilled to have the additions to my rather impressive and growing library. Occasionally, I convinced a librarian from Alexandria to join me and we created a replica of the great library in the infinity room.

The entire Mediterranean was a war zone from the time of Darius to the time of Caesar and beyond. As the heirs of Alexander were primarily in the East, Rome, founded by Aeneas after the fall of Troy, gained prominence in the West. Instead of turning straight north after my book-buying voyages, I turned westward and sailed along the coast of Africa as far as Carthage. Another great mess. The Carthaginians were at war with the Roman Republic, or with a Roman in Sicily, or both. I continued west and sailed through the great rock passage and into the next sea.

Fast forward. I don't remember anything really interesting happening in the islands west of Gaul. Oh, there was Tiona, but I'll get to her later. I know I sailed into the frigid North Sea and settled there with Impi until she passed away. I might have stayed there if it hadn't been so cold. Neither the Scandanavians nor the Britons had progressed to the point of wanting my hand at architecture for temples or palaces. There were some impressive stone circles, though. There were precious few books of any sort there, but I collected what I could, and after paying my respects to Mac Lir, I made my way back through the great rock gates into the Mediterranean, sticking closer to the north shore of the sea this time.

I'm not exactly certain how long it had been since Alexander's death—a couple of centuries, at least. I'd become rather skilled at sailing past the warships of Carthage, Rome, Greece, and Persia. Egypt had withdrawn from the fight and simply held its borders. I used a look-away spell to conceal my ship from others to which I gave wide berth. Mine was one of the few vessels that made its way to Alexandria unmolested.

Rome had risen as the dominant power in the north. They annihilated Carthage and the western Mediterranean was theirs. Their alliances had consolidated their rule into the Seleucid kingdom, giving them control over the eastern shore of the Mediterranean and a shaky alliance with Egypt.

In all this time, there was as much damage being done by pirates on the sea as there was by warships. I made it my unofficial mission to intervene when I saw pirates besetting undefended merchant ships. When I succeeded in freeing a merchant ship from pirates, I was often given some reward from the merchant. A portion of its merchandise, for example. All too often, I was too late to help the merchant and crew when I drove off the pirates. Then I found myself in possession of a ship and its entire stock of goods for trade. It was very profitable.

Unfortunately, it also earned me the reputation of being a privateer.

But I am an honest demon. I can say without blushing that I never attacked a trade ship, but only the pirates I found preying on them. I just couldn't be everywhere at once.

That was how I met Julius Caesar—the third of the great rulers who would influence my life.

I was sailing south through the Aegean Sea and saw a battle raging. It was rather one-sided. The master of the Roman galley lowered sails and shipped oars. The pirates were all over it in an instant. It seemed there was little cargo aboard the galley, but I saw a few men led from it to the pirate ship.

This was something that was becoming more common these days. The Roman Navy ruled most of the Mediterranean by this time. They used galleys that typically had a hundred slaves to man the oars, so they could gain speeds much faster than a simple sailing ship. I noted the pirates stayed tied to the galley for longer than was necessary and eventually, there was a trade of galley slaves made. Maybe twenty were swapped from one ship to the other. Then the pirate ship shoved away from the galley and the galley made quick work of getting away and heading south—presumably to get to Athens or perhaps all the way around the Peloponnese to Rome.

Pirate ships were often older than the galleys. Mine was much older, but didn't require slaves to row it. Most had the upswept bow and stern of the Cretan ships and could cut through the water with greater speed due to their shallow draft. In general, they were more maneuverable than the galleys and hence ideal for piracy. You didn't see many pirates take on a galley, though. Galleys were warships and could throw fire at you or ram you. This one had to be something special.

I observed this from just at the horizon. My eyes are considerably sharper than most humans and two leagues or so to the horizon is not a stretch for me. This gave me the opportunity to sail at the edge of their vision and with the look-away spell on my ship, I was able to keep pace with the pirates until they made anchor at a small island. As the sun set, I took sightings of the stars and where the island was. In the darkness, I sailed silently toward the pirate ship.

I had no need to apprehend these pirates. It appeared they had no cargo of value, but sometimes, a person can be considered as valuable as a shipload of goods. When I was a stade away, I anchored my ship and launched a skiff.

Just as a reminder, I always keep my satchel with the infinity room in my possession, no matter where I go. So, when I leave the ship, the satchel leaves the ship. And when the satchel leaves the ship, everyone who lives in the infinity room leaves with it. I say this to indicate that my ship was completely abandoned. It lay at anchor, protected only by the look-away spell.

I made my way to the pirate ship, gliding across the water silently. They were carousing on the deck.

"And then I boxed in the legion with shields locked as one and spears outward. We simply marched through the them, having only to stop and shake their bodies from our spears," said a voice I took to be a boy's. It had the pitch and timbre of a voice not yet come into manhood.

"Bravo, Caesar!" the crew yelled.

I had little contact with people except when I was in port trading my goods, but even I had heard of the noble who was said to be a brilliant strategist and orator. He was quite popular. Shields locked and spears out, though, was a battle move developed by Alexander's father, Phillip II. I wondered if Caesar had also used the *sarissa*, an extra long spear, to extend the length of his legion's reach in front of the phalanx. Regardless, I wasn't expecting him to sound like a child!

So, that was the cargo the pirates deemed worthy of attacking a Roman galley. Ballsy of them, I had to say.

"Rome will miss me and you will have the money soon," Caesar said.

"It's good you told us to increase the ransom from twenty silver talents to fifty," said one of the pirates. "We'll be wealthy men when we leave here."

"Oh, it's the least I could do for you. When I get back and organize a hunt, I will find you and crucify you."

In his boy's voice, he sounded like he was joking. The chill his words sent down my spine told me that, like Alexander, Caesar didn't have a sense of humor.

As the ship quieted for sleep, I slipped aboard and silenced the pirates. Don't think I slit their throats or anything. I used a deep sleep spell on them so I could locate and liberate their captive. I thought rescuing Caesar might be a way to get on the good side of Rome for a while. Of course, the spell worked too well and by the time I reached Caesar, I found he, too, was fast asleep. I looked to see if there were any valuables on the pirate ship, but only found stale food and sour beer. I left everything as I found it, hoisted Caesar over my shoulder and returned to my skiff. When we were well away from the pirates, the spell broke and Caesar awoke with a start.

"Where am I and who are you?" he demanded.

"Glorious Caesar, I am Bob and I've come to rescue you."

"In a rowboat? I might have lived longer with the pirates!"

"My ship is just here, sire." With that, we bumped up against the ship and Caesar suddenly saw it.

"Nice trick! Can you equip an entire navy with the capability to be invisible?"

"I fear it's not that easy. I'm a simple demon, not a god."

"Well, demon Bob, I command you to take me to Rome instantly!"

"I'm uh... not sure where you get your ideas, your Lordship. Let me say... Well, it just doesn't work that way," I said, startled by his imperious attitude. "First of all, you cannot simply command me and expect me to obey. I am a free demon and serve whom I will. We might be able to reach an agreement on that front. Secondly, I can take you to Rome, quite willingly, but we are sailing. It will be about two weeks before we can get there."

"You can't just pick the ship up and put it down somewhere else?" he asked incredulously.

"If I could do that, what would be the sense in having a ship at all?"

Caesar was as well-educated as Alexander, and just as ambitious. He wanted to know all about my ship and where my crew was. I told him they would arrive with the light of day, but until then, I could sail by myself to get us well away from the pirates by morning.

He had many excited questions about my plans and what I did while sailing around.

"Now, Bob," he said. The condescending tone of his voice was out of place with its immature pitch. "What is it that separates you from common pirates? You *say* you only attack pirates, but then you take what they have and leave them to steal again. You are in possession of goods or people stolen from a legitimate merchant, yet you hold that since you took those goods from pirates, you did not steal them and are legitimately in possession. Are you not simply using others to commit your piracy? You could have slit all their throats last night and the world would be a better place."

"Oh, but my Lord, I would never deprive you of fulfilling your oath to crucify them." The casual snort he made was, I found, as near a laugh as I would ever hear from him.

"Kind of you. What makes you think I won't hunt you down and crucify you?"

"Hmm. That would be an interesting experience, but not one I would prefer. Perhaps instead, there could be an alliance between us. Suppose I made sure the pirate ships I subdued were left where your navy could pick them up and declare justice upon them?"

"Ha! A demon with an aversion to killing. I like that. A noble trait. What else can you provide to me?" he asked.

Hmm. Ask not what Caesar can do for me. Ask only what I can do for Caesar. I would need to be very careful in our negotiations.

"I could tell you stories. I've been around for quite a long time. I traveled with Alexander the Great and could tell you the strategies he used to become the ruler of all Asia from Macedonia to Gordium to Babylon to the Indus River and to Egypt. I know how it was that he could march 20,000 leagues with 40,000 soldiers and bring nearly all home safely."

"Alexander was a pompous upstart," Caesar scoffed. Words from a pompous upstart.

"By the time he was your age, he'd conquered the known world," I rejoined. Oh, that got Caesar's goat. I soon discovered that anytime his accomplishments were compared to Alexander's, he flew into a rage. I'd need to be careful about that.

"The world is bigger now. I'll conquer places Alexander never dreamed of. But your knowledge could be of value. I would like to call upon you at times. Even Pompey has counselors who advise him, but they are all human and see only with human eyes. I should like to have your counsel and the use of your demon eyes," he said. He sounded like a child, but he was a shrewd bargainer and I reminded myself to be careful of what I agreed to.

"Great Caesar, I will give you a means of requesting my presence. If it is possible for me to fulfill your request, I will do my best."

"Bob, that's what I like about you. No oath of loyalty. No solemn vows. We'll have some good conversations."

When the girls started arriving out of my cabin in the morning, Caesar let his mouth hang open. He definitely had a weakness for women. They scrambled over the rigging, cleaned the decks, and brought food to us. Then they got naked and lay around as I guided the ship toward our next stop.

"Are these all demons?" Caesar asked in amazement.

"Oh, no. These are women who have attached themselves to me over the centuries. They come out of my infinity room once every few weeks to enjoy the earth's sun for a day and then return. The next day a different group emerges. I'm never quite sure who has requested duty on the ship for a day. Mostly, Nimia and Josie manage the schedules."

"Amazing. I would like that one for a bit of play time, if you don't mind," he said. I wondered if he was still a virgin. Silly. The man was near thirty years old. I had to remind myself not to be thrown by his voice.

"You may *ask*," I said. "I don't attempt to control what any of them do. Some have husbands back in the infinity room. Some are devoted solely to me. But you must abide by one rule. These women are as free as I am. If you attempt to force one after she has rejected you, she will probably kill you."

"You'd allow that?"

"I don't think I could prevent it. Many of my women have seen war and have been the spoils. They have been raped and men have attempted to enslave them. They have learned to defend themselves, and even naked in bed, they are seldom unarmed. And if that woman failed to kill you for your crime, I would execute you myself."

That slowed his lust a bit. Long enough for me to converse with Josie about sending a few willing women on the next shift.

<hr>

We did not leave the area immediately. In fact, it took nearly two weeks for a Roman galley to appear on a heading toward the island of the pirates. I sent all the women below and handled the ship myself as we intercepted the galley and Caesar hailed them. There was a short exchange during which the galley was prepared to do battle with me, but Caesar gave them a new target.

He had a small chest of silver delivered to my ship for having rescued him and then pushed away, waving to me as they continued toward the island of the pirates. I had a feeling the island would have a number of new Roman crosses by morning.

I hefted the chest and assessed that there were considerably fewer than the 50 talents of silver he'd promised the pirates. Less, even than the 20 they'd initially asked for. It weighted less than a good cask of wine. Ah, well. Becoming ruler of the world requires some cash, I suppose.

26
Battle in the Desert

ONE TIME—I have to tell you about this—I met a man who claimed he ruled the world and I owed him my obeisance. He was, in fact, a powerful chieftain, but he was a little short-sighted. I won his confidence eventually and managed to ask why he felt he ruled the world. He took me to the tallest mountain around and we climbed to the top. It wasn't even all that tall, but he'd built himself a throne on the top so he could survey his kingdom.

"Look!" he said as he pointed out to the sea. He slowly turned in a complete circle and there was nothing but ocean in every direction. "I rule it all!"

"What about the lands across the sea?" I asked.

"Don't be ridiculous. There are no lands across the sea. Those who go into the sea and leave our land disappear forever."

"But how do you explain where I came from?" I asked. It was apparent he hadn't considered the possibility.

"You rose up out of the land and are therefore my subject," he said.

"I assure you, there are lands beyond what you see."

"Then I will raise an army and go conquer them!"

His frame of reference was limited and he raised an army of nearly thirty young men and began training them to go out and conquer the rest of the world. I thought of his thirty soldiers against even one of Caesar's legions and wished I'd left him with his delusions.

I stayed on his little island for a year or more, getting to know the people and... well, you see there was one woman, Princess Agora, who was especially nice to me. Her skin was a rich deep brown and her eyes black as night. And the king had approved our marriage according to the customs of the land. It distracted him from his ideas of conquest for a while.

"You have ruined me for other men, Bob," she said as I parted her legs and lapped at her honey with my tongue.

You probably don't need to hear this, but as a demon, I have the ability to alter my shape in subtle ways, not just in the way of putting on a new body every twenty years or so. When I'm with a woman who is as exciting and receptive as this one, I sometimes lengthen my tongue so that I can thrust it deep inside her. You might assume that being five or six or ten inches inside a woman is a job for the dick. But if you can push your tongue all the way to the end of her pussy, and then curl it back, it will drive her absolutely wild with passion. Agora loved to have me tickle her cervix with the tip of my tongue and went crazy when I tickled her g-spot with it. (We knew about the spot long before a twentieth century doctor gave it his name.)

Oh. Well, if you can't extend your tongue that far and curl it, just stick with your dick. But I assure you, you will never hear the kind of joy my princess expressed at my ministrations. And then she was still just as happy to have my dick in her.

So, I was there for a year or more and she finally agreed to join me on my adventure and I introduced her to the infinity room.

It was too much for her.

Like her father, the king, she thought the whole world could be seen from the top of their little hill. Her transfer to a completely different world resulted in so much disorientation and panic that she was nearly catatonic. She had no idea how vast the world was. It drove her mad. It was the first and only time I ever possessed a woman without her asking me directly to do so. Indirectly, she asked me. It was words like 'Make it stop!' and 'Help me!' I took control of her and gave her peace. It was a near thing, though, and I almost lost her when I had my tongue inches deep in her twat and she called out for God instead of me.

"God! I mean Bob! Oh, Bob! Love me, Bob!"

She got along fine after that, though she was never again comfortable leaving the infinity room for the natural world. She preferred to stay inside the house with my wives and possessions and not even venture into the great out-of-doors in the infinity room. She was truly agoraphobic.

Well, I bring up this little adventure because every ruler I've met is just like Agora's father, the chieftain of his island. He considers himself to be the most important and powerful man in the world and cannot abide having another challenge his position.

Human rulers all want to rule the world. Caesar shared power with Pompey and Crassus as a triumvirate. Each of them wanted to rule the world and, as a result, needed to get rid of the other two. Caesar went north and west to conquer all of Europe for Rome. He even had me meet him with ships on the coast of Gaul and transport his troops to Britain so he could conquer that as well. Much good it did him. The Britons were a cagey people and did not come out to meet Caesar's legions after they'd shipwrecked on the shore. I kept a number of men with me to rebuild the ships so they weren't stranded on the island. Caesar led a legion off to conquer the Britons.

But they didn't stand and fight like the other foes Caesar had encountered. They led him into the forest and attacked from the sides, disappearing back into the brush. When he finally found a town, Caesar negotiated a truce that called the Britons subjects of Rome. He appointed a governor and we all boarded the restored ships to head back to Rome. The Britons snickered at his back and did away with the governor.

Pompey went the other way and consolidated Rome's hold on Asia Minor and the near east. He accepted tribute from Egypt's teenage queen rather than invading the country, and was prepared to push eastward into the Seleucid Empire.

Crassus thought 'the boys' were way too reckless and just sat at home governing Rome while Caesar and Pompey competed with each other to see who could conquer the world. In Caesar's mind, he could complete his conquest of the world by merely defeating Pompey and uniting the two armies. When Crassus died, both made a mad rush back to Italy. Pompey had an edge by getting there first and raised an internal army to defend the city and his territory. Caesar approached from the northeast.

I might have mistakenly goaded Caesar on a bit. He often called me to consult as one of his advisors—one who stayed well away from the political maneuverings of his other advisors and generals. I'd already told Caesar that by his age, Alexander had ruled the world as far as the Indus River and the only reason he didn't rule Rome was because he considered there to be nothing there of value. It made Caesar insanely angry whenever I mentioned the name of Alexander the Great.

I'm afraid that was what happened at a small river on the Italian frontier. I'd come ashore to meet with the man as one of his advisors. They argued back and forth about what should and should not be done. There was something about a law forbidding taking his troops any farther south. I shook my head at them.

"If Alexander were here, he'd take what soldiers would follow him and march south to take what was his. He sacked Thebes because they rebelled against him. It took only days for the rest of Greece to come to his side."

Caesar stood up and shook a finger at me.

"The die is cast then," he said. He left the chamber where we met and, in the morning, took his legions with him and crossed the Rubicon.

And Pompey fled.

I won't go into the details of all the battles and triumphs. You've got a history book, I'm sure. The rest of Caesar's life was marked by making laws and putting down rebellions. He insisted that his front guard ride on my little ship with him as we pursued Pompey to Egypt, only to find out he was already dead. Caesar was incensed against Ptolemy XIII, who ordered the murder, and had the two men who killed Pompey executed. Caesar liked to deliver his revenge personally. Pompey was given a proper Roman funeral and Caesar negotiated his own treaty with Cleopatra.

He had a weakness for particularly passionate and lubricious females—like Cleopatra.

You probably know all about Caesar's affair with the Egyptian queen and how Ptolemy XIII, her co-ruler, besieged Alexandria in an attempt to wrest control from his estranged sister-wife. It was during that siege that my own little ship was burned in the harbor where I was delivering some books I'd collected for the library. I've already told you about how I rushed to the library to save the books. And the librarians.

Without a ship, I was useless to Caesar, and frankly, I'd had enough of him. When he left Egypt and headed up the Mediterranean coast, I stayed in Egypt where there were many other repositories of books.

Which is when I ran into a very sad and mournful Cleopatra, now ruling with an even younger brother, Ptolemy XIV. That didn't last long and she managed to get rid of him as well. She then named her infant son from her liaison with Caesar as her co-ruler.

"You've known him a long time, Bob. Will he come back to me?" she asked as we dined together in her palace. She was still only in her early twenties and as sleek as the greyhound she kept nearby as a symbol of her near divinity.

"Oh, he'll return. Anytime there is a hint of rebellion, Caesar will return with an army. But you must know, he is married," I said.

"He'll divorce her," she declared.

"Probably. But I don't mean the woman who claims to be his wife. I mean he is married to Rome. He will cut down anything and anyone who stands to hurt his Rome and her empire."

"Are you married, Bob?"

That was an interesting question. Nimia and Penelope were my wives. Josie and Pari were my possessions. But there had been many—dozens?—to whom I had been married and outlived. Then there was my harem—concubines, women who had sneaked into my infinity room before I knew it, priestesses of Troy. Oh, yes. Many women.

"My bride was burned in the harbor the night your brother attacked," I said.

"Do you want me to give you a new boat?" she asked.

I laughed.

"How would you like me to set you afloat and ride you on the tides of passion?" I asked.

With any other woman, such an abrupt proposition would have been met with outrage. But Cleopatra was a woman of passion, and if she was not with the one she loved, she loved the one she was with.

I want to clarify that. Cleopatra was not a slut. No, when I refer to a woman as a slut, she is one who will simply spread her legs as a part of any relationship. If you are her husband, you are welcome between her legs. If you are her house guard, you are welcome between her legs. If you are her driver, you are welcome between her legs. If you are the man who bakes bread on the corner, you are welcome between her legs. Helen of Troy was a slut. I was the baker on the corner.

Cleopatra was a woman of passion. Her fire lit quickly and burned hot. Once you had struck a spark to her tinder, the flames could consume you. Caesar found that out. Later, Marc Antony discovered the truth of it. I lit the fire but managed only to get singed a little before she was called to Rome to stay at Caesar's bungalow across the river from the palace.

I've heard people make the assumption that Cleopatra, being the Queen of the Nile, was Egyptian, a people who are generally thought to be moderately dark-skinned. But the line of Ptolemy Soter, Alexander's general, were Greeks and Macedonians. They married Greeks and Macedonians. In fact, Cleo was the first of that lineage who even bothered to learn the Egyptian language, which endeared her to the people. She had pale skin, red hair, and a classic Grecian nose. She might have been carved of ivory, just as My Lady Goddess's statue on Cyprus. She did not always bare her breasts, but she always wore clothes that could fall off with the slightest breeze.

And thus, when I gently blew across her bosom, the gauzy fabric parted and exposed her shapely breasts, capped with hard rosy points begging to be suckled. I obliged. We were dining, stretched out on carpets and cushions in the Arabian fashion. A simple shove with my foot cleared the table from between us, and we fell together right there on the floor.

"Oh, Bob. I had no idea your scepter was fit to rule the world! Bring it to me and rule the delta of Cleopatra." She had a poetic way about her.

I would certainly never rule beside Cleopatra. I was certain Caesar would take that as a personal offense. But as a substitute for him, I ruled between Cleo's legs, and that was a place to be greatly desired. My thick meat parted her delicate, sparsely haired folds and speared her to her depths. Whatever you have read about how desirable Cleopatra was, it was inadequate. Not only was she beautiful with a tight but welcoming pussy for my cock, she was an active participant. She accepted me in the dominant position at first, but when I was not being exuberant enough, she rolled us over and drove that wet snatch down on my cock repeatedly. Between her orgasms and my own, the carpets were soaked. Thinking of her now makes me hard and she's been dead two thousand years.

Over the next year or so, she escorted me to temples and shrines, and showed me where some of the libraries were that had been untouched in a thousand years. When she received the message that Caesar wanted her to visit Rome, she was gone overnight. I was left on the shore of the Nile with naught but the satchel on my shoulder and the memory of her hot pussy wrapped around my cock.

I set about pillaging the libraries of Egypt.

Not all that comes from the primordial mass is good and kind and honest like Bob. Most is not benign. This is my warning to fledgling magicians not to play around with spells and summonings you don't understand. This happened to me on my journey from Egypt through Arabia.

Magi, adepts, sorcerers, and even necromancers have always believed they had to know the name of a demon to summon it. They scoured books (like those I carried in my satchel library) for names of demons and the rituals that would conjure them. And as time went on, they began to *find* names. Amazingly, the names were always in the language the mage spoke. Imagine that!

I believe ninety percent of the known names for demons came from fiction authors and playwrights. And *they* made them up. And if they were especially imaginative, they described the character of the demon and what he looked like. Often in terms that didn't make literal sense, so it was open to interpretation. The demon Trogladach, for example, has a thick impenetrable skull and wields a club the size of a man. He has fiery eyes and legs like tree-trunks. The mention of his name terrifies his victims who quake in fear at him and fall beneath the blows of his mighty club. Uh... that's not a real name, by the way.

The thing is that when a competent mage or a sorcerer with natural ability attempts to conjure that demon, Behold! he appears. And he is *exactly* like the mage imagined him. This is because demons emerge from the primordial mass upon their first successful conjuration, just the way they were imagined.

Undoubtedly, you have seen pictures of djinn, or genies, arising from a bottle or out of a lamp. Ever notice how their lower half is wispy smoke or a whirlwind with no details? It isn't a native characteristic of demons to have no lower extremities. It's the limited imagination of the conjurers. And after a while, it became the accepted way to imagine a genie. The summoning mage didn't think of anything below the waist. Eyes and face are generally nicely detailed. Arms show detail only to the extent the mage wanted a djinn that was strong. Even hair was covered by a turban.

Eventually, those images became ingrained. That was what a djinn was supposed to look like. Therefore, that was the image in mind when it was summoned.

Now Pinaruti, for an inept adept, had an excellent imagination and more than a little artistic inclination. As I went through all the scrolls and papers in his magic room, I discovered he had been drawing pictures of demons and gods from the time he was first sent to the fields to watch sheep. They evolved over time, but he was obsessed with supernatural beings. And that obsession boiled down to one specific form in his later years. The face, though tinted slightly red, was firm and quite handsome. Black hair flowed from the head around two curled horns and down to the shoulders. The shoulders were broad and muscular, the arms looking like the silent guards of the king.

And he did not stop at the waist. In spite of him never drawing a stitch of clothing for his demon, he worked hard on the details below the waist. I'd say he was a little obsessed with male genitalia. There were pages devoted to drawings of the phallus—so much so that I wondered if he were fantasizing about himself or the one he wanted to take him. And then, there were the legs. Pinaruti had spent a lot of time around sheep and goats. There were even sketches of the animals among his early drawings. The legs were an elegant transition from manly thighs to powerful goat legs and hooves. I never had the least problem standing or walking or running because he had rendered those parts so well.

This image was clearly in his mind when he conjured me. He was simply so surprised his spell worked that his heart seized up and he quit this mortal life. I could not complain about the body he had given me, nor did any of the women who had seen it. And I believe I used it well—even when I had to adopt a different outer shell for the sake of getting along in the human world.

I had met some other conjurers over the past two millennia, but had always kept my nature well concealed from them. So, imagine my surprise when I was confronted by a powerful sorcerer out in the midst of the Sinai desert. And he was angry with me! I didn't even know him.

"Demon! You have stolen the books of magic from the great repositories of the world. I demand you give them back! I shall consign you to the flames of hell and take from you all you possess!" the sorcerer declared.

"Kind sir, you mistake me. Any book in my possession was either rescued from destruction or is but a copy of what was before. If you will tell me what book you are interested in, I'll see if I can copy it for you."

"Don't be clever with me, demon. I was in the great library when the harbor fire caught it. I saw you plundering the library and all the librarians with it. I could tell you were a mighty demon and I ran from the library with the scroll I was reading. I have hidden myself for ten years as I read and studied from that one scroll. And now I have found you and demand you return what is not yours," he shouted.

"With all due respect, it's not yours either. I rescued it from the fire. I did not steal it," I protested. "If you take it from me, it is you who are the thief."

"Is that your answer? Then I shall do combat with you. When you are dead, you will yield up your secrets."

"That's not really the way it works, you know. If you truly kill me, I'll evaporate and there will be no body for you to read the memories of." I didn't like the idea at all. There were nearly a million souls in my bag and destroying me would destroy the enchantment as well. I was not going to let him harm my people. I reached into the bag and withdrew the sword of Odysseus, forged by Hephaestus and enchanted by Athena, Goddess of War.

The mage began chanting. I was trying to be fair and not attack unless he attacked me. I should have cut him down immediately. His chant took shape in front of me. He had summoned a very large and very powerful demon to do battle with me. Smart move. The only swordsman I had ever met who might have defeated me while I was wielding the sword of Odysseus was Alexander. I had used it to slay the Scylla. But this demon in front of me was armored and strong and angry. I could see he wore a chain and detected the link to his master. This was not a free demon. This was a demon bound to a magus and forced to do his will. The anger was not directed at me specifically, but filled him in such a way that it would destroy anything in its path.

And he attacked.

I barely missed losing my head with the first swing of his axe. I ducked and dove and ran. Occasionally, I got a strike in or stabbed at some sensitive part. It only served to make it angrier. And the battle went on and on.

I tried to talk to the demon in front of me, but I'm not sure he understood language at all. He seemed to be directed by the continued chanting of the magus. I was fading. He seemed to have a boundless supply of energy and strength. In that, he reminded me of Achilles at Troy. I made a desperate stab at his heel, but narrowly missed the next swing of his mighty axe. I had lost all pretense of keeping my human form. I was fully the ram-horned demon of Pinaruti, swelling to a size that might intimidate a lesser being. But not the unnamed demon before me. I tripped over the satchel I'd dropped on the ground and the monster spotted it. He focused his next blow on the satchel and I snatched it away as he buried his axe in the ground where it had lain.

"Athena, for the sake of Odysseus, bless and defend me," I whispered as I struggled to my feet.

Deus ex machina. It was a term we used in the theatre that meant, 'Saved by the gods.' Literally, it was 'god in a machine.' It came into being during the production of Euripides' Medea. I was still in Athens at the time, acting in the chorus. In the play, Medea had just killed King Creon and his daughter. She taunts Jason (the one of golden fleece and Argonauts fame) from the window of her house, telling him she has killed their children, too. The house is set afire as Jason swears he'll kill her, but just then, a chariot of the gods flies in and Medea is borne off stage. God in a machine—with a huge number of levers and pulleys involved.

I digress.

I felt new strength flow into me. The sword of Odysseus glowed. A voice whispered in my ear, "Sever the chain that binds him."

What? Sever the chain and set the brute free in the world? No one would be safe! But as his axe swung near me and took a chip out of one of my horns, I dove and rolled between its legs. I could see the metaphysical chain that bound the monster to its master and swung the sword with all my might.

The jolt it gave me as it bit into the psychic link stunned my arms. I went completely numb and thought I'd breathed my last. I saw the sword burst into flame and disintegrate in my hands as it bit through the link that bound master and slave.

The monster froze for a moment, roaring at the sky before it turned toward its still-chanting master and advanced. I saw a terrified look in the mage's eye just before the monster sliced him in half and devoured him.

There was a shimmer in the air as the liberated demon turned once again toward me. Its presence, however, had been maintained only by the chanting of the master. Before it could advance on me, it turned to vapor and dust and was gone.

So also, were Athena and the Sword of Odysseus gone.

"You are no longer linked to me, demon," I heard her voice whisper. "The sword is gone as Odysseus is gone. Do not call on me again."

And then I was alone in the desert.

In the twentieth and twenty-first centuries, when I became familiar with movies and special effects, I've often thought that the epic battle in the desert would be a great scene in a movie—perhaps one that traced the life and adventures of the Sword of Odysseus. It would be the final scene as the hero turns away from the place of the battle and goes to join the lover he has protected at the cost of the legendary blade.

Which is what I did. As soon as I could find a fairly secure place on Mount Sinai, I crawled into my satchel and spent several days loving my women and recouping my senses. I came up with a new body, patterned after one of the men in the infinity room, and returned to my journey—not sure exactly where I was or where I was going.

"You see sand. You need to trust me on this, Bob. I see oil. Imagine all this land planted in olive trees, bearing fruit to be pressed into oil. Barrels of oil. It is in the ground and we harvest it from the trees. Enough oil to light all the lamps in the world. And it is ours."

I looked at the fellow I'd come across in the middle of the desert. It took me a bit to recover from my ordeal, and as I wandered deep into Arabia, I'd come across an oasis with colorful tents and banners, as if it were advertising its presence. As I approached the gaily colored encampment, a kid ran up to me, offering me a ride on a camel. A man offered me a ride on his wife. Three people tried to feed me roasted meat on a stick, honey cakes, and cold soup. The place was as noisy as the market in Alexandria. All the while, I was being conducted to the center tent and I had to wonder what kind of powerful sheikh I would meet there.

I met Doug. That wasn't actually his name, but why bother making up another hard to pronounce Arabian name? You'd just forget it anyway. He was happy, as long as he could call me Bob. Sure.

"But it's going to take time and money to develop this paradise, Bob. And that's why I'm offering you this once in a lifetime opportunity to get in on the ground floor. I want you, Bob, to become my partner and my agent. I can tell, you are a man who has connections. You can visit a king and sell him on the idea. And it's so simple, it's genius!"

"What are you talking about, Doug?"

"I want you to buy one share of the future. Now, you might think this will cost you a king's ransom, but I tell you, today only, I can give you a deal that you will not believe. How much do you think this desert paradise is worth, Bob? Five silver talents? Ten? Wait, let me sweeten the deal. Did you see that fine camel standing by the tent when you arrived? It's yours! Now, what do you think? Eleven talents? Fifteen? How about this. We'll include a tent of your own and five beautiful virgins to start your harem. What do you think? Twenty talents? I have a surprise for you, Bob. But first let's have a little dinner and entertainment. Wine!"

He was slick. He paraded women dancing in front of me, two feeding me, another massaging my shoulders and another holding my wine glass. I could see that just a share of the operation here in the oasis might be worth twenty-five talents. I liked Doug! And I liked the dancing girl who was bouncing on my cock.

"Now, let me lay my cards on the table, Bob. I can offer you this one-time deal for not twenty talents. Not ten talents. Not five talents. But for one silver talent. You heard me right. One silver talent."

"How can you offer all this for one talent of silver, Doug? What's the catch?" To be fair, that wasn't cheap. If you were comparing it to the value of silver today, you'd be talking about $10,000-$15,000. A talent of silver weighed around fifty-five pounds.

"You're probably asking yourself, 'How can Doug offer all this for one talent? There must be a catch.' I'll tell you." Apparently, he hadn't heard me ask that question. "You are the catch. I can tell you are enthusiastic about this dream, so I'm going to tell you to go out and sell the dream to two other people. But you don't sell it for one silver talent; you sell it for two. When you sell a share for two talents, you keep one and send one to me. I send the buyer a certificate for his share. This is the beauty, Bob. When you sell two shares, you'll have doubled your investment talents from one to two. Not only that, but you still own your share, which now has a market value of two talents."

"Sounds like mathematics," I said. The wine was really good. So was the naked beauty sitting in my lap.

"When you sell a share, it's important that you sell the concept, Bob. Have you seen the pyramids at Giza? You will be sitting at the top of the pyramid. Your two new shareholders need to go out and sell to two more investors each. Only, wait. They don't sell a share for two talents. They sell the shares for four talents. They keep two talents from each and double their investment. They send you two talents and you quadruple your investment, sending me just one talent of silver per share to generate the ownership certificate. Not only that, but you still have your original share which is now worth four talents, not just one. What do you think of the deal now, Bob?"

I thought the deal was pretty good, just like the talented pussy milking my cock was. He really sold the deal. I gave him a talent for my share.

END OF PART V
END OF VOLUME 1

Bob's Memoir

4,000 Years as a Free Demon

Vol. 2: After Caesar (mostly)

PROLOGUE

H!I'M BOB and I'll be... Yeah, you know the rest. I'm a demon. I've been around for something over 4,000 years. For the last several centuries, I've been looking for a place where I can permanently hide my infinity room and crawl in. This second volume of my memoirs, "After Caesar (Mostly)," is all about how I got to the place where we are today—trying to escape from earth.

There's a lot of story to be told on our way, though. Since you might not have read the first volume, "Before Caesar (Mostly)," I've been told I need to refresh a few things, just so you won't be all "Dazed and Confused." (Gotta love Led Zeppelin.) So, I'll tell you what is what and who is who among those left over from the first volume. Of course, most of the people I've talked about are mere human, so they don't continue in the story unless they've found a place in the infinity room. I do have a passing acquaintance with a number of gods from different ages and parts of the world. I don't brag about that. Most have been congenial, but they operate on a different plane than the natural world.

The infinity room is the result of a panicked spell I cast on an old leather satchel. I needed someplace to stow away everything in Pinaruti's house, including my wives and concubines, before the King of Knossos broke down the doors. (Some trivial thing about me stealing his new wife.) It was the same kind of spell Egyptian conjurers used to fit djinni in bottles. It made what was inside the container larger than what was outside. I had no idea how much bigger!

It seems I have close to half a million people dwelling in the infinity room at the start of this story, including the remnants of a couple of harems I was asked to take care of, some of the sailors who were with Odysseus, a whole lot of librarians—including those from the Library of Alexandria—the priestesses of Aphrodite, and various lovers, concubines, and stowaways. It always seems to be big enough for everyone. Things I take into the infinity room, bring along the memory of their environment and it comes into existence around them. Especially libraries. I love libraries.

And people. When a person enters the infinity room from the natural world, he, she, or they stop aging. I won't say they get younger, but they get healthier and stronger and look younger and fitter. There are exceptions. People who are born into the infinity room seem to age normally—or at least normally for the infinity room. That might be a little slower than in the natural world. It's hard to tell because there is no real timeline in the infinity room. I'm pretty convinced that whatever time is there, runs differently than in the natural world. I've never been able to figure it out.

Let that be a warning to you young sorcerers out there. It is possible to work magic without understanding what you are manifesting. I have a concubine named Chione who is mute because I didn't want her to be able to talk about the infinity room when we were in the natural world. I cast a silence spell and it turned out that she couldn't speak at all. She bears me no ill will, though, and is among the kindest and most loving of my entourage. Just one of many instances in which a spell I cast didn't turn out the way I expected.

Speaking of which, I had two wives in the infinity room as of Caesar—Nimia and Penelope. Nimia was with me back in Knossos when I had to flee the king. I stuffed her into the infinity room and mostly she has stayed there, looking as fresh and young as the eighteen-year-old she was when I first married her. Penelope was once the wife of Odysseus. You know, the fabled hero of the Trojan War. I knew him as a cowardly idiot who got himself killed while hiding in the Temple of Aphrodite in Ilium. I adopted the likeness of his body and all his memories, then set sail for Ithaca. Poseidon made sure I had a miserable time of it, but Athene insisted that since I had Odysseus's likeness and was passing myself off as him, I needed to return to Ithaca and set his house straight. I came clean with Penelope and we left her son in charge and took off. She married me and took up residence in the infinity room, looking fresh and healthy and fairly young, despite her forty years.

Things get a little confusing here because my third wife, Esmeralda, was actually married in the late 1400s, but I told the story in the first volume, even though it was out of order. Lots of this story is out of order. I just keep remembering things and have to write them down. I'd been trapped in the infinity room by Esmeralda's great grandmother and Esmeralda let me out. She was still only a kid at the time, but a few years later, she was as firmly attached to me as any of my other wives.

And then there are my possessions, Josie, Pari, Princess Agora, and Maya. Josie was the first who ever used those magic words, "Possess me!" I did. Now, it is like we think with one mind and we are closer than any other relationship I can imagine. Pari was a concubine in Nebuchadnezzar's harem that he gave to me as a reward for telling him the meaning of his dream. Her harem mate, Chione, was given to me a few years later. But Pari asked me to possess her and I did. I think Chione would have asked me, but she couldn't talk. Oh, well.

I told the story of Princess Agora late in the previous volume, but I possessed her out of desperation. She was going insane and was a near vegetable because she couldn't comprehend a world that was bigger than her island. She's the only one I ever possessed without her asking me, but I gave her the opportunity later to be freed. She declined. She not only stays in the infinity room, she mostly stays in the bedroom or adjoining rooms of my palace there. She's truly agoraphobic.

Let me see. I also mentioned Maya in the first volume. She's Mayan and I met her at the behest of her god, Kukulcán. We were sent on a mission to save as many of her people as we could before the Spaniards got to them. The first thing she did was ask me to possess her, and after I was sure she understood who I was and had a talk with her god and goddess, I did. Of course, that was in the sixteenth century and now we have to go back in time to the first century After Caesar (AC). I'll pick up the story soon after I dropped Issa off in India.

No, I won't do it that easily. I think there are important stories to be told that I just remembered, so I'll start in the 1960s in San Francisco. Don't worry; I'll get around to telling about the other stuff, but this is fresh in my mind since I've been talking about my possessions. That's really all you need to know to understand most of the second volume.

Except that I tend to ramble. Oh, and I love to sail.

Let the story begin. Again.

Part VI
A Woman's Work

Image by ArtnMotions, ID 1851746746 licensed from Shutterstock.com.

27
Unharnessed Joy

>-- ◆ --<

I WAS IN SAN FRANCISCO—Oh, I don't know. Fifty... seventy-five... eighty years ago? Paying attention to dates and time is a pain. Whenever I get tempted to, I find a quiet place to hide and go to the infinity room for a while. When I come out of the room, I have no idea what century it even is. Anyway, this was last century.

As I was saying: San Francisco. I owned a little shop down on Haight Street and was just trying to maintain a low profile in this crazy country. North Beach was too crowded and expensive, so I moved down to Upper Haight. I started off selling liquor and cigarettes. Then I moved into souvenirs as tourists started coming around. Seemed everyone wanted clothes like what my girls wore when they came in to work in the shop with me. So, they started sewing things up in the infinity room and bringing them into the shop to sell. The weather was great most of the year, so the lightweight cottons we wore in the desert weren't out of place. I put a couple of dressing rooms in the shop and before long, I was doing a bigger business selling clothing than liquor. And to prettier girls.

I especially enjoyed going up to North Beach on Friday or Saturday nights and hanging out with the poets and drummers. It was after one of those outings that I remembered a drum I had from way back when I was employed by the god Ninra. I went into the infinity room to find it. It was there, in the back of a store room under a scenery prop from our Greek theatre days. There was a bit of dyed silk from China there, too. I pulled it out and suggested the girls might try something made out of that and they got all excited about it.

Finally, I found Ninra's drum. I wasn't going to take the original drum out into the air of the natural world. I wasn't sure how well it would hold up. But I made a copy of it with my duplication spell and sat to learn to play it. I wasn't very good at maintaining a constant rhythm on the djun-djun, but as far as I could tell, no one who played in the café bars had a sense of rhythm anyway. I guess they were all playing jazz—a little off key and half a beat behind.

I took the replica up to the Beach with me one night and sat in while a couple of poets recited incredibly long poems. People liked the effect of me squeezing the drum between my knees and getting it to change pitch in the middle of a strike. They nodded their heads and said, "Play it, man. Say it." I got the message. They wanted me to contribute some poetry while I played. Shit. Well, like I said, it seems like what you needed in this club was a fast tongue and about any old story. I took a deep breath.

I was floating alone on the deep blue sea
with no work or place I needed to be.
I heard a noise behind me and looked around.
There was a babe there swaying with the rock of the boat
and not a stitch of clothes—covered only by her long blonde hair,
and that was almost no cover at all.
None at all
No cover at all
Just her long blonde hair
And no cover at all.

A girl like this, you don't molest;
just sit and wait to see how she'll move
and if she'll offer a smoke
or drink your wine.
And you hope that heaven
has just answered your prayers.
Your prayers, your prayers
Answered your prayers
And sent you a goddess
To warm up your nights.

Then she stepped into my arms
and I was lost.
And found and lost again.
I tell you this babe took me straight to heaven
And dropped me a million miles back to the sea.
It's a million miles from heaven to sea
But it makes no difference how far you fall
If you've been to heaven
In the arms of a goddess.

But no one believes in the goddess these days.
No one will take the risk to assail heaven.
No one gives sweet offerings of honey cakes
Or chilled goat's milk
to satisfy her appetite wherever it takes you
and let her have whatever you are.
Whatever you are, whatever you are.
Do you dare let that babe know
Whatever you are?
Don't ask me—she already knows.

I ended with a springing note that fell on a silent crowd and was eaten up by the smoke. I think I really had them, right up to that last verse.

>-- ◄◆► --‹

My performance didn't fall completely flat. I had a few new customers at Erosland Boutique. We'd adopted the name 'Boutique' after we started carrying clothes and jewelry. Supplying clothes, jewelry, alcohol, and tobacco had kept a whole country in the infinity room active and producing. People in the infinity room were always working to find new and creative projects. As long as they were working for Bob, their needs were all met.

"You laid some really deep shit on us last night, man," a customer said. I glanced his direction and recognized one of the poets from the café. "Don't let the cubes in the room get you down. They're trying but just can't cut it. Um..." He paused to light a cigarette. "I liked that drum you played. Got any in the shop here?"

That gave me pause. I hadn't thought of selling the djun-djun. It could be another whole industry.

"I can get them. Don't have it today, but later this week," I said.

"Cool. Don't rip me off with the price, okay?"

"Wouldn't dream of it."

I needed to go visit some music shops and find out what a fair price would be for a small drum. I'd done the same kind of research when it came to selling clothes. I had no idea what things were worth in the current currency.

He left and I started meeting more people from the beat café. Some just wanted to hang out and look at the hot mommas who worked in the store with me.

Before any of the girls were allowed in the store or to accompany me to a beat café, they had to learn the language. They only worked a maximum of one day a week, so they didn't get a lot of practice in the natural world. I tested them on the language myself. As years progressed, it seemed that was less important as no one understood anyone anyway. At first, some of the girls sounded like a mashed-up recording.

"Hey, Big Daddy. Cast an eyeball at this neato merch. I bet you've got a hot momma waiting at home and this little dress would really razz her berries. She'll have you out for a little back seat bingo at the passion palace before you know it. I'll clue you, my boyfriend got me one and he had it made in the shade. And that's good because he's usually on a trip for biscuits when it comes to pleasing me. Not this time. I flipped for him. Meanwhile, back at the ranch, give me the bread for this and take it home to your baby. And shoot low out there. They're riding Shetlands!"

I knew what all the words meant and I still couldn't understand her! But they got better at it as time went by and ended up sounding like pretty normal hipsters. Business was good.

Which brings me to the subject I was going to talk about.

>-- ◆ --<

More and more people moved toward the Haight and some of the cafés got a makeover into really hip joints late at night. Daytime they still mostly just served coffee and donuts. The scene changed when it got late. I have to say, I might have helped things change. But the change didn't stop where I wanted it to.

The culture was changing from the beat to the hip and the neighborhood had a lot more kids who really weren't old enough for either smoke or liquor. I had to keep them out of parts of the store and I really hated that. Back in the day, we didn't have all these age laws about who could smoke or drink. Alexander had conquered the Greeks by the time he was eighteen, and believe me, he drank whatever he wanted.

Oh, brother. America was already turning me into a crotchety old man.

So, I went with the flow and expanded the shop out the back door. We got a reputation as a head shop and it was bitchin'. A little ganja, which we grew away from where anyone could interfere, in the infinity room. We also kept an eye out for kids who were on their last legs. It was sad. They came here to turn on, tune in, and drop out. And for some of them, that turned out to be a little more than they could handle.

It was a lot like being a rescue mission—something my harem was very familiar with by this time. We'd pick up a kid who was strung out and had lost her bearings. I always checked on her to make sure she'd fit in with us, but then we took her into the infinity room. Sometimes a guy, too. I hated to take kids that left families and friends behind, but it was really the only choice for many of them. If I'd left them alone, they'd have been dead in days. And after we got them where life had meaning, they were very different people.

Oh, yes. The point of this story. Erosland Boutique became a gathering point for all kinds of demonstrations. I never turned anyone away, so people felt safe and comfortable, even when tensions were high. Like they were with the feminist movement.

It didn't take me long to figure out that 'feminist' was a description of what I'd been all my life. You might say, "Hold on, Bob. You've got a harem of who-knows-how-many women that you have sex with. They all worship you and you say you're a feminist? How so?"

Well, I've always believed that women were self-determinate. I never forced myself on anyone and I always treated my women with love and respect. I didn't expect any of them to do anything I wasn't willing to do—though there were many things they were much better at than I was. All the way back when Josie became my possession, it was her choice and she's never regretted it.

Anyway, when a group came to me and asked if they could hold a rally out in front of our store, I welcomed them and did what I could to make sure it was a safe place for them to have their demonstration.

"We are people! We are not the property of men!" shouted a speaker at the rally.

They'd asked for and we provided a trash barrel for them as they intended to mimic gatherings that had begun after the Miss America Pageant in New Jersey. I found it moderately amusing, but was sympathetic with the cause, nonetheless.

"Women must come together and fight for equality in the workplace, in the government, and in the home. We will shuck off the vestments of bondage and make our place in the world as equals, not as chattel." With that she tossed a mop into the trash barrel. Another woman stepped up to toss a copy of *Playboy* magazine in the barrel. Another threw in a pan. And then one lone brave woman stood in front of the barrel, reached under her shirt, and in a move that had puzzled men for nearly a century, stripped off her bra and threw it in the garbage. There were a lot of cheers, but no one else moved to copy her.

I wholly approved. I couldn't imagine why she should ever need to wear such an instrument of torture. She didn't need the support. The bra only emphasized the minimal size of her breasts, as if they needed the extra layer of padding to be feminine. I thought she looked perfectly wonderful.

That was all there was to the infamous bra burning events. I'm sure one or more were actually burned, just as a few young men burned their draft cards, but they were symbolic. There was no horde of women stripping off their underwear and throwing it on a pyre. One check of the prices of those things and you'd understand why. As the rally broke up—peaceful and celebratory—I went out and collected the trash bin to take to the back for disposal in our dumpster.

"Excuse me," a timid voice said. "Uh, would you mind if I get something out of there before you dump it?"

I turned to find the woman who had stripped off her bra. I reached down into the barrel and pulled it out to hand to her.

"This?" I asked.

"Yes. This is so embarrassing."

"You don't really need it, you know. I can't think of one thing that article of clothing does for you except make you uncomfortable. You're welcome to come in the store and use our changing room if you're really going to put it back on."

"Just like a man," she huffed as she followed me into the store. "To a woman this is a sign of bondage. To you, it's a symbol of sex. Take it off and we're easy. Leave it on and we're frigid. If we're small in the chest, build it up. If we're large, press it together and shove it up and out. A cruel thing invented by men that traps us whether we wear it or not."

"That may be. But you'll find the women here in the store... let me see if there are any who... no... none of the women working here today has ever worn a bra. Ever. In their lives," I said.

"They're all... naked under those flimsy clothes? Aren't they afraid of being raped?"

I turned on her, nearly giving way to my fury at the suggestion.

"If anyone attempted that, I would kill him," I growled. She was taken aback. She didn't go into the dressing room, but came on into the store to look around, the bra hanging forgotten from her hand.

"Sounds rather caveman of you," she said. "Women shouldn't need to depend on men to protect them. We shouldn't *need* to be protected and if we did, we should be able to do it ourselves."

"Hmm. I agree. Watch this." With those words, I slipped up behind Maya, who happened to be working that day. She was a slight girl, about fifteen when she'd entered the infinity room; but that was about three or more centuries ago. Still, I was easily twice her size. I grabbed her around the waist and slapped a hand across her mouth. She reacted at once, slamming a foot down on my instep and elbowing me in the balls. She grabbed my arm and sidestepped, flipping me over her shoulder in such a way that I landed flat on my back with her foot on its way to my nose. She pulled herself up short and threw herself backward and away from me.

"Bob! Why did you do that? I could have hurt you! Are you okay, baby?"

I caught my breath and nodded. I rolled to my side and raised an eyebrow at the braless protester.

"Is that what you had in mind?" I asked.

"That was unbelievable. Are you all right, little girl?"

"Don't insult me, chica. I'm older than you," Maya said. "You put him up to that? You think I want to hurt my man? You should pay for that."

I think Maya was ready to lay her hands on the woman and I was trying to get in a position between them.

"I'm sorry! I didn't know he was going to do that. I just said women should be able to protect themselves. You were amazing. Can you teach me how to do that?"

"Are you going to join us?" Maya asked. "Who are you?"

"I'm Liz and I don't know who you are to join. Is it a self-defense club?"

Ali and Esmeralda were working as well and came up beside Maya and me. They put their arms around us.

"We're much more than a club," Esmeralda said. "We're family. It might be a little too much for you to understand at first. You should get to know Bob a little."

"Are you like, Mormon or something? Isn't that a little illegal?" Liz asked.

"Mmm. More like a commune, I suppose you'd say. Regardless, we're not recruiting. With that said, however, I'd like to get to know you better. You showed remarkable courage at the rally and even in coming into the store with me without your armor on."

She looked down at the bra in her hand as if it were something foreign and she didn't know where it came from. She quickly stuffed it in her handbag.

"Okay," she said suddenly, as if she just accepted an invitation that I wasn't sure I'd made. "There's a great little restaurant just off Grant in Chinatown. It's not expensive, but I can't pay for all of you. I can pay for myself."

"We don't go out at night unless Bob has something special for us. We like to go home after work," Ali said. "Give us a minute to get him cleaned up upstairs and you can have him for the night."

"The night? I... I'm sure I won't need him for the night... I mean, it's not like a date with your husband or boyfriend or whatever he is," Liz stammered.

"Don't worry. You can date him if you want to. Most of us just sleep with him," Esmeralda laughed. "Free love and all that, you know?"

I locked the door to the shop and went up the back stairs to the little apartment above. The girls all gave me a quick kiss, told me to have fun, and went through the gateway into the infinity room. I did a quick clothing change so I didn't look quite like a shopkeeper and went down to join Liz. On the street, I waved down a cab and she gave the driver directions to the restaurant she'd chosen. We went upstairs to find a charming dim sum restaurant. The servers immediately began bringing trays heaped with plates that we helped ourselves to as we talked.

"So, I see that the movement is getting too focused on defining a new role for women instead of freeing them from a life determined by expected roles," she said as we ate.

"Exactly. If you are simply saying a woman has to be something different than she is, you are forcing her into a life path the same as she was before. True choice means a woman should be able to choose to work or to be a stay-at-home wife and mother. Of course, it means that men should have that choice as well. Many are trapped by society's expectation of what they have to be in order to be considered a man."

I believe she was a little surprised that I understood so well what the women's movement was about. It turned out that we got along well, even laughing at each other's jokes. She came home with me and came to my room.

"I'm a fully liberated woman," she declared. "I can choose to have sex with anyone I want to. It doesn't mean I've accepted a life role or that I'm less of a good woman." It sounded a bit like she was defending her choice to herself. Whatever she needed.

"I agree. As two consenting adults, we should be able to do as we please when it comes to a personal relationship," I said.

And Liz definitely pleased me. I had subtly been following the unguarded points of her nipples through her shirt all evening. When the shirt came off, I found them even more delightful. She seemed to think my nipples were just as attractive and spent time tonguing them just as I spent time with hers. She soon found what a talented tongue I had and couldn't believe I would go down on her and lick through her thick red bush.

"But men only want you to suck them off," she said. "They never want to return the favor!"

"Stereotypes, sweetheart. Don't box me in with all the other men you've known," I said as I lapped at her button until she screamed in delight. She was delicious and I vowed that if she allowed it, I would feast between her legs often. When I finally parted the folds of her pussy with my cock, her eyes sprang open as if she didn't know what was happening. She was very vocal.

"What are you putting in me? That can't be your cock! It's huge. Oh, my god! I'm being stretched. I'm so full! Oh! Make me come again! Take me. Fuck me, you monster! Possess me!"

Oh, those magic words. I was a little reluctant, but it was difficult to pass up that kind of invitation from a woman so open to possession. I would need to teach her a little about what it meant to be an independent woman. I'd been there. And she needed to know fully what it meant to be a possession.

I moved into her body, her mind, her heart, and her soul. I possessed her.

28
ON BECOMING A WOMAN

>-- ◆◇◆ --<

THAT TAKES ME BACK to a couple of thousand years ago, which was the whole point of my story with Liz. This was back a few years—maybe a hundred or two—after I'd parted ways with Issa. I'd been in India for quite some time, enjoying the sites and the people. I'd even taken time—with several of my women—to study Buddhism. I could see Issa's hand in that easily. He told me he had been here before and studied the ancient and peaceful religion.

That was a funny thing to me. Budhism is such a peaceful religion, and yet it honors its god of war, Skanda, or Lord Kartikeya. Skanda is the protector of the people and—I shuddered—the slayer of demons. Well, I'd killed one myself once. I determined to simply avoid contact with him.

Given an Indian makeover and some silent observation of customs, I blended in well with the populace and did not try to join the wealthiest or most powerful people. I was a trader. I used my boat to travel from island to mainland with goods needed by one or the other. And sometimes, I journeyed across the subcontinent on foot with a caravan bringing rare items from the coast to the people farther inland. It was a good life and I genuinely liked the people of India.

Occasionally, I would find a woman in a household who felt it was her duty and privilege to provide sex for the guest (me). Mostly, though, the natives of India were respectful of and possessive of their women, so I contented myself with slipping into the infinity room where there were dozens of women eagerly waiting me to bed them.

>-- ◆◇◆ --<

"Buy me, Bob," my lover said. I had gone to bed in the home of my client, Ravi. Not long after, his wife had joined me there.

"I don't trade in people," I said.

"Then buy me and set me free. I will still serve you forever."

"Forever, Lakshmi, is a very long time. Why do you wish to escape from your husband?" I asked.

"He does not care for me. He took my dowry and gambled it away. Then he went to the temple Devadasi and spent the rest there to attract good luck. Since then, he has been a successful trader but prefers the Devadasi to his own wife. I languish in unfulfillment. Only when a guest arrives does he send me to be filled. And you fill me like no other. Buy me and take me away from here."

It was not unheard of. In fact, I'd often purchased slave women I felt were being abused and set them free. Nor did they all immediately submit to me. Some came to me to 'pay me' for freeing them. Those I refused. Some ran away as soon as they were free. And some few had joined my harem when they discovered what a life of freedom in my world could truly be like. I wasn't sure which category Lakshmi would fall into, but it didn't make a difference to me. I negotiated with her husband.

"I can tell you are not satisfied with my offer," Ravi said. "This is beautiful silk, but to trade, I must see a profit. If I pay more, I cannot afford to feed my household."

I noted that he did not say family. Lakshmi told me there were no children in the house and she was the only wife. But he kept a dozen female servants, whom I could only guess served him in the ways Lakshmi was denied.

"I am a lone traveler," I said. Not exactly true since I had arrived with a caravan. "My rugs have no company waiting for me when I set up my tent. I would give you this fine measure of silk as well as five tetradrachmas of silver if you will give me your wife, Lakshmi."

"Bob, Bob, Bob. I would like to take you up on your offer, but other traders in the area would soon hail me as a dishonest man and I would lose all my trade. If you would have my wife in exchange for the silk, that I can give you. But no coins must transfer between us when a person is involved. I am not a slaver and would not be known as one," Ravi said.

"I honor your commitment to honesty," I said. "In honor of that and the fair trade you have offered me, I will donate five silver tetradrachma to the temple of Yellamma in your name. May the goddess grant you your heart's desire."

The deal was done. The temple gladly accepted my donation and I was nearly dragged inside to make a prayer while being drained of my semen, but I passed that privilege on to Ravi who happily spent the next month getting his heart's desire.

"Bob, was I worth so much?" Lakshmi said as she waited naked in my tent.

"Lakshmi, your value has no price. Your freedom was assured as soon as I dropped the coins at the temple. Now you may dress and determine what the course of your life will be from this point forward," I said.

"You do not want me?" she asked near tears. "Am I nothing to a man so wealthy as you?"

"Lakshmi, my desire is to dwell between your thighs. But you do not owe me for the gift of your freedom. You will not be forced into a marriage or a bed. You may travel or find a new husband or even establish your own household. But I will not take you only because you believe you owe me for your freedom. It would no longer be freedom."

She sat on my sleeping rug for a long time as she contemplated what I had said. She made no move to dress, which I found rather distracting. She was a very attractive woman of about eighteen, and for all her claims of abuse in the household, it was obvious she had not been subject to hard labor or to beatings. I chalked it up to emotional abuse of not being valued for herself in his household. I promised myself that would never be the case in my household, with me or with any of my women.

As she sat contemplating her future, I opened a portal into the infinity room and my wives and concubines hurried into the tent with food and drink for us. Of course, they were all as naked as Lakshmi and the woman watched them intently as they went about their tasks, each pausing for a moment of loving kisses and touches with me before she returned to the infinity room.

"Bob, you are a great *ojha*," Lakshmi said, using the local word for shaman or perhaps sorcerer. "I know that you must be pure of heart to work such magic as I have seen. My heart cries out to be the lover of such a man and to bring him joy all his days. I see you have many women who feel the same as I do. I would become one of them. Will you take me to your room beyond this door and install me as the least of all your women?" She prostrated herself in obeisance.

"Rise up, Lakshmi. Let us sit and dine and talk about what may be. Do you not wish to be free to choose any life you might want?"

"Would it not be my prerogative as a free woman to choose a life as a wife to the man I love?"

"Hmm," I said, contemplating the life of a free woman. "In other words, freedom as you understand it includes the freedom to not be free?"

"Is anyone truly free in any other sense? I have thought about this all my life, as I listened to the teachings of a local Brahmin. At one point or another, we choose what we will be bound to or we are forced into bondage. No person is ever free without thought or responsibility save blessed Buddha. To imagine we are, merely points us to a deeper bondage."

"Lakshmi, I think this is the beginning of a beautiful relationship. I accept you and will take you as my wife."

That was a word that brought her great joy and she expressed her joy by pushing aside our table of food and planting herself on my staff of pleasure repeatedly.

For all my sojourn in India, Lakshmi was my wife when I was with people or needed an assistant. Like the other women, she stayed in the infinity room the rest of the time and, as a result, did not age.

>-- ⬥ --<

Which brings me to the point of this story—I think. I was preparing to go out in the bazaar of a large city near the southern tip of the continent. I would be loading my boat with goods to trade up the east coast of India over the next few years. Of course, my little boat held much more than it appeared to, as I could put all my goods in the infinity room and then board the little craft.

Lakshmi was with me and just before I opened the tent, she grabbed my arm.

"Bob! You can't go out there. Your horns are showing!" she cried.

"Oh! How long have I had this body? I seem to have lost track. I'll have to put on a new look. Hold the flap open just a bit so I can see out from the back of the tent and I will choose a new body to model mine after."

I had worked the transformation spell so many times over the past centuries that I had only to fix an image in my mind and with a few words, I could transform to it. I watched out the little gap Lakshmi made in the tent and watched the people outside. I finally spotted a man I thought would be good to replicate. He was obviously a merchant and I always made a few little adjustments on the fly. I began the spell, focusing on the image I wanted to portray.

Just at that moment, a woman passed between me and the man. Normally, that would make no difference because the image was burned into my mind. But this woman was the most beautiful woman I had... Okay, I know you won't believe she was the most beautiful woman I'd ever seen, since I had lain with some of the world's finest women—including the goddess of love and lust herself. But she was so beautiful that it completely stopped my train of thought. She filled my vision with her beauty and as I finished the spell, I felt myself transform. Lakshmi turned to me and suddenly let the tent flap close as she gasped.

"Bob! Ah... What should I call you now?"

"What? Why not Bob like always?" I cleared my throat trying to get used to the treble tones of my new voice. *I might need to adjust that.*

"But... You're a woman!"

"What?" I looked down at myself, past the very nice tits I had on display to the vacancy between my legs. "What?" I repeated. Caught as I'd been by the charms of the woman outside, I must have muttered the feminine form of the transform verb instead of the masculine. There was no mistake that I was, in every detail, a woman.

"What am I going to do now?" I asked myself as I sank onto the rug. My boobs bounced. *Oh, blessed Aphrodite. Is this what they feel like to you?*

"Bob, stop touching yourself. You need to dress appropriately or our shopping day will be wasted."

"Dress. Clothing." I opened the door to the infinity room and my concubines immediately started giggling. They filed through the tent, touching me. I was quite embarrassed and kept making futile gestures to ward them off. Eventually, they got the message and brought me fine clothes. I was nearly ready to go out.

"Bob, we need a man. It is not wise for two women to go through the bazaar unescorted. We could find ourselves on an auction block. Especially, looking as hot as you do. Did you have to become so beautiful?" Lakshmi asked.

"Send me out a man willing to escort two beautiful women through the bazaar," I called into the infinity room. Really, it was ridiculous to think that I, *Bob*, needed an escort. I was sure I could handle myself.

Tony came out of the infinity room. I'd picked him up in Rome as a boy who was being picked on by several others because he was weak and nearsighted from reading so much. I'd asked him if he'd like to join my librarians and learn all the world could teach from books. He gladly accepted and once in the infinity room, blossomed into a handsome and strong youth.

"Wow!" he said when he saw Lakshmi and me. "Ladies, may I escort you through the bazaar?"

Well, that was what we called him for. We toured the area quickly and then went through at a deliberate pace, pausing at booths that especially interested me, and haggling for the goods I wanted. That was a problem.

"Now, young man, I can tell you are a man of sophisticated good taste, just by the women you keep. These rugs you are admiring are among the finest in India. Fine strong weave, and I will make you a great deal on them. Just thirty dinari each and you can take as many home with you as you want."

"Thirty dinari each?" I exclaimed. "The whole lot of them would not bring thirty dinari in Chandra. "We'll give you ten dinari for the lot of them."

The bastard pretended he didn't even hear me. He just kept talking to Tony.

"What you don't see here are the really special rugs I have behind the curtain. Why don't you come inside and have tea with me? We can arrange a good deal on rugs I've imported straight from Arabia," the merchant said to Tony.

"We have plenty of rugs from Arabia already. And every one of them is better quality than this rubbish," I said. "If you don't want to make an honest deal we can go elsewhere."

"I have a tent behind the shop here where you can stow your women while we talk. They won't be too soiled when we are finished and you will have a fine collection of rugs to take with you."

I jerked Tony's arm and he looked at me, suddenly aware of his surroundings. The merchant had been practicing a mesmerizing spell on him and I quickly did my best to reverse it. As Lakshmi and I pulled him away, he still glanced back at the rug display.

"Tony, snap out of it," I commanded. "We'll try that wine booth next. If it tastes good, I might be able to store a few casks of it for later."

"Ah, wine for you?" the next merchant said. "Well, young master, I should ask to see your ID, but since you are in the company of your mother... and uh... other mother, I'll let that pass by. Now this wine is still a bit young. It needs to age another five years, but it's a good vintage. Here, try a taste." He poured a bit into a glass and handed it to Tony. I snatched it away, took a drink, and spat it out.

"This wine has been left in the sun!" I declared. "I swear! Are there no honest merchants here?"

"Perhaps you would like to conduct your ladies to the bakers and grocers. You can leave them there and then we'll have a nice drink and talk business."

I was incensed. The scene was repeated all around the bazaar and we left without purchasing anything. Several had suggested Tony acquire a horse whip.

I spent the night in the infinity room, ranting about how unfair the people at this bazaar were as my wives and concubines looked on and giggled.

"Oh, Mighty Bob," Penelope said bowing to me. "You are two thousand years old. Have you never noticed that women are invisible? Oh, you see us just fine when you want sex, but have you ever once considered having us go out to do the trading? I dare say, I had more experience in trade than you did when we met, but you did not even take me with you to the markets."

"Is that so?" I exclaimed. "I've always treated you with the utmost respect. I ask your opinions. I depend on your advice. Am I such a tyrant?"

"No, dear," Josie said, curling up on my lap. She was naked and I had a typical reaction. Except I had no prick to react with. It was very confusing. My nipples hardened as she caressed my... breasts. "You are simply a man—even though you now have a very sexy woman's body. You should take this wonderful opportunity to let us teach you about how it is to be a woman." Her hand was inside my sari and my breasts were tingling.

"But how will we gather the trade goods we need when we head north?" I whined. What was this? I could actually feel tears trying to fill my eyes.

"You can work another spell on Lakshmi," Nimia said. "Turn her into a man and let her accompany you to the bazaar."

"Thanks a lot!" Lakshmi laughed. "But still, if you turn me into a man, I might get to fuck this beautiful woman you've become."

Oh, fuck!

Let me jump up to the third millennium CE. You know, the 2000s. Surprise! Still around. I have NEVER been opposed to any sexual act between two consenting adults. I figure a person's sexual orientation is the business of no one but that person and his or her or their partners. Born with male genitalia but want to be a female? Cut 'em off and go for it! A woman who prefers women lovers? Lick that clit! A man who prefers male lovers? Suck that dick! Whatever floats your boat, as they say.

So, I could never understand what the issue was about trans men and women in the twenty-first century. Or about gay men and lesbian women. I didn't make it my business to go around looking in everyone's pants to be sure they were what they appeared to be.

Achilles at Troy had Patroclus. They made a cute couple and that may have been why Achilles spent six months in his tent without coming out to fight. And when Patroclus was killed, Achilles went a little insane. He not only killed Hector (and half the Trojan army in the process), but he dragged the body behind his chariot around the city walls declaring his vengeance and grief. It was sheer luck that Paris managed to shoot one of Apollo's poison arrows and hit Achilles in the heel. But that was the power of Achilles' love for another man.

Alexander the Great had Hephaestion. That was in addition to his wife (or wives). He was so moved by Hephaestion's death that he drank himself to death. I could go on and on. Even King David had Saul's son Jonathan. They made a covenant together and Jonathan stripped himself before David and gave him his clothes. When Jonathan was killed (and King Saul committed suicide), David's lament declared, "Your love to me was more wonderful than the love of women." David seated Jonathan's son, Mephibosheth, at the table as if he were his own son.

The stories of women who loved women are older yet. My own women in Knossos were a testament to that, often preferring a woman's touch to a man's—even mine. The Isle of Lesbos, where women from all over the Mediterranean fled when they'd had their fill of men, lent its name to women like Sappho, who loved other women and were thereafter called lesbians. They were honored in Troy and were great allies. The great Amazon warriors had nothing to do with men at all unless they were ready to become pregnant. Then, like the praying mantis, after a man had fulfilled his function, he often lost his head.

What I'm saying is that when I was approached in a nightclub just a few years ago and asked if I would be interested in a very nice young man, I stopped to consider it. I'd long ago learned that a nice young man was a thing to be treasured. I'd just become so accustomed to women that I never considered a man as a lover and probably never would again.

Except during that span of a couple of decades in India in which I was a woman.

>-- ◄◆► --◄

Josie, the little vixen, had my nipples standing upright on my proud, firm breasts. It was obvious that I had never had a child. They were the breasts of a sixteen-year-old, not of a mother. Well, at the time I took Lakshmi as my consort, she had been only eighteen. But she had no children and was not much accustomed to the rites of marriage, even though she was an enthusiastic lover. My woman's body was, using today's vernacular... Well, let's just say I was hot.

I was also ripe for the taking. I wondered how much of my new body was truly a replica of the lady I saw in the market that caught my attention. I was sure she was of the Brahmin caste, as the light color of her skin would be a sure indication. Before I had really become accustomed to the new sensations my body was feeling, Josie had my clothes off me and several of my women were helping her explore my new woman's shape. And, oh! Did their hands and lips feel heavenly! When Josie kissed her way down my body, paying special attention to my sensitive nipples, I thought I would pass out long before she reached the junction of my thighs. I had often bellowed out my release when my cock was deep in a woman who pleased me—as nearly all women I was deep in did—but the squeal that issued from my lips as Josie's tongue first touched my clit was inescapable. Such a tiny bit of flesh to be so sensitive. I imagined every sensory nerve in my tongue, my lips, and formerly in my cock, had taken up residence in that pea-sized nub between my folds.

I wondered, frankly, if I could lengthen my tongue enough to lick my own brand new clitoris. I would never leave my bed. Thankfully, Josie was more than happy to loan me her tongue and I absolutely danced at the end of it. I could recognize the feeling of an orgasm coming upon me. My butt clenched and relaxed as if I were pumping semen into her mouth and my moan reached a pitch never before heard by dogs.

I was not prepared for it to immediately begin to rise again! As a man, the most likely thing for me to do after an orgasm was to sleep. But as a woman, I was ready to come again and again. It was only lack of stamina that caused me to finally fall off the peak and pass out.

>-- ◈ --<

"She's a virgin!" I heard one of the girls squeal from between my legs.

"Don't break it," said another. "It needs to be given to her lover."

"Does her tongue still satisfy as much as Bob's?"

"Even more, I think," said a voice I assumed was remotely attached to the clit I was licking. "I think she's picked up some signals from the way we treat her clit."

"She tastes so much better than Bob," said a voice I assumed had just brought me to my most recent orgasm. "Do you suppose we can get Bob to make his flavor more like this when he returns to us as a man?"

"I simply hope that I can experience what he does when I become a man," Lakshmi said beside me. I squeezed her breast hard and she squealed.

But that was the moment I first realized that the craving I felt in my body was only being aggravated by all the tongue action on my clit and nipples. At some point or another, I would want—no, desperately need—a man's hard cock in my soft pussy. The thought made me shudder and I came again.

29
SPARED BY A GODDESS

I WAS STANDING in front of my mirror, stark naked, looking at a woman I desperately wanted to fuck. Only it was me. This was definitely one of the strangest feelings I'd ever had.

"Are you going to stand there admiring yourself all day?" Pari asked. The Persian beauty Nebuchadnezzar had given me stood in front of the Egyptian Chione, who was unable to speak. It seemed the two were often in that position and I rather thought Chione would ask me to possess her if she *could* speak. I wasn't going to make the suggestion, though.

"My skin is so soft and silky," I breathed. "When I drape the dress over my body, my nerves come alive and I just want to touch myself."

"Mmmhmm. I know that feeling well. But you can't just spend all your time rubbing one off. Or a dozen. You said you wanted to get to the bazaar and... if I recall your words correctly... trade those charlatans into the ground."

"Yes. If they think they can cheat me, they will find they are facing significant losses. Now, give me a dress that doesn't set my nipples on fire!"

"Yes, of course. But who are you taking with you?" Pari asked as she put a lovely bit of silk over my head and ran her hands down my body. I shivered. "You know you need a man to speak for you."

"I can't believe I'm doing this. Is Lakshmi really willing?" I asked.

"You know she would do anything for you," Pari nodded.

"I don't want to push her into something she really doesn't want to do."

"If you let her fuck you while she's a man, she will consider herself the luckiest woman alive. Not that she doesn't already consider herself lucky just to be your wife."

"Well, bring her here and bring Oza for a model. He won't give the youthful impression that Tony does." Also, Oza wasn't the most feminine man around. I thought perhaps I could keep myself from responding to him as a man. Or to Lakshmi as Oza.

The two came in and Lakshmi pouted at me.

"You don't want me as handsome as you are beautiful?" she asked. "Can you at least give me your proud cock?"

"Um…" I considered the size of my cock and that Lakshmi's intent was to put it in me. "Don't you think that would be a little much? You should really have something… uh… more human sized."

"Oh, don't worry, Bobbie. I'll make sure you are ready and it won't really hurt. Will it, girls?" I shuddered at the thought of a cock my size tearing through my fragile maidenhead. I reached out to steady myself against Pari as I came a little. I was not used to being able to do that—or to having it happen to me. As a man, if I orgasmed, I orgasmed. That was it. There was no coming 'a little.' I'd found tremors shaking my body often as a woman that weren't quite full-blown orgasms but had all the signs of being a little one.

"Dear Lakshmi," I said as I gave her a little kiss. "You know that beautiful women are almost always seen with masculine men who are not the most attractive men in the market. Pardon me, Oza. There is nothing wrong with your looks. I just don't want to compete with my companion for who is the best looking now that I'm a hot girl! Now get ready and I'll make the transformation."

They stripped and stood side-by-side. Actually, there was nothing particularly lacking with Oza's equipment. I spoke the spell and transformed Lakshmi into a man. I sadly said goodbye to her graceful shape and looked at the man who stood in front of me. While I watched, both men looked my way and I saw their cocks come to attention.

"Dress," I said shortly. *Oh, my!*

Lakshmi and I gathered ourselves together and exited the infinity room into our tent to go about our trading.

>-- ◄◆► --<

We made some deals. I politely stayed just behind Lakshmi's shoulder and whispered bids to her and instructions for bargaining. Half the time, she didn't need my advice and once she told me to hush. She got a better price than I would have. I was mildly insulted.

"Oh!" I exclaimed, surprising myself with my high voice. I spun in place and Lakshmi turned to see what was going on. "All right! Who grabbed my butt?" I yelled. Everyone in the Bazaar, it seemed, turned to look at me.

"Just ignore it, honey," Lakshmi said. "It happens all the time."

"This happens to you?" I asked in disbelief.

"Almost every time we go out," she said.

"I can't believe it. What kind of animal does a thing like that?"

"A male animal."

"I'll cut the hand off the next male animal who grabs me."

"Please don't," she answered. "I don't know if I could save you and I don't think you want to reveal yourself."

"But he *violated* me!" I cried.

"I'm sorry, honey. Let's go back home and send our carriers out for our purchases."

I agreed, but my feelings were hurt. I couldn't believe I was being treated this way, simply because I was a woman.

I sniveled all the way back to our tent.

Lakshmi was high after our outing. All through dinner she talked about the deals she'd made and the bargains she'd driven. And when I said something and spoke about my contributions, I got a pat on the head or the thigh or the butt and was told I was certainly a good helper. So condescending!

And then, after I'd gone to bed and had a fun little romp with a couple of my girls, Lakshmi crawled in bed with me. And he had a hard on!

"Um... I don't think I can do this, Laks," I whispered as he began petting my breasts and feeling between my legs. I tried hard not to respond, but after the tongues and fingers of my concubines, I was a swamp down there.

"Oh, don't worry, baby. We won't do anything you aren't ready for, I promise."

"Yes, but..."

He kissed me. A man kissed me!

Or a woman I transformed into a man. I fought him weakly for a minute, but he was so insistent and strong. I told myself it was just Lakshmi playing a dress-up game and I should just go with it because we'd get to the part of fucking and it would be me and her, just like it always was, with my cock shoving into her hot little pussy. As soon as I thought that, my mouth opened to her questing tongue and my legs sort of automatically opened a bit. I didn't mean to do that, but I was thinking about the kiss and not about protecting my pussy. Her fingers slipped through my greasy channel and rubbed me just right. I was mounting quickly when she wedged a knee between my legs and started pushing them farther apart. It was so wrong and I just gushed with my first orgasm on the fingers of a man!

"Laks, baby, please don't... Oh, Laks, that feels so good. What are you doing to me?" I was moaning as he started sucking on my nipples and stroking my clit with the bulbous head of his cock. His cock! "Oh, no. Don't do that. Laks, I'm a virgin. Don't hurt me," I begged. At the same time, I discovered my hips were thrusting up at him and his cock was toying right at the entrance to my pussy and he was going to... "OW! Fucking hell! You hurt me!" I screamed.

"Relax, baby. It always hurts a little the first time. All women go through it. Just give it a minute to relax and you'll really like what comes next."

"But I didn't want..." He kissed me again and pushed deeper into my no-longer virgin pussy. "Oh, Laks. Oh, that is so wonderful," I sighed. "You just fill me up and I can hardly breathe."

"I told you you'd like it. Now just relax while I do all the work."

I did try to relax, but every time he pulled back, I felt so empty inside that I thrust my hips up to meet his inward push, feeling him go deeper and deeper into me. I had my eyes closed, so I didn't actually need to look at a man fucking me, but my body was rising to another delicious peak when Laks froze, pressed all the way into me as far as he could go, and started pulsing inside me. I froze as well, feeling the incredible gouts of semen he was pouring into me.

This was good! This was what this body was made for. I started thrusting up at him again and he rolled off me.

HE ROLLED OFF ME!

"Wait. Don't leave. I'm not done yet!" I yelled.

"Sorry, baby. You just knocked me out. I'm too sensitive to keep going just now. Maybe Josie can finish you. I need a little nap and then I'll be ready again."

And the bastard went to sleep!

>-- ◀◆▶ --<

The bastard woke up again in the middle of the night. Twice. When I woke up in the morning, he was lying right there and I had come running out of my pussy and he was hard and... I just jumped on and rode that pole for glory!

I did stop and check my body systems after I got up and bathed. I was definitely sore down there. I wanted to make sure that I could not get pregnant. I discovered the spell I'd used to immobilize my sperm worked just as well on my eggs and there was no chance I could get pregnant. I breathed a sigh of relief.

>-- ◀◆▶ --<

We had to go out and do more trading so we could fill our boat with goods for our trip north. I was a little slow moving when we went to the farthest end of the bazaar and began working our way back. We stopped at various booths and traded for goods like rice, spices, jewelry, and crafted wood items.

We were standing at a tea merchant when two men grabbed me from behind and threw a bag over my head. I struggled and cried out, but I didn't dare use magic out here and reveal that I was a demon. My hands were grabbed behind my back and I was tossed over someone's shoulder where I rode until I was unceremoniously dumped on a floor in a tent. I knew Lakshmi would be coming to save me, so I wasn't really worried.

A voice nearby said, "Strip her," and my fine silk dress was torn from top to bottom and pulled off my shoulders. My arms were held back and a man roughly grabbed my breasts. Then his hand jabbed between my legs and ran through my pussy. "This is no virgin!" he yelled at his companions. "There's dried come all over her." The bag was dragged off my head and a fistful of hair was dragged with it, causing me to scream. He hit me across the mouth.

I know you're asking, "Why didn't you fight back?" All I can say is that it is part of the transformation. I'd always chosen good strong well-built men for my models. I could enhance the strength a little, but it was primarily the strength of the body I transformed to, not the strength I had as a demon. The woman's body was not large and strong, even with the enhancements I did to it. As long as I was in this body, I was a woman and had comparable strength.

My first look in the dimly lit tent told me I was in the hands of a man who was highly experienced as a fighter and kidnapper. Women were bound to poles and frames in the tent, sagging against their bonds. They all looked like they had been beaten and raped. And I could tell we were all headed toward slavery. I only hoped Lakshmi had seen where they'd taken me and was coming with help.

When he'd stripped me, the thug came in contact with my satchel and had trouble figuring out how he'd missed that I was carrying a bag. He opened it to look inside.

"What's in the bag?" the chief of the kidnappers said.

"Nothing valuable. A couple of trinkets and girl stuff."

Unless I opened a gateway into the infinity room, the bag functioned like a normal bag. I contemplated opening the gateway now and summoning help. I drew in my breath and it was knocked out of me by the chief slugging me in the stomach.

"No screaming, bitch. Gag her!" A cloth was stuffed in my mouth and tied behind my head. No! That meant I couldn't speak a spell. I knew very well what happened when a spell was slurred. That was how I came into being. I couldn't risk even the simple spell to open the gateway. My hands were tied behind my back around one of the pole-like contraptions. My struggles did not help. The three men all felt me up, pinching at my nipples and shoving their fingers into my dried pussy. It clenched against the invasion.

"So tight," one said. "Use enough oil and it's still fuckable."

I shook my head and strained against the ropes that bound me, earning myself another slap in the face.

"Boss wouldn't be happy if he didn't get to be first. But that doesn't mean we can't use her mouth. Did you see those teeth? Perfect! She might not be a virgin, but she's definitely been kept soft and smooth."

So, the chief wasn't the highest in the group. There was a boss still to come. I shook my head again, earning another slap.

"Don't you even think about using those teeth on my cock, sweetie. Right now, I could slit your throat and the boss might be disappointed, but he'd be maddest about the mess on the carpets. We don't tolerate biters around here."

He shoved me down to my knees, my hands still tied to the pole behind me. Then he pulled open his trousers to show his erection. I prepared my spell. It would need to be spoken quickly. He pulled the gag from my mouth and I spit out the words. He obviously couldn't understand what I was saying. Nothing happened except that he shoved his dick in my mouth. He was so intent on raping me that he did not see the gateway open behind him and six armed warriors stream out of it. In seconds, the three kidnappers were unconscious.

I slumped forward against my bonds.

"Bobbie. Bobbie, wake up, baby!" I heard Josie sob. I managed to get my hair out of my eyes and felt that my bonds had been released. Josie knelt in front of me. "Are you okay, honey?" she asked. I looked at the scene in the tent. In addition to my warriors, there were a dozen of my women, releasing and comforting the other women who had been bound.

I shakily stood and kicked the chief in the nuts. His still-exposed cock jumped, but had shrunk to nearly nothing. Otherwise, there was no response.

"Lakshmi! Where is Lakshmi?" I managed to get out.

"We don't know. Where were you when this happened?"

"Tea merchant at the north end of the bazaar. We have to find him right away."

My six warriors immediately headed out of the tent and another armed force emerged from the infinity room. Josie led me to a large chair piled with cushions and one of my concubines brought me a dress. The girls were making sure the other captives were dressed. I read the memories of the traffickers while they were unconscious and found they were only three of a dozen or more pirates who were working the bazaar to capture new female slaves for a market across the sea. The captain of the crew would be here as well as other kidnappers before long.

"We need to put this place in order and make it look like the kidnappers were successful and everyone was still bound. Ladies," I addressed the dozen other women who had been released by my people. "We can take you to a safe place. If you wish to return to your homes, you may do so after we clean up this filth. Please follow my wife through that doorway and you will be safe," I said.

They looked a little confused and I realized they were trying to make the word wife, as said by another woman, make sense. Nonetheless, they followed Josie to safety. My women took places at the poles, looking like they were beaten and weary. I sat on the chair at the end of the tent. My warriors arranged themselves around the room where they were concealed. The three kidnappers were stuffed in a trunk in one corner of the tent. I hid the gateway.

We didn't wait long. Lakshmi and I had been making our last purchase for the day and the bazaar was closing up. Voices were heard outside the tent and another ten men brought five women into the tent. They were followed by a man who strutted into the tent between his men and their captives. He focused on me sitting in the chair.

"Who dares sit in my place?" he demanded.

"Mandab, your rule has ended," I said.

"What mere woman would dare...?"

He was cut off by the sudden appearance of my warriors. His startled men dropped their burdens and went for their knives, but were overwhelmed before one could draw. My women quickly moved from their places by the poles to aid the women and escort them to the infinity room. Mandab quickly assessed the situation and dropped to his knees, shaking. His head was bowed to the floor.

"Lady, we are sorry to have offended your grace. We had no idea you protected the women of this region."

I thought he was speaking to me, but his manner of address didn't seem right. My warriors pushed all the pirates to their knees and bowed their heads. I turned behind me and saw a frightful vision. I recognized at once that she was a goddess of as much might and power as any I had known in Greece or Babylon. She had many arms—it seemed the number changed as she reached into nothingness and pulled out heads, which she wore as a necklace. Her skirt was made of arms ripped from her enemies. She carried a sickle-shaped sword that dripped blood and her tongue snaked out of her mouth to scent the air.

"All women are under my protection. You and your rapists are doomed."

I hastened to kneel and plead for my people, but Kali was swift in her judgement. Mandab's head fell to the floor, quickly followed by those of his henchmen. The trunk where I had stowed the first three was sliced in half. Kali gorged on the blood and fastened the heads to her necklace and the arms to her skirt. Then she turned to me.

"You have done well, demon. Take your spoils and depart." With that, she faded into nothingness again.

Around us, we found the tent was filled with treasures, which we quickly packed into the infinity room and then left the bloody scene behind. My warriors followed me as I turned to the docks and found a ship much larger than my own. I'd seen it clearly in the memories I had read. We ran aboard and this time did not hesitate to kill every man we found. Below decks, we discovered nearly thirty women bound and gagged, lying in their own filth.

I opened the gateway again and my women rushed to care for the women and take them into the infinity room to be healed and fed. When we were certain the boat was empty and the slavers were dead, we rushed back through the streets to our tent. Once inside, I left guards on duty and went into the infinity room to assess the situation.

The first thing I saw was Lakshmi, looking surprised. I grabbed his hand and dragged him to the bedroom where my clothes flew from my body as I undressed him.

"I was so worried for you. Come to bed. Fuck me now and assure me this adventure is over."

I did not give an opportunity for response other than to make sure his prick was rigid and my tongue was in his mouth. I bounced on him, crying out my release and frustration. I rolled us so he could pound into my sensitive pussy. I moved to my hands and knees like a mare in season, so my stallion could mount me. I felt his release, not once or twice, but like a continuing torrent filling my pussy and enflaming my lust with his own. My orgasms were uncountable and I collapsed beneath his weight as I released my fear and panic at last.

>–– ◄◆► ––<

I have taken to sleeping more the older I get. I don't know why. I don't get tired or 'need' sleep. But sometimes I just want an escape without getting drunk. I guess that was the case after my misadventure in the Bazaar and with the kidnappers and the goddess Kali. I slept in escape for a long time.

"Bobbie. Honey? Wake up, baby."

I opened my eyes to see the caring and loving vision of my Lakshmi. Yes, I had ridden him hard the night before, but if he wanted more, I was willing to give him whatever he desired. I moved over so he could get in beside me and pushed into the... Lakshmi lay beside me. I looked back up at her/him and again at the man drowsily waking from sexually exhausted sleep.

"Who... Uh... What... Are you...?" I stumbled.

"I just got back. I spent the night searching the area for you until the warriors found me and brought me back to the tent so I could come home."

"Laks. Um... Who...?" I nodded to the man sitting up beside me.

"That's Oza," Laks said. "The man you patterned me after."

"My Lord... Or Lady," Oza said bowing his head to me. "Anytime I can be of service to you, please do not hesitate to call on me. Anytime."

I'd had sex with a man. Not just a woman I turned into a man, but a man who was a man. And I'd liked it a lot. We fucked ourselves into oblivion. What could I do? I kissed him and thanked him for the lovely night. Then I pulled Lakshmi to me and welcomed him back to my bed and my body.

30
ON FREEDOM AND POSSESSION

>-- ⬦ --<

LIZ WAS A FANTASTIC LOVER. Remember Liz? The women's liberationist from San Francisco? You might think that after 4,000 years on earth, I must have had hundreds of women whom I possessed. In reality, there were only a handful. In fact, Liz was only the fifth. Having a woman ask you to possess her is a rare thing, and as a result, those who make themselves my possession are treasures to me.

Josie, Pari, Princess Agora, Maya, Liz. Precious jewels in my crown.

I mean, not like I have a crown, but they make me feel like a prince. Still, Liz needed to know what she had gotten herself into and, yes, I would give her an option out if she wanted it. I expected, as most, that she would be more than happy to find this bondage was the freedom she sought.

When we woke up the morning after our one-nighter, as she called it, she looked at me, rather startled.

"Wow! Did I really just hop into bed with a guy I hardly know?" she asked, pulling the covers up around her.

"Not only that, but you asked me to possess you. And I have."

"Possess? As in own me? Sorry, Jack. Nobody owns this chick," she laughed.

"No. Possess as in take charge of your body and soul and bind you to me for all time," I said. It was actually much more than that, but I figured I should break it to her gently.

"You're kidding. I mean, I could just get up and walk right out of here. You don't possess me. That's ridiculous." She tittered nervously.

"Why don't you do that?"

"Yeah. I will. Don't try to stop me. I'm getting out of here." She didn't make a move.

"Well?"

"Well... Um... I was just thinking there was really no rush, right? I mean, we had a really good time last night, didn't we? I wouldn't mind a little repeat. There's no reason I need to rush off to be anywhere. It's not like I'm married. To you or anyone else. Right?" She didn't make a move to get out of bed, but she did let the sheet drop below her breasts. Now that was distracting!

"Why are you here—naked in my bed?" I asked.

"Oh, that's easy. We had a date... Well, it was more like a pickup, but you treated me like it was a date. And it's not that I'm easy. I don't just sleep around, but I'm a liberated woman who makes her own decisions. I decided I wanted to sleep with you. Nothing wrong with that. You aren't the first guy I've slept with. And so, I'm here. Um... I guess because I want to be. I mean, logic tells me I should run and not look back, but something inside me tells me I belong here. I don't want to leave. Ever. You are... Oh, my god! You possess me!"

"Does that frighten you?"

"Um... It should, I think. But it doesn't really."

"Why do you suppose that is?"

"Because I know... I mean deep down inside, I am positive you will never abandon me, will always care for me, will make my dreams come true, and will be everything I ever want or need. Why do I know that, Bob?"

"Because I will never abandon you, will always care for you, will do everything I can to make your dreams come true, and will be everything you ever want or need. I possess you and I would never want you to be unhappy."

I sat on the edge of the bed and held out my arms. She threw herself into them and hugged me as she began to cry.

"Are you upset, Liz?"

"No! I'm happy. I've never been so happy. You are like a drug and I've already been hooked. I love you, Bob."

"Maybe not yet, but you will. We will love each other like no other love you have ever imagined, just like I love my other possessions," I said.

"Do you have many others? Those women who were with you yesterday... I think I'm supposed to be jealous, but I'm not."

"Only Maya is my possession of those you've met. But Esmeralda is my wife. And there are other concubines."

"Possession, wife, concubines... That implies more."

"Yes, I have a few."

"Like some Arabian sheikh. What are you?"

"I'm a demon."

She was struck silent. She looked at me as what I said fought for a place in her consciousness beside all the things she thought she knew.

"I... I should go. I should see a priest and have an exorcism. My head will start turning in circles. Strange voices will come out of my mouth. I saw *Rosemary's Baby*. I'll have

Satan's child. He'll eat my soul!" she said. She was more and more agitated, but clung even more tightly to me.

"No one bears my children," I said firmly. "The movie was a well-constructed fiction. And I am not Satan. I'm just Bob. And I'm going to set you free."

"Why?" she said in alarm. "Don't you like me? Don't you want me?" She crawled out of the covers and into my lap, hugging me and placing kisses all over my chest and neck.

"Um... Haven't you heard the saying that if you love something set it free? I want you. There is a thing about you that captured my eye, even before you took off your bra. If you want me to possess you after I set you free, then it was meant to be," I said.

"That's so profound. Like, okay then, do it. I'll bounce right back."

"Not yet. First, I want you to know what it is like to be mine."

"So much for women's lib, huh?"

"On the contrary! I hope you will be very liberated."

"How does that work, Bob? How can I be possessed and liberated at the same time?"

"I want Lakshmi to explain that to you. She's much better at it than I am. In fact, she explained it to me," I said.

"Is she possessed?" Liz asked.

"No. She joined me and asked to be a part of my world and of my harem. She is my wife. That is very different. Regarding possession, I'll have you talk to Josie. She was the first and has never regretted it in nearly 4,000 years," I said.

"Wait! Four thousand years? What? Do we like, live forever?" she asked.

"Entering the infinity room from earth slows aging to an almost imperceptible crawl. Now that is not true of those born there. I don't understand the physics exactly, but those born in the infinity room age normally. Or normally for the infinity room, which is still slower than on earth. But no one wants to be a baby for a couple of centuries."

"Oh. I bet," she said. "When can I see this... you called it an infinity room? That's bitchin', man."

"Right." I opened the gateway and half a dozen of my women came through with breakfast for two. Three were naked and three wore clothes appropriate for working in the shop.

"Wow! You asked Bob to possess you as fast as I did!" Josie said as she brought a plate to Liz and sat beside her. Liz started to reach for the plate but Josie started feeding her instead. "I'm Josie and Bob possessed me so long ago, my memory struggles to comprehend it. You'll discover, though, that in the infinity room, time is pretty meaningless. It's not like we celebrate our thousandth birthdays or anything. I'm going to take you into the infinity room and show you around. Don't think you'll see it all. It stretches on, like, forever."

"How did you know I was possessed or that Bob was going to show me the infinity room?" Liz asked.

"Oh. I don't know. I just somehow always know what Bob wants. I think the wives and possessions are all like that. I'm not sure about the concubines."

"How many people are there?" Liz asked around a bite of scrambled eggs and cream cheese.

"Oh, gee! How many are there now, Bob?"

"Mmm. Nimia would know. I think it's around three million. Why bother counting? I'm not Caesar," I laughed as I took a bite from Pari.

"Really? Three million people, like, right through that door?" Liz squealed as she looked around, expecting they might all be in the bedroom at any moment. I guess in a way they were. The satchel was right there.

"Just in there," Josie confirmed, pointing at the open gateway.

"Let me get dressed so we can go. I want to see!"

"Oh, hon, you can get dressed if you want to, but none of the rest of Bob's women are."

Liz closed her mouth and refused another bite until Josie led her through the gateway. I'd catch up later.

>-- ◄◆► --<

Possession, I think, is a two-way street. Maybe I've mentioned this before, but I'm always thinking of new things about it. Like, I might as well say Liz possessed me. Liz, Maya, Princess Agora, Pari, Josie. They were as much a part of me as I was of them. When Josie said she always just knew what I wanted, that goes the other way, too. I always just know what one of my possessions wants or needs. We become that integral a part of each other.

I believe that in some ways, it is a closer relationship than I have with my wives. Nimia seems always to know what is on my mind, but that comes from being married to me for four thousand years. We do communicate mentally with each other, but it is on a conscious level. I think, 'Nimia I need to create a temple,' and she goes about getting together whatever it is I need for the project, but I thought about it *to* her. She might think 'Bob, I really need some long gentle loving tonight,' and she will be the only one on my mind when I'm ready for bed.

Now take the difference with when I opened the gateway in the tent where we were held captive. I didn't have time to think specific instructions about sending warriors or that kidnapped women needed to be cared for. But when the gateway opened, the warriors were ready to charge into the room and my women, led by Josie, were all over the captive women, freeing them and comforting them. She simply knew what Bob needed.

Well, I could feel the sense of awe Liz had at being introduced to the infinity room, and it filled me with the same sensations as she toured the house and harem, the libraries, and the temple. She really didn't even get out of the central district to see the lake or the ocean or the farms or the bushmen or the people from different ages of mankind. It all affected me the same way. I made this thing with a spell from Pinaruti's scroll, but I really had no idea how it all worked.

It made me wonder sometimes, what happened to the people who had been possessed by demons who were then exorcised. Were they happy about it, or did they feel a sense of loss when the demon set them free?

>-- ◄◆► --<

"Now you know exactly what kind of a monster I am," I said to Liz that evening. I brought her back out into the natural world as we called it. "Let's go for a walk and I will set you free."

"Um... Really? I mean, you don't have to, you know. I mean, you've got me and I'm happy, so you might as well keep me," she giggled.

"I want you to be absolutely positive and to know in your heart that it is your choice and you make it freely. The ultimate freedom is to choose to whom you are bound. I don't want there to be any lingering doubt that you might have chosen differently if you'd been able," I said.

"Lakshmi told me about that. She's a cutie. I can't believe she's, like, 2,000 years old. That's just too real. I can imagine just living there with you and all the women forever. Um... I guess I should get dressed if we're going outside." She pulled her clothes on, forgetting the bra. I watched, sincerely hoping she would come back to me, but trying not to project that onto her.

"Forever is a very long time, Liz. Even Lakshmi's 2,000 years is only a drop in the bucket of forever."

We walked up to the top of Buena Vista Park where there was a view out toward the Bay. She held my hand and seemed to find everything around us new and interesting. We paused at the overlook.

"Liz Baker, I set you free. You are no longer bound to me."

I could see the change come over her. There was a difference in the way she stood looking out over the city. She began to shake. She looked around frantically as if she needed somewhere to run and spun to stare at me.

"No! No, this is not what I want! I'm... empty inside. I have nothing but memories and emptiness. Bob. Bob, please, take me. Make me yours again. Possess me!" she cried.

She collapsed against me in tears and I wrapped my arms protectively around her. I let myself flow into her, filling every bit of her mind and soul with my own. I rocked her back and forth and whispered comforting words to her. The three words she longed most to hear and I longed most to say.

"You are mine!"

"Oh, Bob. Take me home. Let me be with you forever. Please, never let me go again," she whispered.

I picked her up and carried her back to the store and up to the little apartment where I felt safe opening a gateway to the infinity room. The bed there is much larger and there were several women who wanted to be on the welcoming committee.

We all rolled into the bed and there was a sexual free-for-all. I know I was mounted several times and I know the last was Liz. Her pussy wrapped my cock in a sheath of bliss. After a frantic beginning, she slowed, sliding up and down my pole with her eyes closed, savoring the sensation as my wives and possessions gathered around us, touching us, and kissing us.

"When you set me free, all the fear and doubt and uncertainty I had known in the world flooded in on me. I felt all the emptiness I'd known in my life. The anxiety of going to school, worrying about finding a date, the struggle for a job, the fear of crossing an empty parking lot, the pressure from my peers to be what they expected. I was so alone and afraid. I never want to feel that again, Bob. Never."

"There have been times when we have all had moments of fear. Even me. We band together to work on overcoming those things. You will become even more filled with love as you stay with us."

"You need to become a man for a while," Lakshmi said with confidence. Liz gave her a puzzled look.

>— ◄◆► —<

And that takes us back to fourth century India. Wasn't that a clever transition?

My experience as a woman and being kidnapped and held helpless by the pirates, lit a flame in me to heighten the protection of my people. To me, that meant better self-defense, no matter what our size or strength. Being a woman should not be synonymous with being helpless. I kept my woman's body for a long time.

We loaded the boat with our trade goods—meaning I stepped onto it with the satchel—and began sailing northward on the Kalinga Sea, generally along the coast. In addition to trading for new goods that we might find, my goal was to learn to defend myself as a woman and to teach all my women the art of self-defense. It was not to be an easy task.

>— ◄◆► —<

You might ask what we traded and why. I might answer.

The infinity room sprang into being at my command, but it was shapeless and empty. The first thing I did was add my house, a duplicate of Pinaruti's house. I furnished it with all the things I could cart out of his house and the whole house seemed to take shape at my command. I don't recall going out to find stones or to make bricks to build it. I eventually added on to the house to make it larger and more comfortable for my growing harem.

But simply keeping a house that we could continually expand, quickly proved to be inadequate for a place to keep my people. They were not all members of my harem. They needed more territory. They needed an 'outside' as well as a house. So, I looked at all that was around us on earth and saw the sky, the land, and the sea. I took fertile soil from the land of Ninra and flung it along the expanse before me. There was land and flowering plants bloomed upon it. I scooped up water from the great river Euphrates and cast it into the expanse. Rivers and lakes appeared and ran freely. I burned sweet incense to the gods and captured some of the smoke. This I released into the infinity room and the sky appeared above us.

As I spent time in the infinity room, I noted other things that were needed and brought samples from earth that would find their place in my little world. I brought seeds and animals, and they grew in the expanse. I brought more people and they built houses, businesses, and libraries. Whenever I saw a thing that amazed me, I brought a sample into the infinity room and it made a home there.

I noted, as well, that when a man or a woman or a couple or a family went out to look for a home, they simply went on a search and they would find what they were looking for. Issa once told his disciples to seek and they would find, knock and the door would be opened, ask and it shall be given. It was truly a fact in the infinity room.

As I traded with the many peoples of the world, I brought samples of new arts and crafts into the infinity room and people there began to practice them. This was why I traded and bought goods wherever I could go. And especially, wherever there were books. I brought books and scrolls and tablets into the infinity room, and my people made use of them.

So, you see, the infinity room took shape through a process of evolution, much like earth did, only I started with things that were already on earth, and so our evolution was much faster. As we sailed north, however, I was looking for a way to protect my people when they ventured into the natural world. I would trade mightily for such an art.

>-- ◄◆► --◄

"Peace be to you, mistress of this vessel," an old man said when we docked a few days north of Lankadeepa.

I had just tied my boat to the dock and turned to find an old man leaning on a staff. I realized I had jumped off the boat wearing my common sailing attire, which was just a scarf tied around my waist. My chest and proud breasts pointed directly at him. Chione saw my dilemma and tossed me a scrap of fabric before she fled below deck—being no better attired than I was.

"Kind sir. Please forgive my immodesty as we labored," I said as I tied the cloth around my chest. "And peace be to you."

"I have been visited in a dream," the old man said. "May I speak to you about it?"

Uh-oh. When somebody gets visited in a dream, it usually means a god is interfering. I needed to be careful, but there was nothing to do but bring him aboard. I whispered a prayer to Morpheus and asked the visitor to please wait on deck while I brought refreshments. I slipped inside the cabin where the gateway was open and arranged for cushions and food to be brought to the deck. He'd already seen Chione so she would serve. Pari asked to be included as she had not been out in quite a long time. Dressed in a more presentable sari, I went out to join my guest and the girls brought cushions for us to be seated. They brought a low table and poured tea, then went back inside to bring cakes and fruit.

"You are a most gracious hostess to an old man," he said. "I am Drona and have come from far away. May I tell you of my dream?"

"Please do. I have some experience in interpreting dreams and will help you in any way I can," I said.

"It was strange and came to me in parts. In the first part, I saw a woman in distress and the mother goddess came to her rescue. I thought, 'It is good that Kali protects the weak.' But then I had another dream and I saw the woman at the head of an army of women, all practicing the art of Kalarippayattu. And I said, 'How can this be that women practice for war?' A voice came to me and said, 'Teach them,' and I knew the goddess had given me a command. Yet I was troubled, for I did not know who these women were or if the command meant that I should teach *all* women, and I was afraid. If I taught the warfare of Kerali to women, I would be outcaste. Men might come for me and make war against the women."

He paused as we sipped our tea. There was no question in my mind that the first dream was of me and he had seen the visit of Kali on the pirates who kidnapped me. But leading an army? I didn't want my women to go to war. I just wanted them to protect themselves. He continued.

"And so, I began to wander, searching for the woman I saw in the dream. My wanderings brought me to this town, far from where my home once was. I slept fitfully and walked as I dreamt last night. In this dream, I came to a house standing alone in the desert. I walked around the house and thought how small it was to be alone in the wilderness. Then, the door of the house opened and I saw the woman and saw that she was only slightly less than the gods I worship. She invited me into her home. This is where I was puzzled, for when I crossed her threshold, it was not a tiny hut in the desert, but a great mansion. People gathered and a great feast was spread. And when I looked out the windows, I saw on one side a city and on the other a lush and green farmland where rice was abundant and animals grazed the mountains. And I thought, 'How can this be?'"

His dream was told in such a perfectly eloquent way that I thought either he must be a practiced storyteller or the goddess was still guiding his tongue as he related the tale.

"But the dream changed once again and this time it was very specific. I was shown a path through this city leading me to a boat on which the princess of the small space would explain to me my dream. And when I awoke, I stood here on this dock watching a goddess incarnate tying her ship. Tell me, oh, mistress of the sea, what is the message the gods have shown me in my dreams?"

I silently thanked Kali for her beneficence. My women would learn from this master. And so would I.

31
THE PRICE OF PASSAGE

ARTIAL ARTS was not the only thing we studied as we plied the waters and traded our way up the coast. I'd heard of other arts, especially the tantras. I was trading in a port near the mouth of the Brahmani when I came across a library. I immediately delayed our plans to sail and spent many days in the library—like many libraries around the world, part of a temple; this one dedicated to Lord Vishnu. The texts were filled with concepts and instructions—some with which I had passing familiarity—and were written in Sanskrit, which was one of the languages I could read without translation.

Since the time of Gautama Buddha, more and more of the ancient teachings had been transcribed to scrolls and collected in libraries. I'd heard of one in the far north, near the Rapti River and planned to find it. An entire university had been established in the north as well and was reputed to have a great library. I resolved to visit it, too.

A young monk approached me and asked if I understood the passages I was reading. I asked in turn, "What is the meaning of knowing oneself? Can one not know oneself?"

"Awareness is the key you are looking for," said the monk. "One may be very *familiar* with oneself, but still not *know* oneself intimately. This is a principle of oneness with the universe and with the gods."

I was intrigued and sat with the monk for several days as we talked. I liked the young man more and more each day. One day he invited me to his inner chamber and suggested we practice one of the texts I had uncovered. We began by sitting on cushions in a more comfortable room than I imagined a monk living in. We faced each other and began by simply looking into the eyes of the other. It was an intense experience and I had to start over a couple of times. I felt he opened up to me and I to him. This was followed by exploring each other with our fingers, tracing the line of the jaw, the curve of the shoulder, the weight of the breast. I shivered a bit at the thought that we had worked our way to undressing almost without comment.

But the young monk did not rush toward my sex, nor I to his. We continued explorations, noticing when my nipples hardened, or his. I traced the bumps that raised on his arms when I swept his lips with my own. I was a pupil, not a teacher in this exploration. He pointed out areas of my body that were tense, and showed me pressure points that would relax that tension. We oiled each other with gingili oil and my senses were opened to his touch. I allowed myself to touch his cock and discover the veins and vessels within that pulsed in my hand. He found places inside me I had not known and I learned about my male self as well as my female self.

When we dressed, we had not had intercourse. Yet I was more euphoric than after any bout of lovemaking I had experienced as a woman or as a man. I returned to the boat in a daze and once in the infinity room, I lay on my bed in silence. As I lay there, unmoving, thinking about my experience, I was shaken by the most powerful orgasm of my life. Not just of my life as a woman, but of my more than two millennia on earth. And I knew I needed to teach this to all my people.

We stayed in that port for more than a year. Each day, I took women with me to study the tantric arts and the young monk was most helpful. While we were there, we duplicated volumes and transferred them to my library in the infinity room.

As we studied, we also discovered Drona, who was teaching us Kalarippayattu, also knew of these arts as an extension of his own. He had been working with select women for some time to introduce them to the sensual side of his yoga as well as the militaristic. The massage with gingili oil—an oil extracted from the sesame seed—was a major portion of the martial art that opened the senses and healed the body.

I had to return Lakshmi to her true form so she could learn the practice and discovered she was the finest of practitioners because she had such intimate understanding of both the male and female bodies.

That started a run which I did not hesitate to allow. From Nimia to the most recent addition to our harem, each woman wanted to spend a day in the body of a man. I granted this wish and during the course of their day, I made tantric love to each of them.

At last, it was time for us to resume our voyage and I found it was also time to resume my masculine form. Each of my women came into my arms before I made my transition, fondly caressing my breasts and my pussy. They all whispered how they would miss my womanly form, but they were eager to have my male form in their bed again.

Transforming from the slight but beautiful woman into a strong and powerful man again, made me feel I had left a part of myself behind and I longed to regain it.

Drona, who had long since been integrated into our society as a much younger version of himself, knew my true nature as a demon. He put a comradely arm around my shoulders after the transition as I complained about having left the womanly part of me behind.

"That is the price of a rite of passage," he said. "You must leave a part of yourself behind. Do not lose what you have learned, and revisit it often. There is nothing saying you need to make a permanent transition. Your wives and concubines would like to switch places on occasion and your life will be richer for it."

"Thank you, my friend," I said. I set my face into the spray of the sea and sailed north.

>-- ⬥ --‹

And that brings me back to Liz. Remember? San Francisco, 1968? That's what this story was about.

Lakshmi had just suggested that Liz spend some time as a man. That was not unusual to us in the infinity room by this time. Since the fourth century after Caesar, each new woman who was added to our harem—I say *our* harem because it belonged as much to the women as to me—was given the opportunity to learn the martial arts, to practice the tantric meditations, and to become a man for a while.

Some declined the opportunity, but those were generally not women (or men) who became part of our inner circle. Often, they found lovers and life mates in the greater world of the infinity room. But those with whom I was most intimate—and especially, those I possessed—were immersed in all three arts.

And so, the day came when Liz said, "I'm ready. But am I supposed to simply pretend to be a man and make love to one of our concubines?"

"No, my love. What do you think of this body I'm wearing?"

"Um... Well, I love you. You could stand to trim up a little bit. I really like a smooth face and chest. I love your muscles. They make me feel safe when I am in your arms. And I love your dick. I mean, I *really* love it."

As she spoke, I worked an incantation and transformed her into the body I was wearing, along with the adjustments she suggested. She was right. I had let this body go a bit with the sedentary life of a shopkeeper. I turned her toward a mirror and she was shocked by what she saw. She did much the same thing I had done when I became a woman. She stared at herself, touching her face, her arms, and her dick. While she examined herself, I transformed myself into a likeness of the Liz she had been. She turned and looked at me.

"Oh, shit! Did we just, like, switch bodies?" She shook herself at the deep sound of her own voice.

"No," I answered. "You are in your body. It is the way you are as a man. And my body—that looks so much like you—is here to be your mate if you will have me." My own voice had raised and softened.

Liz stood staring at me. Looking at oneself in a mirror is not the same as seeing oneself, separate and apart. In the first place, we become used to everything being on the wrong side when we look in a mirror. Left is right and right is left. Looking at oneself from the outside is truly like others see us. She looked down at her growing erection and started to cover it with her hands, jerking her hands back when she touched it.

"I'm sorry. I mean, it just did this by itself. I didn't mean to, like, get hard just because you are standing there, looking at me like... that, and I like you, and you're really sexy, and I want you. I mean, I didn't mean that. *To do* that. Do I really look like that? I'm going to die of embarrassment!"

I laughed and invited her to sit facing me as we went through the tantric rituals of self-examination and examination of our partner. And we made love. For hours. Sometimes doing nothing but looking into each other's eyes and sometimes with him buried in me as deeply as he could be as he bellowed out an orgasm and filled my pussy with his cream.

In the morning, I returned Liz to her own shape. She stopped me before I transformed myself.

"Wait. Please. Let me kiss you and touch you. I feel like I know you better than any person alive. I know how you like to have your breasts touched. I know exactly when you are lubricating in your pussy. I know how to kiss you. And all that means, I know myself."

We kissed and I transformed back into my body that she had so recently worn a likeness of. She giggled when she saw my cock come erect before her.

"I think I know what would feel really good right now." And with that, we made love again.

>-- <&> --<

"I'm going to write a book. Would that be all right?" Liz asked when we went to meet her parents. She cleared out all her belongings and we loaded them up to take to the infinity room. Her parents were surprised that their rebellious and independent daughter had suddenly moved in with a man. I did my best to put them at ease and promised we would come to visit when we could. I might have used just a little magic to calm their fears.

"What are you going to write about?" I asked.

"Well, it will be a book for women about women," Liz began. "I might need to find a co-author, but I'm sure it will be successful. It will be all about how knowing our bodies is a key to knowing ourselves—who we really are. It's just... We need that book."

I smiled and vowed to help her succeed. After all, she was my possession.

>-- <&> --<

Forgive me while I reminisce a little more about India. You see, I'd spent a very long time—close to two millennia—around the Mediterranean Sea. It was where I was born, so to speak. I'd sailed as far as the blue-painted Britons and had nearly frozen in the Northern Sea. I'd put in all along the north coast of Africa. I'd been with Caesar in Gaul and Alexander all the way to India. So, now that I was in South Asia, I saw no reason to hurry. We often put in at a port and either sold or abandoned the boat as I walked through a new part of the country.

I met interesting people that way. I decided to put in for a while and walk up the Ganges Plain toward the Indus. For some reason, I thought that now I had experience in the martial arts, I should stop in to see Issa. I was sure there would be no problem finding him. It's hard for a man like that to hide.

I followed the words of many guides as I walked for years across the land. We had little in the way of threats, and I spent long nights in the infinity room with my lovers. Sometimes the nights went on for what seemed like many days, but I always emerged from the satchel the next morning. One day, perhaps I will understand time. But not today.

The great universities and libraries were not far from the river and I visited each, managing to duplicate their great libraries. I'll tell more about my adventures there one day. I became a student and eventually, a wandering monk, intent on learning.

At a university, I met a man who was very interesting to talk to. He'd have gotten on well with some of the philosophers of Greece. Maybe Pythagoras. I met him once when he was wandering around Mesopotamia. Or perhaps it was Euclid in Alexandria. I forget. But this isn't about him, so I'll move on.

First, you must know that India had a unique numbering system. I found Rome's numbers to be good for nothing but recording totals. To add one to another, you needed to count them all over again. There were few records kept in Rome that were accurate because it was too difficult to decipher the number. Not long ago, I opened a book I found in a library in New York and noted the publication date was MCMLXVIII. I duplicated the book for no other reason than it was the year my precious Liz joined me as my possession. I made a gift of it to her. It was something about androids and electric sheep. But I digress. Again.

In Babylon, we used a numeric system which I started when I was in Bathra two thousand years earlier. It was the number that Ninra and Namri gave for building their temple. It was based on the number sixty. We have time units throughout the day that are still based on that system, as is much of geometry. There are 360 degrees in a circle. There are also 360 degrees around the earth, each divided into sixty minutes. Easy.

But in India, they used a system of nine digits. It was unique because every ten units advanced their value one order of magnitude. Easy.

Now, this man I met at the university was a philosopher who sought to explain the world in terms of numbers. I thought I might talk to him and discover what the secrets of my own world in the infinity room were. Let this be a lesson to you if you engage in magic. You do not need to understand how something works to know that it works. I created the infinity room using the spells and vision that I had in Pinaruti's magic room. But two thousand years later, I still didn't understand how it worked.

This man—Eshan, I'll call him—was wise, but difficult to talk to. When we sat down to discuss anything, he first set a pot of weeds afire and we breathed the smoke. Then our conversations were much more intelligent. (Yes, my friends, ganja has been in use in India for 5,000 years and many great discoveries have been made while under its influence.)

"You speak of hundreds," I said to Eshan. "How many hundreds make ten?"

"No, it is the other way around. Ten tens make a hundred."

"Then we speak of five hundreds and six ones, how many tens are there?"

"There aren't any, so we don't speak of them."

"Write it," I demanded. He wrote '5 hundreds and 6.'

"But why must you write the word hundreds?" I asked. "And how am I to know that 6 is ones and not tens?"

"You cannot write something that is not there!" he exclaimed. We both breathed in more smoke.

"I have been studying the vedas and to become one, one must become nothing," I said.

"Because when we are one with all, we are nothing at all," he responded.

"Ah. If I am nothing at all, then I do not exist. I am not here and we are not having this conversation."

"But I can see you here," he responded. "Therefore, you are not one with all."

"I cannot see me here; therefore, I am one with all and am not here."

"You can't see nothing."

"There should be a symbol that is a placeholder for nothing so we can tell when nothing is there."

I don't remember how long we smoked or who spoke next. I puffed out a ring of smoke and pointed at it.

"Look there. The smoke is in the ring, but there is nothing inside it."

"Hmm. We could use the ring to show where there is nothing," he said. "It wouldn't be nothing, but it would show where nothing is."

And thus was born 'zero.' I swear to you, this is true.

I could have had that same conversation in 1970 in San Francisco. In fact, I might have. I lost track of Eshan when I moved on, but it wasn't long before I began seeing numbers written with a ring in the middle to show what was not there: 506.

I searched far up the Indus for any sign of Issa. At long last, I found a place where an old man nodded and said Issa was no longer there. He led me to a simple tomb that was marked with characters that meant Yuz Asaf, or healer. The man told me that the one I called Issa or Yuza Asaf, meaning son of Joseph, had been a great saint and was revered throughout the land, but that he had died centuries ago and was buried here. He pointed out a carving that had been done of the saint and it clearly showed his feet with nail wounds in them. I supposed that was really the only way anyone could have identified him.

I should tell you about scars on demons. Damage done to our natural bodies is carried through in future manifestations. For example, when I am in my natural form, there is still a chip out of my left horn where the demon in the wilderness hit me with his axe. Issa was conjured in the form of a human and therefore the damage done to his body in Jerusalem was marked on his body forever. When we were swimming in the sea, I saw the scar from where he was pierced in the side. I also noted, by the way, that he was as well-hung as I am.

I was sad that I didn't get to see my old friend again and left an account of our adventure together with the old man. I'm sure he didn't believe me. And I had to admire Issa staging his death (again) and starting over. I had always just moved to a new place and adopted a new identity and a new body. Those bodies led me into all kinds of adventures.

Ah well. Zero Issa.

While I was there, though, I heard rumor of a Buddhist monastery far up in the mountains. I nodded to myself. This Lama, or holy man, the people mentioned would be just the kind of character Issa would put on so he could continue to teach and heal. I decided to journey into Tibet to see if I could find him.

I felt akin to the Tibetans. They considered themselves to be the descendants of a monkey king and a female demon. They also had more than enough legends and concepts to support an ancient kingdom. I journeyed through the river valleys and high into the mountains. Eventually, I found a river flowing southward and I joined it. But I never found Issa.

There was nothing.

END PART VI

Part VII
Temple Builder

32
Nothing of the Soul

>-- ◆ --<

NOTHING IS VERY IMPORTANT to me.

Let me try to rephrase that without getting too high or drunk. Nothing is more important to me than anything. I mean... Pour yourself a drink.

There was a woman on one of the islands of Southeast Asia—I don't remember which one or if that's even the next thing in this story. I just remember our time together.

After we left Tibet and I followed the river downstream to the sea, I bought or built—don't remember which—another boat sufficient for sailing and trading along the coast and among the islands. We'd been sailing in warm waters, putting in at new ports and trading for new and exotic goods we took to the infinity room to propagate there. I remember it as a terrifically lazy time, often having a few of my beauties on deck with me and letting the currents take us where they would. I found a lovely beach and grounded the boat, hauling it up onto the sand and anchoring it solidly to a fallen tree. I opened the gateway and the girls came rushing out to play in the warm equatorial waters of the sea.

Of course, they were dressed as usual—meaning not dressed at all. Nothing. After all, we were on a secluded beach and there was no reason for us to hide from each other. Yes, I was naked as a jay as well. Every once in a while, one of the girls would break away from the others, grab me by the hand and find a place in the sand where we could make love.

As we played and frolicked in the sea, returning from one of my romps, I spotted a woman I could not remember seeing in the infinity room. She was beautiful—of course—brown-skinned as if she had spent all her life playing naked in the sun on this very shore. She was enjoying the company of my women as much as they enjoyed her.

"Bob, this is Ningrum. Isn't she beautiful?" Pari called to me.

"Indeed! Ningrum, I am happy to meet you."

"May I just call you Happy?" she asked.

"Well, you may if you wish. My name is Bob."

"Oh! I misunderstood. Many names in this land are feelings or objects or actions. Like Full Moon, Magical Stone, Dancing in the Rain. You understand?" she said. How cute.

"I see. And what does your lovely name, Ningrum, mean?" I asked.

"Oh, nothing."

I was perplexed, but if someone asked me what Bob meant, I suppose I would have the same answer. Perhaps I was, indeed, Happy to Meet You.

"Do you live near here, Ningrum?" I asked.

"Here or nowhere. I live."

I wasn't sure we were communicating. I checked myself to see that I was speaking and hearing directly mind to mind. Occasionally, I found that I had spoken ancient Minoan to a person who only understood Hindi and I had not bothered to translate mind to mind. There seemed to be no problem with that this time. She blended well with the others—certainly with their mode of undress—and I openly admired her as they played.

>-- ◆◆► --‹

There's always been something a little mystical in my mind about girls and a beach. Perhaps it's an archetype that we all tap into. Just think of being out walking on the beach and meeting a winsome girl with just the wind for a wrap, greeting you with open arms, falling to the sand to make love with the waves lapping at your feet, holding hands as you run in the surf. It's the thing that television commercials are made of. Only it existed thousands of years before television.

I'd had my experiences. Of course, I'd never forget waking up on the beach at Cyprus with Aphrodite riding on my dick and bringing me right along with her on her ascent to pleasure's pinnacle. But there were others as well. When I first arrived at Troy, I beached my little boat just about where the Greeks would land a few decades later. I made camp and was about to open a gateway to get some company for the night when I heard music coming toward me on the beach.

Did I tell you about this when I told you about Troy? No, I don't think so. This was before all the events of that horrid story.

I had gathered driftwood and lit a fire, planning an intimate little party with Nimia and Josie. Anyway, I heard music—someone singing—coming toward me in the gathering darkness on the beach. I was always prepared for an attack, though I had no sophisticated weapons at the time. I felt I could protect myself and my companions pretty well.

As she got closer, the music faltered and I saw her silhouette approaching until the firelight just picked out the scantest details of a shapely young woman in a gauzy gown, looking at me cautiously. Cautious, yes, but not afraid. She continued to approach.

"Greetings, fair one," I said. "Would you share the warmth of my fire on this cool evening?"

"You sound gentlemanly. Are you trying to deceive me?" she asked.

"Lady, why would I have need of deceiving you?" I asked. "I'm a simple traveler who has beached here for the night and hopes to continue in the morning. My name is Bob and I have journeyed far."

"I can tell you have come from far away. And also that you are not what you appear to be," she said. She moved closer into the firelight and I could see the gauzy dress was so light it was almost completely transparent. She was a beautiful young woman.

"What else might I be than what I appear to be?" I asked.

"Hmm. I'm not sure, but I know the gods would not have sent me here for an ordinary man. I have come to this beach under every full moon for five years, expecting to find you. I don't believe you are ordinary at all," she said. "Of course, when I began coming here, I was a mere adolescent with dreams of a great hero coming for me. But you could be a god or a demi-god. You might even be a monster, disguised as an attractive and brawny man."

"Thank you for your compliment. May I say you are a very attractive and beautiful woman," I said. "Please sit and tell me your story. Why have you been coming to this place under the full moon for five years?"

"Okay. I'll tell you," she laughed. "Do you have anything to drink? I think I need to be a little looser to enjoy the full benefits of this night."

"I think I might have something. I've always had a weakness for loose women." I reached into the satchel and Josie handed me a wineskin and giggled. I think I was the only one who heard that.

"Don't get the wrong idea. I'm still pure. So far. I've been saving myself for you."

"For me?" I asked, holding the wineskin for her. "Whyever for me?"

"Mmm. The story," she said, wiping her mouth. "When my first blood came, my father took me into the city to dedicate me to the goddess. One or another of them. I thought my life was over. I would either die a virgin in some holy reclusion, or become a temple whore and part my legs for any and all who would enter. It wasn't my father's fault, exactly. I was a girl and an extra mouth to feed on a poor fisherman's labor. I don't blame him, really. Becoming a priestess of Aphrodite or Athena was an honorable vocation. Do you have any cheese to go with the wine? I'm kind of hungry."

I reached into the satchel and Josie handed me a board spread with cheeses and dried meats and even some bread. The girl, whose name I had not yet learned scooted closer to me and helped herself to the spread.

"Who are you, by the way?"

"I'm Dora. So, as I was saying, I went into the city. I went first to the temple of Athene and the priestess took one look at me and shook her head. 'You don't belong here. The priestesses of Athene are virgins.' I protested that I was a virgin and she laughed. 'Honey, I mean virgins all their lives. You are filled with visions of the man who will take you. Go to the Temple of Aphrodite and talk to the priestesses there.' So, I went to Aphrodite's temple."

"And did the priestesses of Aphrodite take you in?" I asked. I'd heard of them, but in spite of having met My Lady Goddess herself, I had never been to one of her temples.

"No. The chief priestess took me to a room apart from the rest of the temple and sat me down. Then a strange thing happened. It was like she changed right in front of me and I saw the most beautiful woman I'd ever seen. 'Child, I see what you want. You want a love that will forever be young and fresh. You want your hero to keep you like a princess and carry you off to his castle. You want a fairytale romance.'

"I'd never put my fantasy in precisely those words, but I guess she was right. As she spoke to me, I saw a vision of a brave and strong man sweeping me off my feet and carrying me away to his castle where I was pampered and loved for the rest of my life.

"I see and I am inclined to grant your fantasy,' said the goddess, 'but you must do something for me. When you meet your handsome prince, you must convince him to come and dwell in the city for some time. I will then bless you with all you have dreamed of. But you must have him promise to dwell in the city until his goddess comes to him.' What could I do? I agreed and she told me that I was still too young and I must walk on this beach each month at the full moon and eventually I would find you."

"Ah, My Lady Goddess, what have you put in my path?" I sighed. But what could I do? The simple tale was certainly directed at me. "What is the name of this city I must dwell in?" I asked.

"It is called Ilium and lies across the plain to the northeast."

"Then it appears that my boat shall remain on this beach and I shall cross that plain in the morning," I said.

"Oh, that's wonderful! Then we can make love tonight," she said.

She continued eating and sipping from the wineskin, but moved to sit on my lap as she ate. She punctuated her feasting with little kisses on my shoulder and cheek, occasionally landing one on my mouth. I feasted on her beauty, kissing her hair and her neck, and letting my hands traverse her body, parting the folds of her gauzy dress to fully expose the beauty beneath. Her breasts were a feast in themselves, larger than I expected and crowned with very sensitive nipples that I rubbed and squeezed. I found the heat of her sex to be open and well-lubricated, allowing my fingers to dance across her clit. At last, she put the cheese board aside and spread her legs wider welcoming my questing fingers.

"I think I'm loose enough, if you want to make me your lover and promise you will move to the city tomorrow."

"I so promise," I said. And with that, we stretched out on the sand and made love beneath the full moon next to our fire.

Dora was a relaxed lover, seeming to know what came next, but never to have done it. When I broke the barrier of her maidenhead, she gasped a little and then pulled me into her by placing her heels against my buttocks and pulling. I sank into her buttery warmth with a sigh and we began to move together. She was exquisite.

When we woke in the morning, she pointed out the direction to the city and I offered to take her in the infinity room, explaining that it was where my palace was and that she would live forever young and beautiful there.

"Oh, yes, please," she said excitedly. "Take me away to your fairy castle. I'm yours forever now."

Dora was a simple girl. She truly lived in her fantasy and may not have been able to tell the transition from the natural world to the infinity room where her fantasy was a reality. She never had the least interest in returning to the natural world as long as I had promised to go to Ilium. It was an interesting story she told and I thanked My Lady Goddess for sending her my way. I knew that someday she would call on me to repay her for her kindness. Ah well.

>-- ◀◆▶ --<

Back to Bali, or somewhere in that vicinity.

Most of my girls went back to the infinity room when night fell. A few wanted to stay out under the earth stars and make love for the night. Staying out for a night on this peaceful beach was fine with me, especially when Ningrum joined the party. She was sleek and sensual. She danced for us at our campfire and then taught the other women her island dances as well. I got right in there and learned the dances, too. I could feel the feminine energy pulsing through me and nearly transformed to a female version of myself.

But the girls wanted to make love and needed my dick. We made love under the stars on a beautiful clear night by the sea. I made a note to add stars in the sky in the infinity room. When it was safe, I spent my nights in the infinity room, but whenever I had girls staying out all night, I stayed with them.

>-- ◀◆▶ --<

Unless they didn't plan to come back, of course. Then I bid them a fond farewell and provided for them in whatever way was appropriate. That had happened a few times. There are people in the world who have such a strong affinity to their home and to the earth that they simply can't be happy anywhere else. Nimia and I had pretty much decided that wherever the infinity room was, it was not on earth. If that makes sense. When I discovered someone who was unhappy in the infinity room, I did my best to return her to her home.

That happened with Sahar, for example. She'd joined our happy throng back in the days when I was selling oil shares in Arabia. She'd been delighted to leave a cruel man who did not understand the difference between a woman and a pot of oil on the shelf. In fact, he treated the oil more tenderly. She was merely a slave in his household, meant to be used and shared with whom he would. I made her part of the deal when he bought his share and, though I freed her, she rewarded me energetically in bed. I often took her with me when I was touring a city. When I reached Jerusalem, she came to me, begging to be set free. It seemed she had been sold to the sheikh as a child and had always longed to return to her people.

Of course, I let her go. I didn't own her nor possess her. She was with me after I'd set her free. It turned out that she had relatives still living in Jerusalem and her brother welcomed her to his home. It was a very touching reunion. He thanked me for returning his sister who had been stolen from the family when she was a child. She was not more than seventeen when I returned her, so it didn't seem like such a long time to me. But I was happy to have the family reunited and left her with my blessing.

True freedom is to be able to choose our own bondage, as Lakshmi taught me centuries later.

Ah, but Ningrum. That was a different matter entirely. When the girls returned to the infinity room in the morning and I prepared to set sail again, I asked Ningrum if she would come with us and be part of my harem. We'd had a wonderful night as she pleased my girls and pleased me as well. I could still feel the sensation of her pussy gliding down my cock and milking my semen from me. I hoped she would join us.

"Let me show you more of our beautiful islands," she responded. "I will sail with you for a span of days and then you may ask me again."

"Noble lady, I welcome you to my little boat. I will greatly appreciate your guidance through these channels."

"These channels of water and my own moist channels welcome you, Bob."

And so, we set off sailing up and around the islands, stopping at larger ports to trade and talk with the locals. As we approached each port, Ningrum would give me a list of the kinds of things needed by the people there. I would collect appropriate merchandise from the infinity room, and she would assist in bargaining for local goods. She was a treasure and helped me turn a great profit in new items for the infinity room.

That there was a room on my boat that held all my women, my trade goods, and even pastures filled with animals, seemed not to faze Ningrum at all. She happily met any of my harem who came out of the room for the day and handed off goods to be taken back into the room. But never once did she express curiosity about the room or ask to enter it.

And at night, on the deck of the gently rocking boat, we made love. There are few women in the past millennia who could so completely absorb all the love I could give them. I had come to know some women with a profound intimacy that went far beyond the sexual pleasure we shared. Ningrum was not tempered with any limitations on her passion or her joy. It was as if she could immerse herself fully in me and leave all concept of herself behind. The feeling was like...

There was a time once—I believe it was along the African coast, but it could have been on a remote island or even have happened in the Caribbean—when I had made camp along a peaceful shore and my repose was disturbed by a woman's call for help. The distress in her voice made me rush to her aid.

I found she was in a tree, and beneath her, a pack of wild beasts was circling, occasionally leaping up against the tree just inches from where she precariously perched. Don't ask me what kind of beasts. I was too involved in the plight of the woman to decide what species was on the attack. I recall fangs and claws. They were difficult to subdue, even though I cast several sleep spells upon them. The last one seemed to work, but so well that Eisha, the woman in the tree, also was hit by it and instantly slept, falling from the tree. I barely managed to catch her before she landed on one of the sleeping beasts. They were beginning to stir already and I ran for the beach and my boat, casting off before the beasts could catch up with me.

Eisha sailed with me for a few days, pointing me to places along the shore where I would find paths to various villages and warning me against approaching others. She, too, was a voracious lover. It seemed that the more I loved her, the more she desired and if I stayed with her over long, she might seriously manage to drain all my love from me. I have since found that such women have been known in history as a succubus.

And then one morning when I awoke, Eisha was gone. I had no idea where, but apparently, she'd grown tired of our liaison and went to find another. Mostly, I remember her appetite for my love as something more than sexual, but an appetite for something she had been denied all her life.

Still, in the end, she was gone.

>-- ◄◆► --<

"You are not coming with me when I leave, are you?" I asked as Ningrum and I lay wrapped in each other's arms on the deck of the boat. The moon was full and Polaris was barely a dot at the northern horizon.

"You have discovered my secret at last," she sighed.

"I believe you revealed yourself to me, goddess."

"I am only a very minor deity, but I do my best to protect the people of the islands and this sea," she said. "And occasionally I pick up a stray seaman."

"And you are not Ningrum? By what name should I call you, Goddess?" I asked.

"Ah. I am known only as She Who Looks Into Your Soul," she said.

"Yet you told me your name meant nothing," I ventured as she gave me understanding.

"I looked into your soul and saw nothing," she said. "It was comforting to see such vast emptiness. I sort of lost myself in it."

"Then I have become one with all and am therefore nothing!" I laughed.

"Except a very bad punster," she laughed. "Oh, Bob, how I wish I could join you on your adventure and enter your secret chamber. For I see that your soul is empty because you have poured it out for your people."

That gave me pause. The infinity room was filled with all sorts of people. "Filled" is obviously not the right word. There was always room for more. I hadn't even met more than a tenth of those who were there because the others had been born there. In two thousand seven hundred years, the population had grown significantly. Even many of my concubines had children I didn't really know since they were fathered by others. I thought I should possibly spend more time there and get to know them better.

I felt a strong desire once again to find a safe place where I could enter the infinity room and not come out. But if I didn't physically protect the satchel in *this* world, anything could happen to it. Someone might stumble upon it and who knew what they might do. My people were far too precious to abandon them to whatever the world might bring. That is why I kept on the move, carrying my precious cargo on my back wherever I went.

Ningrum was not going to let me dwell on my thoughts for long. In a contest among the deities, she might not have been Aphrodite, but she had the body and mind of a goddess, and she used both to stimulate me and to join with me again. As I slid my cock between her moist nether lips and into her temple, my heart sang praises that there was in this world such a goddess who would love me.

In the morning, I could tell she was preparing to leave. She pointed me toward a port that was rich in spices and flowering plants. We traded and my women were excited about the treasures they brought into the infinity room. And each took a moment to embrace Ningrum and kiss her lovingly.

"Will you continue here, or will you flee to Olympus like the Greek and Roman gods have done?" I asked.

"There is no Olympus for those of us who have survived in this part of the world," she said. "I was born of the sea and to the sea I will return. When people remember and call my name, I will rise again to comfort them."

"It saddens me to think that a goddess has such a fate. I am merely a demon and have no home to return to either," I said. "So, I continue to wander on the earth, caring for my people."

"Oh, Bob, don't sell yourself short. You may have been born a demon, but you are preparing your own palace. Is that not what your friend Issa did?"

"He told his followers he was going to prepare a place for them, but I thought the god of the Hebrews was actually taking care of him and whatever place they would go. He never seemed anxious to collect people for his house. I don't know. We did not speak of that much in our time together."

"You may think of yourself as a demon in *this* world, but your harem—and, indeed, *your* little world—consider you their god. Blessings on you, Bob. May the sea be ever kind to you and the winds blow you to your port of safety." She kissed me again and I reluctantly let her go into her world—so different from mine.

>-- ◀◆▶ --<

As I set sail, it disturbed me that in all the islands I had seen no temple to the goddess. How would people remember and call upon her if they had no physical reminder of her presence? I decided to build a temple. But there was neither abundant rock nor clay to make bricks. Nimia and I spent several days reading in the library until we found a spell I thought would work. Then we set sail back to the sandy beach where we first met the goddess.

We were not expecting her to meet us there again, but all my women flooded out onto the beach to dance the dances she taught us. Then we began piling up sand, moistening it, and piling up more. From this I carved a castle of sand, a home fit for a goddess. Of course, sand is weak. It held its shape as long as it was just so moist and no wetter or drier. When we had built the castle, a home for Ningrum, I set about working the transformation spell that would turn the sand into stone.

We danced around the sand castle for Ningrum and then boarded the little ship to sail off to new lands.

I knew that wind and water would erode the monument over time. There was nothing I could do about that. But to this day, there is still a Castle Rock known amidst those islands.

33
A TEMPLE OF WOOD

S WE SAILED among the islands and up the eastern coast of Asia, I found more and more texts to collect in my library. Various forms of paper had been manufactured throughout Asia for many years. Their inks and the calligraphy of their texts were fascinating. Some were mystical texts, religious, scientific, and some few that were fanciful flights of imagination and poetry. In addition to the texts, I found willing librarians who would come to the infinity room to teach and share.

Buddhism was spreading at about the same pace that we were moving, so as we progressed, I taught martial arts to people who were willing and interested. I found people who could build on these arts and make them their own, just as they built on the religious teachings and made those their own. As the arts evolved, we brought more teachers into the infinity room and my women became masters who went out into my world to teach others. We taught the mantras and meditations, but since there were no gods in our world, they played a role only as teaching legends rather than real people. I even found some mentions of myself as one of the many legends in the greater infinity room. I wasn't sure what to think of that.

I reached the coast of Nihon about the same time as Buddhism. We traded all up and down the string of islands and I taught what I knew. I was summoned at one point to the palace of the prince regent. This prince had adopted Buddhism readily, blending it with the Shinto religion. This made sense to me. I had seen places where a religion was spread by decree or by bloody warfare. In the long run, the gods of that religion were irrelevant to the local people. The stories of those gods took place long ago and far away.

Imagine, if you would, what it would be like if I tried to spread the religion of Ninra and Namri throughout the world today. The stories I told of how the god and goddess had protected Bathra from the invading Assyrians would mean nothing to the people of the southern continent of America where I found myself in the middle of the second millennium AC (After Caesar). And thankfully, the god and goddess had never asked that their religion be spread farther than our valley. We even rebuilt the temples of the other gods who were worshiped there. Instead of conquering other religions, the precepts of the religion were taught to the people and the local gods were maintained. That made sense.

I taught in the palace, spreading the martial arts to the prince's army, and blending in the martial arts they already had. And I had many happy conversations with the prince about how things were in other parts of the world.

"Bob, I think we should have a temple. A temple and a place where the arts can be taught. You know, where Buddhist monks can be trained," the prince said.

"That is a noble endeavor, my prince. We would need a place with good stone and I could build a ziggurat as they have in India."

"We don't have good stone and what we have is used to build defenses. We have a lot of trees, though. Could you build a temple out of wood?" he asked.

That was an interesting puzzle. Most houses were built of wood and the structural elements were sound. I asked leave to study the problem and promised to return to the prince in ten days.

I hiked out to a hill overlooking the site the prince indicated was where he wanted the temple built. There, I found a cave where I could conceal myself and enter the infinity room. Of course, the first thing I needed to do was satisfy the desires of my harem, but I immediately set my librarians to work finding how to construct a temple of wood. Remarkably, they had many examples of wooden structures and the Japanese librarians who recently joined us showed a long tradition of wooden buildings in the country—some very large.

I returned to the prince at the appointed time and showed him the drawings I had made for the temple grounds. He approved and appointed me to be the architect of his new temple.

I had missed building things. I had not been so happy since constructing the pool in Babylon. I employed many people, refusing to have anyone work on the temple who was forced labor. The temple was built as several buildings around a courtyard that connected to the prince's palace so he could attend the temple without leaving his grounds.

When the great gong rang at the temple's entrance just a year later, it was a day of great celebration. Teachers moved in and I moved out, slipping away to my boat on the western shore of the island. I decided to go north and cross Asia by land. We sailed the little boat up a river until it was no longer passable and I sold it to begin hiking north to find what treasures could be located inland.

>--- ◄◆► ---<

Forward a thousand years or so. It seems I've been building things all my life, so it was only natural that in the latter part of the twentieth century, I found a place in North America to build houses. And I've met interesting people wherever I went.

"Now, Bob… Can I call you Bob? Bob, I have just three words for you. These are the most important words you'll hear today, Bob. Term. Life. Insurance. Now I can tell by the look in your eye that you're thinking, 'I'm young. I'm healthy. I'm going to live forever. What do I need life insurance for?' I'll tell you, Bob. This isn't about you. This is about caring for and providing for your loved ones."

I'm not sure why Brenda, my secretary, let him into my office. I'd have to have a discussion with her when we returned to the infinity room. I'd hired her locally, but it didn't take long for her to become a concubine. She still came out on some days to run the construction office.

I glanced at the card he'd handed me. 'Douglas Pierpont III, Licensed Insurance Agent.'

"Do I know you, Doug?" I asked.

"Oh, I get that a lot, you know. Most everyone in town knows me. I've insured most of them. This is a town of people who care for their loved ones, and that's why I've come to talk to you."

I'd left San Francisco in the mid-70s after the Nixon fiasco. The war in Viet Nam was winding down and we were in a booming economy. It was time for me to adopt a new body and a new persona. I'd chosen this midwestern suburb as a place where I could get back to what I loved to do and build things. In this instance, houses. I bought a nice tract of land and got it zoned residential, then started building. The area had been growing out here south of the city and the local authorities welcomed my development with open arms. I had the land surveyed and started putting in the infrastructure within a year of arriving. The city had all the utilities installed and had inspected our streets. We hired local contractors to do the work, all by the book, as the city commissioners were prone to say.

I could have paid for everything at once and had a new neighborhood built by my people in the infinity room in days. But in this country, that was not the way to do business. I hired all union contractors and they knew I personally inspected every project every day. Houses started going up. I had a reputation of building luxury homes starting in the low $40s.

And into my office walked an insurance salesman.

That was something else I had to deal with that was new for me. Everyone wanted their piece of the pie, so to speak. If I chose the wrong supplier, work surprisingly slowed down as half the materials were discarded as 'inferior grade' by my foremen. I was sure Brenda probably knew this salesman and had ushered him in because he was her uncle's wife's cousin who sold her grandfather his policy. He looked vaguely familiar, but I couldn't place him. By this time of my life, I'd met thousands and thousands of people and it wasn't unusual for me to be reminded of an old acquaintance by a new acquaintance. I quickly learned not to say, "You look just like a eunuch I knew in Nebuchadnezzar's harem with a crooked tooth and wandering eye." That usually got a blank stare and a nervous laugh before the new acquaintance excused himself.

"Now, I know you're aware of the accidental death rate in this country. Not a pleasant thing to think about, but people die unexpectedly. You could be walking out on a jobsite and get run over by a bulldozer. It happens."

Was he threatening me? I didn't really think so. Apparently, some guy had been run over by a bulldozer just last year.

"What we're really concerned with here are your heirs. With your financial savvy and good business skills, this housing development is sure to be a success. But without you at the helm, your heirs could be bankrupt in days. That's what we want to protect against. Hardship for your family."

If something like that happened to me, bankruptcy would be the least of my family's problems. In the infinity room, there were nearly a thousand people in my household. Over three million in the world I'd created there. My demise would create a problem that a life insurance policy would not alleviate.

I wondered if I should be looking for a partner who could take over for me if something should happen. It seemed that 'accidents' like Doug described were all too common in America. And the war had taken a heavy toll on the younger generation. But I had no other demons in my rolodex that I could call on for help.

I really needed to get out of here and take my satchel someplace safe. I just hadn't found anyplace yet.

I ended up buying an insurance policy. The guy was a good salesman.

>-- ◄◆► --<

I'd often thought I'd found the perfect place to hide my package and retire. Australia was one such place, but everything there tried to kill me. South America was another. The abandoned city of Machu Picchu was our home for many years, but we couldn't trust it to stay concealed.

And then there was Mongolia. Talk about an isolated and faraway place. No one in his right mind would ever choose to go there.

I started across China, or the Khitan Empire as it was called at the time, near the turn of what we now refer to as the second millennium. For me, it was the beginning of my fourth millennium on earth. I might have continued right across on my westward journey were it not for Fa Zhi.

I had adopted the persona of a Buddhist monk as I made my way westward from the coast. It seemed the monks often traveled alone on undefined missions across the land. I did teach where there were willing students, however. While much of the area I traveled through had a significant shamanistic belief, for most people it was not incompatible with Buddhist beliefs, which did not attempt to replace their gods.

In many of the places I stopped, I built small temples, monasteries, or shrines to encourage the people. Many were studying the martial arts as they learned the mind-freeing practice of meditation.

I had stopped in a small town at an inn to take dinner and hire a room for the night when a small troop of soldiers and courtiers stopped there. They demanded the whole inn for themselves. The innkeeper attempted to explain that I was already given a room.

"He will have to find lodging elsewhere," said the leader of the escort. "This is Lady Fa Zhi and she requires the inn."

"But..."

"Please do not trouble yourself, innkeeper. The fine lady and her escort require your hospitality and I will be fine in the street," I said.

"I detect a condescending tone in your voice, monk," the haughty lady said, stepping forward. "I will have you stripped and beaten."

"If that pleases your ladyship, who am I to object—though I would rather we find some other accommodation for our differences."

"Kill him," she commanded her guards. They drew swords.

Now, I could have gone along with almost anything she wanted, but killing me was not polite. I defended myself and, in a few moments, all her guards lay on the floor unconscious. I bowed to the lady and she stepped back in fear.

"With respect, kind lady, I cannot allow that last order to be executed, so to speak," I said. "I wish you enjoyment of your rooms and your evening meal. Innkeeper, please take this purse as payment for the Lady's entourage and meal." I handed a bag of coins to the innkeeper who bowed repeatedly as he thanked me.

"Wait!" said the lady, not quite as strongly as her earlier commands. "I have mistaken a holy man for a common ruffian," she said when I turned toward her. "I beg you, please stay and dine with me. I need to make amends to your gods."

"Thank you, my lady. I would indeed be a common ruffian if I rejected your kind offer. If it pleases you, let me remove these gentlemen to their sleeping quarters so the servants do not need to step over them."

"You are too kind. Innkeeper, please show the monk where to deposit these men that they may sleep off their... unfortunate drunkenness." I noticed that she did not say their defeat or beating, but left the door open for at least some saving of face in the morning. I picked up two of the guards at a time and took them to rooms in the back of the inn that might otherwise have been used to stable horses. I was not sure.

When I'd taken the last of the six guards to their room, I paused and opened a gateway to call for half a dozen women, modestly dressed according to the customs of the land, to assist the innkeeper in preparing and serving dinner. Most of the innkeeper's helpers had fled at the first sign of a conflict. I then returned to join Lady Fa Zhi.

She invited me to her table, and when tea was brought, she dismissed the server to ritually pour the drink herself. When we were both served, we nodded to each other, turned our heads, covered our face, and drank. Then the food began coming to the table in bowls one after another.

"Your coin has paid for a feast," the lady said, gesturing at her own servants and courtiers who had also been served. "How comes a monk to be so strong and so wealthy?"

"Ah, strength has run in my family for many years," I said, thinking it was not too big a lie. It had been many years. I heard one of my women titter and glared at her. She quickly went to the kitchen. "As to the coin, I have been blessed by the gods to travel this land in order to find a place to build a temple where people may come for peace and education."

"Will that education include the techniques you use in combat?" she asked.

"It is my hope for people to travel in safety and to go about their daily work without worry about being attacked. Unlike many others, however, we recognize our own responsibility in ensuring our safety. Those techniques, as you call them, are a form of meditation practiced all over the south, the islands, and as far west as the Ganges. If one would learn the way of a monk, one must learn not only the words of the tantras, but the movements that free the soul," I said.

"All men should learn such meditation."

"And women," I answered. "There is no reason a woman must be subservient or walk in fear. I would have no woman raped or forced into bondage simply because she is too weak to defend herself."

"That message might not be well-received," she sighed. "I command these men because they fear my father and my future husband. Were it not for that, I would be as weak as any other woman."

Timing is a remarkable thing. At that moment, a band of brigands burst into the inn demanding food and women. They quickly assessed that there were no guards attending the lady and immediately turned to our table.

"Please, defend me," she whispered to me. "Please."

I sat calmly with my tea.

Before the brigands had reached our table, there was a wall of women between them and us. I had selected these women to assist the innkeeper because I knew them to be among the best of my martial artists. The brigands did not know this. They moved to brush the women away and before they knew what was happening, all were laid out on the floor, like the lady's guards had been. I had not moved.

"The women..." Lady Fa Zhi started. I motioned her to silence as the village patrol arrived.

The innkeeper explained what happened and how the brigands had been defeated. The leader of the patrol looked nervously at the women who had returned to serving the guests. They dragged the brigands off, presumably to their execution. I doubted that any would live to see the morning light. I turned back to my companion and smiled.

"These women are not the servants of the inn who fled when you defeated my guards," the lady whispered. I nodded. "Whoever you are, I would enter your service and learn what I have seen."

"Your husband to be might think differently," I said cautiously. Lady Zhi was petite and comely. She had already declared that her father and her fiancé were wealthy and powerful men. Taking on a band of brigands or even a small company of soldiers was one thing. I had no desire to lead my people into a war.

"He will not object. This marriage was arranged for the convenience of getting rid of a younger daughter and my future husband will be relieved not to have one more wife. Besides, I plan to no longer be a virgin in the morning."

>-- ◄◆► --<

I have lived in cultures that value virginity beyond reason, and in cultures that have no regard for the nuisance flap of skin covering a woman's vagina. China seemed to value the virginity of wealthy women and not have much regard for that of the poor—whether they wanted to give up their virginity or not. I have to say, I've been more places like that than not.

Even in the so-called enlightenment of the twenty-first century, women are devalued. An accusation of rape is more likely to be treated seriously if the woman is of a significantly higher social standing than the man. If a poor woman or a woman of color accuses a rich or powerful white man in America, she can expect to be deemed a gold digger or simply out to ruin a man's reputation.

"She asked for it," typically means the woman shouldn't have been born into the lower stratum if she didn't want to be raped.

I don't want to lecture or preach on the subject, but when one speaks about the seven deadly sins, I count murder and rape as six of them. I have held the shattered remains of women who have been raped in my arms as they wept inconsolably or as they withdrew from the world completely, never to be whole again. It is the only crime for which I am a willing executioner.

>-- ◄►> --<

Zhi's offered gift was a treasure I valued in the extreme. I touched it, examined it, tasted it, and ultimately gazed into her eyes as I parted that gate with my cock and paid her all my respect. I slid into her silky depths again and again, making sure she climbed the peaks of passion repeatedly with no regard for my personal pleasure. I was making love to a remarkable, beautiful, and willing partner. What more pleasure could I have?

For her part, Zhi had led a sheltered life and had no experience of men at all. By the end of the night, she was determined to read and practice every page of the *Kama Sutra*. Fortunately, I had a copy. We journeyed together for four more days with her guards warily avoiding contact with me.

Zhi asked where my women had gone and I said simply that I sent them on ahead. People of privilege, I have noticed, seldom note who is serving them. One servant is the same as another. So, when different women helped in the kitchen and served our food on subsequent nights, neither Zhi nor her entourage really noticed.

Let me correct that. Zhi, her guards, and her senior staff didn't notice. She traveled with a number of servants and I could see in their eyes that they wondered how different women left my chambers to serve each night. Of course, I was never seen by any of them either in Zhi's chamber or emerging from it. I was always in my own room when we rose in the morning. That served the double purpose of keeping gossip to a minimum and of giving me time to reward the ladies who had served that day. I always tried to make sure my ladies were satisfied.

At last, we arrived at the emperor's palace.

34
PAGODA

I FOUND THE EMPEROR to be personable. He treated us with the utmost courtesy when we arrived. When Zhi spoke in his presence, however, I was concerned for her safety.

"My Lord Daozong," Zhi said when she was presented. "I bring you greetings from my father, Fa Man-su. I pray that you will find it pleasing to grant my boon of becoming a priestess in the temple of Buddha. I have committed myself to this monk, Bob."

Of course, that wasn't the name I was using in China, but it gets confusing otherwise. This was the telltale point. Would the Emperor grant her boon, or insist she become his wife and execute me? Or execute both of us. What I wasn't counting on was a Khitan tradition of guest prostitution. When a high-ranking official was a guest in another's home, the host was expected to provide his wife or a virgin from his household to the guest for his entertainment. This was the most demeaning of customs, but I could think of no way to spare Zhi after her bold declaration.

"We shall consider your request in the morning, and the disposition of this monk." With that, the emperor dismissed his court. His women took charge of Zhi. I was led to a convenient room deep in the palace where I discovered guards had been placed at my door. I waited impatiently, too concerned to even open a gateway for my women.

It is not often that I find myself too concerned about something to consider having sex with one of my wonderful women. At this time, I had three wives—Namia, Penelope, and Lakshmi—and two possessions—Josie and Pari. And there were about a hundred willing women in my harem which included concubines and women who hadn't decided where they fit in yet, but liked the way I fit in them.

My wives and my possessions were kept exclusively for me. It is not that I demanded it of them, but that they chose that. Well, perhaps it was different with Josie and Pari. I possessed them and their will was mine. It would never have occurred to me to share one of them with another man. I didn't mind them playing with any number of women, but... Let's just say it is the male human in me that prevented me from sharing with other men. I often fought the masculine impulses in me with only moderate success. I, myself, had had sex with close to fifty men during the time that I was a woman. And not all of them were women I transformed. I had no justifiable reason to withhold male sex from my wives or concubines. I simply couldn't fathom sharing my wives or possessions with any other man.

So, the whole idea of guest prostitution baffled me. I noted that the emperor had conveniently reversed it, taking *my* woman for *his* pleasure, and leaving me with none. Not that I'd have enjoyed a woman who was sent to me without her explicit consent. And this night, not at all.

I wondered when it had begun to dawn on me that Zhi was *my* woman. Not that I possessed or even wanted to possess her, but that we had bonded on this journey. I asked myself if anyone would miss the emperor if he suddenly died, or scurried around the palace as a cockroach until someone stepped on him. But Zhi had warned me that this might be a possibility. It would be unlike a man as powerful as the emperor not to take his intended to bed when she got there. Fresh pussy and all that.

Still, I hoped she would be able to talk sense to him. I mean in our favor, of course.

>— ◄◆► —‹

"Monk Bob, stand before us," the emperor declared the following day when I was brought into his presence. I was not chained, but a guard stood on either side of me. "From whence does this name come?" he said.

"I come from the far south where it is a common name—often combined with another name just as Man-su or Ji-lin. Billy Bob is quite common, great Bìxià," I said respectfully. He was pleased and the meeting thawed.

"Bob, my woman Fa Zhi has told me of your plan to build a temple for Buddha and her desire to become Buddha's priestess. How do you plan to build this temple?" he asked.

"With your great lordship's permission, I have plans that I have made for a great pagoda honoring Buddha, as well as grounds and buildings to house his monks and a school for those who would learn the arts of a monk," I said. I presented the scroll on which I'd been drawing plans ever since I left Nihon. I liked the wooden temple I had left there and the dozen or more shrines I had built since then.

"You have built temples before?"

"Many, Emperor. I have built temples of stone, of brick, of wood, and of sand. The material is not a factor as much as is honoring Buddha." Well, technically, I'd only built a few temples to Buddha. But he didn't need to know that. He called counselors to his side to look at the plans and they all nodded in agreement.

"I would have Buddha honored in my town, along with our ancestors and the guardian spirits. How will you build and finance your project?"

"I have found that where men provide freely of their labor, the gods provide abundantly. I will seek laborers among the poor and downtrodden. I will have only those who will freely give of their talents and they will be compensated from the benevolence of the gods," I said. In reality, I could reach into my satchel at any time and pull out bags of the local coinage. This, too, I kept to myself.

"Guards. Maintain vigilance. I will walk in my garden with the monk," he said. With that he led me to a courtyard with gardens that grew rare plants and flowers. I wanted to collect several specimens for the infinity room. We were accompanied by twelve guards, fully armed and looking very strong.

"Bob, you have a reputation already. My people have heard from those who accompanied Fa Zhi that you overcame her guards and that your servants made short work of a band of brigands."

"Stories have a way of growing out of proportion, your majesty. Fa Zhi's guards were at fault for drinking so early in the day when they should have been vigilant. The brigands were taken by surprise and were not very good fighters."

"Yes. And they have been punished. Still these stories must be put to rest. I would know the true measure of a man I employ." I looked at him, understanding his meaning and nodded. He stepped away and turned to the dozen guards who had accompanied us to maintain vigilance. "Kill him," he said.

I may have mentioned, that was a command I really couldn't submit to. A brave guard drew his sword and attacked me by himself. He ended up face down in a pond. The other guards were disciplined and attacked as a single unit, using the best of armed combat discipline. Spears and swords both came at me and I was pressed to disable each of them. I was glad the emperor did not send a legion after me. I stood before the emperor and bowed.

"Soldiers!" the emperor cried out. *Oh, shit.* Heavy shoes echoed from every direction as armed men descended on the courtyard, all weapons pointed at me. "Collect all these sleepers who were supposed to attend and protect your emperor. Take them out and execute them."

The attention of the soldiers was immediately taken from me and they hurried to collect the unconscious guards and carry them from the courtyard. A dozen soldiers remained with the emperor and me. He turned and we re-entered his throne room.

"Bob, I trust you understand that I had to test you. There are disciples of another god who would have simply stood and died. I would have been very disappointed if you had done that. We really do need a temple."

"Yes, your highness. I pray for the easy release of your guards in knowing that to the end they followed your commands." I hoped the message got across that I wasn't pleased, but it didn't make a difference. Their fate was sealed.

"I cannot have people talking about how a single man defeated so many of my armed guards," the emperor said. "I will approve your plans and decree that a temple shall be built next to the palace. The rest is up to you. Oh. And you may have Fa Zhi for as much good as she will do you. She has a sloppy open cunt and is a dead lay. I cannot imagine you will have much pleasure in her. It was like fucking the ocean."

Hmm. I'd found her quite tight around my dick. I wondered at the emperor's equipment. Nonetheless, Zhi awaited me at the doors and we went to begin surveying the area next to the palace for the new Fagong Temple.

>-- ◄◆► --<

It has come to my attention that gods and rulers are quick to approve a site for a temple, a school, a prison, a pipeline, or a capitol building if the location is a problem site. The capitol of the United States was built on a swamp that neither Virginia nor Maryland wanted to deal with. It turned out beautifully and the swamp was no longer there. Unfortunately, development of the site could not ease the muggy heat or mosquitoes—or creatures disguised as politicians who gather there.

Even the Temple of Ninra was planned on land that not only had many poor people living there, but already had a temple, as well. A temple to Ganesh I built in India was commanded in the heart of a slum, intending to displace the poor and clean up the area. All without concern for what would happen to the poor.

I was called upon near the end of the twentieth century to submit plans for building a church in the midwestern city where I was building suburban luxury houses. Well, I have nothing against the Christian god. And the congregation claimed to be followers of Issa—of course, they called him Jesus. The site occupied a full city block just on the edge of the city's worst ghetto. Building there would mean the destruction of a habitat for the poor and people of color. The city had further approved plans to develop portions of the surrounding blocks into parkland. Not parks with playgrounds and jogging trails. No, just manicured lawns and benches for people to sit and meditate.

You might think, *Well, Bob would never have taken a commission like that. He cares too much about the poor.* I'm sorry to disappoint you, but I did take the commission. And I am happy that I did.

I went about it in my time-honored way. Before I began bulldozing apartment buildings and ramshackle houses, I bought up dozens of buildings in the surrounding area, using half a dozen different corporate identities. The city was pleased that these partially empty buildings would be put to use and possibly re-developed with the area improvement. As far as either the city or the church was concerned, we were expanding the zone of improvement and pushing the poor and homeless out farther away from the attractive downtown area.

Of course, I sent my own people into the area intended for destruction and had them move people to new homes in the broader area. It was my intent to keep as many people in the area where their homes were as I could. And I offered all those who would take them jobs building the new church and tearing down the old buildings. My promise to them was that everyone who worked to build God's temple would be cared and provided for.

Of course, I had to deal with unions and labor restrictions. It is amazing, however, how many people were admitted to the organizations when their fees were paid and they were compensated at full union rates. It seems there was no basis for complaint unless I was paying less than union scale. Or not paying the right union boss.

The result, of course, was that the neighborhood prospered. We redeveloped buildings in the expanded area gradually so that people would have better homes. The park area was planted by mothers and children who took pride in the lawns and played on the grass.

And the house of God was built. People who would never be welcome inside its doors still took pride in the beauty of the thing they had built. And when the church opened, with its predominantly white congregation, they found they were fully surrounded by people of color who spent Sunday mornings meeting in the park and singing gospel music.

Some years later, the congregation of the beautiful church filed for bankruptcy and I funded a new congregation of local people to buy the building and move their praise services inside.

>— ◆ —<

The Fagong temple site reminded me of the site where Ninra commanded he wanted his temple. There was already an old and broken-down temple there. Houses had been built right up to its walls and the walls of the palace grounds next door. People tend to huddle together where they see safety, and a temple or a palace has always been one of those places. Perhaps fifty little houses would need to be removed before serious work on a temple could begin. Fifty poor peasants who were right in the palace's shadow. I knew that if the emperor were involved, he would simply set fire to everything in the district and make the survivors clean up the rubble. If there were any survivors.

Instead, I started by sitting on the steps of the old temple and teaching. In addition to Zhi, I brought six of my students from the infinity room to sit and be instructed.

"Zōngshī, how does a poor person improve his lot in the next life?" one of my students asked. She used the highest honorific for me as an ancestral teacher. Over the coming years, I would be known here as *lǎoshī* (teacher) and *shīfù* (master) as well as the high honorific.

"Our lives are like the boards of this temple," I said. "Unless the boards near the ground are strong, the exalted boards on the fourth and fifth level will tumble to the ground. Do not question where the fates have put you now, but strive to be the strongest you can be at the level you are. In this way, not only will you improve your lot, you will make the lives of all those above you better."

"How can we become strong?" asked another.

I stood and they jumped to follow me as I led them in the ancient and more modern forms. The first to join us, of course, were the children. My people quickly ushered them to the front so I could see them and gently correct their form. When we had followed all the prescribed forms, my people brought food out of the temple and fed those who were gathered. Then I instructed people on the cleaning of the temple area and the removal of garbage and rubbish that had collected there.

In all this time, I did not mention my purpose of building a new temple, nor how much space would be required for the edifice. But slowly, over the course of several days, even the surrounding huts had been cleaned and improved. Occasionally, someone who felt threatened by the development would pack his meagre belongings and leave. When that happened, we carefully dismantled their habitation and stacked the wood for future use.

The only thing I had to take to the emperor was the matter of the palace waste. In the mornings, a servant would bring all the night pots to the wall and dump them on the other side. This went unnoticed as long as there was a peasant hut up near the wall with the waste poured in its back garden. When the fresh waste was dumped out in the open, however, it was a different matter.

I made my approach in the most direct way, by leaping over the wall at that point and capturing the unfortunate servant—much to the surprise of soldiers patrolling the grounds. They wanted to apprehend me, but they had all been warned not to confront me. Despite his desire to keep my abilities quiet, the word had spread that those who challenged me ended up dead, either by my hand or the hand of the emperor.

"Who is the person who instructed this servant as to where to empty the sewage?" I demanded. It took a bit, but an officious man who declared himself as the major domo or some such came to demand of me what I wanted.

"Why are you detaining my employee and how did you get into the palace's private grounds?" he demanded.

"I came here investigating why sewage is being dumped into the temple grounds," I said.

"Temple? Ha! That pile of shit is worth only having our shit added to it," he laughed.

"And do you have no sewer into which your toilets run?"

"Of course, we do. But it is all the way over on the other side of the grounds. Why should I have a servant waste valuable time by carrying chamber pots all the way over there? Now clear out and let us get back to our work."

I turned to one of the soldiers who had been watching the exchange and trying to decide whether he should interfere. He was caught between a rock and a hard place as to whether he should permit the intruder or sacrifice his life by challenging him.

"Tell the emperor that Monk Bob wishes to speak to him about the passage from the palace to the new temple," I commanded. The soldier hastened to an official at the chamber of meetings to inform him of my request. I followed to the approach to the audience chamber and soon I was called to the presence of the emperor.

"Monk Bob. I thought we had resolved all design issues. What is so important that you must disturb my meeting?" the emperor demanded.

"Your grace, it seems that an official decree is needed to stop the pouring of sewage from the chamber pots over the wall into the temple grounds."

"Why should I be concerned with where the sewage is poured?"

"Well, it happens that it is being dumped exactly where you have requested a gate from the palace grounds into the temple grounds. Any sewage dumped on that side of the palace will make your visits distasteful at best," I said smiling.

"Call the major domo!" the emperor barked. The frightened man was brought into the chamber. I sincerely hoped the emperor was not about to execute the man, distasteful as he was. "Let this be officially your order. All sewage, chamber pots, and waste of any kind shall be dumped only in the sewer drain and the wall adjoining the temple grounds shall be kept clean and pristine. You, personally, are to lead a cleanup crew to the temple grounds to remove all waste that has been dumped over the palace walls and take it to the sewer. Let this be done!"

The frightened major domo bowed his way out of the chamber and ran to collect a crew and start cleaning the mess of waste that had accumulated over the wall. The convenient dumping ground had been used for a long time. They had a task that lasted several days.

>-- ◀◆▶ --<

It all took time. Each morning, I would come out to the temple courtyard and begin meditative forms. More and more people joined me, some only because they knew we would feed people afterward. Most, however, stayed to work as we leveled the ground and built up the foundation of what would become the new temple.

Just as when I built the temple in Bathra, anyone who worked on the temple was sheltered and fed. We began converting some of the surrounding huts to dormitories where workers could sleep. I seldom issued commands, and then only in the building process. Beyond that, I let the latent pride of the people direct the cleansing of the temple area. When enough area had been cleared, I marked off the boundaries of the temple grounds. Within those boundaries, only the construction I directed was allowed.

Since we spent part of every day in meditation and exercises, it seemed almost as if we were not working on the temple at all. However, the grounds were gradually cleared and the walls arose almost silently. There was never the crack of a whip or the cry of a disciplined slave to herald the construction.

>-- ◀◆▶ --<

"Bob, how are you able to feed all these people?" Zhi asked me as we settled on our sleeping mats.

"Fa Zhi, will you be one of my women and join me for all eternity?" I asked. "For the answer to your question is in service."

"My master and my lover, I would join you and all that is yours if you will but have me," she answered.

That night, for the first time, I took her into the infinity room and she realized I was not just a simple monk building a temple, but I was the life and sustenance of an entire world.

I have seen love in many forms. I have seen suddenly inflamed passions. I have seen comfortable old couples. I have seen utter submission and utter dominance. I have seen the love of soldiers for their general and the love of one soldier for another. I have seen a mother's tender love for her children and a father's protection of his family. But I believe that night with Zhi may have been the first time I had seen or experienced love as utter and pure devotion and adoration.

It was very different from when I possessed a woman. That woman made the choice to become mine and from that moment our hearts beat as one. I had lovers who cherished me and I had cherished many. I had even seen slaves who came to love their masters. But to have a woman worship me in her devotion was beyond my ability to grasp.

Zhi worshiped me with her heart and with her body. She was among the smallest of my women, but she threw herself into the meditation and martial arts training with as much passion as she threw herself into my arms. She learned the art of tantric sex and the meditations that emptied her soul to the universe. When I parted her wet folds with my cock and thrust into her, she was transported to a new plane of spiritual awareness. I could not help but love her with all my heart.

>-- ◄◆► --<

As we loved, the temple grew. Word spread that there would be a new temple and offerings began to arrive from as much as a hundred miles away. Lumber, tile, stone, paper, ceramics, and even rare plants and herbs arrived, often with laborers who followed instructions as to *where* something was to be done, but already knew *how* it should be done.

Surrounding the temple grounds, people planted gardens instead of shacks. Water ran freely through the pools as I pumped it from the river, and it drained through our own sewer system to the waste ponds. When new plants arrived, we separated out samples to take to the infinity room and found a place where they could propagate there as well. In all, the temple grounds flourished. Much more was accomplished in much less time when the people approached the task feeling strong and refreshed after our forms and meditation.

The main pagoda rose six rooftops into the air and above that, I erected a tower as tall as five men, visible from everywhere in the city. By the time it was finished, over a hundred monks had gathered to do service and to train in the courtyard.

Many of the emperor's soldiers came to learn the arts as well. Since these did not labor on the temple, but rather for the emperor, we did not feed and house them. But we did not withhold any of the training from them.

The emperor, of course, was quick to take credit for the temple which he published far and wide as "The Temple Decree of Emperor Daozong," also levying a tax to help defray the expenses of the temple. Most of that tax went to the emperor, not to the temple. In fact, as much as the emperor took credit for being a holy ruler, his administration, as represented by his major domo, was corrupt.

It only got worse after he died. Eventually, I left the temple in the care of the monks and packed my satchel. I bid farewell as I set off on a sacred pilgrimage alone. Some distance away from town, I found a quiet place where I could change my shape and form, becoming a completely different Bob, the monk being gone.

35
In Xanadu did Kublai Khan…

THE MOST REMARKABLE THING happened at the end of the 1960s: A man landed on the moon.

It took me a couple of centuries in the country, but eventually I'd adapted to life in America. It changed so rapidly I had difficulty keeping up at times. I considered myself pretty sophisticated, with a television, an automobile, and a nearby movie theater. But the last week in July, I sat alone on a rooftop for seven days and seven nights, simply staring into the sky at the moon.

I cursed at Pinaruti again for not having given me wings. I would fly to the moon. Or farther. The television and theaters were filled with science fiction movies. People would one day fly farther than the gods of Olympus. I didn't say that aloud. Hubris.

I had never actually flown. Perhaps that is why I spent so many years of my life sailing the oceans. The wind in my hair. The salt spray of the seas. The loving companions from the infinity room. But even in my own infinity room, where I should be able to make any rule I wanted, my feet were firmly anchored to the ground.

And then, ten years after that historic small step for man, Liz came to me and said, "My momma's sick. Can we go visit her?"

I immediately thought of the houses I had under construction and dismissed any thought of staying because of them. I had good foremen and they would work without me for a few days. I'd said yes before I really considered what it implied. Her parents were on the West Coast. We were in the Midwest. I thought of the long car ride ahead of us. If her mother was that sick, we might not make it in time for Liz to say goodbye. I made the heart-shaking decision to fly. In an airplane. I bought tickets and we boarded a ship that took to the air. I was ecstatic! In just a couple of hours, we were in California and Liz joyfully ran to her mother's bedside.

I never regretted that trip. I flew! The feeling of leaving the earth behind us and flying through the sky, higher than any birds flew, was so intense it made me weep. It reminded me of my time with the Khaan.

>-- ◆◆▶ --<

Which Khaan? Well, all of them. It was Chinggis Khaan that I first encountered near the western mountains. He had just been declared the Great Khaan of all Mongols and was riding eastward to consolidate his kingdom. The Mongol Horde followed in his wake, subjecting all to his dominion. And I was somehow in his path.

I was brought before the great Khaan and paid appropriate homage to him. And then we sat and talked. He was a man of uncommon intellect and great wisdom as well. I told him stories of my travels and he laughed at them, because he knew no man could live long enough to have so many adventures.

He was especially interested, however, in the tales of Alexander and Caesar. He had me describe over and over how certain battles were staged and how they were won. He created a large board where I could build models and push troops around to show him how each battle was fought. The big difference between the Khaan's forces and either Caesar or Alexander was that nearly all the Khaan's troops were mounted. They couldn't really lock shields and march forward like the two great emperors did. But he learned strategy and tactics from everything I showed him as he prepared to move toward the Song dynasty in the south east.

The kingdom of the Mongols was a horse-based culture. Not only did they ride them, but they ate them. I was even served a fermented drink made from mare's milk, and it wasn't half bad.

And then one morning, Chinggis Khaan had me mount a horse and ride beside him.

I had been on horseback at times before and I had harnessed a horse to my chariot. I had horses pull my show wagon and had seen Alexander mounted on Bucephalus. But I had never mounted a horse and galloped for an entire day. We flew! It was like sailing across the great plains of Asia.

The Great Khaan captured cities that thought they had time to prepare. He did it by arriving days before they were ready. He swept up their armies and made them part of his own. But the horse brigade always arrived first.

The wind in my hair and the sun in my eyes was the most glorious feeling I had ever known.

And that was the feeling I had when the airplane took Liz and me to California. It was wonderful!

>-- ◆◆▶ --<

"Bob, may you live forever," Chinggis said to me one day as we walked about a city he had conquered near the Black Sea. "I am building a great empire. It needs a great city from which to rule it."

"This city might not be a good choice, Khaan. It is far from the center of your empire and is really not very well maintained," I said.

"These things are true. But I want no one to say of my capital city, 'Chinggis Khaan stole this city from the people and drove them out so he could rule in comfort.' No, I want a city that people will come to and say, 'The Khaan built this city to rule over our vast empire.' I want them to see the glory of the Khaan."

"That is a noble thought, Great Khaan. Where should this city be?"

"Over there somewhere," he said waving a hand vaguely to the northeast. "I know that sounds vague, but I don't know where to build this great city. The empire is vast and its emperor must travel from end to end each year in order to rule it. But he must have a place to call his home in this strange world."

"This would be a great endeavor," I said.

"Make no mistake; I will never see this city. Perhaps you will live forever, but I will not. I am already getting old. I have sons and they have sons. My son Ugedei has set out with an army to conquer Europe. Eventually, some one of my sons or grandsons will rule over the entire Mongol Empire and that one needs to summon his subjects to the most glorious city on earth. You have spoken of the gardens of Babylon. Make gardens for the Khaan. You have talked about the palaces and temples of Rome and Greece and Egypt. Create a palace and temples for the Khaan. You have seen the prosperity of India. Make a place where my heirs can prosper. Do this, Bob. Grant this wish to an old king."

"I will find a place where the Khaans of the Mongol Empire will prosper," I said. "If I cannot live long enough to make this place by myself, I will lay it out so the walls can go up when the Khaan arrives."

"I will tell my descendants to seek a Chinese monk called Bob and follow him to the place of honor. Go now, Bob. I don't know how long it will be."

I left the next morning, separating from the horde and riding the horse Khaan gave me off to the northeast, while he turned to conquer the south.

>-- ◄◆► --<

It was almost fifty years before I had direct contact with the horde again. The second Great Khaan was Ugedei, Chinggis' third son. Where his father had set about conquering the south and pushing into China as far as the sea, Ugedei Khaan set his sights on Europe and the land of Alexander. He annexed most of what is now Russia, all of China north of the Yangtze River, and pushed through the lands of Persia and Asia Minor.

Ugedei apparently missed his father's tale of a city prepared for him. He built his capital at Karakorum, one of the palaces he stopped at during his annual rides from China to Europe. He was poised outside Vienna and ready to attack when he died suddenly. Thrown into disarray, his army withdrew to await the decision of the next great Khaan.

That took some time. Two more Khaans rose to power, a brother of Ugedei and a nephew. But Ugedei's strong influence encouraging trade throughout his empire, kept the empire from falling apart. It took until the Fifth Great Khaan, Hubilai, to create a government that could administer and control the great empire.

>-- ◄◆► --<

Traveling in the general direction that Chinggis had pointed me, I journeyed much more slowly than the horde. I surveyed all the likely places that I might lay out a city of the sort he described. I kept track of my location based on the star charts I always maintained. Released from the pressure of the moving horde, I spent time in the infinity room with my wives and concubines. If it weren't for my knowledge that one day a great Khaan would move through this area, I might have attempted to hide my satchel in this vast empty land and claim it for my own. But I knew that anywhere on earth a person claimed as his own would one day be conquered. I could not risk that for my people.

I had been traveling for a few years, crisscrossing the land, when I came upon a perfect location. There were mountains on one side and a river on the other. Water was plentiful with lakes and springs. The vegetation was lush and materials were plentiful. I paced around the area I would claim and it took me two days to make the full circuit of what would one day become Kaiping, the city of the Great Khaan.

After I had surveyed the land by eye, I set up a place where I could shelter in a cave and opened a gateway to the infinity room. My wives and concubines all came out to view the territory and comment on where the palace would be located and how the streets would be laid out.

"It reminds me of Bathra," Nimia said as she cuddled next to me in front of a fire. "A very lush and green Bathra," she giggled, remembering how dusty and dry the ancient city had been when we first arrived.

"At least we don't need to move people away in order to lay the city out," I said. "I wonder how long it will take before people discover us here and begin to move in."

"Not long, I would say. Have you ever noticed how word of a place seems to travel even when no one has seen it? It is almost as if thinking of a place puts its image in the air and people suddenly speculate that the place must exist. They even draw maps of it before anyone has explored there."

Words like 'not long' and 'suddenly' might have had a somewhat different meaning to Nimia than to people in the natural world. Though she still looked as fresh and lovely as the first time I saw her bathing next door, she was the only person in the infinity room who might say she was older than I was. By a few years. She was still in her early teens when I was summoned. So, after three thousand years, saying 'not long' could mean sometime in the next century.

"My love, lie with me in this cavern tonight," I said gently. "Let your breath mingle with mine and our love be heard before our city is built."

Nimia's mind and body were still as lusty as the teen's she had been when we met. She pushed me back and pulled my robes from me.

"First, my demon lover, I would have you in the shape I first saw you. I want the demon my mistress Ariane laid eyes upon and sacrificed all to be with him. Come, my lover. Come to me as you really are."

And so, I shed my human form and returned to myself. In a way, it was a relief to not be encumbered by a human body, even though I always chose splendid examples of fitness and strength to inhabit. She reached up and stroked my horns—one nicked by the demon in the desert of Arabia. She ran her hands down my chest and arms. She dipped her head to kiss the grand staff that stood from between my legs, and ran her hands down my hairy legs to my very hooves.

Nimia was as fascinated with my demon form as she had been the first time it was revealed to her. And she loved it. I kissed her and tickled at her sensitive points with my claws, careful not to injure her delicate skin with their sharpness. My tongue snaked out to enter her secret valley and dive all the way to its depths, then curl back along the top, sending her into spasms of delight. And then I entered her with my rod. In my demon form, my phallus was what Pinaruti had imagined, which was considerably more than most women could contain. But Nimia opened to me and I sank deeply into her as we kissed and she thrust against me.

We had both participated in the tantric sex games we learned in India. When I was in the form of a woman, she had taken the form of a man and entered me to find a completion she had not experienced before. And since she knew what a man felt when he entered a woman, and I knew what a woman experienced when she was fucked, we judged our responses and built slowly to our climaxes.

When we reached the peak of our pleasure, we both cried out with such passion and pleasure that the water in the cavern split into new streams to enter the valley of our city and the hot baths of the cavern were surrounded with ice pinnacles that reflected light in all directions. The echo of our passion seemed to never die as I emptied myself into her waiting womanhood and she milked me of all my come.

>-- ◀▷ --<

Nimia was also a great help in city planning. She, too, had seen Bathra, Babylon, Troy, Rome, Athens, Carthage, and Alexandria, as well as the great cities of India and Nihon and China. I remember a few hundred years later, she helped me plan the development of houses I built in the Midwest.

"People who own luxury homes want to imagine they have an estate, not just a house," she told me. "Straight city blocks remind them of the common man. They want to believe no one else has as grand a mansion as they have, so they don't want to look next door and see another just like it."

To facilitate her planning, which she had done much of in the infinity room, she enlisted the services of a mathematician in the room and they designed a network of streets that did not run in a straight grid. Each dwelling appeared to be on its own isolated plot where others could not see it. We had to do a lot of grading of the land to get hills and valleys where we wanted them. Adding utilities to the neighborhood was a puzzlement to the city. But when we were finished and had planted trees and erected fences, most people had a view of their property with little or no view of their neighbors. We planted high shrubs along all the streets, so that when a resident entered through the gates to the community, they had the impression they were driving down their own long lane to their home, and not down a street lined with houses just like theirs.

Later developments of the eighties attempted to copy our winding streets, but they did it without changing the terrain or landscaping the homes. As a result, they looked like knotted messes of streets with houses stacked one on top of another. It was a perfect example of the mass production of something that had been a craftsman's dream without any of the infrastructure that a true craftsman would start with. By the nineties, housing developments had returned to straight gridded streets with houses set a uniform distance back and facing the same direction. Beauty proved to be too much work.

>-- ◄►‒‹

In the Khaan's city, I began work, assisted by those who wished to visit the natural world they'd once known and then return to the infinity room. We were not a large crew, but we surveyed and cut and dug and piled. We changed the terrain and put in streets and water and sewer before we built a single dwelling.

Because this was not only a city, but a fortress, I chose to make it perfectly square, about ten miles on each side. The mountains were in the north and the river ran to the south, but several streams ran through the city itself, providing fresh water. We took spare dirt and stone to a pile where the palace would be. Around this, we laid out an inner wall, a mile square, to define the palace grounds. Next to this, I created a modest temple. On the south, we lined up a main gate to a bridge across the river, leading to the gate of the palace complex.

Strategically, one would wonder about having a street running straight for a few miles from the gates of the city to the palace. But all the houses and places of business that lined this street were equipped with a rampart where soldiers could be lined up to shoot down on the street. I shuddered to think of what a killing field that would be should someone have the temerity to attack the palace of the Khaan.

I can talk about all the work as if it were the labor of a few days, but in fact, we worked on the city layout for years. And true to Nimia's predictions, people began to migrate to our city. With more people, there were more laborers. Small businesses grew up. I chose to let the area outside the city grow organically and farms were established with crops and animals. As we had always done, we provided for those who labored. Some worked fields, some tended pastures, and some built buildings. It was turning into a glorious city.

When the envoy of Hubilai Khaan the Great, emperor of the Mongols, arrived to lay claim to the city, he expected to have a siege. Instead, he found a peaceful city of some 20,000 inhabitants, waiting to welcome the king. I continued building, working on the temples, and making sure the houses of the populace were maintained and well-constructed. They were a mix of stone and timber and showed a prosperous front.

Hubilai Khaan arrived with much of the horde at his back.

"Where is Liu Bingzhong, called Bob?" he shouted at the southern gate.

I approached and bowed low. My Chinese appearance was now as an old man.

"Oh, Great Khaan. Welcome to your city. May the gods shine down upon you and your reign. May you live forever."

Khaan dismounted and walked into the city with me, looking in all directions. The main avenue led straight through the center of the city to the inner wall of the royal compound. And in the center of the compound rose the palace of the Khaan.

"Shangdu," the Khaan breathed. "It is good."

There was a bit of chaos that ensued, but the king's envoy had already set up administrative offices and managed the settling of the hundred thousand in Khaan's migrating force with relative ease. I sat with the king at dinner and he offered me food from his plate.

"Bob, this pleases me. How may I reward you?" he asked.

"Great Khaan, if you please, grant me leave now to return to my homeland by the sea that I might die among my ancestors, for I am very old."

"But you can have gold, jewels, women, horses. Anything to take with you," he said.

"What good are these things in a man's tomb?" I asked. "Still, if it pleases you to give me a horse, it would make my journey easier."

Of course, leaving a king is not as easy as saying 'goodbye' and going. Khaan wanted a tour of every inch of his city. We toured the temples where I had trained monks in the martial arts and Khaan immediately wanted his troops trained to fight in this manner. In fact, it took nearly five years for me to leave Xanadu.

In that time, I met the Italian explorer, Marco Polo. Some other time, I will tell you of our meeting.

At last, however, the day came. Hubilai Khaan, the fifth great Khaan of the Mongols, bid me farewell and granted me a horse. I left through the east gate and rode with the wind in my hair toward the coast.

I flew.

END PART VII

Part VIII
Bob Almighty

Image by Bruce Rolff, ID2051686583 licensed from Shutterstock.com.

36
THE LEGEND BEGINS

BEING CAUGHT IN GUABANCEX'S hurricane was not the first time I'd been blown off course by an angry god. Remember Guabancex? After the Spaniards landed in the new world and I got blown in a hurricane to Kukulcán? It's in the first volume. Well, of course, I'd had run-ins with Poseidon aplenty, but...

Let me start at the beginning. I'll tell more about my adventures in China some other time. After my time with the Khaans, I finally reached the east coast of China in the city of Huating, not far from the crossing to Nihon. Once a humble fishing village, now it was becoming a shipping capital with ships from as far away as England and France making it a port of call. It was a perfect place for me to get a ship.

"This is not a fishing boat," the ship owner said. I nodded. It was certainly too small to be considered a shipping vessel, but it did look fast. I could imagine flying across the waves on this little ship. The wind in my hair. The fresh salt spray. And all that.

"Yes, I can see that. I like its features. Looks sleek and fast."

"Well, if you have a good crew, it could win a race among the islands. Can you sail?"

I wanted to tell him I'd begun sailing where the first navy in human history was floated. I'd sailed the Mediterranean Sea, the Indian Ocean, and the Bay of Bengal. Of course, he wouldn't believe that because I had the appearance of being a strong and willful young Asian, out to find my fortune. In truth, I was constantly on the lookout for kidnappers who would grab me to be a crewman on some freighter. I wouldn't mind that so much as I could always take over the ship, but they were too large for my purposes. Some other time, perhaps.

I finally managed to convince him I was a good choice as a boat owner and paid him too much for the little boat. Before he could call anyone to grab me, I'd jumped onto the boat and shoved off. He ran along the docks and shortly, I saw three other boats of similar model cast off and set their sails to follow me.

Well, I knew a few tricks these fellows didn't and set a fresh breeze in my sail, soon outdistancing them to such a degree that they fell back and turned around toward their berths. And I was off and sailing. I set myself generally southeastward and lay back to relax. I celebrated my first night on the open seas with a flask of wine from the infinity room and settled back to enjoy the journey, as I kept the wind in my sail and my hand on the tiller.

I put in at a few South Sea islands and restocked with wine. That's not the subject of this little tale.

Perhaps I drank a bit too much wine. I woke up in the midst of a storm that had the marks of celestial interference about it. It turned out that I'd accidentally strayed into a raging battle between Tāwhiri, the Maori god of storms and the sea, and his brother Tu of the angry face, the Maori god of war (and cunning and the destruction of humanity, etc.) When Tu came upon my little ship, he flung it behind him to get it out of his way as he grappled with his brother. I landed far inland on what I now know as the great island of Australia. My ship, broken in pieces around me, was good only to build a rough shelter to crawl into.

I did not stay in my shelter for long. Too many other beings crawled in with me. It seemed that everything in Australia was devoted to killing me. Snakes, crocodiles, jelly fish, spiders, bears, sharks, and even a giant bird called a cassowary. Anything not intent on killing you will still fight you, including the indigenous people. During the entire time I was in the land of the Australian aborigines, I kept the gateway to the infinity room closed.

Except once.

I looked at my star charts, which were woefully incomplete for this part of the world, and determined that I was far southeast of India. So, I headed northwest, making my way across a land that was alternatively a rich and fertile paradise and a barren desert. It was as I was making my way that I came across an aboriginal tribe that only tried to be dominant over me and not necessarily kill me. I acknowledged my innate inferiority and they then accepted me into their tribe—not quite as a long-lost brother, but more like a scarcely tolerated distant cousin who desperately wants to be part of the family, but keeps getting drunk, insulting the grandfather, and suggesting lewd acts to a married first cousin. Not that I did any of that literally. Exactly. Suffice it to say that my time with the Kalahalakalaka was informative.

By this time of my life, I had met hundreds of different races of people and at least dozens of different civilizations. I discovered that the hundreds of tribes and groups of Aboriginals in Australia were probably the oldest civilization on earth. I estimated they were thousands of years older than my own people on Crete, or any I encountered in Mesopotamia. And they were fantastic storytellers. Ask any question and a fatherly or motherly person of the tribe would sit you down and begin to tell you how it all began.

"When Awa's father sent him to get water from the stream..." a story would begin, and before long, I would discover that two thousand cycles of the sun ago, the spine was broken off a rackarock fish and grew its own body. "And that is how the dreaded dingadocka was created."

When I began to build my boat, I told the people about my voyage across the sea and how Tu had thrown me all the way across Australia. The people were delighted by the story. They wanted to know about where I had been and how I had sailed so far. They helped to build my boat in any way they could and often met until late at night to go over the details of my story and figure out how it fit into their own unique mythology.

I finished the boat and told my adopted tribe that in the morning, I would set sail northward again. When I rose with the sun, I discovered the entire village had been disassembled and packed on the backs of the tribe. They stood by my boat waiting for me. They were not there to see me off. They had packed everything in their village and had even captured some of the less dangerous animals to bring with them when they joined me on my boat. They had to know that the little boat I had fashioned would not hold the seventy or so of their cluster, yet they confidently waited for me to bring them aboard.

I explained that if they boarded my boat, they would find themselves in a different dreamland. They would never return to this dreamland and would live very long lives in *my* dream. They thought this was excellent. So, I consulted with my women and they designated an area far from where our cities were located. I opened a gateway and as the tribe set foot on my boat, it entered into the infinity room. I entered there long enough to explain to them where they were and they nodded and shooed me away to sail my dream.

I paused only long enough to kiss my wives and concubines and possessions, then sealed the satchel and set sail.

That was a long voyage. I intended to make for India, but was blown westward and began a slow crawl up the west coast of Africa toward the Mediterranean Sea. The voyage took a hundred years and I finally arrived in Italy near the middle of the fourteenth century, just as the black plague was taking hold.

>— ◆▶ —<

Let me see. I've told you about Italy and Spain and Columbus. I told you about the Mayan gods recruiting me and my beautiful possession Maya. Well, Maya and I worked our way south until we found the abandoned town of Machu Picchu and there, I hid the satchel and stepped in. We were there for many years and I only came out of the infinity room occasionally to see that the area was still undisturbed. The rest of the time, I spent exploring the infinity room which was truly vast by this time. I eventually made my way to the tribe of Aborigines I had brought from Australia. They had changed their name to Bobbobbob in honor of the god who brought them to this rich land where they flourished. I tried to think how many centuries they had lived in this corner of the infinity room and could not figure it out. Time is so undependable in the infinity room.

To listen to them tell the story to their children, they had lived there many thousands of years, dreamed into existence by The Bob. I was not just Bob anymore; I was The Bob. I was now a part of the creation myth and was deemed the supreme ruler of the gods of this land they now inhabited.

"Bob looked upon the empty land and was lonely. So, he spoke the word of creation and plants and animals grew in the land and there was plenty for everyone. But Bob was still lonely.

299

In all the land he could find no storytellers to speak of him and his mighty works. And so, Bob wandered and found the dreamtime of Ungambikula. Ungambikula had also wandered the earth and found shapeless bundles by waterholes, and under trees, and in the nests of birds. These, Ungambikula carved and gave heads and arms and legs. When they were finished, Ungambikula went back to sleep and humans wandered its dreams. Bob quietly borrowed the Bobbobbob people from Ungambikula and brought them to this land in his dream where they live today."

I was no longer a demon in the hearts of the Bobbobbob. I was the dreamer and sustainer of life.

$$\succ\!-\!-\,\blacktriangleleft\!\blacklozenge\!\blacktriangleright\,-\!-\!\prec$$

I landed in southern California in the early eighteenth century. Of course, that involved having set sail from Lima early in the seventeenth century. That journey lasted nearly one hundred years and was very profitable.

Much has been written about piracy in the Caribbean. It was a major form of trade, engaged in by both privateers and buccaneers as well as general pirates. The difference? A pirate is a private warship that preys on other ships of any nation for its personal gain. Privateers are private warships that have a license from their nation to attack enemy ships and take their cargo. A Buccaneer is a private warship operating in its own interest without any official sanction, but generally does not prey on ships of its own nation.

For the ocean being as big as it is, it is amazing how many ships found and chased down others. There were nearly constant battles at sea and the spoils were taken by the victor. I'd had a fair amount of experience with pirates in the Mediterranean and had eventually operated with a kind of license from Caesar, so I guess I'd been a privateer.

Little has been said, though, about piracy on the Pacific coast of the Americas and on the burgeoning trade routes between the Americas and Asia. Wherever trade is found, piracy will also be found.

$$\succ\!-\!-\,\blacktriangleleft\!\blacklozenge\!\blacktriangleright\,-\!-\!\prec$$

The day came when I decided Machu Picchu was no longer a safe place for us. That's what I told myself. Perhaps I was just itching to move and travel again and made that my excuse. Regardless, I shouldered the satchel and came down from my mountain city. I found a different culture than any I had seen before. Eighty percent of the native population had been wiped out by conquistadores and disease. The Spanish administered the region and silver had become a major commodity.

An entire city in the Andes had been created overnight to mine silver and send it down to the seashore to be shipped back home to Europe. Of course, that wasn't an easy thing to do. In order to facilitate efficiency and a currency of sorts, the silver was first refined and then minted into coins. Spanish pesos became the standard in the trade of silver. After the coins were minted, they were loaded on ships to work their way north to the isthmus of Panama, where they were trundled across the land to be picked up in the Caribbean for transport to Europe—or capture by pirates. It was a difficult journey because the northward journey was against the prevailing winds and the ships had to tack slowly northward. That made them an attractive target for pirates.

By whim of the sea and the wind, a merchant discovered a trade route from Peru to Asia and the Spanish colonies in the Philippines. This proved much more profitable because the ships could move loaded in both directions rather than sailing the faster trip south from Panama empty. Silver pesos transferred to the Philippines were traded for silk and spices which were then returned to Panama or Mexico for shipment to Europe.

Wherever a major trade route is established, piracy is soon established as well.

I intended to buy a ship of my own and see if I could finish my intended journey to India. But buying a ship in this era was a difficult matter. I would have to find a shipyard and build one myself if I wanted to sail the Pacific. Instead, I joined the ship *Sunrise* bound for Manilla as a member of the crew. I thought I might have better luck getting a good ship in Asia.

We were three days out of Lima when we were set upon by a pirate ship. A shot was fired across our bow and the captain dropped sails immediately. It was obvious that the small cannon of our ship was no match for the well-armed pirate ship.

The pirates tied up to the *Sunrise* and boarded us. They drafted the sailors to transport the chests of silver from the *Sunrise* to the pirate ship. I carried a chest of silver across and then had a quick look around. It was a good ship and I was not above stealing from thieves. Once the cargo had all been transferred, the pirates—a congenial lot—helped themselves to a celebratory banquet on the *Sunrise* with the captain and crew. No one noticed I was not among the sailors who had returned from the pirate vessel. I silently cut the ropes and let our ships drift apart. Then I used a simple spell I had learned in my earliest days of sailing and unfurled all the sails on the ship at once. I shot away from the *Sunrise*, leaving both crews aboard it. I concealed the ship with a look-away spell so the *Sunrise* would be unable to follow and then had a look around my new home.

I'd seen the hold where we stored the silver and then inspected the cargo already aboard the ship. I wondered where the pirates planned to take all their bounty. This ship had cabins below deck as well, designed to sleep half a dozen men each. As I examined them, however, I discovered I was not entirely alone on this ship. The pirates had provided for their entertainment by capturing or buying women.

Each cabin had a woman chained to one of the beds. It was plain to see that the half dozen sailors who occupied that cabin shared the woman among them. They were all naked, showed signs of beatings and starvation, and cowered in a corner when I looked into the cabin.

I quickly went into the captain's cabin, which I would use as my own, and opened the gateway. I called out women from my harem to assist the captives. I was sure any approach I made would simply terrorize them more. My wives and possessions led a cadre of my other concubines onto the ship to release and care for the traumatized young women. They led them into the infinity room.

I didn't need help sailing the pirate ship, though I had to stay awake and at the helm. I didn't feel comfortable dropping the sails and sitting in the current while I slept or entertained myself in the infinity room. It wouldn't do to steal a ship and rescue its prisoners, only to be captured by another pirate ship. To keep me from getting lonely, one or ten of my women would come out of the infinity room each night to join me beneath the Pacific stars.

>— ◄◆► —<

"Can you heal their minds, Bob?" Esmeralda asked when she joined me on deck. My fourth wife was loving and kind and just as horny as the first day I met her. But she was troubled by our rescued women. "They are so damaged, most cannot even talk, no matter what language we use to communicate. They have not recognized they are free and stay huddled in a corner of the room we prepared for them. They cling to each other as the only reality they know."

"I wish I had Issa's ability to heal. It is something I have never learned. And I don't know if healing a mind is even the same as healing a body," I answered. I was troubled by the plight of the women as well, and had considered returning to the Sunrise to kill the pirates who had abused them so badly. Unfortunately, or perhaps for my own good, the wind and current ran westward and I would stand little chance of finding them once I hit the eastward currents.

"Could you take control of them as you did Princess Agora?" she asked. Of course, Esmeralda had not been with me yet when I possessed my third woman. She knew it had been done to save her sanity.

"I took possession of Agora because she could not cope with the world *I* brought her into. I was responsible for her condition and did the only thing I could think of to help her. I swear that I will never again possess a person without her will and consent. The people in our world will have free will," I said adamantly.

"But surely there is a part of what you do that could simply be used to ease their minds, Bob." She paused and touched my cheek. She was not going to let this rest. "I know I am pestering you to do something you do not want to do. I... All of us are moved with compassion for these mistreated women. I believe they thought they would simply be drowned at sea when the pirates had finished with them."

"Esmeralda, I have compassion as well. Like all the other women in my household, I created a kind of bond with them when I brought them to our home. I see them. I feel them. I hurt with them. I will think on what can be done. Please tell the librarians to search the books for a means of healing their minds."

Esmeralda kissed me passionately. The matter was apparently not so urgent that she felt she needed to rush back to the infinity room without making love again. I loved the Italian girl I had brought with me from Spain—the one whose great grandmother had trapped me in my satchel for seventy years.

>— ◄◆► —<

I had a real problem dealing with the captive women. I had to stay out on the deck or else equip a crew to sail through the night. We tried bringing them out onto the deck so I could talk to them, but if anything, that set them back even further. They panicked, thinking they were being brought back to the sailors' cabins. One broke free and flung herself overboard.

I did not hesitate to dive into the water after her and bring her back to the ship. I needed every ounce of my strength and I shed my human form to make full use of my demon strength as I swam after her. It took me a while to reach her as the boat was moving away quite rapidly. When I caught her, she was half-drowned and I breathed life back into her lungs with my own breath while I treaded water. When she began breathing on her own, she gasped as she saw me in the moonlight.

"Rest in my arms, child. Bob has you now and I won't let you die."

By that time, the ship, without a captain and with my infinity room on board, was far ahead of me. It took a watch of the night for me to catch up to it, carrying a crying woman in one arm.

My women were quick thinkers and immediately called some of the sailors out of the infinity room to furl the sails and watch with ropes ready to throw to me. Then they took all the remaining women back to their room. They were watching for me as I reached the ship and threw me lines. I hauled the shivering and nearly comatose girl up onto the deck and delivered her into the hands of my concubines.

As long as I had men on deck with me, I decided to sit with them and have a drink of wine as I told them about how the new ship sailed. I restored my body to human form, which put them much more at ease. The ship was larger than any we had used in the past. Even under the influence of the wine, the men grasped the intricacies quickly. It was more difficult to explain the operation of the cannons. None of these men were of an age in which the use of gunpowder was a thing. I decided perhaps I should bring out some of the men who joined me from the Chinese or Mongols to help with the defensive systems.

For the time being, I hoped I did not need to use them.

37
PRAISE BOB!

IT TOOK TWELVE more weeks before we moved into the waters of the Asian islands. I looked our ship over carefully in that time and decided it needed a bit of an overhaul. This had been a pirate ship and might be known in the Asian waters. I went to work, changing the sail configuration and the color of the sails, finding a Spanish flag to fly, and disguising the guns so they were not so obvious. This involved moving them below deck to a special platform I constructed for them that would have portholes above the waterline. The guns were thus concealed from sight, though this meant both cabin space and hold storage were lessened.

The space in the hold for cargo did not bother me since we transported all our cargo in the infinity room. The cabins, however, were a different matter altogether. After having crossed the Pacific staying awake for three and a half months and being on deck alone most of the time, I thought I might take on a small crew for the next voyage. I would try to make sure they were men—and perhaps women—who were likely to want to move to the infinity room eventually. I'd offer them the opportunity in exchange for their service.

We sailed into port in Manila harbor and were directed immediately to the Parian, where Chinese merchants were set to trade and exchange goods for the silver we carried. I called up a full crew from the infinity room for this operation and several women to help with the trade negotiations. Having women driving the deals threw off the Chinese merchants, but they soon accepted them when they found they could neither out-haggle them, nor kidnap them.

There was an attempt at the latter and six thugs found themselves nailed to the door and front wall of the merchant who sent them. I am happy to say, I had nothing to do with that operation. My women acted in self-defense and were never seen harming a soul. We might even have gained a little edge that we would not have had if I had been bargaining directly.

I busied myself with the process of hiring a crew. This involved hanging out in a variety of dockside taverns where there were always sailors enjoying shore leave, and drinking large quantities of *Tubâ*, a Filipino wine made from fermented palm sap. I collected a few dozen pottery jugs to add to our collection of wines in the infinity room. In the long run, they proved to be quite popular to trade in Mexico and we made the wine a regular trade good on our future trips.

Oh, yes. The crew. I was not particularly successful at recruiting experienced sailors, but I found a region of Manila that was populated by women of the night. I found many of these women to be perfect candidates for sailing a ship. Most were unhappy with life working on their backs and many dreamed of escaping to the sea. The women would need to be trained, both in sailing and in martial arts. I was not going to have women on my ship who could not defend both themselves and the ship.

I ended up with nearly two dozen women who listened carefully to what I had to say—spoken mind-to-mind, since I did not speak Tagalog—and decided the life I offered was considerably better than what they currently had. I might have nudged them just a little when it came to believing that what I said was true. I led my new crew, along with their belongings, back to my ship, which we'd christened *The Erinyes*. I had it in mind that wherever we found pirates who had abducted women and enslaved them, we would utterly destroy them and visit vengeance upon their heads. I intended to find the *Sunrise* someplace during our voyage.

We left the harbor and sailed out to sea, following the current that had been charted westward. The eastward current was much farther north than the westward current, but once we reached the continent of the Americas, we could sail south along the coast without a great deal of difficulty. So I was told.

During the first few days at sea, I spent my time instructing the women on how to sail the ship, while Zhi came out on deck to instruct them in self-defense. The women took to both forms of instruction with zeal and soon I had women crawling up the rigging, scrubbing the decks, trimming the sails, and handling the tiller. For a while, I would need to keep one or two of my women on call with them when I disappeared into the infinity room, but I felt that at last I could spend time there to see if I could help the rescued slaves.

I can say that dealing with the women who had been kidnapped, enslaved, raped, and abused by the pirates was not completely unlike dealing with any animal that had been abused. The concubines who cared for them had regained a measure of trust, but that was not shared by any man. I sat in the room with them quietly for some time, just being there. They finally reached the point of ignoring me, which I considered a sign of progress. After an exhausting time of just sitting quietly, I left to go to bed. I made love with Josie and Maya, but it was a kind of sad lovemaking in which we knew we needed comfort more than sex. We slept together.

"Master Bob! Master Bob!" Zhi called as she shook me awake. I sat up ready to rush to the deck if we were being attacked.

"What is it, my precious. What has you upset?"

"After you left the captive women this evening, I sat outside the room meditating to see if I would be shown how to reach them and comfort their minds. As I meditated, I thought I heard your name being called. I pressed my ear against the door and heard the women chanting softly, 'Demon Bob come to us. Demon Bob save us.' Bob, they don't know it is you!"

"Can it really be so simple as telling them I am Demon Bob?" I asked.

"No, it can't. They would not believe you. Remember one has seen you in your full goat glory. They will only believe you if you show them who you really are," she said.

I rose from bed and stood in front of my mirror. My Spaniard body was looking a bit worn and I didn't like it much anyway. I released the spell that kept the form and stood before the mirror in my horns and goat legs with my huge phallus dangling between them. Zhi nodded.

"And here I was afraid I'd frightened the poor girl even more," I said.

"She has apparently convinced the others that Demon Bob is their protector and salvation. You may need to do whatever is necessary, Bob," Zhi said.

Whatever was necessary. When I'd rescued the girl from the sea, what had I said? 'Rest in my arms, child. Bob has you now and I won't let you die.' This was going to tax my acting skills.

I reached the door with a dozen of my warriors and women behind me. I did not open the door; I broke it down. The warriors and women behind me raised a ruckus, demanding to know what I was doing. I shouted back at them.

"Stand away. You have rescued my beloved servants. I will not have them come to harm." I turned and looked at the women who stared at me with awe. Then one at a time, they knelt and pressed their faces to the floor in obeisance.

"My precious daughters. I have found you at last. You were captured and rescued and now I have found you. No one will harm you ever again."

One by one, they lifted their heads and looked at me in all my horny goat glory. Then they began to chant together, "Bob our master. Bob our savior. We will serve Bob forever."

I knelt in front of them and opened my arms. They rushed to me and let their tears flow at last.

"Our master and savior, let us serve you. We are unclean. Take away our filth and let us be your priestesses forever," said one of the women. I quickly identified her as the one I'd pulled from the sea.

What??? Priestesses? My first thought was to refuse such a blatant affront to the gods. But there were no gods in the infinity room. I created it. I populated it and made a paradise. And as far as the women were concerned, this would be a true means of healing for them.

"Listen and hear my decree," my voice boomed out so that all in the outer chamber could hear me. "These are the precious priestesses of Bob. I will take them to the water and cleanse them of their unrighteousness. They shall build to me a temple and shall minister to my people, now and evermore. They shall receive from my people their measure of food and wine. They shall want for no physical thing. They shall be devoted to keeping my light in my temple. Let this thing be!"

Eh. I tried to make it sound godly, but I could see Zhi and Josie in the outer room, holding each other and trying not to laugh. Nonetheless, they led the response: "It shall be as you have decreed, oh Bob."

I led the women out to the pool in the courtyard where my concubines and I had often played. This time, however, I stepped into the water and summoned the women one at a time. I played John the Baptist and immersed each in the water, blessing her and 'making her righteous.' Then I kissed her lips and set her back on the edge of the pool. I swear, she glowed. As I set each of my priestesses back on the edge of the pool, the light from their spirits shone around us. I looked at them and spoke a spell to dry their clothes. Their light shone brighter.

"This is the light that you shall maintain. Whenever you see it dim, you will think of the day Bob dipped you in the water and made you clean, and your light will shine again."

"Praise Bob!" they announced in chorus.

They joined us at the table for breakfast, chatting happily with my concubines and wives and possessions. And then a group of them went out to survey a site for my temple and their home. I transformed myself back into a neutral body and returned to the deck of my ship.

>— ◀◆▶ —‹

I keep getting side-tracked. Well, it *is* all part of the story of how I arrived in Southern California.

Except for one other thing.

We'd been pretty successful on our trade routes for a few years. The priestesses settled into their lives in the infinity room and became special students of Zhi. I wanted them to become so well trained in the martial arts that they would never again fear any man. Zhi attacked the training zealously, finding our original master and having him instruct the priestesses through her. She found practitioners of the Japanese and Chinese variants and taught the priestesses not only hand to hand unarmed combat, but a wide variety of weapons. They were becoming a lethal force.

The Spanish governor in Mexico gave us a manifest that made us privateers under the Spanish flag. Our cargo changed some. The silver production from Peru dropped and they tried to scam the buyers by mixing inferior metals with the refined silver. It didn't take long for the silver buyers in Manila to spot the difference and the bottom fell out of the silver market. Many of the inferior pesos were shipped on to India, where they were simply melted down, refined, and recast as Rupya. Our cargo changed to comestibles, and we carried a lot of alcohol and sugar to the markets in Asia.

The trade goods headed for the Americas and on to Europe changed, also. We carried more ivory, porcelain, tea, and coffee. We took much more in than we traded out, taking new crafts and products to the infinity room.

The first time I took some of my crew to the infinity room, they were overwhelmed with the thought that we carried an entire world on our ship. I hadn't really thought of it that way, but they were delighted to be considered citizens. Thereafter, I would trade out a small portion of my crew on each trip. Some moving to the infinity room and new recruits joining my crew. When we were in port, the women carefully guarded the secret of their gender and appeared to be like any other crew, though happier with their service.

Then on one fateful night, I spotted a familiar ship on the horizon. I had spent only a few days on the *Sunrise* when we had been attacked by pirates. I helped load all the cargo onto the pirate ship and then cut it loose to sail it on my own to Manilla, leaving the pirates and the fairly worthless crew of the *Sunrise* behind. Now, I saw the *Sunrise* ahead of me and determined to get revenge on the pirates for what they had done to my priestesses. Using the look-away spell, which shielded the *Erinyes* from spying eyes, we sailed up within a few feet of the *Sunrise* before we were noticed. I had warriors prepared and they immediately jumped to the other ship, subduing all resistance.

My former captain had thrown his lot in with the pirates and was now second in command to the pirate captain. Most of my crewmates had been executed and those who were left were as bad as the pirates they joined. Below decks, we found another dozen terrified and abused women. I went full goat and summoned my priestesses to care for the women and escort them to the infinity room. The warriors tied up the crew members and then emptied the ship's hold of all its cargo.

I am not normally a violent man—or demon—but these pirates had stepped past the norm by enslaving women and raping them repeatedly. I held a mass trial for all the pirates, pronounced them guilty, and sentenced them to death. We poured oil over the entire ship, including over the pirates themselves. Then we retreated to the *Erinyes* and sent a volley of Greek fire onto the ship. The priestesses, the newly rescued women, and my crew looked on as the *Sunrise* erupted in flame and burned to the waterline. We could hear the screams of the pirates as they were consumed by the fire. When it appeared the fire might not consume all evidence of the ship, my crew bombarded the remains with our cannons until it sank. We were not satisfied until there was not a trace of the *Sunrise* left on the sea.

My crew who was serving and had not yet been to the infinity room were rather awed by my sudden appearance as a demon. However, they were women and they had seen the condition of the women my priestesses had rescued from the ship. They quickly decided they were okay with serving a demon, and affirmed their loyalty.

I resumed a human shape and became their beloved captain once more. In the infinity room, however, I became the demon Bob and baptized my new priestesses to purify them.

>-- ◀▶ --<

We continued to trade, making a circuit through all of south and southeast Asia and the Indonesian islands. I counted heavily on the look-away spell for our protection, but we did have some other encounters with pirates over the years.

It was not unknown for all the crew on a ship to die on the four-month voyage from Asia to the Americas. Such ships were called ghost ships and simply floated on the currents until they were near enough to the major ports to be towed in and emptied. We had found some ships like that and simply removed all their cargo, then let the empty ship continue to float unassisted toward the ports.

However, the phenomenon made it quite easy for us to pose as a ghost ship when pirates spotted us. I was the only one on deck when the pirate ship tied up to us, but they were surprised by the sudden emergence of my warriors. Since all my warriors were highly trained in martial arts, subduing the crew of another ship was usually done quickly and without a shot being fired. Which didn't mean there were no casualties among the pirates, but no one was shot. We would then have all the pirate's cargo transferred to our ship and into the infinity room.

If I found women aboard who were enslaved for the pleasure of the pirates, I went full goat and executed the pirates without further question. The priestesses of Bob would take charge of the liberated women. I had no use for empty ships, so we set them adrift. If it happened that the pirates were merely thieves, I usually let them return to their ship—without cargo or armament—so they could make port somewhere. We never saw them again.

The priestesses developed rituals for the destruction of pirates who captured women. They would chant a death chant to the pirates that might have caused as many of them to die as my sword did. Then they would take the women to the infinity room where I would be summoned to purify them and make them priestesses as well.

As to the pirate ships that drifted to the coast, authorities never released news of the carnage they found on the ships. They simply announced that a ship had arrived with all the crew dead and they were attempting to notify relatives. Of course, there were no relatives of the pirates to notify and we always left a notice tacked to the mast announcing the list of crimes— piracy, kidnapping, rape, and enslavement—and the judgment of Bob having befallen them.

>-- ◀◆▶ --<

After many years—perhaps a century or more—of trading and privately destroying pirates, we heard of a new port in California. This was much farther north than we had traveled before. We collected news of the port of San Diego and made our way there to see if we could do some trading. From there, we worked our way farther north, tacking in the headwinds and found a large bay that was sheltered from all kinds of storms. We tied up the ship at a little island in the bay and created a trading post. It was a quietly flourishing little business that dealt almost exclusively with the natives of the area. Some natives had apparently seen me running around in my natural form and jokingly referred to the island as Goat Island.

I decided this was a good place to settle for a while and we dismantled the ship, moving the cannons into a locked cabinet in the infinity room. The lumber from the ship was used to build our trading post and a small home that looked remarkably like a ship's captain's cabin. The rest of my crew moved into the infinity room to make a new life for themselves.

I found the natives to be a congenial lot and we made many trades and exchanged many stories. I even acquired a couple of new concubines from among them.

All was well.

Until the Spanish arrived.

38
LOVE AND MARRIAGE

OU KNOW, I always loved the San Francisco area—from the potheads to the digital engineers. Sometimes both in the same person. I invested heavily in computers when they first came out and have millions in high tech stock.

But what a learning curve! It seemed like time changed faster and faster once I got to the northern continent of the Americas. It was just the turn of the eighteenth century when I settled on Goat Island. No one asked me for a passport or a visa. I talked to the natives and they didn't object to me settling and trading. That was good enough. If I had wanted, I was rich enough that I could build a temple or buy a boat.

The Spanish came and began issuing land grants. I was unable to convince the governor that I was supposed to have the grant of Goat Island. It went to another noble and I had to talk him out of it. All for a slip of paper that said I was the rightful owner.

The last time I could hide my wealth or the source of it was before California became a state and I dropped into the assayer's office with six bags of gold dust I'd acquired many years before. From then on, I had to track my wealth and make sure it was legally transferred from one entity to another as I changed bodies and identities. I couldn't just walk into the next town as someone else and start over. They wanted a birth certificate, a driver's license, a record of deed, or some other piece of paper that proved I was who I said I was. What a headache.

But, let me see, I was talking about computers. I liked them. I'd already moved to the Midwest before I could acquire one, but I bought one as soon as I could. Then I spent hours playing silly games on it because I didn't know what else to do with it. Of course, Brenda (my secretary in the housing development) insisted she needed a computer to keep track of our burgeoning finances, CPM project plans, customer data, and who knew what else. Until I started writing my memoirs, I still mostly used my computer for playing games and watching porn.

I have noticed that the first use of any new communications technology in history has been pornography. I'm certain the first item written on a piece of paper or animal skin with a brush and ink instead of being carved in a clay tablet with a stylus was an erotic poem from a shepherd who scrawled it with a bit of charcoal on a stretched hide. Or perhaps it was Pinaruti's detailed drawings of a phallus that ended up between my legs. Did you know some of the ancient pictographs found on cave walls show a man and woman copulating?

What was Gutenberg printing before he set out to reproduce the Bible? Pornography! And then he produced indulgences for the church to forgive people for reading pornography.

And when the first camera obscura was used to project an image from one room through a lens onto the wall of another room, what was projected? Nude women, of course! And live copulation. When they figured out how to capture that image on film, I'm sure the first image printed was a naked woman.

Movies? Porn. Video? Porn. Computers? Porn. And when the great World Wide Web was created, the most popular websites available were porn.

I loved my computer.

Of course, with the advent of the internet and the web, we were suddenly connected to people around the world. Before we got social media, we got email. What a delight those early messages from people reaching out to me were. I subscribed to everything. I got news, weather, entertainment, sale bulletins. Hundreds of emails a day.

And in the mass of mail, I received a message that made me sit up and take notice.

Dear one,

My name is Mrs. Peninnah Ariel Dugganaiah. I am a citizen of United Arab Emirates living in Dubai. I was the faithful wife of Mr. Benaiah Dugganaiah, who died of leprosy and venereal disease in the year February 2010. During his lifetime, he deposited the sum of €8.5 Million (Eight million five hundred thousand Euros) in a bank in Brussels, the capital city of Europe. He left me a wealthy and well-cared-for widow.

It has since taken me five years to sort through his papers and close the holdings of his company, of which I was left executrix. In sorting through generations of historical records, I came across a folder marked only, "The Owners." I had to enlist the assistance of Dr. Bernard Lowes, a prominent translator of ancient languages, who wants very much to have the documents I showed him so he can take them to a museum. However, he confessed that the papers were actually a recording of shares in my husband's oil exploration which was begun many years ago by his father's father. Each listing of a share had a notation indicating "no further heirs" after assignments that were recorded through the centuries.

This is true of every share in the exploration company except one made out to Bob. To this share was appended a note that said, "Bob is still alive." Dr. Lowes, of course, laughed at that note, pointing out that the owner would be 2,000 years old, but my husband was a man of honor and I would dishonor him if I did not attempt to locate Bob and present him with what is his.

The documents of the company indicate that the current untapped oil reserves of the company would place the value at over $500 billion US dollars.

I would ask that you come to Dubai at your earliest convenience to claim your share of this company. My husband left me a certain means of identifying the true Bob when he arrives. I have carefully researched your background and believe you have the identifying marks that will allow me to transfer this wealth to your name.

I need your urgent answer to know if you will be able to execute this project, and I will give you more information on how the fund will be transferred to your bank account or online banking. With the love and honor of the ages,

Mrs. Peninnah Ariel Dugganaiah

Well, that set me back a bit. I cast back in my memory a couple thousand years and found a pyramid scheme that would make me rich, according to the trader I'd encountered in the desert. In fact, the sale of shares had made me quite a lot of money in the century that followed, but I never really took the idea of there actually being oil involved seriously.

I set about making travel arrangements.

>-- ◀◆▶ --<

"Bob, those emails are scams," Brenda said. "You are so naïve. They are all designed to milk you for identity information or to get you to pay them huge amounts as an agent to transfer wealth that doesn't exist to you. You can't mean you think this is real!"

"Well, Brenda, think of it as little old me off to do battle against the great scammers of the world, one at a time," I laughed. It was certainly possible that there was some back-alley fellow with an internet account posing as a widow and that the only oil involved would be what was in his hair. But I couldn't help the feeling I had that this could be for real. I would at least go visit the old lady and see if good old Dug had, indeed made me a fortune.

"Bob, you are impossible. Just be sure to pack me in the satchel before you leave. I don't want to be left here without you," she laughed. I promised her I would.

>-- ◀◆▶ --<

I fucking love to fly! I even got a pilot's license in the 90s. Just for small planes, but they were so much fun! At last, I could correct Pinaruti's oversight and have wings.

I'd discovered something important about traveling after 2001: The look-away spell on the satchel only worked for human eyes. The security scanners picked it up just fine. I was pretty nervous the first time I had to pass it through an x-ray machine, but all that showed was the few miscellaneous items put in it without opening a gateway to the infinity room. It still made me nervous to remove it and let it pass through the machines at the airport.

It was a mere fourteen hours to Dubai. Traveling first class included anything I could possibly want, including the flight attendant. When my pod had been made into a bed and I crawled in, she crawled in with me. I booked myself into a fancy hotel and called Mrs. Dugganaiah. She invited me to her office immediately.

The buildings were amazing to me, even having been around for so long. They soared into the sky and out of sight. People were everywhere in the busy financial district. In a way,

I missed the old markets, but I was told Dubai had a bazaar that hadn't changed in hundreds of years. I made a note to visit it.

>— ◀◈▶ —<

"Mrs. Dugganaiah, it is a pleasure to meet you. My sincere condolences on the loss of your husband," I said as I bowed over her offered hand. Her beauty made it a pleasure indeed.

"Bob, the pleasure is mine. Ariah, we'll have tea in my office," she said to her secretary.

I was momentarily distracted as I looked at the secretary. Did she look like my Aria, who died so many centuries ago? The mention of her name brought back the pain of losing her, but I couldn't recall her face. That's sad, but it had been 4,000 years and so many women ago. I told you, I'm not omnimnemonic. Strange what things still are fresh, though.

Mrs. Dugganaiah led me into a very modern office that had a lovely table and sofa where we sat. Her secretary was all smiles as she brought the tea. I assessed my hostess as we waited for the tea to be poured.

I somehow expected her to be an elderly widow. Apparently, Dug had a trophy wife. She was out of her teens, but not midway through her twenties. A burka hung neatly on the back of the door, but she was dressed in a miniskirt suit and a blouse that left her toned midriff bare—a diamond sparkling in her navel. Her heels easily added five inches to her height. She noticed my observation.

"Though a citizen of the UAE, I am a western woman. Doug and I married in Italy. I am not required to wear traditional Muslim clothing. In fact, there are various levels of appropriateness for women's wear here. Many do not wear the face covering, but most adult women cover their hair and ears. You will find western women on vacation in nearly any mode of dress found in the western world, including bikinis on the beach. Since I am now alone, I cover fully when I am not in my office or in my home. When people visit me here, they are the guests and are not privileged to criticize my apparel.

"My only comment would be to say your apparel is quite lovely," I said.

"It looks even better when folded on a bedside chair."

I was a little shocked at her forwardness in that suggestion. But she was a young and beautiful woman, and I could well imagine her folding her clothes neatly beside the bed before she crawled in. With me.

"Do you know how much your email looks like one of the popular scams?" I asked, changing the subject.

"That was quite intentional. I knew that if it fell into the wrong hands, it would be passed off as a scam. In fact, I had to send out several dozens of them in order to get your response. People are becoming more sophisticated about what they respond to in email."

"Well, before you expose any more of the details," I said, meaning the details of the stock, but thinking about the details of her body, "How do you suggest that I prove my identity to you?"

"Show me the goat," she said simply. Whatever she was expecting, it was not that I would transform into the demon in front of her. I kicked my shoes off my hooves and pulled off my shirt before I tore through it. I was unfastening my trousers when she caught her breath and stopped me. "That... that... that... is enough," she gasped. "For now." She stood in front of me and stroked my arms with her hands, examining the claws on my fingers. She reached up and touched my horns, pausing to explore the nick where the monster's axe had clipped me two thousand years ago. She was nearly to my lips with hers when she suddenly pushed herself away from me, panting.

"I take it this was not what you were expecting," I said.

"I thought it would be a tattoo of some sort. Or perhaps a birthmark. This is... so much better." She inhaled deeply and sat on the edge of her desk. She consulted a note. "Now, if you would, please, show me the door."

Once I presented the satchel to her, it became clearly visible and she wondered how she had missed me carrying it. I opened the gateway. Chione and Pari emerged, carrying a tray of cocktails and sweets. I think their nudity made more of an impression on Peninnah than the drinks and sweets or the doorway.

The girls bowed to her, kissed me, and departed. I closed the gateway. Peninnah touched the glasses and sampled a sweet, as if to make sure they were real.

"Will you marry me?" she whispered.

I wasn't quite expecting that.

"Marry you?" I asked.

"It would be the easiest way to expedite the transfer and to be sure there is no question regarding how you came to own the stock. It will be much easier than proving you are the same person who signed the paper two thousand years ago."

"I suppose so," I said. "I mean, yes, Peninnah. I will be delighted to marry you." I'd certainly married women more quickly than that after meeting them. And Peninnah had already seen my natural form and the gateway to the infinity room. Even if there was no fortune to inherit, the prospect of marrying the woman was attractive.

"After the ceremony, you can also show me the rest," she said, vaguely gesturing toward my trousers.

Marrying her was becoming more appealing by the second.

I remember one time... Now this is funny. You never know what the customs are in a strange land. I found an island once while I was sailing and was greeted by friendly natives. It was quite a relief considering the greetings I'd had among some tribes. There were those who preferred to kill anything foreign and never gave themselves a chance to learn about someone new. I guess there are still people like that, right here in America.

Anyway, I was greeted by the shaman and welcomed warmly. There was a huge feast that night with drumming and dancing and acrobatic acts. At one point, as I was sitting in the circle, watching the young women dancing, one of them broke away from the group and began dancing right in front of me. She beckoned me into the circle to dance with her.

Well, I'd learned all the dances that Ningrum taught the women and thought nothing at all about learning the dances of this group. We danced and the steps became ever more suggestive as we moved. And clothes began to fall away. Hers and mine. I had drunk a bit of the local alcoholic beverage, which I cannot even remember the name of at the moment. So, I might have been a little dull in some of my senses when she leapt into my arms and settled herself slowly down on my staff. There, the gyrations of the dance changed, but only slightly. The other women dancing with us surrounded us, just as naked as we were. They touched and kissed and prodded us until we were both gasping for breath. She called out her orgasm to the skies and all the people joined in the noise as I bellowed mine.

Soon, most of the women around us had also been joined by men from the circle and we were all copulating en masse as we danced around the fire. Eventually, the frenzy died down and we collapsed on the ground with my woman still connected at the groin and attempting to bring me to yet another climax, which I gave her. Then we went to sleep, right there where we lay.

In the morning, I awoke to the sounds of the shaman waving a branch over each of the couples who were still lying together on the ground and giving us our wedding blessing.

Well, it turned out that I'd arrived just on the day of their annual wedding ritual. The dance was for all the single women who were ready for a partner to select one from the men and marry him. The dance itself was the marriage ceremony!

There was no sense in objecting by claiming I didn't know what was going on. I'd just fucked her on her wedding night. I had nothing pressing for the next twenty-five or thirty years and Lalapala was a lovely woman who made loving her very easy. But I believe that set the record for the fastest I'd ever gone from meeting a woman to being married.

>-- ◆◆ --<

Marrying Peninnah took a bit of planning and arranging. I was in Dubai for a month, during which time I changed my look and became a citizen of the UAE. Not that they knew that. Over the years, I'd become quite adept at creating a new identity and getting all the paperwork placed in the right hands. It was necessary in the new connected world we lived in. I couldn't just change my look and show up in the next town as a different person. I needed an orderly progression of inheritance and legitimacy. That my lineage never actually existed made no difference, as long as the government involved thought it did. By the time we were married, I'd lived in Dubai all my thirty years, born of wealthy parents who were killed in an epidemic some years before.

As UAE citizens, however, getting married was easy. I had to have a blood test to be sure I wasn't propagating a disease or genetic defect. I'm not sure how all that worked. I just gave a sample of blood and set a spell of cleanliness on it. Whatever test they ran would come out clean.

Peninnah was quite enthusiastic about becoming my wife. She bought a wedding dress and invited her secretary, Ariah, to be her bridesmaid. I asked Oza to stand with me. It seemed he came from some area near here, so fixing him an identity was not a problem. Getting him to quit staring at the buildings around us was more difficult.

We stood before the marriage lawyer and signed our papers. Then I kissed the bride and took her home. We went to her apartment on an upper floor of a very large building. It was the epitome of a rich Arab's domicile in the modern world. She showed me some of the twenty or so rooms in the apartment as she dismissed the servants and sent them home. Then I worked on discovering how good her clothes would look folded beside the bed. The answer...

I never really looked at the clothes except as they came off her lovely body. And then we began some serious kissing and touching. She was a natural at many of the tantric techniques I used with my lovers, wanting to be connected by looking into my eyes as well as having my dick up inside her.

There is something about undressing a woman for the first time. I have done it thousands of times over the years, but each time is unique and exhilarating. I was enraptured with the shape of her breasts, with the two little dimples on her back, just above her pelvis, by the delicate narrow feet, and by the wet and slippery entrance to her sex. She had wanted me to go whole goat, so to speak, but I suggested we save that for another time.

The next day, we entered the infinity room and Peninnah received the full welcome package from my other wives and concubines. She was taken to the temple and my priestesses—there were more than fifty of them now—led her into the water to be purified. They brought her out and massaged her thoroughly, then oiled her body with fragrant oil I didn't identify at once.

Finally, she was brought into a tent I erected outside the temple, and there, she came face to face with the demon. My new wife came so hard her legs collapsed under her. And I had yet to touch her! I led her to a thick bed of carpets, spread with silk and there I made love to her as woman and demon. We were truly married.

We returned to her apartment a day or two later and she began the process of transferring the assets to my accounts. There wasn't that much cash, but a lot of shares of oil reserves. When we were finally ready to start using my wealth, we returned to the US, where I arrived as my grandson and heir to my American wealth.

That was when Brenda (who had stayed in the infinity room and decided not to return to the development) reminded me that I was now the beneficiary of a million-dollar term life insurance policy that I'd taken out forty or so years ago.

The next thing we did was get married again. We wanted to make sure we were recognized under US law as well as under UAE law.

>-- ◄◆► --<

I had a dream. No, not that I was visited by a god or anything. I mean I had an aspiration. It started during the month of July in 1969. I'd failed to find a safe place for my satchel anywhere in the world. I was constantly vigilant and felt like I had to hide in order to join my wonderful harem in the infinity room. Nowhere on earth was so remote and isolated that people couldn't accidentally stumble upon the satchel. But outer space was big enough to get lost in. I felt sure that I could find a way to launch us way past the moon and into space where we could just drift on forever.

American, European, and a couple of Middle Eastern billionaires had begun a space race. They'd all been up in their private space ships already and everyone was waiting for what came next. They were setting up for a tourist industry and were selling trips to space for several million dollars.

One had a good idea to my way of thinking. Mars. I liked the idea because no one would find me for a very long time on Mars. And if I happened to miss Mars and just keep going... Well, the universe was waiting!

Of course, I didn't want to just steal a spaceship, so I decided to invest heavily in it. I traded a bunch of oil shares for a bunch of Space Pioneers stock, which would ultimately pay for the ship I planned to steal.

It would take a while before I could convince my partners that I was the one who should lead the expedition to Mars, but we had time. I wasn't getting any older, so to speak. And, I intended to hand pick my crew.

39
Entering the Modern World

 DIDN'T MEAN to get all involved in talking about Peninnah. It just happened that she walked through the room stark naked and I forgot about everything else. The story, however, was a good segue into how well and how quickly I adapted to the modern world.

Humans have it easy. They live through a period of change over seventy or eighty years and then they die. I lived through four thousand years and am constantly reminded of how easy something used to be that is now very difficult and how irritated I get at things that are simple now that used to take hours. When I have to wait thirty seconds for porn to download instead of getting to see pussy instantly, I get furious. There was once a time when I had to wait until it was safe to go into the infinity room and call a concubine to me in order to see a pussy. What a life!

When I settled on Goat Island—remember the island in San Francisco Bay where I dismantled my boat and set up a trading post?—I hoped to have a few hundred years without contact with so-called western civilization. I was not there long before the Spaniards showed up and claimed everything. That wasn't really a long-term ownership in the greater scheme of things. Maybe a century or a little more. Nonetheless, they built a fort and then they built a mission. Then they introduced smallpox, measles, the flu, syphilis, and a dozen other ailments that will kill you—if you're human.

But after the United States won its independence from England—remind me to tell you about that sometime—there was a steady push of settlers westward. The English were no better than the Spaniards, but they did *buy* the Louisiana territory from the French instead of just fighting them for it. Regardless, the Americans tended to be fiercely independent and adventurous. They didn't care who 'owned' the land, any more than the Spaniards did. They didn't care about the Spaniards' claims either.

I impersonated the head of a wealthy Californio family and received a large land grant from the crown. From this large grant, I willed Goat Island to my grandson and conveniently 'died.' I inherited the island and continued to trade there for another fifty or seventy-five years, until Mexico ceded California and Texas to the US after the Mexican-American War.

Not the least of my trade was in the 'Yerba Buena' so plentiful on my island. In fact, the entire area took its name from the plant: Yerba Buena or 'Good Weed.' The natives had been coming to the island for centuries to harvest the happy herb. The Spaniards thought they had found a new type of tobacco and prepared to harvest and ship it back to Europe. That had some unexpected results. But you see, that area was known for its good marijuana plants long before I moved to Haight-Ashbury.

The city of San Francisco grew rapidly and became a popular port of call for American, Spanish ships going to and from Asia. The city established a very independent presence, even while ostensibly being ruled over by Mexico. Ha! It was just more Spaniards who declared themselves independent of Spain but did nothing to improve the conditions of the natives, either in Mexico or California, aside from raping and impregnating them with half-Spanish bastards.

Don't think by this that I have anything particularly against Spain or the Spanish. All Europeans were pretty much the same. They were God's people and therefore had a right to despoil all of God's creation. When the US won the Mexican-American War in 1848, Mexico was forced to cede California to the US. The only difference locals saw was that the English settlers cared no more for the rights of the Spanish and Mexicans than they did for the natives.

And then someone found gold!

I'd seen booms before. Mention gold or silver and Europeans go crazy. The boom in San Francisco was pretty mild compared to what we'd seen in Peru. I'd managed to stay hidden in Machu Picchu when Potosi became a silver boomtown overnight. It went from a vacant plateau to a city of 120,000 in a year! The gold rush was minor by comparison. But to us who lived there peacefully, 30,000 new residents of San Francisco in two years was a shock. Especially since these were seekers of fortune from the American East and from Asia. The Chinese population increased almost as rapidly as the English population.

For my part, I bought a bunch of goats and set them loose on the island. They were very happy goats, cleaning out the weed on the island. We gradually started to be called Goat Island again and attracted relatively little interest from the mainland because there was nothing valuable there.

We survived, even though I eventually lost control of the island. It was a Spanish land grant, after all, and the American Navy didn't much care about that. They started surveying the island for a fort that would protect the inner harbor. My little trading post was condemned and demolished to make room.

I moved out to the north side of the bay and found a patch of land I could acquire that had no gold on it. I started growing grapes.

I'd really enjoyed my time in Italy making wine. I still had the old family recipes and we'd been growing grapes and making wine in the infinity room for a couple hundred years.

I started a big winery in the valley and began producing wine almost as fast as San Francisco could consume it.

And that's how I met Maureen.

"Don't you come back in here if you've no money to buy your beer!" the redhead yelled as she pitched a big man through the door of her pub to land in the mud in front of me. She wore a dress with the sleeves rolled up showing her well-muscled arms, and was nearly as tall as I was. The fellow in the street got up and turned as if to object, but once he took a look at the redhead standing in the doorway, he grunted and turned away. The woman cast her eyes on me. "Is that my beer? I'm nearly out and I have thirsty men in here."

"Sorry, Miss. I'm a wine peddler," I said. "Fine wine if you'd care to sample some." I had a wagonload of casks of wine that I was selling at any bar or restaurant I could make a sale to. Usually, if they got a taste of what I had to offer, they were happy to buy a cask or two at $50 each.

"What would I do with wine in an Irish pub? Don't you have any good beer? I'd buy anything better than the whale piss they've been selling me." She turned to go back into the pub, but simply grabbed a glass off one of her tables and handed it to me. "Draw me a tipple and I'll tell you if it is any good."

I grinned at her and turned to the spigot on the cask I'd tapped. I looked hard at the glass to make sure it was clean and paused to wipe it out with my towel. I drew the wine and handed it to her. Her tasting was not what I expected from a bar owner. She rolled the wine around the glass and held it up to the light to peer through it. Then she cupped it in both hands and inhaled the aromas from the glass. Finally, she sipped the liquid and washed her mouth with it before spitting it into the street.

"You're a Ginney? This wine was made in the Tuscan fashion. A good wine for that region. You came from Chianti?" she said.

I was stunned. Yes, I had learned winemaking near Firenze in the Chianti fashion. How this Irish barmaid could identify that from washing her mouth out with it was beyond me.

"That's where I learned the art. It was a long time ago," I said.

"Ten dollars for a cask. Bring it into the bar."

"Fifty," I said automatically.

"And what? Think this is Nob Hill? Bring your cask in and collect an eagle for it. Otherwise, climb the hill and see if they'll pay you for your labor." She turned and went into the pub. I motioned to Zhi and Pari to guard the wagon before I hoisted a cask on my shoulder and followed her in.

"Hmm. Strong," she said as I set the cask where she pointed. A barrel of wine weighs about 2,000 pounds, but I lightened them with a spell when I carried them. She didn't need to know that. She looked me up and down in the light of the pub. "And tall. Is everything in proportion, or do you pack like a Chinaman? I swear, the first time I had one of them, I thought I was with a woman!"

I gave her a fully assessing once over. She was tall, broad in the shoulders, and busty enough to overflow the top of her corset. I pulled her to me for a kiss and pressed her against my sudden erection.

"Proportional enough for you?" I asked, releasing her. I thought for a moment she was going to swing at me, but she pulled two large glasses from behind the bar and handed them to me to fill.

"Listen here, boys!" she called to the room. "Bring your glass to the barrel here and let this mountain pour you a pint of red. I guarantee you'll be drunk on your ass before you get to a second pint. A dollar a pull. You put the money on the bar before you get the mug."

She was going to charge a dollar a pint and had paid me only ten dollars for sixty gallons? I frowned at her, but the first mug was in my hand and I started pouring as the money hit the counter. I saw people pushing their way into the pub as others hailed them from the doorway. Maureen, as she told me to call her, examined each coin and dropped it into a box next to her. Occasionally, she stopped to examine a coin and push it back to the customer.

"American dollars only. None of this old Spanish stuff." She kept the line flowing. The coins stacked up on the bar. Maureen would turn a handsome profit from this night.

"You know I won't be selling the next keg for an eagle," I said. "Just so you know."

"Bob, do me just a little favor and when the press gang makes a grab for you, keep the damage in the pub to a minimum. I don't care what you do to them in the street." I nodded and saw the group of rough men in the corner slowly sipping from their mugs rather than guzzling the wine down like most of the clientele.

"Nothing legal about pressing men these days," I said as I continued filling mugs.

"They don't take you into the legal navy, neither," she said. "A privateer or merchant-man who needs more bodies sends his own men out to get them. There's nothing legal about it, but a hundred miles out at sea there's no one to complain to, either."

The moment came when the line had died down that the six roughs approached as if they wanted another pint. Instead, one swung his mug and broke it over my head. The others made to grab me and were surprised I didn't crumble under the force of the blow. I turned and walked out of the pub with the six men hanging off me. I grabbed them and threw them one at a time into the muddy street.

They got themselves up and made to come at me again, when they saw the two slight men at my side. Zhi and Pari were set to guard the wagon and I noticed a row of sleeping men leaned up against the wall on the other side. One of the roughs laughed.

"Oh, the giant needs his little boys to protect him. Well, the master could use a couple of cabin boys to keep him warm at night. Get 'em all."

We were not gentle this time. My women knew nearly every form of martial art from every country of the East. For the most part, westerners only knew how to grapple and punch. Those were moves the thugs never got an opportunity to use. When they landed in the street this time, they were unconscious. A stagecoach came rattling down the street with horses at full gallop and thumped over them, cursing at the idiots for sleeping in the street. They all lived, but they weren't much of a press gang afterward.

I stepped back into the pub to see that the rest of the clientele were mostly asleep or too drunk to move. On the bar, Maureen had two piles of dollar coins.

"There's your cut," she said. "I'm an honest woman and would not cheat you out of a fair share of the proceeds. I just needed to make sure it would be worth it."

"I understand and appreciate your fairness," I said as I moved around the pub collecting empty mugs and placing them on the bar for Maureen to wash—or at least to dip them in dirty water and put them on a shelf.

"You can unload the rest of the barrels into the back room and I'll split everything we make on them. Never turned a pub into a wine bar before. Do you think I need to hang some potted plants around and put cloths on the tables?"

"I could probably harvest some of those leafy things from the swamp if you want to decorate, but I wouldn't put anything on the tables that could be stained by oafs dumping their full glasses on them.

I transferred the last of the barrels into her back room as daylight hit the street, revealing the gang had been removed from it. There were a few more sleepers stacked up against the wall. I opened a gateway wide enough for two more girls to emerge and jump on the empty wagon.

"Have fun, Bob. We'll get the wagon to the barge and leave the rowboat for you," one of the girls said. "See you when you get to the island." I didn't like setting my girls loose outside the infinity room by themselves, but I trusted in their abilities and they seemed anxious to get the wagon out of town. I kissed them each soundly and they took off with the horses at a trot toward the harbor.

There had been no doubt in either of our minds that I'd be back in as soon as I sent the wagon away. She'd turned out the gas lanterns and shuffled all the remaining drunks out the door. She locked it behind me when I entered and hooked her arm through mine to lead me up a rickety stair from the bar to her apartment.

"Isn't it a bit risky living alone above the pub like this?" I asked. One did not often see single women living alone.

"I earned the money to buy this place on my back," she said. "There's a bit of respect for a woman who will throw a man out on his face. They know the only chance they have of playing between these thighs is if I invite them in. Like I'm inviting you. Would you like to play between these thighs, Bob?"

She stripped off her skirt to expose the massive thighs she was talking about and I thanked my forethought that I'd chosen a body as big as this one for my wine-selling venture. I was sure she could crush a lesser man.

Her red hair and freckles proved to be consistent all the way down her body and I parted a thick fiery thatch to dip my cock into her wet and welcoming warmth.

"I'm not a gentle woman, Bob. Let yourself go and fuck me like a demon. I assure you I can take it. And I'll love every minute of it," she said.

I paused to think for a moment, being sure I had not exposed myself as a demon as yet. I was not normally a rough lover. In fact, I tried especially hard to be a gentle lover, ever since the time I spent as a woman and realized how sensitive and delicate a woman's body could be. But riding Maureen definitely brought out the demon in me. I entered her in every way I could imagine and then she suggested a way or two I hadn't thought of. It seemed that any way I took her, excited her. She was right with me every time I filled her with my spunk. When I thought we were done after a marathon day of sex, she jumped on top of me and rode me to completion one more time.

"Maureen, I'd almost think you were a demon yourself! How did you come to enjoy such unrestrained sex?" I asked.

"Oh, you've found my secret. You see these freckles? I earned one for every soul I've eaten in the past 2,000 years. And I've an appetite to take yours as well, Bob. I think I will never let you free."

I could feel a binding spell taking shape around me and quickly muttered a counter spell. Maureen shrieked and I saw her face change shape. Her tongue shot out like the tongue of a serpent and she hissed. Small horns grew from her head and scales appeared on her body. I jumped aside and allowed myself to transform to my demon shape. There was sudden silence as she sat staring at me.

She definitely had snakelike features with the scales and tongue and tiny horns. She still had her prodigious breasts, but I had a feeling if I pulled the sheet off of her, I'd find a tail. I wondered where I'd been fucking. She hissed again and settled back on the bed, gradually shifting to her buxom redhead form.

"Wouldn't you know that I finally find a man who could satisfy me and he wouldn't be a man at all," she sighed.

"You called out the demon in me," I said. "What else could I do?"

"Yes, well, I'm sure you have all the women you could possibly want. I sit in this dingy pub and take tiny sips of the lives I desperately want. But in this world, there is too much danger for demons like us. I was nearly burned in New England, drowned in Ireland. But here, they would shoot me and carve my heart out as they hung me from the gallows. It's a cruel world, Bob."

"Perhaps. I've seen both the best and the worst. I live with my loves and try to be an honest man. I've taken lives, but they deserved to die. It gave me no pleasure."

"You mean you took lives without sucking the souls from their bodies?" she asked in amazement. "You left the best part."

"Souls never appealed to me. Disgusting looking things."

"You're a strange demon, Bob. Now what are you going to do with me? You know me for what I am. The powerful Jesus of Galilee was the last who got the best of me. In a way, I should be thankful to him. I was bound to the body of a mage's enemy and Jesus cast me out. He set me free and I slipped away out of that hellhole and off into the world."

"I knew Issa," I said. "We traveled together a while. I'm nothing like him, but I try to honor him."

"The church is the enemy," Maureen said. "They hunt us when all the while they are the ones hurting people, killing without responsibility, and declaring their words of hate and subjugation."

"I have to say you are at least partially right. I spent a lot of time living inside the religious state of the church and was not happy with what I saw. But most are innocent. Misled, but innocent nonetheless."

"Ignorant slaves," Maureen sighed. "What are you going to do to me now. I'm not a very powerful demon when it comes to other immortals."

"Nothing," I said. "Though if invited back, I might fuck you again. What a hell of a ride!"

"You have a gift for words. Why not get back on and ride me now."

There was a considerable difference between fucking the snakelike demon and the redheaded Irish woman. It wasn't at all unpleasant, though. She'd returned mostly to her female body and parted her legs happily for my invasion. I rather thought the little horns on her head and the forked tongue were charming in an outré way. One thing she had mastered over the centuries was using her body for the maximum amount of pleasure. Now that our cards were on the table, we got along well.

>-- ◀◆▶ --<

I stayed with Maureen for several days, serving wine from the casks I brought. True to her word, she split the take on every mug I poured. Her reputation grew as a purveyor of the best wine in San Francisco. A hotelier stopped at the pub and offered to buy out the remainder of her stock. She looked at me and thought of the amount of money she could make. Before she could respond, I broke into the conversation.

"It would cost you $700 a barrel," I said. The hotelier turned to me, startled by the amount.

"That's more than we pay for any alcohol. It is only the reputation you've gained with this that brought me here. I cannot possibly offer such a princely sum," he said.

"You haven't sampled this wine. Here, let me pour you a measure and let your tongue dance on its flavor." I reached for a glass, but rather than the pint beer mugs Maureen had served, I selected a whiskey glass, about a quarter the size. I handed the hotelier the glass and he went about sniffing and tasting the wine. I noted his approach was not as carefully studied as Maureen's. He didn't spit it out.

"This is a magic elixir!" he said.

"Not quite. We have a vineyard on the north side of the bay where the soil is so perfect, we grow grapes that cannot otherwise be grown in America. My lady Maureen holds the keys to this winery and could be convinced to sell each barrel at just $800. We expect others will be approaching later today, attempting to get the exclusive on this remarkable wine. Your time is expiring."

"$800? A moment ago, you said $700!"

"And just moments from now, the price will go up again. Do you not believe you could sell this vintage for a dollar a glass? The barrel measures over 1,500 glasses the size you hold. And it can be yours for just..."

"$800! I'll pay $800 a barrel! When can we get more?"

"We'll need to get back to the other side of the bay and bring the remainder of this year's vintage. I believe we have one hundred barrels remaining."

"I'll take them. I wish to be your exclusive distributor in San Francisco." He wrote out a check for $3,200 for the remaining four barrels in Maureen's store room. I looked at it curiously and cocked an eyebrow at Maureen. I'd not seen a bank check before.

"I have an account at a bank where this man's check will be honored," she said. "We'll go there directly and deposit our earnings, then leave to get the remainder at once." I grinned at her and she pointed the way to the store room where the hotelier directed his men to load the barrels.

Maureen snorted a laugh when she saw that it took four men to wrestle each barrel out of the store room and up a ramp onto a wagon. When the pub was empty, she locked the doors, put on a very stylish hat, and took my arm to walk to the bank.

40
I LEFT MY HEART...

>-- ◄► --<

’M A POOR COUNTRY DEMON with no particular claim to sophistication. Having been alive for four thousand years did not mean I was all-knowing. Remember? Not omniscient? In fact, I'm sure I've forgotten something significant I should have told you. Still, I felt like a rube when I accompanied Maureen to the Bank of California where she said 'our' money would be safe.

We opened an account for the Goídel Glas Winery and deposited the check and an equal amount in coins from the sales by the glass we'd made that I carried in a heavy canvas bag. Maureen also 'transferred' her personal account of some $2,000 to the winery account. I wasn't sure how all this finance stuff worked, but I figured I needed to equal her investment, so I pulled $2,000 in gold coins from my satchel and deposited it. With more than $10,000 in the bank, we joined the ranks of their large depositors, and Maureen employed the bank as an agent to lease her pub. We left an awed bank manager behind us and I wondered if I would ever see any of that money again.

I took Maureen down to the crossing where the girls had left a small boat anchored for me. We rowed out to Goat Island—I rowed. Maureen sat with her hat and a parasol over her head like a fine lady. The girls were waiting there with the barge and our wagon.

They greeted Maureen with a knowing look and we made our way to the far shore of the bay to drive the team up to our vineyard. Maureen inspected the entire operation, made a few suggestions of how to make it more efficient, and went straight to work on our inventory and accounts. When she was done scratching out numbers with a pen and paper, it appeared that the Goídel Glas Winery was a near million-dollar undertaking.

I wanted to go into the infinity room to celebrate, but didn't trust my new partner not to seal me in it. That was a source of some tension on my part. Issa had once warned me that it wasn't a good idea for two of our kind to be in the same area, so I began working on a plan to return to San Francisco, perhaps leaving Maureen to manage the vineyard where she was instantly happier than she'd been in the city. I liked my time running a trading post and had the idea of opening a store of some sort in San Francisco. I realized that since I met Maureen, I'd let her make all the decisions.

"What inspired you to call our endeavor Goídel Glas Winery?" I asked as we lounged together one night. I'd called it Bob's Wines when I had to give a name. As soon as we were back at the winery, my girls disappeared through the gateway to the infinity room. Except for the trips when I wanted highly trained warriors with me, I did not staff the winery with citizens of the infinity room. There were plenty of laborers available for hire. Once the English arrived, there were many Mexicans and Indians who had been driven out of their homes and needed work.

"Ach! Goídel Glas is who it was that drove the snakes from Ireland."

"I thought that was St. Patrick."

"No! St. Patrick, may his soul burn in hell, was a murderer who went through Ireland centuries later and killed anyone who would not convert to his Catholic religion. There have been hard feelings in Ireland ever since then. It was an Egyptian explorer named Goídel Glas who rid the island of snakes and brought it the Gaelic language spoken there. I know this for a fact as I had fled to the island to get as far from Israel and Rome as I could go. But what was I to do when he drove the snakes from the island? I wasn't exactly human. The man was a good man, and after some negotiations, he allowed me to reside on a small isle off the coast. It was from there that I eventually set sail for America."

"I wonder that I never met nor heard of the man. But then, I spent the first millennium after Issa appeared in India and Asia. I visited the isles of the Britons a long time before that. Did you ever run into a god named Manannán Mac Lir? Fine fellow. We got on well."

"You're the deamhan he spoke of? Liked you, he did. I think that may have been why he was willing to have me on his island. I've you to thank for that. Come here and fuck me again so I can thank you properly."

I did. It was the kind of business partnership that we had.

In many ways, dealing with Peninnah reminded me of the demon woman Maureen so many years ago. I learned a lot about modern finance from Maureen and we agreed that I would open a store in San Francisco and she would stay at the winery. I'd known 'bankers' before, but it seemed they were simply men with money who loaned it out to the poor in exchange for the very lives of the unfortunate. Maureen said it was still true and bankers had eaten more souls than she had. But we were on the other end of the scale now and it was the bankers who owed *us* money.

Well, if it meant someone had to consume the soul of a banker, I'd leave that to her.

Peninnah—You do remember my new wife in the twenty-first century, don't you—knew more about the dealings of high finance than I could ever possibly learn. By this time, I knew how to manage millions in investments and capital. Peninnah knew how to manage billions.

"How do you know this at such a young age, Peninnah, my wife? You aren't by any chance a demon, are you?" I asked as I made myself comfortable between her legs and probed the inner recesses of her sex. She sighed.

"No, Bob. I'm no demon. I'm every bit as mortal as all those other beautiful women in your palace. But my former husband, Benaiah Dugganaiah, married me when I was quite young, not to despoil my virgin body, but rather to facilitate the transfer of all his wealth. He never touched me inappropriately, so you found my sex as pure as it was when I married him. He had many other women to entertain him, which is why he died of leprosy and venereal disease. The doctors couldn't make up their minds regarding which had killed him. But he did like me to run around topless so he could watch my breasts develop. I think he was as proud of that as of my facility with numbers. I learned at his knee, so to speak. He taught my tits. Oh, it was me he taught, but he couldn't seem to keep his eyes off my breasts while he spoke."

"I understand. I have difficulty taking my eyes off your breasts, too. But you are a re-markable young woman, Peninnah. I don't know how I would ever manage this without you."

"Thank you. Tomorrow, we need to lay out a plan for your long-term goals, including where you want us to live. We don't need to stay here because of your housing development. We can divest that or put it under a management company if you want to. We could live anyplace in the world."

"San Francisco," I said immediately. "If we can live anyplace, I would like to return to San Francisco."

"Then we shall begin moving your wealth around and finding a place to live in San Francisco tomorrow," she said. "But that is tomorrow. Tonight, make love to me again, my husband."

I lost myself in my dear wife as I sank into her treasured warmth again. Not only was she beautiful, loving, and kind, but she would let me go live in San Francisco again!

>-- ◄◆► --<

It would not be just if I did not tell you more about Peninnah. I asked about her name and she said it was Biblical, but that Doug had given it to her to make her immigration to Dubai easier. Her real name had been Ariel, currently her middle name. She may have been north-ern European, but she had no recollection of her parents or life before the orphanage in Venice where Doug found her.

I know I have not described every woman in my life in great detail, because I consider what a woman looks like when I am undressing her to make love to be a matter of interest only to the two of us. But Peninnah was a work of art, begging to be described.

She was about five feet and four inches tall, but unless she was in bed, I seldom saw her with less than a five-inch heel on her shoes. The effect was to lengthen her legs and shape them exquisitely. She had light golden skin that spoke of being a sun worshiper, until you saw her naked. Then you realized that if the color was a gift of the sun, she'd been bathing naked in it all her life. There was not the least bit of paleness anyplace one might think would be covered by a bathing suit. The rich healthy tan of her skin was flawless.

Her breasts were full, firm, and round, standing out proudly from her chest, and it was easy to see why Doug had been so fascinated by them. It must have killed him to have them so close at hand and still consider them untouchable. I found it almost impossible to keep my own hands and lips and tongue off of them. The areolae and nipples were only a shade darker than her skin. The pea-sized buds were always hard and erect.

I was not unfamiliar with the practice of depilation, though few of my women bothered with it. The goddess's priestesses had all been smooth, the hair between their legs being plucked from the time it first appeared. My own priestesses, learning of the fashion, also adopted it, but used a razor to smooth the area. Liz—remember Liz? Bra burning feminist of the late 60s?—had always shaved her legs and under her arms, but did not remove any hair around her pubis. Peninnah was completely smooth between her legs and on her mons. Her legs were like silk and her underarms showed no sign of having ever had hair. Even her eyebrows were perfectly and elegantly shaped. She said she'd had laser hair removal and it lasted longer than the practices of waxing or shaving. All I knew was that I never felt the least scratch against my tongue or my cock.

Her nose was straight and narrow, telling me she might have some Greek ancestry in her mixed heritage. She had a narrow waist that flared into beautiful hips and a lovely round bottom.

Her hair, I discovered, was not the dark brown I had seen in Dubai. When we reached America, she had it bleached out to what she said was her natural honey blonde. Her piercing blue eyes seemed like they could look straight through a person and I was reminded of Ningrum in Indonesia, who could look into one's soul. I believe in Dubai, even in her burka, her eyes would have stood out to the most casual observer.

Peninnah did not eschew makeup. I never saw her apply it, but the accent of her eyes, the perfect amount of powder and rouge, and her perfectly defined red lips told me this was an artform and she was an artist.

As to clothing, she loved to show off her smooth toned abs and long legs. So, her tops were always short enough to show ample skin between the top and her belt. Her skirts were never longer than mid-thigh. She had a way of making this all look professional by tossing on a jacket that typically hung from her shoulders to below her crotch, but was always open in front.

My summary, based on 4,000 years of experience, was that she was a walking wet dream.

What was even better, though, was that she knew when to tease and when to stop teasing and get serious. We left the office and spent our nights in the infinity room, where she was a hit with all my wives and concubines. She was fairly worshiped by my five possessions. Though she loved to touch and be touched by all my women, she only turned to me for sexual satisfaction. I found myself falling deeply in love with her.

>-- ◀◆▶ --<

While Peninnah was soft and sensual and loving, when it came to business, she was no-nonsense.

"You want to live *in* San Francisco? Have you *been* to San Francisco lately?" she asked.

"Well, no, not recently. It's been twenty or thirty years, I suppose," I said.

"In order to meet the parameters you've set, we're going to need two or three properties, spread along the Coast. There are no five-acre mansions with a gated wall in San Francisco. Houses are built right next to each other if they are stand-alone at all. To get the kind of views you want, we should look at a penthouse condominium like what I have in Dubai," she said.

We hadn't sold Peninnah's apartment in Dubai. She had suggested that we would probably want houses in several parts of the world in order to manage our empire. We shouldn't need to stay in hotels more than once or twice if we decided to do business in a particular area.

"Wouldn't it be awfully expensive to have houses in so many areas?" Yeah, here's me, Bob the country hick.

"Bob, if we spent a billion dollars on houses so you could have a different house every day for a year, we'd still spend less than two-tenths of a percent of your registered wealth. That doesn't include anything you have squirreled away in the infinity room."

That certainly put things in perspective. There was a guy once...

Well, I was sailing up the West Coast of Africa, you know, after my adventures in Australia, when I came across a very prosperous empire. I was told it was called Mali. When I talked about my voyages around Africa and Asia, I was asked to appear before the king, one Mansa Musa. He was fascinated by the tales of my travels. It seemed his brother had set sail west with 2,000 ships and had never been heard from again. I regretted having not arrived soon enough to join that expedition!

The king was a devout Muslim, a religion I had not had much interaction with before, but I found the basic precepts to be generally in keeping with the honored precepts of most religions. He was also devoted to education and learning and had dreams of creating a great university near his palace in Timbuktu. When he found that I had built temples (I did not specify to what gods), he pressed me for details of how to construct a massive mosque when there was no abundant stone and no trees for wood. I told him I had learned a technique for building out of mud and straw in such a way that the walls would stand for hundreds of years.

At that, the king rolled out plans for his mosque and I agreed to build it for him under two conditions. First, all laborers on the holy structure must be free men who were paid and provided for in exchange for their labor. This, I proclaimed boldly, was to honor Allah who was the only master suited to own humanity. Second, I requested access to his library that I might read (and duplicate) all his books. Both of these things, Mansa Musa granted me.

I discovered in the course of the three years that it took me to build the mosque, that Mansa Musa was very wealthy. His palace was built of imported limestone and polished to a high sheen. Even his slaves in the palace wore gold brocade uniforms. He had paid a poet for the plans for his new mosque the sum of about 400 pounds of gold. While I worked to lay out and build the mosque, I was privileged to stay in a suite of rooms in his palace that was as big as a palace itself. Servants were constantly running in and out to be sure my needs were met. The rooms were adjacent to Musa's library where I often spent my nights.

No one knew the number of binding spells I whispered over the mud walls as they were constructed. I was pleased and at the end of three years, the first services were held at the mosque with the king prostrating himself in prayer.

"Bob," he said as we sat at dinner that night, "it is time to make our pilgrimage to Mecca. We will leave on the next full moon."

That was not what I wanted to do. Going all the way back to Arabia across the desert sounded like torture to me. I had a lot of star charts that I'd studied, and I estimated that by the straightest line—which would cut directly across the largest desert in the world—it would make a journey of some 4,000 miles. The king was excited to make the journey. Me, not so much.

"Your majesty, I have been to Mecca and yearn to return now to the sea. Please grant me your favor to return to my voyage." It was only a small lie. The city had not been there when I was wandering around in Arabia, but I'd been close to where the city would one day be.

"Bob, you have done a great work for Allah. May he bless you on your journey. I will give you twenty camels and six sacks of gold to take with you. Choose among my slaves for twenty of the finest and they shall be yours. You shall have tents and provisions for your journey back to the Coast. Go with my blessing."

It was an easy thing for me to accept six sacks of gold dust and twenty camels. These would go directly to the infinity room when I was able to arrange it. But it was considerably more difficult to choose twenty slaves. In general, Musa treated all his slaves well. They worked hard, but they were fed well, housed well, and were beaten only for cause. I felt he kept with the best parts of the code I'd established under Ninra. But as I slept in the rooms Musa had provided for me, the task was taken from my hands. The servants who had attended me for the past three years gathered by my bed.

"Bob, you have been a kind and gracious master. We love our king, but have come to love you as well. Please take us with you when you depart this palace," spoke Esafa, the woman who had been in charge of my staff.

"Is this true?" I asked. "Do you each wish to join me on my endless journey?" I asked the question of each one individually and read no hesitation in any of their minds. "Then I shall ask the king for his blessing."

As a result, I left Timbuktu for the 1,500-mile journey back to the coast and to my little ship. Along the way, I talked to the slaves and told them of my home and how they could become a part of it, or that they could be free, no longer slaves and I would give them each a portion of the gold dust we carried.

"Bob, there is so much gold in Mali that a portion of what you carry would not last us long here. We would just end up slaves again and might suffer under an unkind master. Take us to your palace and let us serve you there," Esafa said.

I consented and we managed to integrate the former slaves as free women in the infinity room.

I later found that when Mansa Musa started his journey of 4,000 miles to Mecca, he took all his court, servants, slaves, and local craftsmen and their families with him. 60,000 people! Let me correct that. 60,000 men, plus their women and many children. All were dressed in gold brocade. Each of the 12,000 slaves carried a four-pound bar of gold. Eighty camels carried about 300 pounds of gold dust each. He was liberal in giving out handfuls of gold to the poor he met along his route. In Cairo, he gave away so much gold that it destroyed the economy of Egypt for over ten years.

It turned out that Mansa Musa was the richest man who had ever lived, with his worth being estimated at the equivalent of $400 billion today.

>-- ◀◆▶ --<

"Bob!" Peninnah called me back to the reality of our planning session. "You are richer than Mansa Musa! We want to use your wealth more wisely. Let's not go about destroying the economy of America by simply giving it all away. You have a goal to fly to the stars. Let's focus on that. Believe me, we will need homes around the world."

Richer than Mansa Musa! And I knew Peninnah was referring only to my acknowl-edged wealth. Long gone were the days when I could simply reach into the satchel for a hand-ful of gold and pay for whatever I wanted. Now there were taxes and records and accountants and people I didn't even know who were managing my money.

But I agreed to the plan of multiple houses, and the first thing we did was buy a penthouse condominium in San Francisco where I could look out over the bay and the mountains. It wasn't very large as mansions go, but when it came down to it, Peninnah and I were the only official residents. She employed a staff to clean and cook. When they went to their homes at night, I would open a gateway to the infinity room. We would go in to play, or occasionally, some of the women would come out to see the sights of San Francisco.

We bought my five-acre mansion with a wall and gate in Monterey, overlooking the ocean. This was where I truly felt secure in spending time in the infinity room with my lovers and my people.

>-- ◀◆▶ --<

"Now we need to go to work on acquiring your spaceship," Peninnah said. "We'll trade for equivalent ownership in Space Pioneers with shares in the oil fields. With energy being such an iffy investment these days, we need to diversify into a variety of different industries across the board. There are places around the world where we can invest in real estate development and leverage that ownership into technology, communications, and industry so that when you disconnect from earth, no one will actually be out anything."

"Oh, you know, I bought a bunch of technology shares in the computer industry back in the 80s. They must be worth something by now," I said proudly.

"Have you kept transferring the ownership appropriately?" she asked with a horrified look on her face.

"I met this guy who was a financial consultant and he created a holding company for all my stocks. That's the only company I've had to keep transferring to the new me. What was his name? Warren something. Nice guy."

"Oh, my." Peninnah was rapidly tapping across the keys of her computer and looking at numbers streaming by. "Not bad," she said at last. "You chose good stocks to buy and forget about. Apple, Microsoft, Cisco, Dell, Intel. Osborne should have been sold when it was worth something. That comes up to about another half billion."

"Dollars?" I said. I didn't remember investing anywhere near that amount.

"If you want me to convert that into Emirati Dirham, it will take a few minutes," she laughed.

"Wow. Um... while we're at it, I want to sign over my shares of Goídel Glas Winery to Maureen. She won't be going with us and I want her to have clear title."

"Who? I don't see a Maureen among the shareholders."

"Of course. She changes identity as often as I do. I believe she is going by Sylvia Glass now."

"Oh. I see her. Sounds like there's a story to be heard here."

"Demon business," I said mysteriously. I knew she would get the story from me eventually, but I hate just being an open book. Maureen and I owned the largest and oldest winery on the West Coast.

"Now, you need to start actually talking to the chief executive of Space Pioneers and design your ride to the stars."

I took Peninnah home and to bed at once.

END PART VIII

Part IX
What's So Real About Reality?

Image by ProStockStudio, ID1055024000 licensed from Shutterstock.com

41
Integrating the Household

SHOULD SAY A LITTLE about how the infinity room had developed over the past 4,000 years. You'd think that with the different eras and cultures represented there, it would either be a total mishmash of people, or it would be a divided land with people constantly at war. It was neither. There were various areas where people with similar heritage dwelled together. For example, no one was really sure where the Bobbobbob Aboriginals had migrated to. They'd never mixed in with the other cultures. Racially, there seemed to be a pretty even number of black, red, yellow, and white. And there were many among the children and grandchildren who blended all four colors. Religion did not divide people because they soon discovered the old gods didn't exist in the infinity room. I was as close to a god as the room had, and I encouraged people to keep rituals and customs that were meaningful to them and blend them into the practices of others. We had the height of religious and cultural appropriation. By the 2020s, there were well over three million people in the infinity room. No one knew how far over.

It might surprise you to find that we were pretty low-tech in the infinity room. Oh, technology wasn't absent entirely. Each age had its own technology and people who came into the infinity room from that age brought technology or *tech knowledge* with them. We had to figure out how to get television to work in the infinity room, for example. Anyone who arrived from the natural world after about 1950 expected some conveniences and entertainment. But when it comes down to it, technology is driven by war. With no religion, nationalities, borders, or resources to fight over, there was no real cause for major disputes. As a result, the weapons technology we had, for example, was only what we had found and needed when sojourning in the natural world.

"Bob," Nimia said as we toured our little world, "We need a name. Most of our population has no idea what the infinity room is or what it means. The world needs a name so people can refer to it."

"Oh, please, let's not call it Bob's World," I pled.

"No. That, too, is meaningless to most people."

"Well, take the idea to the family and see what they come up with. I'm happy with whatever you decide," I said.

"Leaving your fate in the hands of others might have unexpected results one day, love. Be careful how much power you leave in our hands."

Hmm. That was a warning I would need to consider.

>— ◄◆► —<

Nimia, my first wife. Remember? She had been with me in Knossos when Ariane died. We both secretly wept for the woman who had claimed me on my first exposure to the world. She was justifiably the only person in the infinity room who could claim to be older than me by a few years, but she looked as young and fresh as the nineteen-year-old she'd been when I first opened the infinity room and pushed her and Portia into it. Portia had elected to stay with Bao and age with her and die with her. But Nimia stayed mostly in the infinity room. As my first wife, she was the de facto queen. If there was ever a dispute that arose in the world, Nimia heard it. She typically made the disputants settle between themselves. If they could not…

Let me see. A dispute arose among some of the librarians as to whether the world was round or flat. They meant, of course, the world of the infinity room, not the natural world. They were trying to equate the way things worked in the infinity room with the natural world.

"If you cannot settle this dispute and consider it so important that you must carry on arguing and upsetting the other librarians, then you are required to prove your theory," Nimia said. "You will set out from the palace in opposite directions. If you never meet each other, the world is flat. If by some chance you do find one another, then we can assume the world is round. That is the judgment of Bob."

"But, madam, in either instance, we must leave the library and be gone forever. Even if we meet, we might be unable to ever return," said one of the disputants.

"Yes? So, what is your point?"

"We would be leaving everything we love behind," said the other.

"Yes? So, what is your point?"

"It occurs to me that this might not be important enough to prove. I am willing to put aside the argument."

"And I."

"So be it. Do not let me hear of the two of you arguing about this again, nor do I wish to hear of parties being formed that support one view or the other. Now go in peace," Nimia said. Dispute settled.

Josie had the second most seniority in my household, but she was not counted as a wife. I possessed her—body, soul, heart, and mind. Josie managed my desires. She always knew what I needed or wanted. She was as quick to organize an orgy as a war party. I wanted every person in the infinity room trained in the martial arts and in the tantric sex practices. Josie orchestrated our education program. I wanted the priestesses cared for; Josie saw to it that they received anything they needed. Josie was my go-to girl and right-hand woman.

After masquerading as Odysseus for a decade, I returned to his home and his wife Penelope insisted that she was therefore my wife. I had no objection to this at all. While Penelope was a bit older than the other girls when she entered the infinity room, she was still young and beautiful. In fact, she seemed to have moved back in age to be closer to my other wives and possessions. Penelope was the mistress of trade, both within the infinity room and between the infinity room and the natural world. She kept track of what was needed, what was available for trade, and who could best fill the needs.

My next possession was Pari, a Persian girl given to me from Nebuchadnezzar's harem. She too had responsibilities, managing my harem. No matter how hard I tried, I could not sleep with all of them every night. Not and do more than sleep. Someone had to determine whose turn it was to share the bed with my wives and possessions. Pari was the one.

Lakshmi was my third wife in the infinity room. She had the most experience among all my women in being a man. She'd been a man for the better part of the twenty years I'd been a woman. She was a wonderful relationship counselor and traveled around the infinity room a lot, teaching tantric meditation and relationship resolution. She'd become quite a guru.

And then there was Princess Agora. She was the daughter of an island ruler who thought his island was the entire world. She had gone into shock when she discovered how vast the world really was. Hers was the only possession I'd made without her consent. She was catatonic and far beyond consenting to anything. I brought her out of that state by possessing her and gave her a calm mind. She still did not stray from my house, which had become quite a palace over the millennia. I could almost always find her in my bedroom, fussing about things that didn't need to be fussed about, like smoothing the sheets on the bed or dusting corners of the room where dust never collected. I'd once tried to set her free, but she clung to me and begged me to continue possessing her. I swore, however, that I would never again possess someone without their explicit invitation.

Esmeralda was my fourth wife and was the only one with whom I had endured a 'Christian' ceremony. I disguised myself as a young Spaniard and we went to a priest to be declared husband and wife. Then we'd slipped off into the mountains for a honeymoon. Esmeralda did not return to the natural world after that except on rare occasions when she wanted to see what had happened or to tend to one of my businesses. She and her husband simply disappeared as I returned to the shape of the despised priest of the inquisition.

Maya was as strong-willed as the goddess she had represented when we met. Her Mayan Indian features were distinctive among my wives, and her attitude was unrelenting in support for me. When we'd brought Mayan refugees into the infinity room, she had taken charge of their adjustment to the new life and surroundings. That was a role she continued to fill with new additions to the infinity room for the next five centuries.

And then there was Liz, my fifth—and I believed final—possession. She was an independent women's liberationist of the sixties and seventies. She began writing books on feminism, women's bodies, and twentieth century relationships, which she published up through the mid-1980s, when her parents died. She chose that time to quietly slip into the infinity room and fade out of her public life. Even her parents had begun to suspect something with her not aging past her twenty-two years in the seventeen years we'd been together. There had been a few instances in which she had made guest appearances on television talk shows, but we had to transform her for those appearances so it would look like she was getting older. I assumed that eventually, we'd need to stage her death because just fading away didn't work in this day and age.

Oh, I had also collected Zhi during the Chinese exploration era. I did not count her among my wives or possessions. She had a position all her own as a devotee of Bob. I won't say she worshiped me, but she was dedicated to the service of Bob and all that was his. She was the chief trainer of the martial arts and traveled throughout the infinity room to teach younger men and women born in the room how to meditate and transcend themselves through the martial arts.

And into this mix I brought my newest wife, Peninnah. She was a financial genius and manipulated my wealth in the natural world in such a way that we always had plenty for any project we wanted. We could also disappear and all my wealth would be absorbed by the populace without upsetting any economy in a major way.

Peninnah had no difficulty adjusting to life with my wives and possessions. She was definitely junior to all of them, but was accepted and honored as my primary wife in the new age. She had moved into the infinity room the day after we were married and came out during the daytime when there was work to be done. She was even accepting and tolerant of my nearly 100 concubines, collected over the years. Some of them neared Zhi in their devotion to Bob, like Chione, who might have asked me to make her a possession if she'd had a voice. She was Egyptian, given to me by Nebuchadnezzar, and followed Pari around like a shadow. And some of the concubines were very independent, even having their own lovers and in many cases, families, but always available to the Bob.

I remind you that in addition to these, I had been married many times, but those other wives had not entered the infinity room to live with me forever. Ariane, of course, was my first wife, blessed in our union by Zeus, but she died trying to deliver the monster child I'd spawned on her. Bao was my wife in Bathra, blessed by Ninra and Namri as we stood in the temple on behalf of the god and goddess. Portia, who I took from Drakomaxos in Knossos, chose to stay in the natural world with Bao and died soon after she did. I married Miriam in Israel and was with her until I was summoned to the king's harem. Then there was Delphia in Greece, Cordelia in Rome, and delightful Tiona, a girl among the Britons I married long before my time there with Caesar. Remind me to tell you about her later. Regardless, these were all women who did not enter the infinity room. Most of them aged and died and I mourned them.

And then there were the fifty-two priestesses of Bob who dwelt in my temple.

⟩—◆▶—⟨

Peninnah, I was thankful, got along with everyone. Her comment was, "Of course, a demon with balls like Bob's would need a lot of women. I couldn't possibly satisfy him alone." She had even talked her secretary, Ariah, into entering the infinity room as one of my concubines, and the three of us had some memorable times in bed together. Peninnah grew to love them all.

Except the priestesses.

The priestesses of Bob were a unique group. They were all women and girls we had rescued from various pirate ships. They had been in such a traumatized state that most of them simply cowered in a corner. One had attempted to commit suicide by throwing herself overboard in the middle of the ocean. It had been my rescue of that poor girl that had been the foundation of the priestesses of Bob. She spread the word that I was not a man, but a god. The others prayed to Bob to save them and make them clean. What could I do? I showed up in my full demon form, claimed them as my priestesses, and took them to the pool to be purified. I blessed them and they worshiped me.

I mean that literally. They worshiped me.

And there was a sign when a priestess was accepted and purified. I promise I did not initiate this intentionally. When each priestess had been baptized by Bob, she began to glow. It was the kind of inner light artists since the renaissance have been trying to capture on canvas. I blame it on the infinity room. It must have made them glow when they were purified. And each time we rescued more girls from pirates, they went through the process of indoctrination by the priestesses and when I purified them, they began to glow. At last, there were fifty-two devoted priestesses in the Temple of Bob.

No men were ever allowed in the Temple of Bob. A priestess would stand at the door of the temple, flanked by guards from among my concubines, hand selected by Josie for the duty. It was a great honor. The priestess on the steps would hear the petitions of any men or women who came to the temple. In many instances—perhaps most—the priestess would tell the person to take his case to Nimia for justice to be served. She did not hear complaints of one man against another, nor foolish requests for wealth in a land that was overflowing with wealth. What they heard were petitions for forgiveness, for guidance in a relationship, and for blessings on their families.

Once a month, on the day set by the priestesses... Let me clarify. The term 'month' had no meaning in the infinity room. Time was not cyclical. It simple continued. If you asked a citizen of the infinity room how long they had been there, chances are the response would simply be, "I am here." But I referred to the summoning of the priestesses according to their own internal clocks, as 'that time of month.'

When they summoned my presence, I had to show up in full demon form. If I was in the form of a man, I would not be distinguished from any other man and would be barred from the temple. And, of course, full demon form meant I was nude—as nude as the priestesses who met me to bathe in the temple pool with them. We frolicked in the pool and laughed. There was much touching and teasing among us. I tried to make sure that every priestess got at least one orgasm, and they helped by ministering to each other, as well as waiting for their opportunity with me.

But bathing and touching was only the beginning of the ritual they developed to please me. Once we had bathed, they led me into the temple to a bed positioned on a platform beneath a dome, like an altar. On this bed, they continued to touch me and oil my body until it shone and the goat hairs were brushed to a glossy sheen. Then a priestess would step up on the bed with me. She was the one chosen to receive Bob's blessing on behalf of all of them. With fifty-one other priestesses surrounding us, I made love to the chosen priestess. Since lovemaking was an act of worship for the priestess, I strove to make it as desirable an experience as possible. As much as she worshiped me, I worshiped her. I made sure she had experienced orgasms from every part of her body I touched.

And when my cock pressed into her sex, there was a great sigh of acceptance among all the priestesses. The glow of the chosen one outshone all the gathered worshipers. And when I finally came and loosed my semen into her waiting pussy, the climax was shared by all and so great that the chosen one and all the surrounding priestesses collapsed in unconsciousness. Until the next summoning, the chosen priestess was treated as if she were my goddess consort. Her fellow priestesses fed her, massaged her, and serviced her in any way she desired or they could think of. When time for a summoning rolled around again a different priestess was chosen and we repeated the process.

This was what made it so difficult for Peninnah to accept the priestesses. It was not possible, in her mind, to compete with fifty-two beautiful young women who worshiped me as their god.

>── ◄◆► ──◄

"Bob-san, we are honored with your interest," our host said. Peninnah knew and understood the cultures of our world well and did not push herself into the conversation, even though any deals I made in Japan would be guided by her. My Japanese hosts, however, could scarcely take their eyes off her svelte form. In her heels, she towered above most of the men. Her blonde hair was like a beacon, drawing attention from every direction. And her exposed belly was in constant competition with her breasts for the most attention-getting body part ever.

I don't think I mentioned the piercing. This was in the 2020s, so ear-piercing was common. Other body parts were also often pierced. I once slept with a woman who had her clitoris pierced and loved to have me tug on the post with my teeth. Women were also frequently tattooed. Peninnah had no tattoos, but she did have her navel pierced and wore a diamond in it that was bigger by twice than most women's engagement rings. Since she normally wore a short top and low-cut bottom, the sparkling jewel was a real eye-catcher. Not that Peninnah's belly needed any help catching the eye. But still, there it was.

When she was feeling particularly evil and wanted to throw men off their game, she attached a chain to the diamond and dropped the chain into her skirt. I almost said underwear, but Peninnah seldom wore underwear unless the skirt was so short she was likely to be exposed. Men would spend an entire two-hour meeting fantasizing about where the other end of the chain went. Those were some productive meetings for us.

In this particular meeting, she stayed near me, often draped lovingly on my shoulder, and whispered advice as I negotiated a billion-dollar (¥115 billion) investment in a new resort that would push out into the ocean and attract wealthy patrons in the way the Arabs did in Dubai. We used our Emirates passports to gain entry to Japan, and the executives of this company willingly took our meeting. They listened intently as I talked about adding a 100-story exclusive tower to the resort, of which I intended to own the top floor penthouse as my own residence in Japan. I was still a pretty good architect, though I did not tell our hosts that I had built the oldest wooden temple in their nation.

"Our desire is for the greater honor of Japan," I said. "For too long the princes of the desert have lived a life of ease and decadence that is emulated in every direction. This resort will bring the same prestige to Japan. We believe your company is the right one to build this endeavor and would support it through our investment. You merely need to capture the contract and you will know you have the funding to pursue the endeavor."

As it happened, there were several development companies that wanted the rights to develop this piece of property. The battle had been heated. We'd done our research and chose a company in the competition that was not the largest, but seemed to be above reproach when it came to business ethics.

The battle heated up as it became known that this company had our backing. At first, it was all negotiation and innuendo. The competitors suggested the company we had chosen was not capable of developing such a large project. Then they suggested the company would be unable to get workers or materials.

Peninnah had been busy and had already purchased majority shares in the companies that would supply us under the names of different shell companies we owned. Of course, if they intimidated workers and we were unable to hire, that would be bad, so Peninnah came up with a strategy of enlisting the competitors as subcontractors for various parts of the massive development. I could see even before the contracts were let, the cost overruns would be in the vicinity of three times the original investment.

But money was not my concern. I wanted the company I'd chosen because they had a majority stake in an aerospace supplier that I had already chosen as the most likely to supply Space Pioneers with critical parts. My partners in the space exploration company were worried about the supplier being faithful in manufacturing the parts we needed. Peninnah's strategy was to offer to buy the aerospace company from our Japanese partners when they came back for more money.

I was not counting on the competition escalating to physical threats and violence. My bad.

42
Ninjas

BATHING IS STILL a social activity in parts of Japan and I was invited to join the men of the various companies at a spa where we would spend a few hours being heated, cooled, massaged, and oiled. And given great amounts of liquor and long harangues about why one company was better than another. Peninnah insisted she wanted the experience as well, and since there was a women's wing of the spa, she joined a few of the other wives who had accompanied their husbands. I had no misgivings.

We had been several hours in the spa when the women burst into the outer chamber of the men's area. The attendants, who were all naked women, scattered and ran for cover as it was not common to have women bathing and massaging the men. My name was called frequently. I was nearly dressed, so I grabbed the satchel and went out to meet the women.

"Bob-san. Men burst into the salon while we were having our hair done. They quickly throw bag over Peninnah-san's head and carry her out of the spa. She is kidnapped!"

I was furious and marched out to the outer area demanding to know which direction. A frightened attendant simply pointed up the street.

Back in the fourth century, I had been kidnapped and then my people searched for Lakshmi all night before he was found. After that, I equipped every person I brought into the infinity room and anyone I thought might spend time in the natural world with a tracking spell, so I would know where to find him or her. It had once been important when one of the first rescues from the pirates had attempted suicide by jumping overboard. I'd been able to find her in the ocean under a moonless sky because I was drawn to her.

It took only a moment to determine that Peninnah was being transported away in a car.

Ever since they were invented, I have been almost as fascinated with driving automobiles fast as I am with flight. I was not gentle with the driver of the car that happened to pull up to the curb in front of the spa. I pulled him out of the car, got in it, and drove off. I figured I'd leave a few million yen in the car when I got out.

I drove fast.

In a few minutes, I saw the gates closing on a huge estate where the kidnappers had disappeared. I parked the car I'd borrowed by the side of the road, left ten million yen on the seat, and went on the prowl. There were many guards around the wall of the estate. I was going to need help. I leapt a wall where there were no guards at the moment and followed my senses toward the house where Peninnah had been taken. Once I was near, I called for warriors to help me rescue my wife.

I was surprised when fifty-two black-clad ninjas emerged from the gateway to the infinity room. I enhanced their stealth with a look-away spell and set them loose to clear the way.

I slowly made my way to the house, occasionally stumbling over a body with its head at an odd angle. I wasn't sure who my ninjas were, but they were ruthless. I cast about to see who I had loosed on the unsuspecting kidnappers and smiled when I found who was there. I went boldly into the house and up the stairs with no resistance.

The house and grounds, I discovered, belonged to the chairman of one of the competitors who had openly admired my wife and had made some lewd comments in Japanese to one of his men, assuming I could not understand. Since I did not depend on knowing the language to understand what was being said, I had marked him as mine to punish.

I transformed myself into the full demon and stalked through the house as if I owned it. Which, I contemplated, I soon would.

When I located the room in which Peninnah was held captive, I found she was free and not much the worse for wear. The chairman was surrounded by the bodies of his bodyguards and was held between two ninja girls, while a third held a knife—not at his throat, but at his balls. I approved.

It was hard to tell if the chairman was more frightened by the demon before him or by the prospect of losing his balls.

Peninnah rushed to me and I wrapped her in my arms.

"Are you hurt?" I asked.

"Only my pride and a few bruises," she answered. She was wrapped in a kimono that looked far too big for her. "They ripped my clothes. That was one of my favorite Vera Wang ensembles. And I can't find my shoes. Bob, it was terrible."

I thought she seemed shorter than usual. She was barefoot. I also thought her concern for her clothes with the number of bodies lying around was perfectly illustrative of Peninnah's sense of confidence in me and whoever I sent for her.

"Do not worry, dear. You can buy an entire new wardrobe with what Mr. Yakisoba is going to pay you." I turned to the frightened Chairman. "Let us go to your office so you can sign over the ownership of your company to Peninnah," I said.

"What? You can't take my entire company!"

"No, of course not. Only your stake in it. In fact, no one will even be aware that things have changed, because you will never say anything about it. Peninnah will keep you as the chairman. You will make a good *junior* partner to Fukishina. Oh, and I'll leave you your little estate and your income. I'm not a heartless demon. However, you will need to clean up the grounds. I'm afraid many in your little security army did not survive the night."

We left the chairman, babbling at his desk, after he signed over his shares to Peninnah. His trousers had been slit open and his junk was hanging out. But at least it was still attached.

As soon as we left him, I summoned all my ninjas to me and they returned, with Peninnah, to the infinity room. I leapt the wall, leaving the bodies strewn behind me. It was too bad, but there are certain people you do not want to cross your path if you have abducted and mistreated a woman.

My priestesses were among them.

>— ◄◆► —<

"Bob," sniffed Peninnah when I had returned to our hotel and locked the door so I could open the infinity room. She rushed into my arms. "I'm terrible and selfish and caused you so much grief," she began.

"Shh shh shh," I admonished. "Being kidnapped was not your fault. We let our guard down and I bear as much responsibility as you. I need to ask Zhi to step up your self-defense training."

"I don't mean for that," she sobbed. "I've been jealous and disdaining of your priestesses. In fact, of the idea of your divinity. But it was the priestesses of Bob who came to my rescue. When we returned to the infinity room, they took me to the temple and bathed me in the pool. They anointed me with oil and brought me here to our marriage bed. They are the most precious and wonderful and frightening women in all of two worlds."

"Have I told you the story about how they came to be here and to be my priestesses?" I asked. She shook her head. "Those women endured kidnapping, beating, and serial rape at the hands of pirates in the Pacific. When I rescued them, they were so beaten down, we were unable to reach them at all. Then Zhi overheard them praying to Bob to save them. I had already rescued them from the pirates, but to their eyes, I was just another man. One of the girls threw herself overboard and I jumped in to save her. We were out in the middle of the Pacific and I had to use my full demon form and strength to rescue her. At that point, I was truly their savior Bob. No man is ever allowed to touch them, and they won't even see me if I am not in my full demon form. The first dozen girls were the ones who rescued and helped the next ones. Thankfully, their number never exceeded the fifty-two who are still serving in the temple. I wonder how many poor innocents were out there in the Pacific that we didn't find. But if a woman is in need, has been abused, or is threatened, they are like the ancient furies we named our ship after. They will mete out punishment and save that woman at all cost."

"I will go to the temple tomorrow and make whatever sacrifices they demand. I will praise their god Bob, my husband, and thank them for rescuing me. And I promise, I will never again be jealous of the priestesses of Bob, nor will I despise them."

"Amen," I said.

She looked at me in surprise and we both started laughing. And laughter turned to loving.

>-- ◄◆► --<

Have I mentioned how much I love sex with Peninnah? She keeps herself flawlessly made up and attired (or unattired) entirely for my pleasure. She explores my body, discovering anew every detail of whatever form I have taken. She seeks out my erogenous zones and titillates them in any way she can. Her shape is exquisite and I thank Aphrodite for this treasure of a woman each time my hardened cock slides into her inner passage. She receives me excitedly and works the muscles in her vagina as much as we both work our hips. If she had been created entirely for the purpose of pleasing me, I would call her creator and prostrate myself before her. She is, I have decided, the last of my wives and possessions. I will treasure her forever.

We stayed joined together in loving all night long.

>-- ◄◆► --<

When Mr. Yakisoba offered to become a subsidiary partner to Fukishina in the development of the resort, the offer was quickly accepted and things began to move forward rapidly. Once the plan was approved and the full team was put together, the political machinery moved rapidly. Construction began with surveys and infrastructure the following week. Many of the competitors were further enlisted, following Yakisoba's lead in becoming subcontractors and suppliers. When the foundations were poured, I was relatively certain there were bodies in the concrete footings.

A rumor flew around Japan that ninjas had appeared to take revenge on traffickers and those who would harm women. I might have encouraged that rumor by tracking down a couple of instances where kidnappings had occurred and loosing the priestesses on them. Bodies nailed to a wall were always a warning others paid heed to. And the rescued women and children returned to their homes told stories of ninja warriors who were faster than light and silent as death.

>-- ◄◆► --<

We continued on to India, where we were welcomed as new investors in a support system that could track nearly every object in the sky that had a signal. They were even tracking a few dead objects to make sure the launches of the new independent space companies were unobstructed. It was an attempt at unifying the tracking of space traffic in expectation of an increase in independent commercial launches. No one needed to launch on a collision trajectory with someone else's launch. The traffic system would monitor all extra-atmospheric objects like a massive airport control tower.

As a sign of goodwill, we also started a community redevelopment project and sponsored a dozen different rehabilitation and restoration projects in various cities of India. We focused on paying for infrastructure improvements in poor areas, with the side effect that crime in those areas also went down. Another side effect was how pleased Lakshmi was that we were helping the people of her country of origin, though nearly 2,000 years after she lived there.

And then we decided to do Europe, visiting places I had not been in centuries. We stopped in Rome and Venice, but there was really nothing there Peninnah wanted to revisit.

She appeared at my side and flew in first class with me, even though she'd have been more comfortable in the satchel. But it was necessary to keep up the appearance of being a loving couple on an around-the-world honeymoon during which we were conducting a bit of business, as well.

Finally, we landed in London and I considered taking a little side-trip up to the northern area.

It was a couple hundred years before Caesar led his fiasco to conquer the Britons, when I visited the islands for the second time. The first time, Poseidon had blown me through the channel at Gibraltar and I'd ended up on an island between England and Ireland. At the time, I was masquerading as Odysseus. The lying god of the sea told Helios I'd stolen his cattle. The truth was they were Manannán mac Lir's cattle and I'd bargained for them. When I finally rebuilt my boat, the god of the Irish Sea wished me a good journey and invited me to return one day.

I thought I was paying him a visit, but managed to land on the English side of the sea. It was decidedly different.

The west coast of northern England was heavily wooded and dotted with lakes. I thought perhaps I'd found a place untouched by man, where I could possibly enter the infinity room and just stay for a while as I enjoyed my wives and concubines.

As I was wandering over the hills, I thought I heard singing. It was faint, but I followed the sound and it gradually became louder. Then it stopped altogether and I was lost. I was pretty good at navigating by the stars and had many charts in my satchel, but the forest was so dense that I could not see the stars and had only a vague notion of where I was. Rather than wander around in the dark, I found a soft bed of leaves and lay down to sleep, not entering the infinity room for fear that I would miss some malevolent beast in the forest.

In the morning, I gathered my bearings from the direction of the sunrise, but soon I heard the singing again. It didn't seem so far off, so I decided to see if I could discover who owned the lovely voice. It didn't take long before I came upon a stream with a pool beside a low hill. On a rock at the edge of the pool, with her feet dangling in the water, was a raven-haired beauty with pale skin. She had strands of flowers woven into her hair and ivy snaked around her legs. She wore a gossamer gown, pulled up to her waist as she idly kicked her feet in the water.

I must have sighed or made some such noise when I saw her beauty, because she jerked her head up to glare at me for interrupting her singing.

"Who are you to interrupt Tiona's singing?" she demanded.

"Bob begs Tiona's forgiveness. He was drawn by her lovely voice."

"So is the fawn," she said pointing at a young red deer. "But the fawn does not comment on my music."

"Had a deer the voice of a man, he would sing the praises of Tiona all day long."

"Just like a man to make such a noise," she said.

"I accept your rebuke. Perhaps I could join the fawn and silently listen."

"There is no sense sitting in the mud," she teased. "Come sit beside me on the rock and I will sing you a lullaby."

I crossed the stream and settled near her, but not touching, on her rock. And she began again to sing. I drowsed lazily, letting the music wash over me. Then I started awake. Her music was enchanting. Literally. I whispered a spell to resist all magic and she turned suddenly toward me, ceasing her singing.

"Do you not like my voice? Does it not make you feel relaxed?" she breathed, drawing the word out in a way that would surely make a mortal fall under her spell.

"I find I need very little sleep these days, fair lady. I like your singing so much I wanted to stay awake for it. To drowse during such a concert would surely be an insult to the musician."

"Poo! You're no fun!" she said. "If you stay awake, how am I to lure you into my mound for dinner."

"You might just invite me," I said.

She looked me up and down.

"You are not what you appear to be," she said.

"I daresay, you might not be either."

"Oh, this is me. Your misperception is that I'm simply a human girl bathing in the pond. I'm not human!"

"Well, fancy that! I'm not human either!"

"I knew it! Perhaps you've been sent here to unite our kingdoms by marrying me. We shall rule over all."

"Oh, I don't think so. No one sent me and I bring my kingdom with me wherever I go," I said. "What kind of demon are you?"

"Demon! I am not such a lowly creature. I am Queen of the Fae. At least in this mound I call my home."

"Ah, I see. Well, I am but a lowly creature, then."

"Oh. I didn't mean to insult you. I never thought I would meet a demon. You're rather nice," she said.

"Thank you. I think you are rather nice as well, though I've never met a faerie before. Are they all so beautiful?" I asked. She preened.

"I might be *slightly* more beautiful than most," she whispered. "I *am* a queen, after all."

"Ah, yes. Of course. I am merely a wandering demon, free to travel wherever I desire."

"You mean you'll leave me? We haven't even gotten married or made love or anything! This is not how the stories are told," she moaned.

"Well, I suppose I could make love to you, and even marry you, but I would still leave."

"Um... Well, maybe we could test it and see how it would be. Do you really think I'm beautiful?"

"Very beautiful," I said. "The most beautiful faerie I've ever seen."

She apparently missed my meaning as I'd never seen a faerie before. She practically glowed with the praise. In truth, she *was* very beautiful, and nicely displayed as well. I thought of Aphrodite and wondered if all women of great beauty were so vain.

The thin dress she wore really hid nothing beneath it. She was a slight creature with proportionally small breasts, but her arousal was obvious on them. She had a small patch of dark hair on her mons, but it did not extend down between her legs. Her face was delicately featured with lips that begged to be kissed. In a moment of weakness, I kissed them.

"That is a good test," she sighed. "Do it again."

I did it again and again and again. We tested our compatibility in every position we could think of. My juices co-mingled with hers and ran down her thighs. My lips found hers again and again and we were still making love by the pond when morning came.

"In my land, when you come together three times, you are automatically married," she laughed. "I believe we exceeded our vows."

I believed she'd just made that rule up. Besides, hadn't she said her kingdom extended only to her mound?

"I would happily marry you, my lovely faerie, but I would still depart eventually."

"Be married to me for a year," she said. "We'll do nothing but make love and then you can go."

And I agreed, fool that I am. Of course, Tiona had no intention of letting me go at the end of a year. She was sure I would be a captive of her beauty and sexuality. When I dressed myself and threw my satchel over my shoulder to leave, she rushed to me, falling on her knees before me.

"Please do not leave me, Bob. How will I live without you?"

"My dear Tiona, you shall live as you have always lived, trapping mortal men, and taking them to your magic kingdom. It is not a good thing for two of our kind to be so near to each other for too long. I learned centuries ago that long life together leads to boredom and contempt. I cannot take you into my kingdom and make you mine, any more than you can take me into yours. We are different immortals."

"Very well. From this day forth, I shall sit on my rock and sing of my lost love and mourn you forever."

Her meaning, of course, was that she would kill me and sit on my corpse mourning. I did not let that happen. I wove a shielding spell around her so she could not leave her rath. The sad thing about the spell was that I could not enter it. The spell would not last forever, but I said my goodbye through the veil that separated us and set off to find my boat once more.

In my marriages, I count that one as a divorce. Not a friendly one.

43
A New Palace

I LIKED THE LAKE DISTRICT and thought about going up to see what had changed in 2,000 years, but I guess you'd say in today's jargon, it was an ugly divorce. I wasn't sure I wanted to risk a confrontation. Besides, Peninnah and I received a royal summons to have tea with the other Queen. I guess that wasn't so terribly unusual. We were billionaires and were trotting around the world looking for places to put our money. We'd also made a substantial donation to a local medical foundation that provided services to the poor and underprivileged. I wondered what Her Majesty had in mind.

I found out immediately. We were ushered into a room lined with the Queen's staff and a few notables we should have known. We were presented to the Queen and bowed appropriately. Then a herald of some sort stepped forward with a scroll and read off a list of my charitable contributions around the world as if he were reading the charges in a criminal case.

"Sir Bob, we recognize your contribution to the health and well-being of citizens of the world by investing you as an Honorary Knight Commander in the Order of the British Empire," said the queen.

I bowed my head—low—and she put a nice necklace around my neck. I wondered how many demons had ever been knighted in the British Empire, and then decided it was probably best not to know.

After a brief reception, during which everyone who had been in the room stopped by to congratulate me and shake my hand, we were conducted into a small chamber where a table had been set with tea. We remained standing until the queen arrived and was seated, then joined her.

"You've been very busy, Bob," she said. "A massive resort community in Japan. The redevelopment of entire neighborhoods in India. The support of medical and social institutions around the world. And, of course, your very secretive operations to help end child and sex trafficking."

I was a little taken aback by that and glanced at Peninnah, whose eyes had also popped open. We had kept our work in that arena a secret, following reports of child trafficking, abductions, and missing teens, then moving in quietly to release the children to authorities—usually after there were no traffickers remaining alive in that cell to harm them. I suppose I shouldn't have been too surprised to find the monarch of the British Empire knew about what we had done—or rather what my priestesses had done. I was not about to volunteer any information, though.

"What I am most interested in, though, is your ability to get things built quickly. And so, I am wondering if you would be interested in a commission here in Britain."

"How may we serve your majesty?" I asked. I thought it was a bit unusual for the queen to get involved in a commercial development project, but I was a builder and architect. I was interested.

"I'd like you to build me a new temple... I mean palace, of course. I'm tired of these musty old stones."

"Surely you have many homes to choose from," I said.

"Oh, yes. We are rich in British heritage. There isn't a one of my homes that isn't twice my age or more."

"You do seem to be blessed with longevity."

"Would *you* die and leave your kingdom to *my* heirs?" she laughed. "Nor would I. Perhaps when Will is fifty or so, he'll be ready to usurp the throne from his father. But you can imagine that I am a bit eager to have my new home built so that I can enjoy it for a while."

"Certainly, your majesty. Uh... such a project could be costly," I suggested.

"Not to worry. I started a Go Fund Me and have collected enough to cover the expenses," she said. I nodded. *Really?* "I've had my surveyor locate a bit of crown property that could be developed. But I don't want another stone edifice. If I never see another block of limestone in my life, it will be too soon."

"So, you want a modern palace?"

"Yes. Lots of steel and glass, but it can't look like an office high rise. It still needs to look like a queen's palace."

I nodded and began sketching things out on a napkin. Peninnah gave me a horrified look and I realized I was drawing on a linen napkin with the royal arms embroidered in one corner. Ah, well. I had too many ideas brimming forth to stop.

"Does your majesty prefer straight lines or futuristic curves?" I asked.

"I don't mind round elements in regard to the floor plan, like the towers, but the vertical lines should be straight—even if not perfectly vertical. I can't help but think Gaudí had a vision problem that caused everything he created to bulge like it had just overeaten. As much as I admire their genius, I would not like to live in a painting by Dali, either."

I had to agree about the disturbing image. We left the queen with several sketches, including her own drawings on a royal napkin.

I hoped, frankly, that she lived as long as I did.

>-- ◄◆► --◄

The following days were very busy as I brought in help and negotiated with various unions and contractors. The property just northwest of London was a lovely bit of real estate and we began by constructing a wall around the square mile, then moving inside to construct a second wall that would define the palace grounds. It was a slightly smaller scale of what I had built for the Khaan. I put into practice all I knew about feng shui and much of what was learned in building the palace at Xanadu. While it was a completely modern structure, it leaned more on the design of Asian palaces than European. In a way, it looked more like what I imagined a space station would look like.

The queen approved the designs and we were able to turn the construction over to our crews and continue our world tour, popping back to England nearly every month to oversee the project and have tea with the queen. I believe the project was keeping her young as she didn't seem to age a day. She still looked only ninety.

>-- ◄◆► --◄

People say 'human traffickers,' as if it is a respected vocation. Slavers, I say. I've never liked them and never will. When the slaves are women and children, I like them even less. I know that's chauvinistic of me. Liz has told me so frequently. It shouldn't take a woman or child in danger to make me against slavery. And it doesn't, really. It just gets my goat when it is.

During the unCivil War, San Francisco was a hub of human trafficking. It was the port of entry for thousands of Chinese who came to work the mines and lay tracks for the railroad. Their situation was slavery in all but name. They came willingly, thinking they would earn money to bring their families to America. Most never saw their families again.

Other Chinese were imported to take advantage of the great opportunities in America and found themselves working on their backs in Chinese brothels. Most, but not all, of those were women. American men, I discovered, would fuck anything that was weaker than they were. That was the situation when I found Chin Li hiding in my wagon after a delivery to the Grand Hotel. Just for her to be this far away from Chinatown was a danger to her. My guards, however, had spotted her and hidden her under the seat of my wagon.

Ali, my bodyguard, had been a slave in an African empire when I found her and set her free. From that moment on, she refused to leave my side and joined the harem in the infinity room. She was devoted to the martial arts and founded a cadre of women who would act as my bodyguards when needed. That had been five hundred years ago, but her memories of being a slave were still fresh.

I drove out of San Francisco toward our pier south of the town. I'd lost control of Goat Island during the war, when the army thought they'd build a fort there. It hadn't materialized ten years later, so I still made use of the dock as a waypoint when crossing the bay with my barge and wagon. As soon as we were on the water, I called the stowaway out to introduce myself.

Pardon my continued chauvinism. She was a living doll! No, I don't mean that literally. I mean she was just adorable. Cute as a button. Cute as a bug's ear. All those other exclamations of cuteness. I estimated she was barely fourteen, though my experience in judging the age of Chinese women was notably poor. This girl or woman triggered something in me that was far different than the horny goat was used to. I wanted to wrap her in a cocoon of silk and protect her from damage. I wanted to feed her and teach her. I wanted all the things that Nimia told me later a father would want for his little girl. Oh, my!

It turned out that she was not a little girl. She was twenty-two years old. Her life had been hell and she had run away from a brothel where she'd been kept since arriving in America. There were some questions regarding the legality of her arrival, as well. We found that despite all the regulations trying to bar the Chinese from immigrating to America, there were clandestine operations transporting people from China to San Francisco that were simply ignored by the authorities.

The advent of steam ships had cut the crossing time from the three to four months it had been when I sailed the routes, to a mere four to six weeks. These ships transported goods to and from China. The Chinese in San Francisco still subsisted on a diet that was mostly rice and most of the rice was imported from China. There were also passenger liners that crossed the Pacific and a number of Navy vessels that patrolled the shores. But through that traffic, there were still pirates and slavers who collected passengers—often offering legitimate passage for a large fee—and then stripped them of their wealth at sea and placed them in a network of mines, fields, and brothels to 'work off their passage.'

Li had been one who took legitimate passage and discovered she had signed on to a brothel. While the whites in San Francisco rioted to get rid of the Chinese, they were also quick to patronize the brothels and gambling establishments—and laundries—run by the Chinese. The constant attacks on Chinese homes, businesses, and individuals in the street gave rise to protection gangs that patrolled with the dual purpose of protecting the businesses and keeping their property (slaves) at home.

This all sat poorly with me and I resolved to do something about it.

>— ◀◆▶ —<

Maureen tried to prevent me from taking action. Coming from Ireland, she'd seen the same level of discrimination against the Irish, serving in a brothel herself. But she had no sympathy for the Chinese in the same situation. Racism knows no bounds of decency. She figured that she survived it, they could, too. Of course, Maureen was sapping the souls of her clients, too.

It seemed to me that the best course would be what I had always done: Hide at sea and capture the slavers. The problem was that I knew how to sail. I knew nothing about piloting a steamship, nor did I have one.

With Li's help, we were able to identify the ship she had come on when it steamed into harbor. On close inspection, we discovered it had stopped at a different harbor where its illegal cargo had been rendered over to the network on land. Then, bearing only legitimate cargo to the docks in San Francisco, it had all the appearances of a profitable merchantman.

Li was quite brilliant at setting the strategy.

"Papa Bob," she said as we sat at the table with some of my best fighters. I loved it when she called me that. It had a completely different meaning than when girls of the twenty-first century tried to call me 'daddy.' Li had quickly shown that it was her skill in the martial arts that enabled her to win her freedom. "We can move in silence at the place where people are stored. They will stay there for some days until the ship has left port so it is not implicated should they be caught. If we move quickly, we can overcome the guards and free the slaves."

"And what do we do with these people once we free them?" I asked. That was definitely another problem. They certainly would not be welcome in San Francisco.

"Do you not have *any* place where decent hard-working people can make a home in a new world?" she asked innocently.

"I do not want to force people to leave this world for an unknown world."

"They have already made that decision. Some few have relatives and friends in San Francisco who might want them returned. But most have left behind the world they knew to find a new life and a new world where they can be free." She made sense. I agreed to the venture, and we set out to find the warehouse where the people were kept.

If any authority had been looking, they would have found this place immediately. I had to assume that meant it was profitable for them to not look. We might have problems on that end sometime later, but not this night. This night, twenty of my most capable warriors, led by Ali, joined Li and me to invade the warehouse and disable the guards. It was sickening. Over 300 people were in cramped quarters with barely enough rice to survive.

When we had cleared the warehouse of the guards, I announced what the situation was, with Li helping to explain to those who could not grasp the concept. Perhaps a dozen of the people held captive had family they wanted to join. The others were more than willing to enter the infinity room and start a new life. I opened the gateway and they filed through, welcomed by my wives and concubines, and shown the remarkable world the infinity room had become.

Of course, this was not the only problem to be overcome. It was only a day before workers in the underground trade came to gather slaves for their businesses. Those workers were never seen again. I'd been willing to simply stop their activity and let them go, but it was quickly obvious that the only way to stop it was to end them. Li, my precious little daughter, was a delighted executioner.

Once the slavers had been cleared, we took the people who had relatives to China-town and reunited them with their families. It was not long after they had returned that a rumor began to circulate that a swordswoman of the people had arrived in California and would right the injustices done to the Chinese.

There wasn't much I could do about the rumors, which I honestly had nothing to do with. When the ship arrived again with another 300 Chinese slaves, we acted a bit differently. Oh, we still liberated the slaves and took them to the infinity room, but we also liberated the ship. The captain and his crew met Li. I was suddenly in possession of a fine steamship that still had cargo for delivery to San Francisco. The engineer on the ship, a person we deemed innocent of wrongdoing, gave me a crash course in piloting a steamship. The engineer found a home in the infinity room and emerged only to tend to the engines.

We headed to harbor and there I met the ship's owner. He was disturbed to find that the captain and his main crew had perished from a plague aboard the ship and questioned whether the cargo should be dumped at sea. It didn't take me long to figure out that the ship's owner did not know of the captain's secondary cargo. I talked him out of destroying the cargo. We unloaded with a crew of workers I brought from the infinity room into the lower hold, and we were paid handsomely. I was immediately offered employment as captain of the vessel to take a return shipment to China and make trade arrangements.

I agreed.

It didn't seem reasonable to clean up only one end of the operation. Someone at the other end was illegally selling passage on the freighter to supply the slaves.

>--- ◀◆▶ ---<

I loved Li. Truly as a daughter. She was passionate in her beliefs and untiring in her pursuit of justice for the downtrodden. She was legendary.

For example, while we were in Shanghai, we discovered that most of the agents selling passage to America were legitimately sending people to San Francisco as advertised. It was when a ship was well out into the Pacific that the change occurred. On the other hand, there were some who sold passage to people, knowing they would be enslaved. They often took their client's property in exchange for passage. I let Li take care of closing their businesses.

The legend of the flying sword arose.

She was the best martial artist and especially swordswoman I had ever met except Zhi. The two worked together to hone her skills and Li soon exceeded her teacher.

We stealthily crept up on a steamer out of Shanghai we'd seen loading passengers. It was a freighter and boarded far more passengers than such a ship should carry. I was laden with goods for San Francisco, including enough rice to feed Chinatown for a month. We left the harbor right behind the tramp and I cast a look-away spell both on our ship and on Li and her hand-picked cadre.

When we were right next to the steamer, Li led her squad aboard. She did not kill everyone on the crew, preferring to leave a skeleton crew to take the ship and its reduced cargo on to America. When the crew had been subdued, I boarded the ship and opened a gateway to the infinity room. I offered a return to the real world in San Francisco, but by that time, only a few were interested in leaving my paradise.

When the derelict steamer entered the harbor, the legend of the flying sword was enhanced.

The owner of my ship was thrilled with our cargo. We were transporting twice what the ship had carried under the former captain. After all, we weren't carrying people as cargo. We returned to the sea and worked our way through the treaty ports of China, including Canton, Amoy, Foochow, and Ningpo. We found that with the influx of westerners into China, some of the human trafficking was conducted by whites who sought out young women to supply needs in several countries, not just the Americas.

In each port, we did our best to locate the buyers of children and stop their trade.

The legend of the Flying Sword spread.

Once we freed a shipload of young women, they were taken to the infinity room and given several choices. None wanted to return home, knowing their families would only sell them again. Surprisingly, none were particularly interested in going to America, as they felt it was a country of slavers. We took some few to Hong Kong, where the British were effectively keeping the slave trade to a minimum, but nearly all wanted to stay in the infinity room. I faced a sudden need for men in the infinity room.

We managed to get them, but that is a different story. This is the story of Chin Li, the Flying Sword.

We were in port in Hong Kong when she disappeared. I use that term advisedly. I knew where she was, but as far as our ship and the infinity room were concerned, she was gone. Using stealth and skill, I worked my way into the underbelly of Hong Kong and sought her out. She had acquired a nice but modest residence where she began training young women in the arts.

"There is a great need here, Bob," she said. "I cannot return with you and simply leave these women to fate. Though the prospect of the infinity room is attractive, my life was not meant to be eternal."

"Li, I love you as my daughter and have never regretted saving you in San Francisco, but it pains my heart to leave you here," I said.

"Papa Bob, I honor you as my father and will always strive to make you proud."

"My pride is safe in your hands," I said.

I made it back to the ship and we steamed out of port that night, without having loaded any cargo. I stopped at a port in Japan that was still open to trade with westerners and filled the cargo holds. Then I made my last crossing of the Pacific by steamship. In San Francisco, I resigned as captain and parted on good terms with the owner.

Over the years, I occasionally heard whispers of the Flying Sword from all over the Far East. It seemed Li had trained her army well.

>-- ◀◆▶ --<

It was sometime in the '90s that I was watching TV, looking for re-runs of *Kung Fu*. That show always tickled me, though I ended up yelling at it from time to time because they got some things very wrong. I wondered what would have happened if Caine had ever met Chin Li. Well, if David Carradine actually had the skills he portrayed on television, it would be interesting, but I wouldn't bet on him.

As I flipped through the stations, I came upon a cooking show with a guy who professed to have a dozen girlfriends or more. And he was right out in the open about it. They appeared on his show with him and all seemed very happy. In those years, any relationship that didn't conform to the Christian Right Wing was deemed deviant and unacceptable. They'd lost the battle against interracial marriage, though there were still places where it could get a guy killed.

But to have an open relationship with a harem and have it accepted was something else. I imagined what it would be like to live openly with my wives and possessions and concubines, something we had not really been able to do in the natural world since Knossos. Now that would be the life.

This Brian fellow was said to be quite the martial artist, too. I watched the whole show and came back on a regular basis. There was just something about it that... Well, it didn't have a plot. He just talked to people and cooked food. It didn't have a script exactly, but he did have a recipe. And that was it.

What a life!

44
BELIEVING WHAT YOU SEE

>-- ◄◆► --<

"ᴛLL I'M SAYING, BOB, is there are people who believe this stuff and they are vocal," Doug said. "We have entered a new age of witchcraft. Before the internet, people listened to their doctor, their lawyer, and their preacher, and did what they were told. Now, even the doctor, lawyer, and preacher get what they believe from memes on Meta. We have the most uninformed populace since the dark ages, and they are all proud of it."

I nodded at my contact at Space Pioneers. I'd certainly seen enough evidence of what he was saying. I didn't like where this was going, though.

"What's this got to do with our project?" I asked.

"There are people—Scientists, Bob! Scientists!—who are planning this flight with all the best technology that has ever existed, who still think they're working on a Hollywood script and from the time you get on board the ship until it comes back home, it will all be a production no more real than the moon landing."

"That really doesn't improve my confidence. Wait! The moon landing?"

"You see? Now all of a sudden, even you are doubting it," Doug said in triumph. He was confusing me on purpose. "I have an idea. Now, hear me out on this. I know it sounds a little crazy, but why don't we play into it. We turn it into an outer space family reality show. Kind of a cross between *Lost in Space* and *The Bachelor* and *Survivor*. People eat that shit up," he said.

"You're talking a reality TV show, only we actually blast off into space? Like that cooking show I used to love. No script, just a task and sometimes informative shit about the subject."

"Exactly. We can call it *Bob's Family Goes to Mars*. Maybe a writer can come up with something better. We can start a prequel miniseries as you pick your crew and family and

""",
"""

we introduce the ship. We've got you and Peninnah as the primary love story, but we need to fill out the cast. Or crew. We'll make it an adult viewers show. That will draw a big audience. They should all be women on the crew. Horny women who want to lure Bob away from Peninnah. You need a couple of kids. Um… let's go with young women who could pass as teens. Maybe we can get an android in the mix. Oh, and everyone should be a different color. Black, Asian, Indian, European… you name it. Of course, we'll need some crew in the beginning—also horny women—but we'll dress them all in red shirts so the audience doesn't get too attached to them."

"I don't know, Doug…" I started. I could see possibilities, but also a dangerous amount of exposing who I really was and how many people were actually going on this journey.

"There's more! This puts us in a great position. We get the mini-series out there so people know it's coming. Then season one, you all blast off and deal with whatever emergencies we can invent on the trip to Mars. The season ends with Mars coming into view on your screen. If we've got good numbers and sponsors, we continue through the landing and getting everybody settled on Mars with a bunch of crises you have to handle. Maybe there is a whole tribe of Martians the little Rover never encountered. Any time our numbers lag, we can just cancel the show and we're clear and free to go ahead with our settlement plans. You and a harem of beautiful women, set to populate a new world. In a few years, when we've come out of these dark ages, we can launch a new colony ship to Mars and behold! they'll find a colony already settled and we'll reveal it wasn't a spoof after all. Tell me you wouldn't watch that show, Bob!"

"Um… Well, I'm not sure I have TV star looks. They're always pretty good looking. I suppose the idea and all is good, but the question is, will the damn ship fly? I'm not going to dedicate years to making this series if I don't get to space!" I said.

"That's the beauty of it, Bob. It's all real. We just use the TV show as a cover. Believe me, it will be far better received than 'Billionaire Space Race.' People love a good TV show and don't care how many billions you spend to produce it."

It was a lot to take in. Doug escorted me to the Board Room where the directors were waiting to welcome me to my new place at the table. My conversation with Doug was absolutely thrilling compared to the board meeting. Most of the meeting was about where they were profitable and where they were hurting for supplies. I'd brought some critical materials to the business with the companies I'd acquired on my round-the-world development campaign. I had parts from Japan, tracking systems from India, and an entire factory in Britain we could retool for building the ship without worrying about American engineering standards being subverted by lowest bidder construction. The Queen had even suggested a space travel theme park next to her new space age palace! We could use it as a launch pad.

>-- ⟨◆⟩ --⟨

"It's not a bad idea, Bob," Peninnah said. "And it solves a few problems we have in leaving earth without saying goodbye. A few of us are still 'living in seclusion' after we made the decision to enter the infinity room. Like Liz. Every so often she gets trundled out, made up to look like an old lady, and she makes a statement about women's rights and ownership of their own bodies. Brenda writes Christmas cards to the people in the Midwest. This would give us the opportunity to cast the... I mean hire the crew on our own terms. We might even want to float the idea to a couple of real scientists working on the project and bring them along for the ride."

"It's a one-way trip, Pen. We can't exactly take anyone from outside the infinity room without a full disclosure."

"So, disclose them. Did you read the news this week? Mr. Yakisoba in Japan was admitted to a mental hospital. It seems he couldn't stop talking about a satyr who burst into his house with a bunch of ninjas and killed all his guards. Of course, there was no evidence of foul play or of bodies, because he'd done such a good job of hiding them. So, they admitted the poor man to an institution where he can rave about it all he wants," Pen said. "I've appointed a new Chairman, by the way. I'm afraid that is the fate that awaits anyone we talk to or show the infinity room to who decides to blab about it. People still believe in prayer, but they don't believe in magic. Go figure."

"You have me about convinced," I said. "If we can really control the whole production, then we control the flight. Let's find a decent production company to buy so we have our own people behind the cameras."

Peninnah smiled and went straight to work.

>-- ◄◆► --<

I am not unaccustomed to people not believing what is true. Parse that? There's always someone who doesn't believe the truth. In fact, I've seen more of that over my four millennia than I have seen of people believing the lies. Stop and think about it for a minute. Often, when people believe something false, it's because they didn't believe the truth. Television and computers have made that even easier because we all know how images, video, sound clips, and even the printed word can be distorted, edited, and made up to look like something different than they are. I could probably appear on television in my full demon form, and the biggest reaction would be criticism of my makeup. I went full demon on this guy once... maybe I should tell you about that.

I was sailing around the Mediterranean a couple centuries before Caesar collecting manuscripts and books for the library at Alexandria. I told you about that, right? I stopped in Carthage before the Romans utterly destroyed it. There was this guy named Hannibal, a general of the Carthaginians. The previous general was dead and Rome had withdrawn, satisfied that the war was over. Hannibal didn't think so. I was consulting with him on the conditions at sea, where Rome's navy dominated everything east of Carthage, and told him how much resistance he would meet if he sailed directly from Carthage to Rome.

"Well, I'll cross here into Hispania and march around the coast to Italy. We'll be there before they even expect anything," he said.

"Hannibal, they expect everything. That's what makes Rome great. They've already subdued your allies in northern Italy. Invading by land is a bad decision," I said.

"No. It's logical and works well. We can cross with 20,000 troops and let's say twenty elephants. I have 4,000 cavalry I can put into it. Rome has nothing that can withstand this."

He stayed focused on his maps as I paced around the room. I paused and pointed at the Pyrenees.

"These mountains create a barrier between Hispania and Gaul that has withstood invasion for millennia."

"We can cross them."

"The mountains here are worse," I said, pointing to northern Italy. "They are the tallest anywhere in Europe and are always covered with snow."

"That's impossible. What do they do in summer? Plant crops in the snow? Ridiculous."

I'd had it and converted into my full demon form. I slammed my fist down on his map and yelled.

"I am demon Bob! I've been where you plan to go. You will lose half of everything you take with you."

He scarcely glanced up at me.

"There's no such thing as demons. Nice trick, though. I should have thought about losses in transit. I'll double the number I take with me. 40,000 troops, 8,000 horsemen, 40 elephants. I'll still get to Rome with more than enough to conquer it."

He paid absolutely no attention to me as I strode out of his war room and headed to the harbor. There was a lot of stir and I realized I was still in demon form. I got to my ship and cast off at once. I didn't want to be anywhere near there when Rome got angry. That's when I decided to sail through the gates of Gibraltar and explore the lands of the Britons.

I predicted correctly. Sort of. I wish Pinaruti had thought to add foreknowledge to my character, but I suppose he really couldn't imagine that. I'd probably have ended up like Cassandra if he had. No one would believe me.

Hannibal lost half of everything he started with and only a couple of his elephants survived the Alps. Still, it looked like he was going to be victorious, except neither of us had counted on the Roman Navy sailing in full force to Carthage. Hannibal and his troops had to hurry home some years later to defend his country—something that was futile. Fifty years later, Rome attacked, sacked, and utterly destroyed Carthage, making it a lesson to all the empire about what would happen to those who rebelled.

He had a demon standing right in front of him, declaring he was a demon, and he had the audacity to tell me I didn't exist. Well, I didn't have any sympathy for him when I heard he'd poisoned himself and died.

>-- <&> --<

I could go on with examples. Like the Priest at Chichen Itza who didn't believe in the god he sacrificed to, even when the god showed up and made himself known.

Now here's a puzzle for you. Over the past few centuries, I have heard priests of the Christians argue their proof of God and of Jesus' salvation. I've looked at their evidence, and it required that you believe in their God and salvation in order for them to prove it.

"Why do you seek to prove this," I asked a preacher in Texas once. I'd actually looked the fellow up because I saw a billboard that announced, 'There's proof that God exists!'

"Because now that you see the proof, you must believe!" he announced in victory.

"What does it mean to believe?" I asked.

"You must have faith in order to be saved."

"According to your scriptures, 'Faith is the substance of things hoped for, the evidence of things not seen.'"

I think he was surprised that I had read the scriptures. I had. Not only those, but the entire body of the Jewish Torah and the Talmud, the Mohammedan Koran, the Vedas, the Tao, The Shrimad Bhagavad Gita, and any other book I could get my hands on and put in my library.

"Therefore," I said, "proof is the antidote to faith. If these things are proven, then one need not have faith in them. In fact, one *cannot* have faith if one has proof."

"I disagree!" he shouted. "And I can prove it."

Enough said.

>-- ◄◆► --<

"Welcome to Areola, Bob," Nimia announced when I stepped into the infinity room. She was, of course, naked and I immediately fell to her breasts and started worshiping her nipples. She giggled.

"What is it, my love? What inspires this welcome to worship at your breasts, which I am always more than happy to do?"

"And you are always welcome, my beloved husband. But I refer to your world formerly known as the infinity room."

"What? You've named our world Areola?" I said. I was completely confused. Nimia simply grasped my head and held me firmly to her bosom.

"We—being the wives, possessions, and concubines, consulting with the priestesses—sat together to determine a good name for the world. We asked, 'What is Bob's favorite thing of all?' It took us about thirty seconds to all agree on boobs. But we couldn't call the infinity room 'Boob' or 'Tit' or even 'Breast.' We all agreed that Areola had a more mystical ring to it and was a better name than 'Nipple.' What do you think, love?"

"If you are happy with the name, I am happy to pay homage to it whenever I see it," I said. I carried Nimia away to bed and made sure to show her exactly how much I loved her areolae.

>-- ◄◆► --<

Doug was a brilliant promoter. I think he could sell oil to Arabs. He certainly sold the concept of the Space Pioneers mission to Mars as a reality TV show.

Peninnah bought a producing television company and started slowly training our own personnel from Areola as camera technicians. We kept the company busy producing commercial films and advertising while we set up the arrangements at Space Pioneers. We moved a crew into the labs and manufacturing facilities and began gathering 'color' shots and interviews with the people working on the project.

Over the course of a year in the business, I replaced the executives of the production company with women from Areola. The few men who were seen on set or in the production room were also citizens of Areola and went back there each evening. It was an exhausting year, just getting ready for the start of the series.

Since the part of the crew and staff working on our project were all from Areola, it was no problem for Peninnah and I to live there and not have to maintain the appearance of being in the massive house Peninnah had purchased for us in the hills of Los Angeles. That house was really just a front for the gateway into the infinity room. And to entertain people who were not in the know. It would become the residence of our competitors and the crew during filming.

Doug, of course, arranged the parties.

We filmed a test pilot to shop around, featuring characters from Areola. The big networks weren't interested because they had a backlog of reality TV concepts. One was actually considering a concept for putting a dozen homeless people in a cell and telling them that the last one alive would get a million dollars. Fiction becomes reality. It was beginning to look like I would need to buy my own network when a small cable and online broadcaster took the bait. In Indiana, of all the ridiculous places.

The CEO was a beautiful blonde, closing in on fifty, I suppose. She had the President of the company with her for the meeting and her husband and co-owner of the company. He was a quiet guy, kind of short, and he looked familiar. I shook it off and paid attention to the meeting.

"Let me ask how we're going to get sponsors for this," Rose, the CEO, asked.

I noticed her husband give Peninnah the once-over, but the president of the company was having trouble focusing on business instead of the diamond in Peninnah's navel.

"Of course, you'll get the sponsorship of Space Pioneers," Doug explained. "But that will be our draw for others. We have a couple of high-tech companies looking at buying in for product placement and sponsorship. Nothing sells computers like Scotty picking up a mouse and saying, 'Computer.' His reaction when shown how to move it around on a pad was priceless. 'How quaint.' They sold a lot of computers with that *Star Trek* movie."

"I remember that," the husband said.

"Then there is a special themed resort in Japan that will be a big sponsor. The show is going to be a big influencer for travel. People will be lining up for tickets to Japan. They're already considering expanding to a companion resort in India, America, and... get this... the Queen of England has suggested an adjunct to her new palace. Have you seen that place? She's already selling tickets just to have people come in and tour the palace."

"And who is your production team?" Rose asked. I noticed the sparkle in Pen's navel attracted her eye as well.

"We've been grooming BSE Studios for this show. They've already begun capturing background footage and they produced the pilot you saw. You should see the babes on the production staff. You're aware, aren't you, that we're talking about a TV MA rating here. There are likely to be lots of panty flashes and a few bare boobs in each episode. People love that shit," Doug answered.

"Who's doing the effects, though? Like space travel?"

"This is where it gets good. We're actually going to send a ship up there to film the journey. Of course, it will just be a dummy for the show, but there will be lots of pictures of space filling the screen."

"Boring," said the husband. He was never really introduced or else I'd been too captivated by Rose to hear. "We've seen all kinds of space pictures. Between earth and the moon? Reasonable footage. Beyond that? We've got six months of empty out there before you reach Mars. We'll need some excitement. Near collision with an asteroid. An attempt by Russia to hijack the ship. And... what do they call that stuff when the audience feels the acceleration and changes of direction? You know what I mean?"

"Gotcha. We'll go to work lining up an effects team to glam it up."

The executives looked at each other and nodded.

"You've got a deal," Rose said. "Doug, Bob, Peninnah, I can hardly wait to see the rushes. How soon can we start airing the mini-series?"

>-- ◄◆► --‹

When it came to negotiating with the media, advertisers, and corporate execs, we left it up to Doug. He was a natural.

"Doug, how did you ever get into this business of aerospace, anyway? You seem like a promoter and marketer," I suggested as we greeted guests coming to our first big party.

"Oh, well, that just comes naturally to me. I'm not a scientist or anything, but I've got a degree in physics. Not astrophysics. I'm definitely not a rocket surgeon. But I understand the language well enough that I can talk to people who don't know anything. That's why they put me on being your personal assistant at Space Pioneers."

"Because you assume I don't know anything?" I asked.

"Don't be offended, buddy. You're a smart guy, but we all know you made your fortune in real estate and oil. That doesn't make you an astrophysicist either, no matter how smart you are. I'm strictly public relations at Space Pioneers. Um... Speaking of which, would you introduce me to the blonde with the big tits over there? I mean, Peninnah's nice for you and all, but maybe I could score a little on the side."

I glanced over to Avril, one of the cinematographers from BSE Studios. She wasn't from Areola, though we had our eye on her for later addition. If she was interested in Doug, far be it from me to stand in her way. I thought they might make a cute couple.

45
CASTING CALL

WE HELD AUDITIONS for places in my harem. Don't roll your eyes like that. Anyone who won a place on the crew was going to have a one-way ticket off earth. It's one thing to agree to have sex with Bob and all the other women on the flight. That's an easy choice for most of the aspiring actresses. It's a different thing completely to know it is going to be for the rest of a very long life.

"So, what if you found out it was all real and you weren't coming back to earth?" Liz suggested. She looked almost exactly like she looked fifty years ago, so no one suspected it really was 'that' Liz. She claimed to be a granddaughter.

"Yeah, right," laughed the interviewee.

"Treat it as a serious question."

"I'd sue. I need an acting gig, not a sex slave thing. Really!"

"Okay, thanks for your time. We'll get back to you."

"Wait. Don't I have to fuck him?"

"Not during auditions."

"Oh, shit. I was really looking forward to that."

You get the idea. It was how auditions went. I was beginning to think this was entirely the wrong way to go about casting a crew for our ship.

"So, look. Word on the street is that you haven't called a single person back for a follow-up interview or screen test. The professionals out there figure you're just locking up audition footage cheaply."

"Yet you showed up," I said.

"Five hundred bucks for a screen test and I don't even have to get naked? Hell, yeah."

"So, you had an opportunity to look over the entire concept of the show. What do you think?" Liz asked.

"Well, I look around at you and that Mrs. Bob, and... um... even the camera crew. I figure you've got no shortage of pussy. So, you must be looking for something in particular. I've done my research and it seems there's one question you always ask that gets girls turned down. I'm surprised no one else has figured it out," she said.

I glanced at my clipboard with a copy of her resume and headshot. Deedee Thomas. She reminded me of someone. I couldn't remember who. Okay, so *you* try remembering everyone you've met in 4,000 years! It'll come to me. Or it won't.

"And what question is that?" Liz followed up.

"What if I found out it was all real and I wasn't coming back to earth?" Deedee said.

"And?"

"I'll tell you after we shoot our test scene."

Hmm. I kind of liked this girl. We'd developed a few scripts that we used for screen tests. They were short scenarios and not actually a script per se. We improvised within the scene because we figured the whole point of a reality show was improvisation. It needed to look like reality TV. We borrowed heavily from some classic sci fi for the scenarios. She read through the scenario we'd prepared for this scene and I took my place in the captain's chair. The set was easily three times as large as what an actual ship would be, but it let us maneuver around easily. Deedee took a seat in the navigator's chair below me.

"Captain, scanners are picking up an approaching object," she began.

"Asteroid?" I asked.

"Not unless someone put a motor on it. It definitely shows signs of self-propulsion."

"Put it on screen." We pretended to look out a viewscreen in front of us. "That's approaching a lot faster than anything we have in our data banks."

"And it's coming right for us!"

"Evasive maneuvers, Deedee!"

"It's no use, Captain. It's sticking with us. This is the end!"

With that, Deedee leaped out of her chair and propelled herself into my arms, knocking me back in the recliner I used as a captain's chair. She began tearing at my clothes and her own.

"I can't let it end like this, Captain. Not without showing you how I really feel. I've loved you since the first day I set foot on this ship. I can't die without knowing what it would be like."

By that time, she had our shirts open and slammed her abundant bare breasts into my chest and her lips against mine. Her tongue slipped into my mouth and my hands naturally found their way to her breasts. She would definitely be a nice addition to Areola. Her hands were busy below my waist, working my cock free. She flipped her short skirt up and planted herself on my cock with a fierceness that left me breathless.

"Fuck me, Captain. It may be the last thing we ever do and is the feeling I want to take into the afterlife with you." By that time, there was no question that I was going to take the feeling with me as I thrust up into her amazingly wet pussy and she screamed against my shoulder. I began pumping into her as a buzzer sounded and a computer-generated voice echoed.

"Approaching object has self-destructed. The ship is no longer in danger. Repeat..."

"Yeah," she whispered as she kissed me again. "If I found out it was all real and I was never returning to earth, I'd be okay with that."

>-- ◄◆► --<

It's amazing how much time people spend pretending to be something they aren't—not just individuals, but entire countries. I think the most frequent pretense is religious. One country pretends to be Christian, another Muslim, and another Buddhist. Still another purports to welcome all religions. What is your country pretending to be?

But there are other pretenses as well. Back at Troy, the Greeks pretended to retreat and left a 'gift' of a large wooden horse for the Trojans. The next day, most of Troy had been put to the sword and I had collected all the priestesses of Aphrodite and taken them to the infinity room. Then I pretended to be Odysseus as I shoved off and sailed the Mediterranean, pursued by Poseidon.

Back a few hundred years ago, I pretended to be a Catholic priest and brought the Inquisition to Spain. That sucked. So, what we pretend to be isn't always for the better. And, of course, Hannibal thought I was only pretending to be a demon. Even when we aren't pretending, we are.

I spent enough time in the theatre back in Greece and following Alexander that I got used to playing a part. I kind of regretted that I hadn't trod the boards with Shakespeare, but by that time, I was already in the New World. Regardless, I have often pretended to be something other than what I was. Am. Whatever.

There was this time in Japan... Now, that's worth telling about.

It must have been near the end of the first millennium after Caesar or so—not long before I presented myself to the prince in Nihon and built a wooden temple. I was just exploring the many islands that make up the Japanese archipelago. At one island, I found a village that was beset by bandits and forced to pay a heavy tax each year that kept the people of the village in poverty and near starvation. When I heard of the place, I dressed in the robes of a wandering Samurai, complete with two excellent swords I had purchased and duplicated. I missed having either Ninra's sword or Odysseus' sword. I approached the village.

The elders came out to meet me and plead with me to pass their village by as they had nothing that was not required by the bandits.

"How many bandits beset you?" I asked.

"Honored sensei, there are forty thieves and they keep dozens of slaves, including women to satisfy their lust."

That set poorly with me. Women being kept as sex slaves? Not on my watch.

I retreated from the village and opened a gateway from which I summoned my harem to bring food enough for all the village. I selected six to dress as I did and gave them swords. They were, of course, all highly trained in martial arts since our time in India.

I led the procession into the village, beating on a gong to call all the countryside in for the feast. People were wary. They were more afraid that word of the great feast would spread to the bandits and they would be punished. The vision of the seven Samurai standing at the edge of the village to protect them, and the dozen beautiful women who served them soon calmed their fears and the feast was on.

As expected, the bandits showed up on horseback and attempted to ride us down without even asking what was going on. Let us say simply that none of the bandits remained on the horses that galloped into town and were corralled by my women.

"Samurai? What business have you here? This is our island! Go back to where you came from or face your deaths!"

That was pretty brave talk for a man who had only half his band still standing. Nonetheless, they attacked and we spared only one to lead us back to their camp, so we could free the slaves and women. The place was the size of the village.

When we brought the freed slaves back to the village, would you believe the villagers we had just fed pretended they didn't have enough resources to feed and care for the former captives?—even though most had been taken from their village!

Well, there's no forcing people into a community that doesn't want them. I'd seen evidence of that repeated over the centuries. I pretended to be a simple wandering Samurai and the village pretended to be starving. I led the newly freed people back to the camp where the bandits had enslaved them. There was really nothing wrong with the camp. It was pretty much a village in itself. The land around it was fertile and there were even crops that had been planted by the slaves to supplement what was stolen from the village.

"Now, you don't need to stay here if you think you have someplace else to go," I told them. "I did not bring you back here to make you slaves again. But whoever stays and works will not want for any needed thing. This valley is rich and will provide for you. Your labor is now for yourself."

They weren't exactly sure how I was different from the bandits. The next day, my six other Samurai and I began building a gate for the village. We went out hunting in the mountains and brought back wild goats and other animals we could domesticate and built a pen for them. We tended the rice paddies and pruned the plum trees. Each night we fed those who had worked beside us. We did not feed anyone who did not work. Some begged us but we refused. There was a simple way to be fed and that was to work. Within a week, nearly everyone was working.

A couple of warped individuals attempted to raid the stores of food, but they were met with the sharp point of my Samurai's swords. One fled and took news of what we were doing to the village that had been beset by the bandits in the first place. The other wandered off into the hills and we never saw him again.

We stayed with our new village for several weeks. One of the things they noticed was that whoever was out working would find another person working beside him or her. These people were from the infinity room and took pleasure in helping those who helped themselves. It was a rule of the infinity room and was uniformly obeyed. Work for the betterment of our people and receive everything you needed to live a comfortable and fulfilling life. But at night and meal time, none of the helpers would be seen. The people came to believe the *kami*—Shinto spirits who had once been ancestors—were blessing them. My people pretended they really didn't exist. They never spoke and never touched a member of our new village.

By time to harvest, our village brought in more food than they could consume. And so, on their own, they decided to take food to the village that had been beset by the bandits. They did not say anything, having learned from my women. Instead, they slipped in at night and simply left sacks of rice and butchered meat. Then they silently slipped away.

I could have predicted the response of the original village based on the response of greedy people I'd known for three millennia. And nearly all the people I'd known for three millennia had been greedy. They armed themselves and came to take what they wanted from our village. They found the seven Samurai waiting for them at the village gate.

"Do you think, having seen what we did to the bandits, that you can become bandits yourselves? These people work for their food and they prosper. If you go back to your village and work for your food, you, too, will prosper. Do not think that you can become bandits and take what is not yours. The *kami* protect this village.

As if they emerged from me—actually just from a gateway I'd opened behind me— dozens of my women came out dressed in flowing white gowns and simply pointed at the invaders, gesturing them to return home.

They did so. In a hurry.

And so, we had pretended to be Samurai and *kami*, protecting this village, which, the last time I checked, was still there and still prospering. My women and my Samurai silently slipped away into the hills where I collected them into the infinity room.

>-- ⬖ --<

That was nothing, though, compared to pretending we were mounting a reality TV show on which the participants had been 'hypnotized' to believe they were really going on a space trip to Mars, when they were really on a space trip to Mars and beyond, pretending to be on a TV reality show. I think I said that right, but sometimes it confused me, too.

The parties at Peninnah's and my mansion in the hills were becoming more frequent as the guestlists included Hollywood movers and shakers, politicians, and our growing cast. People judged their status by whether or not they had been invited to one of Bob's parties.

Deedee had been the first cast member we hired. It seemed she was the one who broke the code regarding how to get a part. Afterward, we started finding others who wanted to join. We discovered that, like Deedee, these were what I would call more 'normal' people rather than actresses we'd been sent by the casting agencies.

"I'm not a pro," Deedee had told us after her audition.

She'd left me breathless and I continued to hold her, still embedded in her welcoming depths. Liz and Peninnah pulled up chairs close enough to us that they could touch and pet us as we cuddled. Of course, our cameras were still running and the crew maneuvered for better shots, meaning angles that would expose her breasts and butt.

"I mean, not a professional actress, but I'm not a sex worker, either."

"What brought you to us?" I asked, sneaking another kiss before she answered.

"I'm a grad student at UCLA, studying sociology and group interaction. It's like you've created a whole lab here to study how people exposed to each other on a long-term basis change their perspective in confined quarters." It sounded like the brief for a dissertation.

"So, you really just want to study us?" Liz asked.

"Well, that's kind of a passion, but I think I just drank the Kool-Aid and jumped from observer to participant. I don't know that I'll do a very good job of studying us now," she said. She shifted her hips and I began to harden in her again. She moaned.

"There might be greater opportunities to use your skills than you ever imagined," Pen said. "The ship is much larger than it appears."

"This set makes it look huge already. How big could it be?" she asked.

"Infinite," I said, thrusting up into her again. "You'll discover more than you ever imagined. But for now, you need to keep it a secret. Agreed?"

She clamped down on my cock and rocked her hips back and forth, then began sliding up and down.

"I agree," she panted. "I'm yours to command."

I'd learned my lesson about commanding silence. Chione hadn't uttered a word since she left Nebuchadnezzar's harem—2,500 years ago. We depended on a non-disclosure agreement that would bankrupt a person for life if they mentioned anything about what we were doing on the show or about the infinity room when they'd seen it.

That was our agreement with Deedee. I joined her movements and before long, we'd both moaned our orgasms again.

>-- ⬤ --<

We—officially, Peninnah and I, but where I went, the infinity room went—took a little trip to check on our investment in Japan and moved into the penthouse apartment overlooking the water not terribly far from Osaka. It was beautiful. Our Japanese contractors and architects had made the penthouse a breathtaking example of modern high-end Japanese fashion. It was multilevel with movable screens to divide spaces when wanted, and a very open design when the screens were pulled aside. Furniture was generally low, encouraging sitting on the floor to eat and lying on a low platform bed to sleep.

The bath—separate from the toilet—was large enough for a dozen of us to soak, with separate showers. Of course, there were stools at each shower head so one could sit while another shampooed and washed her. It opened onto a rooftop pool, strictly for my family's use. There were more staff for the penthouse than we had people who regularly used it, and they were housed on the floor below.

While we were there, we held auditions and found a very talented cellist named Rin who wanted to join us. She didn't jump straight to sex, but she was funny and just a bright and sunny girl. And could she ever play the cello! It was amazing. The time in Japan was too short, and we all wanted to spend more time in the wonderful penthouse. I could see that somewhere in Areola, we would be constructing something similar.

We visited our partners in India and one of their software engineers asked if she could audition. Suhani was fun and bright and very suggestive in her dress and actions, without getting naked or actually trying to have sex. I could well imagine a real tease having some prime scenes in the show.

We stopped in England to visit the Queen, who was very pleased with her new domicile. Plans for the space travel theme park next to the palace were well underway and ground had been broken. While we were there, we had a really wonderful dinner of beef Wellington and herb roasted potatoes. This went well with the braised shredded Brussels sprouts. When we were exclaiming about how wonderful the food was, the Queen asked the chef to come to the table. That was how we met Valerie.

"Surely, you will need to eat on this voyage," her Majesty said. "I highly recommend Valerie. She was trained in France, so the food will not all be typical English fare, though she did a wonderful job on that this evening."

"May we have your permission to interview and screen test this evening, Valerie? I'm afraid we are pressed to get back to California tomorrow," I said.

"I'd be delighted," she said. "May I be excused, ma'am?"

"Yes, dear. Go get your things ready and leave with Bob and Peninnah." Valerie left and the Queen leaned in close to us. "I had her prescreened. I think you'll find her a pleasant addition to your crew."

Ah. So, the Queen had taken an interest in providing me with an English girl. It was a good idea and would give us a girl with a nice accent, too. That night in our hotel room we had a very pleasant interview with Valerie—in bed. We found she not only had good taste, but she tasted good, too.

And so the casting went. We returned for more casting in Hollywood and found that we had much better experience and knowledge of what we were looking for. It went much faster.

>-- ◄◆► --<

So now, two months later, we had enough people to launch filming the mini-series. A dozen, make that thirteen young women—by young, I mean they were all from the current era, not from two millennia ago—plus Peninnah, Liz, Penelope, Dezi, and Laine, were ready to join our crew and move into the mansion. Dezi and Laine were both much older than they looked, but they'd joined the infinity room when they were in their teens and stopped aging. They would play our daughters—that is, Penelope's and mine. Penelope was joining as my 'former' wife, still active in the lives of our daughters and determined not to let them leave without her. Penelope was chosen because she was a little older when she joined the infinity room and stopped aging. She glowed with good health and vigor, but looked more mature than Peninnah or Liz, both of whom joined me in their early twenties. No one would buy that either of them was old enough to have teenage daughters. It was borderline with Penelope.

Penelope had the most difficult time adjusting. The twenty-first century was a foreign world to someone of the tenth century before Caesar. We kept her fairly sheltered, but it didn't take long for the cast to all adopt her as their mother figure.

Besides Deedee, Rin, Suhani and Valerie, we'd invited Wendy, a journalist, to be part of the cast, based on an equally positive response to the improvisation during her screen test. She'd been more blatantly seductive in her scene. Granted, Deedee had attacked me sexually, but the scene was played out as one rushed because of impending doom. Wendy had played the part of a communications officer, bringing me a message from control in India. We'd actually arranged a phone hookup to the tracking station in India, who were all enthused about taking part in the audition. Wendy had to relay messages between control and the bridge. She rewrote the scene on the fly, making every line into a double entendre. If what India told her didn't suit what she wanted, she changed the message so it would sound like an invitation to take her to bed. Which it was.

The entire cast and crew were laughing when she started acting as an interpreter. Our crew in India had a bit of an accent. It wasn't a serious issue because they spoke perfectly good English. They just had an accent. Wendy treated it like it was a foreign language and she was translating.

"Wendy, systems are go and you are cleared for launch," Raj said over the speaker phone, following our script. She responded in a perfect Indian accent.

"Roger, Raj. We will be launching shortly." Then she turned to me and spoke in a perfect Valley Girl accent. "Like the guys in India are just waiting for you to get it up, you know?"

"Tell Raj we're in our final countdown," I instructed. She adopted her Indian accent once again.

"The man says he can hardly wait to start his booster. My skirts will be lifting in seconds."

The entire scene was like that with Wendy sometimes hesitating as if she was trying to find the word, as if she was the only one who could understand what the boys in India were saying. Inevitably something blatantly sexual would come out. And she kept up the role right through fucking me on camera.

"Oh, Raj. He's blasting off now!" she screamed.

The guys got into it and began suggesting things to her regarding trimming her tail and increasing thrust. All the way through an energetic sex scene, she kept up the interpreter dialog as if she was following the instructions of the control tower. It was a blast.

And when asked the all-important question, she answered, "I'd be so disappointed if it wasn't real."

Then there was Linda, a school teacher.

Her audition was evidence that we weren't casting based on a sex scene alone. Some of our women did not cut loose with sex in front of the cameras. I wasn't sure about Linda, as we finished the scene in which she was attempting to explain the diagram of the ship to me as if I didn't understand it at all. Which really, I didn't understand. During the scene, without my being completely conscious of it, she worked a kind of sexual magic without ever touching me, or me her, sexually.

She began with a few subtle touches, like guiding my hand to point at a particular feature of the ship, all of which she made up on the fly as if she were a real estate agent giving a tour of a new home. She touched my shoulder. She turned my head to look at her eyes while she explained that the shower was large enough to fit the entire crew and that it was conveniently located just three steps from a ginormous bed. And through it all, she was adjusting her look as well. She let her hair down, took off her glasses, kicked her high heels off, unbuttoned a few buttons. By the end of the scene, she looked like she'd just been ravished. She was panting and when I looked up at her, she moaned and shook as if she'd just had an orgasm.

"I just love these ship plans, don't you?" she gasped.

"That was amazing," Liz said, applauding Linda's performance. We all joined. I hadn't even realized what she was doing until the end.

"So," I said as she caught her breath, "what if you found out it was all real and you weren't coming back to earth?" I wasn't expecting the way she answered.

She finished unbuttoning her blouse, pulled it off, and freed her boobs from her bra. While we watched, she dropped her skirt and panties as well. What was standing naked in front of us was a walking hard on.

"If I found out it was all real, I'd never wear clothes again and you'd never need to ask to have sex with me."

All righty then! Audition successful!

46
CHEESE IT! THE COPS!

WE ATTRACTED A GREAT BUNCH of actresses, none of whom claimed to be an actress. In addition to our sociologist, musician, software engineer, chef, teacher, and journalist, we collected an artist, a mathematician, a race car driver, a pilot, a policewoman (who didn't know she was auditioning when she came in to investigate our operation), an accountant, and a doctor. I had sex on set with four of them. I had sex with two more when they visited the mansion. And six had been very sexual but hadn't jumped on me yet. One had been more reserved sexually than the others, but she was quick-witted and had an incredible screen presence. The plan in the mini-series was to eliminate seven. I was already sorry to be losing them, even before I knew which ones would go.

When we finally had all the participants in line, Doug summoned them all with instructions for moving into the mansion. Peninnah, in her forethought, had designed the mansion so we could feasibly house as many as twenty or more guests. The mansion would be where a lot of the production was filmed. But we'd be doing active training at the company as well. And of course, we had to have some outings as a group and one-on-one.

To celebrate the start of production, we held a big party at the mansion with our actresses, the senior staff at Space Pioneers, a few Hollywood types that Doug knew, and a select few that I brought out of Areola.

I heard a resounding slap across the room that brought the party to silence. I hurried over to where Leroy Reese, the president of Space Pioneers, Inc., was lying on the floor at the feet of Lalonda, the policewoman. He'd made a pass at her and she didn't appreciate it.

Lalonda had surprised us all by really getting into her audition. Apparently, she'd done some theatrics in high school and college, but didn't pursue it as a career. She'd come into the studio based on a whispered rumor that we were producing porn without a permit. She had no official business there, but simply asked if she could watch an audition.

She chose a good time to come in because we had a B-list actress come in with her agent and a contract in hand. Doug intercepted the agent and explained the rules. We would pay $500 for the audition, but required a signed release in advance to use any footage in our mini-series, just like they would have if they were auditioning for *America's Got Talent* or some such. The agent wanted to see a script before he agreed to the terms. It was pretty bland, depending on the actress to bring something to it as part of the improv. He agreed and the actress—Brandy Something, if I recall—signed the contract for the audition. Doug wrote the check, but held it until after the audition.

It was terrible. Hollywood had a cookie-cutter industry in which every actress of minor talent was pressed and molded until she came out white, blonde, and D-cup endowed. I think there was a rule about them not weighing more than 110 pounds—ten of which had to be carried on their chests. They reminded me more of the groupies who were around the theatre in Greece than they did of any real actress I'd met.

We interviewed and the voice was like having a mouse on set. When we got to the improv, she stopped to think for a minute before every response. Nothing like ruining any timing and interaction. We suffered through it. When we asked the big question, she tossed down the script and stormed off the set.

"Bernie! Why are we even here? If I found out it was all real? You've got to be kidding. What do they take me for?"

Doug handed the agent the check.

"You need the money, doll. This is the best I could get without putting you in porn."

"At least in porn they'd appreciate my tits. I think that guy is gay. I'm getting out of here." And they left.

"Well, there went a wasted $500," I said. "We can't possibly even use that footage for outtakes. It was just too boring."

"Excuse me."

I looked up to see Lalonda. She was a nice-looking black woman in a casual suit. I was impressed with how tall she was—at least six feet. Black hair in an afro that matched her dark skin. Good looking and powerful looking. We didn't have anyone like her in our cast.

"Hi. Sorry you didn't get to see a better audition than that. I'm afraid we don't have any more scheduled for today," Doug said.

"Um... I was wondering if this was open auditions. I mean, I don't have a resume or headshot with me, but I'd like to audition. I think I saw what you're looking for."

"We can set up an appointment," Doug said.

"No, we can do it now," Peninnah broke in. "You just said we don't have anything else on the schedule. Everything is set and I'm sure Bob would love to see someone who actually wants to be here. What's your name, honey?"

I would bet that if any of the rest of us had addressed the ebony goddess in that way, we'd have been laid out on the floor, but Pen just slipped into people's inner circle without them even knowing it. Today she was in perfectly fine form with running shorts and a bra top on, the diamond dangling in her navel. The six-inch high heels were quick evidence, however, that she had not been out for the jog the rest of her outfit suggested.

By the time Lalonda had introduced herself, Peninnah had her seated at the table with us for an interview.

>-- ◀◆▶ --<

I'd had dealings with law enforcement during the course of my life—from Drakomaxos's thugs, to State Troopers. I was once stopped by a policeman near Houston who strode up to the car and said, "Do you know why I pulled you over?"

I said, "Well, I'm not a donut shop and I didn't rob a bank, so no, sir, I don't know why." That got me a $200 ticket for what probably would have been a warning.

Most of my encounters have been cordial. One ended with me leaving town just ahead of a lynch mob. One, however, was especially memorable.

No, it wasn't the lynch mob. How could a lynch mob not be especially memorable? They didn't really mean anything by it. It's just that I was a San Francisco dandy in Silver City, Nevada in a gambling hall. And it wasn't even that I was winning a lot of money. It had to do with a banker of some sort in San Francisco going broke and leaving a lot of miners unpaid. Didn't really blame them all that much.

No, the memorable one was far more recent.

I think I mentioned that I liked to drive fast cars. The gasoline engine and automobile were as much an amazement to me after nearly 4,000 years of walking and riding horses as were the mighty steamships after the sailboats I'd been used to. But I was careful. I didn't want to attract a lot of local attention by speeding through the city or getting in an accident. I'm basically a good law-abiding demon.

But as the 80s drew to a close, I was bitten by the bug to buy a new Trans Am 20th Anniversary Model. I suppose I had been influenced by the 1970s movie *Smokey and the Bandit*. Of course, I wanted a black one. But where could I go for a good road test? I wanted something long and straight and flat. What could be better than Kansas?

I-70 runs for 424 miles through Kansas. There were stops for tolls just outside of Topeka, but from there on, it was just over 350 miles to the Colorado State line. I figured that was enough to let the horses out to run.

I filled the tank with gas and entered the freeway in the middle of the night. No sense drawing attention to myself. I rolled up to milepost 350 and floored the powerful car. And I flew across Kansas. I had a notion that I could make it to Colorado in three hours.

I didn't.

A little more than a hundred miles into my run with the needle pegged at about 105, I became aware of flashing red lights in the distance behind me. It didn't dawn on me that they were after me. They seemed to get gradually closer, and when it was obvious the police cruiser had to be doing 120 to catch up to me, I pulled over like a dutiful citizen. The cruiser screeched to a halt behind me and a trooper stepped out of the car and approached me. I'd been drilled on proper protocol for these occasions, so I rolled down my window and placed my hands on the steering wheel with my license, registration, and insurance card in my fingers.

The trooper seemed to take a long time approaching me. I saw the flashlight beam scan my windows and then circle the car. Finally, the light came through the driver's side window, directly into my face. I couldn't really turn to look without being blinded.

"Let's have the license and registration," she said.

She! I'd been pulled over by a female state patrol trooper. I handed her the documents and tried to smile.

"Do you know how fast you were going?" she asked.

I wanted to say something smart, but couldn't think of anything. And I had learned my lesson in Texas.

"Um... My speedometer said 105. Did you get a radar reading with something different?" I asked, genuinely interested.

"I've been chasing you for twenty miles. I had to kick that old box of a cruiser up to 120 to catch you." She sounded angry, but paused in her narration. Then she whooped! "Wow! What a rush! Is your heart beating as fast as mine?"

"I... uh... really enjoyed it."

"I was almost disappointed you pulled over. I could have chased you all the way across the state! You know it's going to cost you. Now that I've got you, I have to give you a ticket. How many miles do you have on this beauty?"

"Five thousand two-eighty. Just broken in, really."

"And you just had to find out how fast it would go?"

"I thought I could make it from Topeka to Colorado in three hours," I chuckled.

"Well, we screwed that up, didn't we? You haven't been drinking or anything serious like that have you?" she asked.

"No, ma'am."

"Okay, I'm only going to cite you for speeding and not for reckless. Once that's done, there's a truck stop five miles on. I'll follow you there and you can give me a full tour of this bird."

I accepted the citation and my documents, still trying to figure out what was happening.

"Don't try to outrun me," she said. "It's only five miles."

I pulled onto the highway and carefully marked my speed at the new limit of sixty-five. She followed right on my bumper with her lights still flashing. We pulled into the truck stop and she motioned me over to the pumps. We both filled up.

"I want to drive it," she said bluntly, while we were standing next to our cars. She wasn't very big, but she'd handled the Crown Vic Pursuit with ease.

"How can we arrange that?" I asked.

"There's a long straight stretch of state highway not far from here. Unlike the freeway, it's not used much and we should have a ten-mile stretch. I'll pull over to the parking area and you can pick me up there." She hopped in her cruiser and parked it beside the café. I pulled up and got out, handing her the keys. She grinned at me and we headed out into the country.

That began one of the most fun nights I ever had in America. She could certainly drive. I'd held the speed to about 105 because I intended to drive it for three hours. She knew the road out in the country for twelve miles and started out like a drag racer. She was 0-60 in five seconds and ran through the gears as smoothly as a pro. After ten miles she let her foot off the gas and coasted the last two miles to bring the speed down to where she could brake. She'd moved the needle to near 140 mph. She was panting after the five-minute drive.

Instead of heading straight back to the truck stop, she pulled into the driveway of a farmhouse. As soon as we were stopped, she jumped out of the car and rushed to my door as I climbed out. And then she showed me what a fast girl was really like.

She hauled me into the house and straight to what was obviously her bedroom. By the time we got to the bed, we were nearly naked. Her panties were drenched and I responded with a massive hard on. Her pussy was a swamp, and I slid effortlessly into it. Our first orgasms were as fast as the speed test we'd just run.

Then we kept our engines revved and pounded at each other for an hour before fading off to sleep.

>-- ◀◆▶ --<

It was a more exhausting night than I'd anticipated from driving. We woke up with the sun coming in the window. I reached for her again, but she slipped away, obviously embarrassed. She grabbed a robe and pulled it around her delightfully naked body, hiding the path to paradise I'd followed the night before.

"You can shower first," she said. "I'll make coffee."

I nodded. Our adventure had come to an end. I quickly showered and she did the same while I drank a cup of coffee. She tossed me my keys and got in the passenger seat, only speaking to give me directions back to the truck stop. She jumped out of the Trans Am and headed for her cruiser.

"You be careful out there and hold the speed down," she said as she got in her car. I watched as she drove away. The only way I had of even knowing her name was the signature on the traffic ticket: Trooper Tracy Holmes. I headed back toward home at a safe speed.

Lalonda's screen test reminded me of Tracy Holmes, so many years ago.

>-- ◀◆▶ --<

"Okay, so in this scene, you are my security officer. A rival space exploration company has managed to dock with us and are demanding we turn our ship over to them. Two of their people are going to come onto the bridge and attack me. Don't worry, they won't hurt you, but you need to decide how to respond," I said.

She nodded and pulled her jacket aside to show her service weapon. She unclipped the holster and looked around the room. She handed it to Peninnah.

"If there's going to be a fight, I shouldn't have this on me," she said. We all breathed a sigh of relief.

We went through the beginning of the scene, which was mostly scripted as we followed the progress of the boarding. Then two of my women burst onto the set and came straight for me. None of us expected Lalonda's response. She did not scream. She did not search for a weapon. She didn't yell for them to halt.

She stepped between Zhi's flying kick and me. It hit her square in the chest.

You need to understand that I often sparred with my women and Zhi was one of the best. We did not pull our punches when we worked out, so Lalonda took the full force of Zhi's kick. I heard the breath rush out of her and thought I might possibly have heard a rib crack.

Zhi was horrified and started toward Lalonda to check her. Bad move. Lalonda swept Zhi's feet from under her and slammed a fist into Zhi's chest that sent her across the room. Instead of attacking me, Lakshmi, the other assailant, rushed to Zhi to check on her. Lalonda stalked toward them.

"Stop! Don't hurt them!" I yelled. Recovering from the shock of what I'd just seen. Both Zhi and Lakshmi raised their hands in submission.

Lalonda pulled handcuffs from somewhere inside her jacket and snapped the raised hands of the two warriors together. She pulled them to their feet and marched them to me. Lalonda stood behind them and put a hand under each of their chins.

"Shall we space them, Captain?" she asked calmly.

"Uh... no. Let's see what they have to say about this unprovoked attack."

"Yes," Lalonda said. "It would be a shame to waste such fine beauty on the eternal black. You wouldn't want that, would you, my beauties?" She forced the girls to shake their heads with her hands beneath their chins. Then she turned their faces toward her and she kissed Lakshmi first and then Zhi—the latter intently. "No. I think we can find much better uses for you. Captain, permission to take these two to my cabin and question them?"

"Cut!" yelled Liz.

Zhi surprised Lalonda by slipping out of the handcuff and turning toward her. The kiss shared by the two women was intense enough to bring us all to a state of arousal.

"Permission granted," Zhi whispered.

We all returned to the interview table and collapsed into chairs. Lalonda dragged Zhi with her and seated her on her lap where she continued to place little kisses on her and ask if she was all right.

"So, what if you found out it was all real and you weren't coming back to earth?" Zhi asked.

"I hope you're coming, too. I need to stop by the station and turn in my badge and gun."

⟩⸺ ◄◆► ⸺⟨

When Leroy chose Lalonda to make a pass at, he was lucky he only landed on the floor.

"Fire that bitch!" Leroy sputtered, holding his jaw. "She assaulted me! I'm bringing charges!"

"No!" I said. "Your job is getting a ship built, Leroy, not groping the crew. The only reason Lalonda hit you was because I was too far away to put you down first."

"I'm going to pull the plug on this whole fiasco," Leroy sulked.

"You forget, Leroy. You're a minority shareholder now. I've left you as chairman of the board out of respect. Don't lose it now," I said.

"You're a devil, Bob. I never should have signed a deal with you."

"True, but now I own your soul."

Surprisingly, Leroy didn't leave the party in a huff. He even managed a quiet 'sorry' to Lalonda and went off to have another drink. I noticed that a Hollywood starlet, who had come to the party with a group Doug invited, was fussing over Leroy, and offering him comfort. Even if he was no longer the majority shareholder in Space Pioneers, he was still a single billionaire. I think she understood this could be the most important audition of her life.

>-- ◄◆► --<

From that point on, we were in production. The girls and the crew had all moved into the mansion. There were cameras running everywhere as we recorded interactions and chit chat. There wouldn't be any challenges for a while because we all had to do one thing first. We had to learn how to fly this ship!

Doug was surprised that many of my staff members were in the sessions as well. Then he got himself busy and trained with the rest of us. We all went through a full astronaut training program. The people who were not from Areola and were not in the know were surprised at how much detail went into the training.

"It's like we are actually going to fly away!" one of the camera people said. We were still using several from the studio who weren't from Areola. "This is unreal." Little did she know...

Everyone was determined to show they were worthy of being kept for the show. I wanted to be sure they were worthy of being kept forever. I think most of the girls we had selected in auditions had figured out that the space trip was for real and there was at least a good chance they would never return to earth.

>-- ◄◆► --<

The first to be cut left voluntarily. It wasn't too surprising as she'd been borderline in her commitment to the real journey. But she'd had such great screen presence I wanted to try her on the show. Rhonda came up to me after we were supposed to be done for the day and pulled my arm around her. As she cuddled with me in a big chair in the family room, I was aware that there were still cameras rolling. I think she was aware as well and had carefully prepared what she had to say.

"You're easy to love, Bob. In fact, I love your wives and all my castmates. Not like I'm going to jump in bed with them, but I still love them. Maybe some of them I'd jump in bed with," she giggled. "I shouldn't talk like that when you and I haven't... well... done the deed. I would if I thought that's all you really wanted. But I guess I haven't been completely honest."

I immediately came on guard and could see alertness on the faces of my women. Not the actresses, but those who were bound to me by our shared experiences. There was a subtle shift in the room as my wives and concubines took up defensive positions around the room, not letting anyone else know there might be trouble.

"Why don't you come clean now?" I said.

"I'm not really without a family or friends," she said. We knew that much through our own investigations. "Specifically, I have a brother who is handicapped. This job has paid really well, and I've been able to provide things for him that social services couldn't do. I convinced myself that I could keep this job and go right on through with it, even if it meant it was all real and I was going to leave earth forever and not see my family again."

"That's a tough decision to make," I said, relaxing a little.

"Yes. Too tough. I didn't really expect I'd get that far in the elimination rounds, but the more I thought about it, the more I realized that if I wasn't eliminated right away and waited till the end to just quit, I'd be taking an opportunity from one of the other girls who really is committed to staying with you. And the thought of not being there for my brother when my parents can't care for him any longer was all it took to convince me that one day I would quit. I send every penny I earn here to them, but it isn't enough... enough to replace me being with them."

Tears were running from her eyes and even though I thought she prepared this whole speech knowing it would be recorded, they were real and I was affected by them.

"So, I need to leave you, Bob. I need to leave all these wonderful people and go home. I can't travel to Mars with you. I can't go anyplace."

"Rhonda, thank you for coming to me and being honest. You know we really care for you and want what's best for you, just like for all the other girls. We'll miss you on the set and as part of the team," I said. "What are you going to do now?"

"I guess I need to find a real job. I've got my degree in accounting and financial management. This just seemed to be a quicker way to earn good cash for my family without dancing on a pole."

"If we can help you, we will. Talk to Doug and get him to introduce you to our HR department. Perhaps there's still a job for you with us, even if you don't launch," I said.

She threw her arms around my neck and kissed me deeply. Then she whispered in my ear.

"Bob, if you really want to, you can undress me here and have sex. I didn't think I wanted to do that, but I do."

"It would be very bad form for me to accept your resignation and then fuck you on camera. Check with Doug about a job."

That didn't really stop us from kissing and fondling a little more before she slipped away from me.

47
WOMEN!

>-- ◄◆► --<

I VISITED OLYMPUS ONCE—or some part of it. I'd gotten to know Zeus early in my life, you know, when Ariane and I were living in a cave that he frequented on Crete. I think I absorbed as much from him by fucking the same woman as I did from anything he said, but he was tolerant of my ignorance and did a lot of patting me on my horns like I was his kid.

Well, if he had fucked one of his women while he was in the form of a goat, I suppose I could have been the result. Those recessive genes come back to haunt you, like they did with the Minotaur.

Anyway, my trip to Olympus was after I'd had my first encounter with Aphrodite. I know that because I recognized her, though we didn't get a chance to talk on that visit. He sat down with me and had some muses or demigoddesses or something serve us a lot of food that seemed to be laced with an aphrodisiac of some sort. While we were sitting there talking about life in the world, we both sprouted erections as we were eating. He sighed.

"It happens every time. If Hera's not around, one of the sprites will lace my food and then come and jump on my cock. It's like a game with them. Of course, I never let one of them bear a child. Hera is actually quite tolerant of the ones she knows. It's when I fool around with someone she doesn't know that she goes ballistic. For a god, I'm henpecked, and I'm a victim of my balls. What am I supposed to do when I've got a hard on and this cute little nymph comes in with no clothes on?"

As if on cue, two little nymphs glided into the room, both naked as the day they were born. They had an ethereal beauty about them as if they might dissolve and float away on the breeze—if there'd been any breeze. They calmly approached god and demon and parted our robes. Then smiling at us, they settled themselves onto our cocks and proceeded to fuck, slowly and languidly. At the rate my nymph was fucking me, this could take forever.

"Now, what I was going to tell you when I called you up here, was that you should always have an exit strategy. I'm already looking at getting out of the deity business, myself. Olympus is big. As big as that infinity room of yours. I'm going to create a nice little retirement palace about a million miles from here," he said. I checked to be sure he was getting fucked like I was. It was hard to concentrate on what he was saying, but he seemed to have no trouble talking about his approaching retirement while being fucked by a truly delicious morsel of immortality.

"Exit strategy. Right," I said.

"Now take a look at this. What do you think of my palace plans?"

He was consulting me as an architect? I'd built a few nice palaces and temples, but nothing along the scale of what he was showing me.

"That's nice," I said. Brilliant conversationalist while I'm being fucked.

"What would you do to improve it?" Zeus demanded. I forced my attention to the three-dimensional plan he was showing me.

"Well, with the likelihood that you'll have a lot of women around all the time, you should include a place where they can go when you don't want them," I suggested.

"When I don't want them?"

"Well, I've found it can be pretty exhausting to have a few dozen women who all want your cock at the same time. I discovered that if I have separate quarters for my harem, with individual rooms for them, then they have a place to go when they really want to get away from everyone," I said.

"When *they* want to get away." Zeus looked puzzled, as if he'd never had a woman who wanted to get away for a while. Well, maybe his goddesses and immortals never had 'that time of month.'

"The truth is that I like a rest occasionally, or just want to be with my favorite for a while. I want all the others to feel like they're wanted, just not right now. So, I tell them they have a retreat and then when the time is right, I make a subtle suggestion that everyone should retreat for rest and rejuvenation."

"I see. So, it's really for you, but you convince them it is for them. Clever. You're getting smarter. Now tell me what else."

"When I did that temple for Ninra and Namri, I put in a big pool out front. I put one in front of the hanging gardens for Nebuchadnezzar and he loved it. It makes the palace look so much more regal. I've put a pool in at my house in the infinity room. The women love it and they're always naked when they're out enjoying the pool," I said.

"That makes a lot of sense!" He turned to the nymph who was posting on his cock. "How would you like to lie naked beside my pool, little one?" She nodded vigorously.

"Now... About your exit strategy," Zeus said, directing the conversation back to me. The palace model disappeared. "I could invite you here to Olympus permanently. You'd need to move before I retire, but you could bring your room with you."

"How soon do you plan to retire?" I asked.

"There are lots of things at work in the world. Let me tell you that becoming king of the gods was no simple matter. We battled the Titans for ten years—just the six of us. When we started the war, we had no hope of winning, but the alternative was to be unmade—returned to the primordial mass. We were joined by several of the Titans who were also ready to rebel against the tyranny of Kronos. I'll tell you, though, chopping that bastard up into little pieces and tossing him into Tartarus gave me no end of pleasure. I tried to reconcile with most of the other Titans, but some were just beyond redemption," Zeus said.

"That must have been a hard time," I said. I was having a hard time holding back coming by this stage and wished Zeus would come to the climax, so to speak.

"The thing is that there will be a succession. Some other god will rise and I'd rather not get caught in a fight like we had, when it's inevitable that I'll lose and a new age will be ushered in. So, I'd say another thousand years or so on earth and I'll close the doors on my palace and just stay there. I never much liked people anyway."

"I see. Gee. It doesn't seem like such a long time. I mean, I'm only about 1600 years old."

"I was just floating the idea by you. The thing is, you need to figure out how to retire as well. And, for your own sake, stay out of the wars with the new generation of gods. They'll ignore you like I ignore Hyperion if you don't raise a stink. Like that idiot Prometheus did. I mean, really, giving humanity fire was planting the seed of our overthrow. There's no stopping what they call progress now. Before long, they'll all think they can ascend to Olympus instead of being content with the Elysium Fields. Or Hades if they're worthless pieces of shit," he said.

"Those are the ones who always seem the most likely to aspire to heavenly places," I agreed.

"Anyway, you need to find a place where you can take your infinity room and retire to it where no one will ever find it. Your little look-away spell will keep people from discovering it for a while, but sooner or later someone will stumble on it and you won't ever be safe again."

I thanked Zeus and saw him wrinkle his forehead, a sure sign he was about to come. With a great sigh of relief, I filled my little nymph with enough spunk to float a ship. She wiggled all over my body in satisfaction and then floated away. I found I was back on my little boat, floating toward my next great adventure in Troy.

Ever since that little adventure, I've been on the lookout for that place I could hide the satchel and crawl in—to retire.

>-- ◄◆► --<

"Do we really have to know physics just to drive the ship? Can't we just put it in gear and floor it?" Julie whined during our training session on astronavigation. Depend on Julie to use that comparison. She was a fast girl. As in a racecar driver. She came to us at the age of twenty-three having already won two Formula 1 championships.

I admitted that the class on astronavigation was a bit of overkill for the cruise to Mars. Most of the class was about determining our timing and trajectory from earth to Mars. But I was laying the foundation for interstellar travel. I wasn't sure how much we'd need after we bypassed Mars and headed to deep space, but I figured we'd better have the course.

"Oh, no, Julie. Don't worry. You're doing great! You know, what we're doing is getting in the driver's seat and figuring out where the gear shift is and how to operate the clutch. Even in a hot car, you have to point it down the track and keep it in your lane. Here, let me show you again," Paul Alford said, sliding his chair up close beside her. Hmm. Maybe it was just a little more than called for to put his hand on hers to guide the mouse. She didn't seem to mind. I tried to stay focused on the task at hand.

When the class was over, we all prepared to go back to the mansion in our private bus. I glanced back when I got on and saw Julie kissing Paul, then rushing to join the rest of us.

Julie was a sweetheart and not at all what you'd expect. She was twenty-three years old and cute as a button. She had rusty blonde hair cut in a bob, dimples, bright green eyes, and beautiful straight white teeth. She was only about five-three and probably weighed 120. But this little girl drove Formula 1 racecars on the track at speeds exceeding 225 miles per hour. She reminded me a lot of the policewoman, Tracy Holmes.

I'd had ample opportunity to get to know Julie's smoothly shaved pussy with both my tongue and my cock. She usually wore a tight sports bra, but when she let those girls loose, she was a real knockout! I tried to understand the feelings of jealousy that I felt a pang of.

I am not overly possessive of my women. Except my possessions and my wives. And in the case of my wives who were not residents of Areola, I had occasionally provided the means for some of them to get pregnant with another man. Like Bao, Esmira, and Cali. My wives in Areola—Nimia, Penelope, Lakshmi, Esmeralda, and Peninnah—were a different matter. They all knew that having children could start aging and the five of them all intended to stay young and beautiful until their demon husband could no longer get an erection. May Zeus forbid.

My possessions—Josie, Pari, Princess Agora, Maya, and Liz—were mine and mine alone. I treated them as the precious possessions they were and did not loan them out. And because they were possessed, none of them ever thought about having another lover. Male lover. Since I often thought about women, so did they.

My priestesses, of course, had set their own rule and thrived on it. Not only did they not tolerate the touch of another man—or any man for that matter—they made love only to demon Bob in his full goat form. They wouldn't even allow me in the temple if I was in human form.

And then there was Zhi. I did not possess her. I did not marry her. She wasn't a priestess. Yet, such utter devotion to me bordered on—no, was equivalent to—the worship of a god. No man entered her mind, and very few women. She loved me beyond reason.

My other concubines and others in the palace, who were occasional playmates but hadn't decided yet where they fit, were free. Most had other lovers and some were even married with nice husbands and families. Once they had children, they began aging and were likely to move out to be with their mates.

So, feeling jealousy when Julie kissed Paul disturbed me.

>-- ◄◆► --<

Later that night, Julie crept into my bed and passionately made love to me. She was an energetic lover, almost as happy to have my tongue in her smooth quim as my cock. Almost. She happily rode on my pole and just as happily lay back on the bed to let me ride her. Any position was a happy one for Julie.

"Now, my love," I said when we were sated. "Tell me what has made you so passionate tonight." *As if I didn't know.*

"Oh, Bob, I'm a horny bitch and I kissed that instructor Paul and now I know you will eliminate me from the crew because I can't remain faithful to you. I don't want to leave the crew. Please, Bob, don't get rid of me." She clung to me and sniffled as I considered what she had to say. Truthfully, I'd considered her a shoo-in for a slot on the voyage. I was ready to take her now. But...

"What about Paul?" I asked gently.

"I really, really like him," she said. "He's smart and handsome and knows racecars. We can talk for hours."

That was significant new information. She'd obviously been spending time with Paul before the kiss I observed today. I wondered if our cameras had footage or if they'd deliberately turned a blind eye. I didn't like the feeling of suspicion. I knew an infrared camera and microphones were even trained on my bed. I'd directed the installation.

"Then how will you feel when we leave earth and everything behind? Do you think you will be able to leave Paul?" I asked.

"Um... Couldn't you make him part of the crew?"

"You think I should eliminate another of the women so he can have her place?" I demanded, a little more harshly than I intended. She cowered next to me and was silent a long while.

"Where do they go at night?" she finally whispered.

"What? Who?"

"Your wives: Peninnah, Penelope, and Liz. And the others who show up each day to work and attend our classes. I see them all arrive at the mansion as if they'd been in your room all night. I see them all come into your room at night. But look. They aren't here. Where do they go?"

"You are treading on dangerous ground, Julie," I warned.

"You could have just told me they have private quarters on the other side of your master bath, you know. But you warned me, instead. I don't think I'm the only one who has noticed. Is that what you intend to do with us? Make us disappear when you eliminate us? Bring us out of your secret pocket to play our parts and then put us away at night? You are training many more people on the operation of the ship than you plan to choose as your crew. And how do you plan to keep the camerawomen on the ship? I've looked at the ship diagrams. They don't show more than the dozen compartments that it would take for you and your family and the six girls you choose to take with you. Isn't there someplace you could put Paul, too?"

It was more serious than I thought. Julie had captured the essence of what we were, in fact, doing.

"Will you do whatever is necessary for me to make this exception, Julie? Paul might choose not to come with us when he discovers the truth. I can eliminate you from the competition and still take you with me. But would you be satisfied with just me? I won't force you, but I'm not sure I can share you, either," I said.

"Bob, you already know I will do anything for you. I'll fuck you; I'll fight for you; I'll leave earth behind for you. Is it such a huge favor I ask of you to let me have my diversion?"

"I need to think about this. It involves more than just you and Paul." Julie settled into my arms and went to sleep.

I did not.

>-- ◀◆▶ --<

Back in my acting days in Greece, I was sort of married to Delphia, a groupie who hung around the Theatre of Dionysus. I say sort of because… Well, it's difficult to describe. It was a theatre thing.

I'd enjoyed her company several times after performances. She was a classical Greek beauty. If you've seen statues of, say, the Caryatids on the Acropolis who support the porch of the Erechtheion Temple—remember I told you about building a temple to Athena for Erechtheus, the king who ruled only the Acropolis and not all Athens?—well, they are perfect images of the ideal Greek woman. I didn't sculpt them. The porch was added six or eight hundred years after I built the original small temple. Most of the Erechtheion Temple was added on, each time another god needed to be honored. Originally, it housed a lovely wooden sculpture of Athene.

As I was saying, the Caryatids are statues of women who support the portico on their heads. Each one stands straight with one knee bent forward as if they were modern-day models showing the latest fashions. Which I suppose they were in their time, modeling the chiton dress so nicely. They are the idealized Greek woman.

And so was Delphia.

This was during the time when women were not allowed on the stage at Athens, so she was backstage to act as a model for building up the male figures who acted female roles so their chiton would fit correctly. I was far more interested in the model than I was in the actor. It turned out she was just as interested in me.

We met after the show and had a very good time. In fact, such a good time that we met after nearly every performance I was in. And one day, we met in front of a magistrate to record our marriage.

But Delphia had a business to run. She'd come into the theatre as a fashion consultant and ran her fulling business outside of town. That's a business where woven wool is washed, shrunk, pressed, and sometimes felted. It stinks and was not allowed inside the city precincts. She also dyed the cloth and often came home after a few days' work with her fingers stained and a strange smell about her. All my work was in town, so she would usually leave after my performance and our night together, and return to her business for a few days, then come back to town to be with me for a few days. It worked well for us, and on days when I had a performance and she was not in town, she had no objection to my choosing another groupie for a night romp.

Of course, I often spent those nights in the infinity room where I had plenty enough groupies to satisfy the horniest old goat.

You might ask how a fuller qualified as a fashion consultant for the theatre. Well, that was the unique thing about the chiton. It was really just a big square of wool. Delphia dyed the fabric and sold it to women, showing them ways to tie, pin, and belt the square into interesting configurations. All those vase paintings and statues you see of Greek women? They're only wearing a square of wool pinned at the shoulder and belted. Delphia's wool was known as the softest available—which was good for sensitive nipples.

All went well in our life for some years when I started noticing a change about Delphia. She was gaining weight. Even as far back as four hundred years before Caesar, women were sensitive about their weight and men learned quickly not to mention it. Delphia had no such qualm.

"I'm sure you've noticed by now, Bob. You really don't need to be so quiet about it," she said as I plowed into her from behind. It was a better position with the belly she was growing.

"Uh, yes. You have been gaining a little weight," I said hesitantly.

"Well, that happens when a woman is pregnant."

I stopped in mid-stroke and did a full evaluation of my reproductive abilities. No. My sperm were turned off. There was no way I had impregnated her.

"Whose child is it?" I demanded.

"You mean besides yours and mine? Well, it's Paulus's, of course."

"Who is Paulus?"

"You don't know? I thought you knew when we married. He's my other husband."

"Your other husband? Since when do you have another husband?"

"Oh, at least a year before I met you. You can't imagine I'd live alone out in the country where my mill is. Bob, are you really saying you didn't know that I have a country husband and a city husband?" she asked in amazement.

I was amazed as well. How could I not have realized she had another man in the country? I was an idiot! Zeus agreed.

"I can't believe you have someone other than me!" I said.

"Oh, come, Bob. You have other wives. You aren't that good at hiding things. If a man can have two wives, why shouldn't a woman have two husbands?"

Well, yes. Philosophically, it made sense. And I truly cared for Delphia. I had heard her mention Paulus a number of times and assumed he was her partner in the fulling mill. I hadn't realized he was her partner in bed. My male ego was hurt.

Of course, things changed between Delphia and me, but not all in a bad way. I gradually became accustomed to fellow actors and friends congratulating me on the pregnancy of my wife. And when little Theo was born, I doted on him as much as any new father, even though he traveled to the country to be with his other father.

I was happy to have never actually met Paulus. But as long as he was out of sight, he was easy to forget about.

Theo grew into a fine boy and I taught him all I could about the theatre, just as Delphia and Paulus taught him about cloth. He was eleven years old when he arrived at my house in Athens alone and crying.

"Papa Bob," he sobbed. "Mama and Papa Paulus... There was a fire at the mill. They were in there. They died."

Oh, no! My precious Delphia! I wrapped my arms around Theo and wept with him.

This story isn't really about Theo. You can ask him for more details if you want. He's still living in Areola. And I'm very proud of the man he became. The story, though, is about having lived through a marriage in which my wife had another husband as well. And it wasn't all that bad. In fact, I still get a little choked up when I think of Delphia.

Perhaps letting Julie have Paul wouldn't be that bad a thing at all.

END PART IX

Part X
To Infinity and Beyond!

Photo by Razoomanet, ID1479962546 licensed from Shutterstock.com.

48
Mission Mars: The Mini-Series

"I NEED TO TAKE my family away for a few days. We have business in Japan we need to take care of and as you can all imagine, adding a dozen women to our household puts some strain on our relationships. We need a retreat so we can work out how to handle our emotions and responses," I said when everyone had gathered in the morning. I'd called Doug and had him bring in our secondary camera crew—not residents of Areola—so I wasn't leaving any of my women behind. As far as appearances went, however, it was just Peninnah, Liz, Penelope, Dezi, and Laine going with me.

"Bob, I don't like this. While the cat's away..." Doug started.

"Part of what I want to know is how the mice play," I said.

"But you'll be off-camera. It will create a hole in the project."

"I've arranged for a crew to meet us in Japan. I'll record everything, but I won't be showing everything. This needs to be family confidential," I said. "However, I think we'll have a surprise for the girls. Please make sure they all have valid passports."

Doug's mouth dropped open and he grinned as the implication dawned on him.

"You're the boss. It makes me nervous to know we're at the halfway point and only one girl has been eliminated. We promised the first episodes to HCEN in eight weeks and haven't started cutting together the first one yet."

"Let's go ahead and cut together the first episode out of the auditions. There's some pretty dramatic footage in that and it should set the stage for what's going to happen in the season. We have to gather the cast before we can start cutting them. And we'll have a solution for eliminations by the time we finish this trip."

I headed for the minibus with the family and our driver took us to the airport, where we boarded the private jet Peninnah had acquired for us. No, I couldn't fly this baby, but I loved streaking across the Pacific in eight hours to Japan. It sure beat my first trip across the Pacific that took four months!

>-- ◄◆► --<

Peninnah dismissed the staff at our penthouse by phone so we wouldn't be seen arriving and unpacking our family into our home. Most had traveled in the infinity room rather than sitting for eight hours on the plane. As soon as we'd checked the penthouse thoroughly, I sealed the perimeter, much as I had sealed the house in Knossos 4,000 years ago. No one would be coming in uninvited. And then I opened the gateway. Free of the inhibitions imposed by working with the actors, my wives and possessions and several concubines and the camera crew came rushing into the penthouse to enjoy the view, the pool, and the bed.

We spent a day just catching up with our lovers. That included time in the temple on Areola in full demon form with my priestesses. I always left the temple feeling exceptionally good. Something about the lethal women who worshiped me just charged my batteries. Or perhaps it was the rituals they performed. Whatever.

I let the cameras run on everything as we went in and out of Areola. Of course, they had to leave Areola in order to download and store the footage and to charge their batteries.

There was no electricity in Areola.

>-- ◄◆► --<

That didn't mean we had no electrical appliance equivalents. I had to give a lot of consideration to this by the time we got to the 1950s. Newcomers expected TV, radio, and even telephones. All I could see was miles and miles of wires and antennae, signal towers, and powerplants polluting the air. But Areola is a magic kingdom. I read a lot of books about power sources and discovered all the usual ones. Water, fire, solar, wind. In every case, something that would be described as magic by ninety percent of my citizens happened inside a device that changed the water, fire, sunlight, or wind into electricity. And if all this could be created through magic, then certainly I could create a power source in Areola that was magical.

After I read up on everything, I found a quiet place where I felt I would be undisturbed for a month and went into the infinity room. It took me the entire month to create the power grid for my capital city. It was a network of forces that I laid out under my bedroom first, because that was the easiest place to generate power. The network spread out beneath the ground and simply began to grow. Soon there was 'power' throughout the capital city. And it continued to grow.

Then I called a meeting of the top minds of Areola, many from the current century. I explained that there was now power and how they could tap into it. It was their responsibility to invent things that ran on that power. If they wanted television, they needed to create a television that would both run on the power in the network and receive the signals from the network. It was the process of learning to use the power grid for various technologies they wanted. The first and foremost was cooking. We'd never been big on fires in the infinity room, but people had learned early on to heat stones with sunlight and cook on them. That had been established about the time I put a sun in our sky.

How did this power get replenished?

Well, what would you expect? Sex! People generate an enormous amount of psychic energy during sex and my power grid simply collected that and spread it through the network. Sex had always been encouraged and was widely participated in throughout Areola. The more people who were having sex, the more power was spread through the grid. That's why I originated the grid under my bed. I spent most of the month I was working on the magic having sex in my bedroom. We generated a lot of power.

Well, as a result, we had the equivalent of television, computers, and electricity without having any of the pollution of generating the power.

The first thing Peninnah had said when I brought her into Areola the first time had been, "Bob, there's no cell signal." Of course there was no cell signal. You could pick up any telephone connection in the infinity room and simply speak to anyone you asked for. What was really missing was contact with the natural world. That's where cell signals were and we stayed separate from that.

>-- ◅◆▻ --⟨

"My beloved wives and possessions—my family, all of you," I said to them when we'd all finally gathered in the penthouse without my cock in one or another of them. That didn't stop us from all being naked, though. "I believe we have come to a crisis point with the whole scheme to leave the planet earth behind and seal ourselves in the infinity room. It has to do with the concept of the 'reality' show and the women we are testing for a part in our voyage."

"You can't bear to let any of them go, can you?" Nimia laughed. "Bob, you've always had that problem. How do you think we got three and a half million people in Areola?"

"I admit that is my problem," I said. "And I hope you know that I love each of you— my wives, possessions, concubines, and many others—beyond life itself. Nimia, you and Ariane first showed me what love and life was all about when I was barely cognizant of the world around me. I fell in love with it just as I fell in love with each of you."

"Have you fallen in love with the cast so soon?" Penelope asked.

"Yes. But even that is not the source of my worry," I said. "I've become aware that the women we are testing for inclusion are at minimum suspicious of our greater presence. I mean Areola, of course. You may have noticed that Julie has developed a close relationship with our training instructor, Paul. She came to me a few nights ago, certain that I was aware of it and afraid that I would eliminate her from the competition because she wasn't faithful. I had to think about that for a while. I don't possess her. I am not married to her. I have no intentions of either one. I have always tried to let my concubines be free to establish other relationships, whether that means my sharing them or having them leave me."

"As long as you don't consider sharing your wives and possessions..." Lakshmi started, then added, "or Zhi or your priestesses, we would have no problem with any concubine choosing to enjoy the company of another man. Some of the girls might not even want to be loved by a woman."

"That is true, but I asked Julie what would happen if she was chosen and we got ready to depart. Would she be able to leave Paul behind and commit herself to our group? After she considered it a while, Julie asked if I didn't have a place I could put him, like with my other staff people and camera crew. She pointed out that you all come to my room at night, but none of you are there if one of the cast comes to call on me. And then that you magically appear again in the morning."

"I could slip out and simply eliminate him. Then Julie could mourn and put him behind her," Zhi said. She reached for her sword, but I held up my hand to forestall her.

"You know how I feel about that," I said. "It is one thing to eliminate slavers and kidnappers. Paul has simply fallen for one of our girls. That's a very different matter."

"One of *your* girls," Liz said. "That's really the problem. You haven't possessed any of them, but you still think of them as yours."

"It's so easy for me to become attached to them. If that was truly all it was, I'd cut her from the cast at the first elimination. No. She brings up a point that is going to be repeated. Others of our camera crew who aren't citizens of Areola, Doug, other trainers and scientists, perhaps even more librarians!"

They laughed at that because my obsession with libraries was only exceeded by my obsession with my women. But they got the message. There were a lot of people we wanted to take with us who weren't in the running for the cast.

"We need to start eliminating girls soon or we won't have a show to broadcast," Peninnah said. "We have to include the eliminated girls in that group you have just named off. I think we are dreading the day when girls get eliminated."

"Exactly!" I said. "What if we offered those girls the opportunity to join us in the infinity room. If we need to, we can figure out a way to disguise the reality of it so we can show it on TV and it will look totally fake. Frankly, I think every single one of them will take the opportunity."

We started talking about it and brainstorming how it could be done. No one questioned whether we should do it. We decided that the more truth we told, the more the television audience would believe it was fake. We even considered having me show up in full demon mode. We'd all come to understand long ago that there was something about my beastly demon mode that triggered incredible desire in women. Perhaps it was pheromones or some other thing in Pinaruti's imagination that had made me irresistible to women when he summoned me. Perhaps it was his own fantasy to be irresistible that he transferred to me as reality. Several of the women in the room had come so hard the first time they saw me in full demon mode that they'd passed out. We shelved that idea for the time being.

Americans—humanity in general—had reached a point of declaring anything they disagreed with as 'fake.' There was no way they would possibly think Areola was real. Even if one of the girls decided she wanted to go back—assuming we hadn't left earth yet—she could talk about what was on the other side of the portal until she was blue in the face and no one would believe her. At best she would be considered an attention seeker. At worst, she'd end up like Mr. Yakisoba.

We then went to work putting together the scenarios and contests for the girls to have. They decided how to introduce Areola and we recorded a tour of the palace just to have on file. It included a lot of naked concubines, but also some of their husbands and children. We would save introducing the demon until we were safely away from earth.

I called Doug and had him load the girls and the crew onto our airplane and be wheels up in two hours. This was the first test to see if anyone dragged the team back and made them late. We would resume filming at our penthouse in Japan. It had plenty of room for everyone, and we had a huge staff to take care of our needs.

The greeting we got when the girls arrived was enthusiastic. In fact, I'd say we were mobbed with hugs and kisses and chattering girls. Each wanted to tell about what they had done while we were gone. The stories competed with their desire to get naked and go to our pool. They were fascinated with our bath and showers and with the huge bed in the master suite.

"Okay, everyone, get ready for bed and then gather out here for a family meeting." Josie, of course, had worked on room assignments and then disappeared, leaving Liz to conduct the girls to accommodations. For myself, I also got ready for bed as if I slept in pajamas! I was also gradually changing my shape to be a little more handsome and perhaps just a little bigger.

When everyone came out of their rooms, it looked like a teenage slumber party. All dressed in their nighties and sat on the floor at my feet as if I was a wise old sage telling stories around the campfire. 'The family' gathered with them as soon as they'd changed clothes for bedtime. I noticed that even the camerawomen were in nighties and wondered if I was going to be able to concentrate on my announcements. I was willing to bet that as soon as I'd finished, bits of clothing would malfunction and disappear.

"First of all, let me say that we, the family, missed you all terribly while we were gone and thought about you every day. We can hardly bear to think of losing any of you. But as you all know, we have to pare the contestants down to a crew of six, which means half of you can't join us."

There were a lot of 'aws' and a few tears as some of the girls were certain they would be eliminated. I could think of no reason to eliminate any of them off the top of my head. I'd really grown quite attached to them. I saw a few girls hanging onto each other as well, and Dezi and Laine were holding a couple of others.

"It's impossible for us to just choose someone and say 'You're out.' So, we will be holding a series of elimination contests. These contests will be held over the course of the next six weeks, and at the end, there will be just six of you left to crew our ship."

I'd watched several different reality TV shows by now in preparation for our taping and knew I was supposed to pause dramatically while the cameras zoomed in on faces for reactions.

"The first competition will begin on Monday. That will give you this three-day weekend to get to know our Japanese staff, the local area, resources, and... the kitchen." There were a lot of worried faces looking at each other. "This will be a test of your domestic skills. You know that we'll be cooped up alone for a long time and we'll all need to take turns..." Dramatic pause. "...cooking. In the next week, you will each cook a meal to serve to the rest of us. That means you need to cook for eighteen, just as we normally sit for meals at the dining table. Our staff will take care of the camera and production crew. You will each draw a ball from the hat Liz is holding. There are six breakfast balls and six dinner balls. Everyone who eats at that meal will score it. We will score based on flavor, nutrition, presentation, and appropriateness for the meal you are serving. When all the scores have been tabulated, the lowest score at the end of the week will be eliminated.”

I saw Julie’s head drop and could see tears falling. I hurried on to the next phase.

“We have categorized everyone in this challenge and are offering one person, who we consider to be the least likely to succeed in any given challenge, immunity from elimination. That means that no matter what she scores, she will not be eliminated in that challenge. For the first challenge: ‘Feeding the Family,’ we have granted immunity to…” Dramatic pause. “…Julie!”

The poor girl just lost it and cried out her thanks and her hope that everyone did great. Everyone knew Julie was the most inept person in the kitchen of all the girls. It was a great moment that would improve our ratings. Doug slapped his hands together and rubbed them. This was what he wanted to happen.

At the end of the week, there would be a second surprise for one of our contestants.

There was a mad dash to the computers as the girls began looking up recipe ideas and making lists for their assigned meals. Julie came rushing to me and grabbed hold of Pen and Liz as well. She was still sobbing.

“I thought… I thought you were just going to get rid of me first!” she cried. “I don’t want to be eliminated. I don’t ever want to be eliminated. I love you all so much!”

“We are doing everything we can to keep people from being eliminated,” Liz said sternly. “But you need to do something, too.”

“I won’t see Paul again,” Julie said meekly.

“That’s not what we’re asking of you,” I said. She looked up at me with a puzzled expression.

“Your task this week is to observe and help at each meal. You should do your best to learn what the other girls are doing and help each of them to do her very best to not be eliminated,” Liz continued. “Do you understand?”

“Yes, mistress,” Julie said submissively. “I’ll do my best to help each of them succeed and to learn all I can from them.”

“One more thing,” Peninnah said. Julie looked up at her, honestly frightened. I think all the girls were both in awe and a little frightened of my newest wife. She always looked and acted perfectly. When she had Julie’s undivided attention, she said, “Report to our bed tonight. I want to eat your freshly fucked pussy.”

I thought Julie might pass out on the spot.

In fact, later that night, with Peninnah’s face between her legs, she *did* pass out.

49
MARIAN THE LIBRARIAN

 T SOUNDS SO CLICHÉ, but this actually happened to me after the big catastrophe on 9/11. Hate that day and all it stands for. Stupid, mindless terrorism in the name of religion followed by stupid, mindless war in the name of patriotism. Twenty years of war, 175,000 deaths, and everything ended up exactly where it started. Just so typical.

But I went to New York with some heavy equipment from the construction site and did my best to help where I was needed. After two weeks there, we were told to go home. There were too many of us for the delicate work of clearing the site and sifting through the rubble for human remains. It was sickening. It was also one of the reasons I felt I needed to get the infinity room someplace safe that was beyond the reach of stupid, mindless religious and political fanatics.

I found a place to store my equipment for a couple of days and checked into a hotel for a shower. I opened a gateway and embraced my lovers, reaffirming life in the arms of each of them.

During my time in New York, I became aware of many famous buildings. Not far from my hotel was the New York Public Library.

Truth? The NYPL is ten times... maybe fifty times as big as the Library of Alexandria. Over fifty million volumes! I knew we couldn't take everything, but I called the librarians out of the secret room and we began shuffling everything we could into and out of the infinity room. We didn't steal anything. We just unofficially checked things out and returned them. While we had them, they went through the replication spell and a copy was made in the infinity room.

I used a combination of spells to keep people from contemplating entering the area where we were working. We moved fast and efficiently so the area moved about every fifteen minutes and didn't disrupt readers and users too much. Everyone helped. Those who couldn't cope with the new and modern natural world stayed in the infinity room and shelved the replicated books. We started in science and technology and continued to work our way through spiritual, religious, and esoteric works. Then history, geography, and biography.

You might notice that we weren't plucking a lot from the fiction shelves. It's not that I don't like fiction! It's just that there was so much of it, I didn't think I could make a dent. We'd collected fiction from many locations around the world. We make choices and sometimes they are right.

And sometimes I cast a spell carelessly and included a librarian inside the bubble where we were working. A librarian who watched me removing and reshelving books with a small army. I was replicating entire shelf units and planting them in the infinity room in random order. We'd need to sort them out later.

Suddenly I became aware of a mousy woman about five-five with light brown fur—I mean hair—pulled up in a tight bun, staring at me over her half glasses, arms folded over her cardigan-covered breasts, tapping her toe quietly on the marble floor—because this is a library, after all. Shh!

"Tell me exactly why I shouldn't have security and police swarming all over here to arrest you," she demanded. "There is something fishy going on here."

"That's an understatement," I said. "Uh... Hi. I'm Bob. And I believe police in this city currently have more than they can handle with actual emergencies and don't need to waste time investigating this. And you are?"

"I'm the librarian. You are stealing my books!"

"No, no. We're just unofficially checking them out in rapid succession and returning them," I defended myself and my minions. "I'm here on a mission to preserve as much human knowledge as I can," I said, trying to sound as philanthropic as I could. She grabbed the book out of my hand that I was ready to reshelve.

"*Sex and Hypnosis: How to Improve Your Sex Life*," she read off the cover. I snatched the book back and put it on the shelf in proper order.

"We're in the self-help section and it was next in line to be replicated," I said.

"Replicated?"

"Yes. We would not take any of your original books without explicit permission. All we are doing is taking them to our replicator, making a copy for our library, and then returning the original," I explained.

"Really? How fast can you make a replica?"

"We turn one around about every five seconds."

"By my calculations, then, you should be finished in about seven years, assuming you remain in the library 24 hours a day, 365 days a year."

"That sounds dreadful. We usually replicate a stack of books at once, maybe ten at a time, but I see that would still take the better part of a year. That's why we aren't touching the fiction section. We had to limit what we can accomplish."

"Why are you doing this?" she asked.

It was interesting to me that her first thought was 'why' and not 'how.' I liked her and made a snap decision that might have changed the course of the infinity room.

"I've dedicated the best part of a very long life to saving the accumulated knowledge of humanity. Even if we succeeded in replicating all the books in the library, we would still only have a droplet in the ocean," I said. She nodded. "Why don't I give you a tour. We'll follow the journey of a book through the Library of Bob." She nodded and I summoned Zhi to supervise and make sure no one else interrupted the flow of our books. Then I took the next book from a shelf and headed to the gateway. She followed me. I noticed that she picked up a book, too. The person behind her loaded a cart with three shelves and pushed it behind us.

"This is a kind of transporter," I said, testing the concept. "It will take us directly to the replication room."

"So, you're an alien," she said, nodding her head. It was almost like she'd been expecting us.

"I guess you could say that in a manner of speaking," I answered.

"It's true then. I've known ever since the towers crumbled two weeks ago the end of the world is coming. Will there be anything left of humanity when this catastrophe befalls us?" she asked. I considered that.

"No. I mean yes. I'm not predicting the end of the world. If one lives long enough, one is likely to expect anything eventually. What I mean is that I don't think I'll be able to continue this project forever, and therefore, I need to get as much done as quickly as I can." We stepped through the gateway and into the replicator room. I laid my book on an invisible shelf and nodded to her to follow suit. She couldn't see the shelf, so she laid her book on top of mine. The librarian behind us quickly loaded up the shelf with the cartful of books he was moving. I turned to him.

"Would you mind grabbing the two we sent ahead of your load? They are in the same sequence as what you have."

"Yes, Bob. I'll take care of it," he said. I think he may have spoken in ancient Aramaic. Marian looked puzzled. Nonetheless, Marian gasped when she saw the stack of books seem to divide and follow two paths. She was even more puzzled when the librarian simply walked between the paths and started stacking the books back on his cart. We followed the path of the replicas.

As we stepped into the next room, Marian gasped again as she saw the books being shelved on replicas of the shelves in her own library that moved along with us. The shelves seemed to be taking on substance out of nothing as the books arrived. My librarians here were shelving the books as quickly as they came through, all understanding the time constraints for getting as many books as possible replicated and in our library.

"This room, as you can see, is a fairly close replica of your library. There is a strange thing about the infinity room. Things brought into it seem to carry a memory of their native environment and create it around themselves. That's the only way I can describe it. The spaces are not always complete, though, since the world the books know is limited to the space immediately around them on the shelves. As more volumes come in, however, the cumulative knowledge of the books expands the space with more detail."

"You sound like they are alive."

"All things, animate and inanimate, carry the memory of their environment. The infinity room is simply a fertile land for that memory to grow in."

"There are books missing. I noticed you weren't taking every book from every shelf," she said, running a hand lovingly over the spines.

"The librarians on collection duty automatically skip over any volume we already have a copy of. I hope that will help reduce the time it takes to get all the best books captured."

"You must have a phenomenal computer system and this wonderful technology that replicates things. Your species must be far more advanced than earth."

"Um... We are actually all of earth. And we don't really have any technology. It's all done by magic. Would you like a full tour?"

"Any sufficiently advanced technology would be indistinguishable from magic to those who were not as advanced. Please. Let me see more of your magic."

I led her into a different room and she identified the room as an old library, probably of the US.

"Yes. This is the San Francisco Public Library as it existed just before the great earthquake of 1906. That was before the current library was built."

"I've studied library history. They lost 140,000 volumes in that earthquake."

"Some were lost. I happened to be nearby when the quake struck and we evacuated as many books as we could before the walls collapsed. Now this next room takes us back a ways. You've undoubtedly heard of the Library of Alexandria," I said. She blanched.

"You can't mean to say... All those precious books lost in the fire!"

"I recruited all the librarians in that library to gather up as many books as they could and get them to safety. Many of our librarians are from that time, including the ones you saw in your replica shelving books. Most have learned English. We don't really have a call for communicating in ancient Egyptian or Greek. The librarians took charge of organizing my library. I'm afraid it was in great disorder prior to their arrival."

"The librarians... are replicas, too?"

"Oh, no. These are those very librarians who tended the library in Alexandria. You see, people and things don't age here. These scrolls are in exactly the same condition they were two thousand years ago." I led her through Nebuchadnezzar's library, the library of Vedic writings, the Japanese texts, and the Mayan texts. Marian was awed.

"Let me help. I want to work here," she breathed. I looked at her and saw tears streaming from her eyes. "Please hire me to help take care of your libraries. I don't care if I never go back to that filthy city again. I could live here among the books forever. Please."

I took her hand and led her outside. It was a beautiful day—as all days in the infinity room were. I'd designed the palace district much the same way I'd designed temples and castles through the centuries. I led her past the pool where there were, of course, a number of concubines lazing contentedly, naked as they always were. Inside the palace, I introduced her to my wives and my possessions, who scurried about preparing a luncheon for us. Before we sat to eat, though, I led her to the magic room, exactly as I remembered it from Pinaruti's house in Knossos. I didn't bring many people here, but I thought she would especially appreciate it.

"This is where it all started," I said. "Actually, where I started, 4,000 years ago. When I had to flee Knossos, I scooped up all the old mage's scrolls of magic and took this room with me."

"It's beautiful in a way," she said, "though a bit... um... primitive."

"To our twenty-first century way of thinking, yes, it is. But this was a house of modest luxury in Knossos. I keep this room exactly the way it was when I came into the world, though I have added areas for the most dangerous magical texts so that people in the libraries don't stumble upon them accidentally and try something that would hurt them."

"You ban books?"

"No. But just as people need instruction on how to use tools, computers, and household appliances, people need instruction on using magic, too. When a person shows the aptitude and desire to learn magic, I will help him or her to study these scrolls. Simply reciting a spell, even if one has the talent to manifest it, doesn't mean they won't be hurt by it. There is one book I have sequestered here that gives very careful and very good instructions on how to turn yourself into an animal. However, the book has no instructions on how to return to human form. It is a book of traps. Turn yourself into a bug and you are stuck as a bug for the rest of your life. Which may be short if someone happens to step on you."

"You've said several times "when you started' or 'when you came into the world.' What are you exactly?"

"I am a free demon, summoned from the primordial mass by an unfortunate wizard who died of shock when I actually answered his summons."

"A demon," she breathed. "I thought demons were mythical."

"Everything is mythical. That's what we all arose from at one time or another." I led her into our dining room and we sat with my four wives. I didn't have Peninnah at the time.

"Wives, Marian the Librarian would like to come and work in our libraries. Perhaps you would like to tell her about what life is like in the infinity room."

I left Marian in the care of my wives and returned to the work of replicating the New York Public Library. Marian quickly joined our force in helping to copy the books and got us access into the rare books collections where we even managed to replicate their copy of the Gutenberg Bible. She did not return to her former life after that.

>-- ◄◆► --<

We didn't immediately read out the results of our cooking competition. The meals ranged from the exquisite to the disastrous. On Saturday night, we all loaded into a bus and were taken to a concert hall where Rin was joined by other members of her string quartet and we were treated to Brahms' "String Quartet in C Minor." It was exquisite and I was so glad we had Rin as one of our crew contestants. After the late-night concert, we went out to enjoy some of the nightlife in the resort where we were treated to a nightclub comedy act with an interpreter. I have no idea if the comedian was any good, but the interpreter was hilarious. Occasionally, she would look at the comedian as if she had said something truly strange and then interpret it in such a way that brought us to tears.

On Sunday afternoon, we called everyone together in the living room of the penthouse.

"We're having a party," I said. "This is a party to honor one of our number who will no longer be with us after today. We've counted the votes and tabulated the results. Now everyone grab a drink and some snacks and tell each of the other women in the contest how you feel about her and how much you hope she is not eliminated."

I'd chosen this method for a couple of reasons. First, I thought the person eliminated deserved more than just to be shoved out the door. And second, I wanted the girls to have a real opportunity to show their bonding and caring for each other. I wasn't disappointed in either instance. The girls did care about each other and showed it in every way they could, without being encumbered by saying goodbye. Eventually, we all sat and the expectations were tense.

Valerie's dinner was, as expected, delectable. She was a chef by profession and knew how to plan a meal and how to judge portions so she had exactly the right amount of food. She also effectively used Julie as her sous chef and assistant. Julie scrubbed and peeled vegetables, set the table precisely the way Valerie directed, and helped serve the meal when we were all seated.

Valerie got high marks all the way around and won the week's competition.

"And now, we have to say goodbye to someone we all love," I said. "The crew has voted and our school teacher, Linda, has lost this competition."

Poor Linda had attempted an elaborate meal that left nearly every pot in the kitchen dirty. It might even have turned out okay if she had been serving dinner. But it was totally inappropriate for breakfast and when the final scores were tallied, she came out on the bottom.

She'd captured all our hearts with her sensual eroticism during the audition and then her blatant stripping and telling us that if she found out it was all real, she'd never wear clothes again and I'd never have to ask to fuck her. Well, we had come very close to fucking, but had never quite gone the last few inches.

After her goodbye party, she came into my study with tears running down her face. I held her gently in my arms and comforted her. No one else was allowed in the room, except the camerawomen from Areola who stayed discreetly hidden. Linda immediately came to me and threw herself into my arms. It could have been a point of recrimination, complaint, or anger. Instead...

"I'm so sorry I disappointed you, Bob," she sniffed. "I really wanted to be the best and be with you forever. Or at least not the worst."

"Linda, how would you like to continue on the journey with us?" I asked.

"Really? Do you have, like, amnesty for losers? Please, Bob, don't tease me. I'd do anything to stay with you and our family," she said.

"It's not quite like that," I said. "In fact, you will find this very hard to believe." I pointed toward the door and opened a gateway that shimmered beside the door. "Linda, the door on the right leads outside where a limo is waiting to take you wherever you want to go.

You will have plenty of money and transportation, literally to anyplace in the world. The driver will give you a ticket and everything else you need. All your belongings will be packed up here and in California and sent to you right away. But if you choose to leave by that door, you will never see us again, unless you happen to watch the TV special."

She froze, contemplating the possibilities.

"The alternative is on the left." The portal began to glow. "I have in my possession a transporter. It is powerful enough to bring everyone in my palace, where they are waiting, to join us when we arrive at our destination. When you walk through that portal, you stop aging. You simply wait for me to call you and bring you with me. I promise, it isn't a difficult wait. But it's all unknown, Linda. You don't know where you'll be. You will never again have contact with the earth you've known all your life. You'll have our dream. It's your choice to make, Linda. Just walk through one door or the other."

Linda didn't say anything. She stood up in front of me and slowly and meticulously peeled off her clothes, just as she'd done at her audition. She left them in a pile on my desk. Then she bent over the desk and spread her legs.

"Any time, Bob. You'll never have to ask to fuck me. Take me. I believe it's all real."

I stepped up behind her and ran a finger through her pussy to make sure she was really ready. With that much lubrication, I was surprised she hadn't already orgasmed. I unfastened my pants and slotted my cock at her entrance and pushed. She groaned as I filled her with more than she'd ever crammed in there before. I pulled back and thrust again, and then she started coming. It was non-stop as I fucked her for a good ten minutes before I bellowed out my own release and filled her with my spend.

After we'd recovered a bit, I pulled myself back and she stood in front of me with come running down the inside of her thighs. She kissed me and turned toward the portal, leaving her clothes on the desk.

"See you on the other side, Bob," she said, and stepped through.

50
NAVEL BATTLE

IT WAS SO EASY to talk about all the things that happened a long time ago. Believe it or not, it's much harder to keep recent details straight with what happened when. But we had an artist who came in for auditions and she was something else.

"Hi. This where you're auditioning for some space race reality show?" she asked.

"This is it," Doug said. "Um... Wow! Do you have a resume and headshot?"

"I, like, took this at Walgreen's. It's all I have, but there are some selfies on my Deviant Art page. I can't believe you guys need paper. Can I email my bio to you? That's all the resume I've got," she said.

I still hadn't gotten a good look at her, but as Doug turned and ushered her to the front of the little studio we were using, I saw Peninnah stiffen. I finally got a look at her and almost choked holding back my laughter.

She looked small, but it only took one good look to realize she was a real hardbody. She made it obvious by the way she dressed. She wore a sleeveless crop top that clearly showed the muscles in her arms. Her bare abs were ripped. The legs that stuck out of her miniskirt were as strong as the set of her jaw. She wore ankle height black boots with thick soles. Her hair was short and curly with makeup that bordered on goth but didn't quite cross the line. To cap it all off, a cluster of rhinestones sparkled in her navel.

Peninnah stood. Her own crop top had short sleeves and her miniskirt might have been a touch longer than what this girl was wearing. Peninnah, of course, did not wear boots, but five-inch spike heels that gave her a good three inches in height over the prospect. And the diamond in her navel was all the competition the contestant's rhinestones needed. Pen walked around the table and stood facing our guest as they stared at each other.

I was ready to move in to separate them and I saw Zhi, our security detail, slipping up behind Doug. Peninnah had taken her martial arts training seriously, but I didn't want to risk either of them being hurt if this tinder caught fire. After just staring at each other for almost a minute while the rest of us held our breath, they started laughing.

"You're just what we need," Pen said. "Come and have a seat and tell us about yourself." Pen showed her to the usual auditioner's chair and then took Doug's place beside her, forcing Doug to come around the table to sit beside me.

"Well," I said when we were all breathing again. "Let's start with names. I'm Bob. You've met our producer, Doug, and my wife Peninnah. Between Peninnah and Doug is Liz, our casting director."

She nodded at each of us in turn and sat there waiting.

"Um... Your turn," I said.

"Oh. Yeah. I'm Artemisia."

"Last name?" Liz asked.

"Nope. Just that. I got it legally changed."

"We try to be pretty informal, girl," Pen said, adapting an accent almost identical to Artemisia's. She was definitely Californian, from somewhere near the valley. "Give us some help here and tell us about yourself and what made you decide to come and audition. You aren't an actress."

"Dang, is it that obvious? Yeah, sure Penny. Okay, I'm an artist. At least I intend to be. I just got out of high school. I'm eighteen, which in California is old enough for any legal activity except alcohol and weed. As if we haven't been smoking since we were old enough to raid our parents' stash. I'd like to go to CalArts, but just tuition is like sixty grand a year. I don't have that kind of money, so I looked for a job where I could get it. This looked like fun."

"You're a body-builder, too, aren't you, Artie?" Peninnah asked. Apparently, it was okay for Artemisia to call her Penny, but she was giving it right back.

"Yeah. Beach bum. I play beach volleyball, too. I know that kind of thing is unusual for artists, but I get a lot of models out there," she said. "And I don't have to take shit from anybody."

We went over the concept for the show, signed the papers and headed for the screen test.

>-- ◆◆◆ --<

You might not believe this, but she wasn't the first Artemisia I'd ever met. And I don't mean the other artist in sixteenth century Italy, from whom this one had borrowed her name. I was already in the Western Hemisphere by her time.

Remember I told you I went to Greece with Xerxes? Well, I kind of got caught up in the flotilla as a supply ship. I sailed with a small unit out of Anatolia. The queen of the area was Artemisia I of Halicarnassus. She was a subordinate of Xerxes, but was also one of his favorite generals. Or Admirals. I never knew quite how to address her, though she felt 'Your Majesty' was appropriate. She led a small fleet of five warships and an equal number of supply ships in Xerxes' fleet of seventy ships that he sailed to Greece.

Of course, most of Xerxes' forces marched by land and had to cross the pass at Thermopylae. That's where the famous battle against the Spartans took place. I'd seen Spartans led by Menelaus at Troy. That's where Helen was married to the king and then ran away with Paris. They were fierce, but what they were doing all the way up at Thermopylae is a mystery. They were part of a Greek coalition that included Thebes, which was much closer.

You remember Thebes. Always contrary and when they refused to pay their tribute to Alexander, he sacked the city and laid waste to it. Nonetheless, Xerxes' army had to pass Thermopylae and the battle there was legendary. During the battle of Thermopylae, Queen Artemisia was distinguishing herself by leading the assault on the Greek Navy in the narrow sea passage to the Gulf of Malia, so we could resupply the soldiers.

Both Xerxes and Artemisia won.

On the other side of the pass, with fresh supplies, Xerxes was gung-ho to press southward and capture the Isthmus of Corinth, so his rule would be established over all Greece. Artemisia warned against it, but by that time, Xerxes was calling himself a god king and couldn't be wrong. He sent the navy around the Athenian peninsula.

I was an admirer of Artemisia. She was a strong woman who was decisive and courageous. Also passionate, if you must know. We'd had some time together in Halicarnassus before the war. I probably wouldn't have joined Xerxes' invasion had it not been for her.

Her husband was dead and her son was a bit of an idiot, so Artemisia had taken over as Queen and ruled until her death—long after I knew her. But I'd been trading up the coast and brought some interesting Persian goods with me. She especially liked the linen that was being woven in the south. It was much softer than the wool she was used to. After supplying her with enough squares of linen to have an entire new wardrobe, we had a nice intimate dinner and I stayed with her for a year or so before Xerxes sent the word to get ready to sail.

We did not marry. Artemisia had a thing against marriage and I wondered exactly how it was that her husband died. But she was a strong woman and I might have been a little more vigorous in my loving than I was with most women. Artemisia uncovered a bit of my secret and knew I was more than just a man. She was not happy that I wouldn't command a warship, but was satisfied that I would bring a supply ship. I believe knowing I was a kind of demon might have contributed to what happened when the Greek Navy sprang its trap at Salamis.

Artemisia had rightly predicted the superior numbers and ability of the Greeks and ended up turning rapidly and heading out of the Saronic Gulf as fast as she could. That did not appear to be fast enough, as a Greek ship was in pursuit and would surely catch her. She took the tiller and ordered her rowers to ramming speed, bearing down on *my* ship! She hit me mid-ship and split it in two. It sank within minutes.

Of course, I was the only one aboard, with all my crew safe in the satchel during any time of conflict. The Greek ship, thinking she must be on the same side, broke off pursuit and Artemisia escaped. If they had known that the admiral with a 10,000-drachma price on her head was the captain of that ship, she might not have escaped.

As far as I was concerned, that was it for me. I'd swum through Poseidon's storms bearing Aphrodite on my back, I could swim to shore here. I made land at Piraeus and eventually ended up in Athens where I discovered theatre!

I didn't hold the event against Artemisia. I didn't really think I could go back to her bed after that, though. I don't give people who try to kill me a second chance.

>-- ◀◆▶ --<

"Bob. Bob!" Liz demanded. "We're ready to do the scene."

"Oh. Sorry. I was thinking of something. So, you're a little young to do a heavy scene..."

"I signed the 2257 form. I know what I'm getting into. Liz said that it would be my choice when the time came, so make me hot and you'll get lucky. Piss me off and I'll let Penny have you," Artemisia said.

Well, we got right into the scene and she handled everything we threw at her in terms of situations and improv. There was even a point where she practically flew across the stage as if she was diving for a volleyball and then did a roll out of the dive to come back up to her feet with no shirt on.

It was obvious that she wasn't a cookie cutter actress from Hollywood. Her breasts were rather small, but there was hardly any body fat on her at all, let alone in her breasts. I kept the scene going to see how far she'd take it and before long she lost her skirt and panties in one slick move while yelling out, "Gravity burst! Everything's coming down." Unfortunately, her panties got tangled in her boots and she tripped, falling on top of me in my chair.

"Cut!" Liz called.

"Before I even blow him?" Artie asked. She turned around and plopped herself in my lap, pulling my hands around her naked body.

"We'll let you look forward to that later," I said.

"Really? I get the job?"

I looked to Pen and Liz. They nodded. Between the jewels in her navel battling Peninnah's and the memory of Artemisia's naval battle, I was sold.

"You're in our cast," I said.

"Oh, cool!" She smashed her mouth against mine for a tongue probing and my hands got familiar with her little tits and muscular ass. I'd enjoy getting to know that more, later.

>-- ◀◆▶ --<

After the cooking competition and 'loss' of Linda, we spent another couple of days decompressing in the penthouse, most of it spent naked around or in the pool. Then we loaded everyone on the plane and headed for India. We had a nice estate home there, near the headquarters of the tracking station. We filmed a tour of the facility where the girls would get training on how our ship would be tracked.

Wendy had been hugely popular with the guys at the station ever since her audition when she translated their instructions into 'English.' They mobbed her and treated her like a princess, sitting her at their stations and showing her all about the system. Suhani, who had been employed there, was welcomed back as if she was the prodigal come home. Which, I guess she was. She'd written a good bit of the software they used.

After the initial introductions and fawning over their favorites, we got some serious training in. The girls were surprised to find that we had a martial arts trainer to work with them. In fact, I'd asked Drona to come out of the infinity room for this session. He'd been old when he entered the infinity room almost two thousand years ago, but he really hadn't aged and was still as vigorous and skilled as he'd been. I think both Lalonda and Artemisia were fooled into thinking they needed to go easy on the old man. They were sadly mistaken.

"Are we all sore now?" I asked. All I heard were groans. It was Sunday night and we were ready to begin our second elimination round. "This is going to be tough. You've all gotten a taste of what it takes to spar in the martial arts. I insist that everyone we work with have an understanding of and at least a moderate proficiency in martial arts. So, we are going to have a tournament."

"You're kidding!" Karla sighed. "I'm already a black and blue belt."

"This is going to be a round robin tournament with nine rounds. You will be competing in three rounds a day for the next three days. You all have received Drona's training and Zhi has gone over the sparring rules. Each pair of contestants will be scored on the items in your folder. You must do your best to win your match. If you do not, you will be eliminated immediately. And that won't stop the tournament loser from being eliminated, so you won't be taking one for the team," I commanded. I was serious, but I didn't think we'd really have a problem.

"Now, we've chosen one person to have immunity from this match. And that person is..." Dramatic pause. "...Rin."

There was a huge sigh of relief from everyone in the room and then a round of applause. Rin had been game to do all the exercises, katas, and forms. She'd worked out hard. But everyone knew she would never hit anyone. To damage her hands would harm her cello playing. None of us wanted that.

"Rin, there is responsibility that goes with immunity," Peninnah said, hugging the girl. "You will join Liz, Penelope, Bob, and me, giving a massage to the five losers of each round. You'll also be the tie-breaking judge. If Drona and Zhi split a decision, your score will make the difference. So, you will need to score every match."

Rin had been enthusiastic about the thought of giving massages, but the thought of judging every one of the forty-five matches was daunting.

>--- ◆ ---<

I was wondering how good an idea it was to massage every loser each day. By the end of the first day, I'd given three massages and it was already looking like Lalonda, Artemisia, and Suhani were going to get very few if any. Artemisia and Lalonda had no losses the first day. Suhani lost to Lalonda in the second round. Marie had lost only to Suhani in the third round, and Julie lost only to Lalonda in the third round. We had four clear leaders and only two had won no contests so far.

I wasn't keeping track of how Liz was assigning the massages, but I had three different girls after the three rounds and ended up with Julie. And that massage ended up with me in

Julie. I had a feeling, however, that my client was not the only one who got a good orgasm after her massage. I hoped that didn't affect anyone's performance.

Day two saw similar results. Lalonda, Artemisia, Suhani, and Marie were maintaining the lead with Julie a near fifth. Eun-ha, one of our smallest girls and our Korean mathematician, was on the table for me after the last round. She had yet to win a match.

"Make love to me, Bob," she pled. "I have a bad feeling about this. I keep thinking I am doing everything right and instead I make a mistake and lose. Please love me. I don't want to lose."

"I don't want you to lose, honey. And yes, I will make love to you, but not because you are a loser. I will make love to you because I love you."

"Oh, Bob, I love you," she cried. I made sure she was very relaxed and was full of my love.

It seemed to do wonders for her because in the first round of the morning, she defeated Julie who had been contesting with Marie for a top honor. Eun-ha was jubilant, dancing around the gym joyfully.

At the end of the day, the judges knew the tabulation of scores. Everyone knew her own number of wins and everyone knew that Lalonda had never been defeated and that Artemisia had only been defeated by Lalonda. They weren't really sure where everyone else fit in. So, after a nice brunch the next day, we had our awards ceremony.

"I think no one is surprised to find that Lalonda is our champion," I announced. We handed her a trinket we'd gotten at the market for prizes. "Nor that second place goes to Artemisia."

I'd had a very nice fuck with Artemisia after her loss to Lalonda. That eighteen-year-old hardbody was something special. She also got an award trinket.

"Third place goes to Suhani, our local girl." She got her trinket and a kiss from each of us. "Fourth place goes to Marie. Fifth place is Julie's."

Now it was getting tense. They all knew how many wins they had and only hoped it wasn't the least.

"In a tie for sixth place, we have Valerie and Karla." Our chef and our pilot. They came to get their trinket and stopped to kiss each other to the applause of the other girls.

"In eighth place, Deedee..." I paused as she jumped up to come running to me. I held her in one arm. "...and Wendy in a tie." Wendy stopped and turned to Eun-ha. They were both crying.

"I'm sorry. I'm sorry," Wendy pled as if she could have changed the outcome.

Eun-ha pushed Wendy forward to receive her trinket, then stood and shouted out, "I won eight massages! And I received them from the most wonderful, loving, and beautiful people I've ever known. And I love each of you. And I'll miss you."

>-- ◆◆◆ --<

I hadn't expected the elimination of our Korean mathematician when we announced this competition. I guess that's just my Americanized prejudices. She's Asian. Of course, she must be good at martial arts.

After her goodbye party, she came into my study with tears running down her face. I held her gently in my arms and comforted her.

"Eun-ha, baby, I want you to watch something, okay? I got this from Linda yesterday."

"Linda? She contacted you?"

"And you, it appears."

I settled into a chair and played the recording on my big-screen TV. The screen came to life with a picture of Linda, lying naked under an umbrella next to the pool at my palace. The shot didn't take in enough to really get an idea of where she was—just that she was next to a pool with a cold drink and enjoying herself.

"Hi, it's Linda," she said. "Hope you haven't already forgotten me. Man, getting eliminated really sucks, doesn't it? Well, look at me. I suddenly have everything I ever dreamed of. Maybe more. I know that you're probably upset—maybe even crying because you have to leave the show. Take a deep breath and listen to what Bob has to tell you. Honey, they aren't being mean to you. Listen and make the decision with your heart. Who knows? Maybe I'll see you again sometime soon." Linda raised her glass to the camera and it faded out.

"You have something to tell me?" she asked. "Besides 'goodbye?'"

"Look over there," I said. "On the right is the door to the big wide world. Waiting on the other side is enough money that you'll never want for anything again. A driver will take you anywhere you want to go. If you want to go to Europe, he'll provide tickets. If you want to get on a slow freighter to Korea, he'll arrange it. But when you go through that door, the one thing you won't have is us—all we've been working the past few months to achieve. You'll never see us again."

"I don't want to never see you again, Bob. I love you. I love Peninnah and Liz and Penelope. I love all the other girls. I don't want to go."

"I have kept some things from people. I'm a lot more powerful than you all think. In fact, I have a transporter. You know, like in *Star Trek*? Beside the door out, is a shimmering gateway that is my transporter. If you choose to walk through that gateway, you will be transported to another mansion of mine. A palace, actually. All of the people you meet in the palace will be joining me when we arrive at our destination. That's a lot more people than the little colony you thought you were preparing to build. You'll wait for a while, but waiting there is easy. In fact, people waiting in my palace do not age. And I visit occasionally. I'll come to check on you and see how you are getting along. I'll make love to you again. Often. But you need to understand that if you choose the transporter, you will never see earth outside my palace grounds again. So, you need to choose now if you will walk out of our lives forever, or if you will walk into the future and be with us forever. Your destiny awaits you."

"You don't like, just kill me if I choose to use the transporter, do you?" she squeaked.

"I promise that neither the door nor the portal leads to your imminent death or suffering."

"I... I choose..."

"Just go to the passage you've chosen," I said.

Eun-ha turned and kissed me and then walked bravely to the gateway and disappeared into the infinity room. I smiled. That worked extremely well. I might not lose them after all.

51
WINNOWING

>-- ◈ --<

SOME OF THE WOMEN who were our contestants were just too much fun to describe. They made me laugh and they made me cry. Sometimes at the same time. For example, there was Marie. I thought at first Marie had inhaled nitrous before she auditioned. Everything she said was funny. Which I thought was really strange. Marie was a doctor. We'd found her in Mexico City and auditioned her on the spot. She was a member of Traveling Doctors and spent three months at a time wherever they sent her. She was due for a new rotation and was able to join our crew instead of taking another assignment.

The scenario for her audition was a space battle in which we'd hear various explosions. We were supposed to act like the ship was being hit by lurching back and forth. We stumbled around almost as if we were drunk.

"Captain, we have to get out of here. We won't have an able-bodied man or woman on the ship if this keeps up. I'm treating them as fast as I can!"

"Keep doing your best, Doctor," I responded. "Weapons, fire port phasers! They're hitting us from every direction." We kept hearing explosions and each time we heard one, we stumbled. She knelt as if to treat a wounded crewmate and when the next explosion sounded, she rolled completely over the supposed body and into my chair. I was pretty sure the first 'accident' really was an accident. Marie stumbled against the chair and her blouse caught on a corner and tore open. She scarcely hesitated a moment before she simply ripped it off and quickly started wrapping it around my arm.

"You've been hit! Let me get this bleeding on your arm stopped."

I nearly forgot to stumble with the next explosion. Marie was braless under her blouse and her large breasts seemed to have a life of their own as she stumbled into me and they wobbled. She next ripped her skirt off and wrapped it around my leg, 'accidentally' opening my pants to expose my cock.

"This calls for extreme measures, Captain. I'll have to kiss it and make it better," she said, sucking me into her mouth. I took another lurch to the side, just to see how she would react next. My cock popped out of her mouth and she looked up at me.

"Oh, my God, Captain! Your mouth is bleeding! I have to staunch the flow of blood!"

None of us expected her to rip off her panties and stuff them in my mouth. Next, she lurched to the side and landed in my reclining captain's chair, pulling me down on top of her. She grabbed my cock and guided it straight into her pussy. That kind of ended the scene, but we continued to rock back and forth on the set as I pumped into her and the explosions continued. I finally spent my load as she screamed, "I'm hit!"

I collapsed forward and pressed her into the chair.

"Dammit, Bob! I'm a doctor, not a mattress!" she called out. That was an effective end to her audition.

>-- ◀◆▶ --<

We headed for London next, with a special invitation from the Queen. I'd been in the new palace several times while it was under construction, of course, but not since Her Majesty actually made it her new home. We were given a private wing as a guest suite where we all stayed together. Valerie was extremely happy to be back home in England and took us all on a tour of her favorite places.

Next to the palace, the British Space Park, BSP, was about to open with some special rides created to give guests the kind of adventures they expected us to have on our ship. Among the rides was a space capsule ride. It was meant to simulate our own command module, though not the entire ship. In fact, the control module was as near to a ship simulator as we had back in California. There were just two seats in the capsule. I would act as the copilot as each of the girls got to 'fly' the ship. The simulator ran a dozen different programs automatically and they were variable in terms of the challenge difficulty. We chose the series that was rated as moderate because I didn't really want anyone to look like a total failure. I knew some of the girls could perform at the highest level of difficulty. Karla was an airline pilot and Julie was a racecar driver. They both had excellent skills on the simulator.

After consulting with my wives, we decided to give Deedee immunity for this contest. We tried to make sure we gave immunity to the person we thought would be the weakest for the challenge. Deedee had not done well on the simulator so far, but she still had to take the test, even though her score would not be announced.

It was a harrowing and exhausting day.

The test was thirty minutes long and the computer scored execution of each task based on response time, accuracy of response, and task performance. We really had no human intervention on scoring this one. As the copilot, I was supposed to be there in case of an 'emergency' the pilot couldn't handle. If we were about to fall into the burning sun, I had the power to save the ship. I was also there to follow the instructions of the pilot. But the task instructions and simulation all came through the headset from the computer to the pilot.

The biggest mistake most of the contestants made was not using the copilot. They inevitably felt they had to do everything themselves, some of which was impossible unless the pilot had four hands and six-foot arms. Karla, of course, knew exactly how to use a copilot. She gave me instructions of what I was to do as fast as the instructions came through her headset. She had a very successful flight.

Julie was slightly behind her in that driving a car is a one-person job and learning to depend on a second person was a new experience for her. From there each girl had her own skills that ranged from barely competent to almost good.

After a long and grueling day, we all wanted to sleep for hours. The girls got to talk to each other about the test and compare their challenges. In all, it was a good team building exercise as well as a test of their skills.

The next day, we had tea with Her Majesty. Everyone was excited, as we'd bought all the girls new clothes for the occasion. They knew this was also the farewell party for one of the girls. After tea—when the queen retired from the room—we would announce who had scored the lowest on the test. She would have an hour to say goodbye to the girls and gather her belongings before coming to see me in my guest office.

I was truly devastated when Rin lost the competition. I was certain her dexterity would see her through, but she simply didn't have quite the measure of skills the other girls had. After being spared from the competition in the last round, Rin simply didn't have what it took to make the simulator challenge.

She came into my guest office, a part of the suite, carrying her cello.

"Bob, may I play for you one more time before I leave?" I wanted to tell her she didn't have to leave, but it would spoil this lovely offer. I thought perhaps her father had arranged for her to audition. I had discovered he was a mid-level manager with Fukishina, and we had put out the invitation to everyone in the company to refer people. Nonetheless, she was beautiful and talented, and she sat in a chair across from me and placed the cello between her knees to play.

I don't have a good memory for music, so I couldn't tell you what it was she played. What I know is that it was so beautiful and sad and uplifting and sweet and passionate that it left me in tears. She put her cello in its case and came to sit in my lap as I held my arms out to her.

"Rin, I have something I would like you to watch. This is from Eun-ha and arrived for you this afternoon."

Eun-ha told Rin that she'd gotten exactly what she wanted in life by simply listening to my suggestions and making her choice. She was sunning herself by the pool, much as Linda had been doing in the first video. I explained the choices and showed her the gateway, right beside the door. I'd been fine-tuning the appearance of the gateway to make it look more attractive each time I used it.

Rin kissed me tenderly and with as much passion as she had shown in playing the cello.

"Thank you, Bob. You have given me the choice of my heart's desire. It pains me to leave you and our wonderful family behind, but I know now where my destiny lies." She kissed me softly one more time, picked up her cello, and walked out the door.

The door! Not the gateway. I wanted to run after her and tell her she'd made a mistake, but I knew that as soon as she was out that door, Doug would be escorting her to a waiting limo and giving her a travel packet.

I sat there with tears running down my face as I remembered the last plaintive notes of her concert. I didn't go out to join everyone else for the evening. I walked through the gateway where Josie and Nimia met me and took me to bed to comfort me.

>— ◆ —<

"Well, Bob, thank you for coming to the palace for a few days. You know, you and your women are always welcome. I almost stole Valerie back again. The new chef doesn't have her touch," the queen said at breakfast. It was just the two of us and I was happy to have a bit of time with her.

"I am always pleased to spend time with you, Your Majesty," I said.

"Now, let's talk turkey, as the Americans say. I want another favor from you."

"Anything I can do," I said.

"I'd like you to take me with you when you go."

Now *that* was something I didn't expect.

"I... um... I mean..."

"Relax, Bob. I don't mean now, and I don't mean on your trip to Mars. Not literally. I'm getting tired of this ruling the kingdom and even being a figurehead. I think you could make a big deal about taking me with you as a stowaway, and just drop me off somewhere on your way to the ship. I could finally disappear and start life over again," she said.

"Do you mean...?"

"That I'm like you are, Bob. I never expected to become queen when I took on this role. The Princess was a sickly girl and I eased her pain on her way out of the world. Then I became her. I'm relatively young in this world—at least compared to one like you. I was summoned in the 1400s, right here in jolly old England. I pleased my master and as a reward, he set me free near the end of his life," she said.

"That was very nice of him."

"Yes. I appreciated it enough that I killed him painlessly. You know, he just made me feel so cheap and used. He could have summoned me to be powerful and take care of his enemies. Instead, he summoned me to be his sex slave. I know you have strong feelings about that," she said wagging a finger at me.

"I do, Madam. I hardly know... How did you discover me?" I asked.

"Just normal reconnaissance and spying by MI6. The thing is that people, even good spies like we have, discount things that obviously couldn't be. I was looking for something different than they were. I saw the pattern of people and research, which took me back quite a distance. The winery in California was the continuous link and when I found that Irish girl who is still running it after what? 300 years? She provided me with the answers I wanted."

Maureen. Sold out by another demon. The Queen professed to have been summoned as a sex slave and not as someone powerful, but she had ascended to the throne, and had obviously managed several identities over the years. I thought at her age, she might well be drawing suspicion to herself at this point and would do well to retire, as it were.

"Oh, don't be mad at Maureen," the Queen chastised me. "I'd already put together most of the pieces, including the existence of your secret hideaway. I'd ask to have you just take me there, but I don't think two of us should share that close a space for as long as we might live. We'd end up killing each other. But just figure out a way to have me die in your arms with my last wish to have my ashes travel into space with you and I'll transform to a harmless production person in the space port and disappear."

"Your Majesty, I will put my mind to work and make sure we take you with us. It might be tricky, but I'm sure we can make it work."

"Good. I've had this body long enough and would like to be young and sexy again. I really didn't mind the sex at all. It was just the slavery thing that got to me. I might see about putting together a group of secret ninjas like you have and do my own prowling around to fight trafficking. Now go back to your women and get thinking. I really need to die sometime in the coming year. Either that or one of my heirs will poison me."

>-- ◄◆► --<

We had to get back to California to run the next elimination round, which would be in San Francisco. I owned an elegant penthouse on Nob Hill that was only slightly smaller than the penthouse in Japan. The girls loved it, and couldn't believe Peninnah and I owned so many properties. We'd actually used very few of them.

"This week, we are going to enjoy some of the classic entertainment of San Francisco and a unique challenge," I said when we all met in the living area. "We are going to the famous Fisherman's Wharf, we'll tour the Ghirardelli Chocolate factory, and we'll eat at one of Liz's favorite restaurants in Chinatown. I'll also give you a tour of Haight-Ashbury and we'll go to the world-famous San Francisco Museum of Modern Art. Everyone will get to ride the trolley, and we'll tour Golden Gate Park, before we board a bus to go across the bridge for a wine-tasting tour of the valley. How does all that sound?"

"Wow! What fun!" Marie said.

"It will be fun, I promise you," I said. "And I'll give you a little historical tour of the city and some of the less-known historical events that happened here. But at the end of the week, there will be an elimination challenge, I'm sorry to say. It will be a weapons decision course in a virtual shooting range. You've all been trained on small arms and on some interstellar armaments. You'll get a chance to test your skill on both. That means that not every target that shows up will be an enemy. You'll need to make a snap decision as to whether to fire or not. Your scores will be tallied based on speed, accuracy, and decisions."

"Oh, shit," Valerie breathed. She'd scored lowest on weapons almost every time we'd trained.

"And, of course, one person will be immune from this challenge. I normally wouldn't tell you this until just before the challenge, but it would cause a lot of unneeded stress while we're trying to have fun this week. So, Valerie will have immunity in this challenge."

We could all hear her sigh of relief as it turned to tears of joy.

"I'll help," she said. "If anyone wants to practice, I'll go with you. I'll encourage you. Anything I can do. Hell, I'll be your target if you want."

Everyone laughed and applauded Valerie. In my opinion, they were expressing the feelings of their stomachs. For the evening, though, clothes were shed and we had the nearest thing to an orgy that we'd had since the girls started this adventure. From eighteen-year-old hardbody Artemisia to thirty-three-year-old doctor Marie, I couldn't find a flaw on any of them. And I checked thoroughly.

In fact, Artemisia rode my cock while Marie settled her pussy on my face and I thoroughly enjoyed both their orgasms. It seemed they enjoyed each other, as well.

Those women I didn't fuck or give oral to, I held in my arms and kissed while one of the other women tended to her. I noticed that my family had chosen favorites from among the girls and they enjoyed them thoroughly. Peninnah got hold of Artemisia as soon as I'd filled her pussy and made sure she was thoroughly cleaned up—with her tongue. Then they might have bounced their navel piercings against each other a while. Laine and Dezi had paired up with Wendy and Karla for a little play time. Liz was with buxom Deedee. And I noticed Zhi was with us, paying special attention to Lalonda. I fully expected Lalonda to ace the decision course. It was part of her job as a policewoman.

Well, we thoroughly enjoyed the week. They were all impressed as I led them through streets, talking about what was there when the streets were made of mud. I stopped in front of a large skyscraper in the Financial District and told them about a redheaded Irish woman who ran a pub in that very location and had thrown drunks out into the street to be run over by a stagecoach. I told them that legend had it, she had a brawny boyfriend who could lift an entire cask of wine on his shoulders and carry it into the pub.

I pointed out the location of the original public library and we strolled up Haight Street and I pointed out the superette that had one time been a headshop for the hippies and as far back as the beatniks. It was all ancient history to our contestants, but I noticed Liz beaming as we walked through our old haunts. She led the way up to Buena Vista Park and told the story of how she'd found the love of her life at the summit. It was very romantic.

Inevitably, the day of the challenge arrived and the girls had to focus on their weapons use. They did well in all respects. Even though she had immunity, Valerie had to take part in the test and surprised herself with how well she did. Being relaxed, knowing she wouldn't be eliminated, gave her the confidence to just cut loose on the course and do her best. I was pleased.

Wendy, however, did not fare so well. She assembled her weapon incorrectly and had to re-do it, costing valuable time. Then in the ship-to-ship weapons simulator, she missed all the targets except one that was friendly. She had been blogging everything about our competition without mentioning who any of the contestants were or where we were. That was hard on her, but we had censorship rights in order to protect the show. It wouldn't be much of a season if we didn't ensure confidentiality before the show started running. I hoped to help her maintain her blogging for the duration of the show.

>-- ◄◆► --‹

"Well, this sucks," I said when she entered my study for her goodbye scene. She was crying as she waved goodbye to the girls in the other room and entered through my door. We played the video, this one from Linda, who was once again sunning herself by the pool, sans clothing. When she'd made her presentation, I pointed out the door and the gateway and asked her to make her choice. She leapt into my arms and wrapped her legs around my waist, kissing me fervently.

"Yes, yes, yes. I'll do anything for you, Bob. I love you. I'm yours. You po..."

I slammed my lips against hers and silenced her avowal before she could speak it. When we'd finished kissing, we were both naked and spent, my cock still plunging into her as we lay on the floor. With her next orgasm, all thought of whatever she was about to say had vanished.

It's not as if I *have* to possess anyone who says to possess her. Not exactly. It's more like a compulsion or an addiction. Once I hear those words, my senses abandon me and I just flow into the person. It was better to prevent her from saying the words.

"I'll see you later," she said happily, as she pranced naked through the portal.

Well, only two more to be eliminated.

52
Happy Days

I GREW UP IN THE '50s.

"But, Bob," you say, "you're 4,000 years old. How can you claim to have grown up in the 50s?" Right. Well, I was recently dead... I should go back just a little further.

Early in the 1900s, after I'd left the vineyard to Maureen and was free, I decided to do a wine tour of France. We'd been in the wine business for fifty years, switching back and forth as to who owned the vineyard. It worked out well, and Maureen was getting the hang of being a neutral demon instead of being evil. I know she still had a taste for souls, but she'd cut back. Her story was quite different than mine and she'd had a hard time adjusting to impersonating humans without killing them.

Anyway, my wine tour in France took the better part of three years, during which time I met Gabrielle. She was a French beauty who happened also to be a vintner's daughter and a very knowledgeable oenophile. I visited her father's vineyard and while tasting wines, got to know Gabrielle, who then mysteriously attached herself to my arm as we toured about a hundred more vineyards and compared notes on what we thought of each wine. I bought several cases of wine on that trip and moved them into the infinity room when I was alone at night.

Yes, I was alone at night. Gabrielle wanted to travel with me and taste wines, but she was a good girl and always had her own room—which frustrated me no end. Which is why I ended up marrying her and then fucking her until my eyes nearly bled. It takes a lot of fucking before a demon's eyes bleed from it. Gabrielle's only comment was to ask why I'd waited so long before I married her.

We finished our tour and I proposed that we buy a vineyard in California and make wine together. She suggested we do that while having sex. I agreed.

So, after a very pleasant ocean voyage, followed by an equally pleasant cross-country train trip, we arrived in San Francisco to take over the vineyard that I recently acquired from Maureen. She'd decided to take a break for a while and go back to Ireland to see what was happening there.

I'd dropped a number of hints to Gabrielle about my not being totally human and she nodded. She had no interest in what I might be as long as I had a usable erection. Which was most of the time.

She patted me on the head and said, "Yes, dear. Just keep your hobby in your den and I won't interfere with it."

My den was in a shed behind the very attractive villa I'd built at the vineyard. Of course, she didn't know I'd built it, because that was years ago. The vineyard had been functioning since the Civil War, some fifty years past. Our Goídel Glas Wines were well-received, and Gabrielle pronounced them palatable. French snob.

Anyway, the US declared war on Germany in April of 1917 and passed the Selective Service Act in May. As a new US citizen, I had to register for the draft and was called up as we were harvesting.

I might have pled for a deferment as an agricultural worker, but I could hardly claim wine was an essential service, though later, I decided it would have been. I reported and with my imported French records, I was made a lieutenant after basic training. I was sent back to France where it was considered my experience in dealing with the French would be useful.

I'll not dwell on my role in that hellish war. Ten thousand Americans a day arrived in France to support the war effort. The losses were high. By the time of the Armistice in November, I was a Captain and was one of the few draftees who were retained in France to help with the reconstruction.

I was given a regional peacekeeping responsibility right back in our old neighborhood. I spent any non-duty time I had acquiring and tasting the local wines, just as I'd done ten years before with Gabrielle.

I was looking forward to getting home and fucking Gabrielle some more, but my departure was delayed when I was shot by an upset local. I will not say if the incident did or did not involve several casks of good wine and his wife. Nonetheless, I ended up in a hospital and made the decision to die there and take on a new identity. I'd done the kind of body swap where I took over the identity of a dead man and disguised his body as my own. That was how I became Odysseus almost three thousand years before.

Thus freed of responsibilities, I spent a few years wandering post-war Europe—a depressing thing to have done. I'd adopted a young look—something noticed by sergeant McAuliffe and his wife when they spotted me. It was mostly to keep myself from being drafted in postwar France. I pled with the Americans to adopt me and thus emigrated to America.

Sadly, the McAuliffes and I 'got separated' soon after reaching their home in Georgia. I decided to switch identities when I discovered the McAuliffes were Southern Baptists and expected me to be one, too. I adopted several identities over the next twenty years and moved around the US a lot. That is a different story entirely. But my brief time as a boy left me with a desire to have that experience, and so I convinced Maureen to pose me as her son, a strapping young lad of twelve in 1951.

Hence, back to where I started this harangue. I grew up in the 50s. Maureen acquired the vineyard from my widow, who was ready to retire and return to France.

>-- <&> --<

The hardest part of being a teen was disciplining myself to act the part of a young teen and not a horny old goat. Fortunately, I had access to the infinity room, where my wives and concubines had a perverse pleasure in sex with a teen boy. And Maureen was always happy to welcome me home from school in the afternoon with wide open legs. Between the two, I was kept from fucking several delectable underage girls.

Until I was sixteen. What a glorious year!

I found school to be quite informational. I was nearly four thousand years old and had never had formal schooling. It was not what I expected at all! They lie! Oh, they talked about history as if they understood it, but half of it was wrong. They simply skipped over the racism in California as if the Chinese weren't still discriminated against. The Japanese had only been released from concentration camps ten years before and many never got their homes and property back. During the California gold rush, more than 150 Mexicans were lynched because they were successful miners. And whites invaded Chinatown in San Francisco to kill eighteen Chinese people because some white idiot choked on a wonton. California had a history of enslaving people without calling it that and I attempted to set the record straight.

I was sent home from school and suspended for a week for causing trouble.

I guess, like students of every generation, I learned to keep my mouth shut. It hurt to see so many of my fellow students accepting what they were told without question. The 'A's they received on tests were a kind of badge of ignorance.

But not everything was bad. I moved into San Francisco to an apartment Maureen rented for me over a little store on Haight Street. Yes, that one. She registered me in public school for my junior and senior years of high school and then didn't really show up again in San Francisco until I graduated. By that time, I owned the store and was using my girls to operate it. I, on the other hand, had a new T-Bird and was a popular date on Saturday nights. I didn't play sports because I didn't think that was fair. It was too easy to enhance my body to make it faster, stronger, and more durable. On the other hand, some of the faster girls at my high school liked the idea of a fast car and a guy with a big dick.

"Bob, I can't believe your mom just takes off and leaves you in this fab pad. She won't be back and spoil our fun, will she?" Bernice said.

I don't actually remember if her name was Bernice. It seemed like such a common name at the time. I'll just call whoever I was with at the time Bernice. I might have to use Bernie for short.

"Mom says I'm sixteen and the trouble I get into is my own problem to deal with. I don't mind getting in trouble with you," I said.

"But if I got in trouble, you'd do the right thing, wouldn't you, Bob?"

I kept kissing her as I opened her blouse to display her very padded bra. There wasn't nearly as much under that as she made it look like. I didn't mind. That was one of the differences between San Francisco girls and Los Angeles girls. Girls near Hollywood were often augmented in order to get considered for parts in movies. The Bay Area girls were usually all natural, whatever they sported. Fashions, however, wanted everything pushed together, up, and out. This bra made her look like she was wearing torpedoes on her chest.

"Do you mean trouble like pregnant?" I asked. "If so, you don't need to worry about it. I had mumps when I was little and it left me completely sterile. I can't ever have kids." It was only a little lie.

"Oh, that's so sad. Does it… all work okay?" she asked, stroking my cock.

I finally managed to get the catch on her bra opened—don't laugh; it was my first time opening one of those—and revealed two absolutely delectable champagne glass breasts, which I worshiped with my tongue and hands.

"I think you'll find it's all in operating condition." She had my cock out of my pants and was trying to get her hand around it. "Now, if you're worried about getting in trouble with your parents, I'll do all I can to get you home before curfew, but other than that I don't know if I can help you with any trouble."

"I'm not worried about that. Right now… um… I'm worried about this. It's huge. We might have trouble… um… I don't think it will fit."

Her skirt was lying on the floor around her ankles as I continued to undress her. I debated leaving her stockings and garter belt on, but she'd put the panties on first and I'd have to unfasten the contraption before I could get them off.

"Don't worry. I won't hurt you. Gee, you're pretty, Bernie. I just can't believe how beautiful you look. I want to make you feel so good you'll forget your name." I was working on the four hooks that held her stockings up and trying not to get frustrated.

"You're so sweet. You know it doesn't work that way for girls. Boys get a big blast and forget about everything else, but it's something girls just do to please their guys."

What? Bernice had told me she wasn't a virgin and I just assumed she knew about sex and pleasure. I was going to make especially sure she had a different opinion about it before our night was over. The stockings finally came loose and I started working her panties down. She pushed away and stripped them and the belt off. Then she jumped on the bed as I finished pushing my own trousers down.

"Are you sure it won't hurt, Bob? None of the other guys were as big as you."

Other guys? It took a while before I found out Bernice was kind of the school bike. Well, she was going to find a new standard on this evening. I started kissing her and let my fingers explore. Hmm. If she was no more turned on than this, she'd never have any pleasure from sex. I worked my way down her body, paying special gentle attention to her breasts. I was sure she'd been mauled a lot, but I didn't think she'd ever been made love to. It was time to bring 4,000 years of experience to bear on this sixteen-year-old slut. When I continued down across her belly and between her legs, she gasped.

"Oh, Bob! That's so nasty. What are you doing? I smell! You'll have me all messy down there. What about hair? Oh, my god! Oh, Bob, no boy's ever... Something's happening to me. I'm going to... Oh, sweet angels!" There was no question in my mind that Bernice experienced an orgasm, and if I were to believe her responses, it might have been her first one ever.

She lay there with her eyes glazed over, staring at the ceiling, and trying to catch her breath.

"You okay?" I asked as I gently petted her. I hadn't moved from between her legs and I kept taking occasional swipes up her slit with my tongue. Yes, she did get messy. Her fluids were thick and creamy.

"What did you do to me? It was like I blacked out for a minute because all my senses went into overload."

"I think I just gave you an orgasm," I said. I took another lick and she shuddered with aftershocks.

"You mean, like come? Like boys do? Did I squirt stuff?" she asked in alarm.

"Not exactly. Some girls do squirt, but it's rare. But otherwise, that feeling is a lot like a boy has when he comes."

"I don't believe you. I've never had a boy pass out when he comes."

"Practice. Boys practice coming from the time they can get an erection until the day they die. You just haven't had enough practice yet."

"Can... you do it again?"

"Oh, yes, Bernie. I was just waiting for an invitation," I said as I resumed lapping with intent and curled my tongue up inside her hole. She skyrocketed into oblivion again and this time I worked my way up and slid into her.

"You're in me! It doesn't hurt! And I'm going to... Do me, Bob. Do me again!"

I did her again and again. And finally, I let loose and poured what I'd been saving for the past hour into her waiting pussy. She came again and passed out completely. I glanced at the clock and saw that it was nearly ten and I needed to get her home. I didn't think she should go home smelling so well-fucked. I went to the bathroom to see what I had available to clean her up. I went to the satchel and stuck my arm in. I was handed a tray with a bowl of warm water, wet and dry cloths, powder, and deodorant. When did my girls learn about that?

I went about bathing and drying Bernice as she lay on the bed, watching me and not attempting to escape, even when I washed all the way back along her butt crack.

"I think I'll strangle my mother," she said at last. I helped her pull her clothes together. "She said good girls didn't enjoy sex, they just put up with it in order to get a husband. She told me it always hurt. She lied to me and I've been making her lies come true every time a guy fucked me."

"Sex is intended to be enjoyed by everyone. It's never just an obligation," I said.

"No offense, but I don't think I should date you again," she finally said as we drove to her house in my T-Bird. "Not that I wouldn't like it. I know I would. But I know that you'll find someone who isn't just an easy lay to settle down with eventually, and if I see you again, I'll just be heart-broken when it happens."

"Bernice, I really like you a lot," I started.

"But you wouldn't have dated me if the guys didn't suggest me. Recommendations. Go fuck Bernice, then you can find a real girl. Maybe they didn't say that all out loud, but you got the message. But that's the old Bernice. I know what I'm looking for now and I won't settle for less. Besides, when the other girls at school hear my report, you'll have them swarming all over you."

"Your report?" I wasn't sure I wanted to be talked about in the girls' locker room.

"Yeah. Good old Bernice will fuck the new guy and tell us if he's worth wasting our time on. It happens every time. Don't worry, Bob. I'll give you a good report. Not as good as it was. No one would believe me. But you'll have no problem getting dates."

I kissed her gently at the door and said goodnight. Then I drove home thinking about what she'd said.

>-- ◄◆► --<

That was kind of how it went growing up in the fifties. In the fifties, I never lacked for a date on Saturday night. Not all dates included sex. There was an unspoken rule about good girls, and even if they thought they would get a good sex experience, they insisted that the first date would include a little light kissing, the second could include petting, and the third—if it went that far—was the earliest that they'd sleep with a guy.

Of course, most also refused to believe that I was sterile, so I had to wear a rubber. But word spread that I was a great date and those that reached the magic number often went several beyond that. I encouraged the girls to not confuse an orgasm with love, and to consider our time together as a learning and testing time, not a lifelong commitment.

There was one who became very attached to me, and I had to sit down and explain the facts of life to her. She was a smart girl named Virginia and had taken a lot of teasing in school about how long she was going to stay virgin. I was surprised to find, after five dates, that she had been a virgin until the night I made love to her.

We'd continued to date every weekend for the next month when I was beginning to feel a little pressure. She'd uttered the L-word once when we were making love and I didn't want it to turn to the P-word.

For having been a virgin, Virginia was very smart and quite lovely. Undressing her for the first time was a breathtaking experience. Her breasts were slightly more than a handful—and I have large hands. Her flaxen hair hung straight to her waist. Her hips were wide and her mound was covered in a mist of fine yellow hair. She was much like the flower girls of the next decade.

When we stretched out to make love, she pushed me to my back and mounted my shaft as I held her breasts in my hands and guided her up and down. There was a slight gasp of pain when I broke through her maidenhead, but there was no question that she was well-lubricated and ready for my invasion. She stared intently into my eyes and rose to her first climax on my shaft before relaxing forward and rolling us over so I was on top.

It was the first time I'd missed a girl's curfew.

>-- ◄◆► --‹

"Bob, I'm not a dummy," she said.

"Of course not," I answered. She hushed me and looked me in the eye.

"We've been together for almost three months. Lovers for more than a month. We hang out together and I've visited where you live when you weren't there. Yes, I was spying on you. I wanted to meet the girls who worked in the shop and I listened to them as they spoke about what a great lover and master you were to them. No, I won't tell you who said what. But I hung out there nearly all of the day I cut school a week ago. The thing is, I know you aren't what you appear to be."

"What else would I be?" I asked.

"Species unknown. Probably alien. Carrying out an experiment on earth, seducing high school girls, maybe taking samples from us for your study. I know you've slept with at least fifteen girls in our school since you got here two years ago. I probably missed some. You're a great lover and every one of those girls speaks highly of you. There's never been a bad breakup. That in itself says you're an alien."

"You've found me out," I laughed. "On my planet it is a disgrace to part with a lover on bad terms."

She looked at me over her glasses and frowned.

"Bob, I want to go with you. I know enough to realize I won't be your only lover. The girls in the shop were very... um... friendly with each other, so I suppose there's a lot of free love wherever it is you're from. But the bottom line is that I want to go with you. One way or another, I want to be part of your world."

Well, that got us into a pretty heavy discussion. It took a lot of planning on our part and I included Nimia and Josie in the planning stages. It wouldn't do for Virginia to simply disappear. We were too well-known a couple and suspicion would land on me right away. We made our plans and when we graduated from high school, Virginia moved into the infinity room. We'd long since broken up in the school's eyes, so the amount of time she spent with me had gone unnoticed. She kept a presence as a student at UC Berkley, a liberal hotbed even in 1959-63. She went to classes, but drove my T-Bird to and from the University. I 'sold' it to her and it was registered in her name. By 1964, she was a force in the free speech movement and civil rights protests.

Then in 1965, she sold the T-Bird (might have been to someone I know) and went to Selma, Alabama to join the Civil Rights March on Montgomery. And that's where she disappeared. To the world. To me, she was back home in the infinity room and welcoming me into her arms whenever she could. During my high school years and a few that followed, she was the only new resident of the infinity room. Of course, during the mid-sixties and later, we began picking up the stray flower children who simply couldn't cope with having turned on, tuned in, and dropped out. Virginia was significant in getting them settled and recovered.

>-- ◄◆► --‹

My point was—there was a point—that the girls in the competition fed off each other like the girls in high school. They compared notes and they arrived at conclusions that defied logic.

By the time of the sixth challenge, they were all sleeping with me on a regular basis. I wondered why I'd never held auditions for the infinity room before.

They all had an inkling that there was a lot going on behind the scenes that they didn't know about, but that being eliminated might not be as big a deal as they were afraid it was. I don't know how they arrived at that conclusion, but it was out there. Probably pillow talk with one or more of the people from Areola. Nonetheless, no one wanted to lose a competition.

I gave Suhani immunity from the sixth elimination.

"This will test your ability to work with each other, to contribute to the plan and execution of the exercise, and to support each other in achieving your goals," I said. "Suhani is going to participate, but she will be separate from the group. She's going to be lost in the mountains."

They all gasped and Suhani's eyes got big when it dawned on her that she'd truly be alone.

"It will be your task as a group to find and rescue her. In some of the places where you will be going, it will be almost impossible to send a camera person, let alone a crew. You will be equipped with body cameras, and there will be drones tracking your progress. An independent team of survival and rescue experts will be monitoring you and evaluating each member's performance. I expect you all to excel in this exercise and it would be impossible for anyone in the family to judge it. The person with the lowest evaluation by this independent panel will be eliminated."

53
Loss

WELL, THE CHALLENGE SUCKED. It was rugged and danger-ous. And surprising. The evaluation that came back was entirely due to lack of life experience and decision-making. Artemisia was eliminated. We were all devastated. She'd acted bravely and put herself at risk so the others could succeed in the rescue, but as a result, she didn't complete the mission. The independent judges ruled this as a loss since the others all reached Suhani and rescued her.

It might have been the saddest going away party we'd had.

I waited in my study for Artemisia and consulted with my wives and possessions. I was to do whatever was necessary to convince her to come to Areola.

I was seated at my desk when she came in, dragging her suitcase behind her. Her jaw was set and I could tell she was only barely holding it together.

"Through there?" she asked, pointing at the door.

"Artie, wait. There's another option," I said before she could reach the door. She stopped and turned to me.

"Don't fuck with me, Bob. I wanted this more than anything in the world. I don't want to leave them. You. Just, don't fuck with me." The dam was about to break.

"You've heard the rumors, Artie. Do you believe them?" I asked. I stood up and came around the desk where I could face her.

"That you'll get us all back? How can you?" she said. "You're broadcasting this on television. You can't just go around making exceptions."

"Yes, I can," I said. "Do you know what I am, Artemisia?"

"You mean a rich playboy?"

"No. I mean did you know I'm a demon?"

"Wait. What? Damn it, Bob! I told you not to fuck with me!" She turned toward the door again and I made a full transformation.

"Artemisia, look at me," I bellowed. The force of my voice stopped her and she turned slowly around. When she turned and saw me as I finished my transformation, bursting the seams of my clothes so they hung in rags, she passed out. I transformed back and picked her up to cuddle in my big easy chair. Unfortunately, I was still naked, but she didn't seem to mind that as she regained consciousness.

"What was that?" she whispered.

"That was me in my natural form. Eventually, we'll expose that to the world, but we can't do it until the ship is ready and we can actually board it and get out of here," I said. "I'm telling you all this—showing you—so that you'll believe that I can and I want to keep you. Forever, Artemisia. Not for the length of the show, but to join with me and my world for all time."

"How can you do that?"

"A long time ago—about 4,000 years—I accidentally created a new world."

"Four thousand years?"

"Approximately. I'm bad with dates. I've been around a long time. It was a couple of millennia before Caesar. But the point is that there are now over three million people in Areola."

"You named your planet 'Titty World?' That is so Bob!" she laughed. At least she was loosening up.

"You know me. Anyway, this whole show and contest and work with the Space Pioneer group is so I can take my world someplace where it will be safe. There is no place on earth where we could remain hidden and secure forever," I said.

"So, you want to take your world, wherever it is, to Mars so you can remain undiscovered forever."

"Beyond," I said. "At the rate humanity is progressing, Mars will not be safe for us for long."

"Us? I'm sure we could stay hidden for a hundred years or more there," she said.

"There is an interesting phenomenon that occurs in Areola. When I bring someone from the natural world into my world, they stop aging. People who are born in the infinity room—that's what I used to call Areola—age fairly normally. Maybe a little slower than the natural world. We've never really done a study. My first wife is nearly as old as I am. Maybe technically a little older. She still looks and feels twenty."

"You'll take me to this Areola?"

"Honey, you showed the very best of the characteristics I am looking for in people I bring to Areola. I couldn't have disagreed with the judges' decision more. You were brave, self-sacrificing, loving, and smart. And not only that, we all love you. I love you."

"Will the others be coming, too?" she asked.

"Unless they choose to leave. I won't force anyone. Rhonda and Rin chose to stay in this world and leave us. Linda, Eun-ha, and Wendy are all waiting in Areola for us to join them. And you'll like it there. Believe me, I've done the best I could to create a paradise and my wives and concubines keep it running that way."

"Will I be one of those?"

"Your decision, sweetheart. I hope you'll be one of my concubines forever."

"Take me there, Bob. Let's go. Take me there and when we get there, strip me bare and fuck me so I'll know it's all real."

"See my satchel over there by the door? Areola is in it."

"Bob!" she whined. "Quit teasing."

"I'm serious. The infinity room is somehow inside that little space and I'm going to open a portal to it right now."

"Open sesame," Artemisia said. She was shocked when the satchel started to glow and the portal sprang into existence. "Shit!"

"Come on, honey. Let's go to Areola."

I took her hand and we crossed the threshold. We were met by Josie and Ali with a small company of warriors who would guard the portal while I was inside. We walked straight into the main square where the pool reflected both the temple and the palace. Several of my concubines were lying naked near it or playing in it. Linda, Eun-ha, and Wendy rushed to Artemisia and hugged her.

"How did you get Bob to come with you? We had to make a big decision and come alone. It was a little scary," Eun-ha said.

"I just asked him to take me here. Wow! Is this all real?"

"It's real and it goes on forever!" Linda said. "And you can get out of those clothes. I haven't worn anything since I took my clothes off in Bob's study. I never plan to."

"I have another task while I'm here," I said. I waited until Artie's clothes were lying in a pile at her feet. Oh, what a delectable bit. "Come, concubine. I want to make love to you."

"Yes!" she said, jumping into my arms. I carried her to the big bed in my room and gave her the full loving treatment. I kissed her entire body. I lapped the honey from between her legs and curled my tongue deep in her vagina. Then I crawled between her legs and while we stared into each other's eyes, I slid deep within her, holding her with my gaze as I gradually worked up speed of thrusting into her. As we reached our climax together, I felt her utter devotion to me grow. This might be another like Zhi.

>--- ◀◆▶ ---<

Even when one has the best benefits of tantric sex at one's disposal, there are times when a couple just wants to fuck. I'd experienced it with all my wives, possessions, and concubines.

Back before his conquest of Gaul and the Britons, Caesar arranged for me to marry Cordelia, a distant cousin. It was a marriage of convenience and an alliance. I asked her point blank if this was what she wanted and her answer was to look at me in consternation and say, "Of course! How could I not want to help Caesar make an alliance he deems important. Take me to your bed and make me your wife."

I thought she was incredibly willing to have her body traded for an alliance, but she proved to be an avid lover.

Religiously repressed people in the After Caesar centuries conveniently forgot how to give women pleasure and they forgot they could receive pleasure. Unlike Bernice and Virginia and nearly every other girl I dated in the fifties and sixties, Cordelia needed no instruction on how to receive pleasure from sex. If I was not tickling the right spot, she made sure I either found it or she took over and found it herself. And she was aggressive in bed.

"Bob, enough with your soft and gentle lovemaking. That's fine sometimes, but right now I just want to fuck. Make me come, Bob. Push that big old dick up my quim and let me have it!"

Yes, well, maybe those weren't the exact words. I never actually learned Latin, but when people spoke to me, I understood what they said and when I spoke back, I planted the idea straight into their brains. Even in Latin there was talking dirty.

I'm sorry to say that Cordelia despised the sea. She absolutely would not board my ship. The closest she would come would be to accompany me to the dock and fuck me there before I boarded to leave. And she would meet me there when I returned to port, no matter how long I'd been gone, and demand to be fucked on the spot.

She passed away about the time Caesar grabbed me to take him to Egypt. What a fuck!

>-- ◄◆► --<

After Artemisia and I made love, we fucked. Several times. Then I had to return to the natural world and take up the role of Bob the Billionaire Spaceman.

We headed back to the mansion in Los Angeles for what I told people would be the final week of filming for the show. We needed a pick-me-up after the decidedly depressing elimination of Artemisia. This whole television thing couldn't end too soon to satisfy me. It was getting to be exhausting.

"This week will be our last challenge," I said. "And you are going to be the judges this time. The task is to do everything together. And I mean everything. I'm having you all move into the master suite with me. You know how big the bath is in that room. So, if one person needs the bathroom, you all go in. When you shower, you all shower. When you sleep, you all crawl in bed to sleep. And it won't just be living assignments. You're going shopping together. You'll go to an amusement park together. To a concert and whatever else you decide together that you'd like to do. Think of this as your last week on earth. What do you want to do? Just do it together. At the end of the week, you'll decide which of you is eliminated."

There was an immediate whispered conversation and Deedee was pushed forward as the spokesperson.

"We'll take the challenge on one condition, Bob," she said. "Our future lies with you and your family. You all have to join us together. You, Penelope, Peninnah, Liz, Dezi, and Laine. Whatever we do, you do it with us."

I looked at the family. They'd mostly been used to slipping into the infinity room at night. This meant they'd all be here for a week—day and night—with the women of the challenge. This would tax all of us.

>-- ◄◆► --<

I had a tendency to treat the show much the way I would have treated a play on the Greek stage. I was supposed to be the leading actor and spend my time strutting around on the stage expounding great speeches of famous personages, while the girls acted as my chorus, commenting on what was happening, giving dire warnings, and praising my cleverness.

It didn't work like that. My crew had ideas of their own. Even Liz was hard-put to keep up with some of the ideas of the liberated ladies who had committed to a life that would leave earth behind—and Liz had practically founded the liberation movement. Among those ideas they brought was the idea of including the family in the last challenge. That had surprised me and I wasn't sure how to handle it, but my wives comforted me and said it would be okay. I suddenly felt that perhaps the odds of five women in the family and seven in the competition vs. little old me were somehow stacked.

Into the breach rides Doug!

I'd been seeing both Doug and Avril with our group more and more of the time. Avril, of course, was carting a camera, but she was the only camerawoman we had who was not from Areola. I'd planned to invite her, but this whole thing with Doug could put a monkey wrench in the works. And the girls had all decided that the camera crew was as integral to our last week of production as the flight crew and the family. They wouldn't get a break from us either. Everyone was given one day to be apart from everyone else and do whatever they wanted to do before the last challenge. I took the opportunity to have a chat with Doug.

"Doug, I think this whole thing might be a little out of control. How are we going to wrap up the series and get out of here?" I asked as we sat in my study with a glass of wine. I thought I might drink quite a lot of wine this week. I planned to spend the next few hours in Areola with my wives and possessions.

"Trust me, Bob. This is great. The women rebelled! What television! Our ratings are going to skyrocket. First, no one is going to believe we are going into outer space to found a colony on Mars. I mean, really. How could we possibly fit all these people onto that little ship? Like, it's not much bigger than your bedroom, right? And we're all going to be sleeping there, doing our camera work, acting out our parts. We'll be clean away before anyone is the wiser."

"Doug, I'm hearing a lot of 'we,' and 'us,' and 'our' in what you're saying."

"Bob, Bob, Bob. Ya gotta take me with you, man. And Avril. Please don't leave us here. Stow us with the passengers in your secret transporter and bring us out as a big surprise. Don't leave us here after all this!" He was impassioned in his plea and I thought quite genuine. I'd had to tell him about my transporter since he would be escorting any women who decided not to go with us and had to know what was happening when no woman emerged to be taken away. Besides, I liked the guy. I didn't agree right on the spot, but I'd already made the leap in my head.

Then there was Paul.

I really wasn't sure when he arrived, but somewhere between a training session and a shopping trip that week, he'd become part of our group and we were all together. I was amazed that with twenty of us living together with no privacy, we managed to get along and not get upset when someone had to stop in the middle of lunch to use the bathroom and we all had to troop up there, too.

Liz really showed her abilities. She set the rules and we all abided by them. The week went by without a single person ever being separated from the others.

It was time to launch the miniseries. It would be the last official function of the group before the girls voted for the final elimination.

>-- ◄◆► --<

"We are here on the flight deck of Space Pioneer 1," an actor we'd hired as narrator said. "In just a few short weeks, this ship will carry our first dozen colonists on their trip to Mars. Crews are working around the clock to make sure this little craft will safely carry our Captain Bob and his family and crew into a new life as extraterrestrials. But how will Captain Bob choose the crew for this historic flight? This special production from the Hearthstone Celebration Entertainment Network will answer those questions. Stay tuned for Episode One of *To Boldly Go*."

"This broadcast is rated TVMA and is recommended for mature audiences only. Nudity, sex, intense emotional situations, and possible violence."

We settled in to watch the episode.

>-- ◄◆► --<

"I can't believe you fucked him in the audition! Were you faking it?" Conversation was fast and furious after we'd watched the first episode. I couldn't keep track of who was saying what.

"Oh no. Once that prick invaded my pussy, I was all in. Well, he was all in, but I knew I was coming. I mean..."

"We all know what you mean now!"

"I can't believe those voices! And keeping it up through the whole scene. Those guys in India were hilarious! I miss Wendy."

"I miss Rin. I hope she's doing okay."

"All the girls. I didn't want to lose one of them!"

"Me either," I said. "The auditions were fun. Losing half the girls wasn't."

"We need to get Artemisia back. There's no reason those bastards should have eliminated her."

"Those early auditions were terrible! Did you intentionally go out and pick girls who were that bad? I can't imagine one of them actually boarding a space ship."

"We had a lot to learn," Liz said. "And it wasn't all about flying the ship."

"Oh, look. They're back with an interview of our lord and master."

The girls all giggled as we listened to the professional narrator/interviewer try to grill me. It had been recorded weeks ago.

>-- ◄◆► --<

"Tell me, Bob. What makes you the best choice to start man's first colony on Mars?"

"Oh, I'm sure I'm not the best choice."

"Then why are you going to choose a bevy of sexy ladies to take with you and leave earth? Why not a great scientist or explorer?"

"Well, I'll tell you. None of them could afford it. I could. Besides, this is an experimental trip to a hostile environment. Do we really want to risk losing one of our great scientists on this journey? They should stay safe while they analyze data and use us to collect samples for them. We'll need them for the future of earth."

"So, you chose beautiful women?"

"I want beautiful ladies around me that I can breed and make founders of a whole colony. I'm no dummy. Really, who would you choose? Our elimination trials helped us isolate the best, strongest, and smartest of the contestants to ensure our colony will be successful. But also, if the whole thing goes south and we're lost in space for all eternity, who's really going to care? You'll watch re-runs, and bitch and moan about the show being canceled. All my money will continue to be used to advance the science of space exploration, and there will be no lack of excited scientists and explorers volunteering for the next mission."

"But you are, according to your own statement, a private corporation. Shouldn't such a big venture belong to the people? Is the government really not involved at all?"

"I can honestly say I have had no official conversation with any representative of this or any other government related to space exploration," I said. "But let me ask you: Are you trying to tell me that a man shouldn't be allowed to spend his money in any way he wants to? It's not like I'm spending my money to get more money. I'm not developing drugs to sell at hundreds of times their development costs. I'm not making loans to people who can never afford to pay them back and will be indebted to me for the rest of their lives. I'm not using my money to develop new weapons to deploy against unknown enemies that will destroy parts of the earth. You may say that my investment in space exploration is not philanthropic, but unlike most investments people make with their money, it's basically benign."

"We've seen the supposed inside of your spaceship and it is tight quarters. Will you all be able to survive a three-month voyage strapped in those little seats?"

"There will be regular exercise routines for all of us and there are spaces in the ship that you were not shown that give us some options regarding privacy."

"Where will you launch from?"

"That location is and will remain undisclosed. We can't risk security or interference. I'm sure there are people who will want to protest, so we'll

put our corporate address at the bottom of the screen and you can protest
there all you want. I'm informed we've even put food vendors and public
restrooms in front of the corporate building to make it safer for protesters.
For your safety and ours, however, we won't allow you near the launch site."

"Are you telling us that not even the United States Government knows where you'll be launching from?"

"Oh, please. The US government knows everything. Didn't you get vaccinat-
ed? And you think the government doesn't know exactly where you are sitting right this moment? Uncle Sam is an alternate identity for Santa Claus.
He knows when you are sleeping. He knows when you're awake. He knows
if you've been bad or good..."

**"I think we get the point. We might owe royalties if you sing that on the air. You've certain-
ly given us something to think about. What can we expect in the next episode?"**

"Everyone went through two months of rigorous training and frankly, that
isn't all that interesting. We'll show enough of it to explain how smart these
girls are and how hard they studied to make themselves part of the crew. But
in the last part of the next episode, we'll show our first elimination round.
You won't believe what happens."

**"That next episode will air Friday night, right after a replay of this first episode. It's all
right here on the Hearthstone Celebration Entertainment Network."**

54
WE REFUSE

"**I CAN'T BELIEVE** you are all still here," I said, looking around at the crew, lying with each other in the family room as we finished watching the episode on TV. During this last week of the contest, everyone had become more casual about being dressed or not. Even Peninnah was running around in a bra and panties. And a garter and stockings with five-inch stilettos. She also had Karla on her lap and the pilot was wearing considerably less. Liz, of course, had never worn a bra after our first meeting, so she was comfortably lounging topless with Suhani, our software engineer from India. It seemed each of my women had found a favorite among the crew. Deedee was cuddled comfortably in my lap without a stitch on as I absently stroked her lovely full breasts.

I should tell you more about Deedee. There was never a question from the moment of her audition about her ultimately becoming a member of my crew and one of my favored concubines. It had been cemented in my mind just a few nights ago as I was visited in a dream, while still resting in the glow of a most satisfying copulation with the busty blonde.

"I see you are enjoying my little gift to you," the voice said. I saw a subtle transformation come over Deedee and I was looking into the eyes of My Lady Goddess Aphrodite, smiling at me. I thought Deedee looked familiar!

"Goddess, is it you that lies here in my arms?" I asked.

"No, love. I have ascended to Olympus and am no longer among the people of earth except in an occasional erotic dream. But the morsel in your arms has been blessed by me to bring you joy and comfort for all your days."

"Please don't tell me you've put a compulsion on her. You know I can't abide slavery," I said sternly.

"No, lover. No such thing. Even in the modern world there are occasionally people who worship one of the old gods. Dear little Deedee was one of those who held me in high esteem and even occasionally whispered a little prayer to me. Often when she was in the throes of ecstasy. In her prayer, she asked me to show her the one who would make her happy for all her life. I showed her an image of you—with me—on a ship in the sea where we made love day and night."

"As I recall, we only made love after Poseidon's storm washed us ashore," I ventured.

"It made for a better story to have us washed overboard as we cried out our passion. Don't spoil it."

"Yes, My Lady Goddess."

"When Deedee saw the scene, she immediately cried out, 'Him! Him! Goddess make him mine!' I had to explain that it would be a shared ownership, but she was all right with that. So, I gave her my blessing and guided her to your auditions. My gift to you."

"Thank you, My Lady. She is a treasure."

"Make love to me, my handsome demon. While she still dreams of my presence, make love to me."

And so we did. At some point, the dream faded and it was all Deedee and me, but it was blessed with incredible satisfaction.

>--- ◆◆ ---<

When I created the infinity room, I had no idea how it worked. I have little more idea today. The most learned physicists in Areola—which I grant you are not rocket scientists—have no idea. They hold that concepts abandoned centuries ago in the natural world are still operational in Areola. What I know is that once a concept is planted there, it takes root and grows. Like our power grid. Well, that was more than a concept. I adapted the idea of ley lines as being sources of physical power rather than of metaphysical power and let them grow underground. But I moved Pinaruti's magic room into the infinity room. I couldn't move the walls and shelves, but the physical objects I could move seemed to build the walls around them. As Nimia—my most trusted companion in my life—picked up an object to put away, the place for that object appeared.

Growth was slow at first. I brought food supplies into the room so Nimia and Portia could survive there, and those supplies never ran out. It was as if the existence of a container for wheat implied wheat in the container. It was simply always there. Of course, when we scattered wheat on the barren ground, it took root and grew. When we brought cattle into our world, they found rich grasses on which to graze. The existence of an oven, implied heat with which to cook. The oven came with the house. The heat came with the oven. I arrived at the conclusion that the existence of a thing implied the environment it needed to flourish. That implied environment then took shape.

When I cleansed and blessed the priestesses, they needed a temple. Now, like in any given city, people tended to cluster around the area of greatest resources so, in addition to my palace and the libraries, other houses had grown up around the pool. But when the temple was needed, it was as if the land in front of the pool stretched out to make room for the temple. I have to say, the temple is modest, even compared to some of those I've built. But it has everything it needs for fifty-two priestesses to live and worship and make love to The Bob.

I have not visited a vast number of otherworldly realms, but I have been privileged to be summoned to Olympus when Zeus invited me to move there. I noticed that his realm seemed to work much the same as mine. When Zeus needed a table, one appeared where he wanted it. When he wanted food, it was brought. When he wanted his dick sucked, some succubus or other came to suck it.

In Areola, even my bedroom was always the right size for the number of us who wanted to be there. The bed, always comfortable for an orgy or an intimate affair. The sailors had water and fair winds. The hunters had game. The planters had fields and crops.

I sometimes also thought that the existence of a thing created a need for it. For example, the creation of the power grid led to the need for power to run entertainment and communications. I'd always avoided laying out a network of roads, as I thought that might create a need for cars—and, while mine were kept in a secret storage room against some time that I might want to get out and drive—I didn't think rapid transportation would be a great benefit to my world.

The big problem was in how I was going to explain Areola to the final crew and get them all to join me there. When I took Nimia and Portia and the three statues into the infinity room as I fled, I didn't really give them much choice. Get in or leave. Later, Portia, Saris, Celeah and Bileah all chose lives outside the infinity room rather than staying there. I collected—or Nimia collected—a few other women for company in Bathra and it was not long after I left Bathra that I collected Josie. Back in those days, the concept of carrying around an infinite paradise in a satchel was easier for people to accept. It was a big world and anything might be possible.

This twenty-first century world was much smaller and fewer things seemed possible. The very existence of our reality television show was evidence that even our plans to escape the confines of earth were not considered really possible by most of the populace. I wondered—and not for the first time—if I would have had better luck just collecting women directly into Areola and going to Nepal to build my own space ship, ignoring physics, and simply making it what it needed to be.

>-- ◄► --<

"The time has come," I said as we gathered in our pajamas after watching the first episode. I use the term 'pajamas' loosely, which was the way most of the scraps of fabric hung on our cast and crew. I saw various members hanging onto each other more tightly than the clothing clung to them. "I really, really hate this part, so I'm going to put a question to you. There are seven of you left in the competition to become the crew of Space Pioneer 1. We need only six. Does one of you volunteer to be left behind?"

I thought I saw Valerie make a move like she would volunteer, but she was pulled into a clutch by the other contestants. There was a subtle shifting of positions and I realized all seven of the girls were in a tight cluster. Sociologist Deedee, Software engineer Suhani, race-car driver Julie, chef Valerie, pilot Karla, policewoman Lalonda, and doctor Marie. I sighed.

"Well, then we have to do it the hard way. I have seven cards and pens. I'll give each of you one. On it, I want you to write the name of the person you think should be eliminated in this challenge. The decision is yours." I handed the girls the pens and cards and directed them to different parts of the room to write their choice in secret. I motioned to Liz to collect the ballots in a box and bring them to me for counting. I thought she wore a rather self-satisfied smirk and couldn't figure out what she was so pleased with.

She collected the cards in the ballot box and brought the box to me. Then she went to join the seven girls, along with Penelope, Peninnah, Dezi, and Laine. I took the box to my desk and sat down to tally the count. I pulled out ballot after ballot and looked at them, puzzled. I turned each one over and looked up at the girls, family, camerawomen, and the few others who had come for the ceremony.

"Maybe I didn't make myself clear. You were supposed to write the name of the one you'd eliminate on the card. These cards are all blank. We'll have to do it again."

The seven women stood and approached my desk. I admit I felt a little worried.

>-- ◆◆▶ --‹

Back long before my time—in fact, near the beginning of Zeus's reign on Olympus—there were seven sisters, the daughters of Atlas and Pleione. They were said to be among the most beautiful and fearsome in all creation. They represented the mother, the maiden, the queen, the huntress, the sage, the mystic, and the lover. It was never agreed upon which was which and they may have shifted in their roles as women are likely to do.

It happened that a hunter named Orion came upon them as they walked through the Boeotian countryside and decided they should be his harem. They fled and prayed to Zeus to deliver them. After seven years, Zeus heard their prayer and placed them among the stars—the seven sisters, or Pleiades.

I had a feeling the seven sisters had just come to face me.

>-- ◆◆▶ --‹

"We refuse," Deedee said firmly.

"We will not vote to eliminate one of our sisters from the crew," Suhani declared.

"And if you decide to send any one of us away," Julie added, "we all go."

I had expected them to be reluctant, but wasn't prepared for an outright rebellion. This was going to be a hell of a conclusion to the mini-series. I did my best to face them, but to look any one of them in the eyes was to invite the tears to flow. In fact, the tears were flowing from all of us. The five in my family, Doug and Paul, the camerawomen, even Zhi and Josie, who had come for the big reveal, were standing around the seven women facing me.

"And that's your final decision?" I asked as if I were offering a million dollars to the winner.

"We're sorry it puts you in a difficult position, Bob," Valerie said. "But we've already lost six women we loved. You wanted to do more than winnow down the number for the show. You wanted to build a crew that would love each other, work together, defend each other and the family. You just got one more than you planned."

"Then I'm going to give you one more chance," I said. "And it's not what you think."

>-- ◆◆▶ --‹

I motioned everyone to resume their seats. This big reveal was going to shock people, and I wasn't sure we'd leave it all in the final episode. Some things the general public just wasn't ready for. I stepped out from around my desk and started removing what little clothing I was wearing. Deedee had gotten me charged up while we watched the episode and I wasn't down to size yet.

"I've not been quite honest with you all," I said. "I am not quite human."

"He's an alien!" Lalonda gasped. "I knew it!"

"Um… not exactly an alien in terms of being from another planet, but not of this world, nonetheless." I began the transformation to my demon self, trying to go slow so they could get used to each bit as it was revealed, and so the cameras could catch and record it all.

"Horns!"

"Oh, my god! I thought his cock was huge before. I have to have some of that!"

"And look at those hairy legs! I just want to pet him."

That wasn't going quite the way I anticipated. I expected some amount of horror. It was possible the pheromones or whatever I emitted were working overtime. I saw a few hands headed for pussies. Even among my women from Areola.

"I am, in general parlance, a demon. I wanted to show you this so you would know and understand that I'm not just kidding around."

I saw Avril moving in to do a thorough close-up shot, examining me from my horns to my hooves, and every item of interest between. If they showed that on the air, it would certainly raise some comments. I started to transform back. There were a few protests, but I thought it was better to get this underway in a body more people could relate to.

"I have a gateway to another dimension in my possession. In that dimension, lies the world Areola. I want us to all go and live happily in Areola. So, you might ask, why do we bother with the whole matter of space travel? Why don't we just go to this other paradise and skip the space travel? That's a problem. As soon as this episode airs in five weeks, people are going to be all over us trying to get into Areola and capture the gateway. The alternate world is located inside my satchel. Don't ask me how that works. I have no idea. I believe, however, if something happens to the satchel, it will or could destroy Areola. That's why I've spent the last 4,000 years moving around and hiding to protect the gateway and the satchel."

"I get it," Karla said. "So, if we fly off to Mars, you should find a place to hide the satchel that humans wouldn't discover for a thousand years."

"That's pretty much it. By then, maybe I'll have another solution. But here's the thing, ladies. If you enter through the gateway to Areola, the likelihood is that you will never see earth again. So, I'm going to give you one more opportunity to back out. Think about it carefully and we'll make the commitment tomorrow night. Got it?" I asked.

They all nodded and I could see each of the ladies, including Avril, converging on the family and the camerawomen from Areola to question them about the infinity room and how long they'd lived there. I saw wide eyes when my wives and possessions told them their ages.

>— ◆ —<

"I see the sense in making that demonstration to the girls, but we need to put off the whole demon/alternate dimension thing as far as the show is concerned," Doug said. "What you did with the other girls is good. We'll just pass the word that when the big announcement comes, it will be a transporter to your palace in an undisclosed location. Work for you?"

"That works, as far as I'm concerned. You really plan to take this into another full season?" I asked. I was getting just a little tired of the whole TV show dynamic. I think the girls were, too. And I'd already exposed the truth to them.

"It's about the technology, Bob."

"What about the technology?"

"Things take longer than they do. We might not make the flight date."

"We've already started airing the series!"

"Difference between real reality and reality TV. We could be as much as a year away from an effective launch date. In that length of time, the whole world could change. We're going to need another season of the competition. Plus, we'll have to up the stakes. The idea of 'once off the show, you're gone,' is blown with this episode. In fact, we have the first transporter to your secret palace in the second episode next Friday," Doug said. "We can do some planning before then, but it will be tense. We'll have to come out with the second season in about three or four months."

"Fuck. I really thought we were on our way."

"Don't let on to the girls about that until we're safely away in the secret palace. They might have something to say about it that we don't want heard."

"Okay. I'll leave the prep up to you."

>-- <◆> --<

I was never that good at deception. I won't say I've never lied. I mean, theatre is just one big lie that people buy into for a couple of hours and then go back to their mundane lives. It's all escapist entertainment.

There was one time—this was back in Italy before I met Esmira—when we had some special entertainment that was all escapist. I'd been working on a moderately-sized church and the work had been extremely hard because the building location was on a steep slope. Hauling the stone from the quarry to the building site was backbreaking labor, even when I subtly lightened the weight of the stone. It couldn't become too light or it would raise suspicion, but I had sympathy for the mules—both animal and human.

The church was finished and a bishop or some mucky-muck from the church was coming to town to consecrate it, a ceremony that would be followed by forty days of fasting and no meat in remembrance of some fast that took place back in Issa's time. Everyone was tired and bemoaning the restrictions to come as we cleaned and tidied the building before the big ceremony. That was when one of the laborers in the church found the scepter and vestments the bishop would use.

"Look at me! I'm his lordship the fucking bishop and I command you all to come and kiss the ring on my dick," the fool called out. Well, the little act soon got out of hand when another fellow found the wine intended for consecration during the service. What they ever thought they would need a full cask of wine for when they only blessed a cup at a time, was a mystery, but the crew soon made a significant dent in the amount to be made holy.

We had quite the party, with a couple of foremen designated to be choirboys and getting fucked in the ass by the pretend priests. Everyone had donned hastily improvised masks so no one knew who the guilty parties were. But no one liked the foremen anyway. Food began arriving at the church as wives and sisters got word of the revels. They all brought meat since none would be allowed for the next forty days and no one wanted their stores to spoil. Of course, there were a number of women who pretended to be other men's wives. It seemed there was a common consent that nothing that happened at this holy party counted and would not be remembered the next day.

A couple of favorite Bible stories were acted out, including Daniel in the fiery furnace, which almost got a fire out of control in the sanctuary. I didn't have the heart to tell them they had the story all wrong. In all, though the acting sucked and the main purpose was drunkenness, it was a moment of escape as Meshack, Shadrack, and Abednego were played out to be the bishop and two priests cast into the fires. Sometime late in the night, people stumbled home and I looked at the detritus of food and ashes in the church. I knew it wouldn't do to have the bishop see this, so I called out a couple dozen of my harem and together we scrubbed the church clean and made sure the bishop's vestments were all neat and tidy.

The next day, of course, life went back to normal, which meant misery and deprivation, but for a night, there had been an escape from life as they knew it.

Where did this start? Oh, yes. Deception. I was going to lie to the girls. Had been lying, apparently. There was no ship ready for us to board and take off in.

>-- ◄◆► --〈

"I've not been completely honest with you all. I have a bit of technology that I've been saving for this very moment. I have a transporter. It has a terminus at a secret location where I have, not only a palace, but a whole community of people I intend to take with me on our trip to Mars. Of course, the ship will only hold so many, so I'll be taking a transporter terminus with us and as soon as we arrive and are set up, I'll be transporting the entire colony to us," I said.

The girls oohed and ahhed appropriately as if this was all news to them.

"Now, you must make your decision. We have to wait for the ship to be ready, which will be after the mini-series has aired." I didn't say how long after. "So, today is your chance to bug out. If you don't really want to say goodbye to earth, there's the door. Beside it is the transporter to my palace. Family, please demonstrate. We'll see you on the other side."

My wives and possessions and concubines all filed through the portal and disappeared. All that was left was cast and crew.

"Deedee. What will it be? The wide world you've known all your life? Or the transporter to a colony that will one day soon move to outer space and never come back to earth? It's your choice."

She went around the room kissing all the girls, the camerawomen and finally me. Then she faced the portal.

"To infinity and beyond!" she announced and walked through.

>-- ◄◆► --〈

One by one as I called them, the girls stood, kissed those remaining and gave a toast before walking through the portal.

"One small step for woman!"

"We do not take a trip. A trip takes us."

"We only live once, but if we do it right, once is enough."

"Don't die with dreams in your pocket!"

"A journey of a thousand years, begins with a single step."

It would make good TV.

"Julie, I'm afraid that leaves you." The gateway began to fade.

"No! Don't leave me, Bob. I'll do anything for you. Please don't leave me behind!"

"What about Paul?" I asked. The physics genius stepped forward. Julie was openly crying.

"Whatever you say," she whimpered. She took Paul's hand and kissed him. "I'm sorry, lover."

"How could you make any other choice?" he said softly.

"Oh, for Pete's sake, you two. Would you just decide which door the two of you are using and go?" I said, laughing.

They both looked at me and then at each other. They didn't even bother kissing the rest of us. They held hands and rushed through the still-open gateway, shouting, "To boldly go!"

I motioned our camerawomen and techs through until only Doug and Avril were left in the room with me. I closed the gateway and shouldered my bag.

"Bob, are you really leaving us?"

"I need you out here, Doug. We're going to have to switch identities for a while."

"What?"

"I need you to be me and go to Japan to the penthouse. Once you get there, you can become Doug again and join me. I'll let you know where. In the meantime, I'm going to masquerade as you so no one follows me as I get Areola to a safe place for a while. We'll decide what comes next after the last episode airs."

"Got it. Um... How do I become you?"

"It's a pretty easy spell. Think of it as switching bodies. See? All done."

Doug looked at me and then rushed to a mirror to look at himself. He looked like I had just moments before. He came back to Avril and me. She'd caught the whole transformation on video.

"I hope you don't mind, but I'm going to inspect this body thoroughly while you're wearing it, babe." She kissed Doug, who looked like me. I waved to them and they headed to the waiting limo. I went around the house and locked all the doors.

Then I went to the garage and fired up my '55 T-Bird, brought out of storage from the infinity room, complete with Virginia in the passenger seat. No one even noticed us leave.

END PART X
END OF VOLUME 2

Bob's Memoir

4,000 Years as a Free Demon

Vol. 3: Current Era (mostly)

Prologue

HI! I'M BOB. I'll be your uncle tonight.

No, just kidding. I'm your friendly neighborhood 4,000-year-old demon. This is the third volume of my memoirs and it will be filled with miscellaneous stuff from the past 4,000 years of my life, as I remember things while trying to sort out what is happening today. It's all very confusing when you have that much trivia floating around in your head.

For example, I was just reminded of the time I saw Roman numerals invented. It was... A story for later. I really need to learn to stick to the one I'm telling now.

I called the first two volumes of my memoirs "Before Caesar" (BC) and "After Caesar" (AC) because I thought Caesar represented the pivotal point that divided my ancient past from my modern past. It was the time that I moved away from the Mediterranean as my base of operations and started East. So, what should I call this third volume? If I have my way, it will be called "Escape from Planet of the Humans." I doubt my editors will let me get away with that one. And if they let it pass, the censors at the Brazilian Forest book selling giant would ban it. Ah well. I'll call this the 'Current Era,' which means roughly 2020+.

You don't need to read the first two volumes of my memoirs if you understand a few fundamental things that I'll go about describing now. However, as an author who considers each of his words sacred, I'll be highly offended if you don't read my magnificent adventures in the other two volumes. Now or later.

First, some 4,000 years ago, give or take a couple of centuries, when I was being chased from Knossos on Crete, I worked a spell on an old leather satchel to create room inside it for whatever I wanted to put there. At the time, I was thinking of things like Pinaruti's scrolls of magic, ingredients that he kept in his magic room, and wine. But in the rush to leave, I stuffed everything I could grab into the bag, including the furniture, the food, my wives, and anything else that wasn't nailed down.

Over the ages, we discovered the infinity room, as I called it then—now called Areola—expanded to accommodate whatever I put in there. And the things I put in it brought the memory of their surroundings, so that when I put sheep in the room, lush pastures grew. When I planted crops, rain fell. And when I brought in people they seemed to live forever—young and healthy. Areola in the Current Era (CE) has a population of some three and a half million. It has its own eco-structure and physics, seemingly unrelated to that of Earth. And it exists conveniently in an old leather satchel that I have worked countless spells on to enhance its durability and invisibility. More about that later.

Among the people in Areola are my five wives and five possessions. The wives are not the only wives I have had over the past 4,000 years. I have married many times, but these are the only ones who have taken up residence in the infinity room. The rest have lived out normal lives and I stayed with them and cradled them in my arms as they passed from the natural world. I have often wept because I loved each and every one of them.

My wives in Areola start with Nimia—with me since Knossos, not long after I was first summoned. Then there's Penelope—formerly Odysseus' wife, but I had been masquerading as the fabled hero for years (a story you can read about in volume one). I met and married Lakshmi, the third of my infinity wives, in India about two or three centuries AC. Esmeralda became my wife just before I sailed with Columbus. She is the great granddaughter of my one-time wife Esmira, who succeeded in locking me in the infinity room for seventy years before Esmeralda set me free. And finally, there is Peninnah, my wife of the Current Era, who sort of came with my inheritance of 500 billion dollars.

Occasionally—not as often as you might suspect—a lover asks or commands me to possess her. Those words are like a compulsion within me. I think I could resist, but I have no desire to. Once she says "Possess me!" I merge myself completely into her mind, body, and soul. I have acquired five possessions in the past 4,000 years. The first was Josephet, or Josie. She was the unwanted daughter of a desert sheikh—a girl I rescued from a well. Back when I was serving in Nebuchadnezzar's court in Babylon, he made a gift of the lovely Persian, Pari. I asked her if she was a willing partner because I will have no slaves. She responded with those wonderful words. "Yes. Possess me."

Let me see. After my voyage with Columbus, I spent a good bit of time wandering the southern Americas, collecting Kukulkàn's people with his priestess, Maya. She happily became my possession at the urging of her god and goddess. And Liz is my twentieth century possession. She was a bra-burning feminist from San Francisco in the 1960s. She has a better grasp of the modern world than all except Peninnah, so is often at my side when I'm dealing with movie scripts and television producers.

I said five possessions and that is only four. Princess Agora is the only person I have ever possessed who didn't specifically ask for it. I found her on an island in the South Pacific and we fell in love. She came with me when I sailed from the island, but was soon overwhelmed by the sense of vastness of the world. She had thought her island was the entire universe. I possessed her to save her from a near vegetative state brought on by acute agoraphobia. I offered to free her again later, but she would have none of it and now seldom leaves my palace in Areola.

There are others who are extremely important and will recur as I tell my story. The first is Fa Zhi. We met in China, sometime around a thousand years AC. She became so devoted to me that it nears worship. She is often my bodyguard and protector and has taken it upon herself to make sure everyone in Areola is trained in the martial arts.

Devotion that approaches adoration is the province of Zhi. Complete worship is the exclusive province of the fifty-two priestesses of Bob. These are all young women I rescued in my days hunting pirates in the Pacific between the Americas and Asia. They had all been captured, enslaved, and abused by various pirates, whom I gleefully destroyed. The girls were in truly bad shape when I brought them to Areola, so I made up a ritual to purify them in the pool. From that moment, they have worshiped The Bob in his temple. They allow no man to come near them, including me when I am in human guise. They worship me only as the horned and goat-legged demon. They also happen to be the most highly skilled of all the martial artists Zhi has trained. They have become a kind of ninja corps and have been called upon over the years to rescue one of our number or to free women and children (mostly) from traffickers around the world. I foresee great things for them before we leave Earth.

Which brings me to the final category of people I will mention by name. I bought a space exploration company and my intent is to get in a rocket ship and just keep going into outer space so I can safely crawl into the satchel and spend eternity in Areola. In order to get things off the ground, so to speak, my advisor Doug developed the concept of a reality television show to select a crew of beautiful women for my ship. He said no one would believe we were really blasting off and the TV show would keep suspicions off us in the name of entertainment.

We selected a crew during the mini-series as a competition. There were complications and I didn't want to lose any of the eliminated contestants. I started taking the 'losers' to Areola if they wanted to continue on the journey with me. All but two elected to do so. When we were down to just seven contestants, I faced a rebellion and they refused to eliminate anyone else from their number and threatened to all walk out if I sent any of them away. Quite the climax to the mini-series. I brought them all to Areola.

The eleven women of my 'crew' are Deedee—a 23-year-old sociologist, selected for me by the goddess Aphrodite; Artemisia—an 18-year-old artist whose devotion approaches that of Zhi; Wendy—a 28-year-old journalist and master mimic of voices; Eun-ha—a 23-year-old Korean mathematician; Suhani—a 29-year-old Indian software engineer; Julie—a 22-year-old Formula one racecar driver; Valerie—a 30-year-old former chef to the Queen of England; Karla—a 31-year-old commercial pilot; Lalonda—a 31-year-old black former policewoman and martial arts expert; Marie—a 33-year-old Mexican doctor with an incredible sense of humor; and Linda—a 27-year-old school teacher. I give you all their ages because once they entered Areola, that is the age they stayed at, no matter how long this story goes on.

I brought a couple of others along from the crew of the show as well. A young physicist named Paul became quite attached to Julie and went to Areola with her. Doug is my friend and producer. I could scarcely leave him behind, though he has to function in the natural world as well as Areola, while we start production of the second season of *To Boldly*

Go. We had to launch a second season to compensate for the delays in getting my spaceship ready to blast off. I'll explain that more as we come to it. And Doug's girlfriend, camerawoman Avril. She's coming, too.

There are many others—concubines and friends and people who were taken to Areola or were born there—and I'll undoubtedly mention them, but you just won't know their backgrounds unless you decided to go back and read the first two volumes. I don't plan to retell stories I've told before. Though I'm sometimes told I repeat myself.

Why are we going to all this work? For 4,000 years, I've been searching for a place where I could hide the satchel and never have it found. But everywhere on earth that I've hidden, I've been found by explorers, conquerors, and predators, and have had to move again. It is becoming harder and harder to keep the satchel from discovery. My look-away spell is fine when it comes to human eyes, but cameras can see the satchel. Airport security x-rays see it. I suspect that if they knew exactly what they were looking for, Uncle Sam could get a close satellite picture of it.

So, I invested in a space exploration company and 'volunteered' to lead the first colonization mission to Mars. My intent was to bypass the red planet and just keep going into space forever. That's why we organized the television reality show to pick my crew of beautiful friendly women for the voyage. Unfortunately, when I had the crew, Doug informed me the ship was not ready and wouldn't be for at least a year. We needed to come up with a second season. That's what's keeping me confused and active now.

With those little bits of information, I think you can enjoy this volume of my memoirs, even if you miss out on all the adventures of the past 4,000 years I've related in the previous books.

Five, four, three, two, one. Ignition!

Part XI
Headaches
and Heartaches

Image Credit: Avishake07, ID2137912169 licensed from Shutterstock.com

55
Dark Chocolate

I AM PASSIONATE about a few things. I'm passionate about beautiful women. I'm passionate about good looking women. I'm passionate about pretty women. I'm passionate about pretty good looking women. And other women, too. But there *are* other things.

I'm passionate about all my people in Areola, and would defend them against all odds. I'm passionate about flying. I still wish Pinaruti had thought to give me wings. That would be so awesome. And I am passionate about fighting sex trafficking and all forms of slavery.

I say all forms and that includes men, women, and children. For example, a few years ago, as I was munching on one of my favorite dark chocolate bars, I read an article about slavery in the cocoa industry. I was appalled and spat the chocolate I was eating into the garbage. We might as well be eating the bodies of the children who are trafficked into slavery in Ghana and West Africa to work on the plantations.

I considered several ways to combat this. The easiest, in my simple mind, would be to loose the ninja priestesses on the owners and slavers in the industry and let them nail a few bodies to the doors. It's become more difficult to launch crusades like that when I have to travel in today's world. The airport scanners can identify my satchel even if the look-away spell is fresh. Of course, they can't see Areola. Unless I open a gateway, the satchel functions as a simple case in which I keep a few papers and innocuous traveler's goods. That's all they see when the bag goes through the x-ray and when the bag is opened to look inside. I am concerned, however, about the effect of various forms of radiation on the satchel seeping into the infinity room. I have no evidence of that so far, but it still concerns me.

Each time I adopt a new identity, I need to create all the paperwork for it. I need a driver's license, birth certificate, passport, marriage certificate, deeds, stock certificates, and bank accounts. It's very complicated to travel anonymously to another country and wreak havoc on the slave trade.

So, I did the next best thing. I bought a cocoa plantation, freed the slaves, and tried to reunite the children with parents when possible. I employed workers to take care of the plantation. I have compared the cost of owning a slave to the cost of paying a fair wage and employing workers. I find it is a wash. I continued to sell my cocoa at the same prices the slave cocoa had commanded. But I soon found the doors closed on my efforts to buy other plantations.

After attacking a few traffickers, I gave up the process for two reasons. The first was that each trafficker I brought down accounted for such a minuscule portion of the children and adults stolen into slavery that it did not seem to make a difference. The second reason was that, as fast and silent and nearly invisible as my ninja priestesses are, they are no match for machine guns, grenades, and other ordnance that falls freely into the hands of traffickers. I'm still working on a solution to that problem. My priestesses are precious to me and I will not willingly risk them in a battle against such machinery.

I fear that the days of attacking traffickers and pirates with swords and knives and nailing their bodies to the wall are all but gone.

Next, I turned to an all-American solution, inspired by a teen whose research paper revealed the amount of slavery involved in the chocolate industry and outlined a means to combat it. I employed him to start putting his ideas in action. We created a small chocolate company and started importing only fair trade cocoa from independent farmers Josh negotiated with personally. I made sure he was supplied with adequate capital to get the ingredients we needed and to ensure it was not slave-based cocoa.

Of course, that only served to make a very small dent in the chocolate market. We weren't even listed on the Exchange of American Chocolate Companies. We got distribution through a local chain of grocery stores and a few specialty shops. But it was our start.

I invested in a chocolatier back in 1855, when I was living in San Francisco. Through ups and downs and several generations of ownership, it had survived and prospered. It had a much better marketing position, and even though it wasn't strictly enforced within the company, it was trying to do an ethical business in a market that was becoming less and less friendly. I increased my stake, and once I'd become the controlling board member, I finished the acquisition and made Josh the chief of the larger company. We began to gain brand recognition and Josh expanded our buying into the markets that were dominated by the slavers. When he discovered an independent farmer was actually owned by one of the big plantations, he cut them off, even if they personally weren't using slave labor in their operation. We insisted on purity in our product and purchased the beans directly.

And then Peninnah came along. When she found what we were doing, she began negotiations with a very large chocolate company and I began acquiring shares in the publicly traded international company. That required a great deal of negotiation as the company was closely held. Ultimately, she was able to exchange the value of our little company for equivalent shares in the new parent and I began pressing the megalith to start sourcing their chocolate in the way we did.

At first, they simply left Josh alone to continue to make his elite type of chocolate. It has since been discovered that our little subsidiary is more profitable by percentage than the rest of the company combined. That might be because the big plantations have seen the guaranteed rates we pay independent farmers and have tried to price their cocoa in the same range. That went over poorly with many chocolatiers around the world.

We've a long way to go. We have begun to make a dent in the slave trade by making fair trade cocoa more profitable than slave cocoa. But even the major chocolatier we own a stake in accounts for only four percent of the world chocolate market. I'm thinking we might still need to invade Africa with a few ninjas and make an example of the worst of the plantations we have found.

Where was I going with this? Oh, yes. My continued passion for fighting the slave trade and human trafficking.

Liz frequently tells me that my prevailing opinions are chauvinistic and it should not take the sex trafficking of women and children to get my goat—so to speak. Yes, I am opposed to slavery of all kinds. I just have a special soft spot for helping the weakest.

Back when Pinaruti summoned me... Remember Pinaruti? He was the hapless and slightly drunk sorcerer who attempted to summon Beelzebub back in Knossos, Crete about 2,000 years BC (Before Caesar) and slurred the name. Much to his surprise, he got me: Beetlebob. (Names have been changed to protect the innocent. Me.) Pinaruti conveniently died of shock when he saw me and unwittingly created a bridge for me to cross into the natural world, a free demon.

I read Pinaruti's memories from his cooling body and discovered his intent was to imprison me in the walls of King Drakomaxos's palace and force me to keep it cool in the summer. Yes, his intent was to make a slave of me. I was horrified! And frankly pleased the old fool had died when his summoning actually worked. But the very thought of slavery has gone against my grain ever since that day.

When I finally convinced Drakomaxos I could build a palace of stone that stayed cool, he immediately wanted to get a bunch of slaves to build it for him. I started my mantra that has been with me for four millennia: A house built by slaves will soon crumble around its owner. In Mania, I made sure that was the case when I was hired to build a palace for the king. Soon after the palace was built for Idiopheles by slaves (and I was safely away at sea), an earthquake brought his palace down around his ears.

Then I was commissioned to build a temple for the god Ninra in Bathra, a town in Mesopotamia. He and the goddess Namri agreed that no slave labor would be used in building their palace. Slavery became anathema in Bathra for centuries.

And so the story goes. I have always been opposed to slavery.

As to sex slavery, this started out as just another form of slavery that I was opposed to. You see, one of the things about having lived a long life is that I have changed. I have learned to adapt to changing mores and to learn from them.

There was a time in certain cultures when women were considered chattel, disposed of by their fathers into the possession of their husbands. In some cultures, women were not allowed to own property, to make friends or even to leave their house. I always felt this was silly but it did not truly sink in that the treatment of women was abhorrent and immoral and a form of slavery until I spent twenty years as a woman. I discovered my weaknesses, my frustration, and my fears. I thereafter made sure that each of my women had the opportunity to learn martial arts to the best of their ability so they would never need to walk in fear.

I further gave those who wished it an opportunity to live as a man for a day and to gain insight into a man's appetites, fears, and power. Most discovered the physical power of a man was not worth exchanging their female bodies for. Some wanted the change made permanent and I happily gave them that wish. There was even an instance back in Bathra when the goddess Namri granted a man his wish to become a priestess in her temple. I got to fuck her once and verified that she was, indeed, changed wholly into a woman.

The thing is that I changed. I became more aware of women as societal equals of men. And when I witnessed women denied that equality, through slavery and abuse, my ire rose to heights unmatched. I once severed the head from the body of one of Odysseus's crew who insisted the woman he captured in Troy was his to do with as he wished. I lost a few more crew members that day as they decided my rules were too hard for them to live by. And I gained a couple of women who chose to live in the infinity room.

I believe that is a fundamental problem with the world as I look around it today. People refuse to change. I include both men and women in that category. They see the problems and are taught the lessons, but they refuse to change. The thought that greater physical strength carries the right of greater social power is so deeply ingrained that men attempt to exercise their superiority by suppressing, abusing, and enslaving women and children.

I am sad to say that this myth is propagated through many of the world's religions, designed, it seems, to maintain a society in which men are considered inherently superior to women and children. This fundamental belief is what feeds the slave trade—especially sex trafficking of women and children.

As a result, I become irrationally incensed when I find captive women and children.

Since the time I discovered the first young girls imprisoned on a pirate ship for the pleasure of the pirates, I have taken as my mission dispatching the offenders as quickly and efficiently—and sometimes as painfully—as I can. My demon morality is not offended by the deaths of slavers.

Those priestesses—the fifty-two very young women I found on various pirate ships over my few dozen years as a trans-Pacific trader—experienced the worst of serial rape and abuse. They were healed and cleansed by me in the pool and became my priestesses. And then they trained harder than any other people in Areola to become an avenging force wherever I pointed them at sex traffickers. They'd once saved Peninnah from kidnapping and rape by completely destroying the personal army of a Japanese corporate president. We now own his company.

The United States experienced a surge in refugees coming across the southern border and, in fact, across both oceans. Rather than taking them in and giving them shelter, they were considered 'illegal aliens' and were arrested. Many parents and children were separated, most never to be reunited. Hundreds were deported, often directly to prisons. That pissed me off. But when I found out what was happening *under* the radar, I went full goat ballistic.

The liberals of the world decried the pictures of children in cages and parents separated and kept in detention camps. Many were announced as deported. But the true story never made the news. I found out only by accident when I was searching for a place in the Arizona desert where I could hide the satchel and crawl in for a few years. I'd also decided to hide out and see what happens when refugees illegally crossed the border out in the desert.

Truckloads of hopefuls were being taken across the border and were stopped and incarcerated on the spot by border agents. Dozens, or perhaps hundreds never made it to detention camps. The desert hides hundreds of bodies of unknown people who came across the border for refuge and were killed on the spot.

Oh, don't let me get the issue confused. I would never accuse the border patrol of murdering innocents. I don't think. It seemed that just before the agents showed up, however, the men who ran the transport lined up the men in their load and shot them. They made the women and children dig in the sand to bury their fathers and husbands. When they spotted border agents coming to chase down the illegal immigrants, the men running the transports always seemed to be able to disappear while the agents focused on rounding up the women and children and putting them in yet another unmarked truck to take them away to detention. The women tried to tell the agents about the murders but were simply pushed into the truck and taken away.

When I witnessed this happening, I took off across the desert in my demon form after the men who transported these unwitting refugees across the border. They were already in Mexico, but that didn't make a difference to me. 'We don't need no steenking badges.' Six men were counting out and dividing the money they'd taken from the refugees. I fell upon them and twisted heads on necks until there were none still alive. I discovered the transporters were called 'coyotes.'

That was how I found out about rescue operations and bullets. This scar I bear on my side is where the one shot that was fired in time hit me. I hadn't been swift enough to avoid it. I was lucky. It hit me in the side and I was in a remote part of the desert where I could hide and enter Areola for a few days to recover. But like Issa still bore the scars of his execution after he'd been resurrected, so I still bear the scar from my brief battle.

When I left the infinity room to have a look around, I discovered the bodies, truck, and money I'd left behind were all removed. I assumed someone had come looking for them. That meant there would be others in this racket that needed to be taken care of eventually. I didn't know when or where to start looking for them, so I prowled around the desert for several weeks before I spotted another delivery being made.

"Where did they take the women and children," Zhi asked me as I was healing.

"I don't know, love," I said.

"Bob, it is good that you destroyed the murderers, though you should have called for me or the priestesses to help you. But killing those men did nothing to help the women and children who were taken away," she said.

"Don't you think they were taken away to a detention center? Those were government agents who rounded up the refugees and took them away."

"Bob, I don't think that's a safe bet," said Virginia. My concubine had been with me since the late 1950s and had continued to be active in the civil rights and antiwar movements into the mid-sixties. She was a pretty savvy young woman, though she'd disappeared from the natural world some sixty years previously. "You said the truck was unmarked. None of the agents accompanied it. How do you know where they were taken?"

So, I watched the scene in the desert play out once again. This time, however, I did not chase after the coyotes. I waited and watched as the women and children were rounded up and loaded in the unmarked truck. The truck went one direction and the border patrol went another, pretending to search for the coyotes. I followed the truck.

It did not stop at any known detention center. In fact, it went straight to a major city and into a warehouse. When the truck got past the rocky and slow part of the desert track it had followed, it picked up speed and it was obvious I would not be able to keep up with it. I quickly went into the infinity room and pulled out my Trans Am. I probably tore the hell out of the undercarriage bouncing over some of that track, even though the truck had picked up speed. I made a note to myself to get a Jeep if I decided to do any more of this shit.

Regardless, I was able to keep up with the truck once we hit the freeway. The look-away spell I had on the Trans Am kept me from being noticed by other drivers, but I knew radar would pick up the car if I encountered a speed trap. I had enough to do to keep out of the way of drivers who didn't notice me on the freeway.

I parked near the warehouse where the truck led me, and started to do some scanning to see what I could find. I brought Zhi, Ali, and two other bodyguards from the infinity room to help keep watch over the action. What we discovered was sickening.

A manager came through the warehouse and checked each room, making notes on the contents. I managed to locate his clipboard when he went into a restroom and discovered it listed the contents of each room in the terms one would use for livestock. Each person in the room was given a number, written on her forehead with a permanent marker. On the sheet, the number was placed in a column with the names of various buyers for the livestock. Some were for shipment out of the country. Some for 'adoption.' And some were designated for buyers in the States.

You might think of the United States as being relatively pure when it comes to trafficking, but that is not so. A study I encountered near that time had said that fifty percent of the world's human traffic went through the US at some point. A percentage of those stayed in the country. The rest were shipped to buyers around the world.

This would be a massive effort. We might manage to assault the warehouse and take out the guards and free the women and children. But to what life? The men they had known were dead. They were illegally in the country. Where would they go? And how would that change the game? We needed to get to the buyers.

The first set was easy. A truck came, loaded women with a few small children, and drove to a dock in Texas. There, the container was loaded on a ship bound for Iran. Before the ship was sealed, I entered, opened the container, and invited the women to come to the infinity room. Maya explained what was being offered in terms the women could understand and they all entered through the gateway.

I returned to the warehouse to await the next load.

I'd missed some and was upset that I'd let so many be enslaved. I was preparing an assault on the warehouse when we got our first big break. The boss came in to tour the warehouse and inspect the stock. He was accompanied by half a dozen buyers who were there to negotiate prices and delivery.

I unleashed the priestesses.

They were prepared for the men with guns and I had provided a look-away spell for each of them so they would not be noticed until they actually made contact. The first contact was with the guards who were outside the warehouse, patrolling in a way that let us know they'd done this many times before. At a silent signal, they all fell with arrows in their throats, eyes, or chests. A second crew of priestesses swiftly moved among the men silently dispatching any who were still alive.

My bodyguards quickly pulled the bodies under a concealing tarp as the priestesses moved inside. They stayed in the shadows and were silent death as they efficiently took care of the remaining guards without a shot being fired. And finally, we came to a room where the men were getting to sample the wares. Women and children were being stripped and presented to the men for their pleasure.

The priestesses of Bob had all undergone similar treatment at the hands of pirates in the Pacific two hundred years before. They did not wait for commands or instruction. Shuriken flew and swords flashed. None of the traffickers were left alive in two minutes as fifty-two furies descended upon them.

Maya, Josie, and Liz led a humanitarian squad from the infinity room, including some of the priestesses of Aphrodite from Troy, and conducted over a hundred women and children into the infinity room.

The priestesses and bodyguards were not finished. Once the women and children were gone, the priestesses hauled all the bodies into the main area of the warehouse and began nailing the bodies to the walls. I noticed they seemed to take particular pleasure in putting a spike through the genitals of each man and into the wall. They swung heavy hammers with long nails. Some were driven directly through the neck and into the wall. Some through shoulders. Some were hung upside down with nails through their feet. Then everyone went into the satchel and I surveyed the area, noting that not a single sword, shuriken, arrow, or knife had been left behind.

I was surprised, however, when I recognized the dead face and blankly staring eyes of a United States Senator among those nailed to the walls. I ran out of the warehouse and drove my Trans Am north to a private spot before packing it back into my bag and getting out a much newer Lexus. This I drove back to my base in the Midwest where I was a simple housing developer.

The only newspaper article I ever saw about the subject was a notice that Senator Truman had unexpectedly suffered a heart attack and had passed away in his home before emergency medical services could arrive. There was never a mention of the others who were left hanging in the warehouse. Or if there was, perhaps I simply didn't know the names to identify what story had been released about them. There was certainly nothing about a warehouse massacre in a city in Arizona.

I had to wonder how high up in the US government the workings of human trafficking were being supported. I really needed to get out of here.

Well, that went way darker than I intended to get in this volume, but I was reminded of all of that when I met a young woman one day as I was doing some shopping for gifts for my harem. They all liked me to bring home new sexy things for them to wear, even though they didn't keep them on for long.

Let me just say that the store was not a major brand. You know what they say: Shop local.

"Welcome, sir. We're happy to have you in our store this evening," a young woman said. There were half a dozen women sitting in a little lounge area—all dressed in very scanty sexy clothes. "Have you ever been to 'Show Me' before?"

"No," I confessed. "I just want to buy some pretty things for my women."

"I'll bet you do. You must have a lot of them, as strong and handsome as you are. You aren't gay, are you?" she asked innocently. "Nothing wrong with that, but I'd call one of the boys to help you. Let me tell you about how we work here."

She proceeded to tell me they were a 'personal shopping' service. All the girls were available to help select and model the lingerie. I could have as many of the girls as I wanted for just $200 each and they would help me select and then model up to five different outfits. They hoped I would purchase something 'off the rack,' in a manner of speaking. I glanced around and saw that prices displayed were well over $100 per outfit.

What the heck. It's only money and this promised to be an interesting new experience. I asked the young woman if she would be my model and she happily accepted the $200 I gave her and hung on my arm as we walked through the very well-stocked store. I was surprised that she actually knew her business as well as how to arouse me. She pointed out several outfits and asked questions about who I was buying for.

"She must be very special that you care enough to shop here. This is one of my favorites. It's soft and sexy. See? No rough seams or scratchy lace. I feel like a million bucks in it, I'm told. Please let me model this one for you."

I agreed. *Wait!* She'd been *told* it made her feel like a million bucks? Wouldn't she know how she feels in an outfit without being told?

She led me to a room with a comfortable chair, table, and small stage. She poured me a glass of wine and told me to just relax for a minute while she changed into the first outfit. Then she took the five pieces I'd selected and disappeared behind a curtain. I heard voices outside our room and wondered how many stages like this they had for customers. It turned out there was a stage for each girl who was working and by the time I left, they all had customers. Of course, that was much later.

"Mr. Bob, this first outfit is one you chose in a royal blue," she said as she mounted the stage in front of me. It was very attractive and wonderfully displayed on her lithe body. "I love how this fabric moves with me when I walk, making that gentle swishing sound that will let you know your lover has arrived before you ever see her approaching. Notice the way it hugs my curves, especially how the fabric falls across my butt and accents the shape. If you are an ass man, this is a surefire way to bring the soldier to attention."

She continued to strut across the stage and pause to pose in various sexy positions. I was very appreciative. Then she stepped off the stage and approached me.

"You can't always tell what an outfit will do for your girlfriend unless you touch it and confirm that she would feel good in it." She guided my hand to touch her... the fabric, as it fell over her butt. "Did you notice that you can see the shape and outline of my nipples without actually seeing through the fabric. She'll love it when you softly caress her breasts encased in this lovely fabric." She demonstrated by guiding my hands to her breasts and rubbing them around so I could feel her hard nipples beneath the fabric. Then she stepped back.

"That's lovely," I said. "I can imagine Maya in it. She'll love it. I'll take it."

"Oh, my! A sale already? You are a wonderful boyfriend. Stand up and help me out of this."

What? I stood and she showed me exactly the best way to remove the little outfit, leaving her bare in front of me. She turned to face me.

"Would you like me to show you the next outfit now?" she asked, making no move to leave until I gasped a 'yes.' Then I watched her bare bottom disappear behind the curtain.

As soon as she was off-stage, a woman I recognized as the cashier at the door of the shop entered the room and took the outfit from me.

"I'll wrap this and have it ready when you are finished here," she said. "I hope you enjoy the rest of the show!"

And thus, the show continued. She arranged the outfits in a way that let the sexiness increase with each piece of lingerie she wore on stage. I bought each of them. The last item was the 'favorite' she had chosen.

I once met an artist who had experimented with sculpting women behind a veil. It was a fascinating technique and when he was finished with a marble sculpture, you swore the veil was transparent in places, showing details of her face, while a fold in the fabric obscured other places. The final outfit Angel, my model, wore reminded me of the sculpture, as it was nearly transparent, exposing her nipples, her navel, and her crotch, though keeping them covered with the fabric. As she moved, multiple layers of the fabric would shift and obscure or expose the view.

Finally, she settled on my lap and encouraged me to pet her wherever I wanted. She even showed me how to get my hand beneath the fabric so I was caressing her skin and bare breasts beneath the fabric.

"I'm afraid this outfit has a very high price, Mr. Bob. But it has accessories that come with it. Do you see the collar I wear around my neck? It's my slave collar. If you snap this leash to the collar, and pay the $1,500 price for the outfit, I come with it. And I promise, *you* will come, too. I will be your sex slave for as long as you will keep me and take care of me. I know you've mentioned Maya and Josie and Liz, and I know you must have others. Add me to your collection. I'm not normally a high-pressure sales girl, but I'm ready for a change and you are the best thing that has come through our door in a long time. Buy the outfit and take me with you, Mr. Bob."

I was so shocked I could hardly speak. She was rubbing at my crotch and I had a finger in her moist pussy as she talked. It was incredibly disorienting.

"You're a slave?" I asked in disbelief.

"Yes. I've been in the lifestyle since I turned eighteen and that's been almost ten years."

Ten years? She didn't look more than twenty at the most.

"I'll buy you and set you free," I said angrily. "And all the others in the store."

"Mr. Bob! How could you? Don't you like us? Me? Would you really throw me out like that? I thought you were special. I wanted you to own me."

"I'm confused. Do you mean to say that being a sex slave is your choice?" I asked.

"Yes. I love it! I don't have to make any decisions. I don't live in poverty. I get all the love and affection I could ever want. My owners have been good men, but I'll probably not be marketable for much longer. Most of the masters want younger women. I thought you liked me."

She started to push away from me and I pulled her tighter to hold her.

"You really want me to buy you? I don't know if I can be a slave owner. I live in a different world."

"Then take me to your world. Even if you remove my collar, I'll remain your slave. Mr. Bob, take this last outfit off of me and make me yours."

I complied, and an hour later I walked out of the lingerie store with my new sex slave—dressed once again in the transparent negligee—to return home and try to explain to my wives how I came to own a slave.

Sometimes, life is very confusing for a simple demon!

5 6
WHEN IS A SLAVE NOT A SLAVE?

OW LEST YOU START THINKING 'Bob is the world's biggest hypocrite,' let me tell you that I did free Angel—under her terms. I took her to Areola and undressed her completely, including removing her collar. Then I gave her the full tour of the palace and city, with both of us wandering around naked, like the majority of the inhabitants.

"When you said you were from a different world, I thought you meant it figuratively," Angel said as we stepped into the pool just to float for a bit. "This is literally a different world than earth."

"We think so. At the very least, it is a different dimension. Everyone here is free. But we all live in harmony in the lifestyle we prefer," I explained the best I could. "Maybe my concubines would be better at explaining. Many were once slaves or lived in societies where the practicality was slavery, even if it didn't go by that name."

"But if I'm employed by you, that's no different than being a prostitute. When I offered myself as a slave, I got no personal gain from it. It was a mission—a kind of ministry if you will. I would be taken care of as good masters take care of their *world*, but I wouldn't get *paid*. Even the little bag of things I brought with me was little more than the necessities and a couple of gifts from former masters. You can't imagine how liberating that lifestyle is," she said.

"Well, I'm not going to pay you," I laughed. "Everyone here works for the good of Areola. As a result, everyone has plenty for all their needs. I make sure everyone is cared for."

"So, in a manner of speaking, everyone here is your slave," she said thoughtfully. I had to think that one through for a while. It reminded me...

Remember when I was with the Great Khaans of Mongolia and China? Most notably, Chinggis Khaan loved to hear me talk of the places I'd been and temples I'd built and the battles I'd witnessed. We sat for hours while I outlined the wars and strategies of Caesar, and sometimes he called one or more of his sons and grandsons in to listen to something particularly important in his mind. Then he asked me to go find a place for his capital city and build it. By that time, I think he was pretty convinced that I was not mortal.

I went off wandering and eventually found the site for Xanadu where I built the city and palace and temple while waiting for Khaan to arrive. Instead, his chief minister or general arrived with 20,000 horsemen, ready to storm the city. They found the gates open wide and the city ready for them to inhabit. When the Khaan arrived, it was Hubilai Khaan ready to take possession. When he was installed and had toured the city, I begged his leave to return east to my homeland 'to die.' He agreed, but said to wait just a bit until he had learned 'one more thing.' The tales his grandfather told had not fallen on deaf ears. Hubilai was fascinated with tales and stories of other lands and customs. He'd been visited by two 'Latin' brothers and sent them back to Europe to get him priests and oil from the lamp at the sacred sepulcher. They'd been gone some years before Khaan moved to Xanadu. But while I was there, they returned.

The brothers Nicolo and Maffeo were accompanied by Nicolo's son, Marco Polo. Marco was the reason I was finally permitted to leave the service of the Khaan. Each time I'd suggested that I needed to leave, Hubilai would agree and say, "Next month," or "Next year." Or, in fact, whenever he grew tired of me.

Marco was a new diversion for the Khaan. His father and uncle were welcome, but Marco soon became the Khaan's favorite at court. He was a bright young man, about twenty years old when he arrived. He had no idea at the time that he and his father and uncle would remain there in the service of the Great Khaan for many years. Khaan sent Marco to me for instruction in the martial arts and Buddhism as the family had failed in the mission to bring priests. The priests they were bringing chickened out and fled back west. Nicolo and Maffeo set up a school in which they taught the seven arts of the West: rhetoric, logic, grammar, arithmetic, astronomy, music, and geometry. In turn, Marco was to learn the arts of the East.

He was a little full of himself, but generally a nice kid. He studied diligently and soon prepared for the first mission that Hubilai would send him on over the next fifteen or so years. He asked my advice.

"The Khaan is dissatisfied with the reports he gets from his ambassadors," I said. "You can be different."

"How shall I differ, *Zongshi?*" he asked. One of the things Marco had going for him was that he was taught respect from an early age. He had another uncle in Venice who had mostly raised him. The Italian Family was very big on respect.

"The other ambassadors the Khaan has sent out came back with a concise factual report on the situation they went to investigate or deal with. They struck a good trade deal for winter rice. This tartar would like to marry the daughter of that tartar. The war at the wall has been averted for now but there is a weakness near Lomein. He *needs* these reports. But he *wants* to know more about them," I instructed.

"He *wants* to hear about the customs in this part of the land that differ from customs in Xanadu. He wants to know what you think of their language, what the people look like, what the fashions are. He wants examples of their art and their music. Even differing religious beliefs and philosophy. These are things the other ambassadors fail to bring back to him, but which you have brought him from Italy. You have told him about the pope and brought him oil from the holy sepulcher. These are the things the Khaan yearns for and they are all things that will make him a better and wiser ruler. You can bring these things to the Khaan." I hoped he took my words to heart.

Marco considered this and went off on his first short mission as a representative of the Khaan. When he returned, he gave his official report and then sat with Hubilai and regaled him with tales of the customs of the people, what vassal had a birthday, who was pregnant, how the peasants were dealing with the water shortage, and even sang a song he'd learned. Khaan was delighted. It turned out that Marco was quite a storyteller.

I chose that time to ask Hubilai Khaan once again for leave to return to my homeland in the East and he granted it at once. He gave me a horse and attempted to press other valuables on me that would have taken a wagon to carry. I politely declined the gifts with the statement that these gifts would do me no good in my grave and should be given to the bright young ambassador, Marco Polo.

The next morning, I rode like the wind toward the East. Three days later, I found a place where I could seclude myself within the satchel and changed my body for one much younger. I renewed my relationship with my wives and possessions and then with my concubines and with my priestesses. Refreshed and ready once again, I proceeded into Northern China and what is now Russia.

In all but name, I had been a slave in Hubilai Khaan's court. I was not 'captive.' All I could ever want was provided for me. I had minimal duties in work that I loved, teaching about the tantras and the forms of martial arts. But I could not leave Xanadu without the permission of the Khaan.

Marco Polo served in Hubilai Khaan's court for seventeen years before his father and uncle successfully begged to be allowed to return to Italy. It was a near thing and they would not have been allowed to leave if it had not been that a certain princess needed to be delivered to a subsidiary king in India. Read about Marco's adventures sometime. They are almost as interesting as mine.

But if Khaan had not had a new plaything to occupy him in Marco Polo, I would never have been free.

Where was I? Ah, yes. Angel.

"Since you consider all here in Areola to be my slaves, then I free you to join them," I said after I'd considered her proposition. "I will expect you to work for the betterment of our world, just as all the others do. Will that be acceptable to you?"

"Yes, master. If that is what it takes to serve you, it is acceptable except for one minor thing. I am a sexual being. If you will not call me 'slave' then I am your sex servant. My job on Areola will be to give you any sexual experience you desire upon your command. Please, Mr. Bob. Use me. P…"

I slammed my lips against hers and took her, right there beside the pool. But I did not let her use the words 'Possess me.' On the other hand, I found she was one of the most creative lovers I had ever had. Every part of her was open for my invasion. And I used every opening. Oh, I made sure she had pleasure from everything we did and we both lost count of the number of orgasms we'd enjoyed. But she explored me in ways I had not used since we learned the tantric meditations. I went to bed, exhausted, with Nimia and Josie at my side. And for the first time that I could recall, I had a nocturnal emission. Yes, a wet dream. It so startled me that I sat straight up in bed and looked down at the mess I'd made on myself.

As I sat there with my sleeping wife and possession beside me, gasping for breath, Angel crept up from the foot of the bed where she'd slept and proceeded to clean me with her tongue as I petted her head and whispered loving words to her. She nursed my cock back to full stiffness and then swallowed it into her throat as I came again. She smiled at me and quietly returned to the little nest she'd made at the foot of my bed.

Angel does not sleep at my feet every night. In fact, she once confessed that she was glad there were a hundred other women to help keep me satisfied because I would exhaust any dozen women with my appetite and stamina. And I heard it whispered that she had found a mission teaching others her techniques and philosophy of being a willing sex slave to Bob. I'm not sure any of my concubines, wives, possessions, or priestesses actually needed the instruction, but Angel had her mission.

I still struggle with the ethics of this situation. I created the infinity room. Or did I? Perhaps I only truly opened a gateway to another dimension that created itself around my desires. Yet, everyone I have brought into the infinity room—with their consent—has found everything they ever need provided for them. They all contribute in some way or another.

I have firmly disproved the idea that people need to work forty hours or five days a week or fifty weeks a year to earn their bread by the sweat of their brow. The one who contributes a new song to our community is as valuable as the one who harvests a bushel of wheat. This is the rule our world lives by. Other than Angel, I don't believe anyone considers him or herself a slave. But as we grew, I needed to continue to think about my relationship to *my* people.

Soon after I brought the mini-series contestants to Areola, Artemisia, the youngest of our crew, came to me with a question. She'd happily discovered that ganja was freely available in Areola. As a result, use was casual and it was mostly used for special occasions. People really didn't need any additional way to relax or feel good. Nonetheless, Artie had indulged, simply because it was available and the idea was firmly ingrained in her from her home in California. She had definitely had a favorite cupcake before she came to talk to me.

"I was wondering, Bob," she began as she planted her naked butt in my lap. I did not impale her, but it was a near miss. She wouldn't have minded if I had. But we reclined comfortably beside the pool and cuddled for this conversation.

"Yes?" I prompted.

"Um... What is the religion here in Areola? Are we going to offend someone by not offering a proper prayer before a meal? Should we be going to church? Are there seasonal rituals? Are you really a god?"

"Whoa. That's a lot of questions. What do you think are the answers?"

"I certainly feel like I've been with a god when we have sex," she giggled. And wiggled. The young artist/body builder knew well what rubbing her hard body against me could lead to and seemed to be headed that direction. I let her drive that part, though I held that firm butt in one hand and petted her breasts with the other. We kissed in the long and languid way that lovers do when they are high. I wasn't, but she was.

"I've never really claimed to be a god," I said. "I'm a simple demon."

"Who has a temple at the other end of this pool with fifty-two ferocious priestesses ready to lay their lives down on your altar?"

"Well, that wasn't exactly my idea."

"Yeah. I heard. The priestesses are pretty open about what happened, where they came from, and how many kidnappers and traffickers they've killed," Artie said. "They also worship you. But they told me straightaway that no one else was expected to worship you. It was something special between them and you."

"That's a good description. I certainly wouldn't want them to go all missionary on me and try to evangelize the rest of Areola," I said. What a catastrophe that would be!

"Yeah, but that's what got me wondering what the religion in Areola is."

"I've never tried to control that," I mused. "When they came into the infinity room, many of the people brought the religion and customs they were born with to the room. For example, did you know there is another temple just a ways from here. Kind of that way," I said, pointing vaguely. "There are another hundred or so priestesses there. I brought them from Troy."

"As in the Fall of Troy? Wooden horses? Achilles? Odysseus?" she asked trying to clear her eyes to take in the concept.

"The very same. I'll tell you all about that one day. But the goddess Aphrodite contacted me and asked me to save her priestesses when the city fell. Not all would come with me, but over a hundred did. They established a modest temple and still carry on the same ministry they did in Troy. Oh, some have left the temple and have married or gone to explore some new area. And there have been some number of people who have joined their priesthood for a time. Essentially, they still do what they were doing in Troy."

"Which is?"

"They have sex with anyone who is lonely, horny, or just wants to have a nice cuddle with a beautiful naked woman. And they do not discriminate based on race, national origin, sex, or religion."

"You mean they are like holy prostitutes?"

"No. The basic premise of prostitution is the acceptance of payment for sexual services. Aphrodite's servants have sex with anyone who needs it or wants it because that is what Aphrodite wanted. Remind me to tell you the story of the Propoetides sometime. They lost their way and began collecting money for the sexual favors they offered in Aphrodite's temple. She turned them to stone. The thing is, the priestesses of Aphrodite all know Aphrodite is not here in Areola. They don't try to convert people to the religion of Aphrodite or of the Greek pantheon. They simply carry out their mission as they have done since before the fall of Troy."

"Wow! That's deep. So, there aren't Christians and Jews, and Muslims and Buddhists and all the others here?"

"Oh, many people have carried their customs into Areola with them and they are widely shared. There is a period when everyone agrees to have a winter festival and they share Christmas, Kwanzaa, Hanukkah, Solstice, um... I can't remember all of them. It's pretty hard to say we do this every winter since there isn't a calendar here. We don't really have seasons. If someone has a desire for snow, they can go to the other side of the lake and up a hill and find snow. If they want fall colors, they will find trees with falling leaves over there somewhere. But they don't really define themselves as Christian or Muslim any more than they define themselves as African or European or Asian. We are who we are. We all know that we entered a different dimension and the gods of Olympus, the gods of India, the god of the Jews or the Muslims, Jesus, or Buddha aren't here. Oh, we may still honor all those gods, but they aren't here."

"But you're here," she said. She started squirming a bit more and soon had my cock in her hand. Not long after that, it was in her pussy. "This," she breathed. "This is my religion."

I have to admit, I wondered if it was my religion, too.

Our conversation put me in mind of my old friend Issa. There were times I really wished I could sit down and talk with him, just to get some advice. Did I really *need* a religion in Areola? Am I doing the right thing by trying to leave earth behind? Does he enjoy sex as much as I do?

I'd looked for him in India three or four centuries AC. I found a tomb in the north that had a statue that was obviously Issa. I think I've mentioned that a demon's body bears the scars of his battles. I've been fortunate. I have a few minor scars. Two where I was shot— one in the side and one in the butt. There are a couple of small scars where I was nicked by a sword. And, of course, the chip out of my horn where a monster demon tried to take off my head with an axe. Issa had distinguishing scars from his crucifixion. Nail scars in his hands and feet. A jagged scar in his side from a spear. These scars were clearly defined on the statue at his tomb.

It was a sad day for me to realize I'd missed him. Of course, I knew he wasn't buried there. It takes a lot to kill a demon and Issa was very good at resurrecting himself. In fact, the old man who showed me the tomb and told me stories about Issa's life in India confided to me that "We know the tomb is empty, but we honor the thought."

I'd met a few demons in my 4,000 years. We don't exactly seek each other out. There was Maureen, my business partner in the winery. We didn't really speak anymore. I'd signed over all my share of the winery to her and she was doing well. She'd finally stopped consuming souls most of the time. There had been a few I was sure she'd taken, but she was almost civilized these days.

Speaking of civilized demons, the Queen was another. I'd had to inform her that our trip to space was indefinitely postponed as the ship was not ready. She'd sighed and then said, "Well, I'll see you around someplace." A week later, I was invited to attend the royal funeral. I went, out of respect for the family. But, like Issa, I knew it wasn't her in the coffin. I had a feeling that if I looked in a brothel, I'd find her catching up on the past forty years without the diet of sex she longed for.

There'd been the monster summoned to attempt to kill me in the desert. He was psychically chained to his master and when Athene instructed me to sever the chain, the demon turned on its master and then dissolved back into the primordial mass he arose from. Not before getting a good swipe at me with his axe.

And then there was Issa. The greatest demon the world has ever seen. Someplace along the line, his followers turned him into a god and created a massive religion around his mythos. I doubted sincerely if he would recognize the practice of the religion. He was certainly moving as far away from it as he could when I last saw him.

And I'd known gods. I'd met and talked to Zeus. In fact, he helped me get my act together when I was only a few weeks or months or years old. Even invited me to come to live on Olympus, but I was still young and adventurous. And if I'd taken his offer, I wouldn't have half the wonderful people who had joined me in Areola.

Then there was Ninra and Namri, the god and goddess of Bathra who selected me to build their temple. I really loved Bao and Portia, my wives in Bathra. It was a lesson in mortality to me.

Aphrodite had taken passage with me from Tyre to Cyprus and I'd had to fight off one of Poseidon's sea monsters before the goddess of lust and love decided to make use of my ready cock to satisfy *her* desires. And she had provided others to me over the years, including Deedee, the buxom blonde I'd settled on first as a member of my crew and then discovered she'd been sent by My Lady Goddess.

Oh, there were others. Ningrum in the Indonesian islands. The war gods Tu and Tawhirimatea in the South Pacific. Kukulcán of the Mayans and Ixchel, their goddess of love and beauty. I'm sure I've forgotten some, but you get the idea. I am accustomed to the company of gods.

In most cases, though, there was nothing really worship-worthy. They were created by the summons of people who needed them and rose to their divine status with the same characteristics that their human creators imbued them with. Like I am with the characteristics Pinaruti gave to me. I have goat horns and legs and hooves, and a goat's sex drive—always horny. Otherwise, rather benign.

I have noticed that as much as the gods thrive on the worship of people, they don't really *care* much about people. They are as lost in their little worlds as I am in mine. When people cease to believe in the same character as the one they first summoned, the gods are somewhat relieved. They can separate themselves and their heavenly kingdom from earth and live eternally with no more thought for the people of earth.

All I really wanted was to do the same thing with Areola. I didn't need worship, but I was extremely protective of my people. I was ready to launch into space in order to keep them safe. I wished I could talk to Issa about that.

It was lonely being a god.

Instead, I talked to Nimia. My first living wife had been my companion since just a few years after I was created. She'd been with me some 4,000 years and still looked as fresh and young as she did when I brought her to the infinity room. And when I was around, she was very nearly as horny as this old goat. I say 'when I was around' because I don't know how horny she is when I'm not around. It seems, however, that all my wives, possessions, and concubines always have the appearance of being fully sated and satisfied women.

"My darling, do we have a religion here in Areola?" I asked.

"Ah, you've been talking to Artemisia," Nimia responded.

"How did you know?"

"She has an inquisitive mind and an undying devotion to Bob. I think she went to the temple hoping she would find a way to worship you."

"Is this going to be a problem?"

"Is Zhi a problem?"

"Zhi? Of course not! She is the most loyal and faithful of any of my subjects. I trust my life to her."

"Exactly. Did you notice that you did not call her a wife, a possession, a concubine, or a priestess?" Nimia asked.

"Well, she's not exactly. She's more like a... a... uh..."

"I believe the word you want is devotee," Nimia said. "There is nothing in Areola or the natural world that she loves so much as her devotion to Bob. You taught her. You loved her. You encouraged her. And the meaning of her life is Bob."

"And you think Artemisia is like that as well?"

"If not today, then tomorrow," Nimia said. "Every thought she has is how to better be Bob's woman. No, I don't mean she wants to usurp the place of any of your wives or possessions. She simply wants to be the best she can possibly be for Bob. She is devoted to you. Please, my loving husband, never break her trust. She has placed her entire being in your hands."

"She's not a possession of mine," I defended.

"No. You are a possession of hers."

57
SEASON TWO

"**ERE'S THE CONCEPT, BOB.** Listen, you're going to love it," Doug said.

My friend and producer had finally come to reside in Areola with his girlfriend, our camerawoman Avril, at the end of the last mini-series. We'd traded bodies when we wrapped up the shooting for the season and he went to Japan while I went to a remote island I first encountered soon after the first millennium AC. Peninnah had acquired a nice little estate for us there and it had been pretty easy to change identities and fly with Virginia from Los Angeles. Virginia had met me at the mansion after the last day of shooting with my T-bird and we simply drove away. When it was safe, we drove it into the satchel and put it away. Easy.

But the final episode was getting ready to air and we had to start thinking about a second season since our rocket wasn't ready to fly. Fine. Go ahead and make sure it's safe. We can wait.

"Tell me."

"Season Two: The Harem Hunter. We're still under the umbrella of *To Boldly Go*, but the season has its own focus. By now, people know you haven't really eliminated anyone. There's no surprise to the show. So there needs to be a new twist. In this series, we follow Bob as he goes hunting for new members of the harem."

"I don't know, Doug. It seems like following my normal daily life will be strange. And what about all the women who wouldn't get chosen? How do we get releases? It seems so complicated."

"Stop whining, Bob. You're going to get fresh willing pussy on every show. Look at this." He hefted a banker's box full of papers onto the table. "This is signed consent forms from over a thousand beautiful women, along with their pictures, history, addresses, and social media accounts. By the end of the first episode, we began receiving 'applications' for next season. I had the staff vet them and get releases from them signed in advance. These are the only ones that followed through on their applications. Get that Bob? These 1,257 signed consent and release forms are the *only* ones who passed our initial review and then signed on. That's out of over 15,000 inquiries! You are a hot property and thousands of women out there want a piece of it."

"You mean... 15,000 women responded to the show and *asked* to become a part of it?"

"Um... not only women. About two percent were men. It's up to you, but I thought that would add an element of intrigue to an episode or two. Even if you don't have sex with them, it wouldn't hurt to have a couple more men in your harem. I mean, that's a lot of pussy for just half a dozen guys to keep satisfied while you're busy elsewhere."

He was right. Over the years, I'd brought hundreds of men into the infinity room, in various capacities. Not the least of those capacities was satisfying the women who outnumbered them nearly a hundred to one. Half a dozen of the men had attached themselves to my harem and lived among my concubines. I counted Doug and the young physicist Paul among them. They could probably use a little help. I sure could.

"So, basically what you're saying is that I stalk these women and when I find one I want, I jump out and say, 'Hi! I'm Bob, the Harem Hunter. Want to go to my world and fuck me for the rest of your life?' And then we see if I get killed by her response."

"Don't worry. We'll have backup for you. But it doesn't need to be that much of a blunt statement. We'll arrange an accidental meeting. She has a flat tire and this hunk of a guy—you—pulls over to help her. They talk and you invite her out. You romance her and get a real feel for her as to whether you want to make her part of the harem. Then, at a time of your choice, you reveal our hidden cameras and tell her you are the harem hunter and would like her to join your expedition. It will be great."

"There are 1,257 applications. How do we decide who gets to be stalked?"

"Bob, this is part of the beauty of the program. You just took eleven beautiful women to Areola from the first season. They should become your review committee. Along with your wives, of course. We can shoot a ton of footage just of the selection process for the applications. That's something we missed in the first season. We had a general cattle call for women and even then, we had to go out and find referrals. This will take the place of the auditions. We can cut in the commentary from the first crew about the women during each episode as they analyze their looks, personality, sex drive, and likelihood of getting along with the others."

"Wow! Okay. I haven't heard any better suggestions. Liz?" I turned to my fifth possession who also acted as the manager of our little production company.

"I think it will work, Bob. And it sounds like something the girls will have fun with. Let me work with them to get them in the mood. But first, you'll have to make the announcement that the ship isn't ready. You've kept that to yourself so far."

"You're right. I'd better go have a meeting with the crew."

It wasn't the first time I had to take bad news to my family and others about a delay. I'd had to explain that I would be staying in Egypt for a while because my ship had been burned along with the Library at Alexandria. Everyone was sad that my ship had been burned, but no one was particularly upset that we'd be staying in Egypt. Whether we were there for a day, a year, or a century, didn't really make any difference in the infinity room. Don't ask me how or why, but the only sign the residents had of time passing was if they happened to go into the natural world with me. At that time, they would become aware that there was a more modern ship, a different mode of dress, and a different language. But none of that really affected them.

This time, however, several of us had been involved in the mini-series production and were marking time until we could blast off from earth for our great escape. The contestants on the last mini-series had lived in the expectation that when the last episode aired, we would actually be boarding the ship.

That night, we watched the dramatic conclusion to the show when the girls all rebelled against the eliminations and demanded that I take all of them. Then I revealed a portal to my 'other palace' in a hidden location. It ended with each of the girls giving their toast to the future and going through the gateway.

"Well, what do you think of the show?" I asked.

"It was so much fun! Will blasting off into space be as much fun?" Deedee asked.

"That's a good question, and it brings me to some matters that I need to discuss with you all. At the end of that episode, after everyone else was in Areola, Doug gave me some bad news. The construction of our ride is woefully behind schedule. It could be a year or more before we can actually board," I said.

"Oh, bummer," Julie said. "We'll just have to stay here in Areola and lie in the sun for a year or so. I can handle that."

That was the most serious expression of disappointment that the girls had.

"When you think about it, our intent was just to blast off and send some expression of excitement and farewell, then all come into the satchel to live here anyway. It's like the schedule was just moved up a year or so and we've already reached our destination," Karla said. "I don't see a problem."

"Good, good," I said as I looked over to my wives. They were giggling. "Well, you can all become productive citizens of Areola, but I have to go back out into the cold cruel world and produce another season of the show. This will need a new twist since we kind of shot our wad on the first season. I can't exactly convince a new crop of contestants that they are going to be eliminated."

"Aw. I'll help," Eun-ha said. "It would be fun to be on the other side of the cameras for a while."

"Yeah, me, too!" they all chorused. This was going better than I expected.

"Okay. I've got a job for you and the family," I said. "It would really be a big help." I put the banker's box in front of them. "There are 1,257 contestant resumes, photos, and release forms in this box. We need to consider which would be the most likely to make a good addition to our world and our crew so we can set up the season. I want them organized in groups of three that I will judge for one slot. That means you shouldn't put all three of your favorites in one contest. Two would be eliminated. On the other hand, you might put someone very low on the list in a competition to make sure your favorite gets chosen. But I won't know what your ranking is. I'll assume that these three are all acceptable to you. It's always possible I'll choose someone other than your favorite."

"What would cause you to do that?"

"Oh, I don't know. Suppose her pussy tastes like honey and I get addicted."

"More likely her pussy will taste like red wine if you're going to get addicted," Wendy giggled. The rest laughed and they started talking about how to go about making the choices and rankings. I excused myself.

Doug set some rules for their discussion. All the resumes had been assigned numbers, translated into English if necessary, and had location information redacted. The group was admonished not to use any names, since the cameras would be running and we'd be taping segments of the discussion when I actually made contact. This was going to be interesting. And, of course it would all change when I actually started interviewing candidates. There was no way around that.

The wives and possessions joined the discussion and occasionally Zhi or a priestess would join in. The priestesses were pleased that we weren't leaving yet. They wanted me to identify more kidnappers they could rid the world of. I thought that was a reasonable request.

Doug handled the publicity for season two, announcing that in the fall I would be hunting for new members for my harem from the 15,000 applications we had received so far. He was very blunt about what the contest would be and that not everyone I met with would even know they'd been taped for television. He invited those who had sent releases to contact us to withdraw if they no longer wanted to be considered.

I didn't expect the result. We received another 15,000 applications! Doug's staff took care of vetting the applications and determining if she should or shouldn't be considered. Rejection letters went out to 10,000. The other 5,000 were sent a detailed rules book, release form, consent form, and asked to provide detailed information and a photograph. I'd been surprised from the first batch how many of the applications came back with full nudes attached.

Perhaps the first line screeners had become better at their jobs and perhaps there were just a different class of women who applied after having seen the entire first season broadcast. The result was nearly 2,000 more completed applications. They were put on hold until the girls had finished their first pass on the original apps. Then they started in again.

Back when I was with Hubilai Khaan—remember that? Around a thousand or twelve hundred years AC—I got to know the adventurer Marco Polo fairly well. In addition to the seven arts and general Christian and Greek philosophy, Marco brought a tale from Europe that I found intriguing and a little inspiring. I cannot verify its veracity, but this, to the best of my recollection, is the way he told the story.

"There are many who tell the tale of the Great Khaan Chinggis defeating the Christian monarch called Prester John. This was about six years before the Great Khaan's death."

I nodded. I had already departed from the camps of Chinggis before he went to war over an insult from the King of Persia. Or the king of a part of Persia. Or a general who claimed to represent a King of Persia. The only thing most of the reports agreed upon was that his name was John.

"Well, I listened to many people in the course of my journey from Italy to Xanadu. We were on the road for three years and within our company, we counted a few Nestorian Christians from India. Their tale was very different than that told in the North. They hold that the name Prester John was usurped from its rightful bearer, who was one of the grandchildren of the Magi who visited Christ's birth in Bethlehem. That same Prester John is variously said to have been St. John the Apostle who was evacuated from the island of Patmos and went to visit the Apostle St. Thomas Didymus."

"You're saying that two of Issa's disciples made their way to India to join Issa?" I asked. Marco was confused until I told him that in India Jesus was known as Issa or Yuz Asaf which means Son of Joseph. Marco was surprised that I possessed this knowledge and I encouraged him to continue his tale.

"Strangely, that would fit. Now this is not scriptural, but there is common belief that St. John, who became known as Prester John, was set to rule a secret Christian kingdom in the East and that he will one day emerge from that location to announce the second coming of our Lord, in the same fashion that John the Baptizer announced his first coming," Marco said.

I remembered back to my meeting with John and being baptized by him, along with the satchel, which I counted as a baptism for all the residents of the infinity room. John had pointed me to Jesus and I really liked him. I'd thought I would set up a bit of a gig like John's and baptize people to point them toward the teachings of Jesus. Then they killed John by severing his head. That freaked me out, if I may use a common contemporary term. I fled from Judea east and as I wandered heard first that Jesus had been killed, and then that he was alive. That confirmed my opinion that he was, indeed, the greatest demon who had ever lived. He joined me at the mouth of the great river and we sailed for some time together until I put him ashore near the mouth of the Indus. I'd tried to find him a couple of centuries later, but found only the tomb and many legends of the great healer and prophet.

"Many men have searched for this secret kingdom, which some claim is in the great wall of mountains called Himavan. All we really know—or suppose—is that this is a fantastic kingdom of peace and plenty, is ruled over by the Christian King, Prester John, and that it is still there, but somehow made invisible to those who are unworthy."

I advised Marco to stick to the official tale of Chinggis' victory over Prester John at Tanduc, as that was part of the history of the Mongols. But I carried his words with me. Had I walked right past the Kingdom of Issa as I made my pilgrimage to find the Lama of Tibet? I thought about returning to the south and investigating, but it was better for me to turn east and set sail. I had been in China and the Mongolian Empire much too long.

Hubilai had built yet another city—Daidu—north of the remains of Zhongdu, a city Chinggis had besieged and leveled to the ground. From there, I traveled along the coast southward until I found a boat that I liked.

On the way, however, I witnessed an atrocity I was told was not uncommon in the coastal areas. It seemed that Korean and/or Japanese raiders held a high opinion of Chinese women and wanted to own one. No, they did not want to marry a Chinese woman, they had their own women for that. They wanted Chinese women just to fuck until they tired of them and then discard—that is, kill them.

The practice of raiding the mainland for sex slaves was established along the coastal waters for centuries, and continued centuries after I had left. I did not discover the extent of the horrors until long after I had left China.

I came across a village—even at this time, a coastal village could have several thousand inhabitants—that was beset by raiders. The men and women were defending their homes and families as raiders cut through the village killing people with their swords. When they came across a young girl they liked, they dragged her back to their boats.

There, along the beach, the men 'tried out' the women to be sure they only took the best. The rest were raped and then killed.

I was furious. I called Zhi from the infinity room and together we cut a swath through the raiders, putting all to death. We liberated some seventy young women. Many were in need of aid. Many more were dead. Zhi and my wives and possessions ministered to the girls and patched them up as well as we could before sending them home.

While we were still working to aid the wounded, girls began returning from the village. They had found their homes burned and their families dead. They begged me to save them once again. We took them to the infinity room and through a long process, integrated them into our female dominant society. We were inexperienced in dealing with so many refugees at one time. The priestesses of Aphrodite proved to be the greatest help as they had all fled together from Troy when I gave them the opportunity.

It was still a long slow process. The priestesses had offered their bodies to men as an act of worship for their goddess. The young Chinese women had their innocence ripped from them at the point of a sword. Let no one tell you that sex is just sex. The circumstances change lives. To this day, many of those young women live together in an isolated area where they quietly farm and go about their daily tasks. My wives and concubines, the priestesses of Aphrodite, and other women, visit them and over the years, most have forgotten the horror of that day in the thirteenth century. But an unfortunate side-effect of the infinity room is the meaninglessness of time. Should anyone mention the natural world or returning to the natural world, these women shake as if the horror had occurred just yesterday. All we can do is care for them.

Six centuries later, these were among the first recruited by my daughter Chin Li to join her as the Flying Sword. The girls took to the martial arts training and Li focused them on the slave traders in China. I believe the stories of the Flying Sword were part of the inspiration that turned my own priestesses into ninja warriors. Prior to that time—that is, the last quarter of the nineteenth century—my priestesses had contented themselves with keeping the light of my temple lit. Then they heard the stories of Li and her cadre of female warriors who went from Hong Kong throughout China, ending many traders and most of the trade in slaves from China to the Americas. My priestesses became anti-slavery warriors.

I intended to tell the story of my journey from China to the South Seas. I told a bit of that story once before, but this is a lesson in magic gone somewhat awry. As if you hadn't had enough lessons in that from my life.

I turned my little ship toward the southeast, easily outrunning three bandit ships that the former ship owner had sent after me. If I hadn't paid him so much for the boat, he would probably not have assumed I had so much more that it was worth sending pirates after me, but that was a short chase and they fell back to their port.

I had no particular destination in mind, but figured I would head south and then back toward the west to find India and the islands I'd once found so pleasant. I saw an island in the distance, and without checking my maps, simply pointed in that direction and raised a wind to send me that way.

Then I leaned back beside the tiller and opened a jug of rice wine. Perhaps I went a little overboard with the wine. Not literally overboard from my boat, but overboard in the consumption. At some point, as I watched the stars spinning in the sky, I passed out. When I awoke, a being was standing over me with his hand on the tiller. I looked around and could not see any sign of land.

"Greetings," I said.

"Oh, you're awake. You must have a strong constitution to resist my sleep spell. But it is of no matter. It will be nice to have company for a while," the man said.

"How may I address you?"

"You may call me A'a. I'm master of the seas in this part of the world."

"My respect to you, A'a. I am Bob."

"Yes. A creature direct from the primordial mass. When I saw your ship adrift, I had to investigate. You were asleep and I just enhanced your slumber a bit."

"I was headed toward an island with a wind in my sail. I'm not sure how I got out here."

"Well, you *are* headed toward an island. There is a wind. I might have altered the course a bit, but I saw that you are a strong and honest creature. I have need of such to help me with a small task."

"How may I assist you, A'a?"

"It's a simple matter of moving some stones. People who call on my name have asked for help in protecting their island. Now, I don't normally get involved in such menial affairs. There are lesser gods that could do this, but I found their requests to be humorous and thought I might just have some fun. Having a helper will confuse them no end," the god said.

He had light tan skin, as if darker skin had been bleached by the salt water. When I looked more closely, however, I saw the glint of reflected sunlight off what could only pass as scales. Upon looking again, they were gone.

"You have a sense of humor," I commented to the muscular god.

"Oh, yes. I spend far too much time quarreling with my brothers not to spend some bit of time having fun. It is a tiring world, even for a god."

"I'm not nearly as old as the oceans," I said, "but there are times when I simply want a place to settle down and stay concealed from the rest of the world."

"I have a place like that! I'll show you once we move the stones," he said congenially. We had a great time as we sailed generally southeastward. That wasn't the direction I'd intended to sail, but I had nowhere special to go. I could take my time. Eventually we came upon an island and sailed around it. I'd put a look-away spell on the boat when I was fleeing from the pirates, and I refreshed it so the islanders would not see us approaching.

"What is that?" I asked, pointing at an oddly shaped rock.

"That is why we are here. The islanders have come from across the sea in the past few centuries. They have reasoned that if they have found this place and it is a lush paradise for them, some others might also find it and take it from them. They have carved great stones into defenders of the island, but the stones all lie on their backs asleep. They are so large that the islanders have not figured a way to stand the stones up. They are sometimes called the sleeping guards or even the lazy guards. With your help, we'll run around the island overnight and stand them all up. People will awake tomorrow morning with their guards standing alert and at attention. I can hardly wait to hear what tales they will create about the waking of the guards." He laughed and I joined him. It was like a huge practical joke.

"How many of them are there," I asked.

"Oh, around a thousand, I suppose," he said. "A good night's work."

Indeed, it would be. We'd need to each stand a stone up every minute through the night. I practiced my spell for lightening a load.

At sundown, the people all retreated to their homes. A'a and I started in the least populated areas and began standing the stones up, digging them into the ground a bit to stabilize them, and moving on to the next stone. A'a brought up a wind and a storm arose to cover the noise we were making and to keep people indoors. I think mostly it was to cover his giggles.

By sunrise, we were standing the last of the stones when I saw a girl—perhaps just twelve or fourteen—near one of the huts watching us. I decided not to mention that to A'a. I wasn't confident of how he would treat a witness. Gods are like that. They prefer to eliminate things that aren't in their plans.

We concealed ourselves near the village and waited for people to realize the great statues were standing all around the island. The people rushed around in near madness, some bowing down before the stones. Then I saw the girl who had witnessed the last erection begin to spin and twirl in front of that statue. Soon people were watching her as a spirit of divination descended upon her. I glanced at A'a and he just shrugged.

"Here is the story we shall tell to our children and our children's children," the girl said. "I saw the great king Tuu Ku Ihu rise up from the sea. He came in a boat like no other this island has seen. Tuu Ku Ihu saw the sleeping guards and he was angry. 'How dare you sleep when you are supposed to be guarding my people?' he yelled. At the sound of his voice, a great wind arose and there was with the king, A'a who made the world. Tuu Ku Ihu consulted with the god and they agreed to wake the guardians and get them up. I saw the great king Tuu Ku Ihu slap the sleeping guard to wake him up. A'a then commanded the guard to arise and maintain vigilance over his village. This, the guard has risen to do and will be vigilant over our village as long as he stands. I, Tuma'a, saw these things happen and tell you the truth. The king and the god awoke these giants and set them to stand guard."

At that the teen spun once more and collapsed as the spirit of divination departed from her. The people carried her in honor back to the village. And that became the story that was told. A'a and I returned to my boat and set sail, both wondering at what kind of spirit had come over the girl.

58
WEALTH

’M RICH in the wealth of this world. By anyone’s standard. Peninnah has told me that in terms of equivalents, I’m richer than Mansa Musa, purportedly the richest man who ever lived. In today’s dollars, his wealth would have been well over $400 billion. I’m up around there, too.

There’s a big difference in the way wealth is measured, though. Mansa Musa’s wealth was in gold. I don’t know that anyone ever calculated the value of his city, his land holdings, his slaves, his wives, his palace, etc. He had $400 billion worth of gold!

My wealth is in various stock holdings which I’ve traded over the ages. When Peninnah began divesting our shares of oil, which I’d invested in just a few years AC, she turned them into real estate, technology, space exploration, manufacturing, and various mining and resource operations. We even have a number of farms and plantations, like those where our chocolate is grown. The value of any of those ventures can rise and fall on a daily basis.

But gold? A bar of gold is roughly 8.5”x2.5”x1”. That’s 400 Troy ounces, or approximately 438 fine ounces. That means, each brick of gold (like the ones you see pictured at Fort Knox) weighs a little over twenty-seven pounds. If we computed the number of pure gold bars represented by $400 billion, we would get around 300,000 bars of gold!

If you just stacked them one on top of the other, we’re talking about a tower five miles high!

When Mansa Musa began liberally distributing his gold on his pilgrimage to Mecca, he destroyed the local economies for more than a decade.

My wealth? Ha! I have a stack of paper, maybe a foot high, that records the shares I own of various enterprises, the property I own, and the bank accounts I have. Each piece of paper has been assigned a value, totaling around $450 billion, but that value varies day by day, depending on the market. I try to always carry some local currency with me when I travel, because you can't buy groceries with stock certificates.

I try to do good with my wealth. Peninnah bought us several dozen homes, many of which I've never traveled to. Some are as small as a little ranch in Kansas or a condominium in San Francisco. Others are as large as an entire South Sea Island. Each property employs a dozen to a couple hundred people to maintain it. I like this arrangement because I don't expect income from those properties, so the money I pay in salaries (and property taxes) goes directly into the local economy.

There are businesses that are 'for profit.' These include our cocoa plantations, for example, which employ people who grow our crops. The people are paid a good standard of living, but even after wages, crop development, taxes, and equipment, we turn a healthy profit on the produce. And, yes, we pay taxes on that. In fact, we also own a share of the chocolatier who buys the beans from our plantations. They process the chocolate into a hundred different products that are sold to various exchanges around the world that distribute to food outlets, and other manufacturers. We make a nice profit on each of those sales. Yes, I pay taxes on that profit, too.

Ultimately, every business I am involved in pays taxes on as many as a dozen different levels for the money it makes. I receive my share of the profit, and I personally pay taxes on it. And I still get wealthier every day.

What about charity? And research? And education? Yes. We fund hospitals, medical research facilities, educational institutions, scholarships, and hundreds of other worthy causes. The only thing we do *not* fund is religious organizations. Of any sort. I've built a number of temples in my life and have insisted on paying and caring for the people who served to create that temple. But I've never paid a priest. I've never refused to pay taxes on any income that establishment receives. And if churches, mosques, and temples around the world were truly not for profit, they would be required to use every penny they take in for good works. Religion should be a net-zero operation, in my opinion. I do not include evangelism in the category of good works.

Why go on about wealth? I'm not a fan. I consider wealth to be a form of slavery, not just for those who possess it, but for everyone they possess. I mean employ. In reality, I believe the women I actually possess are freer than most employees.

Sometime around seventy-five or eighty years ago, I became friends with a fellow I knew only as Bucky. He was quite a thinker. He built all kinds of futuristic structures, and I even recreated a few of them in Areola. Eventually, I included his structural philosophy in the design of my space ship.

He studied the universe and came up with some startling things.

"You've been around a while, Bob. You've seen the world change. We're constantly doing more and more with less and less. Now look at the radio, for instance. Just a decade ago, radios were cumbersome things that were a huge piece of furniture in a person's home. Wonderful things. They brought people news of the world. You might say, they made the world smaller."

Well, I certainly understood that. In the 1770s, I rode a horse for nearly two months to get from California to Pennsylvania, then another two months back. Now people flew from one to the other in hours! It was amazing.

"But look at this radio," Bucky continued, holding out a device that fit in the palm of his hand. "This little thing connects me just as well to the radio stations around the country as that big monstrosity sitting in my living room! What's the difference? We—people in general, not you and me specifically—learned how to make a transistor that's an inch long that would do the work of a dozen big vacuum tubes! And with a battery to operate it, I can carry my transistor radio with me wherever I go. I have much more contained in much less!"

"I see, Bucky. But people still need the same amount of food," I said, trying to come up with something to contradict his argument. "We don't do more with less food. If anything, we have to produce more and more as the population increases."

"But even in food production, our barns and silos are overflowing. Where it once took a hundred acres to feed a family, now we can feed the world on what is produced on our farms. And with farm machinery, it takes fewer people to produce that food. People aren't leaving the farms for the city because the work is too hard. They leave because there isn't enough work there to keep them busy."

"Why do we have so many poor and malnourished and sick?" I asked. "In this country of all places! How can I even begin to take care of people?"

"Scarcity economy," Bucky answered. "For hundreds—maybe thousands—of years, we've held up the notion that people need to *deserve* to live. They don't *deserve* adequate food, housing, medicine, or even safety unless they somehow earn it. That whole mindset of having to earn your way meant we needed a standard of what people were worth. We said time is worth a dollar and a half an hour. But if you're a doctor, it's worth ten or fifteen dollars an hour. If you work putting nuts on bolts all day long in a factory, that's a dollar and a half an hour. If you walk around making sure people keep putting the nuts on the bolts, that's worth five dollars an hour. If you sit in an office 'managing' the process of putting nuts on bolts, that's worth $100 an hour. But who is actually contributing to the gross product? The guy who's putting nuts on the bolts."

"I never used that in any of my times building temples, and don't use that in my infinity room. Everyone who works for the temple in whatever way, eats and is taken care of."

"Even that may be too greedy, Bob. Consider this: The Declaration of Independence says, 'We hold these truths to be self-evident, that all men are created equal, that they are endowed *by their Creator* with certain unalienable Rights, that among these are Life, Liberty and the pursuit of Happiness.' Show me where in that document it says anything about 'if they deserve it,' or 'if they earn it,' or even 'if they work.' We recognize this in our most primitive institutions. A man in prison is still given food, shelter, and clothing. In the least effective way possible."

"The problem as I see it is the whole minimum wage thing," I suggested. "We're still equating people with money. So, instead of guaranteeing a minimum income or wage, we should be guaranteeing food, shelter, and clothing. For everyone, with no exceptions. Sure, if you work for it, you can have better quality food, shelter, and clothing. You can have other things, but your worth as a human is not dependent on those things."

"And education, Bob. How can anyone truly grow as a person unless they have access to a comprehensive education? When a child progresses from elementary to more advanced education, the first thing we ask him is 'What are you studying?' We expect him to answer, 'law,' 'biology,' 'medicine,' 'mathematics.' We expect him to be specialized. But the only great advances in humanity come from those who have a comprehensive understanding rather than a specialized understanding," Bucky said.

That was just a sample of my conversations with Bucky over the years and he made sure I had signed copies of his books for my library. But it bothered me no end. When Peninnah told me I was the richest man on earth, it depressed me. Oh, I was happy to have a new home or ten. I was pleased that we could employ a thousand or ten thousand people.

But it all seemed like a drop in the ocean when I looked at all that needed to be done. I wanted to promote those unalienable rights. I had money. What else did I need?

Of course, none of that applied to Areola. Millions of people lived in my little world, but no one went without any needed thing. And people were valued because they were people. We cared for thousands we'd rescued over the years who could not care for themselves. They still had their needs met and the opportunity to contribute in any way they found. I realized the idea that everyone who works for the temple received what they needed was antiquated and might have been a reasonable concept when I was building Xanadu, but in Areola, everyone ate. Everyone had shelter and clothing (if they wanted clothing). We didn't require clothing and the weather was such that it wasn't really needed. The scarcity philosophy that 'there's no such thing as a free lunch,' was an archaic idea that had no place in our world of plenty.

We weren't really a melting pot, either. People clustered together by background, interest, level of technology, religion, region of origin, and even time in history. When people discovered others they wanted to live with and have children with, then the melding of races and ideas began. But when children came along, people began to age with them. Children grew up and their parents grew old. Eventually, those who had children on Areola or who were born there died.

I still didn't understand how the world worked. Ideas were freely exchanged and the libraries became the centers of our educational system. Whatever one wanted to learn could be learned in the library. The possibilities were infinite.

I'm certain I had a point to make with that whole story. I can draw all kinds of conclusions from it that probably don't have relevance. Even gods who are generally seen as horrific in their worst appearances have a humorous side to them. My time with A'a reminded me of my time with Zeus, only with less fucking.

I also noticed that there are phenomena that the gods don't understand, even in the world they created. A'a had no idea what came over the girl that made her tell the story she did. I didn't mention the fact that she'd seen us setting up the last stone. Perhaps she was just a gifted storyteller and made it up on the spot. It wouldn't be the first time a storyteller saw something they didn't understand and made up a story about it. Read the daily news.

A'a did show me his island getaway. I couldn't see it until we'd sailed right onto the beach. He had quite a comfortable dwelling there and said he just needed to get away from his brothers at times. And it got soggy at the bottom of the sea, even for a sea god. I wondered if Poseidon had joined the Greek gods on Olympus when they withdrew and if so, did he have a sea there to rule over or was he happy to be on dry land?

I will say that since that time, I have searched for the island of A'a on maps to no avail. When satellite imagery became available, I searched all over the South Pacific for an unidentified island and could not find one. I'm sure the imagery would have revealed it, just as airport x-rays showed my satchel. The video cameras saw it, too.

I found reference to an island called Land of Davis after a pirate who had sighted it but did not land. After many decades, reference to the mysterious island disappeared from maps and it is all but forgotten. It is possible that Davis did see the island during a time when A'a was entering or leaving his secret retreat.

I will also say that this story illustrates that gods are capricious. Or perhaps they quickly forget. I encountered the god of the sea again years later (after I'd found another island just at the time of its mass marriage ritual) as I sailed westward and was caught in a battle between the brothers Tawhirimatea and Tu (also sometimes identified as Tangaroa or A'a). That was when my voyage on the Pacific came to an abrupt end. My little ship was cast half way across Australia by the warring brothers.

What brought all this to mind was our refuge while we were planning the next season of *To Boldly Go*. Peninnah had managed to acquire a very nice villa on a Pacific Island and we'd been enjoying relative peace and quiet—mostly just staying in Areola. People did seem to enjoy popping out to see earth's sun and to play on the sandy beach of the Pacific. It was getting to be time, however, when I needed to shoot a test pilot of the concept for the next series. I was going to emerge from isolation yet again.

59
PILOT TEST

"WE'RE GOING TO have fun with this," Doug said as I sat with the family and crew. "The fabulous ladies of Crew One did a great job of sorting and matching up contestants."

I looked around and saw the cameras running. So, Doug wasn't just talking to us, we were actually in the beginning stages of recording the show. I noticed that the cameras were mostly behind us, so they'd be showing Doug over our heads. Avril, however, was in front where she could record facial reactions and... Let's just face it and say she was making sure we had tits on display. She'd been recording the entire process of the evaluation and selection of candidates—hours and hours of recording. We'd discovered something intriguing: In Areola, the batteries for the cameras never ran down. We didn't have to go to the natural world to plug them in to recharge.

"Now, we left a few details out when you were doing the evaluations. Nothing critical that would affect your decisions, but something that might have subconsciously caused some subtle shifts. We intentionally removed the names of the contestants and you have referred to them only by their contestant number. We also removed the location information and had all the applications translated to English. Our applicants come from literally all over the world. And our first set of three contestants you have chosen are from three different continents: North America, Asia, and Australia. This will show how well we can work in coordinating things in a quick and effective way."

There were a number of exclamations and comments about the minor deception, but no one was upset about it. It made sense that they might have rejected someone on the basis of a name or of a country of origin. We'd been heavily North America-centric in our first round having only five of thirteen contestants from countries other than the US. This was almost like a random drawing to find out where we would travel.

"The interviews with the candidates will occur over three days in each country. Bob will need to make a decision quickly after that, assisted, of course, by you lovely ladies. You'll get to see all the footage as it's revealed and I'm sure you'll be cheering for your favorites. So, the initial interviews will all be over in nine days. Then Bob will cycle back through to the women to tell them who he really is and whether they were successful. This might require some fine tuning. We will pay each of the losers, but our signed releases allow us to film them candidly and to broadcast the footage without limitation, regardless of whether they are chosen. There is one caveat. We will not broadcast sex scenes with anyone who is not chosen to move forward without that person's additional release after they know they were eliminated."

"How are we arranging the travel?" Liz asked. "I assume we still need our production crew and cameras."

"Yes and no," Doug said. "I've talked over some of the logistics with Bob and we've agreed on a trial for the first set. Bob will travel alone."

"What?"

"No!"

"He can't leave us!"

"Calmly. Calmly, ladies. Bob will travel with… er… um… the portal. When he arrives in each location, he will summon forth the players needed for the interview, including camerawomen. I have a ground crew already in place in each of the locations, gathering background footage and seeing how aware the contestants are when they are filmed. These will all be distance shots with telephoto lenses. We aren't getting close enough to tip them off."

"When we get to the location, I'll um… use some tech… um… that enables us to move without being noticed by people. I use it to disguise the portal, for example." I was trying every way possible to not say I was going to cast a spell that would make them unnoticed. "It does not shield us from electronic or mechanical recognition, however. We don't blend with the air, so to speak. *People* just won't notice us. That way, the camera crew that joins me from Areola should be able to get in fairly close to the subject and record all our interactions without her noticing."

"Look away, look away, look away, Dixie Land," Karla sang. She was a Georgia girl and I guess they never forget.

"The great thing about this is that we don't need to mess around with entry visas and passports—except for Bob. And he'll be incognito. Once we're inside, we'll stage the operation and make the recording. Then he'll put us back on his shoulder and beat feet for the next location."

It all sounded like it would be easy. It wasn't, of course.

I took our private plane from Tahiti to Honolulu and put it in storage after I'd passed customs and they'd agreed there was nothing in my satchel that shouldn't be. In fact, they'd called in a supervisor, led me to a white room, and emptied everything there was in the satchel, x-raying it again when it was empty.

"All right," said the Customs Officer. "Where is the portal?"

"Really? It's a television effect. Haven't you seen them before?"

"I knew it. All this fuss over a fake TV reality show. The stupid brass have their undies in a bunch over this transporter thing you're supposed to have." He lowered his voice confidentially. "So where did you stash all the babes you had on the show. There were some seriously good-looking women there."

"They were fun to work with. They're all still hiding out in California. We're trying to put together a second season concept, but it's rough going," I answered lightly.

"I thought that palace scene looked like California. Well, if you need a guy to help you manage all the women, call me. You can repack now."

I put my underwear, shaving kit, toothbrush, and change of clothes back in the bag and left the checkpoint. Across the way, I could see agents still crawling all over my plane. I took a Wiki Wiki Shuttle to the main terminal and grabbed a cab to my ocean-front home farther north.

That could have gone worse. I had visions of them tearing the bag apart at the seams. I needed to figure out a way to change the appearance of the bag itself. I was going to change my own appearance, as well. From here, I wouldn't be traveling as Bob.

My problems were resolved through an unexpected means. I stopped at the main shopping area in downtown Honolulu to pick up some clothes. It's a shopping Mecca and people go there from all over the world to buy designer clothes and accessories that they could get for half the price in any big shopping mall on the mainland. But I needed clothes to fit my new image. The image I adopted, in the changing room, was that of a blond surfer dude I'd seen on the beach. The body wasn't quite as big as I'd normally choose, but it was strong, fit, and young. This next part of the trip could be fun.

However, as I was shopping and strolling through the stores, I came upon a display of "The Bob Satchel" by a top name luggage manufacturer. Hmm. I examined the quality of the bag and it wasn't bad at all. Of course, it was made of cow leather instead of goatskin, as my original bag was. If anyone was sharp enough at customs to identify that, the difference would give me away right off.

"That's our best seller!" a bright young woman said as she came up to me. "I mean, it's flying off the shelves. We've sold at least a hundred of them since the end of that mini-series on TV. It's almost impossible to get them now because the manufacturer in Hong Kong can't keep up with the demand. And they're all over. The world, I mean. Look at this copy of GQ. It has pictures of handsome guys like you carrying it from Europe to Asia to America. I've got to tell you, though, most of the guys in these pictures don't look as good with it as you do."

"You don't need to flatter me to make the sale," I laughed. "I'm sold."

"I'm not, really. I mean flattering you to make a sale. Are you a beach bum? It's, like, just my luck to pick out somebody who doesn't have a penny to his name. But I guess you wouldn't be buying this bag if you were poor."

"That's true. $500? Wow!"

"Marcie, our manager, is raising the price another twenty percent, but I haven't got them marked yet. She says no one knows the difference between $500 and $599. Can you believe that? No one's supposed to notice the price went up a hundred bucks!"

"Is this like your career? I mean selling luggage?"

"Oh! No, but I haven't had much luck with my real career, and a girl's got to eat."

"What's the real career?"

"Singer, actor, dancer. Triple threat, they say in the theatre. But live theatre is being undercut by the media. Ever since that pandemic hit a few years ago, people don't go to as much live entertainment as they used to. At least not live theatre. I guess the music venues are still packing them in. I finally thought I had my big break. New show, with good music, and I had the lead. Then opening night—would you believe it?—management came through and told us the show was canceled and the theatre was closed by order of the governor. They kept telling us we'd pick up where we left off, but the playwright died from COVID and the theatre company went bankrupt. The building is in use for corporate meetings and live audience recording of comedians and such."

"Gee, that's too bad. I bet you'd be dynamite on stage. I used to do some performing myself. All classics, though," I said. I didn't say I was in original Greek plays 2,500 years ago.

"Tomorrow and tomorrow and tomorrow, creeps in this petty pace from day to day," she quoted. "I was in that Scottish play in college. We learned classics as much as musical theatre."

"I hope that one didn't have any catastrophes waiting in the wings."

"Only minor ones. I grabbed a drink of water just before going on stage and was choking when I heard the messenger tell me the king was coming. I made it through, though:

The raven himself is hoarse

That croaks the fatal entrance of Duncan

Under my battlements.

Come, you spirits

That tend on mortal thoughts, unsex me here,

And fill me from the crown to the toe top-full

Of direst cruelty!

"I got some nice notices."

"It gives me the chills to hear you talk like that," I laughed. Her voice was really quite compelling.

"It's high school drama these days. You find Shakespeare in specific festival theaters around the country. Ashland, Stratford, Stratford, and Stratford, Canterbury, Cambridge. I am not going to even consider going to Alabama for their festival!"

She struck a dramatic pose and did the same speech in a southern accent, rephrasing the speech in her vision of Southernese.

Thet big ol' blackbird jest cawing itself hoarse

Telling everybody I'm gonna off the King t'night.

I tell ya, bogeyman:

Fuck me raw and fill me up.

I'm a gonna kill that bastid.

"I can just imagine that!" I laughed. "We ought to get together and stage our own down South version. We'll call it That Confed Play. Anyone who says the name is cursed to a life of mint juleps and humidity."

"And wearing a ballgown made of draperies."

We laughed and there was a sparkle in her eye that I found incredibly attractive. I started to speak, but she beat me to it.

"Um... Wanna get together tonight?" she asked. "I mean... I'm not offering to fuck you... yet. But I like you and I get off work here in a couple of hours. We could, um... go somewhere for dinner and talk some more."

"I'd like to say yes, but I never go out with a girl unless I know her name."

"I'm Annie Wolcott."

"That's a great name for the stage. I'm Bob." No, I didn't use my real name, but aren't there enough people in this story without wondering what name *I'm* going by all the time? "Can I pick you up here in two hours?"

"Yeah. I'm single. Unattached. Um... Are you?"

"I have a lot of attachments, but I'm free."

"That sounds like a story to be told."

"Annie, I want those tags changed before you leave tonight," a voice came from the back of the store. "If you're done there, let's get it going so I can update the computer."

"Okay, Marcie," Annie called. "I'll see you in a couple of hours or so," she said to me and scurried off. I left with my new Bob Satchel.

I had the driver take me to my house, half an hour north of the city, and had him wait for me to put my purchases away and then take me back to the city. I changed clothes into something I thought appropriate for an evening out near the beach. Hawaii is not exactly a suit and tie kind of place. Then I spent a few minutes working on the satchel. The new bag was good quality—it had better be at $500. I did some scrunching and forcing, but I managed to fit my old satchel inside, and then worked a little magic to make the two bags fuse together. I opened a gateway to make sure everything was okay in Areola and my wives laughed at me when I told them I was going out on a date. They sent a new camerawoman with me and I worked the look away spell on her and her equipment. I guess this was a good test. I'd had a camerawoman dogging my steps ever since I landed and I was sure my entire shopping spree and conversation with Annie was recorded.

At the store, I finally dismissed and paid the driver, giving him a nice tip. In Honolulu, every place we might want to go was within walking distance. I stood outside the store waiting for my date.

"Oh, cool. A Bob Bag," a woman said as she and some friends came up the street. "Are you him?"

I just grinned at her and pointed to the display in the store window.

"Oh, damn. I suppose all the guys will be carrying them now. Too bad. I'm married, but I'd still put out for Bob." The women giggled and went on up the street, stopping in at a lounge for cocktails.

"Hey, nice bag," Annie said as she came down the steps from the shop. "Think you could stuff me in it and take me for a ride? My feet are killing me."

"I could try," I said with a forced laugh. She just stooped to pull off her shoes as she held onto my arm.

"That's better. Let's walk down by the beach. We can find someplace for dinner and drinks."

That was fine with me. Waikiki Beach was grown over with hotels. It was hard to find an access to the beach that wasn't through one of the massive resorts. She navigated through the maze and found a nice tiki bar with a view of the beach and the ocean.

"I love these funky old-style bars," Annie said. "They make me feel like I just walked onto a television set for something like *Hawaii Five-0*."

"Different than the old days, though. Something like this is more of a caricature of what Don the Beachcomber was when it opened. It barely had stools at the bar. The grass roof was to keep the bartender cool, not the customers."

"You sound like you were there," Annie said.

I shut my mouth. Don the Beachcomber had opened in 1933. I'd taken the ladies of the infinity room there to get a taste of a modern tropical beach which they went back to the infinity room and replicated on our own ocean front. I wasn't sure exactly how big our ocean was. I'd taken some water from the Pacific and started the ocean back in the first or second millennium AC. We often sampled the sand of various beaches around the world to create different experiences at our shore.

"Just a history buff, I guess," I said lamely.

"So, tell me about yourself, Bob the History Buff. I've already decided you aren't a local. Where'd you come from and what do you do?"

I told her I had a small import and export business and I traveled a lot. In fact, I was supposed to leave the next day, but I'd already decided that I'd like to spend another day with Annie before I ran off to interview others. I mean, really, why couldn't Annie have been my first interview. I really liked her.

Annie was a native of New York who got tired of the cold winters and decided to go to college as far away as possible. I gathered there were more reasons than the weather. She mentioned a love affair gone sour. She got her drama and theatre arts degree from the University of Hawaii and had been in Honolulu ever since.

"We created our bubble during the pandemic," she said. "One of the guys was born on the island and we all invaded his family farm on Maui. There were eight of us, plus his family. We earned our room and board by working on the farm when most other people wouldn't or couldn't. It's one of those farms that has always doubled as a retreat center and attracts eco vacationers. The vacationers get to come to Hawaii and in turn they work on the farm. Well, there were no vacationers during the pandemic and the farm work still needed to be done. So, we went there and broke our backs for two years until the all-clear sirens sounded. Brad and two of his girlfriends are still there and hosting the place. His parents didn't make it through the pandemic."

"That's too bad. You weren't tempted to stay?"

"Tempted, but I wanted more in my life than frustrated theatre people turned farmers. I came back to Honolulu and got a job waiting tables as tourists began to return. Then the opportunity at G&B came up and I decided that was better than wiggling my tush from four till midnight, hoping for tips. Marcie's a bit of a slave-driver, but she pays well. And we get a commission. I'm a pretty good salesperson," she laughed, poking at my bag.

"You are, indeed." We stayed at our table and ordered dinner. I'd always had a thing for poke and they served a delicious bowl.

We had another cocktail and then went out for a walk on the beach. She gave me her shoes to stuff in my bag. There was room. We held hands and I soon found my arm around her, my own shoes stuffed in the bag and my trousers rolled up so the surf could play around my toes. In one of those romantic moments I was sure my camerawoman was catching, we stopped for a kiss, silhouetted against the dramatic backdrop of Diamond Head with a full moon in the distance.

"Would you like to come home with me tonight?" I asked.

"Yes, but... I have to tell you something. I really like you and I'd like to be with you for a while..."

"But?"

"Well, I kind of made a commitment and it's only fair I tell you about it. You know that Reality TV show *To Boldly Go?* I applied to be on it. I've heard there were like thirty thousand applicants and they only chose a tiny fraction, but I signed a release and agreement that I'd like to be on the show. That means the star, this Bob-guy, could show up at any time and ask me out. It would be dumb of me if I said, 'Oh, I'd like to but I met this other guy.' I just want you to know that there's a remote possibility—I mean really remote, because what's the chance I'd get chosen for one of his surprise dates?—that he'll show up and take me out and interview me and maybe sleep with me to decide if I'm a good candidate to take to Mars with him. I just want you to know that... I'm willing to sleep with you and have more fun, but I can't make any big commitment right now."

"That's really good to know," I said. What were the chances? I was nearly jumping inside to tell her that I was Bob, but I was sure she wouldn't believe me if I did and that she'd probably stalk off away from me if I tried something like that. "I'm still willing if you are. I told you I need to leave in a couple of days and will be gone for about two weeks. We can both use the time to think it over and decide if we want to see each other again. Fair enough?"

"Fair enough. Take me home, Bob the History Buff, Bob the Importer, Bob the Actor, and whatever other Bob you have in store. I hope one of you is Bob the Great Lover."

I did my best. Annie was a marvelous lover. She was, I found out, twenty-seven years old. She was about five-seven in her bare feet, which when I discovered it, was not the only thing that was bare. Her body was built for a bikini. I wasn't sure how she managed an overall tan like she had, but there was no evidence of the bikini straps anyplace. She appreciated my new body, as well. It was the first time I'd had the opportunity to try it out and I was pleased with the way my new body responded to her. So was she.

We kissed and danced around the room, moving out to the lanai where we overlooked the beach down to the water's edge.

"I'd suggest we go make love on the beach, but I've done that before and it took days to get the sand out of places that were never meant to have sand in them," she giggled. "So, why don't we make love on the bed and then go take a walk in the moonlight before it's gone."

"I like the way you think, Annie." I picked her up as she squealed.

"I'm too big to pick up like that!"

"Nonsense. You're just right. I could carry you in my arms all night long."

"Oh, you sweet talker."

I kissed her as we settled on the bed and then began working my way down her body, taking my time to worship her plump and sensitive breasts. Her nipples stood out straight a good half an inch from the areola. They were just too tempting to latch onto and tease. She squirmed and I continued tracing a path down her body until I parted her legs and played my tongue across her bare mons. Before long, I'd found her happy spot and teased it until she moaned.

"Fuck me, Bob. I want you desperately."

"Soon, love," I said. Instead of moving from between her legs, I inserted my tongue in her love tunnel and licked across the G-spot, tickling it until she screamed with her second orgasm. Then I moved back up her body and pushed her blonde hair out of her eyes where it had fallen as she thrashed around.

I notched my cock at her entrance and swiped it up and down to make sure I was well-covered in her juices.

"Yes. In me. Put it in me, Bob. I want you."

I kissed her deeply as I gradually pressed into her pussy, both of us moaning as I entered her.

"Give it to me. Give me all you have. I'm being stretched more than I've ever been. You're going to ruin me for any other man, Bob. Fuck me!"

I did. I fucked on top of her until she came again. Then I rolled over and she fucked on top of me until she'd peaked again. In addition to being beautiful, she was agile. She swung a leg over me and managed to spin around on my cock until she was facing away from me and I played with her lovely bottom as she fucked her way to another orgasm.

Yes, I know. That's four or five orgasms. I hadn't come yet. I'm not a human. I'm a demon. I was created perpetually horny. I can fuck for hours without coming, and I often do. I wanted to be sure Annie was fully sated before I spent my load. It wasn't that I couldn't turn around and come again, but I've learned one thing about sex in my four millennia, it's that something changes once the man comes in his woman. Even if he stays hard, she can tell the difference if she's paying attention. Annie was the kind of girl who pays attention.

After she'd come in the reverse cowgirl position, I pushed her forward until she was on her hands and knees and I was behind her. And then I rode for glory. I'm pretty sure Annie came twice more before I unleashed my torrents into her welcoming pussy. We collapsed together on the bed and gasped, trying to continue kissing as we were catching our breath.

"You weren't supposed to make me feel like that, you bastard," she whispered. "What am I going to do now? It shouldn't have felt like that."

END PART XI

Part XII
Catch Me If You Can

Image credit: Aura Angel, ID 2106325418, Licensed from Shutterstock.com.

60
SOMETHING MORE

I HAVE SOME experience with South Sea Islands. Might have spent a few centuries there if I remember rightly. I suppose Areola was influenced as much by the South Seas as by the Mediterranean. I loved soft white sand and warm salty water. I loved the clear skies and bright sun. I loved the skimpily clad or unclad beauties playing on the beach.

Well, on one of those islands, I met a kind of chieftain named Hamalamadingdug. For convenience's sake, I'll just call him Doug. Anyway, he wasn't a big king or anything. The island wasn't big enough to have a king. There were only a few hundred or maybe a thousand people. He wasn't even the richest man on the island. The richest man was a woman, and he owned her.

"Why would I want only her money?" he asked. "If I own her, do I not automatically own her property as well?"

"It would be more humane if you only owned her money and not her," I objected. Have I mentioned that I don't like slavery?

"You want her?" Doug asked. "How about if I sell her to you for all the money she owns?"

"Why don't you just keep the money and set her free?" I said reasonably.

"But it's her money and she has not attempted to use it to buy her freedom."

"And you think I would take her money from her to pay you for her? That doesn't make sense."

"Oh, you couldn't do that!" Doug said. "That money is hers. You would have to pay me that amount of money and then I would give you her and all she owns."

"So, if her money isn't yours, what's her value to you?"

"She spends it as I say. But there isn't really that much to spend it on. I provide her meals and shelter, so she doesn't even need to spend her money on that."

I looked at Ilona, the chieftain's wealthy slave. There was something strange about the whole thing. There weren't many slaves on the island. In fact, Ilona was the only one I'd met.

"So, you would sell her for a certain amount of money," I said. "How much?"

"Hmm. I could price her by the pound. We can put her on the scale and you add as much gold as will balance her," Doug suggested.

"I don't think it's very fair to price a person by the pound like you'd price a pig. I don't plan to eat her," I said.

"You should consider it," Doug said. "She's very tasty and enjoys the attention."

"What?"

"What?"

I looked at Doug, gradually realizing he wasn't talking about butchering her. The guy could be rather confusing.

"Okay. What if we price her by the day? I'll sell her to you and you pay me a piece of gold for every day of her life," Doug said.

"Forever? That's more like paying rent," I said.

"No, no, no. Of course not. I couldn't charge you for what is yours. Every day so far. She's twenty-two years old. Let's see: 365 days per year times twenty-two would be... Give me some help here, Bob."

I'm not particularly good at math, but I looked in my satchel and could see Josie through the portal. She was holding up a sign that said, '8,030.' I gave Doug the answer.

"Whoo! Can you count that high? She must be worth all the gold in the world!" Doug said.

"That just shows it's not a good measure of her value. People aren't worth time. People aren't worth money."

"What are people worth?" Doug said. "It's the price of her life."

"Her life is the price she pays for living," I countered.

"Deep," Doug whispered.

I think at the time we were drinking some kind of fermented coconut water. It was a little vinegary and I definitely preferred wine, but this was doing the trick. The trick being getting me drunk.

"Would you trade *your* life for her?" Doug asked.

At the time, I was seriously considering trading Doug's life for her. I don't like slavery and I don't like slavers. There was just something different about this one that made me withhold my vengeance. There were those in Areola who would have killed him first and skipped the philosophical discussion. I glanced over at Ilona, sunning herself naked on the beach. My goat was stirring.

"One of two things would occur if I traded my life for hers. Either I would be dead, or I would be your slave. I don't think either of those is a good trade," I said. "You need to understand that people's lives are beyond price. There is nothing I can pay that is equal in value to the person. They are not to be valued by the pound or by the hour or by any measure of usefulness. They are valued because it is their life. Life is the value and you can't own another person's life!"

I was getting heated up and was taken aback by Doug's snore. My diatribe on the value of life fell on deaf ears. I picked myself up and wandered over to sit down beside Ilona. She smiled at me with brilliant white teeth and bare breasts. Don't ask me how she smiled with bare breasts. That certainly wasn't all of her that was smiling. Or bare.

"Bob, are you enjoying your visit to this bit of paradise?" Ilona asked. "Is there anything I can get for you? Anything you see that you want?"

Perhaps my alcohol addled mind was playing tricks on me. I didn't just blithely go around seducing women who were attached to other men, whether I agreed with the attachment or not. If I chose to have sex with Ilona, I'd probably have to kill Doug. I really didn't want to do that. He seemed so harmless otherwise.

"Ilona, I have been attempting to negotiate your freedom from Doug."

"Freedom?"

"Yes. I believe in the self-worth of all people." I picked up on my diatribe from where I'd left off before Doug went to sleep. Ilona propped herself on one elbow, turning to face me. It was very distracting. She was breathing. "People are meant to be free, to make their own choices, and to determine their own fates. We are not meant to live in slavery. No amount of money can be assessed to pay for a life. I am fighting—figuratively—for your freedom from slavery to Doug."

"Bob. Bob, if your ears are hearing my voice, even as your eyes are devouring my breasts, you need to know something."

I tore my eyes away from the hypnotic rising and falling of those beautiful mounds.

"Yes, Ilona?" I said.

"I am *not* Doug's slave."

"What? But..."

"I'm his wife."

Seldom in my life have I felt the instantaneous shriveling of all that is between my legs. I was certain my balls were crawling up inside me to take up residence next to my kidneys. Wife?

"He... I... thought... He said he was not the richest man on the island, but he had you and you were the richest person, therefore, he was rich."

"That's true enough. He doesn't have much money. We have the beach and the island, and people come to Doug for his ability to settle quarrels and pass judgments. He's pretty good at it. Mostly talks around in circles until people give up what they were arguing about."

"But he doesn't own you?"

"How ridiculous. What's his is mine and what's mine is my own. This idea of freedom you have... I've never heard that word before. You mean living? What you describe as freedom is what we would just call living," Ilona said.

"Yes. Yes, that is exactly what I mean," I said.

"Good. Now, I've not finished my nap. Since you seem to enjoy it so much, why don't you just sit here and watch me breathe while I sleep. We'll all get dinner after our naps."

Of course, I should have just left the island and gone back to Areola where my wives and possessions and concubines and priestesses were waiting for me. But Ilona's breasts were mesmerizing. I sat there all afternoon watching them rise and fall, slightly stretching as she breathed.

Did I mention I like island living?

Back to Annie. I delayed my flight out of Hawaii another day. Annie and I spent every minute together. Of course, no one in Areola would have known anything was amiss if I hadn't had to slip into a bathroom a few times a day to change camera operators. That was when things broke loose in Areola.

"Bob! This is great stuff!" Doug shouted when I stuck my head in the second time. "You picked up a new hottie out of the blue. But you still need to catch your flight to Singapore. One more day. That's all you can spend in Honolulu. We have a schedule to meet."

"She says she filled out the paperwork and signed the releases," I said. "Is there anything I should know about her? Any red flags."

"She was my top choice!" Deedee said. "I know she's in the rotation somewhere. Go tie her down, so to speak. She'll be perfect!"

"But I have to interview three more!" I said.

"That's just this time," Doug reminded me. "If this all works, you'll need to interview at least three every ten days until we have a full season in the can."

"I might die," I said.

"Don't bet on every girl you meet being that ready to jump in the sack with you," Eun-ha said. "The Asian girls aren't that fast. Well, most of them."

"We'll play it all by ear. I'm not out there to set a record for how many women I've slept with," I growled.

"That would be some record to break," Peninnah said, glancing around the pool at all the concubines who were out sunning themselves.

Annie and I didn't just fuck. She wanted me to show her other moves—like on a surfboard. I admit, I had the ideal surfer body. I was strong and tan. My sandy hair looked like I'd just come off the beach. The problem was that I'd never been surfing before. One more new experience.

I managed to get out beyond the breakers and waited my turn for a good wave. I didn't need to wait long. I got on top of the board and caught the swell just at the right time. On the other hand, it took me half way to the beach before I was fully standing up. And no one had told me how to land. I sprawled on the sand with the board lying a few feet away. I looked up to see Annie laughing at me.

I was momentarily distracted by her bikini. Rather, by her body as displayed by the bikini. One reason I hadn't seen much in the way of tan lines is because her bikini didn't cover much.

"You *look* a lot better than you *surf!*" she laughed. "Seriously. Have you ever done this before?"

"Uh... No," I answered truthfully. I'd been afraid I'd need to transform into my demon body if I'd been washed off the board. I really wasn't a strong swimmer as a human.

Annie picked up my board.

"I'll show you," she said. Before I could respond, she'd headed into the surf and started paddling out to the waiting line.

In a couple of minutes, she'd spotted and called her swell. She was on the board, waiting for the water to lift her. I had to say that she reminded me of Aphrodite emerging from the waves on a sea shell. Of course, it hadn't been a sea shell that brought Aphrodite to the shores of Cyprus. She rode on my back. And then she rode on my front.

Annie had perfect balance on the board. She was standing and as she cut into the pipe, I saw something else: Her top was in her hand as she waved it at me. I think every surfer dude was holding his breath as she emerged from the pipe and slid nicely onto the beach. She grabbed the board and ran to me.

"Here! Help me back into this," she laughed. I helped tie her bikini top on and then, much to the disappointment of the other guys, we left the beach.

"I really need to leave tomorrow morning," I said. "I'm scheduled in Singapore next and that's a long damn flight."

"Yeah. I really hate saying this, but I'm going to miss you and hope you'll come back, even if it's just for a little visit," she said. "I'm not going to try to tie you down. You know I applied for that TV show. I'm not quite as enthusiastic about it now, but I'm not going to get in the way of the things you need to do, either. You said you're headed around the world from here. I guess that's what you meant by having a lot of attachments. A port in every girl. I just... Well, if you get back here to Hawaii, this port will be waiting for you."

She guided me once again into her loving pussy and we made love for hours. I didn't get any sleep. I just lay there awake and watched her sleeping, her sated smile enhancing her already beautiful features.

The first leg of my flight was Honolulu to Narita, Japan. It was nine hours flight time, but somewhere in there I crossed the International Date Line and lost a day. After a two-hour layover, it was another seven hours to Singapore. There is little to do on an airplane for that long, even in first class. I did take a little time in the bathroom while everyone was asleep. I locked the door and entered Areola. It was more comfortable there than in my seat, but I couldn't really stay. I went back to my seat in time for the pretty good meal they served in first class.

The meal was a "Japanese Fusion" meal and was easy to eat with chopsticks. It included roast beef with miso pesto, summer vegetables, and crab meat. Then I discovered that was just the appetizer. It was followed by misoyaki salmon, pickled vegetables, steamed rice, and miso soup. The cheesecake souffle for dessert was delectable. So was my flight attendant, by the way, though we did nothing but flirt. When she discovered I was only changing planes at Narita, she quickly brought me another carafe of sake and went to flirt with another solo male passenger.

I have to say the meal served by my Singaporean flight attendants on the next flight was superb, starting with the caviar on toast down to lobster salad, wintermelon soup, seared sirloin, and a dessert cheese platter with my coffee and pralines. The bottle of wine I had with dinner had me feeling extremely mellow and I settled back in the ample lounge chair. The lights in the cabin were turned down and for an unknown reason, my flight attendant perched herself on the arm of my chair and we talked softly for most of the trip. She often smoothed my hair or caressed my cheek and did not seem to mind my hand on her thigh. The cabin only had a couple of others in it, so I guess she could afford the time to pay special attention to one of them.

"You may call me this week and I'll happily show you some of the better sights of Singapore," she whispered as she slipped me a card with her name and number on it. "If you like your hand where it is now, you'll like it better in other places. And I'm not that expensive," she said.

Wait! Not that expensive? Oh, my. She had certainly been seductive in her approach. I guess some flight attendants still supplement their income in the old-fashioned way. She flitted off after bending to kiss my forehead to prepare the cabin for arrival. I looked at the card. Jill Wang. Escort in Singapore, $1000 US per full day.

Hmm. If she was independent and got to keep the money, I might actually be interested. I stuffed the card away and let the fantasy play out in my mind, though I knew my time would be at a premium, just trying to locate and get to know the contestant.

We landed at 3:00 a.m. and I made my way to the Park Royal where I had a luxury suite overlooking the city and bay. There was a lush garden outside my windows and a large marble bathtub situated to look out over the garden and city while bathing. A bit much, I supposed, but I tried to match my lodging with the type of woman I was told I would meet.

Speaking of which, I opened a gateway and my 'production team' flooded into the suite. All eleven of the crew members, my wives, and possessions, Doug, and two camerawomen. This was the big briefing and they all wanted to see what Singapore was like. My cover for this one would be having a suit tailored. It would take three days before the suit was delivered and my contestant, Sue, was in sales. It all sounded reasonable to me and the next afternoon, when she'd indicated in her profile that she'd be working, I headed to Orchard Road.

"Four floors of whores," my taxi driver laughed when I gave him the address. I scowled.

"I'm going to have a suit tailored," I said.

"Oh, sure. But there's no harm in taking a look around while you're there. Everything in this building is for sale. Everything."

I wondered what I'd just stepped into. I held the door open long enough to let my camerawoman in without being noticed and she moved ahead of me to the tailor shop. I breathed a sigh of relief. It was a legitimate business with samples of different styles and fabrics on display.

A chime rang as I entered and my camerawoman slipped in behind me. She moved away from me and a very pretty Chinese woman immediately moved from the counter to welcome me to the store.

"Welcome, Mister. I am Sue and I will be happy to help you choose your new wardrobe. It will be tailored just for you by Mr. Mohan. Did you like the nice Italian style you were looking at when you came in?"

I was looking at an Italian style suit when I came in? I glanced back and realized that watching my camerawoman would have looked like I was interested in a black pinstripe double-breasted suit in the window.

"It's very nice, but I *have* different Italian style suits. I like to collect styles from around the world because I travel a lot. In fact, I'm only in town three days. Will it be difficult to get what I want in that time?"

"I'm sure you could get what you want several times in three days," she said, winking at me. "What did you have in mind?"

"I'd like something that is a little more Asian in styling without appropriating a cultural thing. So, something that has the feel of this region but that I wouldn't be looked down upon for wearing because I'm not Asian."

"Oh, sure. Come and take a look at this. This suit blends some of the best of East and West. You see, it's a five button design with a Mandarin collar. The jacket is cut a bit longer than western jackets, but you'll find the detail and craftsmanship of the inside to be very European. Pleated front pants can be worn with either a cuff or straight."

"Hmm. I do like this," I said as I felt the fabric. "What is this fabric?"

"This is a heavy weight silk. You can just about choose your color. Of course, if you wanted something more Asian, the bright colors, like red, jade green, or royal blue would be in order. If you will mostly wear it in the West, though, we have the fabric in gray, navy, brown, charcoal, and even a fine check."

"I like this. Do you think it would look good on me?"

"This suit would look good *on* anyone who is of a reasonably trim build, like you. Of course, I will reserve judgment as to whether *you* look good *in* the suit. I've a feeling, though, that you would look good in anything. Or nothing for that matter." She laughed at my shocked look. "Come. Let's get you measured up and you can take a look at the fabrics."

She led me to a room that was much like any tailor's fitting area I have seen. I stood on a small platform and she moved a stool up next to me to take my measurements. I was a good foot taller than she was, plus a six-inch platform. Her stool pretty much equalized our heights. And the room was completely surrounded in a hexagon of mirrors, so once a suit was in the fitting stages, I'd be able to see it from every angle.

She measured everything, speaking into a small recorder, and giving all the measurements in centimeters. I believe she spent a bit of extra time measuring my chest and I didn't think the tape measure was even in the hand that felt how firm I was. When she got down from the stool and measured my waist, she definitely tested my stomach to see how tight it was.

"You have hard abs," she said. "Look. I have hard abs, too." She took my hand and placed it against the skin of her stomach. She did, indeed have hard abs, encased in delightfully soft and silky skin. "Okay," she said as she knelt in front of me. "How long do you like your dress slacks? It's fashionable to have them just at the heel of your shoe. Is this the type of shoe you'll be wearing?"

"Yes. At the heel and breaking over the toe, please."

She stretched the tape out and ran it right up the inside of my thigh until her hand was snug against my balls.

"Oh, my. Better give you a little extra room here or something will get crushed. Oh, and room to hang to the right. I assume this is the natural position?" she asked as she ran a hand along the shape of my cock, dangling down the right leg of my slacks. Well, it had been dangling. It was rapidly stiffening.

She jumped up and began writing furiously on an order form, listening to her recorded notes. She pointed me to the fabrics and I went through them carefully, selecting a dove gray.

"Here we have the total," she said, leading me to the counter. I looked over the order. One jacket with two pairs of slacks, five pocket design, incorporating European standard jacket pockets. $700.00 Singaporean.

I pulled out a credit card and she handed me the reader. In many countries I've visited, it is not acceptable for a sales person to handle your credit card. They always hand you the reader and ask that you tap or insert your card.

"Sue, I've had such a good time in the shop with you, would you like to go out this evening? I know that's probably an abrupt way to ask, but I'll only be in town for the three days I mentioned. I'd love to get to know you better."

"Oh, I'd love to. I was hoping you'd ask. We close the shop at seven. Could you pick me up here? We can go upstairs to The Chase to have a drink and decide what else we'd like to do."

"That sounds good," I said. "I'll see you at seven."

"Oh, Mister Bob, I need to tell you to bring cash. Most things in Singapore you don't want to use a credit card for." I made sure I had my card and left to do some sightseeing and shopping.

61
Fair Trade

I REMEMBER MEETING an old man somewhere in Southeast Asia sometime after I'd met Ningrum, the Bali goddess of the sea. We were continuing trading around the coastal villages. One seemed to be quite different than the others. I could say, more regulated.

I had been trading all over the islands of what is now called Indonesia and was told this was a wealthy port of call. I put in at a short pier and was immediately greeted by the old man.

"What is your business in Lontor, stranger?" he asked. He wasn't unpleasant about it but it seemed like a strange greeting.

"Hi there. I'm Bob and I'm a trader. I come with goods from other islands and seek the unique goods of other lands to take with me."

"Oh. Well, that will cost you," he said. "I'm Tenduk. You can call me Doug once we know your association will be profitable for us. Now what kind of goods does your little bark bear?"

I think that's what he said.

"Beautiful fabrics, spices, plants, fruit, and ivory all the way from Bengal," I said.

"That is pretty much what you will find here, as in all the islands. What we need here are heavy metals and jewels. As beautiful as our island is, we lack these things and prefer our exports to be paid for with gold and gems."

"I see. And what is your role here? I'm not sure who you are yet."

"I am the port master. We can't have our island overrun by foreigners, so I monitor all vessels that come in and out. I will tell you if you can trade here," he said brusquely.

"Well, Port Master Tenduk…" I looked around at the empty docks and scarcity of boats in the strait, "it seems you do a good job of keeping people out. I will return to my boat and sail on."

"You owe a port fee," he said. "Certainly, you must have some gems."

"I see." I couldn't help being intrigued by the old man and the scarcity of people in view. We'd sailed around the island and found no other port of call. "I probably have a gem in my cabin. I'll retrieve one for you."

"Very well. But don't try to escape without paying."

"I'm an honorable man, Tenduk."

I jumped aboard my little boat and went into my cabin, where I called out a few warriors to act as guard on the boat and retrieved a bag of gems and gold nuggets from the infinity room. I wasn't completely unaware of how to trade and what I could get. This fellow seemed like a good challenge.

"Now, Tenduk," I said as I held up an emerald I'd collected some years ago in Egypt. "I am willing to pay this fine gem for certain services. It is far more valuable than the cost of moorage at your rickety dock. I will expect that it will ensure the safety of my ship and your guidance to the village so that I may see for myself what goods there might be to trade for. It may be that your island has nothing of value at all. You will introduce me to people and be my assistant."

"I'm much too busy to do such things. I can call a boy to conduct you to the village and I will watch your vessel," he countered. I looked at the empty bay again.

"Call the boy to watch my vessel and report to you if anything is amiss. Then you can guide me personally."

"And you will pay the expenses of our foray," he stated flatly.

I agreed. He whistled shrilly and a young boy in the blush of manhood appeared from his cabin near the beach and ran to us. He was given the job of watching my boat and seeing that no one approached it. I could see that he would attempt to board and explore while I was gone. Well, he'd have a little surprise. I hoped my women were gentle with him.

Tenduk, or Doug, and I headed inland.

The village was hidden just over a rise and was quite substantial. I wondered that they didn't have hundreds of fishermen's huts near the beach, though I had seen that most of the coast was inhospitable. After a brief tour of the town, Doug stopped in a center square and announced loudly that I was a trader and would consider buying what the villagers had to trade. We would be in the little inn. I wondered what a village this remote needed with an inn, but apparently it was the gathering point for all manner of meetings, marketing, and trading.

When we were seated, Doug ordered a meal and wine for us. We were served soup, rice, roast duck, and a variety of vegetables and fruit, making the spread look very appealing. Doug nudged me as the innkeeper held out his hand.

"Pay him," he said.

"How much?" I asked.

"You decide, but don't insult his preparations."

It looked like a very appealing meal and the wine promised to be something new that I might want a stock of. I felt around in my bag and withdrew a small nugget of gold. It wasn't very pure, but would be a handsome price that could probably buy meals like this for a month when it was refined. The innkeeper grinned and bowed, stepping back.

From that moment, people began to gather at the entrance to the inn and were admitted one at a time by the innkeeper to visit my table. They seated themselves across from me and presented what they wished to sell. The old man had been correct in his assessment that most of what they had to trade was the same as the other islands, but I poured each a cup of wine as we sat through our negotiation. Generally, I offered a semiprecious stone in trade for a basket of fruit, a live goat, a nice measure of cloth or some pottery. But then a village woman brought me a flower that was the most beautiful I had ever seen.

"From whence is this lovely blossom?" I asked.

"It grows on a rare stem on the north side of the island," she said. "We call it orchid."

"Can you get me one or two of these stems with the roots intact so I can plant them on my ship?" I asked.

"They are very fragile. I can get two for you, but you mustn't blame me if they die in your care."

"I will offer this piece of gold for these rare plants," I said, drawing out a good-sized gold nugget. It was easily worth three times the nugget I gave the innkeeper. She gasped and bowed to me.

"I will collect the stems and return in an hour." She left the flower in a vase of water on my table.

"Ah! So, you like things of beauty!" Tenduk said.

"Yes. And wine. I would like to buy a cart of jugs of this wine. Can anyone supply that?" I asked.

The innkeeper ran to the door and motioned for an old man to come into the inn.

"This is Sulung," the innkeeper said. "He makes the wine."

"Welcome, Sulung. I am Bob," I said, pouring him a cup of his own vintage. "How much of this lovely wine can you supply me with?"

He pointed out a cart standing by the inn that was laden with jugs.

"Very well. I will take all the jugs on the cart, but you must deliver them to my boat when I go. I have no use for your donkey and cart at sea." He waited for me to offer a price. I fumbled in the bag until I found another gold nugget the size of the one I had laid out for the old woman. He finally grinned.

"I will set out for the dock at once. It will take me longer to get there pulling the cart than it will take you when you have finished your business." I nodded and he left.

There was quite a stir at the doorway and I turned to see a spectacular vision entering the inn. I might almost have thought it was My Lady Goddess, but I knew she was far away.

"Surintan, you mustn't!"

"It is mine to give or sell and will certainly do our village more good if I sell it to a foreigner," she said. The innkeeper led her to our table and I stood to bow before her.

She was young—perhaps seventeen or eighteen. She was wrapped in a skirt of flowing silk. For a top, she wore only a heavy string of flowers of the same sort the old woman was bringing me. I know that it is commonly believed that breasts were not objects of sexual fantasy until around the fourteenth or fifteenth century in Europe, but I had three millennia of learning to love them passionately. I could scarcely wait to become acquainted with these.

"I am called Surintan, though I prefer to use the name Dara while I still can." I heard the words with my ears, but I picked up several meanings as I listened. Surintan could be interpreted as Queen or Diamond. Dara was the descriptive name for a young virgin.

"I am Bob," I said. As I spoke it, I heard the automatic interpretation of people's minds translating it to Budiarto—one who is wise with wealth. I wasn't sure I was that wise. "How may I be of service to you?"

She waved a hand and Doug stood with a little bow. Then he and the innkeeper moved away from us. Apparently, this was to be a private and quiet negotiation. I poured her a cup of wine.

"I can tell from the stories that you are not familiar with our customs, and they are strange to you. You have paid as much wealth for trinkets as our village might normally see in a year. So, I must explain to you that there are customs that might seem very strange to you. On our island, everything is for sale. To give the old woman this piece of gold for her flowers will make her one of the wealthiest on our island. And you gave that price for something of great beauty. Do you think I am beautiful, Bob?"

"Yes, Dara. I find you entrancing."

"One of the chief commodities that women have on this island is their virginity. If a man were to steal that treasure from a woman, he would be executed immediately. But a woman may sell that commodity as she deems fit. I am a virgin because no man has deigned to make an offer for that which I have to sell, assuming he would never be able to meet my price. You have wealth beyond all others. If you were to buy what I have to offer, I could then buy any man on the island to be my husband. It would take me out of the realm of being a seller and into the realm of being a buyer. Tell me, Bob," she said standing and dropping the silk skirt to the floor. She was dressed only in the flowers. "What would you pay for my virginity?"

I was perplexed. I had never paid for virginity before. That is not to say I had never bought a woman and freed her from slavery. Often such women became quite attached to me, refusing to leave. But a straight-out transaction for a woman's virginity...

"And this is the custom of your people?" I asked.

"It is."

"What if I simply gave you the price and let you keep your... commodity?"

"I would be deemed a cheater and a liar and a thief. I would be executed," she said.

"Oh, dear."

"It is a hard lesson to learn for one from outside, but the women of my tribe developed this business many generations ago and we are well-kept and well respected as a result. Again, I ask you, Bob. What would you pay for this precious commodity?"

I tried not to let my cock do the talking for me and failed completely. I put the bag with all its remaining precious stones and gold in it on the table.

"You truly offer a jewel beyond price," I said.

She smiled at me and casually dumped the jewels and gold out of the bag onto the table to count it out. There was a gasp from all around. She scooped it up and put it back in the bag, offering her hand to me.

"When your flowers have arrived, we will walk together to your boat and you may deflower me. I promise, I will be worth every gram of precious stones and gold you have offered."

"Perhaps you should dress now."

"No. My people should see what has commanded such a price as we walk to your boat. They deserve to know."

Not long after, the old woman arrived with the flower stems, potted in soil. I gave her the remaining nugget I had promised her and she thanked me profusely. Then she looked at the pouch of gems in Dara's hand and congratulated her.

Dara took my hand and we walked through the village with the streets lined with people to see her naked beauty. At the boat, my women guards greeted me and quickly left to prepare a bed for me. The boy who had been left to watch the boat turned toward me with a dazed look on his face. I reached in the satchel for a copper coin to give him. He refused.

"Thank you, sir, but I have been amply rewarded."

I turned and gave a copper coin to each of the porters who brought the goods I had traded for. They were all more in awe of the women who took the packages below deck to stow them. I bade the village farewell and picked up my prize to carry her aboard. My warriors disembarked and marched the interested villagers back down the dock.

"I had no doubt that you were a man with many women in your life," Dara said. "It is why I did not offer to marry you. To sell you my virginity is one thing, but I do not think I could live with others sharing my husband."

"I do have wives and concubines," I said. "Dara, if this is too uncomfortable for you, we can simply tell people that we've done the deed and you can return to your home with your treasure."

"That would be stupid. I would still have my virginity intact. The village will look to see the blood on my thighs when I return to them tomorrow. So, for tonight, let us make the most of it and please, try to not hurt me too much."

And from that point on, I made it my mission to make her experience the best I could possibly offer. I caressed her, kissed her, and worshiped her body with my hands and my mouth. When I'd licked her to another orgasm—part of the ritual I was required to do was to look between her legs and verify that she was a virgin—I slowly moved up her body until our genitals met. As I kissed her yet again, I thrust into her pussy and she took my entire length, not with a scream, but with a sigh of pleasure.

"That was not so bad," she said. "Now teach me all the things your women have taught you so when I choose my husband, I will know how to teach him."

I did my best, and we did not sleep that night. In the morning, we ate together on the deck, looking out at all the people who had camped on the beach waiting for her return.

"I would love to take you with me, Dara," I said.

"No longer Dara," she smiled. "I think I shall take the name Intan, or Diamond, and the diamond in this bag will stay with me always."

"Intan, you would be a wonderful addition to my harem and I would take you gladly."

"I thank you, Bob, but now I can truly be free and choose the path I desire for myself. The boy who watched your boat is one I have long wanted to buy, but he could never afford the price of my virginity. Now that your women have instructed him and you have instructed me, I believe I can offer a fair price and he will be happy to become my husband."

"Then go in peace, Intan. Thank you for this precious treasure."

She disembarked and as soon as she was past my warriors they hurried back to the boat and we cast off. She turned and waved at me, then linked her arm through that of the boy who'd watched my boat and they turned toward the village, with people staring to see the blood and come dried on her thighs.

I didn't intend to get so carried away with this little story, but it's important to understand that I was really cut loose on my own to figure out how to 'interview' the contestant in Singapore, and everything I was doing was being recorded. I returned to my hotel room, locked the doors, and went into Areola for a conference.

"She's, um... cute," Liz said when she viewed the footage that had been recorded.

"She was really forward in getting you to ask her out. And she seemed to have a program all set regarding what to do. Nice and safe to go to a bar just a floor above her tailor shop to meet and not reveal anything else about where she lives or really who she is," Peninnah added.

"I don't like her," Artemisia said. "She's used to running things, including all the people around her. I bet she owns that shop and farms the work out to other tailors. She certainly can't expect you back tomorrow for a preliminary fitting if she was doing the work herself. Unless she doesn't sleep. She had no problems accepting a date."

"Bob, just go with it. Take Avril as your evening camerawoman. She's really learned how to disappear and operate a drone, as well as her shoulder camera. If necessary, I can go out to pick her up if there are complications," Doug said.

62
THE DECISION

T SEVEN O'CLOCK, I lost track of Avril as she disappeared into the surrounding shops. She knew how to work with the look-away spell so that she was never in a likely place for people to look. The doors to the shop were locked, so I stood outside in my Italian suit and open collar. About ten minutes after the hour, Sue came to the door and locked it again behind her.

Wow!

She reached up to kiss me on the cheek and take my hand. I had to just stand and stare at her a moment.

Her daytime clothes were professional. She wore tailored slacks that emphasized her narrow waist and a crew neck blouse that just barely touched her belt. It had been loose enough that she could place my hand on her very flat stomach. She'd worn her hair in a tight knot on top of her head and had subtle makeup on.

Her evening wear and appearance were so different from the day that I almost didn't recognize her. She wore a red off-the-shoulder sheath dress that hugged her body like a second skin. The length was just below the knee, but when she turned to show me the outfit, I realized it was slit on the left to mid-thigh. She wore high heel spikes that were reminiscent of Peninnah's favorites.

"I knew you'd change into something nice for the evening," she said. "I'm sorry I kept you waiting, but I felt it was important to try to look as good as you would."

"I think you exceeded that goal quite nicely."

Her straight black hair hung loosely around her shoulders. She took my hand and led me to the escalator to the next floor where The Chase bar was located.

"This bar is a cut above the rest in the building. They frown on girls coming in to cruise, but they'll be fine with us. Since I brought you in with me, they won't charge an outrageous price for drinks, either. At the 'four floors' bars upstairs, they charge double when a guy buys a girl a drink. It's outrageous, but that's their cut." We were seated and ordered martinis. They weren't bad. I noted the bar only stocked top shelf brands.

"So, how long have you been working at Mohan's Tailor Shop?" I asked. "You certainly know your way around a tape measure."

"I've been here five years. I went to a vocational school that taught me all about tailoring and measuring. And it's a good place to meet nice affluent gentlemen. If you were to be here around nine o'clock tonight, you'd see the clientele in the building take a definite swing down the social ladder. That's why all the shops in the building close at seven so we can go home."

"What do you like best about your job?" I asked.

"Meeting people. I like to meet as many men as possible," she said. "Now tell me about what you do."

"I run a small import/export business," I answered. I'd been practicing this repeatedly. I knew my business. "I deal in commodities, so it's not like I'm importing and exporting native carvings or jewelry. I trade in tankers of oil, freighters of grain, ROROs with expensive automobiles."

"Oh, my. You must travel all over the world."

"I've traveled around the world several times."

We continued to chat and sip our drinks for nearly an hour.

"Well, Bob, I always like to have a chat with a gentleman before we move to the next level. I can usually tell when a guy is genuinely a nice guy, no matter what he wants from me. So, I'll be up front with you. If you want the date to continue past eight o'clock, I can be yours until one a.m. for just $500 US. If we decide it will be an all-nighter, that is $800. If we decide that early, though, I'd like to go to my apartment and pick up clothes for tomorrow. I'm sure we'll have a good time, no matter how we decide to spend the time between now and then. I have to leave in the morning by ten in order to get freshened up and back to work at eleven."

"Five hun... Eight... You charge for your time and... uh... favors?"

"Bob, everything in Singapore comes with a price. That's why I told you to bring cash. There are girls who will lie to you and get you to romance them and marry them, but then they will have everything you have. I decided long ago to announce my price up front and then you can leave town on your business trip and never think twice about what you've left behind. And don't think that this mercenary attitude comes with a dead lay. I promise you that you will have a night like you could only expect from the most loving girlfriend," she said.

"That... uh... just surprised me, is all," I said. She'd certainly given the parameters. I gave up wondering what I should do and reached for my wallet. "I think a night with you sounds delightful."

"Not in the bar, Bob. There is plenty of time to transfer funds when we are in private. Did you just want to head straight back to your hotel, or did you want to continue with dinner and maybe a walk along the ocean harbor while we continue to get to know each other?" she asked.

"Oh, definitely dinner and a walk. I would never suggest we do anything else on an empty stomach. Do you have a restaurant you'd suggest?" I asked.

"Oh, Bob, should it happen that you have time to meet any other girls on your stayover, that is a question you never want to ask. There is a list of very expensive restaurants that escorts like to be taken to, but most of them don't know how to behave in one. I do, but I'm not asking for a five-star dinner. Have you had chili crab since arriving in Singapore? It's very spicy, but a signature dish for the city. Usually, restaurants charge from $35 to $50 for it."

"I've not had chili crab in many years. It sounds delightful."

"I know an out of the way restaurant in the Geylang District. It's not far from my apartment, so it will be easy to pick up my bag after dinner."

We agreed and headed out for one of the best meals I'd had in a long time. The restaurant might have been out of the way—and was called simply, "No Signboard"—but the food was wonderful and the atmosphere was vibrant, both inside and outside the restaurant. I wondered that she actually lived in what was reputed to be the most popular sex tourism area of Singapore. We passed three brothels on the way to her apartment. She asked me to please wait in the lobby while she ran up to get her bag. She was down in a flash.

"I keep my bag packed in case I need it," she smiled. "Now, how about that walk, my love?"

Her little endearments had become more intimate as the evening wore on. Knowing we had all night, we didn't rush to my hotel, but walked along the harbor, stopping to see the lion fountain, and continuing around the Marina. It was very colorful. Sue was leaning on me more and more and I finally woke up to the fact that she was walking in those impossible high heels. I called for a cab and swept her up in my arms to meet it and get her off her feet.

"Oh, Bob, you're so gallant." She leaned in to kiss me for our first real kiss of the night. By the time we got to the hotel, she was practically in my lap. "This is a good hotel," she said. "They don't ask questions when a young lady accompanies a man to his room."

"I just thought it looked nice and comfortable," I said. "I hadn't really thought about inviting a young lady to my room."

"I should walk as far as the elevator, though," she said as we got out of the cab. "It's not good to raise too many eyebrows by being carried."

"Certainly, sweetheart. Hold tightly to my arm and I'll support you."

"Thank you, love."

It wasn't long before we were at my suite and she looked around appreciatively. Somehow, however, I didn't think it was the first time she'd seen a hotel room of this caliber.

And that is where the evening got very interesting. Yes, we made love, but Sue knew how to turn a man on far beyond simply getting undressed to show her exquisite body to him. She continued to talk to me as we undressed each other, caressing me in delightful ways that did not immediately focus on my cock. Of course, she got to that and gasped a little when she couldn't fit her hand around it.

"Many Chinese girls would run when they saw this," she said. "In fact, my mother only worked in Geylang and never slept with anyone except Chinese men. I got over that racist idea the first time I slept with an American. I am one of the few Chinese girls who would stand a chance of getting you all inside me. Would you like to try that, Bob? Would you like to see if all this wonderful cock will fit in my little Asian *yinhu?*"

The answer to that was obvious and before long I was stretched out on my back as Sue managed to stretch herself around my cock. She was focused, but still relaxed as she managed to get me completely in her. And incredibly tight. I was afraid we wouldn't be able to slide at all, but she provided all the lubrication needed to make the passage easy and stimulate the maximum pleasure. And she was right about it being the best *fake* loving experience I'd ever had.

We did not fuck all night, but we did a lot of those little things that lovers do, like sitting with a plate of cheese and fruit I had ordered from the all-night room service between us. We laughed and stole little kisses. We talked. And we made love.

"What do you hope for in the future?" I asked her.

"Oh, impossible dreams. I dream that Prince Charming will find me and fall in love and I can pretend to be in love for the rest of my life with a man who treats me like a princess and provides for my every need. I'd only have one man that I had to spread my legs for and I'd do it willingly for the rest of my life. It's what I know how to do best. But I also know it won't happen, so I'm saving every penny I can with a goal of retiring alone in five more years. You'd be surprised how profitable my line of work can be. I have a good savings account."

"Why do you think you'd have to live alone and that Prince Charming would never find you?"

"Oh, he might find me, but once he knew what I do for a living, he'd never rescue me. You know that old movie *Pretty Lady?* Lies. All lies. I'm so used to pretending to be in love that I don't think I'd recognize it if I actually was. I even applied to that *Bob* television show, *To Boldly Go.* I figure that if he accepted me, I'd never want for anything again, and I would happily let him fuck me as much as he wanted. I doubt it would be that much because he's got so many women. I'd just be one of them, taking my turn when it comes around. I suspect that's what most of the others do. I mean, why would anyone really fall in love with him and still be willing to share him with a hundred other women in his harem? And when he found out I'm really just a whore, that would be all. Although, maybe he'd just pay me enough to make my dream of living alone securely for the rest of my life a reality."

"That's somehow rather sad," I said.

"Don't let it get you down! That's not what this conversation or this night is for. Let me show you just what he'll be missing."

With that, Sue proceeded to make sure I was ready to mount her and opened her legs wide.

⤜≻⧟⊙⊙⊳

I paid for two more nights with Sue. I could have just left and forgot about the suit and all, but I *did* like her. She was a very convincing actress, though I don't think she was used to having the same guy every night. The third night the conversation and the actions became repetitive. I recognized the exact whine she used to indicate she was coming, even when I knew she wasn't. I had a feeling that the next guy—tomorrow?—would hear the same intimate stories and that in a week, I would not even be remembered.

So sad, but that night, I caught a flight to Sydney, Australia.

I will not dwell with such detail on the next two contestants. I found the next one, in Sydney, on a long walk in the park. She was pushing a baby stroller. The toddler was about two years old. We chatted a bit as we walked along and I found she was a single mom, desperate to do anything to ensure the safety of her son. I didn't need to even ask her about her dreams. She told me that she was sure that when The Bob met her little boy, he would be so moved he would sweep them both up and take them to his palace, because what would a new colony on Mars be like without children?

Amy was a sweetheart and I saw her two more times. I just couldn't imagine bringing a child to Areola. I'd done it once before. My son. Well, the son of my wife and her other husband. When the two of them were killed in a fire in Greece, a few centuries BC, I'd taken Theo into Areola, but only after we'd lived several years in the natural world as I traveled around Greece performing. So, he was a young man when I took him to Areola and didn't really bring that time of growth that seems to age parents with him. Now, more than two millennia later, he was still a striking and talented young man, often carrying on my life by staging plays in Areola.

But to bring a toddler into Areola? That would take some thinking.

I moved on to Toronto.

The little coffee shop in which I found barista Louise had posters of *To Boldly Go* along with photos of me and all the women on the first show posted all around the shop. There were also signs that said, "Bob, I'm ready to go. Take me!"

Louise was wearing a button on her uniform that said, "I'll boldly go!" She was quite attractive, but during the time I was in the shop, four men tried to convince her that they were Bob. She laughed at all of them, including the bald paunchy man who said he was in disguise. I thought all four of the men had a pretty high opinion of themselves to try to pretend to be me. One even had an ID that just said "Bob." I wondered how many of *those* were floating around. When I finally got up to the counter, she looked me up and down.

"I suppose you're Bob, too," she sighed.

"Oh, no. I just want a cup of coffee."

"Really?"

"Well, I'd like to take you out tonight, too, but right now, just coffee."

"That's refreshing. So, if you were to take Louise out on a date, what would you do?" she asked, pointing at herself.

"Well, first, I'd try to find out what Louise likes, then see if I could arrange to do that. Failing that, I'd ask her what would be second best. I'm sure we could find something agreeable."

"Hockey. The Maple Leafs are playing tonight. Get good tickets to that and I'll go with you," she laughed. I took my coffee and left to make some calls. An hour and a half later, I walked back into the coffee shop and approached the counter.

"Louise, I'd like to take you out tonight. Do you like hockey?" I laid the tickets on the counter and she nearly jumped the counter to hug me.

"Yes! Yes! I want to go with you! Bob will just have to wait and come for me tomorrow!"

I did take her to the game and she was very into it, but she talked all the time. All I ever did was nod or shake my head. When I took her home, she leaned across the seat and gave me a quick kiss on the cheek, then hurried out of the car and into her apartment building.

I caught my flight back to Honolulu the next morning.

I was excited to get back to Honolulu and, I admit, to Annie. I'd had dates with four women on this trip and there was no question that I would choose Annie to come with us. If she'd agree. Before I contacted her, I had a strategy meeting with the crew, wives, and possessions.

"I agree," Artemisia said. "I never really liked the girl in Singapore and we'd know she was pretending all the time."

"I thought Toronto was a bit of an airhead fangirl," Karla added. "That she'll be just as happy with an autographed picture."

"I had a lot of hope for the woman in Australia," Lalonda said. "She seemed so simple and down-to-earth. And even though she somehow failed to mention her son in any of the applications or forms, it was a sweet story and it wouldn't hurt us to have a child along for the ride."

"Are you sure we're going about this the right way with you pretending not to be The Bob?" Liz asked. "Maybe being right up front about it would have been a better approach. I'm afraid Annie's going to be really upset about being deceived. She's fallen in love."

"That's what makes her the best choice," Nimia said. "That and Bob's in love with her."

"Each of them tickled my fancy in a way. I'm sure that if Annie hadn't come into the picture, the decision would be between Sue in Singapore and Amy in Australia. And I'd have just left it up to you all to decide. But I *want* Annie. What do I need to do to get her?" I asked. It was a stimulating conversation that went on all night, with frequent interruptions for loving. The next morning, I called Annie and made arrangements to meet her for lunch.

I drove myself this time. The car wasn't particularly fancy, but it had room for Annie and me in the front seat and a camera crew in the back. So far, we'd depended on one person to operate both a handheld camera and a drone. This was going to be too intense to assume one operator could get everything.

"Bob! You came back!"

"I told you I would, Annie. I'm here for you."

"I was so worried. I missed you."

She proceeded to show me how she'd missed me with a kiss that nearly melted the sidewalk.

"Let's just get some carry-out food and go back to your beach house. I just want to be with you."

"I'll do anything you want to. We don't need to rush."

"I want you to read this," she said, handing me an envelope. It was addressed to our studio back in California. Inside the envelope was a short letter asking that her name be removed from consideration for a place on Bob's crew.

"Um... About this, Annie..."

"If you'll have me, Bob, I'll send this letter and we'll be together. I don't want anyone but you. If you feel the same way I do, let's go to the post office and mail it."

"Well, what if I told you *I'm* The Bob?"

"Oh, honey, please. I've already fallen in love with you. Don't make things up just to convince me. It would cheapen it so much."

"If you met The Bob, how would you know it? You know he won't come around looking like the guy on TV."

"Yes, but... Well, first there would be cameras. I signed an agreement to be recorded any time I'm with The Bob because it's part of the television thingy. And second, there would be the satchel with the transporter. And The Bob never goes anyplace without his wife Peninnah and his... um... producer, I guess, Liz."

"And how would that make you feel if you saw all those things?" I asked.

"Well, kind of self-conscious, I suppose. I worked up all kinds of ways that I'd react so I could stand a chance of being coherent. Even rehearsed a speech or two. But, Bob, that doesn't matter anymore. I just want to be with you—even if you do have a port in every girl."

"Okay, look. This might sound crazy, but I'd like you to take my picture. Let's see..." I quickly checked around for the cameras and chose a location. "This looks like a good place. Just get out your cellphone and look at me through the screen as you take a picture."

"Okay, but you're being a little weird just now," she said. She got out her cellphone and hit the camera button. She looked at me to take the picture. "No. Not there. Someone's flying a drone around and it keeps looking like it's right over your shoulder. Move to the left a little." She looked up from the phone. "Wait. It's okay. I don't see it now." She looked back at the camera. "Now it's back." She looked around over the top of the camera. "What's going on? I can see this thing through the camera, but not when I just look up."

"It's a kind of stealth technology. It can deceive the human eye, but it can't deceive electronics. Your camera sees it, but your naked eye can't."

She scanned the area with her camera and stopped when she saw Avril.

"There's a camerawoman!" she exclaimed. Avril waved at her but, of course Annie could only see her through the camera lens. "Bob... What's this mean? I'm scared. There are people and machines around that I can't see unless I'm looking through my camera."

"You said that one of the ways you'd know I was The Bob was if there were cameras around."

I was afraid Annie was going to hyperventilate. She looked faint.

"Come on, love. Let's head for the beach house," I said.

I led her to the car and as she was getting in the front seat, the camera crew quickly got in the back. When I closed the door, she jerked around at the apparent sound of the other doors closing. She didn't see anything, but when I got in the car, I could tell she was getting her camera ready. I didn't say anything. Suddenly, she swung around to the back seat with the camera raised in front of her. And screamed.

"Bob! There are people in the car with us!" She lowered the camera and then jerked around to face forward. "I'm going crazy."

"No, love. You're not crazy. They follow me everyplace I go. Like you, it's part of my contract."

"So, The Bob hires you to go out and find girls?" she asked. She was not computing the reality of my unreal existence.

"Well, I had to work out all sorts of contract things with the production company. If I'm going to be out meeting people, they have to record it for the show."

"You don't really look much like The Bob," she said. "Maybe you should take me home."

"I intend to," I said, intentionally ignoring her meaning. I pulled up to the beach house and got out. The other doors opened at the same time as hers and she squeezed her eyes shut. We went inside.

"Okay. What about the satchel?" she demanded. I patted the bag hanging from my shoulder. "I know that bag. I sold it to you. That's not The Bob's satchel."

"Amazingly, with very few alterations, I found it to be the perfect size to fit the real satchel inside. No one has even thought to look beyond the obvious when I went through airport security because they see so many of them now." I set the bag on the table, opened it, and pulled the real satchel out of it. She shook her head.

"Very funny. You're a good mime," she said.

"Here, will you hold this for me?" I turned with both bags in my hands and she held her hand out to take the new satchel. Instead, I pressed the old one into her hands and she could immediately see it as well as feel it in her hands. She nearly dropped it. I steadied her hand.

"All of a sudden, I could see it and feel it. Like one of those magic shows!"

"Except if you'd been looking through the camera lens, you'd have seen it. Same stealth tech. So, let me see, you wanted to meet Peninnah and Liz," I said.

"No! Wait! I... I'm not sure I want to know. I fell in love with this Bob. I don't trust that I'll love The Bob. What if everything is different? What if The Bob's other wives don't like me? I'm scared, Bob!"

"Annie, my love, don't be frightened. This Bob fell in love with you, too. I wouldn't do anything to hurt you. But the world is a much bigger place than most people imagine. In it, there are beings like me, who can change their look, hide things from the human eye, and even open a gate... or a transporter to my palace. What I'm asking, Annie, is that you just continue to love me and come with me on a great adventure that will last us both the rest of our very long lives."

"Take me to bed, Bob. Take me to bed and love me like you loved me before you left on your trip. I want to know for sure that you are *my* Bob. Then you can convince me that you're The Bob."

That was an easy enough request to grant. We made love for hours and I tried to make sure she knew it was me and that I loved her.

63
THE GAME

"ARE YOU READY, LOVE? Will you come with me and be with me from now until forever?" I asked as we watched the sun rise over the ocean in the morning. I held her in my arms.

"Yes, my Bob. I will be with you forever. Let me meet Peninnah and Liz, and take me away to your palace. Oh. Should I dress?"

"No one else does." I set the satchel on the lanai and opened the gateway. Annie sagged against me as Peninnah and Liz stepped through into the natural world. Liz was simply nude and barefooted. Peninnah had high heels, hose, and a garter belt on, with her huge diamond dangling in her navel. Liz rushed to Annie and hugged her.

"I'm so glad you're coming to join us!" she said. "Oh, Annie, this must have been such a stressful time for you."

"Welcome to our family, Annie," Peninnah said. "I hope we'll be very happy together. Everyone is waiting to meet you."

"Everyone? Here?"

"It would be easier if we went there," I said. "Annie, would you go with me to my palace and meet the rest of my family and friends?"

"Yes, Bob," she said draping her arms around my neck. "Please take me." I lifted her up and followed Peninnah and Liz through the gateway.

Let me tell you about one of the most fun times I've ever had, just being normal playful me. I know that sounds like a non sequitur, but the whole process of convincing Annie with her cell phone reminded me of this time a few years ago.

A game came out that kids played on their cell phones. I use the term 'kids' loosely, because I saw people of every age waving their phone around and throwing imaginary balls at imaginary creatures. The app used the camera on the phone to create the background and superimpose these creatures in your real-life environment. Then you could use features of the app to capture and train the creature.

We had enough commerce between Areola and the natural world that some of the citizens would come out of the satchel just to play for a while, then we'd all go back to Areola. I intended to just play with my own people, but things got complicated.

Half a dozen of the young women who wanted to play came out in a small city of about thirty thousand people with a couple of college campuses, which made the area perfect for creature catching. We had several cellphones we supplied for our people when they came into the natural world and all were equipped with the game.

I watched them play for a while and discovered several others as we walked through town and across campus who were all playing the game. Occasionally, we'd hear a cry of excitement as someone would yell, "By the streetlight over there!" and players would suddenly converge on the area trying to capture the creature that had been spotted. There was a lot of giggling and running around.

I got a bright idea and decided to have some fun of my own.

By this time, I knew that my look-away spell didn't work on electronic devices. I'd been through enough airports and put the satchel through enough x-rays that it was pretty obvious. I slipped off where I was pretty sure I couldn't be observed and changed into my full demon form with the horns and goat legs and hooves and... I didn't think about other things that were exposed. I cast a look-away spell on myself and went out to have some fun with my people.

I scampered down the block where they were playing and ran across the street in front of them.

"What was that?" one yelled. "Did you see it just run by?"

"It looked like Bob! I don't see him anywhere."

"What kind of creature is a Bob?" a nearby gamer asked my girls.

"Oh, um... Over there! Standing in that doorway!" I was lounging casually near a building on campus. Suddenly, there were a dozen phones pointed my direction.

"I see it! I'm throwing."

Of course, the net they used in the game was virtual and only snared virtual creatures. I took off running and had at least a dozen players chasing after me. I had only intended to play with my women, but once I was spotted through a camera lens, I was fair game for all.

There were boys playing the game as well as girls, but most of the players were female. The guys tended to be—I think the most common designation was 'geeks.' As far as I could tell, they were the smart ones. There were a lot of good-looking girls out there that they got to hang with.

We were having a great time! I could move faster and more agilely than the kids playing the game. A bunch would be chasing me and I'd slip around a corner and come out behind them. Eventually, someone would yell, "Where are you going? He's over there!" and the flow of the chase would change directions.

We played for more than an hour and some of the kids had to get to class or to other obligations. A few of the hardcore gamers were on the prowl but I was easily avoiding them. It was about time for me to change back into my human form and collect my girls. I backed around a corner and tripped over a girl coming from the other direction. Of course, when a person comes in contact with an object protected by the look-away spell, they can see it. I was staring straight into the eyes of a very startled young woman. It was an anime moment as I discovered I had both her breasts in my hands and she slapped me hard!

"No, no! It was an accident. I'm sorry! I didn't know you were there," I explained.

"I tried to tell them you weren't part of the game," she said. "You smell good." Her nose twitched.

"You can smell me?"

"Yeah. I caught the scent when we were chasing. I have a good nose."

"You do, indeed."

We heard the sound of players coming closer.

"I really need to get going."

"In here," she said, grabbing my hand and dragging me through the doorway.

"Where are we?" I asked. She kept a firm grip on me.

"Basement of the girls' dorm."

"I should probably not be in here."

"No one can see you unless they're pointing their camera at you. That's how you fooled everyone into thinking you were part of the game."

"Well, yes, but it was just for fun. My girlfriends are out there playing and I need to collect them and go home."

"Hmm. More than one girlfriend? Where's home?"

"Oh, it's, um... a ways from here."

"I'll bet. You don't look like what I imagined a technologically advanced alien to look like. I'd guess you are from a different plane of existence. The physical manifestation of a thoroughly metaphysical creature," she said.

"Uh... You might say so."

"Studying the correlation between metaphysics and physics is my aspiration. Can you show me this other world you come from?"

"Well... Aren't you scared? I'm a demon!"

"You smell good. I don't mean just pleasant, but like a good being instead of an evil being. What do we need to do to go to your world?"

"Well..."

She seemed to have answers for all her own questions.

"Okay, then. Here's what we'll do. We'll head upstairs to my room. You call your girlfriends and have them come to room 270. If you need to change bodies or something, you can do it there. Come on." She kept hold of my hand, having not let go since she slapped me for feeling her up. That feeling was very nice for a girl with a slight and short body like she appeared to have. "By the way, I'm Sally," she said.

"Pleased to meet you. I'm Bob."

"Much better introduction than the first time. Though it did have its moments. That is a huge cock you had between my knees."

"Yeah. Sorry about earlier."

"Nothing you could do about that. You didn't really have to start squeezing my boobs. Though, it wasn't that bad. Does everyone in your dimension run around naked?"

"It's an option."

"Wow! That's getting as much chatter out there as you just appearing and disappearing all the time. No one can believe the game would put a character in that was hung like that. You know, little kids play this, too."

Great. There would be rumors abounding about the goat-legged creature with a huge dong running around campus. Then I realized that someone might have snapped a picture of me and moaned.

We got to her room and she started stripping.

"Wait! What?"

"Well, if it's an option in your world, I'm in. Ow. I hate bras."

Yes, the breasts she exposed lived up to all the expectations my hands had built up in me. I called the girls and gave them the instructions. Then I transformed.

"Wow! The human side lives up to the demon advertising," Sally said.

"Thanks." I reached in the satchel and grabbed some clothes. I distinctly heard Josie giggling.

"If we're just crossing to your dimension, you don't need to get dressed. I don't mind."

"Um... the girls can all return to Areola, but I have to take the satchel someplace safe before I can join them."

"Uh-oh. That's going to be a problem. You're like clearly visible now, even when I take my hands off you. You can't just walk through a girls' dormitory and out the door. I assume others could see you, too. And if you were back in your other shape, everyone out there with a game will be hunting for you. Hmm."

"You seem very intent on solving problems. And it looks like you are all packed for a trip."

"Oh, yeah. I was leaving today. End of term and I'm escaping the lecherous Professor Arnold. He promised to help me with my thesis if I stopped by his house this evening. I did some investigating and he's a *propredator*. That's a term I coined for my paper. It's a professor who preys on innocent students to satisfy his perverted lusts. His thing is bondage and beating. No, thank you."

"How do you know I'm not a pervert?" I asked.

"Oh, I know you're a pervert, but you're not a predator. Like I said, you smell good. Professor Arnold smells evil. Three girls this year left school after private conferences with him. I suspect they were raped, but they wouldn't speak to anyone. Apparently, he figures that showing up at his house is consent."

"I think he might need a visit from a demon," I growled. She looked at me speculatively. Just then there was a knock at the door and Sally let my five girlfriends in. They all stopped short when they saw she was naked.

"What could I do?" Sally said innocently. "I brought a naked demon into my room and suddenly, I was naked, too."

They looked at me quizzically and then started laughing.

"Don't worry. It happens all the time. A lot of girls have a spontaneous orgasm when they see Bob in his full demon glory. Are you one of us now?"

"I'm coming to your dimension with you."

"Wait a minute. Did I say you could come to Areola?"

She looked down at her own bare nipples.

"I'm ready."

"When people come to Areola, they stay there. Usually forever. Those who leave never mention it or talk about it. I try to never take anyone there who would—well, be missed in a bad way. By parents or children or friends and lovers."

"Oh, no worry. My parents are crazier than I am. Can you believe they named me Salvadora after an artist?"

"That explains it. Sally, I mean." I really meant that it explained how crazy she sounded.

"My bags are packed, so everyone is expecting me to walk out the door and leave school. My parents never expect me home after term. I'm not even sure where they're traveling right now. The last I heard, they were trekking through Central Africa collecting native artwork. As to friends and lovers... well, what you see is what you get. Let's go!"

"We still have the problem of me getting out of here," I said.

"That shouldn't be a problem," Dora said. She'd been with me for more than three thousand years and only rarely came out of Areola to play games. "Just transform yourself into her body. Pick up everything and walk out with us in the satchel."

"Hmm. That might work," I said. "Sally, how do you think your propredator would like a life-changing visit from a demon who looked just like you?"

"That wasn't the way I was thinking of you having my body, but sure. What do I do?"

She was still standing in front of me stark naked, so it was easy to fix her image in my mind. I worked the transformation spell as she stared with an open mouth.

"Could I borrow your clothes?" I asked.

"Um... Yeah. I don't think I'm ever going to need them again," she said handing me the clothes she'd just taken off. I dressed as Sally gave me the particulars about where her professor lived. I opened a gateway and all the girls went through into Areola. I hauled Sally's big rolling suitcase behind me with her pack on my back and my satchel over my shoulder. Then I just walked out of her room, downstairs, and out the door.

Now here's a little lesson about not making assumptions. Remember the old saying, "Assume makes an ass out of u and me?" Well, when I was in touch with Sally, I read her memories of the propredator and he was genuinely creepy and sinister. So, hauling her suitcase, backpack, and my satchel, I walked nearly a mile to his house and rang the bell. He seemed a little surprised to see me but invited me in.

"You said you had some material for my paper you'd help me with before I leave town."

"Oh, yes, yes. Of course. I was surprised to see you carrying your suitcase. I was afraid you'd misinterpreted my invitation. But you are just packed and ready to leave campus, aren't you? Bus to catch?"

"A friend is picking me up."

"Oh! I hope you didn't give him this address!"

"No. Of course not. I'm no more excited about letting anyone know I came here than you are about it. I was sure we could wrap things up quickly and I could be on my way."

"Yes, yes. Please come into my study. Let me show you... my references."

I left the suitcase and backpack in the hall and followed him with just my satchel. I was surprised when he didn't proceed directly to offering me a drugged drink or some such.

"Very unusual line of research you have explored during your time here. Not many people make the connection between different planes of existence—alternate dimensions, if you will—and the sightings of various mythological creatures over the ages. Now this volume in my library is not widely available. It narrowly escaped the burnings during the Middle Ages when the church was determined to purge the world of everything that did not uphold its doctrine. So many things were lost during that time. This manuscript was probably copied by a monk who couldn't read, but carefully copied the shapes and forms of the words, adding his own decorative doodles in the margins."

He handed me a volume that must have originated around a thousand years AC. Then he snatched it back.

"We need to take proper precautions," he said.

He set the book on a reading stand and handed me a pair of cotton gloves, donning a similar pair himself. Then he began to recite an incantation I recognized as one that warded a circle. In this case, his entire house. So, I was dealing with a sorcerer. Interesting. I tested the barrier, but it was strictly to keep things out, not to keep things in. I whispered a personal protection spell of my own and silently sent a message to Josie that I might need my sword.

"Now, look here," he said, opening the volume and pointing at a page. "This author has clearly described two common origins for all the mythological creatures we have ever encountered. The first is imagination. He describes many of the creatures as simply coming from the imagination of a powerful sorcerer—or several—summoned from what he calls the 'primordial mass.' The other source is from alternate dimensions, much as you describe in your working thesis. These creatures include many of the ancient gods, some of whom bred and made tiny monsters themselves. I think of creatures like the Minotaur of Crete, for example. He points to evidence from all over the world—a world that seems much broader than what any individual might experience."

I could feel the memories of Sally, contained in this body, starting to make her salivate as I read through the manuscript. She—I?—was even lubricating, it was so exciting.

I felt his hand stroke down my back.

"Of course, you can't read it. The Sanskrit text is ancient and this must have been copied many times. But we can sit just over here and I will read it to you." His hand slid on down to cup my butt. Ah, so this was his game. Dangle a fruit that is irresistible to his victim and seduce her into his lair with it. I was nearly vulnerable to the temptation myself as I scanned the page and looked at the range of books on his shelves.

"It says here that these other dimensions may be opened with a gate of sorts, but it doesn't give the spell. Have you discovered that as well?" I asked, ignoring his hand on my thigh sliding under my skirt as I read.

"You understand the words? My, you are a remarkable girl. Perhaps we can make a little trade. I will let you copy this manuscript if you will let me... enjoy your intimate company during that time."

I heard his zipper being lowered and turned to see his erection sticking out of his pants. He'd worked his other hand under the leg band of my panties and was determined to get to the promised land.

"Yes, you just continue reading and pay no attention to me. It's a fair trade, don't you think?"

I pulled his hand out from under my skirt and turned on him.

"It would be for most ordinary girls," I said. I began pulling off my clothes so I didn't ruin them for Sally. I'd need clothes when I left. The propredator gasped.

"Oh, yes. Oh, so much better than I imagined. I will enjoy you so much I might just give you the book!"

"That would be so nice of you," I said when I was naked. "I think, in turn, that I shall enjoy you, as well." With that, I transformed into my full demon form. The poor professor fell back on his sofa, his stiff cock wilting as he stared at mine.

"You're... ah... What..."

"A demon," I supplied. "I don't usually have an appetite for paunchy old men, but I could turn you into a sweet young girl—a virgin, I think—and then we'd have a very good time."

"No! Please. I didn't mean any harm!"

"You didn't? By my count this makes the fourth impressionable college girl you've lured into your lair this year and offered something she found irresistible in exchange for her body. They couldn't all have been seduced by your library, which I compliment you on. I would guess you have a chemistry lab in this old house, too. Perhaps even a particle accelerator that you conjure up when you need it. Unfortunately, when the girls leave your clutches, they become overwhelmed with a sense of shame and guilt that drives them away from the college. I'm guessing another of your spells to be sure she leaves and doesn't look back. Am I right?"

"They've all been furnished with letters of high recommendation and have taken their studies, along with the results of their research here, to respected institutions. I didn't intend for them to suffer. I just need to enjoy a nubile young body occasionally."

"Occasions are becoming more frequent, though, aren't they?" I asked. "How old are you, sorcerer? Old enough to have rescued this manuscript and others on your shelves from a fire in a scriptorium a thousand years ago?"

"Yes! Yes, I'm old. I've used the spells I found to keep myself young through the ages by sapping the essence of young women during sex. But look at me. It's not working. My body is aging. I'm going to die."

"That's rather human of you," I said.

"I *am* human! Or, at least I was human when I started this."

"Well, I have a deal for you now," I said. He continued to watch the tip of my cock as I kept it at full erection to intimidate him. He actually licked his lips! "I will show you the spell that opens another dimension where you can enter with all that belongs to you. There you can create the reality you want, including, I suppose, an army of horny nymphs to keep you satisfied. Now, I can't guarantee it will be paradise. That depends on how you approach the new dimension. But it will be yours. In return, you will let me copy all the books in your library and you will never re-enter this dimension. Is that clear?"

"Yes. But it will take you forever to copy all these precious manuscripts."

"No. I have librarians who can take care of it in an hour or so. Now, do we have an agreement?" I conjured a contract and a knife out of thin air. I don't usually show off like that, but he needed to know what he was dealing with. He read the contract, in the same language as the book he'd shown me, and nodded.

"I sign here?" he asked.

I handed him the knife.

"In blood."

Okay, so I was being overly dramatic. I didn't technically *need* the scrap of parchment once he'd agreed, but he had his preconceived notions.

As soon as I had the parchment in hand, I summoned a crew of librarians from a gateway I opened to the satchel and they immediately began transporting and duplicating the books. It was a treasure chest waiting to be read!

In return, I asked Nimia to bring me a copy of the original manuscript from Pinaruti's library that showed me how to create the infinity room. I explained the process as well as I could and warned him that if he took anyone unwilling to his alternate dimension, I would personally find and unmake him. It's amazing how compliant he was. He sat on his sofa for the hour it took my librarians to duplicate his library and read the Pinaruti manuscript.

"It may take me years to learn how to do this."

"Try to do it without preying on young women," I suggested as I returned to Sally's form and put on her clothes. "Professor Arthur, I bid you a good day." I walked out of the room, picked up the suitcase and backpack, and left a bewildered old sorcerer in my wake.

64
THE SEARCH

"YOU SHOWED HIM my naked body?" Sally screamed at me when I told the tale of the wicked sorcerer.

"I didn't want to ruin your clothes when I transformed," I explained.

"Ha! Who needs clothes in Areola?" she asked, then spluttered in laughter. Indeed, she was sitting in front of me with nothing on but a smile.

"Well, I'm afraid that if you'd gone there yourself, he'd have done much more than see your body. His thoughts were really quite disgusting. I don't think there is any part of you he wouldn't have used. What's more, by the way your body was responding, you'd have let him and not thought a thing about it until you had left and started feeling guilty and dirty."

"You could feel what I feel in my body?" she squeaked.

"The transformation spell, when I'm in direct contact with the person I'm mimicking, is very complete. I considered letting him do exactly what he wanted."

"Gross. You could feel me getting turned on?"

"Yes. And you, too, have a very good smell."

"Don't let him tease you too much, Sally," Josie said as she sat with us. "One day you should have him transform both of you and you can make love to you as if you were him. Did I say that right?"

"Never mind," I said. "No one said anything about Sally and me having sex."

"Wait! You don't want to have sex with me? Was there something so disgusting about my body when you were in it that makes me repugnant?" she asked.

"No. Not at all. We just haven't discussed that... or even if you will be staying in Areola. Now here's what he had for you," I said, changing the subject. I presented the old manuscript to her. Nimia leaned toward her to look at it as well.

"This is… in a foreign language," Sally said. "How would I have gotten turned on by that?"

"I can translate for you," Nimia said as she began reading from the page. I could visibly see the change coming over Sally. Her nipples hardened, a flush spread across her face and chest and her breathing sped up. And there was a delicate aroma of an aroused woman emanating from beneath the table.

"Um… Nimia, I'm not, like, into girls, but if you want me to eat you while you read, I'll figure it out. My god! I do have a scent!"

"Told you," I said. "Now, about your stay in Areola."

Nimia closed the book so Sally would pay attention to me.

"A different dimension," she whispered. "It doesn't feel any different."

"We need to figure out if you are a temporary resident or permanent. I'm not saying you need to decide this instant, but I'm not willing to show you any more of Areola if you are going back to the natural world and leaving us. You have your life ahead of you in the natural world and could write your thesis. I'd even give you an exact duplicate of this book. It might take a while for you to get it translated, but you would have source material."

"I could go back to what you call the natural world and be considered a crackpot and lunatic. I'd be ridiculed in every academic institution in the world and would end up stacking panties at Walmart. No thanks. I want to stay here. I would like to send a message to my parents to let them know that I'm safe but not coming back."

"Many of us have had to keep in touch with our families back home for a while. I popped in occasionally until my parents died and I still get trundled out to do presentations occasionally. They make me look like an old woman, though," Liz said.

"Wait! You're *that* Liz?"

"Mmmhmm."

"Please, Bob. Let me stay in Areola. Let me be… one of your concubines. Have sex with me. Make love to me. And let me study the nature of alternate dimensions from inside one."

I smiled at her. What could be better?

Being chased around in a game was not the first time I'd been chased. Might have been the most fun, though. And Sally proved to be both an enthusiastic lover and a great researcher. What I know about the infinity room now, I mostly learned from her.

Let me explain.

Assertions, denials, speculation, diversion. Conflict, rebellion, revolution. It's all about libraries.

I know that comes out of the blue—doesn't everything?—but it's important.

I've been fascinated by books and scrolls since the day I came into existence. I found half a dozen scrolls in Pinaruti's magic room and read them repeatedly. Whenever I could gain a scroll or book, I did. I imported massive libraries and, when possible, librarians into the infinity room where we recreated both the volumes and the surroundings. Then Marian, our modern-day librarian, began the process of collecting all the digital media she could find, including papers, magazines, books, movies, and websites. Our scientists found a way to power readers for that information. It's all quite remarkable.

But one thing the best libraries have always been is 'public.' Any individual can gain access to the words in a library. And perhaps our library contains more dangerous words than any other library that has ever existed. It has never been restricted. And so, when a person chooses to study a subject in depth and learn all he or she can learn about it, they are free to do so, and our staff of librarians, who probably know more about what is in the library than any other human could possibly know, will help direct that curious individual to the books that will impart that knowledge.

Including magic.

I had always considered magicians to be a part of my world. I had never consciously imported a magus to the infinity room, but the knowledge was there in our library should anyone choose to learn it and have the talent to apply to it. Oh, and understand the language it was written in. You see, magic is much like—oh, say basketball. You can read everything about it; you can understand every technique and strategy. But if you don't have a talent for it—the physical strength and coordination—you still can't hit the basket. Certainly, with more practice, you will become better at it. But practice and knowledge alone will not make you a great basketball player. The same is true of magic.

I, being a magical creature, have a gift for magic, and still, I have as many spells that go afoul as that are successful. Witness poor Chione, bless her. She has not said a word since the day I thought I was casting a spell to keep her from talking about the infinity room. She certainly never has.

The talent, knowledge, and practice to become a truly powerful mage is a rare thing—especially when there are no experienced magi to learn from. But just because the odds are one in a billion, doesn't mean that one of ten million won't possess it.

Sally was a mage.

And when Nimia read and translated the ancient words to her, they always ended up in bed together. Sally came to us an exclusive heterosexual and progressed to being not quite so exclusive. But no one pushes her. She just gets involved and can't help herself.

Eventually, I did swap bodies with her so she could experience what it was like for a man to make love to a woman. I'd have to say she was far more enthusiastic about loving either sex after that.

So, back to the more or less present. I was getting ready for my second foray into the natural world in search of a future crewmate. That's what this was all about, right? We had agreed that I needed a little more flexibility. Living and working with the original crew contestants had been a growing experience, and it took us weeks to develop the relationship that turned them into such a tight and cohesive team. It didn't seem that three days was enough to make a positive decision. For example, I'd have left it up to the other crew members to decide between Sue and Amy. Instead, I happened to find Annie. I needed an out.

I figured that some of the women I would meet would be eliminated from consideration immediately, but that others might need more time to grow on me. I would no longer be limited to making a choice among three, but would continue to travel and interview and repeat visits to some before I chose one. That would be good, but I wanted to spend some time getting to really know Annie better before I went out again. We stayed in the beach house—well, the satchel stayed in the beach house. Annie and I stayed in Areola most of the time, though I emerged each day to make sure the guards were changed and everything in the natural world was okay.

After a week that we lightly called a honeymoon time, I was surprised it was Annie who told me I needed to get some more footage in the can.

"Bob, we have a mission and getting more people for the crew is necessary for the television series," she said. "You need to get out there and hunt down some more women. And maybe even some men."

"Are you tired of me already, honey?" I teased. We'd made love every day and I'd taken her exploring in some of the less accessible areas of Areola.

"You know better than that, Bob. But I'm a member of the crew now and we've been meeting about the second season. You need to be out there."

"Yes, you're right, I suppose."

"Oh, Bob. It would be wonderful to imagine it was only you and me that mattered. But you have five wives, five possessions, eleven other crew members, fifty-two priestesses whom I adore, and at last count there were seventy-three concubines in the harem, but I'm informed that number changes almost daily. And in addition to those, or included in those are other women who have a very special relationship with you."

"Oh?"

"Don't be dense, honey. Zhi, your warrior. Marian the Librarian. The little research mage Sally. Social engineer Virginia. Dora, who took you to Troy. Doria, who was part of your spoils of Troy. Chione, from Nebuchadnezzar's harem. Ali, the former slave in Musa Massa's court. A whole bunch of priestesses of Aphrodite who say *you* are their god now. A woman named Srininx who has a bronze colored breast. I could go on and on, and you know it. This world is filled with women who adore you and would open any passage for you. But the crew is still working hard to become the best possible crew to sail your ship into space, and I need to take my place among them. Don't worry. I'll always be in line to make love to you when you return."

Well, she was right and I took the list of women and locations with me as I set out for another trading mission. It would be exciting.

"It's time for Bob to return to the US," Doug told me. "You need to make some appearances to announce that you are working on season two of the show, since the ship is not yet ready. There will be questions and maybe some laughter, but you should be able to move around fairly easily. I think you should take Peninnah and Liz and me with you to the mainland. And Avril—to film, you know."

I knew. Avril and Doug were quite an item. But he was right. As my producer, he should be seen as well. I took the appearance and identity of The Bob and we headed for the airport and our private plane. We still had to go through security and scans, but nothing seemed amiss. We just got on the plane and left for the mainland.

One of the things I stocked up on were satchels. If anyone was thinking they could snatch and grab my portal, they'd need to figure out whose satchel to grab. We all carried one and I didn't use a look-away spell on any of them.

I saw a great movie about that once. Man in a bowler hat who steals a priceless work of art and suddenly there are several dozen men in bowler hats with a portfolio like his wandering around. Fun movie. We were prepared for something similar. Doug would be my foil. Once we were airborne over the Pacific, I worked the transformation spell that turned him into an image of me and me into him. That way, I could keep hold of the real satchel while he took the heat for possibly carrying around alien portal technology.

When we got to LA, a customs agent boarded the plane and went straight to Doug. After several minutes of arguing, Doug was led to the customs desk with his satchel, while I protested that this wasn't an international flight and Customs had no right to be inspecting our personal property. You can imagine how far that went with TSA and Border Control.

Doug came out of the terminal looking a little bedraggled, but in good spirits. We picked him up in our limo and drove to the mansion, which had not been in use since the first season selections were made.

"I was really afraid they were going to rip the bag apart at the seams searching for 'the portal.' I kept the protests up. Even demanded to speak to my Senator," Doug said. "I told them I'd left the portal at my palace and didn't intend to use it anytime soon. They finally gave up and sent me on my way. Oh, the tampons in the bag were a nice touch. I just told them I was carrying some things for my wife."

We congratulated him on making it through customs and we switched body transformations back to our own likeness in the back of the limo.

When we got to the mansion, I pulled out bug detectors from Areola and we all swept the house. I had Avril check all our camera installations to make sure they were ready to record for the show. Of course, as she was checking, she found one camera that had been tampered with to send its signal to a receiver off-site. She also found two other cameras that were not part of our setup. *They'd* been in the mansion in my absence.

We neutralized all the bugs we found and set all our own cameras to play an endless loop of the rooms. That was the best we could do for now.

Doug and I had meetings and interviews for the next few days.

I'm afraid it was not to be a time of peace and quiet. I expected to need to work, but I wasn't quite expecting the crowds that followed me around everywhere. Most of the time they were peaceful and friendly. Occasionally, there was a mob of protesters against our show, against leaving earth, against sex, against science, against the government, against the church, against taxes, against medicine, against vaccines, against women... It seemed there was a crowd against just about everything. There was even a crowd against natural grains and whole food. Somehow, they all figured I was the right place to protest.

On the other hand, there were crowds—mostly women, though not exclusively—who cheered and held signs that said "Pick me!" "I'll boldly go!" "Let me port with you!" "Official Space Cadet." I'm not sure that last woman understood what her sign said. Which was appropriate. And, within the crowds both for and against, I could see hundreds of Bob Satchels. They'd become quite the fashion accessory and even high school students carried them.

"Tell us about your new show," Elaine Frost, the newest host on a late-night television show asked.

"Well, it's season two of *To Boldly Go*. But we kind of shot our wad on the first season because we thought we'd be leaving earth at the end of the season and would be sending season two back from space. So, we've had to change our format considerably. I'm going out to personally interview contestants," I said.

"How many contestants are we talking about this year?" Elaine asked.

"This is unbelievable, but we've received 30,000-plus applications to be on the show. I'm sorry to say that for many reasons, the vast majority were unacceptable. But the crew selected in the last show, along with my family, have reviewed over 5,000 and have sent out letters of commitment. We have received some 2,000 responses with signed consent forms and releases to use footage we shoot of them candidly on the show."

"You can't mean to say you'll be 'interviewing' all 2,000!"

"I doubt it. That would probably take us into season five, at least, and I hope to be long gone before then. I'm sorry to say that I'll get as far as I get. I can't hope for more than that," I said.

"So, it seems like doing a personal interview would be a good way to get a lot of innocent women into bed with you," Elaine said skeptically.

"Well, it would be if I was recognizable. But I'm pretty good at changing my appearance."

"You mean makeup and such?"

"Oh, sure. But do you remember that movie a few years ago where the guy put on a mask and suddenly had a rubber face?"

"It's hard to do special effects when you're live."

"Yes, but that actor reduced the number of special effects that were needed. He has a rubber face. A couple of adjustments and he's a different person. I have the ability to do some of that, too. Then with a little makeup, I'm someone totally different."

"I've got to see this. Audience, would you like to see Bob demonstrate?" Loud applause indicated their answer.

Elaine looked at me with a raised eyebrow. I suppose she expected me to make a funny face at her. Instead, I started doing facial expression stretches—yawning, raising and lowering my eyebrows, squinting and popping my eyes open, and shifting my jaw from side to side and in and out. While I was doing the exercises, I worked a few magical transformations on my face, careful not to go overboard. I pushed and pulled at my face, and covered it with my hands.

"I hope this worked," I said with my face covered. "I usually work in front of a mirror."

"You mean all those funny faces you were making were your disguise?"

"No, this is." I uncovered my face and the audience gasped. I hadn't gone overboard, but I was more square-jawed, my nose was narrower, my mouth a little smaller, and my eyebrows closer together. I looked like a different person.

"Whoa! Where did Bob go and who are you?" Elaine said.

"I call this one Dean Larson," I said. "Add a blond wig and I'm good to go."

"Cameras, can we get a split screen with one of our earlier shots of Bob and what he looks like now?" Elaine asked. The audience saw a big screen with the two Bobs side-by-side. When you looked closely, you could tell we were the same person and looked like there had just been some really good makeup applied. The audience applauded.

"How do you do that?"

"There are forty-three muscles in the human face. The real trick is to be able to isolate and flex each of them independently."

"I've never seen anything like that."

"This is a little difficult to hold," I said. "Can I go back to myself again?"

"Uh... sure. Does it take all the same gyrations?" Elaine asked.

"No." I shook my head violently back and forth, making a noise like I was spluttering. When I stopped, I had returned to my normal look.

"That was truly amazing. If you hadn't been sitting right beside me, I wouldn't have believed it." She paused for more applause. "So, you'll be in disguise and supposedly the women won't know who you are. Anything you'd like to tell them?"

"Yes. A couple of things. First of all, I will never, *ever* force myself on a woman. Don't feel like you have to accept every overture from every man because he might be Bob. That's not what I'm judging my interviewees on. It's all going to be based on how good our chemistry is with each other. If you didn't reply with a consent form and release, I won't be approaching you at all. Second, not every man who approaches you will be Bob in disguise. Exercise normal precautions that you'd use upon meeting any guy who sparks an interest in you. Third, I will *not* try to lure you into an unmarked van on the street. There are very real traffickers out there and until we get to know each other, you should exercise good dating protocol, including letting a friend know where you are, staying in well-lit public places, and keeping information about yourself confidential. I don't need your social security number, driver's license, or bank account. I already have that because it was on the application form. Don't give it out freely."

"That's really good general dating advice, Bob," Elaine said. "I see our time is about up. Is there anything you'd like to add?"

"Yes. This is to the men who think this is an opportunity to exercise predatory behavior, or want to pretend they are Bob and see where it gets them. I spent $100 billion last year on the show and on spacecraft development. My investments are growing so fast that I still have over $500 billion. That's $500 billion I can spend to chase down and eliminate traffickers and predators who think they can cash in on a woman's desire to be on my show. $500 billion I can use to prosecute frauds and impersonators. $500 billion that I can use to track you down to the ends of the earth and make sure you never hurt another person again. Beware. You've been warned."

I delivered that line standing and staring straight into the camera. There was stunned silence on the set for a moment and then a standing ovation from the live audience. I waved at them and left the stage.

65
THE EXORCIST

IZ AND PENINNAH, of course, were always with me when I was out in public talking about the show. Doug was usually nearby, but he had responsibilities that took him to other offices or studios as he got us geared up for production. We had to verify that we were using union employees and were paying union scale, or we couldn't be broadcast. Our contacts at HCEN told us they'd had to comply with the union standards eventually, though they'd managed to fly under the radar for several years as providing educational internships.

We were usually pretty friendly with people. Police and security services made sure fans didn't get too close to us as we went from the studio to the waiting limo.

As we made it to the limo, I became aware of a man on a step stool with an amplified megaphone preaching to the crowd about the evils of my show and the perversion of Bob. I paused to listen to him as he railed on. As loud as he was, I was sure he was breaking some kind of noise ordinance. No one moved to stop him, though.

"Women *boldly go* into his lair and are never seen again. He preys on the dreamy-eyed, making them victims of his perversions. I tell you, he is an emissary from hell and has possessed those women. Do not render yourselves into his devilish lair. Stand firm upon the word of God and resist this temptation."

I was thinking about replying to him, but Peninnah grabbed my arm and pulled me into the limo with her. We headed back to our hotel and ordered dinner sent to our suite. We always did that rather than simply stepping into the infinity room and eating. Hotels became suspicious if you never ordered food or ate in their restaurants. This week it had been much easier to book a downtown hotel than to commute out to the hills to the mansion.

As soon as dinner had been delivered, I opened a gateway and half a dozen others came out of Areola with additional food to join us. Peninnah and Liz went back to the palace for the night. That, too, was typical as they did not like to spend the day in the natural world and then the night, too. They were concerned that they would start aging. I believed the room had a rejuvenating effect on them as they looked as young and fresh as the first day I met them.

We were finishing dinner when I decided to tune in on the television for the evening news to see if we were mentioned.

"At the bottom of the barrel for entertainment news tonight, Bob is causing quite a stir as he announces plans for casting the coming season of *To Boldly Go*," said the news announcer, Delilah Samson. "According to an interview and press release from Bob's Studio, the entire second season will be done candidly, with Bob in disguise and secret cameras recording every interaction as he travels the world looking for additions to his harem crew. But not all reactions have been positive. Here's a report from our woman on the street, Lily Lalane. Lily?"

"Thank you, Delilah. It's hard to tell if Bob's announcements about how to behave with a new man, his threats against men who try to imitate him, or the denunciation of his entire being by Rev. Ronald Richards of Bethany Consolidated Church of the Holy Grail is at the top of the news tonight. Rev. Richards preaches regularly to crowds nearing three thousand people at his megachurch, but has taken his ministry to the streets to reach out to the people who throng after Bob."

"I tell you, this Bob is the devil incarnate," Richards said in the interview. "He thinks the world has sunk so low into depravity that it will sit idly by as the flower of humanity is plucked and destroyed. Oh, we can all get a little wistful about the promise of wealth, sexual gratification, abundance, and gluttony. But down that road lies the gates of hell. Bob must be stopped and the women he has captured must be freed from this cult that has risen around him."

"So, you believe the women have not gone willingly to be on his show and compete for inclusion in his space journey?" Lily asked.

"I believe they have been bewitched, enchanted, and possessed," Richards said. "They might think they have entered his lair of their own free will, but once there, like a fly on a spider's web, they discover there is no return—no way out. They must have the devil within them exorcised."

Maya grasped my arm and buried her head on my shoulder. She was shaking and sobbing.

"Don't let him near me, Bob. He is like the Spanish priests of so long ago. They exorcised demons by burning people at the stake or cutting their heads off. Don't let him, Bob. Please don't let him near us."

"I won't, my sweet love. You were given into my care by the god Kukulkàn and the goddess Ixchel. You asked me to possess you and I entered every fiber of your being. But that is a two-way street. At that same moment, you entered every fiber of my being and we became one heart. I will protect and defend you to my last breath."

Over the years, I've met various priests who practiced exorcism on people mostly possessed by the priests. Nor were they all within the so-called Christian religions. It seemed in every religion, there were those who felt anyone who disagreed with them must be possessed by an evil spirit.

I'm not saying no one ever was. I'd met people possessed by demons. I mean people other than the women I possessed. Most seemed to be living in a mutually satisfying relationship. There were some who had been possessed by demons ordered by a conjurer to torment them. I know Issa had encountered some like this. In fact, he cast Maureen out of a fellow she'd been confined to and she fled from the area as soon as she was free. She didn't enjoy it any more than the guy who'd suffered from her.

But most of the people exorcists practice their rituals on aren't possessed at all. They simply disagree with the exorcist's peculiar brand of religion. During the Spanish Inquisition, when I was traveling as a priest, the majority of those burned as demon-possessed were simply Jews who refused to convert. That doesn't mean there were never Jews who consorted with devils. The Kabala has instructions in it. Solomon was dead before I made my way to Judah and was taken to Babylon, but it is said that his wisdom included how to tame a demon.

Experience told me, though, that the loudest denouncers of evil were those who practiced it. Pick any preacher or politician who makes a stand against homosexuality, child abuse, adultery, trafficking, or any of the deadly sins or ten commandments, and you will find a practitioner or a person wishing he was and lying in wait for his opportunity.

Take Ahman, for example. I ran into him in Southeastern Africa, sometime after I finished my time working for Ninra and Namri. In general terms, I was still pretty much an innocent in the ways of the world. I knew there were good people and there were bad people, but I didn't expect them to affect me much. *Nobody* would care about me.

Ahman was nobody.

I was a stranger, just wandering through the world, but Ahman saw me as an opportunity.

"Bob is a danger to our children and our women," he whispered. "Why is Bob always alone? Where does Bob go at night? Why is Bob so secretive?"

It was a primitive area and an even more primitive time. There was always the possibility of a raid by one village or sect on another to get something the other had—food, animals, women, children. There wasn't much commerce that used tokens, though occasionally a gem was discovered that inspired a certain amount of lust.

Anyway, when a young woman of the village disappeared, most people mourned her a little, but assumed she'd been stolen by another village in the night. Shit happens. Sometimes, they'd mount a raid of their own and steal a woman or a child to replenish their village.

But Ahman whispered just a hint.

"It might have been Bob, you know."

Most people shrugged it off as unlikely, though some amount of interest was shown in where I went at night. I had to be especially careful where I hid the satchel and crept into it to spend time with my precious Nimia. We tried to spend a lot of time together because otherwise she was almost alone in the bag. I say almost. I recall that she'd enticed a couple of other women into the bag with her, but over the course of a century or so, some would stay and some would go. I was never sure how many she'd attracted.

When another woman went missing, Ahman whispered again.

"Why would the other village want another woman so soon? It must be Bob. He's too secretive."

Then a few men from a neighboring village showed up one day and demanded their women back. They accused the village of stealing too many of their women and would kill all the men in the village if they didn't return some.

"We haven't been on a raid. You took two of our women!" an elder declared.

"We've taken no one!" the elder of the other tribe protested. "Who else is there?"

"There's Bob," Ahman whispered. "He might be behind it."

It didn't take long before Ahman was no longer whispering. He was speaking out loud about the evils of abducting women and each time, he would point at me as if I was the perpetrator.

I could have just left. Then, a thousand years or three thousand years later, the story of the demon who stole women in the night would still be told and used to explain abductions and all kinds of other atrocities. I waited and watched. And then I saw Ahman creep away in the middle of the night.

He made his way to a cave. It was so difficult to find I wished I'd discovered it to hide the satchel in. Inside, Ahman had nearly a dozen women, tied with vines so they couldn't escape and gagged so they couldn't cry out. Of course, they couldn't eat either, which didn't make much difference. Ahman wasn't feeding them. They were getting weaker by the day and one lay dead in the back of the cave. All Ahman did was use them. When they became too filthy or starved to satisfy his desires, he stole another woman from one of the villages.

I went full goat. I stormed into the cave and knocked Ahman out. I didn't kill him. It wasn't my injury to revenge. I untied the women and they fell upon the unconscious man, tearing and disemboweling him. He awoke only long enough to understand his predicament and scream. When they had completely butchered the man, they sat, weeping. I had Nimia and her women bring out food for them and minister to them.

When morning came, I showed the women the way to the village and they dragged the remains of Ahman and the body of the dead woman to the center of the village. There, they began to wail.

The village awakened and rushed to see what the uproar was about.

At first, they thought Ahman and the woman had died rescuing the others, and swore to hunt down Bob. But it did not take long for the women to set things straight. The village sent a runner to the next village and asked them to come and witness the return of the women. One young woman was selected to tell the story, and she was quite a story teller.

"That man took us from our beds in the night and carried us to his burrow in hell," she said, pointing at Ahman's corpse. "He tied us and raped us. He starved us and we were his slaves until hunger killed us. But then when this man came to work his evil on us last night, Tiger followed him," the young woman said. I wasn't sure how she got a tiger out of my goat. "Tiger swore at that man for being cruel to his own kind and starving us. Tiger tore apart that man until there was no part recognizable and then Tiger cut our bonds and freed us from this demon of the night. Tiger gave us food and told us to bring that man to the village so the village would know how we were harmed by that man."

"It wasn't Bob?" an elder spoke. "Where is Bob?"

"Bob is here," I said, standing from among them, having returned to my human shape. "It was never Bob. It was Ahman."

"Well, our women are back home," said one of the elders. "We needn't worry now. Ahman is dead and all is well. We will make wives of these women."

That did not go over well with the women.

"What? You will deprive us of our freedom now that we have been freed by Tiger? You will rape us in your huts and starve us until we die? We will not return to the way things were. We will not be your property and live in fear for our lives. We will not bear your children or cook your meals or kneel before you while you plant your seed. We will go and find Tiger and we will serve him. He was the one who saved us, not the worthless men of these villages," the young woman said.

The rescued women seized spears and stones and backed away from the center of the village. When the men made to pursue them, other women of the village attacked them from behind with rocks and sticks. Then they rushed to join the women leaving the village.

The remaining men shrank back when they heard a Tiger's roar from the jungle.

That left me with a great deal to do. I couldn't just let the women wander away in the jungle. They could find a real tiger out there and be worse off than they were. I stood before the men and spat at them.

"May your manhood shrivel and your villages die," I cursed. I turned and followed the women.

As soon as we were out of sight, I got in front of the women and appeared in my goat form, leading them through a gateway into the bag. Nimia awaited them with her women and saw to it they were fed and cared for. She discovered whether any wanted to return to the natural world, and most did, but not to the men they had left. I carried the bag inland and found a peaceful and isolated tribe. Sadly, mortality was higher among women in their tribe due to poor birthing conditions.

I had Nimia come out to help improve their success rate, and then those women who wished to return to the natural world came out, willing to replenish the number of women in the tribe. There were then more women than men in the tribe and so a kind of matriarchal society grew. They called themselves The People of Tiger.

After spending some years there, helping the society become established, improving their water supply and sewage removal, and seeing that the imbalance between men and women didn't become a problem, I picked up my satchel and headed back eastward, where I built a small boat and made my way north along the coast of Africa once again.

That was just a story the current situation reminded me of. Something told me the one who was protesting the most was the most likely to be an offender. Centuries of experience seemed to bear this out.

I bundled everyone but Zhi and Artemisia back into Areola and the three of us went out hunting. I chose these two for many reasons, but not the least of them was their devotion to me. They were devoted but not possessed. Should it happen that the preacher attempted an exorcism—which I doubted would work—I didn't want to risk one of my possessions. For now, the five of them would stay in Areola until I assessed how big a threat this was.

It wasn't difficult to find where the preacher lived. His mansion was every bit as big as mine in the hills. The difference was that mine was meant to entertain dozens of people *inside*. It was actually rather modest from the outside. His was meant to be seen from afar. I very much doubted that anyone who belonged to his megachurch had an idea of just how he lived.

We prowled around the grounds and discovered several cars and a panel truck waiting. Drivers were with the cars, but we didn't disturb them. We had nothing against the church's board of directors meeting with the preacher, if that was the case, and certainly their drivers would be harmless.

When we got inside, we saw that no one could possibly be harmless.

Yes, we got inside. Even though my look-away spell that I'd been using for millennia didn't leave us undetectable from electronic devices, Artemisia, Zhi, and I had developed many ways to circumvent alarm systems. Zhi and I had developed our tech when I started unleashing the ninja priestesses on traffickers. Artemisia was a natural at it, excelling in the physics and electronics aspects during our rocket school training. We avoided most of his alarms and disabled others.

When we got inside, we found a hedonistic palace made for the pleasures of the flesh. And Reverend Richards was taking great pleasure in them.

Well, he was *in* one of them. Others were attending him in various stages of preparing for him to be in them. Now, I can't really be judgmental about a man with any number of women ready to please him. Or any number of men for that matter. Reverend Richards had both. But there was something I didn't like about the scene. Every one of the sex objects wore a collar. And it wasn't just a necklace collar or a collar from the lifestyle. I don't argue about the lifestyle either. I recognized these collars for exactly what they were: slave collars.

And each had a blinking light on it, which told me they were undoubtedly equipped with some kind of electronic system, most likely for tracking, but possibly to administer punishment as well. I could see red burns on the necks of two or three.

All told, the right reverend was entertaining half a dozen men with over a dozen of his slaves. We stayed quietly in the background witnessing to make sure we understood fully what was going on.

"What did I tell you, Ronnie old boy? This new batch has been trained by the best. The drugs and the shock therapy keep them compliant to your every wish," said a broad man sodomizing a boy who was definitely underage.

"Oh yeah. I like this," the preacher said. "She lubricates on command. And you're sure they're all clean?"

"Clean and sterile. No fear of disease or pregnancy to spoil your fun."

"How about the pain quotient?"

"Oh, they'll take it. They don't like it at all, but they'll submit. Hell, if you commanded one of them to slit her wrists while you fucked her and let her bleed out, she'd do it. They can't resist."

"I'll take them, but you'll need to remove the last batch from the playroom downstairs. Two didn't make it. The others are pretty much used up."

I'd heard enough. I nodded to Zhi and Artemisia and in a few seconds, all seven of the traffickers—including the preacher—were unconscious. I worked a releasing spell on the collars and they fell to the floor. I couldn't do anything about the compliance of the slaves, but at least if I missed something, the slavers couldn't punish them with the collars. I examined one of the collars and was shocked to find that they contained an explosive charge as well. I put a binding spell on the seven slavers and left Zhi in charge so that the slaves didn't attack them. The slaves seemed unaware that anything had happened as they continued in whatever activity they'd been engaged in when we arrived. A look in their eyes told me they weren't home.

In the basement, we found a horror. Another dozen slaves lay chained to the walls and various pieces of torture equipment. Two of them were dead. All bore scars and open wounds. The room was filled with various dungeon equipment, most of which was used in the more radical forms of torture and bondage.

I didn't hesitate. I opened a gateway and my concubines flooded out to care for the tortured slaves as I released their bonds. They led the slaves—or in some cases carried them— to Areola. When all were gone, I took Artemisia back to join Zhi and our captives.

She was having a bit of difficulty controlling the slaves as whatever commands they were under began to dissipate. I opened a gateway again and concubines took charge of the freed slaves and led them away as the slavers looked on. They had awakened from their nap, but were still under the effect of the binding spell that immobilized them.

While the gateway was open, I called forth the ninja priestesses. I could see a flicker of recognition in the eyes of one of the men as he realized this meant he was about to die. Rumors in the underworld of the black-clad glowing ninjas had been whispered for a few years as we'd cleaned out various nests of traffickers and freed their prisoners. I selected that one to read the memories of. It was possible he could lead me to more of his kind.

It is hard for people to believe, but thirty-five million people worldwide are hurt by trafficking each day. And more startling, fifty percent of sex trafficking goes *through* the United States.

His memories were disgusting, but they revealed another level of his organization. And the 'trainer' who created the slaves for the market. That one would receive a very special visit one day soon.

I shook my head in disgust, trying to clear the filth from it. Then I turned to the preacher.

"What is it that makes you think you can cast demons out of people when you are worse than any demon I have met?" I demanded. I freed his tongue to answer.

"By the power of the Lord Jesus Christ, I command you to release me and to depart from those you have possessed!" he shouted.

"Hmm. Not going to happen. Where's your authority? Show me your documentation," I yelled back.

"I have the power of holy writ behind me."

"Not good enough. Nothing in the Bible gives you the power to cast out demons."

"Jesus sent his disciples into the world with authority to cast out demons and unclean spirits."

"He gave that authority to his twelve disciples and later to Paul. He never said anyone else could have it. Even Paul, who wrote half the New Testament in his letters, never mentions casting out demons. You have no such authority. And when your church finds what you have concealed here, paid for by their loving donations, you will have no authority there. And when you lie in a prison cell, the next to be gang raped, you will be powerless to stop them."

I could see a change come over him. I half expected it and was prepared. I strengthened the binding spell as he struggled against the bonds.

"You have no authority over us either, Demon Bob," a different voice issued from his mouth. "You cannot fight all the demons of hell. I will..."

His voice was cut off with his head.

I had suspected he was not completely human, but I couldn't act on the suspicion at once. I'd intended to kill him as soon as I found out he was trafficking. But knowing he was a demon left me few options in how to deal with him. Removing his head and burning it was one of the effective ways of killing a demon. I set the body and head aflame. My priestesses, glowing like avenging angels, set upon the six remaining traffickers and nailed them to the walls of the preacher's torture chamber. Their particular signature for the purging of sex traffickers.

The last of the men died, choking on his own genitals.

Part XIII
Candidates

Image Credit: imasecret, ID 269287313, licensed from Shutterstock.com

66
CLEVELAND BOB

I FELT PARTICULARLY DISGUSTED when I'd finished at the preacher creature's house. When the flames died in his torture chamber, the ash dissolved into dust and evaporated into the primordial mass from which he had come. I collected Zhi, Artemisia, and the priestesses into Areola and left, getting back to the hotel before morning. Once there, I locked the doors and entered Areola where the priestesses met me and bathed me in the pool and in the glow of their light.

The victims we had rescued were in various conditions, some having not fully transformed into the automatons the traffickers were trying for and others having gone so far into a different head space that there was nothing we could do for them but purge them of the drugs and return them to the natural world, usually just inside or outside a hospital that could care for them.

Why? Why not care for them in Areola?

Those brought into Areola ceased aging, no longer subject to death. It would have been cruel to keep them trapped in their damaged minds forever. At least in the natural world, they would age and die and be released from their pain. It was the best I could do. I truly wished I could heal their minds, but they were beyond the reach of even The Bob.

On another occasion, Sally, Eun-ha, Julie, and Deedee joined me for dinner in my hotel room. The latter three were contestants in the first season. Sally was my mage. She was just beginning to try working spells, but complained that she was making no progress in Areola.

"You know, everything is just perfect in Areola," Deedee said. "There are times when it is a relief just to come out into this flawed natural world and have a bite of a steak that was overcooked by an inattentive chef."

We laughed and all had a taste of the too well-done meat. It was true that we seemed to never have a meal that was lower than our expectations in Areola. And that was true whether the person eating liked rare meat or well-done, spicy or mild. In a way, I was reminded of Aphrodite. I pulled Deedee to me and began to caress and kiss her.

'Why the juxtaposition of Deedee and Aphrodite?' you ask. Well, I'd had a dream of Aphrodite the week before our final elimination challenge of the first season. I'd been making love to Deedee and the visage of My Lady Goddess came over her. I knew there was something familiar about Deedee that attracted me to her. She'd been blessed by Aphrodite and shown how to find me. She was my special gift from the goddess.

But as for why I'd been reminded of My Lady, it was related to why she was the most beautiful image of a woman the world had ever seen. Now, if I lined up one hundred men and asked each to describe their vision of the perfect woman, I would get one hundred different descriptions. Oh, the same would happen if I asked a hundred women. Some would be redhead, some blonde, some brunette. Some would be black, white, Asian, Native American, Latina. There would be tall, medium, short, and ridiculous. They would have breast sizes from nearly flat to impossibly huge. The same would be true of their butts. I guarantee you that no two descriptions would be close to the same.

Still, every one of those men would look at Aphrodite and pronounce her perfect, the very image of the most beautiful woman in the world as they would imagine her. I think it had to do less with the goddess herself and more with the image each man would project upon her. She would always be perfect. Of course, Paris *had* to say Aphrodite was the most beautiful of the goddesses—even without the bribe. She was exactly what he imagined beauty to be.

I'd once asked Sally to look into that aspect of our world and she reported that, as far as she could tell, our world was shaped by the projections of its inhabitants. Essentially, Areola had no fixed shape at all. Each individual found exactly what they considered perfect. And that extended to the food, as well. I agreed with Deedee that there was something refreshing about sampling something that wasn't perfect occasionally. It certainly heightened our appreciation of that which was.

And all that line of reasoning ended up with a very naked Deedee on her hands and knees on the sofa as I plowed into her hot wet pussy, which I found was just perfect.

"Cleveland," I said. "This one looks intriguing."

I looked at the crew and my family and they nodded. They'd presented me with a list in some semblance of order that would let me jet around the world again interviewing the candidates and recording the show.

May Abernathy was the candidate in Cleveland.

It took a couple of weeks to get everything set up, but Doug had a good cover for me. I was a new resident of an incubator office building. It was a concept in which new companies could rent discounted office space that included janitorial and support services. He confided that he'd found a person trying to organize a space and funded him, so I was essentially renting an office for my import/export business from myself.

Nonetheless, May had started a janitorial service and hired a small staff of maids who cleaned four office buildings in the office park and got free office space in our building in return for cleaning ours. I landed in Cleveland and became a desk jockey named... I'll just go by Bob for convenience's sake. Just understand that I didn't register the business under my name. I was not The Bob in Cleveland. I was just Cleveland Bob. You'll get used to it.

"Oh, good evening. Are you Mr. Bob? I was told today a new company opened in this office. I'm May and I'm here to clean," said the sturdy brunette in my doorway.

By sturdy, I mean she was solidly built. With her sleeves rolled up, I could see the muscles in her arms, and it was a cinch that she was not petite. But she was nonetheless attractive and had a bright smile.

"Oh. Hello, May. They told me I should expect you to come in tonight. I've just been... well, working, obviously. I didn't realize it had gotten so late," I said.

"No problem. I can come back a little later. I don't want to interrupt your work. I'll vacuum last."

"Thank you. Could you tell me how this works? I'm still new at it all. You just come in and clean? How frequently and what do I owe you?" I asked.

"You don't owe anything for me. Unless you need something special done."

"Special?"

"There's some kind of marketing guy on the third floor who gets carried away and I have to scrub the marker off his window. He just starts writing his plan and outlining campaigns and uses every available surface. Washing windows is something we do once a month. If you need it more often, that will cost you."

"I see. But normal cleaning each night, like emptying the wastebasket and vacuuming the floors is just included?"

"Yes. Of course, if you really like my service, an occasional tip is nice, but not expected. Same with Christmas gifts, but that's a long way away," she laughed.

"I've been so focused on my travel arrangements that I guess I really didn't listen that well during the introductory orientation. Secretaries are the same, right?"

"Sort of. You'll find a lot more services they offer are in the extras category. Telephone answering, message taking, and greeting visitors is in your package. If you dictate letters or need someone to type up a proposal, that service is extra."

"I see. Thank you for taking the time to explain. Sometimes I get confused."

"That's not at all unusual. The concept has been around a while, but in order to work, a big investor has to basically underwrite the operation in hopes that there will be a big payout when your business matures. Import and export, your door says."

"Yes. It's funny. I never even see what I'm shipping, but I still travel all over to make deals. I'll buy a shipload of grain in the Midwest, sell it to a broker in the Middle East and buy a tanker full of oil there to ship to Florida. That kind of thing."

"You just buy these things?"

"It's more like brokering. I find a client in the Middle East who wants the grain and I negotiate the pricing and delivery parameters with the grain producers in the Midwest. The only part of the transaction I see money from is my commission. Which is usually pretty good."

"Wow. Uh... Sounds really interesting, but I should let you get your travel plans made and I should get back to cleaning. See you later."

Introduction accomplished. I set about stage two, which was emptying and breaking down all the boxes Doug had shipped to me for my 'new office.' Everything was well-organized, so by the time May got back to my office, I had a stack of boxes to take to recycling.

I timed things right so I was backing out of my door with a stack of corrugated in my arms and bumped into May.

"Ah. We meet again. I was just trying to get these boxes out of the way so you can vacuum. I'm sorry, but there's a lot of paper dust in there."

"No problem. This is my last room for the night."

"Can you tell me where to take all these for recycling?" I asked.

"Oh, just leave them. I'll get them out to the loading dock."

"Loading dock? It's no problem. I don't want to create extra work for you. I'll take them down. Can I take anything for you?"

"Really? Um... If you *want* to. Let me dump your baskets and you can take my bag of recycling with you." She quickly added the few scraps of paper I'd thrown in my recycling basket to her bag, tied it off, and handed it to me. "If you use the first set of stairs, the dock is right at the foot of them. The recycling dumpster is to the left of the dock. Don't let the door lock behind you."

"Thank you. This won't take but a minute."

It took a few minutes and I was afraid I would miss May by the time I got back from juggling the flattened but still unwieldy boxes. When I got back to my office, she was just winding up her vacuum's cord. The office was spotless. My desk had even been wiped down and everything on it was arranged tastefully.

"If you leave papers or anything related to your business on your desk, I won't touch it. But if it is just your decorative items and office supplies, I'll dust them and make sure everything on your desk is clean."

"You're so efficient. I guess I can close up for the night. If you're off now, I'd happily buy you a drink. I'm so wound up and excited about having an office that I could use a drink to settle down. For three years I've been running my business out of the front seat of my car and my briefcase."

"Oh. Well, I don't usually. But... um... give me a minute to stow my things in the janitor closet and I guess I'll join you, just to celebrate your arrival." She glanced at my desk and then took off for wherever her janitor closet was. I grabbed my hat and satchel and was locking the door when she returned.

"There's a little after hours bar across the parking lot if that's okay with you," she said. "We might even meet some of the other late workers from the office park there."

"Sounds great."

We got to the little bar and there were a couple of other office workers that May stopped to introduce me to. She was obviously known and liked by everyone. We sat at a table and ordered drinks.

"So, Mr. Bob, I noticed that you have a pen set in recognition of service to Space Pioneers. What did you ship for them? Have inside information on where their launch is going to be?"

"Oh, no. I'm afraid not. I arranged a shipment of parts that were urgently needed from Japan to Texas. I think, frankly, they could have sent an email and gotten them just as quickly. But my company expedited the customs process and made sure the correct tariffs were paid, so I suppose we did our part," I said.

"It's too bad about their delay. I could have told them they wouldn't blast off on the schedule they'd set," she sighed.

"You could? How's that?"

"They're going about it all wrong. I appreciate the idea of wanting to keep their launch location a big secret, but everything I've researched indicates the ship they are building is way too small to be effective for interplanetary travel. Maybe for resupply and communications, but not for colonization. Even if The Bob has a portal, like he says he has."

"You doubt that?"

"I'm a physicist. There are a few things I understand about things like instantaneous travel from one point to another," she said.

"I thought you were a janitor!" I said.

"I own a janitorial service company and I clean offices in our building in exchange for an office and services myself. But I've got a PhD in Physics with a thesis on orbital escape velocities. Their little ship can't carry enough fuel to escape from Earth's gravity well and power a flight all the way to Mars. And they have to understand, of course, that it's a one-way trip because they won't have enough fuel to get back, even out of the weaker gravitational field of Mars."

"Wow! What are you doing cleaning offices?"

"Check the job boards tomorrow for employers seeking a Doctor of Physics with a specialization in orbital mechanics. Oh, there are jobs for scientists with my qualifications, but they aren't engaged in space travel. NASA is still a good old boys network, no matter what you hear about the training of female astronauts. Did you know that even in the sciences, women are paid less than 80% of what their equally qualified male counterparts are? Don't get me started."

"Well, how about going to work for Space Pioneers? I hear they have a good reputation for women in the business."

"I haven't managed to get anyone to return a call from Space Pioneers. That's why I joined the applicants for that TV reality show. Stupid, really. It's not like The Bob would ever look twice at me. I know I'm a nerd and I'm... a little bigger than most of the candidates he's had on his show. And I don't just sleep with a guy because he's rich." She kind of laid that on the table and looked at me until I'd met her eyes. "I'd never be able to get out of bed if I did that. I just want a chance to show my stuff," she said. She might be self-conscious about her size, but I saw absolutely nothing wrong with it. I'd love for her to show her stuff.

Okay, I needed to tone down my runaway libido and really think about what she had to offer.

We headed back to the offices—me to my car and just before we parted, I said, "May, I really liked spending a little time with you and appreciate you making a couple of introductions. I am leaving tomorrow afternoon for a week… eight days. Is there a chance we could get together again when I get back?"

"Hmm. I guess so. Just something light. I'm really not at a stage in my life where I can consider anything serious. Okay?"

"That's great. Let's plan for a week from Friday evening. I'd just like to sit and talk for a while. Nothing serious. You sound like a great friend."

She waved as I opened my car door. I held it open long enough to let my camerawoman crawl in before I slipped in.

"She didn't say anything about being a PhD in physics in her application," Paul said as Julie sat on his lap. He'd read through the apps with Julie when they weren't screwing. Or when I wasn't screwing her. He was our resident expert in Astrophysics.

"I'd just hire her on the spot," Karla said. "What kind of an idea does she have that will get us into space faster?"

"I'm not sure it will be faster," I said. "But it should be interesting to discover. I was careful not to probe too deeply when we went out."

"What a loaded word," Deedee said as she settled into my lap. "You can probe me deeply, lover."

That was a great thought. In fact, it was how I spent most of my night in a hotel room in Cleveland before I caught my flight to Europe the next day.

I flew in business class to Amsterdam and first class from Amsterdam to Bucharest, Romania. I found the flight attendants to Europe to be less flirtatious than the ones I'd encountered flying to Asia. I suppose it all depends on who is on your flight. I'm sure there are both flirtatious flight attendants and strictly-business flight attendants of all races on every airline.

My reservation in Bucharest was not until the coming night, I discovered, so I quickly booked a luxury hotel for the weekend, even though I was supposed to be in a Rent-a-Bed room in a private dwelling. My hostess, the next candidate, owned the apartment and kept one room she called her "Bohemian Flat" for Rent-a-Bed guests. If things were too uncomfortable, I would return to the hotel.

Once in my Executive King Suite, I locked the doors, opened a gateway, and went to Areola. We all strategized how the interview should proceed. It was a bit unusual, I thought, to book a room in the home of my candidate. But I supposed that I might learn more about her in this short time than I would if just stumbling upon her on the street and trying to get a date.

After we had worn ourselves out with our strategies, I took Penelope and Princess Agora to bed with me.

I realize I have told you a great deal about the contestants on the reality TV show and the love affairs I've had, without telling you about the wonderful wives and possessions I have. Penelope was my second wife in the infinity room. She was the wife of the Greek, Odysseus, and when I was pretending to be him, I had to rescue her from the predators that styled themselves as suitors for her hand. They were despoiling the palace and land. Athene requested—required??—me to get rid of these uncivil bastards and rescue Penelope, ensuring that Odysseus' son was placed on the throne in Ithaca. I confided in Penelope and she pressed me to take her away with me and let her become my wife. I agreed.

In the TV show, Penelope played the role of my ex-wife and mother of my two daughters, while Peninnah was my much younger trophy wife. Even though Penelope had been nearly forty when she entered the infinity room, much of her youth and vigor was restored simply because her health was made perfect. She didn't really look old enough to be the mother of a seventeen and an eighteen-year-old, even though she was well over 3,000.

She was a brilliant manager of our internal trade relations in Areola, just as Peninnah managed our trade relations in the natural world. And she was a marvelous lover. Being Greek, she enjoyed some less conventional sex acts and was always ready to welcome me into her back door. Personally, I'd just as soon put my cock in her pussy, but I do try to accommodate her anal predilection. It's been good for us for over three millennia.

And this night was no exception. She lifted her ass in the air and placed her face in Princess Agora's pussy. It was an open invitation and I accepted. It wasn't so much the aperture in which I was lodged as the vigor with which Penelope fucked me. She drained me so well that it took me several minutes to get back up for the princess.

Princess Agora was the daughter of an island king who believed his island was the entire world and he was the ruler thereof. When I announced that I would be leaving on my little boat, the princess had implored me to let her stay with me. I think she believed I was just going to sail around the island and she would always be able to see her home. When we sailed out of sight, she began to panic. The panic turned into a full agoraphobic onslaught that left her nearly catatonic. There was nothing I could do to restore her. So, I took her to the infinity room and possessed her. She is the only woman I have ever possessed without her consent. I did so to save her sanity and swore I would never do it again.

I've mentioned that when I possess a woman, we become one mind and one heart. She has her identity, but I have it, too. With my possessions, I seem to always know exactly where they are and what they are doing, what they need, and what they want. With Princess Agora, I experienced a bit of her fear of open places and had to work at overcoming it.

I offered to set her free and she begged me not to. She stayed in the palace, most often near or in the bedroom. I asked her once how she preferred to spend her time and she said simply, "I see the world through your eyes. I could never go out there, but when you are in the natural world, I see a dreamland that is quite entertaining."

I see. I think.

Agora had no phobias about sex. If I had been fucking her, she probably would have been fine anywhere I took her. She totally lost herself in the sensations of being my mate. And, as with my other possessions, I believe there was a feedback loop that let us both experience a bit of what the other was feeling and experiencing. It was quite magical and we made love for hours.

67
THE ERINYES

FOUND the Bohemian Flat the next afternoon and followed the instructions for entering through the door with a dog flap and climbing the three stories to the
top floor. Tassa greeted me there and welcomed me into her apartment.

"Just drop your bag there and let me fix you a cup of coffee. We'll sit and talk. I want
to know all about you," she said.

"This is a lovely flat," I said, joining her in the kitchen.

"You have the run of the living room, kitchen, bathroom, and your own room, which
I'll show you shortly. Please don't enter any other rooms as I have a couple of boarders and,
of course, my own room."

"That is quite a little business," I said.

"Oh, it isn't really a business. This was my mother's flat and when she died it was
just me here and was very lonely. I started letting out rooms just so there would be company
occasionally. Now what brings you to our lovely city?"

Speaking of lovely, I will say that Tassa was a young woman under thirty—I'd have to
look at the application to get her exact age—and was elegant in a way that I learned to expect
of most women in Romania. She wore a skirt and a blouse with a large bow at the collar. Her
hair was just less than shoulder length and beautifully styled. Her fingers were nicely manicured and painted red, a color I noticed on her toes as they peeked out from her open-toed
high heels. Her makeup was perfectly done. As I observed her, I noticed my camerawoman
of the day scanning her as well.

"I am in your lovely city on business, but came to spend the weekend first. I thought
that taking a Rent-a-Bed would give me an opportunity to see the city without being fed a
false image," I said.

"That's very good of you. So many people come to Bucharest, to see the Parliamentary Palace and to see the grave of Eugene Ionesco, who is actually buried in Paris, or to attempt to meet Nadia Comaneci, who actually lives in Oklahoma in America. People have so many misconceptions."

"Where would you recommend that I go to see the real Bucharest, eat good food, and meet people?" I asked.

"There are many places. I have a little map here with various walks that you might take, with sights that are worth seeing marked on it."

She proceeded to unfold a map that she had obviously drawn on and annotated. She highlighted routes as we talked and I assured her my preferred transportation was by foot. We sat there drinking coffee for over an hour before she showed me my room.

"Keep your head down. The ceilings are low on this end of the apartment."

They were, indeed. I could stand up straight in the center of my room, but the ceiling soon sloped down under the eaves. My feet in the bed would be only a few inches from the ceiling. Fortunately, the head of the bed had a ceiling high enough that I could sit up.

"Tassa, I'm wondering if I could hire you." She caught her breath. "Hire you to guide me on some of these routes. Show me your favorite places and let me see Bucharest through your eyes."

She tilted her head quizzically.

"I have often been propositioned, but never hired as a guide. Please do not think my service would include anything else. If we can agree to that, I would have no difficulty accompanying you on some of these walks. They are my favorites."

"Would one hundred leu per day plus meals and treats along the way be adequate?" I offered twice what I'd rented the room for. She smiled.

"That would be excellent. How soon would you like to leave?"

We agreed to head out immediately and had a wonderful time as she described to me a city that she certainly loved. We walked for miles and I was concerned about her feet in her high heels. She seemed to be impervious to strain, though, much like Peninnah.

It was a lovely day. We had dinner and wine in a local restaurant and when we returned to the apartment, she bid me goodnight and went to her own room. I retired to the Bohemian flat.

In the morning Tassa took me to the Orthodox church she attended—an historic building that had been one of the few left in the hands of the church during the communist regime. We dined at out-of-the way bistros, listened to very Bohemian music, and drank vodka. We were a little tipsy when we returned to her flat that evening. She paused at my door and gave me a little light kiss on the lips. I was ready for much more.

"Bob, I think you are a wonderful man and would probably be a good lover for the right woman. And I thank you for the opportunity to show you my fair city. But I must tell you that sex doesn't interest me. I don't mean sex with *you* doesn't interest me. Sex *at all* doesn't interest me. With anyone—male or female. I've tried, but it isn't that I can't get turned on, it's that I'm just not interested in it. I hope you will understand and not attempt to pressure me. You would make a very good friend."

She left me at my door and went to her own room. Was this the infamous 'friend zone' I'd heard mentioned so often? Hmm. As I thought of it, I really didn't mind. Tassa would, indeed, make a great friend.

I will not bore you with my adventures in Pakistan or the Philippines. In one instance, the woman I met would not speak to me because I was not Muslim. I wondered what she thought The Bob was. The Filipina woman was ready to move with me to the United States at once. With her mother, aunt, three sisters, and a cousin. I was very happy to return to Cleveland. Alone.

I made some calls and then planned out my date with May. I really liked her and I was waiting in my office for her when she arrived to clean Friday evening.

"Oh! You're here!"

"Yes. Sadly, I didn't have your phone number with me. We didn't set a time this evening, so I thought I'd just stay here until you showed up."

"Bob, that's a weak excuse. You could find my contact information through the office building. But it doesn't make any difference. I really wasn't expecting you to call. I was only half expecting you to show up tonight. I'm kind of pleased you did. Give me half an hour to finish my chores and I'll be back and ready. And I'm starving. I didn't get a chance to break for lunch today. I switched rotations with one of the girls from building C, just in case you were here and I needed someone to cover the rest of my offices tonight. Give me thirty?"

"Absolutely. I'll find a place for dinner."

I hadn't asked May what she'd like to eat, so I took a wild guess and made a reservation at a highly rated Italian restaurant near the water. I was ready to go and my camerawoman was ready to slip into the car with us. May arrived and we headed out to eat.

This time, I probed a little more deeply regarding her concept for the colonization of the planet, and a ship that would get us there, careful not to ask questions that would seem like I knew too much. It was so tempting to just say "I am The Bob and I want you!"

"It's simple, really, but I suppose they're trying to cut costs. We used to have a space station up there in orbit 250 miles above the earth. That still wasn't enough to keep it from crashing into the atmosphere when the alliance fell apart and the station was abandoned. I wish we'd been getting ready for a colonization trip back then. Rather than risk it crashing down on a populated area, they blew it up and most of the pieces burned upon reentry. But conceptually, they had the right idea. Launch a core into orbit and then keep delivering parts, one ship at a time, until you've built a ship the size needed to hold a colony starter. Equip it with a rocket engine and transport fuel for the journey. Atomic fuel. There's no sense fooling around with liquid fuel for a ship this big. They could even conceal its capability by sending a ship up to 'move it to a higher orbit' every few months. Once we have an orbit at about 400 miles, breaking out of Earth's gravitational well is a relatively simple feat. Even for a ship that is estimated to weigh 20,000 tons, we could bust out of the gravitational well with no more thrust than it takes to do a lunar landing, and be happily on our way with an atomic engine."

"Do atomic engines work?"

"Nearly all the serviceable submarines in the world now are atomic powered. There's no reason it wouldn't work. And I'll bet even on Mars we could find fissionable fuel. It just seems like such a waste to keep redesigning and building a ship for a dozen people when that won't even begin to get us to a colony."

Well, I had information that she didn't, regarding how much three and a half million people weighed. But conceptually, I liked her idea.

"I know some people there. May, how would you like to visit Space Pioneers?" I asked. Her eyes got very big.

The Bethany Consolidated Church of the Holy Grail did not fall apart when it was discovered that several dead men had been found in their preacher's torture chamber and the preacher had disappeared. Instead, they doubled down on him and the church grew in membership.

"It is obvious to anyone who looks that our beloved Pastor Ron has bravely taken to the underground to visit retribution on those who would harm God's people," said a deacon in the church. "He laid a trap for these criminals and they fell into it. I would not be surprised if forensic evidence emerged that one of those filthy men was Bob."

Well, that was disgusting. Perhaps I should have left more evidence. But, the disappearance of 'Pastor Ron' served to keep all attention off me. I was not considered a person of interest in the case. Oh, when I got back to the mansion, I was visited by a detective wanting to know if I'd seen the man. They were following up a lead that suggested he might actually be one of my own people. There was no evidence linking us together other than his preaching about my evils. We'd never met and I never mentioned him.

I've seen it happen before. Seems the world goes in cycles of denying what is plainly in front of them.

People can't view the recent past with any perspective. They are still caught up in living it. So, let me go back a few generations. In the Civil War... Um... No, people are still living in that past. Let me go back further.

In American history, much fuss is made over the Mayflower arriving at Plymouth Rock and the pilgrims founding a new settlement. You've probably heard the romantic tale of John Alden going to Priscilla Mullen to propose on behalf of Myles Standish. Her famous line, "Why don't you speak for yourself, John?" is known to us through the poem of Henry Wadsworth Longfellow, who lived from 1807 to 1882. Understand? Poem. Not an eyewitness accounting.

We are led to believe through this poem and popular 'history' that the Pilgrims were religious refugees coming to the new world for religious freedom. In reality, they were roughly the same as the Spaniards invading the Caribbean and South America. They used religious zeal to fund a trip in search of gold, jewels, and wealth. They would come to America and convert the natives to their religion in return for all their wealth.

We are told of the kind natives who helped the strangers through their first winter and celebrated the first Thanksgiving with the kind pilgrims. We are not told that Myles Standish was a murderer. He invited the native chiefs to parlay in one of the new cabins the

Pilgrims built. Then he closed the door and killed them all, burned the cabin, and blamed it all on the evil Indians who were attacking the village.

No. The Pilgrims were righteous and God-loving people, spreading His word to the heathens. Myles Standish was the protector of the Pilgrims who made it possible for them to establish their village. John Alden was a poetic master of the language who...

Let me just say that we double down on the lies even when the evidence is right in front of us. We deny that anything bad was occurring or that our cultural heroes were anything less than what we wanted to believe of them.

History is not true. I know. I lived there. What you believe tells me nothing about what is true. It tells me only about what kind of person you are.

That's why it is getting harder and harder to choose people to join me in the infinity room—Areola. It isn't about whether they are nice people. Hitler was nice to Eva Braun. Until he killed her. Standish was nice to the Indians. Until he killed them. Columbus was... Never mind. Columbus wasn't nice.

The problem comes down to what kind of person he or she is deep down inside. Does he believe he is superior to everyone else (or even most people)? Does she use sex as a tool to manipulate people? Do her religious beliefs send everyone who disagrees with her to hell? Is he willing to sacrifice you for money? Or just for a better deal? These are all things that *nice* people will do.

Reverend Ronald Richards could preach love and reconciliation in his church and gain thousands of followers, but at his heart, he was a demon-possessed man who had sold his soul for money and the pleasures of the flesh.

Not every rescue the priestesses made was *quite* so bloody. Some were simply reported to proper authorities. But try finding who to report 200 sex slaves on a barge in New Orleans to. Yes, you can call the National Human Trafficking Hotline at 1-888-373-7888. And if you or someone you know is a victim, *call it right damn now!* But they aren't equipped for rapid response when there are 200 victims involved.

In the US, nearly three-quarters of a million people are *reported* missing each year. Many, I'm happy to say, are quickly found, but 3-10 thousand each year are not found. There are nearly 100,000 active cases of missing persons. Of that number, 35% are under the age of 18. Back in the late '60s, I was responsible for some of those who went missing. I collected them off the streets just before they died and restored them to health in Areola. All elected not to return to the natural world. They were looking for Nirvana and found it.

We found that barge, and it was a mess. I'd read it in the mind of the trafficker at the preacher's house. I'd like to say it was a foreign entity transporting boys and girls into the US, but this was a US-based mob I'd been tracking for some time. They specialized in collecting runaways, homeless, and abused teens.

Once they had a barge full, they towed it out into international waters and held an auction. Most of their cargo would be sold to bidders from around the world. The leftovers were discarded into the ocean.

I'd never been able to locate them before they set sail.

This time was different. But we needed help to rescue the children.

I called the FBI from an anonymous phone that could be tracked to our location. I wanted them to find it. I explained that I was about to liberate two hundred captive children from a barge in New Orleans and even gave them the pier number.

During the time I was on hold, I unleashed the priestesses. There were alarms on the barge, of course, but even after we set them off, the kidnappers could not locate us as we moved stealthily around the barge. I went room to room, delivering concubines from Areola to aid and feed the kids.

I said we were not as bloody as the previously related affair. Well, not quite. About half of the two dozen guards on the barge were dead when they were nailed to the side of the barge. The priestesses had advanced in their technology and in addition to their traditional weapons, they carried air cartridge-powered nail guns. The other dozen guards were needed as witnesses. They watched as their comrades were displayed.

I personally checked all the enemy for demons or signs of demon possession. Finding none, I approved the priestesses to complete the job. The remaining dozen were nailed next to their comrades, often with nails through body parts they thought were safe. All they saw were black clad ninjas who perversely glowed with an inner light.

I collected all the ninjas and the concubines who were assisting the prisoners, dropped my cellphone (still on hold), and fled into the night. I took up a post on a roof nearby where I could see as the first local policeman arrived to check things out. He was frantically on his radio, urgently requesting backup as there had been a massacre on the docks. When they entered the barge and discovered the kids, their tune changed.

"Angels came to bring us food and water. They said not to be afraid because help was coming for us," a fourteen-year-old girl told investigators.

"Demons!" declared a critically wounded man in the hospital. "Angels of death rained down upon us and made us pay for our sins. We couldn't see them at all as they killed and captured us. They glowed in the dark when they had us all and seemed to get brighter with every nail they drove through our bodies. I wish I'd been killed instead of living to witness their retribution."

Most importantly, the twelve men we let live put the finger on another fifty who had not been present that night. I ripped the memories from their minds. They included two of their chief operators who organized the auctions, and the 'trainer' who was due to arrive the next day. I would be ready.

The Furies had struck again.

It was the second time I'd heard one referred to as 'the trainer.' It was believed he could take any woman or child and turn her into a compliant sex slave overnight. Slaves trained by him were highly valued. Of course, this mysterious trainer never showed up the next day. If he even got within a few blocks of the dock, he'd have known things weren't right. Something about police cars and yellow tape and ambulances.

Reading the guards had provided other clues, though. We found out about a yacht located in international waters, prepared to receive the merchandise for the auction.

It had been a long time since a ghost ship had floated toward the shore. I let the authorities sort out who the bodies belonged to. Their crimes were written out and nailed next to their bodies. I've often wondered if that yacht was ever sold again.

68
INTERNATIONAL BOB

I PROMISED MAY that I knew several people at Space Pioneers and could get her in to see them. She was doubtful at first, but I convinced her with a first class ticket to Houston where the main offices were. Doug met us there. She recognized him from the television show.

"I'll take it from here, Cleveland Bob," he said, using the name I'd adopted for my travels. "We'll give you a call and let you know how things turn out." He led May to a conference room. I went into a bathroom and transformed to The Bob. Twenty minutes later, I entered the conference room.

May gasped when she saw me.

"Hello, May. I'm Bob," I said. "We've had a lot of applications to be on the show, but I think you're the only one that tracked us down here."

"It uh... wasn't really me who did the tracking. The import/export guy I met in Cleveland made all the arrangement. If you don't mind, this uh... Doug didn't give me a chance to say a proper goodbye. I'd like to see Bob again."

"That's not a problem. I hope he was civil and decent to you."

"Oh, yes. I've never met someone quite like him. I really like him, you know. I mean, I'm sure I'll like you, too. I did apply to be on your show."

"And so you are," I said, pointing out the cameras in the room. She caught her breath again.

"So, tell me about your design for a space station that would fly away from earth. Do you have drawings? Specifications?"

"Yes," she sighed. "They're probably too much for the budget of a television show. I was hoping to talk to the people at Space Pioneers because maybe they could get funding for it."

"I see. You didn't know I'm the majority shareholder in Space Pioneers."

"You are? I thought that president fellow, Leroy Reese, founded and owned it. He's always in the news as the spokesperson."

"Yes. He runs most things on a daily basis. The Mars Mission is all mine. So, tell me more about yourself."

We got into quite a conversation. Many of the things she was telling me were a repeat of what she had told Bob of Cleveland. But there was significant new information, as well.

"It's almost impossible for a woman to get a hearing in the science and technology arena. And what's worse, using just a first initial is as much a red flag to reviewers as a woman's name. Their first assumption is that it is a woman trying not to appear to be a woman. I have to ask, did you ever select a woman for your crew who wasn't sexually active with you? That seems to be the expectation."

"Actually, that was never intended. It has worked out that way in a majority of cases, but I don't bring women to Areola just to have sex with me."

"Areola. You named your palace after a woman's nipple."

"The women named it. I had nothing to say about it."

"I see. So, what do I need to do to get selected as one of your crew, if it isn't sleep with you? I mean... You're nice. I'm pretty sure it wouldn't be a hardship to sleep with you. But I'd like to be valued for what I can contribute, not for my collection of holes," she said. "Um... Besides, as nice as I think you are, I'd kind of like to see where the relationship with Cleveland Bob goes. I do like him."

"I'm glad to hear it. I will make no demands on you, but understand that Bob has responsibilities traveling around the world. Your base of operation will be here in Houston," I said.

"My base of operation? You mean I'm hired?"

"I expect you to head up the design team for our space station cum interplanetary colony ship. Can you handle that?"

"Yes! Yes! Oh, thank you, Bob. Uh... Do you mind if I call Cleveland Bob and tell him the good news?"

"I'll step out and give you privacy." I immediately headed down the hall so she couldn't hear my phone ring.

Let me tell you about Mia in Firenze. I know that's a jump, but it's the next thing on my mind. It started with a conversation I had with Doug on that visit to Houston.

"It would be awfully damn nice if you could just open a gateway to and from Areola whenever and wherever you wanted to without depending on the satchel to function as your portal," Doug said. I would leave him in Houston, as I headed off to Europe. There were just so many loose ends. We'd hired nearly a thousand non-Areola personnel to work on the production of season two, in addition to those special individuals who were jumping in and out of Areola from my satchel.

"You mean open a gateway to Areola from wherever I happen to be, regardless of where the satchel is? And open a gateway from Areola to anyplace in the natural world? I don't know if that can be done, Doug. Areola is kind of in the bag."

It was an interesting concept and I don't know why I'd never thought of it before. I had often thought of Areola as being *in* the satchel, so I needed to be where the satchel was in order to protect Areola. This would be a completely different understanding of what that meant.

"Bob! Did you hear me?"

"Sorry, Doug. You just got me thinking. What was it?"

"Yes, but the big problem today is that you need to be in Italy on Sunday to meet Mia D'Angelo. She's going to be touring the cathedral in Firenze, compiling historical notes for the Società di Antropologia Religiosa. She is a member of the Order of Shebites, a non-monastic order of nuns and outspoken critics of the Pope," Doug said.

"I'm going to interview a nun for a place in my harem?" I asked in disbelief.

"Yes. But don't get in the habit," Doug laughed. I just groaned.

"Unlike many of our contestants, her life reads like an open book," Doug continued. "She's been in the news since she was fifteen and told the pope that he was wrong about the church's stand on celibacy and the acts of priests through the ages had proven it. She quoted Paul in saying 'Better to marry than to burn,' and that she sincerely hoped the priests who abused nuns and children were burning in hell."

"And they allowed her to become a nun?"

"The Order of Shebites snatched her up immediately, rushed her off to their chapter house, and helped her refine her position. She is actually vacationing to conduct her research for the Society of Religious Archaeology. The Shebites are devoted to the acquisition of knowledge and wisdom and take their name from the Queen of Sheba, praised both in the books of Solomon and in the Koran."

"Wow. Am I up to this?"

"Only time will tell, Bob. Good luck."

I didn't have a problem talking to the nun. She wasn't naked. Sister Mia D'Angelo was a pleasant woman in her late twenties with a real thirst for knowledge. She was making notes as she walked through the duomo. I paused beside her and looked up at the duomo.

"It's amazing, isn't it?" she asked. "Every brick cut precisely to the measurements needed to create the eight-sided dome."

"One hundred fourteen and a half meters from the floor to the top of the lantern above the dome. You know that's more than the length of a football field!" I responded.

"Oh, my, you know your architecture, don't you?"

"I studied this particular cathedral extensively." I cut myself off before I added, "as it was being built." She would definitely not understand my being in Firenze when the cathedral was built. I'd intended to come back and help with the dome, but just before I headed that direction, Esmira managed to trap me in the infinity room.

"What can you tell me about it... uh...?"

"Bob," I supplied offering my hand. She took it warmly.

"Mia." No last name. No 'sister' or other honorific. Just Mia.

"Well, let me see. You probably know there was a competition to see who would become the architect/builder for the dome. The walls had already been erected and it remained for someone to engineer the dome. DiCambio had actually built a model of the dome that was fifteen feet high, right over there. But the engineering had never been done at the scale of this dome. Before or since. Brunelleschi won the competition to engineer the dome, closely contended by Ghiberti. There was some competition by two patrons of the architects that resulted in Ghiberti being awarded an equal sum to Brunelleschi's."

"I have read that the two architects were not only competitors, but were close friends," Mia said. "Ghiberti even took over the construction when Brunelleschi became ill."

"It was an illness, I believe, that was feigned, specifically to get his rival out of the way," I said. Mia looked at me sharply for an explanation. "You see, the tools we would use today to measure and cut the bricks of the outer shell had not yet been invented. Simply measuring the model and scaling up left quite a lot of variances. After laying several courses of bricks, modifying the sizes by a technique he did not share, he feigned his illness and begged his dear friend to continue his work so the dome would be completed. Ghiberti took over, but did not have the technique for making the courses turn out correctly. After a year, he gave up in frustration. At that time, Brunelleschi miraculously recovered from his illness and came back to work, finishing some years later. The dome, I'm told, was finished before Brunelleschi's death in 1446, but the lantern was constructed after."

"And what was this special technique that Brunelleschi used to make his course of bricks fit perfectly and that Ghiberti could not do?"

"There were some ingenious techniques, like the double wall, the chain supports, and the herringbone laying pattern, but exactly how he fit the bricks and kept them from caving in, he never revealed. I have studied the structure and all the most scientific data concerning how the dome was built and how it stands. I believe there was only one way he could have managed it, given the tools and measurement systems he had."

"And that was?"

"Magic," I whispered. Mia's eyes lit up.

"Mister Bob, why don't we have dinner together. I would like to explore this a bit more with you."

"It would be my delight, Miss Mia."

"I'm doing research for a report on the anthropology surrounding the great cathedrals of Europe," she said when we were seated in a trattoria. "I look at the local culture and glean as much as I can about the people I find. The evidence of the gothic and new romance styles of cathedrals from about 800 to 1400 AD puts them at the same level as the great pyramids of Egypt in terms of the mystery of construction," Mia said.

"How so?" I asked. "I've seen the great pyramids and they are at a scale far above the cathedral."

"Yes, but what intrigues me is that neither society had the *technology* to build them. Here in Firenze, there weren't even enough trees to cut to build a scaffold high enough to reach the dome."

"And the scaffolds they had shook and were as likely to collapse or pitch a man off them as to help in the construction," I said, remembering going around the building muttering binding spells to hold the scaffold together. "Another of Brunelleschi's inventions was a platform anchored into the dome as it was being built."

On one of those nights, I became aware of someone following me. I turned suddenly and found a young man. As soon as he was discovered, he rushed to the scaffold and attempted to rattle the joint I'd just bound. He turned back to me.

"Teach me," he said. It was a simple request. "O Angel of the Lord, teach me to bind the blocks of this temple in honor of the Most High." Okay. Not a request. A prayer.

I would have expunged his memory and walked away, but I had a strange feeling inside. It was as if Ninra was speaking to me out of the past.

"Teach him."

That was not a request. It was an absolute command. I pulled the scrap on which I'd written Ninra's spell to bind the bricks of his temple. It was essentially the same spell I'd used when building pagodas in China and holding the scaffold up in Italy. I sat with the young man all night long until I was certain he had the spell correct and just needed to go practice. Then I commanded him never to reveal it to another.

"I didn't even think of that. Imagine even building a wooden scaffold out of today's lumber materials that would reach a hundred meters in the air!" She paused to scratch a note in her journal. "When I look at the tools that were used and the precision of the scale, I have to believe that some sort of supernatural assistance was available for the construction. Even if it was only to guide a man like Brunelleschi in inventing tools like the *lewis* for lifting stones, he had divine help."

"Or demonic help," I suggested. She stopped abruptly and looked at me long and hard.

"Are you a Satanist?"

"No. Not at all. I merely suggest that supernatural help might come from a number of non-human beings. We call it divine if it comes from the God of the Christians."

"And demonic if it comes from the God of the... uh... Romans," she laughed.

"Or from any other being summoned from the primordial mass and imbued with such power as the summoner grants it."

"I do not believe in superstitions of that sort."

"What sort of superstitions do you believe in?"

"I... Don't twist my words. I'm not superstitious."

"Do you believe in prayer?"

"Of course."

I simply held my hands up to present the case in point.

"Prayer is not the same as magic. Its answers come from God."

"And how, exactly is that different than a... Roman praying to Jupiter and receiving an answer?"

"All answers come from God."

"Then God might answer in any form? If Brunelleschi prayed to a god of masonry for an answer to lifting the heavy blocks and the God of Christians answered, how would he know the difference? And therefore, I submit, if he prayed to the God of Christians for an answer and the god of masonry answered, is that not, too, God's will?"

"I have debated these very points within the sisterhood. But to acknowledge any other god than our Lord is heresy and I have trod dangerously near that in many instances," she said.

"Like the celibacy of priests?" I asked.

"Are you an inquisitor?" she demanded. "I have treated fairly with you and have answered honestly, decrying heresy."

"I am not of the church in any way," I said. "I am not here to examine you on its behalf. I merely recognized you from... it must have been twelve or fifteen years ago. Quite a write-up in the news."

"Thirteen years. The Sisters of Sheba gave me refuge and helped me formulate challenges that would not step over that line. They gave me a superb education."

"Yet, you are still seeking another answer. One that does not seem to be found in the stones of the cathedral."

"You seem to know me so well, Bob. I am on a quest for knowledge that seems to be officially denied and buried so deeply that people no longer think it exists," she said. I poured another glass of wine, pleased to see it was from a small vineyard east of the city. Some things are more durable than even the temples we build.

We continued a stimulating chat that covered cultures and customs of a thousand years. When at last, I paid our check and we rose to go, we had put away two bottles of wine along with our meals. It was a beautiful night.

"Bob, I hope you don't think me too forward, but I would like to see you again," she said as we were ready to part ways.

"I would enjoy that," I said. "But are you permitted a liaison with a man, Sister Mia?"

"I did not ask to sleep with you," she said. "Though, were that to happen, I don't believe my vows would interfere. I seldom find a *man* with thoughts as deep as yours. Most merely recite their catechism and are done with the conversation. You seem to have a depth of experience I would like to tap into."

Yes, I actually thought she had depths I would like to tap as well. I wisely did not give that thought to my tongue.

"Then I would be delighted to go out with you whenever and as often as you would like," I said.

"Good. Let's meet at the museum tomorrow afternoon. I want you to explain what magic you believe might have been used in the construction of the duomo."

"It will be my pleasure, Mia," I said.

Then she surprised me by moving close and kissing me on the cheek. She tittered a bit, then turned to walk away.

It might sound like I just flew from Houston to Italy, and had only those two stops as I sought out talent for the next show. I'd been to Georgia, New York, Calcutta, Hong Kong, Brisbane, Rio, and Moscow. It was going to be a very international show, but I was having to spend a day between each stop just recovering in Areola and getting my head in the space for the next girl on the list. I watched recordings of my previous encounters and reviewed with the crew and family what I should be doing next.

I ended up back in Houston, which had been a regular stopover on my trips to see May. She was happily working on her designs for our space station/interstellar ship.

"How's it coming?" I asked. I was still carefully maintaining a separation between The Bob and Cleveland Bob. As The Bob, I was getting daily reports on the progress and had made a few calls to smooth out the path for her. I let it be known that this was what I wanted and even the scientists grudgingly reviewed her designs, eventually becoming confused about them.

"Oh, it's great, but I miss you. The preliminary station plans passed review, but now the hard part is to get the finals coordinated with all the departments that have to contribute to it. It seems like every time I need something, Presto! it appears. I was having difficulty with a materials list and this girl, Sally, shows up and introduces me to a new alloy that another division of The Bob's company had developed. I have no idea how the stuff is made, but I had it run through various stress tests and it's the lightest and strongest alloy that's ever been manufactured. I guess it's exclusive to our ship. It's good that it will be so light. We'll still have to shoot tons of it into space to build the station."

"That sounds great. How about the power plant and engines?"

"Presto! An atomic engineer appears on the staff. He's got some interesting concepts about compressing atomic fuel and channeling off only as much power as is needed at the time. I can hardly believe his estimates on output. It's hard work and I'm crunching numbers absolutely all day long, but I'm so excited, Bob. Let's go to my place."

"Are you sure, May? I mean, The Bob is doing all this stuff for you and is really making things happen for you."

"I won't lie to you, honey. If I'd met him first, I probably would have fallen head over heels in love with him. But it's hard to do that when I'm already head over heels in love with you."

"Then let's go to your place, lover," I said.

69
TRYING NOT TO LIE

$\mathcal{I}$ THINK IT WAS all the traveling around the world and all the keeping different characters straight as I met women that made me do what I did with my next contestant. Or it could have been the setting in which I found her. Sonia Lind was a twenty-seven-year-old PhD candidate in archaeology, completing her thesis at the Çanakkale University in Turkey. Yes, an American woman with a Swedish name, studying in Turkey. What's more, she was completing her dissertation while assisting on further excavations of Troy.

"It's been years since I was last here," I breathed as I stopped to look at a bit of rock she was examining. She started and looked at me, then snorted.

"Couldn't have been that many years, could it?" she asked. "You can't be more than thirty."

"I look much younger than I am," I sighed. "Who wants to go around looking like an old man?"

"O-kay," she said. "So, when was the last time you were here?"

"Hmm. I think it was with Alexander. He had a great fascination with Achilles and Patroclus. I showed him where the tomb was and he and Hephaestion placed flowers there."

"I've heard that story, but while there is evidence of many wars in this area, there is nothing that points to an actual tomb of Achilles or the legendary battle of Troy," she said.

"Oh, there was, indeed, a battle of the Greeks against the Trojans over the trivial insult of Paris stealing Helen away from Menelaus at his very wedding. I've no doubt you disbelieve it because Homer made a mash of it and Virgil did little better. I brought Homer here to show him the site, but he was far more interested in heroes and gods than in history."

"*You* brought Homer here. *You* visited with Alexander. *You* are such a liar," she laughed.

"I assure you I am telling the truth, but you could never write it in your thesis. If the stones could talk, they would tell you the story," I said.

"Really? What story would this stone tell, oh instructor of Homer?"

"Ah. This stone once knew Helen intimately," I said. I could say that about nearly any stone in Troy.

"It is not shaped like a dildo. Or as contemporary archaeologists like to say, 'a ritual object of unknown use.'"

"Oh, no, of course not. But this stone was part of the structure of the master's bed in a household of Ilium."

"So, this was part of Paris's bed?"

"No. This was part of the bed of a local baker."

"Now you have me intrigued. How did the bed of a local baker know Helen of Troy intimately?"

"She was a slut. One of the things that got her so excited about coming to Ilium with Paris was that it was a whole city of men she hadn't yet fucked."

"Oh, come now."

"Seriously. She ran off with Paris so Menelaus would not discover that his new virginal bride was anything but virginal. While she was in Ilium, she discreetly worked her way through every man she came in contact with. Including the baker."

"So, Helen was a slut, hence her favor with Aphrodite."

"Shh. Please do not refer to My Lady Goddess as a slut. A goddess of sex and lust, yes, but not a loose woman. I can think of scarcely twenty men and gods Aphrodite had sex with. In a life of thousands of years. I don't know how she managed such restraint. I couldn't. Helen would have sex with twenty men in a month."

"Usually, such beautiful women withhold sex from men in order to control them. They don't need to sleep with so many."

"Need in the sense that you use it is very different from raw lust. Helen simply never saw a man she didn't lust for. With the possible exception of Menelaus," I said.

"You seem to have great knowledge of the intimate affairs of Helen of Troy. How did you get this 'knowledge?' I'd like to know."

"I was the baker," I said. Sonia started laughing and then touched me. She basically started patting me down and I wasn't sure if she expected me to return the gesture.

"You seem solid enough, so I don't think you are a ghost of Troy," she laughed.

"No. I survived."

"Right. How?"

"I masqueraded as Odysseus," I said. "He was killed in Aphrodite's temple as I was collecting the priestesses on request from the goddess. I took on his shape and memories and was able to escape on his boat. That was a disaster, let me tell you."

"Oh, so now you were the great hero, Odysseus!" Sonia laughed.

"The great hero Odysseus was a figment of Homer's imagination as it was fed and fueled by Athene. The truth is that the Odysseus whose memories I grabbed from his cooling body was a coward and sneak. When the Greeks captured the city, many Trojans fought back. To escape the fighting, he hid in the temple of Aphrodite, hoping to get a little action from the priestesses. Being horny was one of the few things we had in common."

"So, let me see, ten years of sailing around?"

"Constantly tormented by Poseidon and trying desperately to rid myself of several thoroughly disgusting crew members. Finally left the last lot of them on Circe's island where she kept them as pigs and I continued on alone."

"I don't believe a word of what you are saying, but I love listening to your stories!"

"I could entertain you with them all night. Several nights. I collected a lot of stories in 4,000 years," I said.

"Oh, you *are* an old man, then. How did you get to be 4,000 years old?"

"By living for 4,000 years, of course. Ever since the day the inept sorcerer Pinaruti summoned me from the primordial mass," I recalled. Whether she believed me or not, it was actually rather refreshing to be able to tell the truth about my life instead of living a long series of lies.

"Summoned from the primordial mass? So, what are you, then?"

"I am a free demon, compliments of Pinaruti's untimely death."

"The only thing I find truly demonic about you is that you're a consummate liar." We walked through the ruins to the edge of the old city and I looked out at the lush farmlands below. Farmlands that were once the bloody battlefield of the Trojan War. One of them. "I can see you thinking up another story. The death of Hector? Achilles? The fabled horse?"

"Well, it's a rather long story if you want it all. Are you certain you have time?" I asked.

"Time seems to be all I have at the moment. I've hit a stall on my dissertation and need to take a few days' rest. How about starting with dinner in Çanakkale. Café du Port?"

"How convenient," I said. "The hotel I'm staying at."

"Hmm."

I had a car waiting, so we didn't need to wait for the tour bus. This was the only sure way I could get a camera person along with me in cramped quarters. We'd already installed remote operated cameras in both my room and hers. Of course, she didn't know about that.

Dinner was lovely, with plenty of wine to accompany our meal. Then there was a luscious dessert with Turkish coffee. Then there was luscious Sonia.

"Bob the Demon—you know Bob doesn't sound like a very demonish name," she giggled.

"For the protection of the innocent, especially me, I have never used my demon name. Only the sorcerer Pinaruti has ever spoken it," I explained.

"So, how does one go about commanding you. Who owns you?"

"I am a *free* demon," I said haughtily. "No one owns me. I am not bound to anyone."

"Hmm. I bet I could disprove that given enough time."

"Well, come with me and you will have all the time there is."

"Oh, no. I know that trick. The only time that is, is now. Therefore, to come with you would give me only this instant."

"This instant repeated hundreds, thousands, millions of times," I said. "That's an interesting concept in Buddhism. All time is now. All things are one. To be one with the universe is to empty yourself of all and become nothing."

"I would expect a demon to be more versed in Western thought than Eastern," she said.

"That is only a Westerner's viewpoint. You assume that because your church makes such a big deal about demons and there is so much literature about demons, that we are a Western concept. But every culture in the world has some concept of demons. They may not be called that, but they are creations summoned from the primordial mass, generally to do the will of their masters," I explained.

"But you claim to have no master. How convenient."

"For me, yes."

"I'm just a wee bit tipsy, but the coffee has ensured that I will be awake for a long time yet. Are you up for having a late night with me? Perhaps all night?"

"Sonia, I can think of no better outcome of this encounter."

We chose my room. It was on the top floor and had a small balcony overlooking the harbor. I also had a double bed. When I'd checked in before going out to meet Sonia—accidentally, of course—I had worked the basic spell on the bed that I'd always had on my beds. It would become as big as was needed or desired. A few touches from my wives and possessions made sure the room was equipped with everything I might desire. There was champagne on ice, fruit and cheese, coffee, and an assortment of chocolates, all kept at a perfect serving temperature.

"You must at least have good connections to get this room. The option for this didn't even appear when I booked mine. Two single beds, shower, toilet, and sink. I don't really have a desk, but there is a chair that I can sit in while I write. This is quite comfortable."

"How did you end up in this hotel rather than staying at the University?"

"I like my privacy. I have a study grant that allowed me to rent a decent room and this hotel has a nice monthly rate, even better than the individual rates. I do spend a bit of time at the University, but I came here more for the atmosphere than for the facility at the University. I just wanted to get a feel for the area I'm writing about."

"What part of the Trojan War are you writing about?" I asked as we finally settled back and started kissing. I'd chosen to settle into the comfortable chair by the window instead of rushing her to bed. She lounged easily in my lap.

"Oh, I'm not writing about the Trojan War in particular. It is a sociology paper I've titled, 'The use of gods to justify war and carnage throughout the ages.' Troy just happens to be an example in which we have an array of powerful gods lined up on either side. Did you ever notice the gods themselves never directly participate in the battle?"

"Yes. It would be a kind of sacrilege to suggest that a god stooped to personally bloody his hands in a war. The god is used to whip the people up into a killing frenzy."

"Yes, exactly. I intend to show... Mmm. Yes. I'll show you that, too," she murmured as I cupped her breast.

"I've an interesting theory about that. In fact, it has to do with the creation of gods themselves. If you take the example of Ninra at Bathra..." Her lips closed on mine and interrupted my train of thought as thoroughly as I'd interrupted hers.

"Tell me about fascinating god theories in the morning, Bob. Make love to me tonight."

That was a suggestion I was only too happy to take. I was sure that in a saner moment, tomorrow or the next day, she would wonder at how brazen she was in coming to my room and asking me to make love to her. She might blame it on the wine. Personally, I thanked Pinaruti for whatever it was he had done in creating me that made me so attractive to women. It seemed to have nothing to do with what body I was shaped into. I could always find a woman to make love to.

We rolled around on the bed and moaned our pleasure as our clothing landed in piles on the floor. I exposed a body that was utterly delicious. I kissed my way down over full round breasts and teased at her nipples with my tongue. They were soon fat and hard as I continued my way southward.

I believe men often jump from the breast to the vagina, forgetting about all the delicious female flesh that lies between. I find that on many women, no matter their body type, this is an extraordinary erogenous zone. I've known women to climax just from having their abdomen caressed and kissed. Case in point, Sonia. She was gasping for breath before I ever reached her cleanly shaved pudenda.

I would need to remember to tell her about how hairy Helen was. That would entertain her. Tomorrow.

I wanted to milk out multiple orgasms from her while the coffee was keeping her jazzed up. Licking her clit, her pussy, and her asshole all drove her crazy, but when I inserted my tongue in her vagina and curled it up to find the spot on the roof of her canal I knew was there, she began tossing and humping and screaming so loudly that I withdrew momentarily to put a spell of soundproofing on the room. Then I dove in and licked until she was nearly comatose. She tasted heavenly.

When I moved up her body and nudged at her opening with my cock, she pulled at me.

"Yes. Fill me. Fuck me. Put it in meeee!" she squealed as my cock spread her channel and filled her. "Oh, my god. You fill me so much. I'm coming again. Oh, god, Bob. Do it. Pound me. Po..."

I slammed my mouth against hers and shoved my tongue in so she couldn't finish that thought. In that position, I fulfilled her other desires, pounding another orgasm into her before unleashing my own. I continued kissing her as we came down from our climaxes.

"Never," I panted, "ask a demon to possess you. We tend to take that very literally. I want you, but I want you as a free woman, just as I am a free demon. I want you to be able to pursue your dreams. To write your paper. To live your life. If you can live it with me, then I want you to come with me and see the stars."

"What? What are you talking about?"

"I'm Bob. The Bob."

She passed out.

70
BACK TO ITALY

I THINK YOU'VE BEEN holding something back from me, Bob," Mia said on my next visit to Italy.

There were lots of things I was holding back. And Mia was certainly holding a little something in reserve as well. She hinted at intimacy, but never quite got there. For my part, there were so many possible answers to that suggestion that I thought it best to just keep silent and let her proceed.

"I've looked into a couple of the references you gave me on temples built with magic. I must say it isn't at all what I expected."

"I've tried to give you some appropriate examples that I felt illustrated the concept. Of course, I'm not making an outright statement that magic was involved, only that it had the appearance of something magical," I defended myself.

"But I think you know," she said. "You've carefully avoided claiming the exact knowledge, but your statements about how such buildings were created have led me to believe that you know more than you've let on. I believe you know—or think you know—the actual magic that was used. Say to enchant the bricks of the duomo in Firenze or of the excavated temple in Mesopotamia. You want to avoid a witch-hunt, as do I, but I want to see the magic used. I want to know for sure there is a power that moves through the earth that is greater than our feeble minds have comprehended. Show me, Bob. Show me how the spell was cast on bricks to make them more durable and to weld them together."

"Ah. Well, Mia, it's like this. I don't know for sure that the magic still works. It hasn't been used in centuries," I said. "It seems that as technology is developed that supersedes what could have been done by magic in a different age, the magic falls into disuse and then finally disappears altogether."

"For example?"

"It was said that certain sorcerers and witches could fly and get to a place far away faster than any pursuit. Well, now all we need to do is get on an airplane. Who needs to fly? Though, I admit that I've sometimes wished I could fly, even though I have a pilot's license for small planes."

"But from that, I detect that you *do* know the spell, but haven't tried it," she persisted.

"I have access to certain ancient manuscripts which purport to have that knowledge."

"And you can read them."

I nodded. I was thinking it might be time to tell her I was The Bob, but really, the only thing that I'd revealed about The Bob that could be considered magic was my portal. And that was shrouded in mystery and widely supposed to be a television special effect.

"How about if you show me yours and I'll show you mine." I think she meant 'spell' but I was certainly willing to exchange glimpses of other things.

"I think it calls for something special," I said. "What would you say to a weekend away with me to someplace very private?"

"I would say yes under one condition," she said.

I assumed she was going to put a stipulation on how intimate it was.

"And that is?"

"We could go away for a nice weekend someplace very private if we were already in an intimate relationship, don't you think? Why don't we go to your hotel, Bob?"

"F.! Gotcha!" I called. "H! Has anyone seen G?" I got hit in the back of the head and a message came up: 'Game Over.' I took off my goggles and turned to Sally. "What was that for?"

"New realism I've built into it. Now if you get hit in the game, you get hit in real life," she giggled.

I had a feeling she was just using that as an excuse to hit me! She could be very physical at times. Sometimes that was a very good thing. I pulled her into my lap and before long one of those times was taking us to a peak as I thrust into her.

"Oh, Bob. I need to figure out how to build *that* into a game," she panted.

"People would never stop playing," I said. "When are you going to name those characters instead of just having them labeled with letters?"

"I'll get around to it. This is only a pastime I use to unwind after I've been studying," Sally said.

"And how are the studies going?"

"I think I'm making progress," she said. "Nimia has been a great help, but every time I think I understand something, we end up having sex."

"That can be a problem."

"Naw. I like that as much as studying. Nimia knows more about all the magical stuff in the library than I ever will," Sally said.

"She told me to ask you about this. She said that while you were working on the portal research, you came upon various binding spells like the one we used for bricks back in Bathra."

"Oh, yeah. It was cool. And the librarians brought me five other scrolls that had similar spells and a manuscript from the Middle Ages. I did some comparisons and it looks like the fundamental elements are all the same, but there are different invocations used. It was a bit of a rabbit hole that I dove down, but I've got my head back in multi-dimensional portals now."

"Right. How would you like to have a discussion with another researcher who has been looking at how the structures of the fourteenth century were created without the aid of modern tools and technology? She could use a little demonstration of how the spell works."

"I'd love to meet and talk to her," Sally said. "But just because I can read the spell, doesn't mean I can work it. I um... tried," she said as she tucked her chin down on her chest.

It wasn't against any laws to practice magic in Areola, but no one had unveiled any real talent for it. Areola provided all the magic they could want. Actually, they worked magic, but didn't recognize it as such. Developing a screen and network to project entertainment onto was considered science and engineering. The thing was that they used little understood foundations of Areola that were decidedly outside the science of the natural world. Their science and engineering were built on Areola's magic.

"Hey," I said, lifting her chin so I could kiss her. "Why don't we try it again in the natural world. It might just be the environment."

"Hmm. Dimensional interference," she said. "This could help in my study of dimensional portals. If the sorcery of one world doesn't work in another world, it might mean the portal sorcery would be different in Areola than it is in the natural world. Let's do it!"

I laughed and left Sally to her plans in Areola while I caught a flight to New York.

I was ready to rename the whole mini-series *My Double Life*. Only I'd need to have it be triple life or quadruple life. I was leading so many lives as I met and dated these women that I was sure I'd mess up and be the wrong Bob at the wrong time.

Fortunately, there were some who were an instant 'no.' Like the racist Lorelei. She wasn't the belle in Georgia, but the boutique owner in New York. I walked into her shop with Lakshmi on my arm, out for a day of sightseeing and shopping. I thought we might find some nice gifts for the girls in this shop and get to know the owner informally as well.

After a few minutes of being ignored, I started toward Lorelei to ask a question.

"We really don't carry any ghetto clothing here," she snapped, looking at Lakshmi. "Just look at the posters around the shop and you'll see what our girls should look like." I glanced around. There were full-size posters of women in the lingerie offered for sale in the shop. Every one of them was white and blonde. I hadn't seen a display like that in years. Something grated against my sensibilities. I turned to her.

"I see. So, you only cater to women with huge oversized tits. Well, that definitely brings our business to a close."

Lorelei huffed.

"You're a decent looking guy who obviously has money. You could have any one of those white girls on your arm. You don't need to eat dark meat."

That was it as far as I was concerned. I reached in my pocket for a business card. It was simple and I'd not had a reason to use one before now. On the front, it had our show logo and a smiling picture of me in my other guise. It said, "To Boldly Go, starring The Bob." On the back, it simply said, "You have been eliminated." I took Lakshmi's arm and led her out of the store as Lorelei spluttered behind me.

The thing is, if she watched the show and applied to be on it, she had to know that I had all races on with me. Whatever her intent, I didn't plan to even show her shop or mention her name on the show. She didn't need any advertising from me.

I took Lakshmi to dinner on the rooftop of our hotel where we could watch the lights of the city come on. It was lovely.

I'd promised Mia a long weekend away to show her the spell for binding and adjusting the sizes of the bricks used in precision building, like the duomo in Firenze. I wanted to be well away from the city for our weekend, so I picked Mia up in Rome and we headed out to one of the islands where I'd rented a villa. It was beautiful.

"Are you sure you didn't invite me out here just to take advantage of me and plunder my womanly charms with your big plunder stick?" she giggled as I wrapped my arms around her on the balcony overlooking the Mediterranean.

"Mmm," I said as I kissed up her neck and around her ear. "Plundering your womanly charms has a certain attractiveness to the sound. Perhaps I should change plans and just focus on that."

"No, no. Binding spells first, then plundering."

I turned her so I could capture her lips with mine and kissed her passionately.

"Maybe a little plundering before spells would be a good thing," she whispered. I carried her to bed.

Who would ever have thought that a 4,000-year-old demon would ever get so much pleasure enjoying the love of a twenty-seven-year-old nun? Mia's order did not hold to the celibacy of nuns or priests and thought it ridiculous to pretend to it when few abided by it. I whole-heartedly agreed and Mia welcomed me into her body as happily as any lover I had ever had.

After we had made love all afternoon, we then walked to town for dinner and drinks at an osteria, owned and run by a local family for some centuries. Then we walked back to our villa. I'd gone into the cellar at the villa when we first got there and opened a gateway so Sally and a few others could enter. They stayed out of the way until we'd left for dinner, then it seemed they'd decided to party and were all playing in the pool.

"Bob? Who are all these women? I thought it was going to be just me and you for an intimate weekend."

"Well, I invited Sally to join us because she has the scroll I wanted to show you and has studied it most recently. She decided to bring a few friends. Don't worry. I'm sure they won't bother us."

"Not as long as we can keep our eyes off their naked bodies out there. Should I be concerned?"

"No. If your eyes stray to them, they will probably display themselves more prominently for your viewing."

"Oh, my."

"Sally!" I called. "Please join Mia and me in the salon."

Sally's light brown hair had become even lighter since she joined us in Areola. Not quite blonde, but light brown. Her slight, five-foot-two frame was an ideal foundation for the prominent breasts she sported. I rather thought those had grown a bit since she'd come to Areola, so perhaps she'd been remaking her self-image over the years. She grabbed the scroll and walked into the salon as if she were a six-foot model on a catwalk. She stepped between Mia and me and gave me a quick kiss on the cheek. Then she placed the scroll on the table.

"You just carry around an ancient scroll with you as you stroll nakedly through the world?" Mia asked, a bit perplexed.

"It has a kind of preservation spell on it," Sally answered. "When we put it away at night, it sort of rejuvenates itself, I think. I'm studying what occurs when one crosses from alternate dimensions into and out of the natural world. You smell good. Did you and Bob already make love? You did, didn't you? Mmm. Just smelling you makes me horny."

"Sally," I reprimanded her gently. "We're here to talk about the manuscript and the binding spell that was used on the temple... or cathedral, I mean."

"Yessir. You're Mia, right? I'm Sally. Let me show you what I found. I chose this manuscript because it's in Latin, so you can probably read it. It takes me forever to get through a Sanskrit manuscript without help."

"So, you think this actually works?" Mia asked after Sally had unraveled the spell for her and told her how it was supposed to work. In the meantime, she'd also managed to wiggle onto Mia's lap and get her clothes partially off. Studying these manuscripts just affects certain girls physically. I hadn't seen this side of Mia before as she talked about the spell and softly caressed Sally's breasts.

"I haven't been able to make it work, but Bob thinks it might work here in the... uh... Italy. My special area of study is really interdimensional portals and multidimensional crossovers."

"Oh, that sounds fascinating. I wish I had time to study everything I want to."

"I do! That's one thing about being with Bob. You have all the time in the world," Sally said. She kissed Mia and both girls moaned. I poured another glass of wine for each of us.

"Let's try it. Do we need to cast a magic circle or something in order to put it together?" Mia asked. Her head was filled with magical rubbish.

"Bob?" Sally asked.

"I don't think so. You cast a circle to protect you from outside forces, or to confine magic inside so it doesn't leak out. In some instances, a circle might give a sorcerer some extra focus for his power. If Brunelleschi worked this while he was laying bricks in the cathedral, he couldn't have used a circle."

"What will we use to bind together?"

"I found a couple of loose bricks in the garden," Sally said. "Uh... earlier when I was exploring."

"You've been here ever since we got here, haven't you?" Mia accused.

"Um... sort of. We tried to stay out of the way." Just then, seven naked nymphs came in out of the moonlight by the pool. I think Mia had forgotten they were there. They filed by and kissed me and Sally before going up the stairs. What a lovely sight that was.

"Guest room," I said to Mia. She nodded slowly. She looked strangely at one of the nymphs and I realized Julie was among them. The darkness and the excitement about their experiment kept Mia from recognizing one of my crew from the first season.

Sally led us out to the patio where two bricks were lying on a table. Mia immediately picked them up to examine them, pushing them against each other to see if they would stick. When she was satisfied they were not rigged, she faced us. The only thing she was still wearing were her panties. She seemed to have just noticed and shrugged.

"Okay. I'll hold them together and you work the spell," she said to Sally.

"No!" I said. "Set them down over there on the patio. We'll stay behind the magic worker. You don't want to accidentally be in the path of her spell."

"Ew! I can imagine. Okay." She set the bricks down touching each other on the patio and stepped back behind Sally. I stepped up and put an arm around my little scientist mage.

"I think you can do this. Remember what the manuscript said about putting your will behind it as you chant the spell. Do you remember all the words?"

"Yes," she said weakly.

"Just focus on the bricks and when you can feel them with your mind and everything else fades away, point at them and chant the spell."

"Okay, Bob. I can do this."

I stepped back beside Mia, who had decided wearing panties wasn't necessary. She put her arms around me and we watched my little apprentice. We weren't sure anything was happening, but Sally was gathering her focus. We saw her hand gradually come up to point at the bricks and heard the low chant of the spell. It wasn't long and she repeated it to make sure she had it correct, then dropped her hand.

"Is that it?" Mia asked. "No bolt of electricity or flash of light?"

"That would make it a worthless spell if you planned to work in secrecy as you were laying bricks," Sally said as she sagged against me. "Did it work?"

Mia went to the bricks and gingerly touched them as if they might be hot. Sensing no surprises, she grabbed the edge of one and pulled at it. It didn't move. She pried at the other and it didn't move. She pulled at both of them and they refused to budge.

"They're stuck!"

"That was the intent," Sally said. "It worked!"

"Yes, but they aren't just stuck to each other, they're stuck to the patio. I think if you moved them, the whole batch of bricks under them would move. This is amazing. They could have built the whole dome like this if they had a little more control."

"Thanks," Sally said. "I'm so tired."

"Oh, you poor thing," Mia said, running to embrace her. "You did it. You worked a magic spell." She started raining kisses all over Sally's face and lips. "You're wonderful. Wonderful."

"I'll take her to bed. I think she needs some sleep," I said. I scooped Sally up in my arms and she snuggled against my chest.

"Our bed, Bob," Mia said.

END PART XIII

Part XIV
The Bare Facts

Image Credit: Maisei Raman, ID32435272, licensed from Shutterstock.com

71
MY RECORD WITH STRIPPERS

"**H**EY! COULD YOU use some help?" I called out the window into the rain. A wet blonde lifted her eyes and turned toward me.

"I can't get these lug nuts off!" she said. "I should be able to fix my own flat, but I think they put them on with one of those hydraulic torque wrenches."

"I'll be right with you."

I questioned the wisdom of causing a flat tire on a rainy night with limited visibility. I backed up and pulled in behind her, turning on my flashers. From this position, my headlights shone on the work area as well. I took the wrench from her and checked the jack to make sure the car was stable. She'd blocked the wheels and the tire was not quite off the ground. Classic instructions for changing a tire.

"Go ahead and get the spare out. I'll have this ready in a minute or two."

She opened her trunk and wrestled the donut spare out of the back while I loosened the lug nuts. As soon as they were loose, I raised the jack so the tire was off the ground, finished removing the nuts and took the tire off. She rolled the donut to me and hefted the heavier tire into her trunk. I placed the spare, finger tightened the nuts, and lowered the car so the tire was touching the ground. Then I finished tightening the nuts with the lug wrench. I released the jack, put it in the trunk, and collected the chocks.

"Remember, you can't drive fast with these spares. Don't go over thirty-five. There's a station up about three miles on the right. I'll follow you with my flashers on."

"You don't really have to," she said.

"My girlfriend would never forgive me if I didn't," I said, nodding back to my car where Annie was peering out through the windshield. I could see our contestant visibly relax when she realized I was with a woman. "I'm Bob, by the way."

"Oh. Roxie," she said holding out her dirty hand to shake my equally dirty hand. She looked at them. "Well, I guess neither of us can get the other any dirtier. Or wetter. Thanks for the help and for following."

She got in her car and as soon as she pulled out onto the highway, so did I.

The service station, of course, had only a night attendant on duty. He couldn't do anything about her flat tire. He was really only a cashier for the limited supply of convenience store merchandise.

"I'm sorry," he was explaining to Roxie. "I don't even have access to the garage and the tools. Joe will be in at eight tomorrow morning. Oh, hi, Bob. Annie."

"Problem, John?" I asked my confederate.

"This poor lady has a flat and needs it fixed. You know Joe doesn't get here to open the shop until eight. I was trying to explain that there isn't anything I can do," he said.

"Oh, you poor honey!" Annie said taking over. "You're drenched. Do you at least have a change of clothes you can wear?"

"Not even. I was just headed to a friend's house in St. Joseph. She got called away to tend a sick mother and I told her I'd get there as soon as possible to take care of her cats. All I packed was my personals. It's still a hundred miles away. I can't make that on a spare."

"Come home with us for the night," Annie said. "Bob's house is just a couple of miles from here."

"I don't know. It's kind of dumb to just go home with strangers. Even if you're known by the locals," Roxie said.

"Is there someone you can call?" I asked. "Call to let them know where you are and what happened and that you're at Bob and Annie's house. Here's the address. And here's my phone number."

"I guess that would work. Do you think it's safe to go with them?" she asked the cashier she'd just met. He nodded.

"Bob and Annie are always rescuing someone. Or something. Couple of weeks ago they stopped here with a cow they'd found wandering on the highway. We found the owner. They're dependable."

"Well, if they saved a cow, what do I have to worry about?" she laughed. "Are you sure it's no trouble?"

"No trouble at all," Annie said. "I'm sure I've got something in Bob's closet that will fit you. I haven't been living there very long, though, and usually just on weekends. Let's get you home so you can get a hot shower and some dry clothes."

"Thank you so much, Annie." She pointedly left off thanking me. I think she didn't really want to acknowledge there would be a man at the house. Well, we'd made contact. We'd have to wait and see how the interview went.

"Take your time in the shower, Roxie. You need to warm up. I'll make us some hot chocolate when you're out," Annie said as she ushered our guest to the bathroom.

"What about me?" I pouted when Annie returned to the living room.

"Why don't you go take a dip in the pool and dry off in the sun in Areola?" she asked, giving me a deep kiss. "Or I could just take you to the bedroom with a towel and make sure I've gotten every drop of water off you."

"I don't think I should leave with our guest in the house. And don't forget we have photographers everywhere. I don't want to leave them here alone. So, I think option two is the best bet. And you know very well it was my first choice anyway."

We went to the bedroom and I stripped out of my wet clothes. I turned to find that Annie had also stripped out of hers, even though they weren't that wet. I didn't mind at all as she moved up against me and worked at removing all the water from my body without actually ending up with it inside her. That latter failed as I ended up leaving quite a large liquid deposit in her.

We heard the shower shut off and quickly went about pulling clothes on. Annie made do with just a pair of panties and a robe. The panties were to keep her from dripping come all over the floor. I managed a pair of comfy jogging pants and a sweatshirt. I met the ladies in the kitchen and Annie suggested I start a fire. In the living room.

With the blaze roaring, the ladies joined me in front of the fireplace and Annie handed me my cocoa. Delicious.

"So, tell us all about yourself, Roxie. You're on your way to St. Joseph—down in Missouri?—to take care of a girlfriend's cats. Where from?" Annie asked. Roxie's application led us to believe she'd be much more comfortable in the company of a woman than a man, so I let Annie take the lead.

"I live in Des Moines. Joan and I met in high school, but she got a great job offer and moved out here. We're close enough to the same size that we can wear each other's outfits. Um... clothes."

"What do you do in Des Moines?" I asked.

"Um... I'd rather not say. Company confidential."

"Oh, sure." That was strange. Her application said she was a temporary secretary, living on her own since she was eighteen.

"We're just lucky we happened to have a house out this way," Annie said, changing the subject. "Why are you out here instead of the interstate?"

"They're doing highway maintenance on I-35. The report said there was a three-hour delay. I decided to cut over and keep driving instead of sitting in the car waiting."

"What a bummer. You were probably closer to help out here than on the interstate, though. That's not a very populated route," I said. Doug had done a great job of setting up the repaving project through a generous donation to the state highway department. The rain was an added bonus.

"Have you lived out here all your life?" Roxie asked. *Hmm. Acknowledgment that I exist.*

"No. I worked for a few years in the building trades. But I didn't like building in developments, so I decided to build a house for myself. That led to another and another. This one is only a year old."

"Um... different houses in different places?"

"It's great. If the weather gets bad in one location, he just moves to another place with better weather. It wouldn't surprise me if he decided to move from here because it was raining," Annie teased.

"Wow. I suppose you've got a different girl for each house, huh?" Roxie said. She was trying to be playful, but I detected a note of... was that suspicion?

"Oh, no," I said, giving Annie a kiss. "I take 'em with me."

"You must be rich if you can afford to flit around the country rescuing damsels in distress," Roxie said.

"I just made some good investments that left me able to do what I love. I love to build things," I said.

"So, Roxie," Annie came to the rescue again, "what kinds of things do you like? We know that Bob likes building things. I'm into acting, though I don't have any gigs right now. Meeting Bob kind of interrupted my plans."

"I can imagine. Um... well, I like all the things girls usually put in want ads. Walks on the beach, romantic dinners, dancing. I'd even drink a piña colada. It's getting harder to date these days. Lots of guys will say they like the same things, but their idea of the beach is the local YMCA pool," Roxie laughed.

"Yeah, and how about that romantic dinner at Mickey D's?" Annie joined her. "I do like to go dancing, too. What's your favorite group?"

"Um... uh..." Roxie looked at me and then seemed to make a decision. "I'm not into that kind of dancing, exactly."

"Ballet?" I offered. Dense as always.

"I'm an exotic dancer. I work at The Gold Standard in Des Moines. I knew I couldn't keep secret that I'm a stripper. I never could. That's why my parents threw me out. I can't keep my mouth shut about it. I love to dance," she said. "I suppose you want to see now." She stood up.

"No. Sit down and relax," I said. "You've been through a lot tonight. There's no reason for you to feel like you have to work, too."

"I'm sure it's great, Roxie, but if we decide we want to see you dance like that, we'll come to the club and pay the cover," Annie said. "How about another cup of cocoa?"

"Oh, Annie! You're both so nice. I thought it would be so much more difficult. Please don't just write me off because I'm an adult entertainer. I have other skills as well."

"Come on. Let's make cocoa and you can tell us all about them."

The girls went into the kitchen and I sat there staring at the fire. This was an interesting turn of events.

I was on the hunt once—this must have been back in the late nineties, before everything got so technologically sophisticated. I headed for the Pussy Cat Lounge in Biloxi, Mississippi. I'd tracked a series of kidnappings to the town and was looking in all the low-life places I could find.

Let me start this back a step with a disclaimer. I have nothing against strip clubs, strippers, exotic dancers, or sex workers of any sort. Those arts have been around for the entire four millennia plus that I've been alive, in every single culture I've encountered. And I've met some truly wonderful entertainers in locations around the world. When a club is on the up and up—drug free, coercion free, and the performers come to work of their own free will, are well-compensated, and protected—I'm happy to let them be in business and provide this ancient service to humanity... mostly men. But when I find performers who are hooked on drugs, forced into prostitution, and generally abused, I get very upset.

Now I had nothing directly against the Pussy Cat Club. Perhaps it was a little seedier than some and run-down, but it had a long history in the town. When I got there and paid my five-dollar cover, I was 'encouraged' to buy a beer as well. They came two at a time. I carried them to an empty table near the back of the room to get a feel for what was going on.

Entertainers came to the stage, danced, and took off their clothes. Then they made the rounds of the customers to collect tips and offer private dances or just to sit and chat for a bit. One dancer, Noel, came to the stage and was particularly good. And good-looking. It was always hard to tell how tall a girl was with the platform shoes that were fashionable on stage, but she was nicely shaped. As she revealed more and more of herself, I saw the shape was nicer and nicer. And it looked like she was performing just for me. She constantly looked across the room at me and was sure to turn so I got a good view of what she was uncovering. I think that must be a real art of strippers—to make that kind of connection with all the men in the room. I assumed.

She finished her turn on stage and slipped backstage to dress again and then came out to tour the floor and collect tips from the guys who weren't sitting up at the tip rail during the performance. I watched her out of the corner of my eye and eventually she got to me. I thought I must be the last guy in the room she talked to. I held a ten up and she pulled her panties away from her waist.

"Why don't you put that right here in my moneybox," she whispered. She had a wad of cash in her fingers and several bills in the waistband of her panties or her garter, but I hadn't seen anyone else tuck a bill quite so intimately into her 'moneybox.'

"Thanks for a great performance," I said.

"I'm glad you liked it. I did it just for you." Now that was a good line. There were probably thirty guys in the club at the time. Several were in uniform. "I got here at the same time you did and saw you head in the door. I thought to myself, 'That guy is mine tonight.' I even warned the other girls off. I want to celebrate my birthday with you."

"Well, happy birthday," I said. "Can I buy you a drink?"

"Oh, yes. I had a sip of my birthday present from the girls in the dressing room. So how about Jack on the rocks?" She flagged a waitress who hurried to our table and took the order. A drink for a girl was twice the price as one for a man. Noel whispered to the waitress and she giggled. "I told her to tell Will at the bar not to water it down. I want a good strong one. They do that, you know. It's really nice because a girl can accept a drink or two from a guy and not get uncontrollably drunk. But I want to celebrate and let go."

When the drink arrived, I gave the waitress the money and a good tip. Noel called her close and gave her a kiss. The waitress squeezed her boobs.

"You behave tonight," she said. "I'll be watching."

"Don't be a spoil sport," Noel responded. "But thanks."

"I'm glad you all look out for each other," I said.

"Yeah. There are a lot of weirdos in the world. And some strange things going down. We can't be too careful. But we like to have fun, too, and I want you to be my fun. Want a dance?"

"Sure," I said. I pushed my chair back expecting the usual table side dance. Instead, Noel grasped my hand.

"Bring our drinks. We'll go to the quiet area."

The quiet area proved to be an elevated floor at the back of the bar with a curtained railing about three feet high. Along the wall there was a long bench seat with tables spaced six or eight feet apart. Two girls were down to nothing but a G-string as they worked a single guy over pretty well. When I sat, I noticed the riff-raff on the main floor couldn't easily see up and into the private dance area. We could be seen from the sound booth, though. Safety. I approved.

"Thirty," she said. I quickly grasped that she needed thirty dollars for the dance. It was twice the price of the table dances on the main floor. "Up here, we get three nice intimate songs and then we can sit and rest for a while. Okay?"

I nodded and when the music started for the next song, she began her dance. She was sensuous, and piece by piece her costume came off until she was in just her G-string and was grinding against my cock. I was glad I'd worn loose fitting slacks.

When she finished her dance, she did not sit next to me, but sat on my lap. Then she started fiddling with her under bra. In this club, the dancers wore 'a costume,' top and bottom. Under it, they wore a very flimsy, see-through bra and a G-string that was barely there. On stage, they went completely nude, but in private dances, they were required to keep the G-string on.

"After a dance, we're supposed to at least put our under bra on. They watch to make sure we get them on within one song after the set," Noel said. "So, I'm going to fiddle around with this thing for another minute or two. No sense hiding the girls from you before I have to."

I agreed completely. The girls were two nice-sized snowy mounds capped with rigidly hard nipples that had recently been brushed against my lips. I'd love to take that a little further, but the men were not allowed to touch the girls. The ladies could touch anything they wanted, but not so the men.

Eventually, those sensuous points disappeared beneath the bra, even though Noel continued to wiggle her mostly bare butt against me.

"We're going to auction the lot of the girls for private dances, now," the DJ said.

"Oh, shit," Noel said. "I don't want to do this."

"Then don't."

"All dancers to the stage for the auction. All dancers."

"Can you give me a fifty?" she asked. "I promise, I'll make it worth it." Wow! That was a steep increase. But frankly, I wasn't in a hurry to lose her warm company in my lap. I handed her a fifty.

"All dancers for the auction. Noel, Amber, Starlight. To the stage." The two dancers who had been dancing for the guy a few seats down from us got up and headed for the stage. The guy slowly followed, adjusting his trousers. Noel held up the fifty and waved it.

"I don't have to go up if I've already got a premium customer," she said. She relaxed onto my lap. "Now we can just wait here until the auction is over and then have your dances."

She picked up my hand from where it was sitting beside me on the bench and held it. Then she explained the rules as the DJ auctioned off the girls, and guys bid for their favorites. First high-bidder got his choice of the girls. The next high bidder got second choice. They kept the auction going until the last girl went for the minimum fifteen dollars and just led her guy back to his table to dance for him there. On the main floor, the girls didn't remove either their under bras or G-strings.

"Here's the deal, Bob," Noel explained. "I'm not a whore. I don't fuck the customers and you aren't allowed to touch me. Unless I put your hand somewhere. Anywhere *I* put your hand, you can enjoy touching, but keep it subtle. I'm not going to get your dick out and play with it or suck it or fuck it. If you come in your pants, that's fine. Like if I put your hand here on my stomach, it's okay for you to stroke and squeeze my stomach." She demonstrated and I felt the muscles rippling beneath her skin. "If I put your hand on my butt, you can squeeze and pat it. Don't spank. I get really angry when I'm spanked." She demonstrated by moving my other hand to her butt, which I thoroughly enjoyed squeezing. "If I put your hand on my thigh... well, you get the idea, don't you?" she said while guiding my hand to stroke up and down her thigh, moving it slightly to the inside. Then she slipped her hand between us and gave my cock a squeeze through my trousers. "I'm glad you're getting turned on, because so am I."

Yes, she was a real seducer. This was already worth the fifty dollars. The auction ended and the dancers moved to various stations with their customers. Then the music started. It was a three-song set again, which meant about ten minutes. This time, however, Noel wasn't wearing her costume, so the first piece she lost was the under bra and she rubbed her breasts up my chest then whispered in my ear.

"I haven't been with any other guys tonight, so if you happen to get my nip in your mouth, it won't be like you're kissing every other guy in the club." She nibbled a little on my ear and stuck her tongue in it while I continued to stroke her thigh and her butt.

Then she turned to face me and I dropped my hands to the side rather than try to move them around with her. She straddled me and moved my hands to the outside of her thighs as she leaned into me. One of her pert titties made contact with my lips and I followed what I thought was her instructions and stuck my tongue out to lick it. She sighed and shifted to the other side. I gave that tit equal treatment and added a little suction between my lips. Noel began to gyrate on my cock, sliding up and down with just my trousers and her G-string between us. Then she shifted her position slightly, putting one leg between mine and the other outside. She started rubbing up and down on my leg.

"I don't usually get so turned on when I'm dancing," she said. "But it's my birthday."

I figured that was as good an excuse as any. Especially when she moved my right hand from her thigh and set it palm-up on my thigh. Her gyrations moved her pussy ever closer to my waiting fingers and soon, she was riding on my hand. When the third number began, she reached down and pulled the G-string aside and I felt the wet evidence that she was indeed turned on.

She'd told me I could move my hand around the area she put it, so I did, sliding my fingers up into her moist channel and then out to find her clit and begin squeezing and circling it.

"Oh, yeah. You know what to do there," she gasped. She returned her face to my ear and began nibbling again. "Do it. Make me come."

I did. I manipulated her clit and plunged into her pussy, hearing her get closer and closer to her peak. Then the music ended.

"Almost. Almost. Keep going. I'm almost there." It took only a couple more flicks of her clit until she gasped and moaned into my ear. Then she quickly shoved my hand out of her pussy and repositioned her panties. She began working on her bras and tap pants. She stood up and leaned in to kiss my other ear.

"Thank you, Bob. That was a great birthday present. I need to go catch a shower and get ready for my time on stage. I can't get out of that. I hope you enjoy the rest of the show and your night, but you'll never meet anyone else like me."

Well, she was right about that. I returned to a table on the main floor and ordered another beer.

72
STOPPING TRAFFIC

IT WAS ABOUT MIDNIGHT that night in Biloxi, when I saw what looked like a signal pass between a couple of tables. The men at both tables stood and headed for the door.

"Don't leave now, boys," the DJ announced as some others started to rise as well. "It's shift change and to start things off we have fresh talent on the main stage. This is Darnelle!" A blonde stepped onto the stage and began dancing energetically as a few of the men sat back down. I'd seen what I needed to, though. The coincidence of the table I was watching leaving right at the shift change got me moving.

Outside, I didn't see the men. I stepped around a corner into the shadow and released the ninja priestesses. I couldn't imagine the guys trying to snatch the entire shift of over a dozen dancers, but I could well imagine they'd try for one or two. The priestesses disappeared into the night in all directions. I just watched. It wasn't long. I saw the girls start to leave through the stage door. A bouncer accompanied them to see that they'd all make it safely to their cars. Then two shots rang out and the bouncer fell. Instead of running back inside like they should have, the girls all knelt around the bouncer and I saw a dark van move toward them. One of the girls finally ran inside, presumably to call an ambulance and police. One backed away and turned to run to her car. That was when the van moved, cutting the dancer off from the others. The door on the far side of the van opened and the dancer was grabbed. The girls around the bouncer didn't even notice. The van pulled out of the lot and the tires squealed. Then it came to a sudden stop.

I didn't need to look inside the van to see what happened. I saw the door open and three of my priestesses leave the van with the kidnapped dancer and lead her quickly and quietly to me. Of course, it was Noel.

"Are you okay?" I asked.

"What was all that? Where did these black knights come from? That van... it's a bloody mess. I think I have blood on me. Was this your doing, Bob?"

"These are my... warriors. We knew something was going down tonight, but I didn't know when and where it would happen. I'm guessing you were specifically targeted and your car may have been tampered with as well."

"I headed toward it because the lights came on. I thought I'd pressed the key," she said.

"Here's the question, Noel. Do you want to stay here and keep doing what you're doing? Do you have people you can go to? If you stay, you'll be asked a lot of questions by the police. That's fine, but they won't believe anything you say about us."

"You're like a secret service," she breathed.

"Very secret," I said.

"What alternative do I have? I was teasing guys intensely all night. You know that. None quite as intensely as you, though."

"That's your job. All the girls were teasing guys. But that's not an invitation to kidnap them."

"My boyfriend," she said angrily. "He has my other set of keys."

"What?"

"I've been watching for him all night. He said he had a surprise for me. He sold me!"

"That's likely. We'll need to investigate."

"God, what can I do?"

"You can go with my warriors if you want to. You can just lie low for a few days while we try to sort things out here and see if your boyfriend was involved. If you want to go, we'll have to leave now."

"And then I can come back?"

"Yes. Just remember that whatever you see when you're with us, you won't be able to talk about. I mean, you could, but no one would believe you."

"I'll go with you," she said.

I opened a gateway and the priestesses came running from every direction to dive through as the ambulance and police cars came skidding into the lot. I slipped away into the shadows.

"I think your house is haunted," Roxie said when she and Annie brought me cocoa and rejoined me by the fire back in Iowa. The memory of Noel was still fresh in my mind thirty-some years later.

"Really? What makes you say that?"

"I distinctly felt something brush against me and thought I heard a step when I was putting away the sugar. Of course, when I turned to look, there was nothing there," she said.

I glanced toward the kitchen and saw a camerawoman raise her hand and shake her head.

"Annie, are you playing tricks on our guest?" I asked lightheartedly.

"Oops! You caught me," Annie said.

"No way. Annie was on the other side of the table from me. She couldn't have touched me unless she had a rubber arm and that would bring up worse speculation than the house being haunted!" Roxie laughed.

"So, you speculate the house is haunted. I promise you that no one has died here that I know of," I said. "We could do some checking to see if there are other hauntings reported in this area."

"I might do that," she said. She yawned. "Wow! I'm really beat. If you don't mind, where can I sleep?"

I think she expected us to say 'with us.' She seemed a little disappointed when Annie said she'd show her the guest room. I breathed a sigh of relief and motioned the camerawoman to the bedroom. There, I opened a gateway and let her back into Areola. Annie shook her head.

"She is suspicious of you at the moment. I need to stay here for the night. I can go home tomorrow," Annie said.

"One of the camerawomen got trapped in a corner and brushed against her escaping. We're lucky she didn't get a glimpse of her."

"Yes. But Roxie is a sharp cookie. It's like she always expects something to be going on."

"It comes in her line of work. She has to be hyperaware of where customers' hands are, who is coming up beside her, and where she is all the time."

"You sound like you know a lot about strippers," Annie laughed as she stripped off the last of her clothes and posed before me. I thoroughly enjoyed the sight and picked her up to carry to bed.

"I've met one or two."

Back when we were cleaning up the mess in Biloxi, I was having some difficulties getting information and following up the incident at the Pussy Cat Club. It seemed the handgun used to shoot the bouncer had been held by a low-ranking army officer who was driving the van. Sometimes, I wished the priestesses were not quite so thorough in eliminating threats.

But there had been only three other men in the van that snatched Noel. I'd counted six leaving the club together. That meant at least two and possibly more were at large. Plus the boyfriend.

And we had no information regarding where they were taking her. It could have been to a private party where they'd rape and murder her. It could have been to a transport vehicle that would get her out of the country. There were so many unanswered questions.

And the Army base recalled all soldiers and locked down when the police told them of the bloody body of the officer.

Acting on the information given to me by Noel, I tracked down the apartment of the boyfriend and found it cleaned out. He was missing. It seemed like he'd left long before the caper at the club went down. I was in Biloxi for a month before we finally cleaned out a nest of traffickers who were mostly taking women out of the country and into South America for the entertainment of the dictator of a Banana Republic. They were being paid well, but none of them lived to enjoy their spending. The story released *said* that revolutionaries had killed the dictator and burned his house. A dozen henchmen involved in the trafficking ring had been in the burning house. The women were all returned to their homes or found a place to stay in Areola. Many had been originally trafficked by family members and chose not to go back.

But Noel was one of the ones who did choose to return to her life in the natural world. She asked to be dropped off in Southern California where she had contacts for a job and could set up as if she'd always been there. I agreed, of course. I wasn't enslaving anyone, but I was a bit disappointed by her choice.

"I'd like to dance for you again before you leave, Bob," she said.

She'd seemed quite comfortable with the nudity in our household and was often lying out by the pool in nothing. I'd made no inappropriate advances toward her because I didn't bring her to Areola to fuck. And she quickly saw that I had no lack of beautiful women to sleep with. We did, of course, meet and talk frequently as I pulled together the remaining parts of the operation in Mississippi and South America. It appeared that she was just one of many slated to make the trip south. She was gratified when I told her the boyfriend had unfortunately been in the dictator's house when it burned.

She asked me to visit her at the club she was headed to, which I did. It was a similar setup to the Pussy Cat Club but a little more upscale. She danced on the stage, getting delightfully nude.

"Did you see my new moves, Bob?" she asked. "One of the girls is a real pro on the pole. She's teaching classes. It's all about how you leverage and counter the forces that let you get into positions that don't seem possible."

"It was very impressive. I should have had you give lessons to some of my women while you were visiting."

"Oh, I did. Now, let's have a dance."

The price at this club was thirty-five dollars, paid to a fellow checking names and ID before we were allowed into the more discreet area. It was not quite as exposed as the main floor, but Noel was all over me in our three-song set. Panties stayed on up here, but the rules on touching seemed to be more about what the girl would allow than what the club rules stated. Noel allowed me ample opportunity to play with her breasts.

"You're hard and I'm wet," she whispered in my ear as she stroked my cock through my slacks. "Let's get a VIP room for half an hour." I agreed.

Half an hour in a VIP room was $300, paid to the concierge. Noel had come to the desk with her top still in her hand. I paid the fee and the concierge gave me a card giving me admission with no cover for the next time I was in town. Noel took my hand and led me to the room the concierge said was hers for half an hour.

This room held a sofa and an end table with a very low light on it. It was blocked off from the hall by a very heavy curtain that we pushed aside to enter and then Noel straightened to be sure we were not visible. Amazingly, the room and drape also blocked out nearly all the sound from outside the room. Soft music was piped into it.

"The rules are different in California, Bob. Just relax and let's have fun."

The fun began with Noel undressing me and spreading a towel on the sofa to sit on. In a few seconds, she was as naked as I was and began her dance. The light was so low it was difficult to really see her lovely body, but she made sure the experience was far more tactile. She did many of the same moves from when she'd danced in the lap dance area, but they were very different when there was no clothing between us. Her wet pussy slid up my engorged cock and then she continued to stand straddling me until she could push her pussy right at my mouth. I knew what to do with this and held her by the butt cheeks as she nearly collapsed from my tonguing of her clit and g-spot.

When she'd recovered a moment, she moved down, catching the tip of my cock at the entrance to her pussy and then slowly impaling herself on it. When she was fully seated, we began kissing as she slowly slid up and down my cock. We made love in that position for several minutes when she whispered, "Time's about up. I'm ready if you are."

With that, she sped up and I recognized the clenching of her pussy on my cock for the orgasm it prefaced and let go of my load, spraying into her well-prepared chamber.

"Noel, your thirty minutes is up," a voice said over the speaker system. She quickly dismounted and handed me my clothes as she threw hers on. Before the voice announced again we were in some semblance of order and left the room.

"Wait for me before you take off. I'd like to cuddle a little before we say goodbye."

I found a quiet spot in the club and settled in. About twenty minutes later, Noel came out in another outfit and settled close to me on the bench seat.

"I wanted to thank you, Bob, for doing what we've been unable to accomplish."

"What? Saving you from those traffickers was no problem. I'd have done it for absolutely any one of the girls."

"I know. Just um… look at this," she said. She opened her purse enough for me to look in and see the shield she displayed. "I'm a special agent with the sex trafficking task force of the FBI," she said. "Don't panic. I just accepted three hundred dollars to have sex with you and I still have your semen in my pussy. I can't do anything to bring you up on any charges or to arrest you for anything."

"I have to say, that's a bit of a shock."

"When you found me in Biloxi, I'd been under cover for three months, attempting to track down where women were being trafficked to. I saw the opportunity closing in when Jack was shot at the club. He's fine, by the way. Another agent, and he was wearing protection. I put myself in a position away from the other girls and just like I planned, they pulled up and grabbed me. Then all hell broke loose and ninjas appeared out of thin air. It was all over before I even had an opportunity to react. Then your offer came and I thought perhaps you were part of a rival operation."

"I'd been following the trail of a missing woman in Chicago," I said. "I don't let go of one of my own unless she asks to leave."

"Like me. So, our investigations crossed paths. Your ninjas did such a thorough job in the van that I thought the best course for me was to become your hostage. Guest. I have never been treated so well anywhere in my life. Thank you and please express my thanks to your wives and concubines. I wish... really wish... I could just stay with you. But I'm needed out here and when you showed me the devastation in South America and I met the women you rescued, I asked you to drop me here where I had an established cover and contacts."

"Noel, about Areola, you can't ever..."

"Bob, no one will ever know from me about your secret palace. I couldn't direct them to it if I told anyone. I have absolutely no ill will to you or your people. If I did, we wouldn't have made love. I'd have just killed you."

"That would have made me very uncomfortable," I said, breathing deeply.

"Yeah. Well, I'm heading back to the Bureau tomorrow to see where the next trail leads. Maybe we'll cross paths again someday. If we do, I might be ready to retire."

Noel gave me a light kiss on my cheek and disappeared back into the dressing room. I left.

I was in the kitchen drinking coffee and looking at various news and weather reports when Roxie came into the kitchen, dressed in one of my oversized T-shirts and, I presumed, panties. Annie had equipped her with whatever she needed for the night and this seemed to be her choice of nightwear.

She stumbled to the coffee pot and poured herself a cup.

"Up early. I suppose you're eager to get out of here."

"Oh, not so much," she said. The T-shirt she'd chosen was a vee-neck and way too large for her slight frame. It fell off one shoulder, hung up on the rise of her breast. It was apparent by both the bare shoulder and the obvious nipple outline beneath the fabric that she was braless.

"It's still raining. We can call Bill and ask him to get your tire fixed as soon as he can. You probably picked up a nail or something," I suggested.

"I left my keys with the clerk so he can pull it in where it's dry to work on it," she said. She lightly touched my head as she walked behind me to get to the refrigerator. Then again as she went to a seat at the table. "I called Joan and she said to wait until it was safe to travel. The cat can be on her own for a day without a problem."

That was news to me. I knew we didn't have a cell signal out here. I'd talked to Doug on the landline. I tried not to respond to her declaration.

"That's good," I said. "This weather isn't projected to let up until eight tonight. They're calling it the drought-breaker. Problem is, of course, that the ground is so dry they're afraid there will be more run-off than soaks into the ground."

"It seems like every four or five years, we get 'the storm of the century' out here in middle America. Sometimes it's snow; sometimes it's rain; sometimes it's wind. Doesn't make a difference. Four or five years later we get the storm of the century again."

"Well, you're welcome to just hang out here for the day. I don't think we have anything particular planned."

"I hope to get to know you better," she said, reaching out to put her hand on mine. "Much better."

Now that was a difference from her response to me the night before. She seemed afraid to be in the same house with me then. I recognized the touch. It was the same way that a stripper touches a guy when she's trying to get him interested in talking, buying a drink, or having a dance.

"Hey! Are you putting the make on my boyfriend?" Annie said, coming into the room and seeing Roxie's hand on mine.

"Not exclusively," Roxie said. "I wouldn't mind sharing with you a little, though."

"Uh... Where does all this sudden interest come from, Roxie? Last night you could hardly stand to be in the same room with me," I said.

"Too sudden? Damn! I was afraid of that. I've always been lousy at the transitions. It's either shy damsel in distress or wanton seductress. I never manage anything in between." She sat staring at her coffee. Annie gave me a curious glance and then shrugged and got her own coffee.

"You just surprised us," I said.

"Does that mean I'm out of the running?"

"What?" Annie and I said at the same time.

"I should have known it was too good to be true. Stranded on a stormy night and who should come along, but The Bob and one of his harem? I was so afraid that I'd blown it by being too reserved last night that I overdid it this morning."

"What makes you think I'm The Bob?" I laughed.

"Oh, it wasn't that hard to figure out. When you work in the business like I do, you learn to read people pretty well. I knew you weren't just who you said you were when that John at the convenience store was talking to you. It's one thing to treat a customer courteously. It's another when the customer is your boss."

"That's pretty amazing," Annie said. "Do tell us more. Bob, you could have a good time with Roxie and then tell her she didn't meet the qualifications."

"I don't think so. Did you hear what The Bob said about hunting down fakers? Not going to happen here."

"You two are so good. I'm pretty sensitive to things. Even when you stopped to change the tire, I had the feeling we were being watched. Then when you pointed her out, I figured it was just Annie who was watching, but the feeling persisted. In the C-store, I thought it was just the security cameras until I saw how John looked at the two of you. He doesn't have much experience, does he? Nice guy, but I could see he owed some kind of intense loyalty to Bob. When we got to the house here, there was the ghost touch. I'd heard about your stealth technology. I didn't turn fast enough to see her, though. When I said I talked to Joan this morning, you didn't miss a beat, even though you know very well there's no cell signal out here. I bet that's only in the house and two steps outside there would be a good signal. Plus, there's this." She held up her phone and showed me a picture of bare feet.

"Whose feet?" I asked.

"You tell me. She was in the hall when I came out of my room. I had my phone in my hand to see if I could get a signal, but then I thought I'd just take a picture of the place. As soon as I switched on the camera, I saw the feet. I didn't raise it up to see any more of her. I could tell, though that she was moving backward to keep me in focus. I remember signing the document that said all my interactions with The Bob would be recorded candidly." She sat there looking at us and smiled. "Well, how'd I do?"

That was a good question. Roleplaying for the purpose of seeing who a person is might be okay, but I really don't like outright lying. I could probably convince her I wasn't me, but eventually she'd find out I *was* me and be very upset that I lied to her when directly confronted. I guess I needed to come clean.

I leaned over to kiss Annie, then opened a gateway. She blew a kiss at Roxie and stepped through to disappear.

"Well, that nailed that," Roxie breathed.

"Mmmhmm. I guess we should just formalize the interview now. Hi. I'm Bob."

Her response was not quite what I expected. She whipped the T-shirt off and stood in front of me in all her naked glory.

"Uh... Not that I mind your naked body, but it's not required at this stage," I said.

"After all this, if I don't at least get to fuck The Bob, I'm going to be broken-hearted," she answered. She circled the table and seated herself in my lap. "Now, what kind of questions do you have for me?"

73
ON THE GO

YOU MIGHT NOT BELIEVE this after all this time, but I'm still not that good at talking to naked women I don't know very well. I'm not a natural seducer. I think that comes from Pinaruti's legacy. Since he didn't know how to conduct a conversation with a woman, he imbued me with a certain level of irresistibility. Fortunately, not so much that every woman I meet instantly wants to fuck me, but enough so that if they want to fuck me, they'll make the first move. Sometimes I actually turn them down.

But just talking to a naked woman who has suddenly plopped herself in my lap and invited me to interview her—while her hands, mind you, were constantly caressing my arms and touching my cheeks—left me a bit tongue-tied.

"Yeah. Um... Why did you decide to apply to be on *To Boldly Go?*" I asked. Somehow, my hand had found its way to cup her delightfully full breast with its hard nipple pressed into my palm.

"It's a long story. Joan and I decided to become dancers while we were still in high school. We even practiced dancing and stripping with each other, and got kind of involved, so that's how we discovered sex. We even had a little party once where we invited some classmates over and danced for them. It gave us good practice at controlling where guys put their hands and what we'd allow them to do. We got a reputation as being real cock teases, which is exactly what we had set out to do. When we turned eighteen, we went to a club and applied. Most of the boys we knew weren't old enough to go to the club, since it was a bar and restricted to twenty-one and older clientele, even though they let eighteen-year-olds work as dancers."

"Sounds like you got everything you wanted."

"Mostly. When my parents found out I was dancing, they kicked me out. No discussion. They're hyper-religious and absolutely would not tolerate having me as a stain on their reputation. Joan and I got a room one of the club managers was renting and moved ourselves to Des Moines. We were happy, even, to pay the rent with a weekly fuck for the manager. It was only until we got on our feet and could get a place of our own. And it was easy. I pulled down around a thousand a week after the club took its fee. And we both decided we could create a good cover for ourselves by working as temporary secretaries. So, I work wherever the agency sends me four days a week. Three nights a week, I dance my ass off and rub guys' cocks through their pants until they pay me."

"And you like what you do?" I asked. She had managed to get a hand between us to do a little rubbing on me as she talked. I discovered her legs had parted in an open invitation to explore.

"Yeah. But that's the difference. Joan and I do it because we love it and that's what we always wanted to do. But there are lots of girls who are there for less positive reasons. Some of them got hooked on drugs and started stripping to pay for the next dose. A lot of them pick up johns while they're dancing and that inevitably leads to STDs or arrests for prostitution. Some of them are just desperate because they made a mistake in their lives and figure the only asset they have left is their tits. And there are some who were coerced."

I stiffened in a bad way and Roxie petted at my chest, saying "Down boy."

"I have no problem with a woman choosing whatever path she wants to take," I said. "I have a great deal of problem with people who force a woman into a path."

"I think we've all heard that message loud and clear," Roxie said. "And here's the thing, Bob. I'm here of my own free will. I'm naked in your arms with your finger in my pussy because that's where I want to be. There's something perverse in me that just wants to fuck you. Though, you know you could bring Annie back and we'd have a really good time. But I don't expect you to choose me for your crew. What use would you have for a stripper in space when you've already got a dozen or more women who run around naked all the time. Guys don't pay me because I'm the most beautiful woman they've ever seen. They pay me because I'm the most available right now. I don't know how I could ever become the most available for The Bob."

"What is it you really want, then?"

"Joan and I have put together a pretty good-sized bankroll in the five years we've been dancing. But it's not enough. What I really want is for you to bankroll a buyout of my club. I want to get the druggies off drugs. I want to free the girls who are being beaten by a boyfriend at home if they don't bring home enough tips. I want to turn our club into a refuge for girls who love what they're doing and will enjoy every minute they're in my club. Like I do. You know, we could get this big boy out to play now," she said, squeezing my cock.

I did a lot of flying around the world to collect my next crew. I needed at least a day of rest in Areola between trips. While there, I watched recordings of my previous encounters and reviewed with the crew and family what I should be doing next.

And I didn't have sex with all of them. Not like with Roxie. Once it was established that Roxie didn't want a permanent place on my show or my ship, and had a very reasonable request for me, we went to bed.

No, that's not quite the order. We fucked on the kitchen table. Then we went to bed and fucked there. Then we fucked in the shower. We fucked in front of the fireplace. Eventually, I lit a fire and we fucked in front of it again. We ran outside while the rain was still pouring down and then fucked on the front porch with water dripping off us. Annie *did* join us and we fucked all together before Roxie finally got her car and left. In the meantime, Peninnah went to work and bought a strip club in Des Moines. When Roxie got home, she had a new job.

"We really missed the boat when we investigated Roxie," Doug said when we got together again.

"You investigated? I mean, that's okay if you withheld info from me as a surprise, but it was a bit of a shock when she revealed she was a stripper," I said.

"Well, the girls ranked them, including how genuine they appeared to be, but it's obvious we aren't getting deep enough. It's not like we can call their references. We completely missed your Doctor of Physics in Cleveland. She's getting along great in Houston, by the way, but really misses Cleveland Bob. I told her I'd put in an order for something that would bring him back to Houston."

"Houston is a big adjustment for her," I said. I knew she'd had to fly back to Cleveland the make arrangements for her business there.

"Bob, we've got a problem," Doug said, getting down to business.

"Great. Words I always want to hear. What this time?"

"The interactions between you and the women for this season are great. Some great scenes. Just great."

"Doug?"

"Yeah. Well, the show is flat. With the exception of May, we have absolutely no interaction with the concept of getting a space ship off the launchpad. And she still doesn't know Cleveland Bob is The Bob. In season one, we had the thirteen women in direct competition with each other. They were learning how to fly the ship. They were competing in contests of strength, smarts, skill, and generally being a nice woman. But in the cuts for this season, all we have is Bob trying to decide whether a woman should join his harem. They've never even met any of the others. We need some interaction between the women you are selecting and the crew already onboard. And your family. So far, we have reality, but we don't have a show."

"Hoo. Well! I don't know what to say. You're the producer. What do we need?"

"I think we should start off by arranging an encounter between them. Maybe one or two at a time. See how they get along together. Give them a challenge they need to work together on. Invent some more positions for crew members. The way I count it, we've got eight women and one man. Ten's a good number. So only one more selection. Then we need to get things happening. You know they're harem material. Find out if they are space ship material."

"Okay. I'm going to come home. I've been flying around the world for two months. I need to crawl into the bag for a while and get something organized with my family and crew," I said. "I'm tired."

"That's good, Bob. Come home. I'd like some time in the bag, too, you know?"

"Yeah. You've been great, Doug. Sorry so much in the natural world depends on you. It's vacation time."

I headed for LA and the mansion where Doug met me. He had a happy reunion with Avril and I invited the crew into the mansion to all be together with me. We had a wonderful and loving time. They all had comments to make about our nine new candidates. Half of them still didn't know they'd been with The Bob.

"Gwen is so quiet. Will she be able to hold her own in the group?"

"Mia wants the magic. She thinks she'll become a wizard."

"May is already designing a whole new generation of spaceships. Do you think she'll ever actually want to leave Earth?"

"Tommy is pretty cute. You didn't sleep with him. Are you thinking of bringing him along just for us?"

"I have never seen anyone so happy as Sonia. I mean, just happy with life. And she still thinks all your talk about being a demon is a joke."

Comments went on, carried on by several girls while I made love to others and then shifting smoothly to the others. No one got to sleep until late the next morning.

"So, what we are thinking is that we call all the contestants who qualified and invite them here to the mansion. We have a little get-together and then start training everybody on the ship operations that we learned. But in the middle of the process, there's an emergency and we all have to work together to save the ship or the show or each other or something," Lalonda said.

"What kind of emergency?" I asked.

"Maybe there's a hurricane," Eun-ha suggested.

"We can't fabricate that," Wendy said.

"How about a strike that takes all the workers off the ship? Then we all have to take over building it," Suhani offered.

"Maybe you could build a spaceship, but I wouldn't be good for anything but holding someone's coffee while she did the work," Artemisia said. "How about if the government tries to take over the project and we have to fight them off?"

"A foreign government, of course," Karla said.

"Or the mob," Linda said. "Like they find out Bob's been messing with their trafficking and decide to get even."

"Oooh. That would work."

"We need to plan this event out carefully. One thing we've learned in the past is that if we plan one kind of emergency, it turns into another," Doug said. "We need people to have their roles and to be buddied up with one of the candidates, so we know they are all kept safe and in line. We'll be the ones in the know, but they will think it's really happening."

Before long, we had the skeleton of a plan in place, but it needed a lot of work and we needed to get on it. It was definitely going to be a working vacation. We decided to go back to Japan and move into the penthouse for a while. We'd work things out there and start calling all the contestants.

We made a big deal about our travel plans. The cast and family all needed to be seen traveling to get ready for the next season. The girls on the crew hadn't been seen in public since we finished taping the first season, almost six months ago. We checked everyone's pass-port and made sure we were ready, then headed for the airport. Everyone carried The Bob Satchel. We took Avril as our traveling camerawoman, but I'd let others out when they were needed. Avril couldn't hope to cover everything 24/7.

Twenty-one of us boarded our private plane after having passed through a rigorous security check that did not seem to be the same for other private jets. Every bag was scanned, opened, and searched. The plane showed evidence of having been taken apart and put back together again. The government really wanted my 'portal.'

Japan was no better. Customs inspected every garment the girls brought with them. Paul, Doug, and I were searched thoroughly. I'd taken to answering questions with a new phrase and it seemed to be having the desired effect.

"Bob-san, how does your portal work?"

"It's magic," I responded.

"How do you make the girls disappear?"

"It's magic."

"How will your spaceship be powered?"

"It's magic."

When we got to the penthouse and the staff greeted us with an elaborate dinner, one of the girls asked, "How do you make simple rice taste so good?"

"It's magic," I responded before the chef could answer.

"Bob, do you think it's a good idea to respond to everybody by telling them, 'It's magic.' I mean, that's what it is, isn't it?" Doug asked. "Aren't we giving away something that should be kept secret?"

"Two things, my friend. First, I spent an entire week trying to convince Sonia I was a demon. She still thinks that's a big joke, even after she agreed that I must be The Bob. Everyone believes magic doesn't exist, so telling them something is magic is just saying 'I won't tell you.' Secondly, the governments are looking for some kind of super technology. An old saying is that the science of an advanced society will appear to be magic to a less advanced society. Our reality is that the science of Areola is magic. I can speak the absolute truth and they can interpret it correctly and still not believe it. I say it's magic and they assume it's a highly advanced science that needs to be learned—or stolen. They are right and completely wrong."

"How is research coming on opening a portal from any location?" Peninnah asked.

"Nimia and Sally are convinced that Areola is not in the bag," I said. "They believe the bag has become a focal point for me to create a gate, but theoretically, I should be able to open a gateway from anywhere, with or without the satchel. I haven't been able to do it, though. Apparently, I'm being blocked by the ingrained pattern of seeing the satchel as my access point. I'm not sure how to overcome that."

"The idea of putting a few thousand satchels out into the world was brilliant. It's getting so that border patrol sees them as a nuisance they need to inspect because everyone wants the portal. If one actually showed up in a bag, they'd be so shocked they wouldn't know what to do," Doug laughed.

"That was one of Peninnah's brilliant ideas," I said. "She measured my satchel and created a pattern, then sent it to a manufacturer in Korea. They started turning them out by the hundreds and when they hit the market, they were an instant success. The Bob Bag, or Bob Satchel was advertised on all the episode reruns of the first mini-series. When I bought one in Honolulu, Annie told me the price was going up 20% that day because they couldn't keep them in stock. $600 for an old bag!"

"You can't get one for less than $750 today," Peninnah said. "Which has had the added effect of having them in the hands of many very wealthy people who use airports and are highly offended by the kind of security they have to go through. There's a lot of pressure on TSA and other inspectors to back off. There was a rumor that said the bags would be banned from all international flights, but it got so much pushback that they dropped the idea."

"My wife is more than a financial genius," I said proudly.

"Oh, don't think this was all to take the pressure off of you, dear husband. We've made $2.25 million off our share of the royalties. It's been a very profitable endeavor."

The next thing on our task list was to call all the contestants I'd approved and bring them to Los Angeles for training. The task fell to Doug as producer of the show and he had to do some fast talking to get them all to agree. There were some who couldn't believe they'd ever been interviewed by the Bob until Doug sent them a video clip. Then they needed to be convinced that they should come from Turkey, Italy, Australia, India, the UK, and various places in the US to LA. Doug booked each of their flights while they were on the line and sent them first class tickets. May, in Houston, needed a call from Cleveland Bob and The Bob to convince her she should take time off her design duties for the space station to participate.

Eventually, the date was set and all the arrangements were done. We had one more loving night in Japan and boarded our plane back to LA.

A week later, they began to arrive. Gwen, a pharmacist (or chemist) from Scotland. Abby, a professional golfer from Phoenix. Mia, a researching nun from Italy. Sonia, a PhD student from the US, studying in Turkey. Amy, a single mom from Australia. (The girls got me to reconsider her.) Tommy, a musician from LA. Ranisha, a jeweler from Chennai, India. May, a physicist from Cleveland working in Houston on our new spaceship design. And finally, Annie, an actress I met in Honolulu who now resided with my concubines in Areola.

I think the only people who had never had a doubt that I was The Bob when I told them were those we sent a rejection note and check to.

Over the next week, we welcomed them all to the mansion and had a relaxed and enjoyable time with everyone getting to know everyone else. We talked about the schedule, training, filming, and socializing. We were in the midst of a martial arts demonstration by Zhi and Artemisia when one of the staff burst into the room.

"Bob, there are men here who say..." she was cut off as a man pushed her aside, backed up by several others in black vests.

"FBI. Bob, you're under arrest. Please come peacefully so no one gets hurt."

74
ARRESTED DEVELOPMENT

THIS, JUST SO YOU UNDERSTAND, was not according to the plan. In the plan, we'd have a couple of weeks of training before we staged a kidnapping of two or three of the contestants and they'd have to all work together to rescue the others. It was a little on the cliché side, but the whole series was over the top.

Instead, I had my hands cuffed behind me and was being read my rights.

"What am I being accused of?" I asked.

"Suspected trafficking and illegal travel under forged passports. There's a charge pending from the IRS as well," the agent said.

"Well, thank goodness you got here instead of them. That could be serious," I laughed. He didn't think it was funny. He spotted my satchel on the desk and grabbed it.

"We'll take this along as evidence." I wasn't worried about fake passports. I'd been traveling most recently as The Bob, and I no longer used separate documents when I had a different identity. I cast a 'glamor' on my passport so that it would look like and read as the person I was traveling as. But all the stamps were in the same little book. "The rest of you should consider yourselves under house arrest and will be questioned shortly."

"Not without legal representation," Doug shouted at him.

I saw Zhi and Artemisia move toward the display of weapons and shook my head. I turned and followed the agent with another on either side of me. I whispered a look-away spell and Avril fell in behind us. I hoped she and her drone could keep up.

Do you know how Roman Numerals came to be? This is bizarre, but I saw it happen during the time I was plying the waters of the Mediterranean almost eight hundred years before Caesar. Rome, under Romulus, was still in its infancy and war parties were often sent out for various purposes, including getting women for their mostly male inhabitants. They used various methods for this, including trickery. You can read all about the rape of the Sabine women in your history books and their story is as good as mine.

Anyway, one war party, under a particularly vicious lieutenant of Romulus, met stiff resistance and instead of pursuing the battle, fled. This was a shameful practice for the proud and warlike Romans, who were going home without spoils or women.

The lieutenant lined up his troops to see how many he had once they regrouped. Keep in mind, we are not talking about legions here. We're talking about a large war party which had run from its battle. The lieutenant walked down the row of soldiers counting them. When a soldier had been counted, the officer struck a vertical line down his breast-plate. At every tenth soldier, he drew an X. When all had been counted, he had a row of soldiers marked IIIIIIIIXIIIIIIIIIXIII... He then told the soldiers next to the ones with an X to turn and kill that unlucky bastard. This, he said was punishment for all of them for turning to run instead of fight.

I should mention, the soldiers marked with an X did not go down willingly and it was not only those who died in the melee that followed. The next day, the lieutenant led his men into battle. His men sacked the city, ran off with the spoils, and kidnapped the women. It was interesting to note the lieutenant was killed in the battle.

Hence forward, the ninth soldier was known as IX, the tenth as X, and the eleventh as XI. That was not only the beginning of Roman numerals, but the lieutenant recorded the first decimation of his troops. The symbol V for five was not added until years later. The system for adding and subtracting the cumbersome numbers came mostly from the Etruscans.

It was three hundred years before a General exercised the punishment on an entire cohort and by that time it was already common usage to talk about something being X-ed out.

You don't need to believe me. I use this as just another illustration of a leader of a trafficking circle being X-ed out himself. I had no intentions of joining that number.

I saw the drone enter the van in which I was transported. Avril didn't make it, but I knew she'd figure a way to get close and maneuver the little bug to wherever I was. This would make some good television eventually, I was sure.

Once at the headquarters, I was led to a room and seated. I assumed I was here for observation while they looked at my belongings. I was still for an hour before two men came into the room to question me. They did not look nice.

"Where are your other passports?" one demanded. I remained silent.

"When were you last out of the country?" asked the other. Still silent.

"You *are* going to talk to us, you know."

"The rights that were read to me indicated I had the right to representation. When my lawyer gets here, I'll happily answer all your questions."

"You might be here a very long time before any lawyer shows up. Who knows what he'll find left in your cell when he comes to talk to you? We might even forget we arrested you at all. So, no one will care a bit if we do some damage to that television face of yours."

He came around the table with intent and one fist raised. I mumbled a spell and the cuffs dropped to the floor. He didn't hear them hit before he swung and I grabbed his fist before it made contact.

"No!" I said. I was still seated and he was struggling to get his hand out of mine. I muttered another spell and the handgun the other agent was raising suddenly became too hot for him to handle and he dropped it. "I will sit here quietly and wait for my attorney. We'll do this the right and legal way or I'll consider myself free to go." I released the agent and he found he couldn't close his hand on the grip of his gun.

"You're making enemies of the wrong people, buddy," he growled. "I was only interested in your illegal entry and exit from the country. When Agent Dean gets here and starts asking about trafficking, things won't be as comfortable. Whatever tricks you're using won't fly."

"Then let me get my lawyer and we'll have a nice conversation. You have my belongings, including my passport. You can check my visas and stamps."

"Oh, we have. We want to know what technology you're using to fake those stamps when you are traveling under a different name."

I looked at him blankly.

"Let's go, Jack. They should have that bag torn apart by now." I blanched. That got his attention. "Yeah," he grinned. "We'll find whatever it is you're concealing in there."

I've been held in a dungeon before. Not a pleasant memory. Not at all like being locked up in the infinity room for seventy years. It was during my sailing years on the Mediterranean.

Most of the islands in the middle sea were inhabited by that point and ports were well-known to sailors. I docked at an island west of Italy, expecting to do a lively trade and hoping to uncover some manuscripts for my client in Alexandria. And, of course, for my own private library.

I have to say that I attach no mystic premium to the idea of a manuscript having been penned by a specific sorcerer or historian. If I can get an exact duplicate of it, I don't care if the author ever saw that copy. So, I seldom keep the original. Even at this time, I was delivering originals to Alexandria for the library but was making a replica of each manuscript before it was delivered.

Nor did I make the mistakes of later booksellers. Sometime in the middle of the fifteenth century, a goldsmith alchemist in Germany started printing books, most notably, the Bible. He was a poor businessman and had his secrets. His partner was a thief, like many good businessmen are. Just before the project was finished, the partner sued the printer for embezzlement of funds and was awarded the entire operation, cutting the inventor out of all profits from his invention and years of labor.

But, like many businessmen of that ilk, he schemed for a way to make the most profit from his product. He found himself in possession of somewhere between 150 and 180 unbound copies of the book, a situation that would commodify it very quickly. His solution was to load a cart full of the unbound pages and drive off to France, where he felt the people were less sophisticated than those in Germany. Here, he attempted to sell the books as original manuscripts—a product that would command the equivalent of a five-acre vineyard.

Upon examining the books, the elders of one village noted that they were *exactly* alike in every detail. Their conclusion was that they had been created through witchcraft. They went out to capture and burn the bookseller, who escaped from France, missing a few of his Bibles, and made his way back to Germany. To our knowledge, he promoted the new technology from that point forward and Pope Pius II wrote that he had seen pages displayed in Frankfurt to promote the work and the new printing press. Ultimately, Gutenberg was recognized for his contribution by the Archdiocese of Mainz and was given a retirement benefit through the remainder of his life.

I digress. I was inquiring about books to be purchased on this island when the local lord heard about me. He sent a detachment of his soldiers to search my boat for contraband and confiscate it. Upon finding nothing on the boat (all my goods were in the infinity room) he presumed I was a trickster and fraud. Better than a witch, I guess. He had me imprisoned until I could pay a hefty fine. His assumption was that I could pay no such fine and therefore he would confiscate my boat.

He was quite surprised when I demanded to be brought before him to pay the ransom on my boat and buy my freedom. I placed a sack full of Greek coins on his desk and demanded my freedom. He chastised his guards for having not investigated fully and invited me to dinner. The purpose became obvious. He needed to know if I had more coins to buy manuscripts.

I complained that he had already cost me my earnings and I would suffer great hardship to find things I could trade up for the price that was in that pouch. I told him a cockamamie story about my voyage and expeditions and having a small home on Crete where the rest of my wealth was secreted. He felt badly enough that he gave me half a dozen books from his library and sent me on my way.

Among those books, which I'm sure he considered worthless scrawlings, was a manuscript that included several spells for protection and defense that I've found useful ever since. One was the very spell for releasing shackles that I used on the handcuffs in the FBI interrogation room.

I was led to a private cell and locked in. They didn't cuff me, and it was a different agent who led me to the cell. I wasn't sure, but it might have been the janitor.

"Does it even do any good to lock the door?" he asked as I went into the cell.

"Not really, but it will help them rest better in their offices," I laughed.

"Well, if you decide to raise Cain out there, remember, I'm Jimmy. I'm one of the good guys, okay?"

"Sure. But I'm really not who they need to worry about, Jimmy."

"Yeah. I've been told the other agents have already been ejected from your mansion and some high-power judge is asking questions as to why we've moved to arrest you. Right now, it's an argument between that judge and the one who issued the arrest warrant. I'd guess there will be a Senator or a congressman or maybe even the President of the United States involved. Video footage of your arrest has already played on a dozen television stations. Did you get anything to eat?"

"Uh, no. Don't go to any trouble, though."

"There's a pizza shop next door. One with everything?"

"That's always been my goal," I said. He left and I glanced toward the drone that had entered my cell with me. I wondered how long before the footage from our conversation would be on television. I supposed, however, that as soon as pictures from inside the facility were shown, the agents would be coming through here with a bug sweeper and the drone would be found. I considered just revealing it.

I had no idea what was going on outside at the moment. I could feel all my women moving, but hadn't figured yet where they were or what they were doing. My effort to contact Peninnah mentally had failed. We had always had the weakest psychic link of all my wives, just because she was the newest and it hadn't grown so strong as the others yet. But the others were in Areola and would be unable to help unless I opened a gateway.

I didn't think I'd left one open or the station would already be flooded with ninja priestesses of The Bob. It made me nervous, though, to think that they might literally tear apart my satchel. I wished Sally had progressed further in her research. Maybe she could open a gateway.

Or Nimia. Nimia had more comprehension of the ancient scrolls than anyone, but to my knowledge, she'd never worked a spell. She hadn't been out of Areola in at least three thousand years and I wasn't sure the spells would work in Areola. Spells seemed to be a means of affecting the natural world. In Areola, the magic was active all the time and specific spells weren't required.

I'd been pondering the nature of magic and the world for quite a while when my jailer arrived with a pizza and a large soft drink bottle.

"Sorry it took so long. We had to figure out how to do this," he said. "I couldn't bring you a glass bottle of wine, so we dumped and washed a soft drink bottle and poured the wine into it. All our reports said you prefer wine."

That was nice of him. And the pizza was great. I sat and chatted as I downed the whole 'family-size' pizza.

"You said the agents had been ejected from my mansion," I said. "I hope no one was hurt."

"Egos were hurt aplenty," he laughed. "Nobody knows quite what happened. There were eleven agents inside your mansion, supposedly trying to question the others who were there—none of whom would say a thing. The next thing they knew, they woke up in a pile on your front steps. The door of the mansion was locked and no one even knows if anyone is still inside. The little tidbit of how they all suddenly went to sleep and were stacked outside wasn't on the video the TV stations all got." He shook his head. "I'm sure glad I wasn't on that detail. My entire assignment is just to watch over you. Some responsibility, huh? Maybe I should audition to be on your show."

"Stranger things have happened. You know we have a guy on this season. Local musician. Nice guy. I think he'll add a lot to the crew."

"I thought you needed some more guys on the show. It's a real fantasy trip to think of you with all those beautiful women, but it doesn't seem practical."

"How did this whole investigation start, anyway?" I asked. "We never seemed to be anything more than a television show to most people. Why the sudden interest?"

"Conspiracy theory. You ever hear about this guy who made a whole bunch of conspiracy documentaries a few years ago? Started with the Kennedy assassination and included things like the moon landing, alien abductions and Area 51, nuclear power conspiracy, seven rich people who run the world, and the Masons who are really Jews running Hollywood and trapping stars who are never able to leave, a la 'Hotel California.' Well, he's an old man now but he still talks and there are always those who will listen to a good conspiracy theory. He claims to have evidence collected during his investigations of all these conspiracies that suggests you are a very old alien who has been abducting the best of America's young women to people a planet that was destroyed in some holocaust a million years ago. He cites the disappearance of kids off the streets during the hippie era, raids on sex slave operations that don't actually release all the slaves, the Bermuda Triangle, and the rigging of elections in the past few decades to keep a steady flow of fresh blood to repopulate your lost world."

"Wow! I must be like Superman," I laughed. Like most conspiracy theories, this one had a few grains of truth in it that made me nervous.

"Well, some guy who used to date a woman who ran off and disappeared got wind of the theory and started raising a ruckus. He has the ear of some pretty powerful people in Washington and with your big show to select more crew members than could possibly fit on your little ship, he whipped up a frenzy and got a judge to listen to him who is known to be a fan of conspiracy theories. Hence, an arrest warrant. But no one knows what to look for. Things like your portal and the handcuffs falling off you really just add to the plausibility."

"That's all just special effects," I sighed. "Even the handcuffs were an illusion. David Copperfield could do it."

"Well, that's the news. I need to go sign the log book and indicate the prisoner has been fed."

"And a damn good pizza, too," I said. I took another swig of wine and lay back on the cot.

"What part of a 'No Contact' order do you idiots not understand?" a woman was yelling down the hall. From a long way away. I guess my sensitive ears were picking up distant voices in the otherwise silent jail. "You're messing with an important asset and now *I* have to go apologize to him for *your* stupidity."

"We got a warrant!" a voice I recognized as one of my interrogators yelled back.

"Who got it? You're being led around by your nose. It's been revoked. And the entire episode has been broadcast on television already, making you look like incompetent fools as well. Eleven agents asleep on his doorstep? That's just brilliant! Open this damn door."

"We can't just let all these people through!"

All these people? Now thoughts were beginning to filter through. Peninnah was here. And Doug. In fact, the whole cast and crew, including camera women, were inside the FBI building. Outside, there were at least a thousand protesters. Oh, yes. This was a media circus.

"And give me that bag," she yelled as the door opened. Ah. She came marching down the hall leading a small army of my people behind her. I had to think, though, about who the lead woman could be. I didn't recognize her. She definitely wasn't one of mine.

"Bob," she said as my jailer friend unlocked the door. "I did not want the first thing I said to you after we met again to be 'I'm sorry.' Please, forgive the oafs. Here's your satchel. Agent, is there anything else?" she asked the jailer.

"No, ma'am. Everything he had with him was in the bag."

"Let's go. Ladies, if you can all follow me downstairs, we'll take a bus back to your home. With my apologies."

"Thank you," I said. "And Agent Jimmy, thanks for the pizza."

"No problem, Bob. Have a good day."

75
JAIL BREAK

*I*T'S A LOT EASIER to break out of jail when you are led by an FBI agent than it is if you are all on your own. I'd had that experience a few years ago. I was on the street just minding my own business when police rounded up everyone they could see and carted us off to jail. Ali was with me and when she protested physically against the treatment, I had to step in to protect her and things got a little out of hand.

Now, let me tell you that I am not a person who just naturally dislikes police. Most are good people who are out there doing a very difficult job, sometimes under less than proper orders. That goes for every level of law enforcement. But they have a very high profile, and when one abuses his position, often all of them suffer.

That's what happened a few years ago when what should have been a routine arrest in Minneapolis turned into the murder of the suspect, protests, and nationwide riots. It was exacerbated by a quarantine during a pandemic, shortages of supplies, a constant flow of disinformation from leaders through the media, and a new epidemic of racism and fascism.

I don't speak ill of the police in this instance because there was a riot in progress and they were doing the best they could to restore order. And I couldn't just unleash the priestesses because there were no clear good guys and bad guys. Some of the people arrested deserved to be. I didn't think Ali and I deserved to be. We just happened to be there.

Okay. We happened to be there on purpose. A number of years ago, I'd built a church in a community that displaced a lot of people. They were people I created low-income housing for in the neighborhood. When the people of the church realized they had not managed to completely eradicate the poor from the neighborhood, the church gradually died. I funded a local group to buy the church and it became a neighborhood center that happened to have church services on Sundays. Good people. I wanted to be sure everything was okay in that community, so Ali and I went into town.

The neighborhood appeared to be safe, though tempers were as hot there as anywhere else in the city. In their instance, they wanted to protect their community, just as I did. When a local news report indicated the riots were spreading in their direction, they mobilized and created a human barrier between the riots and their neighborhood. The human barrier included blocking off the streets with parked cars and lining up to meet the rioters if they got that far.

They did get that far, chased by the police. Trapped between the community's barricade and the police, things got violent and the police loaded everyone they could into vans and buses with their hands zip-tied behind their backs. I had to struggle to reach Ali and get tossed into the same bus.

There wasn't anything I could do there because of the number of people jammed in the bus. We were shuttled to overcrowded jail cells and then processing began. That was when the police suddenly realized I had a leather bag under my arm when they thought they'd removed everything like that from the prisoners. They decided to take it.

I decided not to let them.

I didn't have many options. First of all, Ali had been with me for around seven centuries. She didn't have any ID. My ID didn't exactly look like me. I'd made a few subtle alterations to my appearance when I visited the community, darkening my skin and making my features look a little more like Ali's. Not like my driver's license at all.

There was a spell I'd only used once years before that caused temporary paralysis on all it affected. Unfortunately, the more people it was used on, the shorter its duration. Then they resumed whatever they were doing before. I spoke the spell and everyone in the room froze, including Ali. I shoved her into the bag. One problem solved. I quickly moved to the exit, just as people in the room were beginning to stir. I changed my appearance as I walked out so I was a white guy no one noticed as I walked down the street.

It was a near thing. I managed to get back to my car and drove out of the city. Then I went into the satchel and joined my wives and concubines in Areola.

We stayed in quarantine for the next several weeks before I came out and started the construction business up again. I was pretty tired of city living, and that was about the time Peninnah's email arrived for me. I was sure I had a way out of the Midwest.

In LA, a decade later, twenty-five of us followed the female FBI agent down a few flights of stairs to a waiting school bus. As soon as we were all aboard, it started moving. It came out of a parking garage a block away from the FBI office and headed us toward our mansion. I wanted to ask some questions, but I had family, crew, and contestants all over me.

"What did you do?" I finally got to ask.

"It was Sally," Mia said.

"Sally?" I was momentarily confused until the little researcher's head popped through the crowd.

"I did it, Bob!" she proudly announced.

"How did you get here?"

"I was in the mansion to meet Mia when she arrived. When all the Fibbies busted in, I used a sleep spell I'd been practicing. It worked great. They all just collapsed where they were standing."

"So did any of the rest of us who were near them," May said. "I still don't understand how you did that."

"Well, we woke you up right away," Sally said. "Then we just stacked the agents up outside, got in a couple of their vans, and drove down here."

"By that time, Doug had already uploaded the video of the whole incident and when we reached the FBI building, we started the protest. It didn't take long to gather more people," Peninnah said. "Doug's still at the mansion handling the phones and the stream of our rescue. Not all of it is going online. We got some great footage for the show."

"And you all worked together to come and rescue me?" I asked.

"Amazing where a pram will get you," Amy said. The single mom from Australia had her little one in her arms. "When I told them I wanted to see my man Bob right now, the whole place got chaotic."

"Mia had the entire Catholic Diocese flooding the phone lines with demands for your release," Ranisha said. "I'm going to design and make her a new cross. I have just the right jewels to do it."

And so the conversation went. It wasn't quite as daring an operation as raiding sex traffickers (or as bloody), but my new contestants had combined with the family and crew to bring together a protest and a rescue.

We got to the mansion and the bus let us off in front, then drove away.

"Darn it! I didn't get a chance to thank that woman agent and find out who she was," I said as we crowded back into my study. I started to feel like I was in an episode of *The Lone Ranger* in the last scene. *Who was that masked man?*

"I'm right here, Bob," she said. "Don't tell me it's been so long you don't recognize me."

I'm just not omniscient, omnipresent, or omnimnemonic. Remember that last word I coined in Volume 1? Probably not. It means all-remembering. I'm not. I have over four thousand years of experience crammed into a very modest amount of memory space.

I once forgot the name of that mischievous god who runs around playing tricks on people and messing up plans. I've had a feeling that he's been tormenting me lately because I still refuse to remember his name. It would be just like him to manage to delay construction of my space ship.

Where was I? Oh, yes. In Areola, I don't have a problem remembering people because they mostly don't change much. Yes, I think Sally lightened her hair and made her boobs grow a little, but she was essentially unchanged from the time back in the second decade of this millennium when I found her in a game.

On the other hand, people in the natural world change. They age. They collect their own scars and worry lines. I don't recognize them right away. For example, after leaving San Francisco in the seventies, I went back for a high school class reunion sometime before the turn of the millennium. Virginia thought it would be funny to go back, but she had been listed as 'missing, presumed deceased' in the reunion directory. I decided to take her as my date with an assumed name and a slightly different look.

We walked into the reunion, picking up our nametags, and I looked around for anyone I knew. I'd dated a lot of sweet girls in high school and they were all quite satisfied and satisfying. Like Bernice. She'd gotten the surprise of her life when she discovered girls could enjoy sex.

I looked around the room of around three or four hundred people to see if I could spot her. All I saw was a sea of old people! Yes, I'd added age to my character but not *that* old! And Virginia looked like a movie starlet I'd picked up as a trophy wife. We both wandered around the room, looking at nametags to see who was who. When we finally found someone we knew, they looked at me like I was a complete stranger.

We didn't stay late.

It took me a minute looking at the FBI agent before it dawned on me. The last time I'd seen her, she was a nineteen-year-old stripper working undercover for the FBI. She'd made very sure she couldn't arrest me by fucking me in the private room of the strip club. And it had been very good!

"Noel," I breathed.

"Real name Lacy White, though that sounds more like a stripper name than the one I assumed. I'm the special agent in charge of a trafficking task force. While I've followed you for a few years, I managed to get a strict hands-off order when it came to any investigations of you," she said.

"Why would you do that?"

"I needed you. There are some things I just couldn't get close to without risking too many lives. I knew I could pass information on to you and you'd take action. Then my team would move in to clean up what was left."

"The Border Patrol," I breathed. She nodded.

"We had statistics that said over three times the number of people were crossing the border than official estimates. And those people were never heard from again. My initial assumption was that the Border Patrol was simply eliminating the refugees and burying them in the desert. That region has very little in terms of tourist traffic. I've been through it a number of times myself and never saw anyone but Border Patrol doing their jobs."

"That's what I thought until I saw the murders the first time," I said.

"Think back about how you found out about the suspicion that it involved trafficking," she said.

"No. I was out of the country. Peninnah and I were just getting started on buying our various homes," I said.

"And a real estate person you met when doing a job for the Queen mentioned what she thought was going on with the illegal immigrants in the US. She was really talkative and went on about conspiracies and top government officials in the US and UK who were engaged in trafficking," Noel said. I guess I should get used to calling her Lacy.

"I remember it was when we were surveying the ground for the Queen's new palace and were looking for a place nearby. That agent had a theory about everything, but something about the Border Patrol just struck a chord with me. I had to investigate," I said. Lacy wiggled her fingers at me. "No, that couldn't have been you."

"No, it was a counterpart in British MI5."

"But how did you know that was me? I... changed between when I saw you and when Peninnah and I came back."

"You were the very devil to spot. I must have watched a thousand hours of airport footage. I saw you leave Chicago for Dubai, but once there you suddenly disappeared. Whole new identity. And you proceeded to come back and 'inherit' the business in the Midwest."

"What gave it away?"

"The bag. I knew you never went anywhere without it. We'd examined it pretty thoroughly and when I spotted it come through customs on video, I zeroed in on you," she said. "That's when I managed to get a hands-off order. It was obvious that you were an expert at identity change."

"But why would you give me the hints about the Border Patrol and trafficking of illegal immigrants?" I asked.

"We were being stonewalled," she said. "We knew something was going on, I'd seen suspicious behavior out there in the desert myself, and every time we tried to get permission to move on it, we were blocked by this technicality or another. It all seemed to point to one high-ranking government official."

"A senator who died in the cleanup."

"That removed a whole lot of obstacles. I wasn't sure when you would strike, but I had cameras strategically located around the facility. I checked them each day and watched the secret ninjas infiltrate the warehouse as guards and traffickers hit the ground without appearing to have noticed their presence at all. The next day, we moved in and found all the refugees gone and the bodies of the traffickers and the Senator nailed to walls inside. Very effective, and something we couldn't have done. We were ordered to keep it covered up, but photos leaked out to certain parties who became very afraid to have anything to do with the business."

"But you haven't supplied all our leads to traffickers. We..." I cut myself off before I confessed to anything. She didn't need to know about Reverend Ronald Richards.

"What happened to the preacher?" she asked, jumping on my thoughts. "We were able to track down the chain of command for the traffickers in his house, but there has never been a sign of him. Are you holding him at your palace?"

"No. I wouldn't take anything like that into my... palace." I'd almost said world. Fortunately, all the video that was being shot was by *our* camera crew. We could edit out anything we didn't want publicly known. "He was actually very insubstantial. He simply disintegrated into a wisp of smoke."

"The burn marks on the floor," she whispered. "Bob, I hope I'm not too late to the party, but I've never stopped thinking of you since our time together more than thirty years ago. I want to take you up on your offer to move in with you."

"You really want to leave the Bureau and the world? You know we're planning to fly away into space and not return."

"Yes. After."

After?" I asked. "After what?" Lacy dropped all forms of professional demeanor and ran to me, wrapping her arms around me. A few of my companions went on high alert but it was just a hug. A desperately passionate hug.

"After one more mission," she whispered. "I'm all alone on this, Bob. I need help and you're the only one I know who I think I can trust."

"You mean your agency is involved?"

"I'm afraid so. If I can pull this thing off, I'll need to disappear. Permanently," she said. "But Bob, please tell me I didn't wait too long. I know I'm not as young and... nubile as so many of your women are, but I won't be a burden, I promise."

"Lacy, I would take you at any age. I'm so happy to see you. But you need to tell me all about what the problem is," I said.

"I'll do that, Bob, but we should do it without cameras, or at least off the record for the show. This could be sensitive. Alone, except, of course, I know you're never alone," she said.

"Doug, you're in charge of debriefing everyone on the day's activities and having a good conversation about what everyone did. I'm taking Lacy to the palace for a bit to talk. We'll leave from my bedroom." I hooked my satchel over my arm and escorted Lacy upstairs to my bedroom. There, I opened a gateway and four of my warriors came out to guard and protect the satchel while I was inside. Then I took Lacy to Areola.

END PART XIV

Part XV
It's in the Bag

Image Credit: imasecret, ID 2134813893, licensed from Shutterstock.com

76
GATEWAY

"IT'S SO BEAUTIFUL, like I remember it. I feel younger and freer just being here," Lacy said, holding onto my arm.

We headed for the pool and before I'd finished speaking to one of the concubines to ask for refreshments, Lacy was naked with her clothes piled on the pool deck. She stretched out on a lounge chair. It had been thirty-some years since I brought the nineteen-year-old stripper/undercover agent to Areola while we cleaned up the traffickers who were preying on various strippers in Mississippi, among other locations. The last of those traffickers had perished in a fire in South America, along with the dictator who had ordered the supply of women. Lacy had definitely matured in that time, but to my eye she would still make a phenomenal entertainer. I certainly enjoyed looking at her trim body.

I decided it was my home; I could be naked if I wanted and joined her. My concubine brought us cold drinks and fruit.

"Now, perhaps you can tell me what is going on," I suggested.

"I've been working on sex trafficking for all my adult life. I'd been rescued from a trafficker before you found me and was recruited by the FBI to help them track down others. Most of my job was being vulnerable and hoping one of my so-called partners would be there to step in and save me when someone made a move. But during that time, I studied hard and passed several exams that led to me becoming a full-fledged agent by the time I was twenty-three. I'd kept track of you through nefarious means over the years. I might as well tell you, I put a tracking device in your satchel. It worked rather well."

I was shocked. To think that it had been so easy to deceive me and track my whereabouts. I never went anywhere without the satchel, so it was a sure thing that she had a record of everywhere I'd been in the past thirty years.

"I had you declared my asset immediately, and got a hands-off order from the Director to warn everyone to stay away from you. I've had that renewed regularly, including updating it with your new identity. I actually got credit for a couple of particularly bloody takedowns of trafficking operations during that time and before long, no one in the agency would work directly with me. When I said I head a task force, you should know that I meant I *am* the task force. For fifteen years, I have been compiling the data that shows a major trafficking operation in the US. Way beyond Epstein's little island. I have attempted to bring some known forces in to stand trial, but somehow those people have all ended up dead while in custody."

"Like Epstein," I said.

"I started keeping all my records secret and have had a few scares that my own life was being targeted. Lately, that's been more often than I care to admit and I went into hiding a few months ago. Marching into headquarters and demanding my asset today—or was that yesterday? I don't remember. Anyway, it was the first time I'd been seen or heard from in that time. I think some of them were hoping I'd been killed. So, you see, I can't really go back now, but I could be all that is keeping you from being harassed non-stop."

"What can we do about that?"

"Become heroes. I have the locations and the names of over a hundred traffickers, currently holding nearly ten thousand women and children for transport and sale. That's not all the people involved, but those are the ones I've ID'd."

"So many," I breathed. "I thought the traffic across the border had slowed after our raid down there."

"It did. The largest percentage of unauthorized immigrants in the country are not from Mexico or South America. They are from India and the Philippines. There are a good mix of other Asians as well. After the fiascos in Russia blew up in their faces, we saw a spike in Eastern Europeans making their way to the US. Most of them entered the country legally. But then they disappeared in the system. Some 40% of legal visitors to the United States overstay their visas. Over half of those are located and either renewed or deported. But close to half a million a year now are never located. It takes less than one percent of those people to become a profitable commodity, especially when mixed with the usual kidnappings and disappearances off the streets."

"Are they all in one location?" I was seeing a nightmare of frantic abductees all trying to reach safety through Areola. And how many people would be employed to guard the product? It was baffling.

"No. They are scattered at a dozen different locations. That is why I need your help. I think we can take them all out in a single night if we do it correctly."

I listened to her idea that would include revealing her as orchestrating the raids and then disappearing into Areola forever. I saw a few flaws with her plan.

"Lacy, you've mentioned eleven different locations. There's no way we can make all those in one night. Five on the East Coast, three in the South, and three on the West Coast. You'd need a hit team in position for each of them. Then we'd need to time it right."

"We have your ninjas," Lacy said. "They're more than a match for any of those goons. If we time it right, we can get the higher ups in the sweep as well. And no loose ends. One thing working in this line for thirty years has taught me is not to waste time with judges and trials. Go in, clean them up, and nail the bodies to the wall. Dress me up like one of your ninjas and when we finish, I'll unveil myself in a video as the one responsible. I'll instantly become America's most wanted, so I'll need to disappear."

"That still leaves us with transportation. And I'm not sure I want to put my priestesses in that much danger. Something could go wrong."

"Transportation? You can just transport us in to the coordinates and then out to the next location before anyone even knows we're there."

"I see. You have, unfortunately, a misperception about my portal shared by most of the world's governments. I can use it to go back and forth to here in Areola. When I come here, I have to leave warriors guarding the satchel so no one can get to it. The whole idea of going into outer space has been to get the satchel and the gateway somewhere safe where no one can get them."

Lacy looked at me strangely and shook her head.

"Can we just send a satchel to each of the locations? That would work."

"No. The gateway is in the original satchel I've been carting around for 4,000 years," I said. "I can't open a portal anywhere else."

"4,000 years. You've been at this a long time, Bob. But you haven't had the original satchel for months."

I was stunned. I jumped up and dove through the gateway back to my bedroom in the mansion where I surprised six warriors standing guard with my nudity and that of Lacy following closely behind me. I grabbed the satchel and opened it up. I kept all kinds of things in the satchel. I was a business man and carried around plans, reports, and daily necessities. It wasn't wise to go jetting off around the world with no clothes. I usually had spares in the satchel and hauled around a suitcase as well.

I emptied all the contents out on the bed and then worked the unbinding spell that had made my original satchel part of the new one I'd put it in. The satchel fell apart, but the original bag did not appear. I looked at the pieces. There was even a tag inside that said 'Made in Korea.' Once the satchel was in pieces, I found the tracking device that had been inserted between layers of the leather. But no bag from Knossos 4,000 years ago.

I ran downstairs and checked six other bags to see if the original satchel was in them, all with the same results.

"What? How? When?" I sputtered. And if I didn't have my satchel, how was I getting back and forth to Areola?

"When the new line of bags came out, we compared them to every image we had of your original bag. We bought and prepared half a dozen. The boys upstairs were convinced that the portal was part of your bag, so we took the opportunity to swap your original bag with one of the new ones. Just transferred all your stuff over. Then they took your original bag to the lab and disassembled it, looking for any trace of technology in it. The only thing they discovered was that the lining of your bag was a lot older than the outside," Lacy said.

"My original bag has been destroyed?"

"The intent was always to return it to you in the same way, but they never managed it. They restitched everything and got it back in the original condition. If it's that important, I could probably get it back."

"How have I been traveling back and forth to Areola," I asked. Sally approached us.

"That's great, Bob! It means you've been opening portals wherever you happened to be without actually having the prop you thought you needed," she said. "I knew it would work. Areola isn't in the bag!"

"We thought for a while that you must have gone into manufacturing bags to seed portals wherever you want them, but I like this... um... Sally's interpretation best. You could just open a portal to anywhere."

"We don't know that," I muttered. "I need to go back to Areola and think for a while. You're welcome to stay here. Or come to lie by the pool. Your clothes are probably still there."

I looked around. Where could I open a portal? I'd always focused on the satchel. I spotted one lying on the other side of the room. I focused on it as I said the opening spell and a gateway appeared. I went through with Lacy and Sally following, and closed the portal.

I'd had a close brush with death when a conjured monster attempted to sever my head with an axe. I have a nick in one of my horns from that. I hid out in the mountains of the Sinai for a few years. I went into the infinity room and let my wives and possessions and concubines soothe my shattered nerves with wine and sex. A very effective combination, I've found. I emerged refreshed and energized and ready to meet the world again.

That paled beside the utter panic I had when I lost the satchel and feared I had lost the infinity room forever. It was at the end of the American Revolution. I don't think I've ever told you about that.

I traveled East when I heard the colonists had begun a war for independence against England. What a horrid, dirty time that was. I'd been upset when I found the fledgling colonies had begun importing African slaves. I'd journeyed in and around Africa for some time.

I don't know if you are familiar with it or not, but when I left Bathra back four millennia ago, I took with me one of the native trees to plant in the infinity room. I liked the odd-looking tree and just wanted a few. When I was sailing out of the Persian Gulf and into the Arabian Sea, I went down the Coast of Africa for a ways before I headed back up into Mesopotamia. I came to a peaceful and lush island—another of the many places I thought I would be able to hide indefinitely, but was soon dissuaded as immigrants from the mainland crossed to it and settled.

By that time, I'd been there some years and decided to plant some of my special trees as a kind of memorial to my life and loves in Bathra. They were very happy with this climate, but when settlers arrived and I knew I would need to move on, a man came to me and asked me what these strange trees were. Remembering my beloved wife Bao, I said, "These are

Baobob trees. Always care for them and they will provide for you as they did once for Bao and Bob."

Then I headed back up the coast and into Mesopotamia.

Even then, I hated the concept of slavery, with my own near enslavement to Pinaruti still fresh in my mind. I wanted to get slavery banned in the fledgling country of North America as I'd been unable to do in the southern continent.

I found many sympathetic ears among the northern delegates to the congress. Its most noted accomplishment to date had been drafting a declaration of independence. I'd read the words when a copy found its way to me in California, and I rejoiced. "We hold these truths to be self-evident, that all men are created equal, that they are endowed by their Creator with certain unalienable Rights, that among these are Life, Liberty and the pursuit of Happiness." This in a nutshell was what I believed.

I journeyed to Philadelphia even though California was the property of Mexico and not part of the new nation. My hope was to influence the delegates to ban slavery in all its forms in their new constitution. The American independence was a threat to the Spanish in California. They looked at their own rule of the Mexicans as being somewhat tenuous and feared a similar revolution would disrupt their privileged position and the profitable trade routes to Asia.

Which, ultimately, it did.

Sympathetic ears were hard to come by among the southern delegates. The celebrated penner of the Declaration was off in Europe and I discovered that even he was a slave owner. "All men" seemed to be defined as "Males of English and European descent." It was not interpreted in the broader sense of "humanity" or "all people." While in Philadelphia, I was asked to take various letters to General George Washington.

I gladly took the task so I could meet with the General and plead my case against slavery in this new nation.

It was a case of bad timing. The British overran Philadelphia and Washington with around 10,000 American troops camped at Valley Forge. It was quite the city that had grown up nearly overnight. I was ushered into the cabin Washington and his generals had set up as a headquarters. He read the missives I brought, cursing the British for driving the congress out of Philadelphia and swearing he would take it back in the spring. He immediately penned a letter and told me who to deliver it to. Before I left, I pled my case for the abolition of slavery in the new nation.

"Bob, let us fight one war at a time. My slaves are quite content and well-cared for. None of our states prohibits slavery, though some of the legislators here in Pennsylvania are talking about doing that. This country is scarcely civilized and you want to ban the one factor that makes us gentlemen instead of common laborers," he said.

"But these are people, unjustly taken from their homes and brought in captivity to America. The declaration says that all men are created equal…"

"Men, Bob. Not Negroes. God placed some men in servitude to others. Perhaps in another day and age, slavery will become a thing of the past, but I cannot give time or energy to your cause while I have an army to feed and a war to win. If we don't win this, we shall *all* be slaves."

I left for Philadelphia with the letters for hidden members of the congress. And there, disaster befell me. I was captured by the British.

As soon as they trapped me and put bindings on my arms, of course, they discovered the satchel slung on my shoulder. This they snatched from me and would have had just cause to hang me if they'd found the letters. I had, however, secreted them away in the infinity room, only to be brought out when I was ready to deliver them.

This, however, did not prevent them from throwing me in a stockade and taking off with the bag to who knew where.

I was desperate. I was in a prison, which I could surely break out of if I chose to, but I had no idea where the satchel—the infinity room—was. I needed to get out and find it quickly. I could sense its direction, but could not tell how far it had been taken.

In the morning, I was led before a general and he passed judgment. He determined that there was no reason to have been in the direction I came from other than as a spy. Therefore, even without the letters, I was to be hanged.

I think I've mentioned my aversion to being killed.

There was nothing to be done but defend myself. I transformed, bursting the ropes they'd tied me with and clubbing the guards so soundly they were unconscious in an instant. Then I faced the general with my horns still growing.

"You mistake me, General," I growled. "I am neither American nor a spy. What have you done with my satchel?"

"I sent it as a gift to Earl Cornwallis in New York," the frightened general stuttered. I read his thoughts regarding the route his courier would need to take, then bellowed and struck the general so hard he, too, was unconscious. Looking around the small room, I decided on one of the sleeping guards who had been particularly nasty to me and transformed myself to look like him. I dressed myself in his clothing and then worked a second transformation so that he looked exactly like I had when I was captured. I put my rags on him and left on a horse tied outside the garrison.

Later that morning, another man died in my stead. The general never dared say anything about a demon appearing before him.

From thence ensued the greatest panic I had ever had. I knew what route the courier was taking, but had no idea how far ahead he was. I pushed my horse to its utmost in order to catch him, just as he sought a boat with which to cross the Hudson River into New York. The poor fellow never knew what hit him as I knocked him from his horse and snatched my satchel.

From there, I ran for the West. I'd had my fill of America. As soon as I was out of range of any civilization, I entered the infinity room, transformed myself once again, and left to resume my journey of some months back to California.

As soon as I was safely on my island, I hid the bag and went back to the infinity room, where I loved my women and drank my wine until the panic that had driven me from the general's cabin all the way to California had subsided.

My head was swimming with the revelation that I had not had my satchel for several months, and had, in fact, been going in and out of the infinity room from all over the world.

I left Sally and Lacy behind and ran directly to my magic room, shedding my human form, to contemplate what these revelations meant. I'd been there for some time—hours? days?—when my dear wife Nimia entered the room with me. She brought sweet cakes and strong coffee. I might have preferred wine, but Nimia was probably wise in her selections. She was the only person of all my wives, possessions, and concubines who was ever allowed in my magic room, a perfect replica of the room Pinaruti had summoned me into 4,000 years ago.

"What is it, my husband? What has you so troubled?" she asked. "Perhaps my mind or my body can help you."

"My loving wife, you are the most constant thing of my life for four millennia. How I love you!" I said. I drew her to me and simply held her in my arms.

I wept.

I had never quite understood the Christian writings when they said, "Jesus wept." I understood now. I understood how he must have felt when he faced the loss of all he knew and loved. The realization that if I had known the satchels had been switched, I would never have succeeded in opening a gateway, filled me with horror. I could have lost all of Areola. Anyone who was not in the natural world with me would have been cut off forever.

I told Nimia of all this and of my fear that I would be unable to get back to Areola without a satchel to focus my endeavors.

"I see," Nimia said. "Even though you know now that not only can you open a gateway from anywhere, but have done so, you still fear that you will lose something by not having the satchel with you."

I nodded.

"Then carry a satchel with you," she said. "You know without a shadow of a doubt that you can open a gateway through any satchel. You've been opening them for the past several months. And you just destroyed the satchel you'd been using and used a different one to get here just now. So, the next time you open a gateway, carry the satchel through with you. Look."

She pointed at a corner of the magic room where I saw an old dusty satchel lying. The room had recreated itself so thoroughly in Pinaruti's image that it had even reproduced the old satchel I'd enchanted.

"My beautiful, loving, and insightful wife. I depend upon you to balance my life and keep me sane in these insane times. Make love to me, Nimia. Make love and tell me what I should do about Lacy's request."

Nimia is the only woman I have ever made love to in the magic room.

77
PLOTTING THE FINALE

I HAD TO DO a lot of testing. I grabbed a satchel and slung it over my shoulder, then opened a gateway back to my mansion and stepped through. I had the satchel still over my shoulder, but when I stepped through the gateway, there was still one on the floor in my study. So were a couple of dozen women there and Doug was trying to keep them calm about where I'd disappeared to. They were surprised to see me back.

Naked.

In full goat form.

So many things to remember.

I said a little spell and transformed to my Bob persona.

"Aren't special effects just incredible?" I said as if I had just entered for my own comedy special. "I once saw a guy just evaporate into thin air. And he wasn't even on TV!"

My original crew were all laughing. They'd seen me in full goat form already and figured I was just some kind of morphing alien. The new contestants were a little shaken. I reached into the bag and Josie handed me a pair of pants and a shirt.

"Well, that was exciting," I said. "You all know from watching last season that I possess some super technology, including a portal that I use to get to and from my secret palace. I carry it around in my satchel. Only I just discovered that I haven't had that satchel for months! And don't worry about me exposing that right now, because we haven't even started airing this season and we're recording the final episode now. By the time it airs, we'll all be safe and sound at my palace. Assuming you all want to go. One of the things you all need to think about tonight is whether you really want to make this commitment to leave Earth, because once we enter the portal to my palace, you will rarely if ever see *this* earth again."

There was some murmuring as the new contestants started asking the first crew what it was really like. Of the new contestants, only Annie had actually seen the palace and understood that it was actually in an alternate dimension.

"Bob, are we going to be safe there?" Mia asked.

"Absolutely," I said. "That's what this whole adventure is about. Making sure my palace is safe from intrusion and destruction. It's also about keeping it a perfect world. Well, maybe not perfect. But it's pretty damn nice."

"That's for sure," Artemisia said. "Bob, you know I'm with you. I'll follow you into outer space. I'll follow you to Timbuktu. I'll follow you to bed. Give me any task and I'll do it. Just let me be with you."

That girl. Zhi had always had a special place as my devotee, but Artemisia had joined her fully. With those two women, I didn't need worship, I didn't need marriage, I didn't need possession. They lived for me and I wanted to keep them happy for the rest of our very long lives.

"Okay," I said. "In the next few hours, I want you all to put together a strategy for rescuing a whole bunch of enslaved women and children. I'm going to give you a list of resources that we can use, but we'll need to execute it in eleven different cities in one night. Yes, it's going to be a bit hairy, but we have 'technology' that no one else in the world has."

"Bob, why don't you just share that technology with the police or that FBI chick who was here? Why do you think you have to be the one to do this rescue?" Sonia asked.

"Well, there are a couple of reasons. My tech doesn't work with any other tech on this planet. In fact, to use it, a person would have to unlearn four thousand years of human science, and then study for a thousand to learn how to use it. The only person I know who has made the leap is Sally, who jumped back home with me and will be back later. Ask Mia what Sally can do."

"I saw her weld a bunch of bricks together with a few words," Mia said. "I examined them before and after. It was incredible. And we all saw her put everyone to sleep."

"But my tech is also fairly incompatible with the most advanced human technology. For example, I can make my satchel invisible to the human eye." I set the bag on my desk and cast the look-away spell. "In this room, you all just saw the bag disappear. On television, people are going, 'What's the big deal? I can still see the bag.' Well, the problem is that my stealth technology only works on the human eye. Electronic devices, including the video cameras, can see it just fine. I demonstrated this once to Annie. Honey, lead them through the exercise."

"Sure, Bob. Everybody get out your cellphone and turn on your camera. Then start scanning the area on Bob's desk."

The whole cast and crew got out cellphones and started looking. They were looking over the tops of their devices and then at the screen. Amy got up and came to the desk. It was fun to watch her looking at her phone while she reached out her hand to feel for the satchel. When she touched it, she gasped.

"Now I see it. It's... wait... it's gone again." She touched it again. "I can only see it when I'm in contact with it."

All the girls and Tommy had to get up and follow their cellphones to the desk and touch the bag.

"You see the problem. I have stealth technology, but it can be detected by human tech. That is one of the things you need to consider in your planning of our rescue operation. Another tech I have is the portal, but it may be that I have to have a satchel at each location I want to port to. I'm not going to indicate why, but at the moment, it only seems to work when one of these satchels is present. Yet the FBI, and probably other organizations around the world, have torn the satchel completely apart, down to the threads that hold it together, and can't find any sign of the portal. We need to consider this."

"And finally, we need to deal with the very real possibility that the bad guys who are holding these sex slaves might be—no, *are* willing to kill us to keep their slaves. And, of course, we have to figure out what to do with ten thousand women and children we intend to rescue and what to do with their captors. I'm going to leave you to work on planning this effort as I take off for a while to scout the locations. I'm not sure how long this will take, but I know that once people enter the cycle of slavery, they don't have much time to be rescued before they are sold off and transported out of our reach. With the idea of a rescue mission in the air, we can anticipate that the bad guys will start to anticipate it and may start moving their merchandise to other locations sooner rather than later. Your mission, if you accept it, is to beat them to the punch and rescue these people who are being trafficked."

I looked around at all the cast and crew and saw them beginning to nod as the ideas started coming. I picked up the satchel and slung it over my shoulder as I had done thousands of times in the past and opened a gateway. I stepped through, taking the satchel with me, and closed the gate behind me.

I was back in Areola and Lacy was waiting for me.

"Excuse the old goat in me, but I really liked you naked," I said.

"We finish this raid and I promise I will live the rest of my life naked for you, Bob."

"It's that important?" I tested her.

"It's that important."

"You've visited each of the locations from a safe distance, right? I'm going to need to borrow your memories of those places."

"Take them, Bob. I give you permission."

I looked at and memorized each of the eleven locations, then opened a gateway and popped into the first East Coast location in Massachusetts. At first glance from the rooftop where we arrived, it looked like any other shipping port. Lacy led me to the edge of the roof where we peered over at a dock.

"In there," she said.

I wanted confirmation and checked all around for surveillance devices. There were the typical security cameras overlooking the dock and a traffic camera at the gate. I fixed a point on the roof in my mind and opened a gateway. We popped back to Areola and then I opened the gate to the rooftop. We stepped out near the door from inside to the roof. I did another check for surveillance, hoping the look-away spell I'd cast on the two of us would be all that was necessary. I took hold of the doorknob and whispered an unbinding spell.

The whole door came loose, which was not my intent. I only wanted to unlock it. We listened carefully and I moved the door aside so we could enter.

We could see what we needed to see from the top of the stairs. The warehouse was filled with cages. In the cages were women and adolescents. They quietly sobbed. It was all I could do not to summon the priestesses immediately, but Lacy gripped my arm and I backed out, replacing the door, and putting a temporary binding spell on it. Lacy and I flashed back to Areola and I swore.

"Whoever has imprisoned them will die!" I declared. "Let's go to the next one."

I opened a gateway and we were in the restroom of a small coffee house. We listened and as soon as we were sure the way was clear, I released the look-away spell and the two of us walked to the front of the shop and ordered coffee like any couple out for a morning stroll.

In fact, we were in a popular tourist area of a historic seaport on the north side of Long Island Sound.

"This looks like a typical New England tourist spot," I said. "Even a college here."

"Makes it much harder to locate the prison," Lacy said. "It's actually on campus."

We walked across the lawns of the old college.

"The mansion of the founder on the edge of the campus is deserted. Supposedly. It was closed five years ago because it was deemed unsafe and in need of structural abatement. No one has come forward with the money to do the restoration and renovation but it's on the national register of historic places, so it can't just be torn down. Right here, on the college campus, over two hundred sex slaves are housed and transferred on a constantly rotating basis. This quiet little community is a hub of international sex trafficking, right under the nose of the proper and respectable people who live here. The good thing is that there is very little external security and it is all routed through the college security office. Inside, the guards are well armed and brutal. Rumors of late have indicated the house is haunted. In reality, it has an entire warren of underground rooms that date back from the American Revolution," Lacy explained.

I snapped some pictures of the beautiful campus and the mansion as we strolled by. We entered a classroom building and saw signs that pointed to campus police. After scouting by and seeing the unattended video monitors of the campus, we slipped into a bathroom. I opened a gateway to Areola and we left.

"Do we have to return to Areola each time we move to a new location?" Lacy asked.

"I don't know," I said. "I was doing it automatically."

We went to the next location, which was an old warehouse on a US Air Force Base.

"This is a difficult one. An Air Force general is leading the operation here and uses storage facilities on the base. Containers of people are moved out into cargo planes and flown to other locations. I don't have a good record of where they go. The hardest part is that the outside guards here have no idea what they are guarding. They're just airmen on duty. There's no way those inside can be unaware, though."

It was sickening, and some of the tightest security I'd seen. It was a US Military installation.

I focused on the next destination and we had a little jolt before we arrived at a plantation in Georgia. I surmised that the jolt was us passing through Areola without stopping. That would work. We kept traveling all day and all night, as we made the loop around the coastal areas of the United States. Massachusetts, Connecticut, Delaware, Georgia, Florida, Louisiana, Texas, Texas, California, California, Oregon. When we stepped back into Areola, I was sick at heart and eager to get moving. Lacy's stories of what was happening at each staging point and who was involved were almost unbelievable if I hadn't seen the evidence myself.

It was time to see what was happening with my TV show cast and crew. I'd sent video of each location to them from my cell phone. I wondered what they'd done with it.

"Two issues we can deal with right away," May said. "We have the technology to jam video signals and cellphone signals. Zero bars. Doug took care of ordering plenty of supplies for us and we expect them to get here by noon today. That PREMO service is great."

My family, cast, and crew were all dressed in camo outfits that reminded me of the kind of thing you'd see in an old B-movie of sexy women as jungle fighters. There was a lot of flesh displayed and even with the look-away spell on them, I thought they needed to paint up the rest of their bodies. I'd help with that.

"But, aside from Artemisia, Lacy, and Lalonda, none of us are well enough trained to take on all those people," Sonia said. "Peninnah told us a story about having been kidnapped in Japan and how the black-clad ninja priestesses of Bob had rescued her. I'm not sure about our Bob having priestesses who worship him, but I'm willing to accept their help when it comes to mowing down the bad guys."

"It seems you've mastered the art of opening a portal from and to anywhere," Liz said. "So, transportation to each site shouldn't be a problem. You should transport in with the electronics team and let them do their thing to block transmission. Then move in with the ninjas and clean out the bad guys. Any one or all of us will help nail the bastards to the walls."

"We have the problem of other technology picking up our movements, like motion detectors, that could send a signal to police or to other bad guys. That would make it bad if we were going from one to the next to the next," Amy said. I was really happy I'd reconsidered the single mom from Australia. She always had ideas. In and out of bed.

"What's the answer to that problem? We can move quickly from location to location, but probably not faster than the speed of an electronic signal. Plus, it is going to take a while in each of these locations to clean things up, no matter how quickly and efficiently we mop up the bad guys," I said.

"Here's what we're thinking," Tommy said. "It will only take two or three of us in each location to take out the surveillance. Preplant us. Take a team of two or three of us to each location, maybe with a bodyguard or two, and as soon as everyone is in position, we take out all the surveillance at once. That way they won't be able to communicate with each other. And don't hit them in order like you did when you surveyed the sites. They need to be so confused they don't know which way we're coming from."

"And take out the military installation first. They have the most firepower and pose the greatest risk to the whole operation," Ranisha said.

"I might be able to take out more of their surveillance," Suhani added. "I think we can depend on the guys in India to do exactly as we want. I built a backdoor into the code that would let me disable any satellite we focused on. That means the base would go dark."

"We don't want to take out the entire American military surveillance system. That would be perilous for the country. If we can limit it to that base, I'm good with that. I'm not happy about leaving people in locations without me present, though. And if I leave two priestesses in each location as guards, that would nearly cut our attack force in half," I argued.

"What about those guards?" Julie asked. She pointed to the side of the room where Ali and five warriors were still standing guard over an empty satchel. "I've met a lot more people in Areola than the priestesses who are trained in martial arts. Maybe not as honed to an edge as the priestesses, but surely enough to have guard duty. Zhi could take on an army by herself."

"And has," I said. "Get everything we need here and be ready to move tonight. I think we should take out the big installation here in California first after the military base. Then hit a South base location next to keep them wondering where we'll strike next. But we have one more problem. What do we do with all the freed slaves? Put your minds to that while I go rally the troops in Areola. Lacy, you should stay here with the cast and help get things organized. There must be some law enforcement people we could depend on."

She nodded. I opened a gateway and transferred to Areola.

78
SOMETIMES AN ALLY

YOU KNOW, it's not always Bob against the world. Or even Bob against some upstart king or emperor. Sometimes, I'm actually asked to intervene and become an ally. That happened back after Caesar was killed and Augustus became the ruler of Rome. That was also before I encountered the demon in the desert. I was deep in the Nubian Desert somewhere between what is now called the Nile River and the Red Sea, searching for a temple.

Cleopatra had told me where there were several ancient temples. She was extremely well-educated and spoke several languages. She was the first of the Ptolemys to learn the Egyptian language and was fluent in hieroglyphics, which she taught me during our time together. While her ancestor, Ptolemy I, founded the great Library of Alexandria, Cleopatra was a patron and great promoter of the library. I think it was for that reason that her brother/husband attacked and burned the building, even as I was rushing to evacuate as many scrolls and librarians as I could. I am still upset about the number of scrolls that were lost in that fire—some of which I had personally transported to Alexandria. Those, at least, had already been duplicated and stored in Areola.

Regardless, Cleo told me of a temple far to the south. She'd never traveled there because things were not always at peace between the Egyptians and the Kushites. However, she believed the temple of the god Amun was located there and may have been ancient when people first settled in lower Egypt. It took me a while to find the place. There was no trace of civilization there and I thought it must be buried under mountains of sand. It was quite by accident that I stumbled upon a fissure in the rocks and having passed through it, I found myself in a cool dry temple that was also quite empty. No books.

But it was certainly interesting. I had some of my people come out and begin copying the writing on the pillars and walls. It was a job that would take them a few weeks and they returned to the infinity room each night to sleep.

As I worked myself deeper into the temple, which I verified that like Cleo had suggested, was dedicated to Amun, I was impressed. This had been built near the same time I was building the temple to Namri and Ninra, but was much more substantial as it used stone, much as I had on Crete for the king's palace. But farther into the depths of the temple, construction methods changed. I could see that much of the temple was made of the same kind of sand bricks I'd made in Bathra. I had to wonder if this was a common technique that all the gods knew and graciously passed down to me. These bricks were older than I was!

It wasn't the first time I'd encountered a structure that was older than I was. The great pyramids were already half a millennium old when I was summoned into the world. But as I descended—yes, the path definitely sloped downward, even though spacious rooms had level floors—according to the descriptions I found, the temple dated to at least a millennium before my birth!

Originally, the god had been called Atum and was the creator of the world. My librarians informed me that according to this creation story, the world was covered with water until a mound—the very mountain we were inside—was thrust up out of the waves and on top of it was Atum, who created a man and his own wife and then the rest of the world.

Wow! I was impressed and bowed in reverence before the god, who might have had some remnant of presence in the ancient temple.

While my head was bowed, a light moved ahead of me, guiding my path until I came to a wall that moved when I pressed my hands on it. Behind that wall were coves stacked with ancient scrolls. The librarians carefully removed them and put them through the duplication spell. Then they reverently replaced the originals on the stone shelves where they had resided for thousands of years. They did not immediately dissolve into dust, so I had to assume the god was protecting them and would continue to do so.

We backed out of the room and the wall silently sealed itself before us.

I don't know how long we spent in the temple. Not much had changed when I emerged, except the presence of a beautiful woman as black as the night, sitting on a horse with a dozen spearmen behind her.

She immediately jumped from her horse and knelt before me. The spearsmen dropped to one knee.

"Rise! Rise!" I called. "Whatever you may think, I am not your god and will not take his worship!"

That was a dangerous thing to say, but I'd been in the presence of an ancient being, I was sure, and I would not upset him. There were places I'd been where such a declaration would have meant my instant death. If I wasn't a god, then I must be an enemy. Not so with this woman. She rose at once and faced me.

"I am Amanirenas," she said. "Queen of the Kushites."

"Bob. Free man and wanderer. How may I help your majesty?"

"I had a dream," she said.

Oh, shit! Whenever someone starts a conversation with the words "I had a dream," you can bet some god or other has a task for you. It had happened to me too frequently. Who wanted me for what now?

"Please, come in where it is cool and we will have refreshment and stories," I said.

She followed me back into the temple. She motioned her guards to stay outside, but I waved them in. Whatever journey had brought her here on a horse, her spearmen had made on foot. That was just the reality of royalty.

Once inside, I subtly opened a gateway and my women appeared with cool goats' milk and honeycakes. The spearmen were in awe. The queen did not acknowledge them.

"Now, your majesty," I said as we sat on chairs my women brought us. "Tell me about your dream."

"You must know our circumstances first," she said. "We Kushites are a proud people. We have withstood the advances of the Ptolemys, the Nubians, and many others. But now, the Romans have decided they should collect a tax from us. They occupied our Northernmost city and demanded payment. We owe them nothing."

"But you paid?"

"Ha! We took back our city and put the Romans to the sword. We took the head from their statue of Caesar and buried it in our temple where the people walk on it every day."

"What Caesar is that?" I'd heard Julius was killed by his own senate and Marc Antony was now bedding Cleopatra.

"One called Augustus. He defeated the Egyptians and marched south on us."

I'd once met Augustus, or Octavian as he was called then. Caesar introduced us at my wedding to his cousin Cordelia. I thought he was a nice boy, but like most of his family, he was rather greedy. He was only a teen, but the only person he considered his better was Caesar. Caesar recognized him and openly declared that he adopted Octavian as his son.

So, that was who had come to attempt to tax the Kushites. They'd responded by chopping off the head of his statue and burying it where everyone would walk on it. That probably pissed off the emperor.

"In my dream, Amun Re told me to come here and make an alliance with the one I found here. Caesar's Egyptian Governor Petronius is on the march and has sworn to enslave us. O, Bob! Every man, woman, and child in Kush will die before we are enslaved!"

That got my goat. I would die before I saw them enslaved as well.

"I have traveled with Alexander, Xerxes, Julius Caesar, and even greater generals," I said. "I will help you lay out a strategy and will be your comrade in arms."

We set about creating a strategy and went out to meet the Romans.

One should always consider the character of one's allies. I learned that. Amanirenas was devoted to her people and their independence. She was a ferocious fighter and, from what I could see, a just ruler. But she was not a nice person. She was vicious.

Our strategy was to feint an attack on a city occupied by the Roman army and then flee, leading a chase deep into Kush. Here, the queen's army knew the terrain and instead of standing to fight, like other armies did, we set ambushes. The fighting was intense. The Kushites had inferior arms and inferior numbers, but they were, perhaps, the most devoted army the Romans had ever faced.

In a strategy I borrowed from the Britons, who outmaneuvered Caesar without him even knowing it, we whittled away at the numbers, killing most of the enemy. A few of the enemy were sent back to report what they had seen, but only after being forced to watch others of their living comrades fed to Amanirenas's pet lions.

She wasn't nice. But she didn't enslave anyone.

She paid for her courage. In one battle, an arrow found her right eye. She was blinded in that eye and bleeding, but when she threw the arrow back at the one who shot it, I gave it a little boost in speed and accuracy. It killed the archer who shot her. Then, she turned and led her army into the battle again, driving back the Romans.

The battles went on for three years and both sides lost hundreds of warriors. Seeing that both the Romans and the Kushites were equally damaging to the other, Amanirenas sent to the general and proposed a peace. The Romans agreed and ultimately withdrew into Egypt and repealed all taxes on the Kushite cities.

The one-eyed Queen Amanirenas led the only country and army that stood victorious against the Roman legions. She became a legend in both countries.

You're probably saying, "Well, Bob, what kind of lover was she? Was she as vicious in bed as she was on the battlefield?"

I have no idea.

After the peace treaty had been signed, I bid the queen farewell. When you have seen a woman feed a living man to her lions, it significantly reduces the libido. I was glad she had saved her country from slavery to the Romans—we had saved it—but I felt no desire for her. She thanked me with some valuable jewels from her country and I left to continue looking for libraries and ancient books.

Okay. That was on my mind when Lacy made her proposal. There was a significant difference, though. When I fought at the side of Amanirenas, no one from Areola was risked. I had very few people in my world who were warriors. Those who were laid down their arms when they entered the infinity room.

Lacy was asking me to bring my precious priestesses into the natural world, along with the contestants and crew of our show, and send them with our little bit of magic and our ninja skills against a heavily armed and vicious predator. There was a reason it took only a few hundred guards to watch over ten thousand slaves.

Getting the priestesses and fifty more skilled warriors ready to launch an Earth invasion was less problem than I imagined. I appeared before the priestesses in my full demon form and explained what we'd been asked to do. One of the priestesses stood as the others hummed. I recognized it as the priestesses uniting their minds. I had no idea how they did it, but in this state, when one made love to me, all of them participated and orgasmed when she did. When they spoke in this way, it was the voice of all of them in one mouth.

"I was unclean. I was a captive, raped, beaten, and starved. I was unfit to live in this or any world. My one desire was to die," said the spokeswoman. The others nodded and rocked as they continued to hum. "Then The Bob came and took me from the dungeons of filth and purified me in the pool of life. He made my light glow with his love. I placed my life in his hands. Now he tells me there are others suffering at the hands of pirates and asks if I would go where he could command me. I will go and free the captives. I will bring them to the blessed land of The Bob. Let this be so!"

Well, fuck! that was short and definitive. They knew the risks and they rose to meet them. Fifty-two fierce warriors who would leave no slaver standing.

There were others. Zhi and Ali brought warriors with them who were more versed in modern warfare through their frequent visits to the natural world as guards for me, my family, and the satchel. They even knew how to use firearms. I didn't think any of them had actually killed a man with a gun, but they were willing. I soon had another contingent of fifty who would go with the contestants to disable the communications and security devices at each location.

And the camerawomen. Doug had used a couple of dozen camerawomen from Areola in filming the show and contestants. Many were trained in the use of drones as well. A crew of camerawomen would accompany each attack to show the world what happened on this fateful night. All I needed next was to arm my priestesses with more than their swords, knives, shuriken, and bows. We definitely didn't have enough firearms, and I wasn't sure they could use them if we did have.

In Areola, when there is a need, it somehow always gets fulfilled.

An inventor in our community who had come from the construction industry when I was building in the Midwest, came up with a tool to help the priestesses with their task. He created a nail gun that didn't require an air compressor. Previously, they had used a kind of nail gun powered by a cartridge of compressed air. But the cartridges didn't last long. The new nail gun was something like a staple gun, but had a hair trigger and shot six inch spikes. The priestesses were so pleased with the new tool that they almost touched the poor guy when they blessed him. They holstered their nail guns and glowed with the fierce light of The Bob.

I went to see Nimia and Josie. Of course, my other wives and possessions were with them. I'd brought Peninnah and Liz back with me from the mansion. There were still things I needed to resolve. I wouldn't do this without their agreement.

"We are not as eloquent as the priestesses of The Bob," Nimia smiled. "Still, we are as committed as they are. We cannot know of this atrocity without acting to end it. Yes, Bob. We should do this, and we should make Lacy one of our own."

"What do we do with the slaves?" I asked. "If we leave them after killing all their guards, others will just show up and enslave them. I'm not sure we can even trust the police. Certainly, ICE would be a poor choice. I suspect many of them of being complicit in this."

I really couldn't see transporting ten thousand women into Areola. I wasn't sure how that would improve their lot. They must all—or at least some—have homes they wanted to return to. And some might be badly damaged and beyond our reach to heal.

"Bring them in and quarantine them in a welcoming environment. Make sure they are fed and bathed and tended to medically. Then sort them out after the operation. You could return any of them to any place in the world since you know how to open a portal now," Nimia said.

"I will organize a welcoming committee," Maya said. "There are many people in our world who remember what it was like to be snatched out of the world they knew and brought to this one. This would be one of the times that the flower children of the sixties would be good to use. Some of them still think they are tripping out in the best trip ever."

"Bob, excuse me, but there is a priestess of Aphrodite at the palace asking for an audience with you," Oza said. He was one of my most faithful retainers and had been attached to the household since before I reached India.

"By all means bring her in," I said.

The priestesses of Aphrodite. That was another resource we hadn't thought of using. I hadn't even mentioned them to the contestants. While they were known for providing sexual comfort, it was not all they did. Few people on Areola actually needed sexual comfort very often. These priestesses had expanded their mission to include counseling and guidance. It was simply another kind of comfort.

A beautiful naked woman who had served in Aphrodite's temple in Troy approached and knelt before me.

"O, Bob. I have received a message from my goddess Aphrodite and beg leave to deliver it."

"Yes, yes. How is My Lady Goddess?" I hadn't heard from Aphrodite in a year. She'd managed to send me one of my favorite contestants, Deedee, during the first season of our show. She'd last appeared to me as I made love to Deedee.

That should have given me a clue regarding what happened next. The priestess crawled into my lap, kissing her way up my chest to my lips and then sliding down to impale herself on my cock. I think all messages from Aphrodite are delivered in that way.

"Bob, I can only maintain this link briefly," the priestess said. I looked into her eyes and saw before me the most beautiful woman in the universe. Aphrodite had taken over. "Zeus has blessed your operation. He has granted me permission to bring any of the women who would serve me to Olympus. Like in Areola, they will always be cared for and treasured. There are many who were captured because they still pray to me and I would not have them suffer further for my sake."

"That is wonderful, My Lady Goddess. I thank you and I thank Zeus."

"There is more. I have a gift from Apollo." She gave me a quiver of arrows that materialized in my hand. "These are arrows enchanted by the bright god of the sun and poetry. It is the same enchantment used by the Trojans and anyone struck by one of these arrows will die. Yes, that includes any strike of the arrow, whether or not it would be deemed fatal otherwise. Like when Achilles was struck in the heel by the arrow of Paris."

This was an incredible gift. I would be armed and able to help my warriors in the battle. As I moved in the priestess and we approached our climax, the quiver of arrows transformed itself into a modern handgun and holster.

"The gift of Ares is to make the bow of Apollo into something more manageable in the natural world today," she gasped. "Oh, Bob! I have missed you! Fill me!"

I had no difficulty granting her request and as my orgasm faded, so did My Lady Goddess. I kissed the priestess tenderly and she smiled, making no move to dislodge herself. I guess I didn't mind. I was making no move to get rid of her.

On Areola, we had all the pieces in place. We still needed to get the plan together with our contestants. I headed to the mansion, half expecting our contestants would have fled. I was gratified to find them all gathered around the table with a plan for how the rescue would work. The rescue would become the final episode of our season two reality show.

I wondered if they understood that this was real, but Lacy had been with them through all this and they were definitely ready.

79
TO BOLDLY GO

’LL TRY NOT TO BE too graphic about the raids that released ten thousand women and children (plus a few men) and ended the lives of some three hundred traffickers, including an Air Force General and a dozen airmen, a US District Judge, a high-profile evangelist, a dozen men in ski masks, a South American general, an Arab prince, a high-ranking airline executive, and two other billionaires. I was thankful my business partner in Space Pioneers was not among them, but it wouldn't have made a difference if he was.

We dropped our logistics teams at each of the eleven locations and they confirmed readiness. We intentionally did not tell them what order we would attack the installations. In fact, Lacy and I decided the order as we carried out the purges. The actual attacks took the least amount of time. Communications and video were shut down at all locations at once. As soon as they went dark, we struck the military installation where a dozen freight containers were being loaded for transport on a C-5 cargo plane. Each container had fifty people in it. There were another two hundred containers still in the warehouse. We made it just in time, but it was a bloody battle and we had to evacuate the slaves at the same time we were taking down the guards. Any guard or airman who seemed not to know what was being transported, Sally cast a sleep spell on. In one instance, that put all fifty of the people in the container he was moving with a lift to sleep as well. The guards inside the warehouse who knew they were guarding human traffic were dispatched, along with the General who was directing the operation. The airplane pilot and crew were put to sleep.

Compartmentalization in the ranks meant that the vast majority of those involved had no idea they were moving human traffic. But the ones in the inner circle were not only aware, they were profiting. I was glad that the same compartmentalization let us reduce the number of casualties.

Those bodies, however, were nailed to the side of the aircraft. We moved on with the entire operation taking about half an hour.

We struck the opposite coast ten minutes later. This operation was larger, as the shipment was going by sea to South America. Some forty casualties were nailed to the walls and 1,100 women and children were transported temporarily to Areola for processing. As expected, we were finding it took longer to transport the victims than it did to clear the traffickers. The priestesses of Aphrodite, most of whom had not been in the natural world in nearly three thousand years, cast a blind eye to the environment and focused on moving the freed slaves to Areola to get them food and medicine, clothing in many instances, and safety.

The college in New England went very fast. It had the fewest slaves for transport at about 150. Only ten bodies were nailed to the walls of the old mansion. Then we were on to Texas. As the night wore on, we found the guards more watchful. Being out of communication with the outside world made them suspicious and wary. Resistance was stiffer and our great advantage was the look-away spell and the silence of the priestesses' weapons.

And so it went, down to the last target hidden near where our raid on the Border Patrol had taken place years before. And we had to deal with Texans on this one. The guards were better armed than at any of the other installations and were on alert. Their communications had been down for ten hours. They didn't wait to see a target, but when they heard a noise or sensed a presence, they shot. A priestess next to me was hit and I returned the shot with my own Apollo-blessed weapon. I knew I hit the scum and didn't wait to see where. Any wound with one of Apollo's arrows was fatal. I opened a gateway and carried my priestess through, where Josie, Pari, and Penelope took charge of her and pushed me back through the gateway.

I went a little wild. My gun blazed at every guard I saw, cutting down a swath of them. And when I broke into an office and found a man using a collar to shock a naked woman into obedience, I knew I'd found the fabled trainer. I kept him alive just long enough to transfer the slave collar to him and then detonate the charge that effectively removed his head. Lacy nailed his body onto a suitcase full of money lying on the floor where he fell.

As soon as we had the 700 slaves from this location transported to Areola, I shepherded my team through and closed the gateway. Then I rushed to my wounded priestess, shedding my clothes, and transforming to my full demon form.

She was lying next to the pool where Marie, our doctor crew member from the first season, had rushed to her. She worked feverishly, removing the bullet and attempting to stanch the bleeding, but it was to no avail. When my priestess saw me, she weakly raised a hand toward me and smiled. I grasped her hand and the light within her brightened. I thought all the healing magic I had ever read to her but nothing seemed to work. The light faded and died as she did.

I took her up in my arms and waded into the pool with her, bathing her body in the warm water that was stained with her blood. I cried and wailed, cursing myself for having let her come to harm. The other priestesses stripped off their black robes and joined me in the pool, surrounding us, their light nearly blinding those who stood around the edge of the pool.

I wailed my grief.

"This is a precious priestess of The Bob!" I called out.

My voice echoed throughout Areola. Even the Bobbobbob people from Australia in the farthest corner of Areola heard me and told the story. My voice may have been heard in the natural world as well.

"She has known kidnapping, rape, abuse of all kinds, and yet she came to me and was cleansed. She was baptized in the pool and her inner light glowed with love. And when she knew of others who suffered as she had, she donned the garb of a warrior priestess, took up her sword, and bravely went to rescue them, whether at sea, in the air, or in any other place the criminals were to be found. And one of those criminals shot her before I killed him. She gave her life for the salvation of 10,000 others. For that and for all her devotion to The Bob and the cause of freedom for the enslaved, for having loved me and had faith in me, I love her! I will love her to the end of time. Beloved priestess and lover of The Bob, I release you to the primordial mass from which all life arose until that time when I, too, may join you there."

As I spoke, her body dissolved into dust and smoke and was carried away on a breeze.

The operation took longer than one night. From the mansion, we sent photographs and documentation from Lacy to FBI headquarters. She signed them all "Special Agent Under Cover Lacy White." She included photos of her badge and her face so it could be matched with records. So far, no one was questioning whether Bob had anything to do with the mop up overnight. It looked like Lacy had raised a small army and coordinated attacks all over the country.

In Areola, we did our best to comfort and heal those we rescued and then return those who wanted to go to the natural world. When the women and children started showing up at various law enforcement offices and social services centers, they each carried a photograph and evidence of where they had been held. And that's when the story of their remarkable escape began to get bigger. They talked about a glowing light that entered their prisons, destroying the evil men who held them. They spoke of being transported to a holding area where they received medical attention and food and were given a choice of what they wanted to do next.

Some bore letters from others that stated they had chosen to stay in hiding and not return to the lives they had before. Some wrote accusations against other people who betrayed them or even sold them to the slavers. An ever-widening dragnet developed as people were brought in for questioning and many charged, awaiting trial.

Of the women who chose to 'stay in hiding,' close to two hundred chose to accept Aphrodite's offer, including half a dozen of her priestesses from Troy. The other priestesses of Aphrodite promised to keep her love alive in Areola. And there were some who simply wanted refuge and chose to stay in Areola. If they were able to adapt to life in our world, we accepted them. Some we turned away because their underlying attitude and personality simply would not mesh with our society. And some were so damaged from their treatment and trauma that we had no choice but to release them into institutional care in various places around the country.

Of course, the government wanted to know where the vast number of undocumented women and children came from. The INS and ICE both came under investigation. There were, of course, some who used their positions to feed the traffic themselves. Mass deportations did not always wind up in countries they were supposed to. Just as the immigration raids had done, several dozen officers were pulled from their jobs and offices. Others quickly stood up to accuse those they knew.

And with the mention of being transported to a holding area, someone made the connection to The Bob. Hadn't he shown a portal in use to his secret palace? Hadn't they wasted thousands of man-hours on trying to capture and investigate that portal?

I avoided contact as much as possible by simply staying in Areola. Doug and a few of his assistants made regular trips to the mansion, from which he handled the mail, email, text, and phone messages. Our non-Areola staff in LA and Houston kept things running and we began releasing the episodes of season two when we got news that the first materials transport ship was finally ready to launch into orbit.

Under May's direction, we began transporting materials for the space station colony ship to orbit. And then we all gathered together to watch the first episode of season two.

We watched the first episode, that included the original crew sitting around like goddesses to decide who should be included in the second season competition. It included several different candidates, some of whom would be surprised to find they'd been considered. Those who were eliminated received a nice check for their screen time and I knew for a fact some of them could really use that extra income. So, the first episode left everything open as to who would be selected. There would be more people introduced as the season went on. Our actual acceptance rate had been about one out of thirty. It just wasn't easy to find compatible harem members.

"This all seems so tame compared to what we just went through," Ranisha said. She was a jeweler from Chenai, India and one of the ten people selected during the competition.

"It is tame, but did you notice the fire in Annie's eyes?" asked Gwen. Gwen was a pharmacist, or chemist, from Wales.

"I loved the way the camera caught that glint when they were talking about trafficking," Mia said. "I hope something like that came across during my time on camera."

"We had a lot of opportunity to catch it when we were talking about the possible use of slave labor to build cathedrals and temples," I said. "Your fervor was something you all were judged on. It came out in each of your interviews."

"I was so worried," May said. "I wanted to like The Bob, but I'd fallen in love with Cleveland Bob and just didn't know what to do. And then I couldn't believe they were the same person. Do people still believe you do those persona changes with just makeup?"

"We may never know," I said. "The capacity for people to not believe is beyond my ability to comprehend."

"Out of all the people who you interviewed—I think Liz said there were 300 candidates who were contacted—were we really the only ten who had that kind of hatred for trafficking and enslavement?" Abby asked. I'd interviewed her first on the golf course where she was a professional and she'd told me about her own near brush with trafficking.

"No. There were many others, which made the selection process that much harder," I said.

"Like Roxie in Kansas," Annie said. "I was ready to bring her to Areola on the spot."

"Why not?" Tommy asked. He was a bass player in LA who flitted from gig to gig but hadn't landed in a band full time.

"Roxie had her own mission to fulfill," I said. "She was already engaged in a fight to free dancers who were coerced or forced into stripping and prostitution. We fund her efforts, but she didn't want to leave her mission to join ours."

"It was a common theme, wasn't it?" Sonia asked. She was the PhD candidate studying in Turkey. "You asked me about how I viewed the gods' interaction at Troy."

"And?" I prompted.

"Bob is different. The Olympian gods didn't care about the people they sent to battle. Oh, they had favorites like Odysseus and Paris, but mostly they didn't care about a hundred thousand soldiers they whipped into a frenzy to do battle on the plains and die for them. The gods, all the way through the history of the world, used their devotees as if they were disposable slaves. The soldiers died for their god and some vague promise of a post-death reward. Religion is slavery," Sonia said.

"The priestesses worship The Bob," Maya said. "But they don't blindly obey him. They created their own mission to rid the world of slavery and sex trafficking. If Bob had used some other means to handle the slavers in the last raid, the priestesses would have been broken-hearted. Even the one who died in his arms. Their mission was to free others as they had been freed."

Everyone took a minute to acknowledge the sacrifice of my precious priestess. I still had tears whenever she was mentioned.

That night, I had nine women in my bed, and Tommy. No, I didn't screw Tommy—not this time. But the musician was surprised to find how completely he was accepted into the cast, including being accepted into several of their pussies.

It was a long night of celebrating and I indulged in a deep and sated sleep afterward.

Mostly, the new members stayed in the mansion during the run of the show. Lacy stayed in Areola except when we were viewing and discussing each episode. An FBI agent came to the door of the mansion and politely asked if Lacy was in the mansion. We simply shook our heads and he turned around and left. No show of strength. He looked at the candidates who had marched on FBI headquarters in Los Angeles lined up behind me and just backed away from the mansion.

Five weeks into the airing of the show, when I'd made a big deal about how we used the portal to take candidates to the palace in Areola, I received an ambassadorial invitation from Washington, DC. They decided to take a different approach than previously and invited me as a representative of 'your country' to have a private conversation with the President of the United States.

I debated long and hard about this and eventually decided to take her up on her offer.

I did not arrive in a limo.

I only partly trusted the offer to parlay with the President. There were still too many people who were as interested in seeing me captured as they were in seeing me sign a trade agreement. Lacy White had been put on the FBI's most wanted list. As soon as they figured out that I assisted her, I was sure I would join her in that august recognition.

At the appointed time, I stepped through a gateway onto the presidential seal in the oval office and waved at the doors to seal them. No one but the president was in the office and to say she was startled would be an understatement.

"Madam President," I said. "Greetings from Areola. I'm not here to do any harm, but hope we can have a civil discussion of things that affect both our worlds. I am Bob."

She took a deep breath and took her hand off the button that would have called secret service in from all over the building. They couldn't have gotten in, but it would have made an awful racket and I'd have left before they started tearing down the walls. She stood.

"On behalf of the United States of America, I welcome you to the Oval Office, Bob. Do you mind if we record this meeting so I can review it with my advisors?"

"A wise decision. Please allow me to assist." I removed the look-away spell from Avril and she appeared nearby with her camera running.

"Color me impressed," Madam President said. "Why don't we have comfortable seats to discuss our countries and the ways we might open diplomatic relations?"

She waved me toward one of the oval sofas and seated herself opposite me, carefully avoiding stepping on the presidential seal where I'd appeared.

"You obviously have technology at your disposal that would benefit the United States. What does the United States have that will benefit... Areola?" she asked.

"Areola has very few needs. We are slightly more than another country. Areola is here. All around us. It is a different dimension of the reality you know. There are things we hope to gain from our association and there are things I believe we can provide to you, even if our technology is beyond the reach of your scientists at this time."

"A different dimension. Do you mean we are sitting together in Areola at the same time as we are sitting in the oval office?" she asked.

"Sort of. The idea that no two things can occupy the same space at the same time is erroneous. All things occupy the same space at the same time. If we were in Areola, however, we would be sitting beside my pool, surrounded by the beauty of the palace, temple, and libraries..."

"I hope I can visit one day," she said before I'd finished.

"Naked," I finished.

"You think I would be naked, too?"

"It is possible. Nudity in Areola is the equivalent of a business suit in the Oval Office."

I'd carefully dressed for the occasion—or rather, Peninnah had dressed me—in a respectable business suit. The president took a moment to collect herself while considering the proposal to visit Areola naked.

"What does it take to set up a trade negotiation between your people and mine?" she asked.

"We have little that is needed. You know of our work in the space industry. We still intend to launch on a colonization mission currently slated for Mars. However, without access to Areola, such a small mission would stand no hope of survival. Therefore, we have also begun construction of a satellite that could be turned into a colony ship. It is far larger than any space ship that has yet been built on Earth."

"Where is this being constructed?"

"In orbit. We have launched materials that will be used in construction and expect the shell construction to move along quite rapidly once we have enough materials. We are using exclusively labor from Areola for the construction as many of the materials are only found there. The colony ship will be slightly more than a kilometer in diameter and capable of transporting some ten thousand people. Once it is lit, it will be clearly visible from Earth."

"A kilometer in diameter? Surely that would require tons of material and many journeys to supply such a ship."

"And hence my first offer. We have developed an element in our dimension that is far lighter and stronger than any metal found on Earth. Yet it can be fabricated into nearly any usable object." I reached into my bag and retrieved a bar of metal to hand to her. She took it, hefting it and even attempting to bend it. "We call this Areolium and would be willing to offer it as a trade good and to train workers in its use."

"This is an amazing thing. May I give this to our scientists to analyze?"

"Please do. As I said, the element is unknown on Earth. I'm not even sure it will fit on the table of elements."

"You have indicated that there is little we have that is needed in Areola. What would you like us to trade for this commodity?"

"I would like Lacy White to be removed from the list of America's most wanted and all supposed charges against her dropped."

"That is... unexpected. Perhaps you are unaware of the carnage she left behind in liberating some sex trafficked women."

"Some three hundred sex traffickers were eliminated in a single night while liberating over *ten thousand* slaves. Brutal, yes. Some might even say barbaric. Once they have analyzed it thoroughly enough, your investigators will realize Lacy could not have effected this endeavor at all, let alone in a single night. I have extended asylum to Lacy White and she has accepted permanent residence in Areola. But her reputation does not deserve to be dragged through a court battle when she has merely stopped a shameful trade in kidnapped women, some men, and many children. These people were destined for short lives of degradation and disgust. Such enslavement is anathema to Areola and to me personally. When discovered, I will not hesitate to eradicate it. Anyplace in the world."

I spoke a little more strongly than I'd intended, but with each word, I remembered my precious priestess dissolving in my arms as she rejoined the primordial mass. The president fingered the bar of Areolium and considered what I said before nodding.

"I will discover what I can do to eliminate all investigation into the matter of Lacy White and to expedite the trials of the accused traffickers arrested in the aftermath of that dark night. I don't know what it will be, yet."

We continued to talk and I alluded to my library and its contents. I also mentioned that there was no reason our space ship needed to be owned and controlled by Space Pioneers, but that I was not comfortable giving it into only the hands of the United States.

"What about the portal technology," she asked. "You must realize by now that it has been sought after by dozens of nations."

"That is one reason I am loath to release it. However, the other reason is equally important. Your science and my science are fundamentally incompatible. A researcher would need to unlearn four thousand years of scientific development in order to learn to work a portal. I'm not saying that such people don't exist, but in most instances, they are not the people you would want to share that technology with."

"So, you're saying it is magic," she laughed.

"I was recently informed by my crew that any form of sufficiently advanced science and technology would be the same as magic in another less advanced society. We can call it magic if you like. That's what I call it."

Our conversation ended after less than half an hour. She returned to her desk and I stood on the presidential seal in the middle of the carpet. I waved a hand and the doors of the oval office burst open with secret service and drawn weapons as I stepped through a gateway and disappeared.

80
FINALE

*I*T WAS DONE. There was an official recognition of Areola by the United States Government. And with that recognition came a Presidential Pardon for Lacy White. She sent a note of thanks to the President and an official resignation to Lacy's boss at the FBI. Then she and I went to bed together for the first time since her reappearance.

"You know, I can't complain about our first time together," she said as I filled her welcoming vagina. "But I hope this time we can take a little longer and really enjoy the experience. Thirty minutes was just too short a time for our first time together."

"Not to mention less than ideal circumstances," I said. "I was not expecting to engage with you in quite that manner when we went into the private room at the club."

"I wasn't sure I would have the courage to do it. Other girls talked about the fucks they'd had in the private rooms, but I'd never done it. It all seemed more commercial than what I wanted our first time to be."

"You are a beautiful woman, Lacy. You were then and you still are. I came to love you during our time working together."

"And look! In just the short time I've been in Areola—you'll have to tell me if it has been a day or a thousand years. I honestly can't tell—my boobs have gotten firmer. They're almost what they were when I was nineteen and trying to convince myself that being a stripper was a valid way of serving my country."

"Did you know that Nimia is 4,000 years old, by natural world reckoning? And she has the same difficulty telling time that you do. It's irrelevant here. The priestesses have been with me 400 years and all still look like the gentle beauties I baptized on their first day here." I was a little wistful, I guess.

"Oh, Bob, I'm so sorry your priestess was killed. She was so beautiful and so devoted. What was her name?"

"Well, that's one of the unusual things about the priestesses. None of them has ever spoken her name. They all declare themselves simply 'Priestess of The Bob.' I can't even go into their temple unless I am in full demon persona and not a trace of human in me."

"Perhaps not tonight, but soon, I'd like that full treatment. For now, just love me some more. I am so happy not to be living under cover for the FBI."

Lacy was not the only person wanting my time in the wake of our rescue and the recognition by the government. We were sent an ambassadorial committee of four women who, of course, wanted a tour of Areola.

It was very funny. They came to the mansion—by appointment—and were shown to my study. I opened a portal to Areola and they took a deep breath and stepped through. The first thing they did upon arrival was undress! The president had carefully instructed them on protocol. Indeed, everyone around the pool was naked and I stripped off my clothes for the tour as well. They were only a little uptight, but they relaxed as we continued through the buildings and they got used to seeing naked people.

They didn't get the whole infinity room tour. They were shown the palace and grounds, the pool and temple, and the libraries.

They were impressed that in what looked to them like a non-technological society, we had a form of television and telephone. They were all a bit disconcerted, however, that their cell phones didn't work in Areola. Perhaps most impressive of all to them, however, was their tour of the Library of Alexandria and the story that went with it.

"This treasure that you have collected may be worth more than all the alien technology you can offer," Erin Flynn, leader of the delegation said. Sometime along the tour, she had taken my arm as we walked. "We would definitely like to arrange a repatriation of the volumes of this library to the new Library of Alexandria in Egypt. It would go a long way in cementing relations of Areola to the rest of the human world."

"I think we can arrange that," I said. "However, like other things, I believe the process should be undertaken over the course of a number of years. The sheer volume of historic information contained here would overwhelm most libraries. Our librarians have had many, many years to come to grips with what is here."

I did not mention that some of the librarians were from the original Library of Alexandria. They had no desire to return and I had no desire to paint Areola as an eternal fountain of youth. There were already applications coming to our office in the mansion for tourist visas. I didn't think I was going to allow tourism at all.

And, of course, the committee wanted to interview some of the women who had elected not to return to the natural world after their ordeal. When they departed, none of the committee members had dry eyes.

"Bob," Erin said as we neared the end of their tour. "We don't know all the customs of your world. We've all seen your interviews this season on *To Boldly Go*, though. If it is customary to seal our friendship with sex, I am willing and available."

I was not really sure if that was an official offer or her own spur-of-the-moment suggestion. I rather thought she was hopeful.

"While Areola is a world with a lot of sex in it, no one is *ever* under obligation. It is not a transaction and is not expected of residents or visitors," I said. "We even have a temple to Aphrodite here and the priestesses there make it their mission to physically comfort and entertain anyone, male or female or other, who feels in need. There has never been a case of rape in Areola. If there was, the perpetrator would have been unmade."

"Killed?"

"More. Completely disassembled and returned to the primordial mass," I said. She shivered and pulled herself closer to me. She was as close as we could get and still be able to walk.

"We would like to establish an embassy here. Can you tell us how to acquire land on which to build so we can have a full-time ambassador here? We'd also like to establish your mansion in LA as an official embassy of Areola to the United States. Of course, we would welcome your establishment of an embassy in Washington, DC."

"Things don't actually work that way here," I explained. "No one acquires land. No one owns any. People have homes they found that are perfect for their purposes and just moved in."

"But how do you collect taxes?" she asked.

"There are no taxes in Areola."

"How do you fund things like the raids on the slavers?"

I led her to the pool and as if I called—which maybe I did—the fifty-one priestesses of The Bob filed out of the temple and into the pool. I shifted my form to the goat-legged demon they loved. Erin gasped at the transformed body she was still holding onto.

"Every person who participated that night was a volunteer. Our force was the fifty-two priestesses of The Bob. There are now fifty-one. One of my precious priestesses was killed by a trafficker and I will mourn her forever."

"You did all that with these girls?" Erin asked.

"There is no force greater than these women," I said. "You will see it in our finale."

Erin hugged herself to my demon form and inhaled deeply. I escorted her to her clothing before I took them back to the mansion. The other three women in the delegation—the president obviously knew who to send—had scarcely said a word, but they all huddled close to me and inhaled my scent.

At the mansion, we agreed that the US embassy to Areola would be established in a mansion next door to our LA home. And we were now an official embassy to the United States.

I still don't believe you're a demon, Bob," Sonia said. I had been one hundred percent truthful with her about my nature since the day I met her and she still wouldn't accept that I was a demon.

"I don't know what I could possibly do to convince you, my love. I've been completely honest with you." She'd even been present when I was in full demon mode and carried the lifeless body of my priestess into the pool.

"Don't try. I know you believe that is your nature. But I have seen more since becoming one of your women than any demon could possibly hope for."

"What is that?"

"Bob, look out at this incredible world of Areola. I won't say there are no arguments and no pain, but look. Everyone here is cared for. There is food for all. If something is needed, it can be found. There is good, healthful, and productive work for everyone. Even if it is not perfect, it is as near to Utopia as any human dwelling is likely to be. You are not a demon, Bob. You are a god."

That statement made me shiver. In my experience, gods get crucified. That's what happened to Issa.

"Did you know that in the United States and in several other countries, including Japan, India, the UK, and Turkey, there is now a 'Church of Bob?' They profess to believe in you and offer the hope that you will take them to Areola where they will live happily ever after."

"Oh, dear Zeus, no!" I said. "I don't want a church. How can they offer something I have not offered? I'm not going to start moving random people into Areola."

"Do you think a visit to the churches would help? You could tell them outright that you aren't sanctioning their religion."

"My experience is that none of the gods actually sanctioned the religion that grew up around their legends. Ninra, Isis, Athene, Aphrodite, Yahweh, Buddha, Issa, Mohammed, Confucius, Zeus, and now Bob. They were all called into existence by the devotees of the religion, not the other way around. And when the devotees cease to adhere to their principles, they close the gates on their world and fade away from even the memories of the churches and temples."

"Well, you needn't fear that in Areola. The world would cease to exist without The Bob. Now, make love to me again before the others get here."

We had a boatload of work to do to get ready for the season finale. Part of the process was dealing with our construction of the new space station/starship. As soon as it became known we were in negotiations with the US regarding ownership of the ship, a dozen other countries wanted in on the deal. We finally put a structure in place that would continue Space Pioneers as the majority shareholder, but would sell shares to other countries. By letting everyone know that The Bob would continue to be in charge of the construction and management, the shareholding countries were reduced to participation according to the number of shares they purchased. And we strictly limited the maximum number of shares any country could own, so they couldn't just buy everyone out.

I knew that wouldn't last forever as the idiots who govern the world's nations would constantly be in contention with each other over who got the best deal, the most seats, and highest prestige. The structure wouldn't be ready for habitation for five years and not ready to move from orbit for another five after that. There could be an entirely different world order by then. It was why I'd been devoted to leaving.

"Are you really going to launch toward Mars with Space Pioneer 17 the day the mini-series concludes?" my favorite interviewer asked. Elaine Frost dominated the late-night TV schedule. I was always happy to be on her show.

"It might not be that day. There are a lot of details we still need to work out. We will be launching five missions at the same time, Elaine. We will keep the details secret as to what is on each of the ships as they launch. This is to protect the crew and the groundcrew from danger. We don't mind protests, but we want people kept safe. In fact, I'm told we have full facilities for a large crowd at our Houston headquarters where people can come to protest in relative comfort. There will be cooled tents, restroom facilities, food vendors, and medical aid available. I encourage people to use that location for their protests as others are considerably more remote and unable to handle large crowds."

"You're being awfully friendly to protesters."

"It's a right and a privilege. Really, we just don't want anyone hurt."

"So, what can you tell us about the selection process that is going on in your show? Are you really going to take even more women with you to Mars?"

"The season was created because our ship wasn't ready at the close of the last season. We thought we'd be gone by now. But the selection has included much more than the entertainment you see on the show. Our crew found a mission and they were and are completely devoted to it. We finished recording the season a few weeks ago and everyone selected has been undergoing rigorous training since that time. Everyone who boards the ship will be ready to fly," I said.

"Is there room?"

"By this time, everyone knows that I have portal technology that I use to cross back and forth into my home, Areola. Once aboard the ship, I will open a portal to our home and everyone will return to Areola to make the trip in relative comfort. I'll leave a portal on the ship so that when we land, we can transport back to the ship."

"I mean, is there room for me?"

"Oh, Elaine, how I wish you had applied. I understand, however, that our network affiliation would be damaged by that move."

"Well, it was worth a try. Any other hints you can give us?"

"Just one. The final episode of *To Boldly Go* will be intensely graphic and is not meant for people with a weak constitution. It is both a grueling test of the finalists and an explicit message for people who persist in thinking they can get away with human trafficking. We *will* find you and *eliminate* you."

"That sent shivers down my spine. I can't wait for the last episode. Safe journey, Bob, and to all you contestants who are or were vying for a place on Bob's ship of dreams."

Even with the frequent warning, I don't think anyone was truly prepared for what we showed in the final episode. We had surveillance footage from Lacy's frequent trips to scout the locations and that I had taken when the two of us surveyed the sites. Then we had brief footage of our team of ninjas and the rescue with a scrolling tabulation of how many traffickers died in each location, how many people were rescued, and what our losses were. Finally, it showed me in full demon mode releasing my priestess into the primordial mass.

It concluded with me in my office, looking like a human. Much to my surprise, the cast and crew had presented me with a new flag of Areola which hung behind my desk. It was highly stylized, but to anyone who looked closely, it would obviously be a breast and nipple.

"We may journey to the farthest stars, but we will still eliminate trafficking in humans wherever we find it," I said, looking into the camera. "If you believe you can continue to trade in human flesh *anywhere* in this world, I encourage you to live each day as if it were your last. Believe me. One of them soon will be."

I stood from my desk and grabbed my satchel.

"If you'll excuse me now, I have an appointment." I opened a gateway and stepped through.

We didn't end the show there. It shifted to a live broadcast from a luxury yacht in the South Atlantic. We had the time displayed in the lower corner of the screen so people could see it was live. It showed four women led naked into a room where men lined up with drinks and proceeded to start fucking them.'

Then, the camera showed a light appearing in the room and I stepped through, still in the suit I was wearing behind my desk. Behind me came the glowing priestesses. I used the paralysis spell on everyone in the room then moved with the camera and the priestesses further into the ship. There we saw the room where dozens of women and children awaited their call to service. They were guarded by two men who had their pants around their ankles as they held a gun to the head of a woman giving them a blowjob.

This time, the priestesses struck and the men fell. Priestesses of Aphrodite came through the portal and ushered the women into Areola. By that time, the people in the lounge were thawing and looking around to see what happened. When they saw us return, they pulled the women in front of them to act as a human shield as the two guards who had brought the women into the room swung their guns toward us. They did not get a shot off, but fell with knives and shuriken sticking in their bodies. The women were quickly released into the care of our people and ushered to Areola. Some of the priestesses moved onto the decks and began silencing the armed guards permanently.

The men in the room offered to sign confessions and we filmed each of them signing their names. Then the priestesses nailed them to the walls of the lounge and tacked their confessions to their chests with a nail through their hearts. I went on deck and my priestesses gathered to retreat into Areola. My camerawoman and I left last. The clock on the screen showed elapsed time of eight minutes and thirteen seconds. The screen faded to black.

81
LAUNCH

"**B**OB! BOB!"

"Huh?" I said groggily. It had been an active and exhausting night satisfying all ten of my new crew. I rolled over and pulled a pillow over my head.

"Bob! Wake up!"

"Bob's not here," I muttered and went back to sleep.

"BOB!"

"What?" I growled sitting up in the big bed in the palace. The nine beauties and one man were still sleeping next to me. No one else was there. My little 'sex slave,' Angel, crawled up from the foot of the bed and sucked my cock into her mouth.

"Bob, I need to talk to you."

I'm not completely unfamiliar with head talk. My possessions and my wives, most notably, can carry on conversations with me in my head. But this didn't sound like any of them. And they should be the only ones who could reach me in Areola.

"Who is this?"

"It's Issa, Bob." That gave me pause. I hadn't seen Issa in 2,000 years, in spite of looking for him all through Asia a thousand years ago.

"Right. Who is this really?"

"Really, Bob. It's Issa."

"How did you manage to reach me? Are you in Areola?"

"No. Areola, by the way. I like that name. It suits you."

"Thanks, but..."

"Just listen up for a minute, would you? I don't know how much time I have to talk. This connection is tenuous at best."

"Okay, okay." I wiggled my way out of bed and gave Angel a quick kiss before I went into the magic room to have a private head-to-head talk with my old friend Issa.

When Issa and I traveled from Mesopotamia to India, we had a great time together, sharing about life and philosophy. He called me 'brother' and that made me feel special. We shared a lot with each other as we drifted along in a gentle breeze that seemed to move our craft always toward where we needed to go. He taught me a lot about the philosophy of Buddha and tried to teach me to turn water into wine. That was a disaster. If he turned water into wine, I could replicate his bottle and get the same results. But fill my bottle with water and let me try to turn it into wine and it wasn't drinkable. I might have inadvertently killed some fish when I poured it overboard.

He couldn't teach me to heal, either, though he acknowledged that my infinity room seemed to have healing powers and to keep people there forever young. He said it had to do with the primordial mass I spoke of having been created from.

"The Jews just called it mud," Issa said. "Or if you go way back, they referred to Earth and water as being 'without form and void.' It might be that the people taken from the natural world to your infinity room are separated from the primordial mass in some way but the people born there are part of your world's mass. The mass from which you create things in that world."

I still didn't understand how the infinity room worked, but I shared the spells with him that I'd used to create it and to open a gateway. He wanted to practice, but there was no convenient container to put an infinity room in, so he put off working the spell until he had a good place to do it.

I was really sad to see him go when he headed up the Indus and I continued down the west coast of India. But he said it wasn't good for two of our kind to be in the same place for too long. A couple of centuries later I tried to find him and kept finding traces of where he'd been, but couldn't locate him.

"Let me in, Bob," Issa said when I'd settled into the magic room to converse with him.

"In where? Where are you?"

"Behold I stand at the door and knock."

"Oh, Jesus!"

"Your front door, Bob. The door to the swanky mansion embassy in Beverly Hills. Let me in before I attract the attention of the cops or the constant security patrols out here."

I opened a gateway to the mansion and ran to the front door. There was a shriveled bald man there, walking with a long stick.

"Issa?" I asked. He nodded. "Well, come in. Come in. Let me get us some wine." We went into my study and I opened a bottle of Goídel Glas's finest. When I turned back to him, I found a man about thirty, dressed in jeans and a sweatshirt. He looked a lot more like Issa than the old man at the door.

"I've been in the country on a diplomatic tour and decided to stop by to see you when I saw your final episode air last night."

"Diplomatic tour? On whose behalf?"

"Oh, they ask me to come around occasionally because the Dalai Lama is still respected as a leader of Buddhism."

"You're the Dalai Lama? Come on. I came through Tibet a few centuries ago and met the Dalai Lama and he wasn't you."

"No. Of course not. I was sorry to miss you, though. I only ever serve one lifespan at a time. Then I switch it off to various others so I can go into my own infinity room and have a rest for a couple of generations."

"So, you did create one. I probably walked right by it and didn't know it was there."

"That's true, but it was too early for us to meet face to face. I was still getting organized. Prester John has always been a little pigheaded about how things should be run. And Mary is still giving me advice on dealing with people."

"John the Baptizer?"

"No, Bob. That John died. I haven't raised anyone from the dead. The one time I tried, the guy stunk to high heaven and he died again a year later. I won't put anyone else through that. John my disciple was the last of the apostles still alive when I finally found him on Patmos. He was near to being a raving lunatic from the isolation. You should have seen some of the things he'd written."

"I read Revelation."

"That was just the part I let remain. The rest of his writings were completely off the wall insane. I figured Revelation would give people something to worry over for a few thousand years."

"And Mary?"

"My beloved. I'd given her directions on where to meet me, so as soon as she could separate herself from the disciples, she made her way to me in India. Would have been a miserable eternity without *her*!"

"That I understand. Without Nimia, I'd have been lost more than once."

"You've got a treasure there."

"So, what brought you to see me? You're not upset about that preacher I got rid of, are you? He was possessed and had no desire to shake the demon within him. Now that fellow was truly ugly."

"No. You know how I feel about killing things, but I don't see any way you could have redeemed the situation. I came to talk about your show and what you plan to do."

"So, you're a fan, too?"

"No. I just caught the last episode of season two last night. Brutal, but I had to cheer. This has to do with you taking the infinity room—or Areola—with you into space and leaving forever."

"You want to come along? Bring your infinity room and we'll sail off into the big black."

"I can't. And neither can you."

"What?"

"You can't leave, Bob."

"Issa, I've been planning this for years. It's the best solution. I can finally go into the room and not worry about anything outside."

"You don't get it, Bob."

For some reason, he sounded like Zeus telling me how to keep a palace cool millennia ago. Same frustration.

"I guess not," I admitted.

"*Areola is not in your bag.* It's a dimension of Earth that is different, but compatible. No matter how far you send the bag into space, Areola is still here," he said.

I should have known that. Even when I started opening gateways from other locations, I still thought of Areola as being in the bag stuck in an evidence container someplace in the bowels of the FBI building. Like that movie *Raiders of the Lost Ark.* Or maybe they'd taken it to Area 51. It just didn't compute with me that it was tied to Earth in some way.

"You can carry around a bag as a crutch, but you can open a gateway to and from it anywhere. It exists in the same time and space as the natural world. It's you that needs to stay here. Without you, Areola would cease to exist."

I was beginning to get a headache and poured another glass of wine, which I downed before I answered.

"So, Areola is One with All."

"And All is Nothing," Issa repeated. "We can have what appears to be eternal life in our infinity rooms, but in reality, when Earth fades back into the primordial mass, so will our alternate dimensions. I believe, however, that attempting to separate and go off into space would separate you from the mothership, so to speak, and that would be catastrophic for both Areola and the natural world. It would most certainly return you all to the primordial mass."

"Well, shee-it! That kind of puts a damper on things. Our whole intent is to do a live broadcast of our launch into space. The ship is almost ready."

"Here's what you do…" For a minute there, he sounded just like Doug. No. I knew Doug was asleep with Avril in a room of the palace.

Issa outlined a plan for me to go ahead and blast off with the crew and everyone, then to just open a gateway into Areola and disappear from the ship. He said leaving a satchel behind on the ship would be a great inside joke. I wouldn't even need to tell anyone that we weren't traveling into the deep. No one in Areola would know the difference.

"Knowing you, though, you'll keep popping back into the natural world for another four millennia, just to see how the human story turns out. That was a nice touch in the show to pop into a ship in an unrelated part of the world and drive the point home.

"I've been popping in and out over the centuries to see what happened. That, and I've been shopping for other residents for Eden. You must know how difficult it is to find people in the natural world you want to spend eternity with."

"I haven't had that much problem. And you have millions of followers around the world. It can't be that hard to find true believers for your kingdom. Eden, you say? I have to say, it's more original than Areola," I said.

"Fitting names for both our kingdoms. You've met Christians, Bob. How many of them would you want to spend eternity with? I've decided to cut off the total at 144,000. I thought John was crazy when he proposed that number, but I'm still several thousand away. Which brings me to another matter."

"Whatever you want, Issa. What can I do for you?" I asked.

"In your most recent raids, I found a few people who I'd looked at and would like to take to Eden. I can still hear their prayers crying out to me. Let me take those few people from Areola to Eden where I can care for them."

"Of course! *Anyone* who wants to go with you will be welcome to emigrate. Why don't you come with me and choose the people you want?"

"You know, I've always wanted to visit your place. Is it true that the priestesses of Aphrodite will do anything with a man?"

"Or with a woman," I said.

We chatted on as I opened a gateway to visit the refugees.

Of course, after my meeting with Issa, I had to keep secret that we weren't actually going to leave Earth. I needed a simulator in Areola that was so exactly like the real thing that no one would know they weren't actually viewing the real thing. We scheduled five launches that day from different bases that would carry supplies to the construction site. One of those ships would continue into space. It would look like we were on it.

We started our live broadcast as my private jet touched down on an island in the Aleutians. When the only thing you are doing is creating a launchpad for a rocket ship, you can construct a lot without being noticed. I was sure the site had been spotted by US, Russian, and Chinese satellites, but they were also watching the half dozen other sites we'd created and put rockets on. Still, as soon as we started our live broadcast, the clock started. I knew people would be after us.

We did an orderly progression of our crew to the launchpad where we crossed the bridge to the capsule. But the capsule remained empty.

I created a gateway from the gantry directly to the simulator I'd created on Areola. We'd done a lot of training sessions here, so everyone was really pleased with how accurate the simulator had been to the real thing. None of the crew realized they'd ported directly to Areola instead of walking into the real rocket ship.

The countdown progressed. Then we all felt the g-force as the rocket blasted off. It had been a simple thing to mimic the acceleration on Areola by manipulating the ley lines.

"Space Pioneer 17, this is control in India. We have logged your launch and are following your trajectory. Everything is looking clear."

"Thank you, India Control," I said. I nodded to Wendy. She grinned.

"India Control," she said in a perfect duplicate of their accent, "Captain Bob says thank you. You know he doesn't always speak our language clearly." There was laughter through the speakers.

"I hope we can follow along when it is next time to trim your tail," the guy laughed.

"Space Pioneer 17, this is launch central. We have separation of the launch rockets and log you as thirteen minutes until you approach the construction site. Second stage rockets will fire in twelve minutes and twenty-eight seconds."

"Copy, launch control. This is Space Pioneer 17 and we are comfortably relaxing until docking. You could send the flight attendants in with drinks and snacks now," I said.

"Bob, you don't really have flight attendants on board with you, do you?" our startled launch coordinator asked. He no longer knew what to think or what was real.

"Well, not that we'll let get out of their seats before we leave orbit and head toward Mars. This weightless stuff is going to take some getting used to."

"Affirmative, Captain Bob. All systems have been checked and conditions are go."

"Holy shit, Bob!" our guy in India yelled. "We've detected a missile launch from the South Atlantic. It looks like someone is firing at you. It's on an intercept trajectory."

"Julie, Lalonda, activate defensive systems. Prepare to shoot the hostile out of the air."

"Affirmative, Captain. Defense systems are active. Laser point defense is tracking incoming object."

"Captain, tracking has identified the object as a US nuclear missile fired from a submarine in the Atlantic. Contact in one minute thirty-seven seconds," Wendy said.

"Hold steady on course, Karla. Weapons lock on target."

"Weapons locked and loaded," Lalonda said. "Optimum range in twenty-two seconds."

"Fire at optimum range," I said.

The seconds ticked down and we held our breath.

"Lasers fired. Direct hit. The missile has been detonated. No damage to SP17," Lalonda said.

"Bob, when did you have weapons installed on that thing?" a very shocked voice said over the speakers. I immediately recognized Leroy, our company CEO.

"Didn't you read the spec, Leroy? I'm sure it's there. Can't send a ship out into the solar system undefended."

"Here comes another, Captain," Wendy said.

"Prepare to answer fire on that submarine," I said. I was pissed.

"This one was not fired from the submarine. India Control cites China as the source. Wait! Here's another, tracking from Siberia."

"What is this? Every power gets one shot? Weapons status!"

"Primary lasers are recharging. Ready in thirty seconds."

"Are you tracking bogeys?"

"Affirmative, Captain. Optimum range for Bogey 1 will be two seconds after recharge. That will leave us exposed to Bogey 2 before we can recharge again."

"Deedee, Artemisia, activate secondary defense weapons," I commanded. I wasn't liking our sendoff at all.

"Secondary defense weapons are online and ready."

"Target Bogey 2."

"Targeting."

"Bogey 1 entering optimum range," Lalonda said.

"Fire at optimum."

We waited a second until India Control gave us the signal.

"China missile has been destroyed," Wendy relayed. "Russia missile is still on target."

"Bogey 2 entering optimum range for secondary defense."

"Fire at optimum."

We all thought we felt a shudder go through the ship as the plasma bottle was fired to intercept the missile.

"Russia missile has been destroyed," Wendy relayed. "Sky is blue."

"Defensive weapons go to standby. India, watch for activity from any satellites in our area."

"SP17, you are seventy-five seconds from the construction site. Prepare for docking," launch control said through our speakers.

"I'd still like to know where those weapons came from," Leroy demanded. "We assured the government we were a peaceful unarmed mission."

"Which made us a target for them to easily pick off and claim it was a malfunction," I growled. "Change in itinerary. We are bypassing docking and head directly for Mars. Ready for second stage rocket fire."

"Burn in three, two, one. SP17 is leaving orbit on slingshot trajectory."

"That's a thing of beauty to see," India Control said. "Perfect exit from orbit. Tracking on planned trajectory."

"Captain, troops have arrived at Launch Site. We will be overrun shortly. Well, maybe we have a few minutes. It seems Russian and Chinese troops are also landing and they might have a conflict of interest. All we can do is lock the doors and hope."

"Affirmative, Launch Control. We'll pick you up shortly," I said. "Karla, engage override of Launch Control. We're on manual from now on. You have control."

"Affirmative, Captain. I have control on manual override," Karla said.

"Stand down from battle alert," I said. "Ladies you just proved all the training was worth it. Congratulations."

"Can we go to the pool now?" Julie asked.

"Signing off from Space Pioneer 17," I said. "We'll leave the bag here so we can reboard when we get to Mars." I made a show of leaving a bag on the deck as everyone ported directly to the pool from our simulator. I switched to the remote camera on the real spaceship that simply showed a shot of the bag in the empty capsule.

Of course, it would throw the world into a confusion of debate as they argued about whether any of it was real.

The five rockets that launched in sync with us docked with the construction site. Robots unloaded the cargo and moved it to the proper places. We were still supplying Areolium for the construction in space and the robots were working well. Soon, shuttles would begin carrying people to the station to do more of the work. That would be interesting to watch. Most of the supplies were delivered via portal, direct from Areola.

We were free.

Like Issa told me, I can't keep my fingers out of the natural world for long. We were free in Areola and it wasn't long before people there began forgetting about our mission to Mars, the television show, and other things of the natural world.

We ported the launch crew to Areola before any of the competing armies broke through, so all they found was an empty control tower in which all the equipment and computers were dead.

The ambassadors to the United Nations from the three big powers appeared on the steps of the Areola Embassy in LA and apologized for the misunderstanding caused by their firing of an aerial salute to our journey. No harm intended.

Right.

I figured I'd pop in and out every few years, partly to manage the selection of colonists and partly to check on the condition of the world in general. I figured we would be making some more raids in the future.

You see, I had a new contact doing the scouting for me. Lil was a sexy young society girl in London who knew the ins and outs of everything, it seemed. As well she should. She'd once been the Queen. She'd staged her death and managed to escape and return to her demon form, which had been created specifically to sexually please the eighteenth-century mage who conjured her.

She'd set about creating her own network of spies who had spread out across the world. And they were looking for any sign of trafficking. Having essentially been created as the mage's sex doll, Lil was well acquainted with being a sex slave. She hated the trade as much as I did and had often made sure my tracks were covered when we made a raid.

Now she was sending me information. I had every intention of carrying out additional raids so that the traffickers would know that the launch of our ship didn't change anything as far as my resolve to end the traffic.

And, in fact, my resolve was not ended. Very little had changed other than I spent less time in the Natural World. I was busy in Areola. I had five wives, five possessions, fifty-one priestesses, twenty-one crew members, and more concubines coming in and out of the palace than I could count. I spent almost as much time in bed, satisfying the needs of my women, as I did being useful in Areola.

Why not? After all, our entire power grid was based on sexual energy. I was just doing my part.

END PART XV
END OF VOLUME 3

Interview with the Author

For this Signature Edition of *Bob's Memoir: 4,000 Years as a Free Demon* we're happy to welcome award-winning author Karlene Petitt as the interviewer. Karlene is the author of the airplane thriller series *Flight For....* She has also written and published several non-fiction works on airplane operation and safety, including her doctoral dissertation.

Karlene is a retired Delta captain living in Seattle. She is type-rated on the A350, A330, B747-400, B747-200, B767, B757, B737, and B727 aircraft. She holds a PhD from Embry-Riddle Aeronautical University in Aviation, with a focus on safety, and MBA and MHS degrees. She has flown and/or instructed for Coastal Airways, Evergreen, Braniff, America West, Guyana, Tower Air, Northwest Airlines and Delta. She spent 21 years training airline pilots, was instrumental in training program development at multiple airlines, and has over 40 years of flying experience. Dr. Petitt is now an aviation safety advocate, and aviation safety expert working with Aero Consulting Experts (ACE) and numerous law firms. She is a mother of three grown daughters and a grandmother of ten who is working on her golf game.

Karlene Petitt: When I heard the name, *Bob's Memoir: 4000-years as a Free Demon*, I was thinking historical fiction. And while there is a lot of history, what genre would you call this? As they say, what shelf do you put this on?

Devon Layne: I suppose I need to classify this in case it ever makes it to a shelf in a mythical brick and mortar bookstore. Some people have called it Historical Fiction and it bears many hallmarks of the genre. Bob lives a very long life and often interacts with historical personages, both human and divine. There is a lot of fiction in that category that simply has a character added into the historical record who makes his own observations. In this case, Bob.

But Bob is more active than most of those characters, interfering with their adventures. As such, it would usually be called Alternate History Fiction. But most of Bob's interactions don't change the outcome of historical events. It isn't a 'what if' kind of genre, for example, 'What if Caesar hadn't crossed the Rubicon?' It's more like, '*Why* did Caesar cross the Rubicon?'

So, where is my imaginary bookstore going to shelve it? Because it involves a mythical creature's view rather than a human, it will probably be shelved in a new category like Historical Fantasy. The last volume, in fact, mostly takes place in a future where Bob is much more active in writing the history.

KP: So, Bob is probably every man's envy and every woman's dream. He is funny, compassionate, and witty. Who is the real Bob? How much of you is Bob?

DL: Well, aside from not being 4,000 years old...? I suppose many of Bob's beliefs and his philosophy comes from me. It's very hard for me to write things that don't agree with my own philosophy. So, when you read about Bob's view of religion, politics, slavery, women's rights, and other issues, that is mostly my world-view poking through.

When I publish a book like this, I put a warning on the copyright page:

This is a work of adult fiction. The story and characters are fiction. Any incidental mention of places, historic personages, products, or organizations are the property of the respective owners. This book contains content of an adult nature. This includes explicit sexual content and characters whose beliefs, actions, and comments may be contrary to your religious, political, or world view. Perhaps this story will entertain. Perhaps it will take you to a similar time in your own life. Perhaps in rare instances, it will enlighten. The content is inappropriate and in some cases illegal for readers under the age of 18.

I believe that part of being allowed to read 'adult fiction' is not just reading about sex, but being able to read about beliefs and actions that are contrary to one's religious, political, or world view is a requisite. People who can't read that without becoming incensed at either the fictional characters or the author should be banned from reading adult literature.

Regarding every man's envy and every woman's dream, there's certainly none of me in that! And I hope the readers understand that *Bob is not human!* He does not have man/woman relationships and no one should envy or desire what he has.

KP: I found fascinating the amount of historical accuracy. When reading something about Caesar, Alexander the Great, or facts of a particular war, I wondered, *is that really true?* because I'd never heard of a detail. I would research and ultimately discover everything I investigated was true. This leads me to the next question, how many years did you spend researching historical facts, or do you just have a strong grip on history? And more so, how much liberty did you take with fictionalizing the facts of history?

DL: I am not a history expert or historian. I enjoy history—most of the time. What I don't like is the recitation of specific viewpoints about historical personages. Bob ends up in Spain and leaves with Christopher Columbus in 1492. While there, he lives through the Inquisition. He hears Christopher proposition Queen Isabella and get himself banished from court for two years. He is a thoroughly disgusting person who promised gold and slaves to his crews and 'taxes' to the monarchy. Yet until just a few years ago, every elementary school child was taught "In fourteen hundred ninety-two, Columbus sailed the ocean blue. He had three ships and left from Spain; He sailed through sunshine, wind, and rain." A few years ago, we began to break the bonds of this false history narrative and credit the natives with Indigenous People's Day instead. But this year, the country was officially back to celebrating Columbus Day and his near annihilation of the tribes he met.

So, when I thought of sending Bob with Columbus, I did a huge amount of research about Columbus, the Inquisition, and Ferdinand and Isabella. Most of it was pretty sickening.

I had other, more general resources. My dear friend Jason loaned me a book he'd had since his school days called *The Timetables of History: A Horizontal Linkage of People and Events* by Bernard Grun. This remarkable 850-page book covers the entire human timeline in a chart format that is divided into columns of different topics like science, religion, culture, medicine, art, geology, etc. When I determined an approximate date and location of Bob's travels, I checked the book to see what was happening in that region about that time. It was a great starting point.

Of course, I mostly attempted to be true to known history, but it was surprising how much history I discovered that was *not* generally known. And a few times, I took liberties with what was 'known' but not really proven. We know that Artemisia rammed one of her own ships in order to escape from the Greeks. We didn't know that Bob was the captain of that ship and that he escaped by swimming to Greece. A lot of the book was stories I made up to explain things that weren't 'adequately' understood.

KP: The interesting thing about this series is that some might call Bob and his sexual behavior depraved and immoral. Yet Bob's belief in the fairness and equity of society, how to treat people, anti-slavery, and how he takes care of those who participate in caring for others, is beyond moral. Was this an intentional, to show the opposing values of judgement of sexuality with respect to morality to challenge the question what is morality?

DL: It actually upsets me a little that stories that contain any amount of explicit sex must be labeled 'erotica.' Now, Bob is a *very* sexual being. He was created perpetually horny and attractive to women, in any body form he adopts. So, there are some very erotic parts of the story. I estimate, though, that it is less than ten percent of the total. And the sex scenes are by and large respectful, kind, possibly passionate and usually loving, even though they involve many people over his 4,000 years of history.

I'm afraid I know—and I think you know—a lot of people for whom the mere mention of a sexual act or reference results in an obscenity label. I'm sorry for those people.

Bob is your every day, slightly horny, happy-go-lucky—mostly lucky—demon. None of those words imply immorality.

When he was first summoned, he discovered his summoner intended to seal him in the walls of the king's palace with the task of keeping it cool. He was horrified by the thought that he was meant to become an eternal slave, and rejoiced that the adept was so shocked when Bob actually appeared that he died of heart failure on the spot, freeing Bob across a bridge formed by his body.

But aside from Pinaruti's intentions to enslave Bob, he had really imagined a demon that was all of the things he wasn't. He was attractive to women, always happy to satisfy them, well-hung, and basically harmless.

I think the intentional showing of opposing values with respect to morality comes from purposely ignoring those ideas. I don't share them, so why write about them?

KP: There were many powerful lines throughout. Two of my favorites: *"People can't view the recent past with any perspective. They are still caught up in living it."* and *"People refuse to change. I include both men and women in that category. They see the problems and are taught the lessons, but they refuse to change."* Would you relate these statements to current issues, and if yes, how so?

DL: Between when I originally wrote the series in 2021-22 and this 2025 Signature Edition things I thought were bad have gotten much worse. It's been only five-and-a-half years since George Floyd was murdered in Minneapolis, sparking protests and riots nationwide. Everyone thought we were past that issue, but today masked and unidentified federal police pull people from their cars, jobs, and homes without warrant or identification. How soon we forget. In the second edition of Volume 3, Bob and Ali were arrested in Chicago during the George Floyd unrest and had to escape.

The whole 'never forget' mindset is sometimes a contributor to the idea of still living in the pain and hurt of history. I could point out the Israeli and Gaza conflict that dates back three thousand years or more. But the constant 9/11 memorials and tributes ensure in the US that those horrific feelings of being attacked and scared are renewed at least annually. We never let go of them and continue to relive that history all the time.

Bob's complaint about people not changing is based on his admission that his own behavior and outlook changed over his four millennia on earth. The standard that he knew in 2,000 BC (Before Caesar) was that the strong ruled and women and children were chattel. They were weak; therefore, they *belonged* to the men. Over the years, Bob changed and realized that was a poor characterization and led to a kind of slavery. He changed—especially after he spent twenty years as a woman in India just a few centuries AC (After Caesar). But all we need to do is turn on the news or scan feeds and we can see that there is an overwhelming number of men who still believe they have the right to regulate women's bodies, financial prospects, family life, marriage, inheritance, home responsibilities, and mental health. They haven't changed. They are still living in 2,000 BC.

KP: There is very strong theme throughout the book of Bob's abhorrent feelings toward slavery, and in the final book examples of sex trafficking. I found myself haunted that the military was involved and the truckloads of people brought over the border followed by children digging their fathers' graves and then sold into the sex trade. How much of these present time facts on sex-trafficking are true, and what do you hope to accomplish with this theme, if anything?

DL: There are many things—problems, if you will—in the world today. Being concerned about one of those things doesn't mean that you aren't concerned about anything else. But if I had the ability to solve just one thing out of all the problems in the world, I would end human trafficking. That's not just sex trafficking, but slavery, deportation, custody battles, illegal adoption, and many other avenues that can be seen as human trafficking.

As I've mentioned, Bob was summoned from the primordial mass to be a slave, confined to the walls of the palace to keep it cool. There is never a moment in his life that he doesn't abhor slavery.

You see, slavery and trafficking aren't about sex. They're about power. They are the way one class maintains its position above another or how one person imposes his will on another. I'm sorry to say, I include most employer/employee relations in this category. Essentially, the corporation sets a value on a person's life on an hourly basis. And for some reason, we accept that some people's lives are worth $7.00 an hour while other people are valued at $1 million an hour. This is a means of human trafficking.

I know many people will disagree with this specific definition—after all TANSTAFL. I'll let them disagree. We live in a world of abundance where no one needs to be denied the "unalienable rights" spelled out in the Declaration of Independence: Life, Liberty, and the Pursuit of Happiness. It isn't about who deserves them.

Bob saves people from trafficking all through the three volumes and takes them to a world where everyone finds everything they need. But it is his time as a trader on the Pacific and his battles with pirates that brings him face-to-face with the young women and girls who were kept in the ship cabins for the pirates to satisfy themselves on. Bob ultimately finds a way to heal them by purifying them in the pool and making them his priestesses. They become his Erinyes, or the Furies. They are merciless when dealing with traffickers.

I have known a few people who were trafficked and escaped. I have seen what it has done to them. I would stop it if I could.

The statistics I cited regarding the number of missing persons and the amount of trafficking that goes through the US each year are researched statistics, not made up. When Bob and his crew make the big rescue of 10,000 people, I tried to point out that there was no echelon of our society that is not involved in trafficking. Military, religious, political, educational, criminal, corporate, entertainment, law enforcement. This is a travesty that we have the power to end, if only we would. We can't even get the files from a known trafficker released because they might implicate well-known people.

KP: Last comments?

DL: Yes. *Bob's Memoir* is intended to be light and funny and perhaps a little sardonic. I don't avoid tough subjects because no one who has lived for 4,000 years could possibly have avoided them. I hope people are entertained and perhaps challenged a little.

ACKNOWLEDGEMENTS

THIS SERIES OF THREE VOLUMES takes place over a span of 4,000 years or thereabouts—time that I have not actually lived myself. There were many people who influenced the writing and the adventures.

I'd like to start with my stalwart editors, Pixel the Cat, Old Rotorhead, and Cie Mel, as well as my alpha reader, Les. These guys were vocal about what they liked and didn't like and helped me through several renditions.

Jason supplied me with a book that was a timeline of the world, divided into topics like science, arts, politics, religion, and philosophy: *The Timetables of History: A Horizontal Linkage of People and Events* by Bernard Grun, based on Werner Stein's *Kulturfahrplan*. ©1946, 1963 by F.A. Herbig Verlagsbuchhandlung, Eng. ©1975 by Simon and Schuster, SBN 671-21682-1 Library of Congress 73-7704 foreword Daniel Boorstin, 850 pages. Jason happily pointed out additional resources like a graphic map look at the adventures of Marco Polo.

When I first conceived of the idea for this book (at Bob's insistence as I was driving one day), I told my friend and story consultant Doug about it. His response was, "So Bob is just your everyday, slightly horny, happy-go-lucky—mostly lucky—demon." That became the catch-phrase as we sat around the campfire and dreamed up adventures for Bob to have. Doug and I are now separated by miles and ideologies, but I remember fondly those evenings sitting and brainstorming Bob's adventures. His only request was to have a cameo in the book, which I gave him repeatedly.

Finally, my thanks to Dr. Karlene Petitt who took the time to read all three volumes and compose questions for the author interview preceding. It seems that thanks is scarcely word enough for the years of mutual support we have shared.

Without all these special people, *Bob's Memoirs* would never have been a possibility. My special thanks to you all.

Devon
Layne